BEIJING ODYSSEY

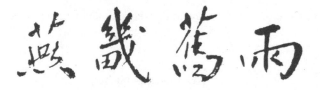

Based on the Life and Times of Liang Shiyi, a Mandarin
in China's Transition from Monarchy to Republic

Steven T. Au

Mayhaven Publishing

While based on historic figures and events, this is a novel; a work of fiction.

Mayhaven Publishing
P O Box 557
Mahomet, IL 61853
USA

First Edition—First Printing 1999
1 2 3 4 5 6 7 8 9 10
ISBN 1-878044-68-0
Library of Congress Number: 99-74554

Liang Shiyi, a First-ranked Official in Beijing, December 1911

Contents

The Ultimate Conciliator

Edict of Abdication of the Last Emperor, 1912
Liang Shiyi's name is next to the last on the left.

Foreword

On the west side of Tiananmen Square in Beijing stands the Great Hall of the People with its huge auditorium and exquisite reception rooms. This hall has been made famous by televised meetings on special occasions for foreign dignitaries. On the east side of the square is the Revolutionary History Museum where historical events in China were organized and interpreted through the eyes of peasant revolutionaries. To the north, Tiananmen (Gate of Heavenly Peace) provides an imposing wall with a row of archways leading to the Forbidden City, once a palace for emperors, shrouded in mystery, and now a public museum. Since the opening of China to the outside world in late 1970's, Tiananmen Square has been the center of attraction for foreign tourists.

Inside the Revolutionary History Museum, are displayed pictures and artifacts depicting the rise and fall of past dynasties. On display in the room describing the overthrow of the Qing Dynasty in 1912 is an edict of abdication of the last emperor. Led by Yuan Shikai, the Prime Minister, all ministers in the emperor's last cabinet affixed their signatures on the edict. Second from the last, is Liang Shiyi, the Minister of Posts and Communications, known to be the key negotiator for the terms of abdication.

Liang Shiyi had the impeccable credentials of a traditional Chinese scholar-official, but he was best known for his unusual talent in finance and public administration. His uncanny skills allowed him to survive in Chinese politics. Although he was an official of the imperial court to the very end, he was a sympathetic listener to the cause of the revolutionaries, and was eager and willing to reconcile their differences peacefully. During the early republican period, he was the chief secretary of the President and eventually became the Premier of the republic.

Liang Shiyi was involved to some degree in every major political movement of his lifetime. He was no doubt an ultimate practitioner of realpolitik but his thoughts and actions were always guided by the Confucian tradition. His civility without malice earned him respect, even among his detractors.

From 1916 until his death in 1933, Liang Shiyi maintained a home for his extended family in Hong Kong, where he was a political exile three different times.

Because of his prominence in international politics, several governors of Hong Kong befriended him.

A reminder of Liang Shiyi's reverence to his Chinese roots was an encounter with Cecil Clementi, then Governor of Hong Kong. This little-known history is enshrined on a Chinese-style stone arch (paifang) at the entrance to the Qingshan Temple on Castle Peak of the New Territories in Hong Kong. The inscriptions in front of the arch tell a poignant story.

Cecil Clementi was scheduled to retire as Governor of Hong Kong in 1930. A year earlier, some Chinese philanthropists in Hong Kong were planning to build a Chinese-style stone arch at the entrance to the Qingshan Temple. To honor the retiring governor for posterity, they asked him to write a few suitable words for engraving on the horizontal header of the stone arch. Since Governor Clementi was noted for his fine Chinese calligraphy, he wrote four large Chinese characters signifying "famous hills in the fragrant sea," and signed his name in Chinese.

These philanthropists also asked Liang Shiyi, who was then living in Hong Kong, to compose a couplet for inscription on the sides of the arch. Responding to the request, Liang Shiyi wrote these lyrical words:

> From the tower above shaggy roofs and trees, the sound of a bell
> penetrates the world below in a clear night;
> Overlooking such beautiful lakes and hills, when will the old man
> with a tin cane return to the central plain.

Upon completion of the arch, the governor and Liang Shiyi along with other honored guests were invited to attend the dedication ceremony. When Governor Clementi saw Liang's couplet, he was perplexed. Knowing the subtlety of Chinese classical poetry, he thought the last statement might allude to the question of when the colonial territories would be returned to China. In a harsh voice, spoken in Chinese, he protested to Liang, "What do you mean by 'lakes and hills' and 'return to the central plain'?"

At that time, Liang Shiyi was avoiding an arrest warrant issued by the Chinese Nationalist government in Nanjing. He had no reason to wish his safe haven to be taken away. Yet he could not suppress his yearning to be true to his Chinese roots. Realizing how sensitive the British in the colony were to the anti-imperialism rhetoric uttered by Chinese officials and students, Liang Shiyi was ready with an adroit answer.

"In bygone days, elderly Buddhist monks carried a tin cane when they crossed the rugged mountains," Liang Shiyi explained. "In this context, the old man with a tin cane refers to a Buddhist monk, not a political leader; and the central plain refers to the Nirvana of the Buddhists, not the vast expanse of China. While the phrase 'rivers and hills' may convey the notion of territory, 'lakes and hills' does not." Then he added: "The first half of the couplet describes the serene view from the tower as a devoted monk rings the bell on a clear night to proclaim his faith to the downtrodden world. The second half implies that even a devoted monk may wonder when he will give up such attractive surroundings and return to the Buddhist paradise. Isn't that an appropriate couplet for a Buddhist temple?"

Whether or not Governor Clementi believed this explanation, he knew that he could not win against such an elegant argument. He gamely acknowledged Liang's wisdom as they parted.

Sixty-seven years later, Liang Shiyi's hope and Cecil Clementi's fear finally played out to an international audience when Hong Kong was returned to China on July 1, 1997.

A search for the life and times of Liang Shiyi is more than an exploration of past history. The sentiment of "This is my own, my native land" is so ingrained in the Chinese psychic that it overflows to the Chinese who live beyond the Chinese borders, and continues to influence their thoughts and actions. Even those who have experienced tremendous sufferings in their native land often share the ethnic pride while deploring the injustice. The key in understanding this paradox requires the unfettered examination of the Chinese cultural, social and political legacy.

This novel is based on the life of Liang Shiyi, a colorful Chinese politician whose career mirrored China's changing political fortune in a crucial period of Chinese history. He was the symbol of a group of devoted officials who struggled to hold the country together during years of painful resistance to foreign domination and economic erosion. He was dubbed the "god of fortune" by his contemporaries. To his critics, he was manipulative and Machiavellian. In their eyes, he could not rise above his conservative background and instincts. But even his critics conceded that it would be difficult to imagine Chinese politics in his time without him.

Liang Shiyi lived from 1869 to 1933. Much had changed in China and yet much remained the same. This novel includes significant events in Chinese history. While some dialogues in the novel are direct quotes from recorded documents, others are constructed from imagination of what might have reasonably been said by various characters. Most historical events actually took place, but their descriptions have been dramatized.

The names of people and places in China were translated according to the new Chinese standard romanization (pinyin). In conformity with Chinese practice, the family name of a person precedes the given name. A few names, historically well known, are preserved in the old style.

Many publications about that period, both in Chinese and in English, have been consulted in writing this novel. The major references, together with pertinent commentaries and the Chinese names of people and places referred to in this novel, are also appended.

I wish to thank all who have provided assistance and encouragement to me in various stages of gathering materials and writing this novel.

Steven T. Au—1999

The Chinese-style Arch at the Entrance of Qingshan Temple in Hong Kong

The Scrupulous Mandarin

Russia
(Soviet Union)

OU

Urumqi

Turfan

Kashgar

XINJIANG

GANSU

Dunhuang

QINGHAI

Xinning

XIZANG
(TIBET)

Lhasa

NEPAL

BHUTAN

INDIA

Calcutta

Map of China
1870-1927

0   Miles   400

MYANMAR
(BURMA)

SIAM
THAILAND

Chinese Diplomatic Mission in India, 1905
Left to right: Liang Shiyi, Counselor; He Yugao, Secretary; Tang Shaoyi,
Special Envoy Plenipotentiary of the Mission; General Herbert Kitchener,
British Army Commander in India; and Zhang Tianbo, Counselor

The Long Journey

"Beijing is so cold and windy in early spring. I'm not used to it," Liang Zhijian complained to his son Liang Shiyi, as he sat shivering within the crowded confines of their room in the Sanshui Hostel.

Shiyi rose from the wooden chair facing his father and rummaged among the contents of an old black chest. "Perhaps an additional jacket will keep you warmer," he said, handing his father a quilted cotton jacket.

Zhijian pulled the jacket tightly around him and tucked his chapped hands in its padded sleeves. "I hope our trip will be worth all this," he grumbled. "I wouldn't relish such an ordeal again."

It was the early spring of 1894. Liang Zhijian, a native of Guangdong Province in south China, had traveled to Beijing to take the national civil service examination. He was fifty years old and was exhausted from the trip to the national capital and his extensive preparation of study for the grueling exam to which he had just subjected himself. Before becoming eligible for this competition at the national level, a candidate had to first pass the examinations at the county and then at the provincial level. Liang Zhijian was late at this game, having passed the provincial examination only the previous year.

His precocious son, Liang Shiyi, had traveled with him, and had taken the same examination after having passed the county examination at seventeen and the provincial competition at twenty. However, when young Shiyi proceeded to take the national examination, he had failed twice. Now at twenty-five, he had made a third attempt. The stakes for passing the national exam were high. Both father and son were anxiously awaiting the results.

"Uncle Hongzhu should be here any minute now," Shiyi said to his father. "When I met him yesterday on the street, he told me that he would visit us today before dinner." Uncle Hongzhu was a third cousin of Zhijian and two years his senior.

Zhijian nodded. He was relieved to have something other than the recent exam to think about. "Your Uncle Hongzhu is an inspiring example of success for his clansmen. Even though we are only remotely related, we live in the shadow of his glory." Indeed, Liang Hongzhu had passed the national examination in 1883, and

15

became a member of Hanlin Academy, the prestigious National Academy of Eminent Scholars.

Shiyi, too, wanted to be distracted and talk of his Uncle Hongzhu was welcomed. "I'm happy Uncle Hongzhu followed the footsteps of other successful clansmen from Sanshui County to provide subsidies for this hostel. We're indebted to them for this inexpensive place to stay in this windy city."

Zhijian looked away from his son and scanned the little room. "Hongzhu lived in this hostel while preparing for his national exam." His eyes came back to his son and narrowed slightly. "I wonder what Hongzhu would think of your radical ideas on political reform."

Shiyi heard the implied criticism in his father's voice and expected severe comments to follow. A sudden knock on the door made him jump to his feet with relief. "That must be Uncle Hongzhu now," he said. Swinging open the door, he was greeted by a middle-aged man dressed in a heavy blue cotton gown.

"Good afternoon, nephew," Liang Hongzhu squinted against the darkness of the room. "I hope you've both recovered from the stress of your examinations."

Shiyi helped his uncle remove his coat.

"Yes, yes, come sit and have some tea," Zhijian said, welcoming his cousin. "We have survived. I was just about to tell Shiyi, though, that in the exam he took too radical a position to support a new policy for political reform."

Hongzhu thanked Shiyi for leading him to the room's most comfortable chair. After settling himself in, he turned to Zhijian. "Everybody inside and outside of the imperial court now speaks of political reform. No harm is done by your son's exposition on this subject."

Shiyi's face reddened with pleasure, while his father's face flushed from a different emotion. Mindful of his manners, though, Zhijian held his tongue and offered a plate of dried plums to his cousin, who took one. After setting the plate on the table next to Hongzhu, Zhijian nervously passed a hand through his graying hair. "I grant you that political reform is a timely topic, cousin. But radical ideas may offend the imperial court."

Before Hongzhu could reply, there was yet another knock at the door. Shiyi opened it and quivered at the sight of the messenger who had run all the way from the Ministry of Rites. Short of breath, the messenger stammered, "I've arrived…with the news that you asked me to bring, sir. The names of…of…those who have passed the national examination have been posted at the Ministry. Your's, Liang Shiyi, is among them."

It was customary for the Ministry of Rites, which administered the examination, to publicly post the list of successful candidates according to the official ranking of their performances. Even the successful candidates were often embarrassed by the low ranking of their names in the presence of their peers. The unsuccessful candidates would feel terrible humiliation. Shiyi and his father were no exceptions. Thus they had arranged a messenger to report the results to them.

Shiyi's father was silent. Shiyi thanked the messenger and asked him to wait. Through the tense silence of the room, he crossed to a low nightstand next to his bed and lifted from the drawer a small leather bag. He extracted two coins, returned to the door and handed them to the messenger. Then he leaned forward and asked, "Is there…any other news?"

"No, sir. None at all." In this case, no news was bad news. Without further exchange, all those present understood that Liang Zhijian had failed.

* * *

The elaborate system of civil service examinations had originated more than a thousand years before, and had been modified periodically during the course of several dynasties. The system was inherited by the Qing Dynasty after the first Qing emperor was enthroned in the Forbidden City in 1644.

The Qing emperors were descended from tribesmen in China's northeast frontier who called themselves Manchu. However, because Chinese were predominantly ethnic Han, they regarded the Manchu tribesmen as foreigners. The Manchu rulers were ever conscious of their outsider and minority status. The early Qing emperors studied Chinese diligently and were able to read Chinese petitions without having first to have them translated into their native language. This tradition of becoming "more Chinese than the Chinese" became the pride and joy of subsequent rulers. They generally upheld Chinese traditional values and social structures based on the teaching of Confucius, and assiduously wooed the intelligentsia loyal to the previous Ming Dynasty. By using both carrot and stick, the Qing rulers incorporated millions of Chinese into the Manchu ranks to administer the vast area they had conquered.

Civil service examinations were used to instill the Confucian ethics in the ruling class and became an important vehicle for selecting capable and reliable administrators at all levels of government. This system of examinations was one of very few government operations meticulously carried out with safeguards against favoritism or corruption.

The examinations, at all levels, were held regularly and the dates were announced far in advance to allow time for travel. Special examinations were also authorized on important state occasions. So as to avoid even the appearance of favoritism, the examinations at the county level were administered by the Education Commissioner appointed by the emperor. The examiners at the provincial level were appointed from distinguished national officials who had no previous assignments in this particular province. The examiners at the national level were ministers and senior advisors in the imperial court. All examination papers were anonymous, with the names of the candidates sealed at the corner of the papers, and the graders were held incommunicado for the duration of the examination. Only after the grading was completed would the seals be broken to disclose the results.

The method of competitive comprehensive written examinations for selecting civil servants so impressed the Europeans in the early nineteenth century that the system was later introduced into the British Civil Service. No such compliments could be applied to the contents of the examinations, however, which prescribed a narrow scope and rigid style of essays and poetry within the established limits of Confucian propriety. The meticulous craftsmanship required to take, never mind to pass, the examinations was so demanding as to make the mastery of the styles of Shakespeare's plays and sonnets pale by comparison.

The difficulty in learning these skills was compounded by the absence of schools in the modern sense. Only private academies with tutoring service were available in most towns and villages, and these services were offered to men of all ages. Often, young boys from wealthy families got a head start while self-made grown men played the catch-up game in the same one-room schoolhouse. No certificate or diploma marked the accomplishments in these private academies. Recognition came only with the passing of the escalating levels of rigorous government examinations.

For all its idiosyncrasies, the competitive examination system was an accepted way to assure a skeptical populace that opportunities for upward mobility were available to those who were studious and willing to conform to traditional Confucian values. Although the journey to success was long and risky, it was a viable channel for those who were considered the best and brightest, and it helped pacify those who would otherwise have nothing to hope for. The low success rates at each level of examinations would insure the prestige of the well-earned degrees. More importantly, such degree holders were automatically elevated to an elite social group officially recognized by the government and willingly accepted by society.

An ambitious but unlucky man might fail many times, virtually waste his entire life. Liang Zhijian would never admit that he was trapped in such a scheme. He could at least point to his successes at the lower levels. But at the age of 50, the highest prize still eluded him.

* * *

As Liang Shiyi got the good news from the messenger, his thoughts wandered back to his childhood when his father first taught him to read. To the delight of his father, he could recite long classical lyrics without missing a word at the age of four. Under the tutelage of his father until sixteen, Shiyi absorbed the Confucian classics as his daily diet. By then he had already passed the first two steps in a three-step county examination. He was poised to take the last step toward the first official recognition.

One day, in the summer of 1884, a family friend came with his son for a visit. Pointing to Shiyi, he said to Zhijian, "It will be mutually beneficial if your son and mine study together under a great master." Four years younger than Shiyi, his son, Liang Qichao, was a prodigy. Young Qichao and Shiyi became friends and studied together under the same tutor.

When Zhijian decided to send Shiyi to study under other scholars, he told his son, "It is time for you to learn the intricacy of calligraphy and literature. You should study attentively under the great masters." This strategy paid off handsomely, for in late 1886 Liang Shiyi passed the last hurdle of county examination and received the Xiucai (comely talent) degree.

In celebrating the wedding of Emperor Guangxu in 1889, a special provincial examination was authorized. Shiyi took advantage of this extra opportunity to take this exam in Guangzhou, the provincial capital.

Shiyi recalled the experience. Each candidate was locked in a cramped 5-ft by 5-ft cubicle for ten days with only two short breaks between sessions. The flickering light from an oil lamp on the desk in the cubicle often disturbed the concentration of the serious scholar at work. Without bed or adequate toilet facilities, the only way to get a rest was to take short naps in the sitting position with the head resting on the desk. One welcome distraction was a knock at the door for meals that would then be pushed through a small hole on the door. The penetrating odors in the cubicles would impede the inspiration of all but the most determined candidates to compose a lyrical poem required for passing the examination. Shiyi took this hardship in stride, and was successful in gaining the Juren (learned man) degree.

Shiyi was pleased to learn that his friend Liang Qichao had passed the same examination. So did another acquaintance, Liang Boyin, who was four years older than Liang Shiyi. All were young and brilliant and, despite the family name, were unrelated. These three Juren degree holders were dubbed the "Three Liangs of Guangdong" by their friends and admirers.

Buoyed by his success in the provincial exam, Shiyi lost no time in preparing for the national examination to be held in Beijing the following spring. Liang Boyin was not ready for the ordeal and did not join him. Surely Liang Qichao would want to go for the next degree in a hurry, Shiyi thought, since this boy wonder was the talk of the town for receiving a Juren degree at the tender age of sixteen. He was wrong. Qichao would not compete this time because his father thought he was too young for the strenuous journey to Beijing.

With full commitment, Shiyi went to Beijing in 1890 for the national examination, but failed. Passing through Shanghai on his way home, he found many translations of Western books on a variety of subjects. Intrigued by these new ideas, he spent all his pocket money to buy them, especially books on political institutions and economics. Upon arriving in Guangzhou, he decided to devote most of his time to self-study of modern subjects not normally taught by the tutors. A year later, Qichao and Boyin would join him to search for practical applications of their knowledge to political reform.

In one of their study sessions, Qichao surprised his two friends by telling them, "I shall no longer continue to take higher examinations since they will drain my energy for more important pursuits. I have heard about a new political reform movement led by Kang Youwei. I am very excited about his approach of appealing for public support to force the imperial court to act. I intend to study under him for a while."

Shiyi was quite aware of Kang's unorthodox views but he was not persuaded by Kang's radical ideas. "And you are determined to follow this course, Qichao?"

Qichao nodded. Boyin remained silent. But all three knew their paths were turning from one another.

Unfortunately, Liang Shiyi again failed the national examination in 1892. Returning home, he decided to become a tutor in a private academy in Guangzhou to earn some income, but he had not given up his dreams. He was even more eager to study translations of Western books, and he never took his mind off the next national exam. He was delighted when his friend Liang Boyin joined him to prepare a third time for the examination. This time, he felt he would not fail.

* * *

It was a bittersweet moment as Shiyi stood in front of his father and his uncle Hongzhu to receive the good news in the spring of 1894. All the agony of defeat experienced in the last few years suddenly seemed to evaporate.

For a few seconds, Shiyi wasn't sure what to say. Uncle Hongzhu coughed in embarrassment for his fifty-year-old cousin. But Zhijian straightened his shoulders and managed a smile for Shiyi. "I now have at least a Gongshi for a son. That is indeed something to celebrate. Let us do so, and be happy."

Shiyi's eyes moistened. Uncle Hongzhu noticed and, in a bright and forceful voice interjected, "We must not stay up too late," Clapping Shiyi on his shoulder, he added. "Remember, you're now eligible for the palace exam, only six weeks away. You must study, study, and study some more."

Shiyi groaned at the truth of Uncle Hongzhu's words. He had cleared this particular hurdle only to train for the next. And it would be a difficult task indeed.

The palace examination in the Forbidden City was the final screening of successful candidates for the national exam of the Gongshi (presentable scholar) degree. It placed a premium on artistic calligraphy and flowery literary style. Although the emperor was presumed to appear during the palace examination, no candidate ever saw him. Any attempt to look at the emperor without invitation or permission was strictly taboo. It wasn't worth the risk. Those who survived this exam process would be given the Jinshi (advanced scholar) degree.

Liang Boyin, who had also passed the national exam, came to Sanshui Hostel for a visit. When they had a moment alone, he whispered to Shiyi, "I don't have the flair for artistry. I'll pass up the palace exam."

"You did very well in the national exam." Shiyi encouraged him. "You are so close to the top. How can you give up this rare opportunity? Boyin, you must give it a try."

"I'm fearful of the palace exam," Liang Boyin replied. "I can't help it."

* * *

For Shiyi, the long journey in the quest of scholastic eminence finally came to an end when he passed the palace exam. Boyin was one of the first to congratulate him for receiving the Jinshi degree. "You have earned the title of Hanlin—Eminent Scholar, Shiyi. I'm impressed and proud to be your friend."

The ranking of Jinshi degree holders was of utmost importance. It was the basis of selection for members of Hanlin Academy, where the scholars would be groomed for the most lucrative appointments in government.

They strolled along the street, stepping carefully to avoid the mud. "How do you feel to be an assistant compiler in Hanlin Academy?" Boyin inquired.

"I'll be glad to chronicle the major events of history for posterity—at least until I receive a high calling."

The Patriarch

Liang Zhijian brimmed with smiles at the news that his son Shiyi had finally become a member of Hanlin Academy. He wanted to forget the embarrassing moment in front of his cousin when they learned that Shiyi had passed the national examination that he had failed. This day it was easy to comfort himself. "Did I not give my best to bring about this glorious day?" He expounded. "Did I not prepare you, Shiyi, for this moment? The entire family wins today, and my own old age is secured— because of your success. I would not have wanted it any other way." True, he could have been more generous in judging his son before the results were known, but teaching one's offsprings was the inalienable right and solemn duty of a responsible father. His son could now do great things with the new-found fame. In his buoyant mood, Zhijian counted the blessings that were deemed just rewards for the moral upbringing and hard work of his ancestors and himself.

* * *

Liang Zhijian was born in 1844, the only son of Liang Ruji who descended from generations of peasant stock in Gangtao Village in Sanshui County. Liang Ruji toiled in the rice paddies in his youth while struggling to study in his spare time under a sympathetic tutor. After age thirty, he passed the county examination, even ranking first among the successful candidates, the first in his direct family lineage to receive a Xiucai degree. In a society in which scholars were held in higher esteem than farmers, artisans and merchants, Liang Ruji was finally elevated to the elite status of gentry.

Two avenues were open to degree holders in government examinations. Those who sought and received a government post became officials; others who did not join the bureaucracy remained scholar-gentry. The members of scholar-gentry were a sort of reserve who could become officials when opportunity arose. They usually resided in their native villages as community leaders until they were appointed to official posts elsewhere. For someone like Ruji, who gained a Xiucai degree in his thirties and had no connections, the choice was limited to being a scholar-gentry in his village where he could offer tutoring service in a private academy. But he was quite satisfied with that role and made no attempt to seek official positions or to take higher examinations.

Beijing Odyssey

"I'm quite fortunate to have come this far. It is now up to you to go further," Liang Ruji told his son Zhijian.

"Yes, Father. I'll try my best," his son replied earnestly. From then on, this promise became the obsession of Liang Zhijian.

Gentry life was not all rosy, at least not for someone with only a Xiucai degree but no family fortune. Giving up farming on two acres of rice paddy, Ruji collected meager rents from a tenant farmer to supplement his income from private tutoring. Occasionally he received honorariums for performing other services befitting a gentry member. Although his calligraphy did not attract any buyer for collector's items, he was sought after to compose couplets for wall posters to commemorate special festivities such as weddings and birthdays.

A scholar-gentry, Ruji was exempt from conscription and from some taxes. Most important of all, he was protected against transgressions from local people and officials as gentry members were immune to actions taken by the magistrate without approval from officials at a higher level. He performed indispensable functions in his village, from the arbitration of disputes to the promotion of public works. By virtue of hard work and good deeds, Liang Ruji served as an important link between government officials and the common people, even though he was not on the public payroll. His inner satisfaction came from the knowledge that he was well respected in the community.

Liang Ruji was not averse to simple living and high thinking, but made no pretense of glorifying a scholar's indifference to material comfort by forsaking worldly success. He spared no expense to send his son Zhijian to study in a private academy. Liang Zhijian was slow to catch onto new ideas, but he was obedient and studious. Once he absorbed the Confucian ideas as orthodox views, they became part of his soul. When it came to defending the Confucian values, he had the tenacity of a bulldog.

"You will be happy all the time if you are content with your lot in life," Liang Ruji advised his son on reaching adolescence.

That struck a chord of resonance in Zhijian, who had learned this lesson from his tutor. "Yes, Father," he responded warmly, "I'll remember the admonition of Confucius that I should be as aloof to wealth and glory gained from injustice as watching the floating clouds yonder. I'll honor my parents and ancestors by doing only righteous deeds to succeed in life."

To insure the succession of the family name, Ruji wanted to find a bride for his son when the boy reached 19. He entrusted this important task to his wife who spread the word to self-appointed matchmakers. These women were social gadflies and the sources of village gossip. For a handsome fee, the matchmakers could operate as efficiently as present-day realtors who quickly provide lists of suitable prospects. They also knew the rules of the game and were sticklers for social etiquette. They would recommend only the daughter from a gentry family for a gentry son. To bolster the authority of their recommendations, they utilized astrology to determine the compatibility of a match from the birth dates and times of the boy and the girl. The parents from both sides often accepted the recommendations of the matchmaker unseen, but not without a thorough background check of the prospective brides or grooms.

A matchmaker of good repute responded to Liang Ruji and his wife. For their son, she chose a girl of 17 from neighboring Nanhai County. She was the seventh child of Pan Mingxun, a minor official under the Provincial Military Commissioner. "Do you want to have a glimpse of the girl?" the matchmaker asked Liang Ruji's wife. "If you do, I can arrange an elaborate pretext so that both sides may happen to be in the same place at the same time without actually meeting each other."

Liang Ruji's wife shook her head. "Not really, as long as you give me the full details of the family and the names of their friends and neighbors. You know that we want to check her family as far back as three generations to see whether there were criminals or hereditary conditions which could cause malformations or incurable diseases." The matchmaker went away with relief. In due course, the match became a reality.

On the wedding day, the bride's family rented a sedan chair decorated in red silk with a front screen to hide the bride's face. The groom arrived at her home in a very plain sedan chair to welcome the bride. He got out and bowed to the bride's parents and then he and the bride left in their separate sedan chairs—in tandem. The magic moment came when the groom opened the screen of the bride's sedan chair at his own home to see the bride for the first time. Liang Zhijian was pleased to find a beautiful and gentle woman.

The wedding ceremony took place in the groom's home with the groom's parents presiding. When Zhijian and and wife were pronounced husband and wife, the couple kowtowed to his parents. As a symbol of her obedience, the bride served a cup of tea to each of her in-laws. Then Zhijian introduced his wife to his three sisters, two of whom were married and had come home for the occasion with their husbands. No one from the bride's family witnessed the ceremony. They had to wait until the third day after the wedding when both bride and groom would go to her home to celebrate with her parents and relatives.

Like all new brides, the first duties of Liang Zhijian's wife were to her in-laws, not to her husband. Since his unmarried sister lived at home, it was easy for his wife to discover the likes and dislikes of his parents from this sister. "How does this dish taste to you? Would it be better served hot or cold?" she often asked Zhijian's sister while preparing the meals for the family.

Liang Zhijian and his sisters were very lucky that their father took a permissive attitude in bringing up his children, not a common trait for most fathers. But their mother was very strict, also uncommon for most mothers. Generally the children were raised in an atmosphere in which conflict was suppressed, sex was taboo and emotional distance was maintained. Through the paternal but benevolent guiding hands of Liang Ruji, the two generations appeared to live harmoniously together.

Apparently, however, no one was aware of the torment of conflicting thoughts between career and family in the mind of Zhijian. He did not want children to distract his concentration in preparing for the county examination. But he also knew how strong the wishes of his parents were to have many grandsons to protect the thin family lineage. In any case, he would not want his father to support the expanded family while he buried himself in books. There was no easy solution, but his desire for a career finally won. Nothing should be left to chance if he could help it. With characteristic forethought, he began four years of self-imposed sexual abstinence, a prudent decision. No one but his wife had an inkling of his plan.

Because his mother often wondered aloud when she would have a grandson, Zhijian's well-meaning sister told his wife: "Mother is very concerned about your health. Is there any food or medicine that can help you in conceiving a baby?" Zhijian's wife had listened to this tune so many times in so many variations that she grew sick of the words. With her proper upbringing, how could she disclose the most intimate secret between husband and wife to her sister-in-law? And yet, if some explanation did not get back to her mother-in-law, would the old lady get the wrong idea and try to find a concubine for her son? While Zhijian might be very proud of his strict discipline, his wife was driven to tears.

In more ways than one, 1867 was a watershed year in the life of Zhijian. He finally passed the county examination. Like his father, he ranked first among the Xiucai degree recipients in the county. After making plans to secure a regular income through tutoring, he also decided that the time had come to raise a family. Sure enough, his first son was born the following year but their joy was shortlived. The baby died at two-months old.

"This is a difficult time for both of us," Liang Zhijian told his wife after the burial of their firstborn, "but we must restrain our sorrow to not cause even greater sadness to my parents."

"We have waited so long for our first child," his wife sobbed in her reply, "and now we have lost him. I don't know what your parents will think." She was very much afraid that her mother-in-law might blame her for the misfortune.

Fate intervened. Zhijian's wife gave birth to another son in the spring of 1869. They named him Shiyi. His grandparents watched him grow to a toddler before Liang Ruji succumbed in 1871 and Grandma Liang died the following year.

In observance of deep mourning, Zhijian visited the graves of his parents frequently, sometimes for days in a row, and practiced sexual abstinence for one year after each death. His wife breathed a sigh of relief from the pressure of having more sons. She could now give undivided attention to Shiyi and a daughter, born just before the death of her father-in-law.

* * *

Liang Zhijian began his tutoring service in 1867. He rapidly gained the reputation of a stern and methodical teacher. Probity seldom deserted him. How could you build character without strict discipline? What would the world be without moral order shaped by leading citizens of impeccable character? Like-minded parents flocked to his private academy and entrusted their heirs to him for a thorough

Confucian education. "It would be folly if I did not give him a chance to study under you." "Find the man in him." "Don't spare the rod." Time after time, these words of trusting parents echoed in his ears.

By 1870, Zhijian had saved enough money from tutoring to embark on a journey to nearby Jiujiang in Nanhai County to study under Master Zhu Ciqi, a well-respected Confucian scholar in south China. Zhu Ciqi was particularly noted for his exposition on the political history of China and the application of such scholarship to public affairs. Liang Zhijian was greatly inspired by this great teacher and enjoyed the association with many bright and budding scholars in Zhu's circle. This pursuit was interrupted twice by the deaths of his father and mother, but after several years of devoted study under the master, Zhijian was left with Zhu's indelible influence for the rest of his life.

As a strict disciplinarian, Zhijian believed that sex was for procreation and not for recreation. Although he could not utter the word "sex" to his students, he found ways to get across the idea through the use of examples in the guise of filial duties. He was emphatic that in the mourning of one's parents, a man should not share his wife's bed for one year. Some curious students would try to test the seriousness of this assertion by quietly matching the mourning periods for his parents and the birth dates of his children. "Perhaps ten months, not quite one year, according to the terms of normal pregnancy," reported one estimate. Piously, Zhijian had already spread word that his third son, who was born after the death of his mother, was a premature baby who did not survive the first week of infancy.

At the invitation of a friend, Zhijian went to Hong Kong in 1880 and taught at a private academy there. He took his eleven-year old son Shiyi along, but left the rest of the family in his native village. He thought that it was time for Shiyi to learn more about life in the real world. They left this colonial city four years later when Zhijian set up his tutoring service at a private academy in Guangzhou.

* * *

When Liang Shiyi reached the age of 18, he had already passed the county examination. To celebrate his success, his parents, as Zhijian's had done, would present him with a wife! In 1887, his parents selected as his wife a girl two years his junior, the daughter of a minor official named Gao Zuoqing in Nanhai County. His wife had small bound feet—"three-inch golden lilies"—which were supposed to make a woman physically and artistically appealing, causing her body to move seductively while walking. It also symbolized the confidence of her well-to-do family that she would not have to do any hard labor in her life. In some ways she was spoiled by doting parents, but their expectation was not misplaced. Since her husband showed great promise early in his life, he would doubtless bring her all the material comfort of her dreams.

Since Shiyi seemed to be secure in his gentry status and could look to a bright future, his parents had high hopes that they would soon be grandparents. At the moment, however, his mother was more concerned about her own pregnancy as she told her husband emphatically, "This will be our last child, whether the newborn is a boy or a girl."

Later in the same year, Zhijian's youngest daughter was born. Some matchmakers, who had purposely not been asked to arrange his son's marriage, circulated the village gossip that it was shameful for a woman to have sex with her husband when she was old enough to have a daughter-in-law. One loudmouth even dared to add, "His wife should get him a concubine if that is necessary to satisfy him." With the gift of sensing the imminent danger, Zhijian's wife quickly proclaimed that from now on the childbearing duty had passed on to the next generation.

Altogether Liang Zhijian's wife obligingly bore him nine children—five sons and four daughters. While all four of their daughters lived to adulthood, their sons did not fare as well. Since their first and third sons died in infancy and their fifth son, Shixin, died at barely 20 years of age, only their second son Shiyi and fourth son Shixu would ultimately carry on the Liang clan. However, Zhijian was quite content with the status quo without expanding his family further. He eagerly anticipated his role as a patriarch surrounded by his children and grandchildren, as he would receive his much-deserved rewards in the not-so-distant future.

The Precocious Son

Unlike his father, Shiyi was quite ready to raise a family at the time of his marriage, since he had been assured the life of gentry. He enjoyed diversion and, rarest of all among serious scholars, humor. However, his wife was a serious and humorless woman. At first she was coy and evasive, but later became dominating and resentful. Liang Shiyi felt that if he could not satisfy her with love, he would at least respect her wishes. After passing the provincial examination, Liang Shiyi spent most of his time studying with his friends in Guangzhou while his wife stayed in his native village. His failures in two national examinations did not endear him to her since they meant more study sessions, more time away from home and less attention to her. Even after he became a Hanlin scholar, he was still far away in Beijing.

One thing that set Shiyi's wife apart from most women in the village was her air of superiority. She liked to be addressed as taitai (madam) by her neighbors, and took great pleasure in the symbol of her status when her husband addressed her as Madam, the one and only wife in his life. At the celebration of her husband's ascendancy to the Hanlin title, she told some neighbors, "Some day I will be my husband's furen (lady)—when he makes the grade." The neighbors were shocked. What a presumptuous statement! To ordinary citizens, "furen" was nothing but a polite way of saying "Mrs.", but to those attuned to the official etiquette in Beijing, furen was the title for the wife of the first-ranked official conferred by the emperor. Even though her husband had become a Hanlin, he was still far from reaching the goal of a first-ranked official.

One fine morning in late spring of 1894, Liang Shiyi left his father at Sanshui Hostel and reported to Hanlin Academy. With him were several of his close friends who also had received the Hanlin title after passing the palace examination. They were all Cantonese except Guan Mainjun who hailed from Cangwu in the neighboring Guangxi Province. A short figure among his taller friends, Guan Mianjun was deferential to them. He said to Shiyi, "I feel quite out of place here as I know no one in the academy who is from my home district. I envy those from other counties which can boast many successful scholars and support large hostels in Beijing."

"We always regard you as one of us." Shiyi stated the obvious. "The people in Cangwu speak Cantonese. And we see eye to eye on many great issues of the day.

You must naturally join forces with us.

"That's true," Guan replied thoughtfully. "And I often find myself in need of a friend to guide me through the labyrinth of this capital city. I'm weary of rounds of official activities associated with this new position. I truly appreciative your support.

Shiyi smiled. "I'm new here too. We must act cautiously, but we don't have to be so timid as to limit our own experiences."

Hanlin Academy was a unique institution whose primary function was to provide literary and scholastic underpinnings to official activities. Members of the academy were ingrained with the spirit of noblesse oblige—to whom much is given, much is expected. Shiyi and Mianjun were in awe of the academy's venerable tradition and the excellent opportunity for training in officialdom.

The top officials were two chancellors. A number of readers and expositors who prepared materials, recommended lectures for imperial affairs, and performed official ceremonies at Confucius temples, reported to them. There were also compilers and assistant compilers who were selected from the new Jinshi degree holders. Their duties were to draft edicts and to compile official documents.

As assistant compilers, Shiyi and Mianjun held the lowest possible positions. That was the fate of all new members, except the three top-ranking Jinshi degree holders who were immediately appointed compilers. Each assistant compiler was assigned to a mentor who would monitor his progress. He was allowed a maximum of three years to prove he had satisfied all criteria for promotion to compiler; otherwise he must seek employment elsewhere. The salaries for compilers and assistant compilers were very low. Their hope was that in positioning themselves near the center of power, they might be in line for a good job they could otherwise never have secured.

The ambitious young men who had gained honor, but neither power nor wealth, by becoming compilers in Hanlin Academy usually did not rest their feet at the academy for very long. They looked to the successful members of the past in projecting their own future—if they could find the right connections. For a long time, the Grand Councillors, who were chief advisors to the emperor, had to be Jinshi degree holders and often had a Hanlin background. They usually held concurrent appointments as heads of ministries or other important offices. Even during the late Qing dynasty, when this practice was sometimes ignored, the Hanlin title holders certainly had the edge in gaining the most coveted positions.

* * *

After the first day at the academy, Shiyi went to the Nanhai Hostel to visit Liang Boyin who was still uncertain about his own future. Boyin was delighted to see Shiyi and told him about the job prospects, "I have talked to Li Duanfen, Minister of Punishments. You remember that he was the chief examiner when we took the provincial examination? He was sympathetic, offering me a position of seventh rank or, with luck, even sixth. But he must check with the Ministry of Civil Office first."

"I remember Li Duanfen very well, indeed. Shiyi continued. "He was a Deputy Minister sent from Beijing to administer the provincial examination in Guangdong in 1889 when we 'three Liangs' made such a big scholarly splash. Li Duanfen has a reputation of being reform-minded. I admire him greatly. I hope you'll get the chance to work for him."

"Yes. I hope. But I'll have to be patient in order to gain a foothold in the vast bureaucracy."

Shiyi was quite aware that examiners, like Li, were eager to promote capable and patriotic young men to serve the country and at the same time to build up their own influence. It was through such connections that networks were often built. They knew that the men raised from obscurity would be forever grateful to their mentors.

Shiyi and Boyin also knew that all government appointments coordinated by the Ministry of Civil Office were classified by official ranks—first rank the highest and ninth the lowest. High officials of first to third ranks were appointed by the emperor himself. Those from fourth to seventh rank were recommended by the Ministry of Civil Office but had to be approved by the imperial court.

Because of the suspicion of Manchu rulers toward Chinese, the imperial court of the Qing Dynasty had adopted an elaborate "quota system" of checks and balances between Manchus and ethnic Han Chinese. Even in regional and provincial administrations, the pattern of checks and balances prevailed. When a Manchu was appointed governor-general with jurisdiction over two or more provinces, the governors under him were usually Chinese, and vice versa. There were considerable duplications of official functions in the organizational structure to ensure that the emperor would be the ultimate arbitrator of state affairs. Exerting personal authority at every level, the Qing Emperors had cultivated their power to the zenith of absolute monarchy.

* * *

After watching Shiyi's successful entry into Hanlin Academy, Zhijian felt it was time to return home to Sanshui. Shiyi would go with him. Since the imperial court regarded filial piety as the foundation of loyalty, it was easy for Shiyi to receive a leave of absence from the academy to accompany his father home.

"I've made the necessary arrangements to go home with you," Shiyi told his father. "This trip will allow me to express my gratitude to our ancestors at the ancestral hall in our village."

"Perhaps it's all for the best," his father replied with relief. "You've been away from home often to pursue your career in the last few years. Now you'll find time to raise a family." Zhijian thought his son had neglected this duty because of the burden of the examinations. Of all the unfilial acts, the most serious one was in not leaving a male heir to continue the family lineage. This was a good time to remind his son who had brought up the subject of honoring their ancestors.

Shiyi thought only about the solemn ritual of paying respect to his ancestors in his native village. Such an event would be an occasion for his clansmen to celebrate not only the high honor bestowed upon him but also the glory to his clan. Perhaps his father's pain at having failed the national exam would be eased.

That strategy worked. As soon as Shiyi and his father arrived home, the villagers staged a colossal event for the celebration of the success of their native. Zhijian was indeed very proud. The enthusiasm for this occasion exceeded even the event staged for Uncle Hongzhu when he became a member of the Hanlin Academy eleven years earlier. In such a joyous mood, Zhijian was able to put his own failure behind him.

Nothing received a higher priority in a clan than the encouragement of budding scholars who could become high officials in the provincial or the national capital. With influential clansmen in high places, the interests of the clan could be protected against transgressions from corrupt local officials or other clans.

Clans or lineage organizations based on family descent through the male line played a vital role in rural China. They were particularly strong in the south where the family land holdings were larger. Although the Chinese farmers divided all land equally among their sons, the lineage organizations often held large plots of common land that provided income for maintaining the ancestral hall and for supporting local causes and charities benefiting their clansmen.

Most clans viewed the promotion of candidates for government examinations with enthusiasm. The promotion meant the entire village was honored and the honored candidate became a celebrity, whose ongoing achievements became increasingly newsworthy. Many forms of support were provided to these candidates, including stipends and travel allowances, with the expectation of a final payoff. The candidates could not help but feel deeply indebted to such favors. When Shiyi became a member of Hanlin Academy at the age of 25, the hope was high among his clansmen that he would reach the very top.

* * *

When all the cheers subsided, Shiyi turned inward to assess his personal life. Seven years earlier, his parents had chosen a very refined girl from a respectable family to be his bride. Shiyi and his wife had remained childless. The situation became intolerable as there were no more excuses for the delay. Because of his wife's hot temper beneath her serene surface, it was difficult for Shiyi to approach her on the subject. Now in his hour of scholastic triumph, he decided to come directly to the point: "Madam, don't you think that it's about time for us to have a son to continue the family line?"

The reply was not what he had hoped. "Yes, but you are going back to Beijing to assume your new position soon. I don't think that I can manage to live in a strange city with a young child. On the other hand, if I am pregnant and stay here in the village without you, my life will also be unbearable." Then she suddenly sprang another surprise on her husband, "Why don't you take a concubine who can serve you in ways that I can't? She can bear a son for you."

In a society in which sexual intimacy was considered an unpleasant duty by most respectable women, the suggestion of a concubine for the husband was often a way out when a woman either had enough sons or had given up hope of having one. However, his wife was still young. In the absence of any proof of infertility, it was a puzzle why she would suggest a concubine. But Madam obviously had her own rea-

31

sons. She knew that the pressure of finding a concubine for her husband would come sooner or later from the in-laws. She might as well be generous and accept the credit. She also knew the habits of high officials in Beijing. Once they became well-to-do, they would frequent the houses of disrepute. Why not let him find a healthy girl who could bear him sons instead of squandering his energy in those terrible places?

The Madam was confident, being a solid Confucian scholar, her husband would provide her the respectability and authority of a wife in the family with all the associated privileges even as he sought sexual pleasure with another woman. And his father would see to it that she would be well treated, according to the Confucian tradition. There was no point in her husband discussing it further. She had made up her mind.

Shiyi consulted his father, as his wife had anticipated, about what he should do in such a serious matter. The criteria in searching for a concubine were quite different from those for a wife since only poor families would allow their daughters to become concubines. Most concubines were subjected to the whims of the wife unless the husband favored a particular concubine by ignoring the convention. In a society in which most aspects of personal life were prescribed by the imperial court, only the wife of a court official could be conferred a rank commensurate with the official title of her husband. A concubine could gain an official rank only when her own son became a successful official and secured a rank for her. But then he must simultaneously secure an identical rank for his father and his father's wife so that they would not be out-ranked by the concubine. Madam was secure of her ongoing position.

The matchmakers would look for a healthy and good-natured girl who could fit well with the Liang family. They did not hesitate to brag about the bright future of being the concubine for a man with the highest scholastic honor; a man whose wife was childless. "This is an extraordinary opportunity for a girl with refined qualities. If she plays it right and produces many sons, she can reap rewards beyond imagination," the matchmakers would tell the families of promising prospects. Though it would be extremely helpful, beauty was not the first criterion. Any man who looked for a woman of beauty alone would know where to find her without the benefit of matchmakers.

In the summer of 1894, Shiyi took a refined girl from the Pan family in nearby Shunde County as his concubine. Unlike his wife, this concubine had "loosened feet," a sign that her parents had at one time attempted to practice foot-binding on her but later abandoned the tedious effort. In the old days, this would have been an admission of declining family fortune, conceding that the girl might not be able to avoid hard labor. Lately this was a practice of "emancipated" parents who abhorred the inhumanity of foot binding. Shiyi's wife addressed this concubine as A'er (number two) as she would address a servant, and her husband recognized the admonishment. But their neighbors politely called her er-tai (second lady).

In a simple ceremony, A'er kowtowed to Madam, as well as to her husband and his parents, to acknowledge her humble place in the family. Shortly afterwards, Liang Shiyi journeyed with the second lady to Guangzhou on their way to Beijing.

Devils From the Ocean

It was very hot in Guangzhou in August 1894, when Liang Shiyi arrived with his second lady. But hotter still was the temper of the public in greeting the news of the declaration of war between China and Japan over Korea. China was totally unprepared for war, and the reported initial setbacks stunned the populace in this southern city. Guangzhou was a hotbed for rabblerousers. It was here that the Opium War against Great Britain had started fifty-five years earlier. The people viewed with alarm the latest fiasco of another war. Patriots and progressive elements clamored for political reform to save the country. One of the most outspoken critics of the imperial court was Kang Youwei, then based in Guangzhou.

Amid this frenzied atmosphere, Shiyi left his second lady in the care of a relative in town to prepare for their trip to Beijing and to visit his good friend Liang Qichao whom he had not seen for almost two years. They sat in his study, fanning themselves and talking of old times. When it seemed appropriate, Shiyi approached a tender subject. "Qichao, I'm on my way to Beijing. I hope you will come next spring for the national examination. You should not waste your talents by staying away from the center of action."

To his surprise, Qichao replied: "Both Kang Youwei and I will storm Beijing and try for the Jinshi degree next year. You know that Kang passed the provincial examination and received the Juren degree last year."

Shiyi nodded, "I know. My father also passed that examination. I'm glad the two of you have changed your minds."

"We have no choice," Qichao explained. "We have thought through the strategy for political reform carefully, but no one in Beijing would listen to us. We have to establish our credentials by passing the highest level of government examinations."

"That has been my position all along," Shiyi said. "Even though the civil service examinations fail to prepare qualified officials to meet the challenge of modern world, it is important to go through them to reach the top before you can influence public policy."

"We still hope to educate the public through persuasion," Qichao replied. "Kang Youwei is planning to start a newspaper soon. I think that we can do both."

"I hope you assess the situation realistically," Shiyi cautioned. "If you make one false move, you will be crushed and all your effort will be in vain."

"Unfortunately, our country is in a very perilous situation. There's no time to waste on personal consequences." Liang Qichao spoke with the impulsiveness of a 21-year-old.

Since Shiyi was four years older, he always treated Liang Qichao as a younger brother. Sensing the frustration of Qichao, he persisted in his unsolicited advice, "Qichao, the arduous quest for peace and prosperity for China requires patience and understanding. There is no short cut for success when the nation and its leaders are not ready."

At sundown, the evening breeze cooled the air. They shared some food in a near-by restaurant. Their conversation extended late into the night. There was much to say, much to consider.

"The hour is late for saving the country, Shiyi. Not so long ago, China considered itself as the center of the universe surrounded by barbarians. China's very name, zhongguo, means a 'central nation' with an ethnically cohesive population and a universal culture."

Shiyi agreed. "The early Qing rulers gave special personal attention to state affairs, as exemplified by the wisdom of Emperor Kangxi, the dedication of his son Emperor Yongzheng, and the energy of his grandson Emperor Qianlong. Even the fine porcelain vases and artistic vessels we now prize attest to the high status of culture under those rulers."

Qichao sipped his tea. When he spoke, Shiyi sat back and leaned against the wall, prepared to listen. He recognized a change in Qichao's voice, his need to expound on his thoughts.

"Toward the end of Qianlong's reign, when he toured the empire through the grand canal as far south as Lake Tai in the Yangzi River Valley, the social and economic problems growing in the midst of peace and stability were evident."

The deterioration of living conditions in China had been exacerbated by the rapid rise of population to 300 million in the 1790s. While China benefited from the expansion of foreign trade, Western traders who purchased large quantities of silk and tea and other goods were eager to sell their manufactured goods to China. In 1793, King George III of England dispatched a special mission to Beijing, ostensibly to congratulate Emperor Qianlong on his birthday, but in reality to promote trade and diplomacy.

Shiyi nodded and took another sip of his tea. He wondered, briefly, if A'er was comfortable in the company of his relative.

"Are you listening, Shiyi?" Qichao was bemoaning the attitude toward trade and official missions from Western maritime powers to keep all foreign traders from having contact with the Chinese population and to prevent all foreign officials from having any contact with Beijing. "The court's determination to keep the Yangguizi—devils from the ocean—out of China symbolized the Chinese mentality of complacency."

Liang Shiyi sat quietly and thought before responding. "I'm very proud of our Chinese cultural tradition, Qichao. And the Qing officials have shown some short-sightedness in these matters. With hindsight, it is easy to see that China lost the golden opportunity to open itself to the West during the reign of Emperor Qianlong. We are now paying dearly for such a mistake."

"Yes," Qichao responded in agreement. "We would now be dealing with the Westerners on more or less equal footing. But the inward-looking imperial court would never allow that to happen."

* * *

After they had dinner in a restaurant, Shiyi went to the home of his relative. He was greeted by A'er but he was still lost in reflection about the fate of China. He thought about the war with Britain over opium which had such an important impact on China and its people.

"May I share your thoughts, husband?" A'er asked, moving about in the candle-light.

He looked at her. She smiled back. He wondered if she would understand. Did she want to know more about what this new life meant?

He sat across from her. "If you want to hear what I am thinking, I can tell you. I don't want, though, to keep you from being interested in other things."

"I will never be disinterested in other things," she said. "I am lonely here. I will be happy to hear your thoughts."

"I was thinking of the history of our country, what happened before you and I were born, but the night is sweet and tempts me with other thoughts."

"I am in full attention."

* * *

At daybreak, Shiyi heard a noise outside the room. "Are you awake?" Shiyi recognized the voice. Fortunately, his relative, who owned a herbal medicine shop, had already left for work. That saved Shiyi the embarrassment of this inconsideration to his host. He climbed out of bed and threw on his robe. "I thought you weren't coming back?" he said to Qichao, opening the door."

"I needed to talk to you. There's so much more to say, and our time together is fleeting."

"Fleeting?"

"I could not sleep well last night. We have only a few more days together."

Behind them in the half-light of the morning, stood his second lady. Shiyi introduced her to Qichao.

"We'll have tea and some biscuits, Shiyi said, looking at her. He admired the light on her skin and the silky darkness of her hair.

Qichao took a chair near the window. Clearly, he was ready to talk. He lamented the inaction of the imperial court to deal with foreigners over half of the century. Indeed, in the last third of eighteenth century, the foreign traders were allowed to deal with the local authority here in Guangzhou, but were permitted no further north.

By then, the complexion of trade at Guangzhou began to change as private traders from Britain were engaged in the lucrative traffic of opium smuggling while regular trade, under official auspices of the East India Company, declined. When Emperor Daoguang ascended to the throne in 1821, opium had superseded regular goods as the British import to China. The emperor was eager to shore up the declining fortune of his empire and decided the opium trade must be stopped. In December 1838, he appointed Lin Zexu as Imperial Commissioner to end the opium trade in Guangzhou.

Shiyi glanced at his second lady. She sat very still, waiting for the water to heat. He didn't know if she understood what Qichao was saying, but she asked no questions.

"Lin Zexu was a man of impeccable character." Qichao finally came to someone he could cheer. A Jinshi degree holder who had served in Hanlin Academy, Lin was the powerful Governor-General at Wuhan. After the new appointment, he immediately positioned himself in Guangzhou to deal with the problem. Commissioner Lin was very much aware of the new technology in British warfare and sought to learn more about the Western maritime powers. He hoped to avoid a clash with Britain through moral exhortation, including appeals to Queen Victoria, all of which went unheard. In March 1839, Lin ordered foreign traders to surrender all their opium in three days and sign a bond pledging not to engage in the illicit traffic in the future. He never once mentioned, nor ever intended, to offer monetary compensation for such immoral import. If his order ran directly against the economic interest of foreign powers which were behind the opium trade, so be it. On June 3, 1839, in the presence of high officials and foreign spectators, Lin supervised the destruction of over 20,000 cases of opium.

A'er carried a tray with two cups of tea and some biscuits to her husband and his friend.

"The people of Guangzhou were jubilant as they thought that they had scored a moral victory. However, the British government lost no time in striking back against Lin's actions." Qichao seemed to waver between jubilance and despair. He recalled the first salvos of British naval power and technology struck China in June 1840. Bypassing Guangzhou, the expeditionary force sailed north and inflicted blows on the interior of China. The war went on intermittently until the formal Treaty of Nanjing was imposed by Britain upon China at gunpoint on August 24, 1842. The general tenor of the treaty included an indemnity for military expenses and for the destroyed opium, opening of five ports to trade, cession of Hong Kong, and a fixed tariff to preclude future protective custom duties imposed by China. The treaty also allowed British Consuls to have jurisdiction over their own subjects and allowed British warships to anchor at five ports to protect commerce. It further gave Britain the most-favored-nation status whereby China would grant the British whatever rights might be conceded to other powers at a later time.

Shiyi was striving to be polite, but already the room had grown oppressive. A'er noticed the beads of sweat on his brow and brought a small fan to him. Swinging the tiny fan in his hand, Shiyi said. "I appreciate your enthusiasm, Qichao, but I have had enough of the history of China."

Qichao ignored him. His face was flushed and his eyes wide. Shiyi knew it was useless to interrupt. "After the opium war, the Chinese national psyche changed from boastful superiority to humility and shame. Over confidence gave way to despair. Nothing seemed to work to fend off the foreign devils any more." After a pause, Qichao continued: "The opium war against Britain not only exposed the political ineptitude of the Qing court but also the attitude toward the foreigners. The worst of all was the finger pointing after the debacle which lasts until this day."

Shiyi sat quietly for awhile. His second lady mirrored his solitude. Finally he spoke. "It is painful to trace the deterioration of our beloved country. Guangzhou has been a constant reminder of the best and the worst of the Chinese people in confronting Westerners. They are patriotic, but also ignorant. With the best of intentions, the people of Guangzhou caused the serious diplomatic dilemma for the Qing court."

Shiyi dipped his fingers in a small bowl his second lady had placed on a table beside him, and wiped drops of water across his forehead. He was growing impatient with Qichao. He gestured to the tea, as if to give his friend a respite, but Qichao continued his discourse which was familiar to both of them.

After signing the Treaty of Nanjing in 1842, four of the five ports were opened on schedule to foreign trade, residents and consulates. When the French and the Americans requested similar treaties granting them most-favored-nation status, the Qing court prudently complied with their requests. However, the residents of Guangzhou steadfastly refused to admit the British in to the city. The stubbornness of the people in Guangzhou became the nagging "Canton-city question" to the British. Out of common interest in expanding trade to all parts of China and in demanding a resident minister in Beijing, all three Western nations proposed opening negotiations in 1854, but by that time, the officials were in no mood to grant any extension of foreign footholds in China.

Qichao got up and paced for a few moments and then walked to a chair and sat down. Both men leaned back against carefully placed cushions. At this early hour, the heat was overwhelming. It was difficult to find a comfortable space.

After a few moments, as if conversation would distract them from the heat, Qichao began again: "The British and French governments formed a joint expeditionary force in 1857 which successfully stormed the city of Guangzhou and captured the governor-general stationed there. What a shame!" Having settled the Canton-city question, the expedition proceeded north to demand satisfaction from the imperial court.

The Russian government had sent an emissary as a mediator for the conflict. After much negotiation, the Treaty of Tianjin was signed in 1858, granting all the Western requests. However, Emperor Xianfeng, who had ascended to the throne in 1851, remained opposed to the establishment of diplomatic missions in Beijing in spite of the treaty. Running out of patience, the Anglo-French forces charged into Beijing in 1860 and burned a Western-styled summer palace in a Beijing suburb. The emperor had taken refuge in another summer palace in Rehe and had left his younger brother Prince Gong to take charge of the peace settlement. On October 24, 1860, Prince Gong accepted the Convention of Beijing dictated to him, which included the cession of Kowloon Peninsular north of Hong Kong harbor to Britain. Claiming its reward for mediation, the Russian government secured a Supplementary Treaty of Beijing by which the Russians won extensive new territorial and commercial concessions and the benefits of most-favored-nation.

Shiyi loosened his robe and added sadly: "This interlocking most-favored-nation treaty system became an ironclad bondage which choked any hope China had to shake off foreign controls for a long time."

Shiyi reached again for his tea. It was cold and tasteless, but it was cool to his tongue. He hoped Qichao had completed his thought, but knew his friend could always find more to say.

As if on cue, Qichao began again. "Just look at the deterioration of the Qing empire. It fumbled time and again. Worst of all, the opium trade sapped the vitality of a large segment of our society and the unequal treaties have eroded the economic foundation of our nation. That's why it's so important to educate the people if we want to stop the downward spiral of our country," Qichao said in a defiant tone.

With sweat streaming down from his forehead, Qichao took a handkerchief to wipe his face as he continued, "Unless we can make great strides in modernization, China will stay in the dark forever while the outside world moves ahead without us."

"I understand," Shiyi commented. "Even now few high officials understand the root cause of our weaknesses. We should not be afraid to trade with foreigners if it serves our self interest. We need to influence the officials of the imperial court when we get to the inner circle of the ruling elite in Beijing."

"But the high officials are paralyzed by inaction." Qichao moaned. "Just see what has happened in the imperial court in the last twenty-five years. We must mobilize the people to take action."

Although he didn't speak, Shiyi recalled more of China's past. Emperor Xianfeng died a year after being forced by the Anglo-French forces to flee to Rehe. Because his wife was childless, he was succeeded in 1861 by his young son from a concubine, who was a woman of remarkable ability and scheming mind. With the assistance of Prince Gong and the head of the Imperial Guard, Manchu General Ronglu, this concubine wrested power from two other princes by the sheer strength of her personality and intelligence. She made Prince Gong the prince regent, and pronounced herself and the wife of the late emperor co-regents of the young emperor. As Empress Dowager Cixi, this strong-willed concubine exercised the real power behind the throne in the thirteen-year reign of Emperor Tongzhi. In early 1861, Prince Gong advised the imperial court to set up a new Foreign Affairs Office (Zhongli Yamen), and to appoint himself the Director. The Western diplomats finally had a channel of communication to the Qing court.

In his own way, Shiyi also had his eyes on modernization. He said to Qichao, "I recognized the importance of modernization when my father took me to Hong Kong in my early teens. Some of the things in the British colony impressed me. I liked their municipal management, the clean streets and efficient garbage collection. But I also sensed that the British looked with contempt on the Chinese. My father used to say that he often heard the snort of foreigners when he lived in Hong Kong."

"Your observation of the attitude of the Westerners is true," Qichao agreed. "Now even Japan joins ranks with the Western powers in seeking special privileges in China. With the Sino-Japanese war, Japan has finally got an upper hand to force its way in China."

Qichao leaned forward, saying earnestly to Shiyi, "Our ideas of saving China from ruin are very similar. Why don't you join the reform movement of Kang Youwei?"

Shiyi was silent. He had not resolved many conflicts in his own mind. After long deliberation, he replied, "Our goals are the same, but the means we choose are different. I don't believe political reform will get anywhere when you openly challenge those in power."

* * *

The next day, Liang Shiyi invited Liang Qichao to visit his relative who ran the small herbal medicine shop. The relative had a back room in the shop where Shiyi's second lady could rest comfortably while waiting for Shiyi. As Shiyi and Qichao walked past a vendor hawking watermelons, they quickened their pace to avoid the flies hovering over a puddle of melon juice. When they got to the pharmacy, the storefront was filled with people waiting to pick up prescriptions. They overheard one customer say to another, "We used to be invaded by the Xiyanggui (devils from the western ocean) with red hairs and green eyes. Now even the Dongyanggui (devils from the eastern ocean) with our culture and our race are doing the same thing to us."

Emboldened by this remark, another customer went further: "It took the army so long to get rid of Taiping, even with the help of the foreign devils. How can you expect the Qing army to resist Japan?" The two customers were reminiscing about the Taiping rebellion that began in 1850 and was ultimately suppressed in 1864, with the help of a mercenary army led by officers from the Western maritime powers. Shiyi and Qichao looked at one another. Making such comments in a public place was daring since the comments bordered on punishable treason. But the people in this southern city seemed to be able to get away with it. Perhaps the officials themselves were not as loyal to Beijing as they professed.

Inching their way through the crowded storefront, Shiyi and his friend went to the back room where his second lady was waiting. After greeting her, Shiyi turned to Qichao in the privacy of the small room. He sighed, "What we heard in the storefront, Qichao, is the discontent of the people. It's far more serious and widespread than the imperial court in Beijing realizes."

The second lady looked from one to the other politely, but she pretended, again, not to listen to their conversation as she was not supposed to be interested in men's affairs. Deep in her heart she wished that she could understand what her husband was talking about so intently.

Qichao took a chair in the corner. "The map of China resembles a mulberry leaf. Now the leaf is shrinking as if it were bitten by silkworms. There's no end in sight." But he added, "When people in the street speak openly, there is hope that someday the entire nation will wake up to meet the challenge. Our children and grandchildren may yet live in a better country because we have labored to make it so."

The next morning, Shiyi and his second lady left Guangzhou by boat. Their immediate destination was Hong Kong, but they had begun a journey into the unknown. This was Shiyi's fourth trip to Beijing, but her first trip beyond Guangzhou. When they arrived in Hong Kong and transferred to an ocean liner heading for Tianjin, they saw many Westerners waiting to board the same steamship.

"Don't be frightened," Shiyi whispered. "Not all foreign devils are bad. You may even meet some of them."

"I would not care to," his second lady answered, "I have no reason to want to meet them." She appreciated his humor but didn't know how to reciprocate.

"You don't have to worry about that. They will be in the staterooms for the first class, and we will have to be satisfied with separate sections for men and women in the third class." She looked at him. "I'm sorry. This voyage is not a romantic setting. We must take a third-class berth." Shiyi wondered how his second lady would manage by herself while they were at sea.

Since there were no railways connecting the major cities in China at the time, the most reliable means of transportation was by foreign steamship that sailed from Hong Kong to Shanghai and then to Tianjin. Although the steamship sailed along the coast in relatively calm water, Shiyi's second lady was seasick and stayed in bed most of the time. They met in the hall at meal time but she could eat hardly anything. She now appreciated why Madam didn't want to go to Beijing with her husband. But Shiyi himself was able to enjoy his meals, and he read books to pass the idle hours.

After arriving at the port outside of Tianjin, it would still take a torturous ride over land by horse-drawn carts to Beijing. They survived the last leg of the journey on land without a glitch.

A Surprise Interlude

Liang Shiyi and his second lady arrived in Beijing in late September of 1894. They immediately checked in at the Sanshui Hostel. The hostel consisted of several groups of single-story buildings inside a large compound. The largest group of rooms surrounding the front courtyard was operated like a hotel for single men only since women would not be admitted to the common areas and dining facilities. Several other groups of buildings, accessible by narrow lanes in the rear, were operated as rental apartments of variable sizes for families. At a moment's notice, the staff in the hostel could assemble the necessary household helpers for the renters of furnished apartments. Liang Shiyi and his second lady moved into a small apartment and started their new life in the capital city.

To the dismay of the second lady, the household helpers could not understand, let alone speak, Cantonese. Since she could neither understand nor speak Mandarin, she was immediately confronted with problems even in getting the daily necessities. Using her husband as an interpreter when he was available, but mostly taxing her own ingenuity, she often relied on gestures to make her needs known. She soon got along and even picked up a few words of Mandarin—difficult for a woman who could neither read nor write.

"You've adjusted very well," Shiyi told her one day, "The helpers genuinely adore you, particularly your high-pitched Mandarin. It sounds like music to them."

"I'm certain you are mistaken," she replied. "I can hardly survive without being laughed at all the time."

"They don't laugh at you," he added. "They laugh with you." He watched her for a few minutes. She looked away, still a bit uncomfortable when he looked at her. "You should learn to read and write some simple words. Most of the male members of the staff know enough words to communicate with you in writing, even if you don't understand each others' dialects. I'll start teaching you five words a day until you understand one thousand commonly used words."

"Is that possible?" his second lady asked.

* * *

Shiyi was concerned with the flood of bad news about the war with Japan. As soon as he settled down in the apartment, he sent a messenger with a note to Guan Mianjun, asking him to stop by Sanshui Hostel as soon as convenient. Before reporting to work, he wanted to find out what was going on in Hanlin Academy during his absence.

The same evening, Mianjun responded to his request. Holding a lantern in his hand, he had come in the darkness of the night to brief Shiyi about the most urgent task now pending in the academy. Mianjun was the very soul of discretion, and made it a point never to take sides politically. Liang could count on his unbiased opinion.

"Two petitions to the throne are being circulated for signature in Hanlin Academy," Mianjun began. "The first is a petition to recall Prince Gong from retirement to take charge of the national crisis, and the second is a request to censure Li Hongzhang for inadequate preparations in the war against Japan." Then he added, "What a twist of fate that Li Hongzhang is now placed in such a terrible position! What can Prince Gong do?"

Shiyi frowned. "Li Hongzhang tried to save our country but failed. It's difficult to see how Prince Gong can do better, given his record in the past. The situation of our country is not unlike that of a chess player with a very weak position. If you don't want to be a player, you may end up as a pawn on the chessboard. They wanted to be players and got their chance to perform the impossible mission. They will be judged for what they did or didn't do to make a difference."

Guan Mianjun was apologetic. "I haven't thought of it in these terms. That's why I refrained from placing my signature on the petitions circulated in the academy. You'll have to decide for yourself when you're asked to sign these petitions."

* * *

Li Hongzhang owed his meteoric rise in officialdom to a surprise interlude in Chinese history when almost one-third of the population in China was ruled by a self-proclaimed Christian king from Nanjing, the capital of several former dynasties. This revolt was led by Hong Xiuquan, a charismatic leader with a new vision and strong religious faith. He had organized the oppressed in the villages to shake up the establishment in Beijing, as the Qing army had been too weak to fight the populist uprisings in the decade after the Opium War. Unlike previous uprisings, which were quickly suppressed, the Taiping Rebellion, as this revolt was known, was the most serious challenge to the authority of the Qing court.

Hong Xiuquan started out like most ambitious young men of his time by trying to gain the gentry status through civil service examinations. Although he completed the first two steps in the county examination, he failed the last hurdle four times. After the second failure in 1836, he ran into an American Protestant missionary in Guangzhou, whose Chinese assistant pressed upon him a collection of translated passages from the Bible. When he failed for a third time the following year, he fell ill and had a strange vision of a venerable old man and a middle-aged man he called brother in his delirium. That dream meant nothing to him until he opened the

Beijing Odyssey

Christian tracts and read them seriously after his fourth failure in 1843. He envisioned that the two men in his earlier vision must be God and Jesus, and he himself must also be a son of God, the younger brother of Jesus.

Hong Xiuquan began to preach his message publicly and to baptize converts to his new brand of Christianity. Believing that a prophet was without honor in his native land, he went to a rugged region of neighboring Guangxi Province to recruit new converts. Although he later took a trip to Guangzhou to study the Bible, one of his converts and former schoolmate stayed there and formed a Society of God Worshippers. When Hong returned to Guangxi Province in 1847, the God Worshippers had already won more than 3,000 followers.

Hong recruited followers from all walks of life, with the greatest appeal for the poor and dispossessed. These included local miners, frustrated scholars, oppressed merchants, and others who contributed a variety of expertise to the cause. Among them were five brilliant military strategists who became the backbone of the fighting forces and important political leaders. Two of them had the most unlikely backgrounds: Yang Xiuqing, an illiterate, orphaned charcoal maker, and Shi Dakai, a member of a wealthy local landlord lineage. By 1850, Hong's movement finally attracted the attention of the authorities. Qing troops were sent to oust him but were badly defeated.

In January 1851, the God Worshippers made a formal declaration of revolution at Thistle Mountain of Guangxi Province. Hong Xiuquan was proclaimed "Heavenly King" of Taiping Tianguo (Heavenly Kingdom of Great Peace). Within two years, the Taiping forces moved into the Yangzi River Valley even though they were forced out of their original base by the larger Qing forces. In their trail, the Taiping forces won recruits through fiery proclamations, and eventually seized a large amount of booty to enrich the treasury, and stockpiles of arms and boats to boost a string of incredible military successes. In March 1853, Hong's army captured Nanjing, and Hong moved into a former palace of the Ming Dynasty to formally assume the role of Heavenly King.

The policies of Taiping were radical by any measure. The asceticism advocated by their faith required the segregation of the sexes in communal living and absolute bans on opium smoking, prostitution, and use of alcohol. They also instituted social reforms including the abolition of private ownership of land, the unification of the military and civil administration, the equality of men and women, the adoption of the solar calendar, and the propagation of Christian faith according to Hong's interpretation of the Bible.

After reaching Nanjing, Hong Xiuquan settled down to a soft life instead of following the momentum to press northward to Beijing. He yielded the de facto power to Yang Xiuqing who tried to boost his own authority by convincing the Taiping followers that he was the Holy Ghost, God's own voice, more powerful than the brother of Jesus. Worst of all, the Taiping leaders did not practice what they preached. They accumulated vast wealth and kept a large number of concubines, all contrary to the declared policies. Hong forbade people to read the works of Confucius, but he himself even explained his Christianity in Confucian terms. In a power struggle among the top leaders in 1856, Yang Xiuqing was assassinated in a palace coup and Shi Dakai escaped from Nanjing shortly afterward for fear of his life. Deprived of his most talented advisers, Hong Xiuquan faltered as a leader with no plan to advance his original goals of revolution. In 1859, his young cousin Hong Rengan, who had lived in Hong Kong, made his way to Nanjing and was named prime minister by the Heavenly King. But the vitality of the regime was too eroded to be arrested by his valiant efforts.

* * *

Shiyi vividly remembered the story of the Taiping Rebellion told by his father who had some first-hand experience of the movement. His father had said to him on numerous occasions, "But for the loyalty and sagacity of Zeng Guofan and Li Hongzhang, the Taiping rebels would have wiped out the traditional Confucius heritage and forced the outlandish culture on the Chinese people. Don't ever forget their valiant effort to defend the Confucius values and the Qing court which upholds these sacred values."

Indeed, the people ultimately rallied against Taiping when they were frightened by the extreme nature of its religious claims and social restrictions. Since the vested interests of the gentry were so intertwined with those of the Qing court, the Taiping forces encountered opposition from local militia, organized by the gentry throughout central and eastern China, to defend their homes and lands. The most active resistance came from the voluntary Xiang Army organized by Zeng Guofan, with the tacit approval of the Qing court. In May 1860, Zeng Guofan was given the jurisdiction of all military operations over four key provinces in the Yangzi River Valley near Nanjing. Upon his recommendation, the Qing court also authorized Li Hongzhang, his most trusted assistant, to organize a new voluntary Huai Army to supplement the Xiang Army.

With the Taiping forces poised to attack Shanghai and its vicinity in 1861, the only effective defense was provided by the voluntary armies organized by Zeng Guofan and Li Hongzhang. As the Taiping regime turned out to be inefficient and arrogant, particularly with its leaders adamantly opposed to opium import, the Western powers had everything to lose by not supporting the Qing court, from which they had extracted numerous treaty concessions. A mercenary army led by foreign officers was organized by British and American interests in Shanghai to fight alongside the Chinese to prevent the seizure of Shanghai by the Taiping armies. This "Ever-Victorious Army" was led first by an American adventurer, Frederick Ward, and after his death, by the British officer Charles 'Chinese' Gordon. When Hong Rengan's grand strategy to regain the upper Yangzi River Valley failed, the last hope of the Taiping regime was dashed.

In July 1864, Hong Xiuquan reportedly committed suicide, and the Heavenly Kingdom, which had lasted from 1851 to 1864, perished with him. His supporters were either slaughtered, or captured or committed suicide. Even Zeng Guofan was forced to report in awe to the young emperor: "Not one of the 100,000 rebels in Nanjing surrendered themselves when the city was taken, but in many cases gathered together and burned themselves and passed away without repentance. Such a formidable band of rebels has been rarely known from ancient times to the present."

Empress Dowager Cixi had assumed power in 1861 when the battles raged in the Yangzi River Valley. She had a better grasp of the changing world than the princes she disposed. She was too shrewd not to recognize the major contributions, as well as the potential dangers, of the voluntary armies organized by Zeng Guofeng and Li Hongzhang in the defense of the Qing dynasty. The Manchu officials at Qing court were alarmed that the system of checks and balances began to tip in favor of the ethnic Han Chinese. However, after the Taiping Rebellion, Empress Dowager Cixi entrusted the rehabilitation of China to Zeng Guofeng. With Zeng's death in 1872, Li Hongzhang inherited his unfinished tasks. After Prince Gong lost the favor of the empress dowager in 1880's, Li Hongzhang gained even more power and became the undisputed guiding spirit for restoring peace and stability to China.

* * *

Shiyi was in a mood of introspection when he said to Guan Mianjun, "The imperial court has ignored the suffering of the people for too long. The top officials do not seem to have learned a lesson from the Taiping Rebellion. Perishable food usually spoils before the worms infest. The Taiping leadership had done themselves great harm before the forces allied with the Qing court could overwhelm them. As our country suffers from so many defeats inflicted by foreign powers, can we not trace them to our own ignorance and incompetence which invited at least some of the troubles?"

"I'm afraid it will be a long time before peace and stability will be with us again," Guan said, getting to his feet. "Good-night, Shiyi. And good-night to your second lady. He walked slowly toward the moonlit courtyard, hoping he would find the night air a relief.

A Question of Responsibility

When Liang Shiyi went the next morning to Hanlin Academy to report his return to duty, he was greeted by Zhang Jian, whom Shiyi knew only slightly but admired tremendously. Jian ranked first in the Jinshi class of 1894, and was honored with the unique title of Zhuang Yuan (Valedictorian). As the newly appointed compiler, he was the center of admiration.

"I come to see you about two petitions to the throne with the hope that you will agree to co-sign them," Jian remarked after making some small talk. "These petitions are intended to ask the throne to improve the war effort against Japan."

"Who sponsored these petitions?" Shiyi asked.

"Xu Shichang is the prime mover in preparing these petitions. He has a good sense of what should be done," Zhang replied.

Indeed Xu Shichang was a savvy politician among the compilers, having received his Jinshi degree eight years earlier. Unlike Zhang Jian, he was not noted to be an outstanding scholar, but he was a good observer and manipulator of people and events. After gaining tenure in the academy for many years, his career went nowhere for lack of attractive posts that were available to him. Clearly the senior members of Hanlin Academy did not initiate the petition which could jeopardize their standing in the ruling circle. Only the compilers and assistant compilers took the matter in their own hands to vent their frustration. Without ranking officials for sponsorship, the petition must be submitted to the Censorate for transmittal to the emperor.

As Shiyi took a quick look at the contents of the petitions, he did not like their accusatory tone, but understood their dramatic effects. The first was to recall Prince Gong from retirement to take charge of the national crisis, and the second was to censure Li Hongzhang for inadequate preparations in the war against Japan. Li Hongzhang had been the principal architect of major domestic and foreign policies for over a quarter of a century, but he acted at the pleasure of Empress Dowager Cixi who wielded the real power. On the other hand, the relations between Prince Gong and the empress dowager had been alternately hot and cold. His record of accomplishments when he was in power was mixed, but in the past decade he had simply been on the sideline.

46

Beijing Odyssey

Not wishing to look for a scapegoat, Shiyi asked Zhang Jian, "Are there any concrete steps other than a change of the top advisor at the imperial court that can be proposed to mitigate the disastrous consequences of this war?"

Zhang Jian seemed to stiffen. "Xu Shichang knows what he's doing. He tries to sail with the wind. Otherwise the Censorate would block their transmittal."

The submission of a petition to the throne was a serious business. The refusal of the Censorate to transmit it was probably the least of worries of the petitioners. If the petition transmitted to the throne aroused the wrath of the emperor, the petitioners could receive severe punishment, including exile or death. It was reassuring that the prime mover of these two petitions understood that. Shiyi realized, too, that no petition could fault the emperor, much less the powerful empress dowager. By blaming Li Hongzhang, while proposing Prince Gong as a viable alternative, the petitions would at least alert the imperial court about the popular discontent.

"I'm inclined to sign these petitions," Shiyi finally told Zhang Jian after an initial hesitation. "Give me a little time to think it over."

"Come to see me when you're ready," Zhang replied, walking toward the door.

After Zhang Jian was gone, Liang Shiyi spoke to Guan Mianjun, "What a terrible bind we're in! These petitions probably will not do much good. But what else can we do?"

"Has it occurred to you that Xu Shichang might be using this opportunity to advance his own career?" Mianjun asked. "He would attract the attention of those in power if these petitions could reach the throne."

"I have faith in the integrity of Zhang Jian," Shiyi replied. "He doesn't need to call attention to himself. He's already famous as the valedictorian of our Jinshi class."

"But he's fifteen years older than you or me," Mianjun said. "Given his experience in life, he can be a valuable friend or a formidable foe."

* * *

Prince Gong and Li Hongzhang were important players in the court of Empress Dowager Cixi when she came to power in 1861. Cixi understood that China could not survive without modernizing its institutions, even though she herself would be vilified for her initiatives. As a first step, she approved Prince Gong's proposal to establish the Institute of Common Languages (Tong Wen Guan) in Beijing in 1862 for training interpreters of foreign languages. More importantly, she entrusted the major thrust of modernization to Zeng Guofeng and Li Hongzhang under the banner of the self-strengthening movement. However, the advocates of modernization in the movement were primarily preoccupied with the establishment of a military-industrial complex to produce modern weaponry for national defense. They generally regarded Chinese culture as superior to Western culture except in weaponry, and refused to accept the idea that a Western political system might contribute to the modernization of China. Even so, these advocates had to fight every inch with the reactionary old guards in the imperial court.

As a pioneering industrial project in 1865, Zeng Guofeng established the

Jiangnan Arsenal in Shanghai. In what was then considered a bold move, Zeng employed a young man named Yung Wing (a.k.a. Rong Hong) as an agent for the purchase of equipment in the United States. Yung Wing had gone to the United States as a teenager and in 1854 was the first Chinese graduate of Yale University (or, for that matter of any American university). Besides playing varsity football while at Yale, he married a Yankee schoolteacher. When he returned to China, his credentials and personal outlook were so different from other government officials that it was a giant step in trusting him to hold a job of importance in the government-sponsored enterprise.

After this initial and limited experience, the Qing court saw the advantage of employing Western-trained technicians. Beginning in 1872, a group of teenage students was sent annually to study abroad by the government, signaling its willingness to adopt Western technology, if not Western culture.

In 1870 Li Hongzhang was made Superintendent of Trade in Tianjin for the northern ports (Beiyang), a post which was created in parallel with the Superintendent of Trade in Shanghai for the southern treaty ports (Nanyang) in the 1860's. Through Li's skillful handling of foreign affairs in Tianjin, the Foreign Office was very glad to use him to forestall and minimize diplomatic activities in Beijing. With his concurrent appointment as Governor-General of Zhili Province, which included Beijing, Li was able to build a strong diplomatic and military base of influence. In fact, he took over many functions of the central government for a quarter of a century.

Following Zeng Guofeng's legacy, Li Hongzhang established the Nanjing Arsenal in 1867, the China Merchants' Steam Navigation Company in 1872, a naval academy at Tianjin in 1880, a military academy in the same city in 1885, and the Beiyang fleet in 1888. Over 90 percent of the modernization projects were launched under his watchful eye. To raise money for expanding the military industrial base, it was also necessary to develop profit-oriented enterprises such as shipping, railways, mining and telegraph under a government-supervised system. A new breed of officials was recruited to manage these enterprises.

In the decade after suppressing the Taiping rebellion, there were signs that China might yet shake off the lethargy of the recent past and forge ahead. Some optimists even dared to hope that the self-strengthening movement in China might produce results similar to the Meiji Restoration in Japan in 1868, which brought that country into the modern world.

* * *

Unfortunately, that scenario was overshadowed by the intrigues in the imperial court. Empress Dowager Cixi was deeply involved in a power struggle when her son Emperor Tongzhi died without an heir in 1874 although Tongzhi's wife was expecting a child and might yet produce an heir. Under the imperial law of succession, a nephew of the late emperor should be chosen as his successor. If the new emperor was a child, Tongzhi's widow would become the empress dowager during the minority of the young ruler. The Empress Dowager Cixi quickly used her usual strong-arm tactic to forestall such a possibility that would completely strip her of power. Against all arguments based on the imperial law, she preferred a first cousin of the late emperor, whose father, Prince Chun, was married to her own younger sister. She took the necessary precautions to cope with any opposition by enlisting the military support of the Manchu general Ronglu, the head of Imperial Guards, and of Li Hongzhang, who posted the troops at strategic locations under his command as Governor-General. During the deliberations of the Imperial Council, she played one prince against another since their sons were all eligible to be the successor. Finally she announced her choice and dismissed her opponents before they could organize any opposition.

Guangxu was four years old when he was selected by his aunt as heir to the throne. As soon as the choice was approved by the Imperial Council under Cixi's watchful eyes, the frightened princes and grand councillors petitioned the two empress dowagers in Tongzhi's reign to assume the co-regency of the new emperor. However, as long as the widow of Emperor Tongzhi lived, there remained the chance that she might give birth to a son to complicate the succession question. That problem was resolved conveniently three months later as she reportedly committed suicide. Empress Dowager Cixi no longer worried about competition.

Even though Empress Dowager Cixi won the fight over the succession, she was bruised and lost the support of several powerful princes. Prince Gong had fallen out of favor with the empress dowager because of his involvement in the execution of one of her favorite eunuchs who was known to be corrupt. Prince Gong was gradually eased out and finally dismissed in 1885. Despite her political victories, Empress Dowager Cixi grew more suspicious and conservative, trying to retain her own power at every turn, and surrounded herself with flatterers and eunuchs. She diverted funds for military preparations to private use, notably allocating the funds for the navy to construct a new summer palace with a marble ship in the lake.

When Emperor Guangxu announced in 1886 that he would assume his own rule after reaching majority in the following year, the empress dowager could count on the boy's father, Prince Chun, to suggest tactfully the postponement of his takeover. For good measure, Empress Dowager Cixi tightened the noose on her nephew further by arranging his marriage in 1889 to her favorite niece. With the intermarriage of two cousins, the son of her sister and the daughter of her brother, her clan was in full control of the court. She would never allow Guangxu to forget that he owed everything to her. She was not about to give up her power even after Guangxu reached adulthood when the regency should have ended. Throughout his life, Guangxu felt nothing but resentment toward his terrifying aunt and was greatly annoyed by his wife who always acted in her interests.

Without the support of Empress Dowager Cixi, the modernization movement could only inch forward. In the atmosphere of corruption in high places, the industrial enterprises under the state-supported capitalism bred bureaucratic inefficiency, corruption and nepotism. These industries, counted on to support China's military power, were in a tattered state. The foreign powers were able to wrest several tributary states from China—Liuchiu (Ryukyu) to Japan in 1874, Annan (Vietnam) to France in 1885, and Burma (Myanmar) to Britain in 1885.

Korea was a far more important tributary state to China than others because of its proximity to Beijing, and was regarded as a vital part of the Qing empire. After the Meiji Restoration, the Japanese government made a number of aggressive moves in Korea. When Li Hungzhang was ordered by the Qing court to be in charge of Korean affairs, he quickly used diplomacy to open Korea to the West to counteract the rising influence of Japan. Li urged the Korean government to enter treaty relations with Western powers. He also strengthened China's position in Korea by assigning a young Chinese military officer named Yuan Shikai to train the Korean army. With six Chinese battalions stationed in Korea, this young and brash Chinese officer dominated the politics as well as military operations in Korea.

In 1882, the United States signed a treaty with Korea recognizing its independence, and within a few years, similar treaties were signed by Korea with Britain, France and Germany. In 1884, a group of pro-Japanese Koreans staged a coup, but was soon defeated by the troops of Yuan Shikai. Realizing the detrimental effects of Western influence on its secret plan of making Korea its protectorate, Japan adopted a policy of encouraging China to strengthen its control in Korea on the assumption that it would later be easier to dislodge China than Western powers. Li Hongzhang fell into this trap by appointing Yuan Shikai as the Chinese Resident Commissioner in Korea, establishing a period of Chinese supremacy in Korea.

By 1894, Japan had sufficiently modernized itself to challenge China in Korea. At first Li Hongzhang was determined to find a diplomatic solution. When all hopes failed, he finally acceded to Yuan's urgent request for reinforcement. Unfortunately, one of the British steamers chartered by China, under the escort of three Chinese warships, was sunk by the Japanese Navy on July 25, 1894, and 950 Chinese soldiers were drowned in the Korean Bay. On August 1, China and Japan declared war on each other. Although the war was in effect a contest between the two countries after a generation of modernization, China was no match for Japan either on land or at sea. For all the bravado of other regional leaders in China, they did not commit the military resources under their control to the war effort. Only the voluntary Huai army organized by Li Hongzhang took the brunt of fighting in Korea, and his Beiyang fleet fought at sea with disastrous results.

* * *

It became moot to ask the question who lost the war against Japan, as Liang Shiyi well knew. Would the empress dowager now reverse herself by allowing Prince Gong to come out from retirement and take charge of the war effort? Would she leave Li Hongzhang to twist in the wind after his many years of devoted and faithful service? Those in Hanlin Academy who were willing to place their signatures on the two petitions had more than a passing interest.

When Shiyi recalled the conversation of the two customers at the herbal medicine shop in Guangzhou, he was more convinced than ever that this was an opportunity to express their sentiment of protest. He went to see Zhang Jian and boldly placed his signature on both petitions.

Zhang Jian was pleased. He spoke to Shiyi as a contemporary, "Just between us, I don't think this is the time to ask who lost the war. Both China and Japan started to modernize about thirty years ago but Japan has succeeded in making great strides while China has moved at a much slower pace. Many wrong turns have occurred in China during those years."

"I couldn't agree with you more," Shiyi responded. He could now count Zhang as one of his friends. The first petition received 57 signatures, and the second one 35. Obviously fewer people wanted to offend Li Hongzhang. It remained to be seen whether the petitions would produce any results.

Then Zhang Jian turned to Shiyi and said, "This is not the time to seek a position of influence in the government. Just look at Xu Shichang who is still waiting after eight years. When the things calm down, I intend to return to my hometown to develop the local industries."

Shiyi was surprised at Jian's disclosure. Some compilers, for financial reasons, left the Academy for the first low-ranking position available. Others preferred to wait longer, and used their connections in the academy to get a higher position in spite of temporary deprivation. But Zhang was the center of envy among his peers. He could afford to follow neither path. At the age of forty, he did not want to waste any time in Beijing. He was well known among the high officials. They would summon him back if a fantastic opportunity should arise. His family was wealthy enough to allow him to become an industrialist in his home base. He really had the best of both worlds.

"Whatever you decide to do when this war with Japan is over," Shiyi replied, "you will be important in advancing the cause of modernization of China."

"Thank you," Zhang Jian said. He accepted this sincere compliment without blushing, for he indeed envisioned himself to be nothing less than an important figure in this juncture of Chinese history.

Act of Defiance

In November 1894, Prince Gong was recalled from retirement by the imperial court to head the Foreign Office. It must have been a bittersweet moment for him even though he was confronted with an immense task of negotiating a peace settlement with Japan. He immediately initiated a move through the American minister to forestall total naval defeat, but Japan refused to go along. In the end, it was Li Hongzhang who went to Japan to negotiate the best possible terms to end the war. He proved to be indispensable in salvaging the pieces from the ruin.

Shiyi was reading a letter from his brother Shixu when his friend Liang Boyin dropped in for a visit. "I just learned that my father will come to Beijing early next year in another attempt for the national examination," Shiyi told his friend.

"I thought your father had given up the examination and would just rest on your laurels. Boyin was quite aware that the father of a favorite official could be awarded the same, or even higher rank, as that official by the emperor. He expected that Liang Shiyi would eventually be in a position to honor his father in that way.

"It's a matter of principle with my father," Shiyi said. "He's not interested in the title associated with the officialdom. He spent his whole life studying and teaching Confucianism. He still wants to prove his scholarship."

"I passed by here to let you know that Qichao came to town yesterday." Boyin told him. "Maybe we can get together soon."

"I would like to see him again," responded Shiyi. "I'll leave the time and place of meeting to the two of you." On that note, Boyin left for another errand.

After Boyin was gone, Shiyi thought about his father who'd had a hard time a year earlier when they traveled north together. This time he would be without the care of a family member. Even after arriving in Beijing, he would find the weather in early spring unpredictable. If he did not choke on dust, he would get stuck in the mud. And the dampness would certainly bother him. It was not a pleasant prospect.

* * *

Although he had anticipated a rough journey for his father, Shiyi was shocked by the exhaustion on his father's face. A'er, Shiyi's second lady, immediately sent a servant to buy a hot-water bag for Shiyi's father to keep him warm during the days

52

and a new quilt cover, stuffed with feathers, for the chilly nights.

"Father, welcome. I know it has been a rigorous trip. You must rest. A'er will be happy to look after your needs."

"I had to try one last time, Shiyi. I will prove to them, this time, that I am a worthy scholar." Shiyi had never noticed so many lines around his father's eyes. And there were lines that extended down his father's face. Shiyi had never thought of his father as aging. Now, he could not deny it.

Soon after the examination was over, it was announced by the Qing court that a peace treaty with Japan had been signed by Li Hongzhang at Shimonoseki on April 17, 1895. Shiyi heard the news and was eager to hear the details. His father did not comment immediately.

Liang Boyin stood in the doorway. "Have you heard anything about the results of the national exam, Shiyi?"

"I expect there will be an announcement soon," Shiyi answered.

"Kang Youwei and Liang Qichao have come to Beijing with more on their minds than the national examination. I have arranged a meeting with them in your favorite restaurant this afternoon."

"Yes." Shiyi was thinking of his father. He wanted to be with him when the results of the examination were announced. He wanted to reassure him that if he failed, honor would still come to him.

Shiyi continued to stay with his father long enough to be polite and then spoke with A'er. "Please make my father comfortable. I must meet Qichao and the others."

Shiyi pressed into her hand a flower he had picked in the courtyard. He wanted her to know he would miss her and that he appreciated her efforts on his father's behalf. She nodded. He is a good and considerate husband, she thought.

* * *

Kang Youwei was furious. Despite the gray skies and slight mist, Qichao sat on a bench outside Shiyi's favorite restaurant, looking dejected. When he saw Shiyi, he called, "Have you heard?"

Shiyi understood and nodded. "Where is Kang Youwei?"

Qichao looked back over his shoulder. "In there, embroiled in an argument with the proprietor. He has been told to keep quiet."

"Why?"

"Because he wants to address the group about the peace treaty."

Shiyi walked past Qichao and into the restaurant. Qichao followed. Kang Youwei was standing in the middle of a small group of people waving about some papers.

Shiyi heard Qichao's voice behind him. "Youwei lost no time in capitalizing on the anger of the Juren degree holders who have just taken the national examination. While we wait in Beijing for the announcement of the results, we are all his captive audience. He has prepared a ten-thousand-word petition to the emperor and mobilized the Juren degree holders to support his cause. It urges the Qing court to reject the peace treaty and to fight on while initiating institutional reform."

Shiyi turned to look at Qichao. "You speak as if you are not among the group."

"I certainly am. But I don't need to prove it in front of the crowd."

"How was your exam?"

"Not good. I doubt if I will pass."

Shiyi pulled Qichao off to the side. "Perhaps you are mistaken. I didn't feel confident when I took the exam."

"It is more than that."

"Will you join Youwei in his cause?"

"Yes. That's all I have left."

"Please be careful, Qichao. You're a brilliant scholar. There will be other ways for you to demonstrate that. Please, be careful."

* * *

Liang Qichao dropped by Sanshui Hostel two days later. A'er informed him that Shiyi wasn't home and tried to avoid waking her father-in-law from his nap. To her surprise, Liang Qichao asked to see Liang Zhijian. She had no choice but to receive him graciously. "Please, sit and rest. I'll speak to Shiyi's father." She appeared in a moment with tea and some small rice cakes.

Liang Zhijian finally came out to greet Qichao. As he suspected, there was something important for such a visit. "Do you have news of the examination?"

"No. I'm helping Kang Youwei circulate a petition to the throne. All Juren degree holders, here in Beijing for the national examination, are being asked to sign. I hope you will join us."

Zhijian took a quick look at this petition. He sat next to the window and leaned toward the light. There were signatures already on the document. He recognized several. "I came here principally for the examination." He explained to Qichao.

Qichao nodded. "I know."

Zhijian sat reading the document. Qichao sat in silence, waiting.

"Well written."

"Yes. And with passion." Qichao responded.

"And with passion," Zhijian repeated.

Qichao sipped his tea and reached for a rice cake, glancing at Shiyi's father.

Zhijian placed the petition on the window sill and looked up. "I spoke briefly with Shiyi about the treaty, and about this petition. It was to be expected."

He sat for a few more minutes, quietly looking at the lilac bush brushing against the window pane. Without looking at Qichao, he said, "Shiyi will be here soon."

Qichao swallowed and took another sip of tea. "I can't wait too long."

Liang Zhijian hesitated, and spoke his second daughter-in-law's name—barely above a whisper. "A'er." She appeared from behind a curtain, as if she had been waiting expressly for that purpose. "I will need my pen and ink," Zhijian stated.

She disappeared again, and carried back a beautiful lacquered box. She opened it and Zhijian lifted a brush pen and a small pot of ink, setting the pot on the sill beside him. Carefully, he added his signature, not out of conviction, but because he could not refuse this brilliant son of a good friend. "I wish we could do something more useful than submitting this petition," he said as he held out the petition to Qichao.

Eventually 603 signatures were collected from the candidates for the national examination. Since only officials with third rank or higher could address a petition to the throne directly, others had to submit them either to a ministry or to the Censorate for transmittal. The officials of the Censorate were entrusted with the power to impeach, criticize or praise any official or policy, openly or secretly, to the emperor, as well as receive petitions from plebeians. Although none of the signatories of Kang's petition were high officials, the sheer number of signatures from highly respected Juren scholars were expected to impress the Censorate which was supposed to serve as the "eyes and ears" of the emperor. However, the response was disappointing to many and devastating to a few, among the latter, Liang Qichao and Kang Youwei. The officials at the Censorate refused to present the petition to the throne. The language, they felt, was too blunt and too emotional. The petition died a premature death.

* * *

Liang Qichao sensed the first sign of unfavorable results in the examination when he learned that a messenger had reported Kang Youwei's success. Undeterred by traditional inhibition, Qichao went to see the results himself and confirmed that both he and Liang Zhijian had failed.

Rumors spread quickly among the intellectual circles that the chief examiner, Xu Tong, had targeted Kang Youwei for failure because of Kang's outspoken radical ideas for reform. Since all papers were anonymous, Tong could only look for the one with unorthodox views and an eccentric style for which Kang was famous. When the examination results were announced, Kang was successful because he had been wise enough to disguise his feelings and wrote his paper in strict conformity with traditional Confucian morality, an accepted style, but one that did not accentuate his true skill. Kang did advance to the palace examination in which the chief examiner had some leeway of recommending the ranking of the top candidates to the emperor. Even though Kang received the Jinshi degree, his ranking was so low that he was denied the opportunity for an appointment to Hanlin Academy. He only managed to obtain the lesser position as a sixth-ranked secretary in the Ministry of Public Works.

Liang Qichao stopped by Sanshui Hostel again, primarily to console Liang Zhijian who was in a state of despair. Shiyi, trying to cheer his father, took time to extend his regrets to Qichao, "If Kang Youwei could fool the chief examiner, why didn't you do the same?"

Liang Qichao's reply could only have come from an idealist who had already accomplished so much at the age of 22. "My exam paper was quite critical of the action of the imperial court and was probably identified by mistake as Kang Youwei's work. That, at least, saved the examiner the trouble of a witch hunt. My paper, intentional or not, was part of the diversionary tactic." Then he added, surprisingly cheerful, "As long as Kang Youwei succeeded, our movement will not be deprived of a powerful leader. When he gets to the center of power, I will be by his side."

Qichao's faith in Kang Youwei was unbounded. Shiyi wondered if Qichao had delayed taking the national examination for six years, after receiving the Juren degree so young, so that he could be a right-hand man under Kang. Purposeful on not, it had certainly come to pass.

* * *

The submission of a petition, instigated by a firebrand and signed by a large number of Juren degree holders assembled in Beijing, was regarded as the first mass political movement of the intellectuals by its supporters. It was an act of defiance that could lead to the immediate attention of the imperial court, or could cause the signatories to be hanged together. Neither happened. The movement was suffocated by the high officials in the Censorate and the momentum collapsed. The major flaw of such mass movement was that the Chinese intellectuals aspired to be a part of the ruling class. Ordinary citizens simply regarded the actions of these scholars as a squabble between those who were impatient while waiting to grab power and those already in power whose self-interests were threatened. The movement lacked support of the general public even though the general public was just as angry about the outcome of the war with Japan.

Some regional leaders also urged the imperial court to reject the peace treaty and continue to fight. However, they provided no more clues than the Juren holders on how the war could be won or a better peace treaty could be secured. Their public outcries only served to embarrass and humiliate Li Hongzhang. Under pressure from Japan, the Qing court ratified the Treaty of Shimonoseki on May 8, 1895. Under the terms of the treaty, China ceded Taiwan, Pescadores, and Eastern Liaoning peninsula in Manchuria to Japan, in addition to recognizing Korean independence and terminating its tribute to China.

* * *

As the terms of the treaty gradually sank into the minds of the court officials, it was widely recognized that China simply could not survive with a medieval political system. Even Empress Dowager Cixi wanted political reform, so long as she continued to retain full control of the state affairs. She was supposed to have retired to the summer palace after 1889, but she impressed upon the court officials the filial duties in the Confucian teaching. They understood that Emperor Guangxu must obey her wishes. Behind the scenes, two powerful court officials, Weng Tonghe and Xu Tong, each of whom sensed the opportunity to gain the upper hand over the other, quietly vied for the leadership of the court-sponsored reform movement.

Grand Councillor Weng Tonghe was a conservative Confucian scholar, a valedictorian of his Jinshi class, and was tutor to the boy emperor for twenty years. He began to introduce some translations of Western publications to the emperor after 1889, and was considered to be "reform-minded," a derogatory label in the minds of the arch conservatives at the court. Weng held many important concurrent posts, including Minister of Revenue. He was in a good position to influence the emperor, while maintaining good relations with the empress dowager. He knew that the support of both the emperor and the empress dowager was absolutely necessary. He cautiously promoted a moderate reform to improve administrative efficiency, relying on Chinese moral and ethical values as the foundation while accepting Western devices and implements of war.

Grand councillor Xu Tong was the leader of the reactionaries, and knew that he was no match for Weng Tonghe in an intellectual duel. However, he recognized the ambition of Zhang Zhidong, Governor-General at Wuhan, who could be his ally in wresting the leadership of the reform movement from Weng. Zhang Zhidong was also a conservative Confucian Scholar who gained a regional power base through his promotion of profitable industries. He was impatient as well as ambitious, attacking the foreign policy of Li Hongzhang as appeasement. To provide an effective shield against conservative attacks on his clamor for reform, Zhang Zhidong coined the slogan "Chinese learning for the foundation; Western learning for applications" which reaffirmed the superiority of China's moral tradition while conceding the supplementary role of Western science and technology. Xu Tong sought to bring Zhang Zhidong to Beijing to lead the reform movement, but his move was blocked by Weng Tonghe.

* * *

Shiyi watched the political development in the imperial court from the sidelines. He was discouraged by the subtle and not so subtle struggles for power by different factions in the court after Li Hongzhang was quietly eased out by the empress dowager. He was convinced more than ever that political reform could come only through the efforts of insiders with access to the center of power. But under whose leadership? He did not want to get on the wrong side of power struggles even as he was determined to be a player in the reform movement. He admired the sagacity of Zhang Jian more than ever as he, too, concluded that this was not the time to actively seek a position in the government.

Fortunately, Shiyi had done well in a very short time as an assistant compiler and was therefore promoted far ahead of schedule to the rank of compiler. As such, no time limit was set for his tenure and he would be assigned various duties related to compiling official history. He could wait out the perilous time in the safe haven of Hanlin Academy.

Liang Zhijian finally came to the realization that his own long scholastic journey had reached the end of the road. He said to Shiyi, "I've had my share of examinations. At my age, I have neither the energy nor the desire to come back again for another try." Shiyi was greatly relieved. He would now take an indefinite leave of absence from Hanlin Academy to accompany his father home, again. He intended to stay in his native village as long as necessary, until his father could return to a normal life.

When Liang Boyin heard about Shiyi's recent promotion to compiler, he dropped by to express his warm congratulations. Shiyi led him to the courtyard where they sat under a beechnut tree and shared tea and rice cakes. "Will you try to approach the Ministry of Civil Office to see if there's a suitable position for you?" Boyin inquired.

"No, my first duty is to accompany my father home. Although I'm eager to do something to effect political reform, this is not the time to get into the action. I'll wait it out in my native village for a while."

Zhijian joined them, walking slowly, his head bent in thought. Boyin stood when he saw him. "Shiyi says you are returning to your village. I'm happy for you. You've spent all your life teaching and practicing the moral principles of Confucianism. Those of us who have benefited from our association with you wish you a well deserved retirement."

"Thank you." Zhijian agreed, looking up at Shiyi and Boyin. "And my son deserves a rest. He has much to do before he leaves this long road of public service."

Liang Boyin looked at the father and the son. He knew what he heard was true. He bade them good-bye.

Introspection

"Shixu, go help your father and brother," Liang Zhijian's wife shouted to her teenage son as she looked out the window and saw her husband getting off a sedan chair carried by two coolies. Shixu responded quickly, dropping the book he was reading and running to greet his father and brother.

Shiyi and his second lady were walking behind the sedan chair. A coolie walked behind them, carrying the luggage on two ends of a bamboo pole resting on his shoulder. They were on the last leg of the journey home from the wharf where they had disembarked from the boat that brought them from Guangzhou. It was a bright sunny morning in July 1895.

Zhijian's wife greeted them with a big smile at the door. Zhijian was not happy at this homecoming since he had again failed the national examination and had decided to give up his life-long ambition. But his wife was truly relieved. "It was a burden on you." She said. "Now you can find time to think about what you want to do—to continue teaching in the private academy or do something else for a living."

Life in the village had not been easy for Liang Zhijian's wife, who had to take care of their younger children with very little help. The village did not have a store. The farmers brought their vegetables to an open market on the main street every five days, and meats every ten days. Since cattle were not bred for food, the only beef available was from buffalos, and then only when the animals became too old to plow the land. Pork was the main source of meat, but the cuts were usually very fatty because of how the pigs were fed to increase weight. It didn't matter to Zhijian's wife. Most women did not eat beef out of their gratitude to buffalos which helped with farming, and they disliked the fat in the pork. Even the men who liked meat, and could afford it, did not eat meat often. Most families raised a few chickens or ducks in their own yards for dinner on special occasions. Tonight would be a very special occasion. Zhijian's wife prepared a home-grown chicken for a sumptuous dinner to celebrate her husband's return.

Shiyi did not share his father's sense of failure, but found the reunion with his wife quite delicate. This was not the first time he had returned home after a long absence—in fact it was the fourth time since their marriage. However, he was accompanied this time by his second lady who was practically a stranger to his wife. How could he show his wife that, except for his mother, she was still the most important woman in his life? Proper etiquette would rule out any emotional outburst in front of other family members. With mixed feelings of tenderness and cordiality, he spoke in a subdued voice, "I trust that you have been well, Madam. A'er can now take over the household chores to give you a rest." His second lady, who stood behind him, then awkwardly muttered a few words of respect to Madam.

Not to be outdone, his wife replied loud enough for all to hear, "You need not be concerned about my health. I hope that you can now stay home comfortably for a while after your long trip." Madam was an expert in putting up a serene facade, particularly in front of her in-laws, as she was every inch the lady she wanted to be. She also knew how lucky she was that her husband treated her deferentially with the acquiescence of his mother. Most mothers-in-law vented their own frustrations at their daughters-in-law, even as they doted on their daughters. Liang Shiyi's mother was considered a saint by her neighbors since she treated her daughter-in-law so kindly. They didn't know how she had suffered under her own mother-in-law earlier years.

After the dinner that evening, Zhijian's wife spoke to him privately about the marriage of their third daughter. She had made some preliminary inquiries through a matchmaker who had recommended a young man of the Lu family in neighboring Nanhai County. Without any delay, Zhijian garnered all the facts from his wife and eventually gave his blessing to the marriage, which would take place in three months.

By tradition, the wedding ceremony was to be held in the groom's home and the newlyweds would come back to the bride's family for celebration only on the third day after the wedding. The parting of the bride from her family on the wedding day was always a source of sadness for the bride and her mother. Some mothers would warn their daughters : "You might as well enjoy your freedom for the last time under our roof. When you get married, you will trade freedom for security. You can raise your standing gradually in the eyes of your in-laws only with the birth of each son. After the passing of your mother-in-law, you may be free to run the household, but you will still be subjected to the tyranny of your husband."

Zhijian's wife was prepared for such an occasion. She asked her two older daughters to come home and stay for a week. Their oldest daughter, who had been married into the Ou family in Nanhai County, brought along her three-year-old daughter, their only grandchild. Their second daughter, who was married into the Lin family in the next village two years earlier, was also on hand for the occasion. The presence of the extended family not only brightened the wedding day, but also made the celebration on the third day a truly happy family reunion.

Shiyi discovered quite recently that his second lady had become pregnant. He was debating with himself how to break the news to the family without hurting the feelings of Madam. He decided to make the announcement without causing a big fuss at this joyous occasion. Picking up his three-year-old niece, Shiyi told the little girl, loud enough to be heard by the other family members, "You are going to have some competition for the attention of your grandparents. Your aunt will soon have a baby, too." The unexpected news, though subtle, electrified the entire family.

At the same time, Zhijian received an invitation to be Chairman of the Chamber of Commerce in Beihai County of Guangdong Province. Zhijian was not noted for his business acumen, but his Juren degree would lend prestige to the organization in dealing with local officials. After long deliberation, he decided to accept the position and to take his son Shixu with him. Tall and mature for a 16-year-old, Shixu was delighted at the opportunity to travel, which so far had eluded him.

Zhijian's wife was so used to Zhijian's absence from home that she was not surprised at his decision to leave the rest of the family behind in his native village. She was just glad that he was pursuing a new career that would help him forget his repeated failures in the national examination.

"I have labored on the Confucian scholarship all my life," Zhijian told Shiyi as they parted. "Now that I'm giving up teaching, the torch is passed to you. I trust you will not disappoint me."

"I will try. You have taught me well, Father."

Since childhood, Shiyi had heard much of his father's affirmation of faith in Confucianism. In his youth, Zhijian acquired his view of Confucius from Master Zhu Ciqi, a traditionalist in the late Qing period who had many followers in south China. He was noted for his bent on political philosophy, presumably blending the best of the past and avoiding controversies in his teaching. His reputation was enhanced by the support and patronage of then Governor-General at Guangzhou.

As a historian, Shiyi was struck by the twists and turns of Confucianism through the centuries. He understood, far better than his father had taught him, the political and social forces which shaped the Confucian doctrine. Yet he upheld the orthodox Confucian view of respect for authority. Liang Shiyi took to heart that he must work through the existing system even as he tried to effect political reform. As he examined the past, he could come to no other conclusion.

* * *

Confucius was a political philosopher born in 551 B.C. In an era of feudal states, he was one of many philosophers who tried to convince contemporary rulers to reform the world. He won recognition as Grand Master Kong (Kong Fuzi, which became Confucius in Latin). Confucius edited a vast number of ancient books that presumably recorded a remote and legendary period of enlightened government in Chinese history. His conversations with his students, in the form of Socratic dialogues, were recorded in the Analects. Among his followers, Mencius (Latinization of Meng zi, or Master Meng), who lived in the third century B.C., was noted for his eloquent exposition of Confucian philosophy that man by nature was inherently good, and only lapsed into evil through lack of education. Thus the education of youths in proper Confucian moral principles became the first duty of scholars and parents. In some respects, the contributions of Mencius to Confucianism were no less than those of Apostle Paul to the propagation of Christianity.

When the First Emperor of the Qin Dynasty conquered all feudal states and unified China in 221 B.C., he adopted the ideas of the Legalists, a contemporary philosophy which advocated a legal system based on force and severe penalties. The First Emperor ordered the burning of ancient books and the burying alive of Confucian scholars. When the Qin Dynasty was overthrown, less than two decades later, the ancient classics were salvaged from oral versions or hidden private collections of scholars who had escaped the persecution. The succeeding Han Dynasty, in theory, established Confucianism as the state doctrine, but in practice upheld Qin's autocratic system of government based on the Legalists.

Though officially suppressed, the undercurrents of the Legalists created a curious and long-lasting contradiction in Chinese society. On the one hand, society was based on the rule of moral authority and governed by an elite that honored learning above anything else. Justice and benevolence were prominent in the official doctrine of government, but were absent in the legal tribunal; force and severity formed the basis of the legal system for ordinary people, a legal system based on fear as the only deterrent, a legal system that exercised cruel and barbarous penalties. Scholars and the elite were not subjected to such cruelties, except when they committed crimes against the ruler. Such dichotomy passed on from dynasty to dynasty even as Confucian scholars refined and reinterpreted the Confucian philosophy.

As the Confucian concept of human nature colored the organization of Chinese society and the governance of the state, the Confucians took the approach of exhorting personal virtues rather than building lasting social institutions. The rulers were supposed to have derived their tenure by the "mandate of heaven," which would be withdrawn if they failed in their virtues. By suppressing all other competing philosophies, the Confucian moral principles became the foundation of proper human relationships between individuals: between the ruler and the ruled, father and sons, elder and younger brothers, husband and wife, and mutually supporting roles of friends.

In the late Han Dynasty, a prominent Confucian scholar, Zheng Xuan, bundled the ancient texts together as the Five Classics. He also grouped together the Analects, the teaching of Mencius, plus two selections from other ancient books into the "Four Books." The Five Classics and the Four Books became the basic precepts of Confucian canon needed for leading a moral life. With the support of subsequent rulers, the interpretation of Confucius by Zheng Xuan and his followers became known as the Han School, which dominated as the orthodox doctrine for over ten centuries.

In the 12th century, Confucianism got a new theme under the influence of several celebrated philosophers in the Song Dynasty. Zhu Xi, the last of this group, synthesized their works to modernize Confucianism and present it as an ethical system divorced from supernatural sanctions. The followers of Zhu Xi, known as the Song School, argued that Zhu Xi did not invent anything new but only grasped the true meaning of the ancient classics that had eluded the scholars of the Han School. An emperor in the late Song Dynasty declared that only Zhu Xi's interpretation could be admitted as the orthodox Confucian doctrine. Modern Western scholars call this doctrine Neo-Confucianism. If Zhu Xi could know that his work is called anything but orthodox Confucianism, he would protest from his grave.

The early Qing emperors adopted Zhu Xi's teaching as the state doctrine, but rejected the extreme individualism as advocated by some of Zhu Xi's subsequent followers. In 1672, Emperor Kangxi decreed a Sacred Edict based on Confucian philosophy as the foundation for the governance of the state. The edict was later incorporated as a part of the county examinations that all candidates had to memorize verbatim. The local gentry, imbued with the maxims in the edict, were required to deliver court-dictated lectures twice a month to insure that Confucianism would be spread to the people at the village level.

Zhu Ciqi, under whom Liang Zhijian studied, was a master of Confucian orthodoxy according to Emperor Kangxi's Sacred Edict. His popularity was derived as much from his touting the official lines of the Qing establishment as from his charismatic personality. To Liang Zhijian, this orthodoxy was the dogma that he would never question. He simply ignored the existence of other interpretations.

Not all students of Zhu Ciqi took the cue from the master. Kang Youwei, too, at one time studied under him. After he left Zhu's circle, he developed an independent line of thought and reached the conclusion that Confucius was a social and political reformer who would not hesitate to upset the status quo. Kang's ideas attracted a large number of followers who wanted radical political reform.

Liang Shiyi was aware of his father's dogmatic instinct, but he never desired, nor dared, to dispute his father. If his own interpretation of Confucianism seemed radical to his father, it was pale in comparison with Kang's utterances. Liang Shiyi never strayed very far from the orthodoxy and did not appreciate Kang's outright use of Confucius to challenge the actions of the imperial court. He could live with his father's admonition with a clear conscience.

* * *

Just before Zhijian left for Beihai, Shiyi was approached by the Fenggang Academy in his native county to become its principal lecturer. The academy had a long and glorious past, and was poised for renewal. Shiyi's presence would add tremendous prestige to the academy. The timing of the offer could not have been better since Shiyi had intended to stay in his native village, at least until the birth of his first child. He accepted the offer with great enthusiasm.

It was a strange irony that Liang Zhijian, the perennial scholar who could find a Confucian quotation for every human endeavor, suddenly became a worldly man; while his son, Shiyi, a man of action in the national arena, would now be confined to teaching in his native village. Shiyi comforted himself with the thought that it was probably for the best. His father could now apply the Confucian moral and ethical principles to the affairs of men.

As Shiyi assumed the position of principal lecturer at Fenggang Academy, he wanted to improve the learning skills of his students and to project a kinder image of teachers. Traditionally, the students were asked to copy and then read aloud passages from the classics to facilitate memorization. At the start, he told his students, "Don't copy long passages from the classics. Instead, analyze them and jot down the pertinent points in an outline form. Submit a critique to me for review tomorrow."

He followed up by asking stimulating questions and soliciting answers from his students. "Can you give me an answer?" Shiyi would plead. The students looked at each other in surprise while he gently probed the depth of their understanding.

"We're not used to such an approach," one of his students boldly explained. "Can you go slow with your new ideas?"

"Of course," Shiyi replied. "I shall be patient in waiting for an answer. Don't be afraid. Eventually you will get used to it."

Two months later, this same student came to thank him. "Your innovation has improved my comprehension tremendously. I express the sentiment of my classmates as well when I say that you will long be remembered as a legend in the academy."

* * *

In February 1896, Shiyi's second lady gave birth to a daughter who was named Houyin (Good News). Some neighbors thought this was a cruel joke since most families would consider the birth of a daughter bad news indeed. Another one added: "Why fuss with the name of a daughter? It would make no difference any way." He was referring to the custom that a young maiden was known as a daughter of her father, a married woman as the wife of her husband, and an old lady as the mother of her sons—never by their own names!

Not to be outdone by the second lady, Shiyi's wife announced that she too was pregnant. Shiyi was happy for her. A son was born to her in August, but the infant died in less than a month. Shiyi tried to console his wife with a subtle message, "Madam, don't be overwhelmed by your sadness. Now that you have broken the barrier of child-bearing, there will be more sons in the future."

After one year at Fenggang, Shiyi decided to return to Beijing to resume his duties at Hanlin Academy. He wanted both his wife and his second lady to accompany him this time. So he brought up the subject with his wife.

"A section of the new railway from Tianjin to Beijing has just been completed," Shiyi informed Madam. "The travel to Beijing will be more comfortable than before, and I hope you'll go to Beijing with me."

Much to his surprise she agreed. "Yes, I will go with you if I can manage to take a maid who is willing to come along." Madam was now eager to get another chance to produce a son, but was afraid that she might not be able to find a servant in Beijing who could speak Cantonese dialect.

"Of course, Madam," Shiyi was sympathetic. "I'll leave this matter to your discretion."

In January 1897, Shiyi and his wife, his second lady and one daughter, plus a maid, whom they called Mai San, were on their way to Beijing.

A Rude Awakening

"This place is really miserable." Shiyi's wife complained to no one specifically, but her discomfort made those around her anxious. Shiyi and his family had barely set foot in Sanshui Hostel when Madam experienced the inconvenience of their new home in Beijing. She suffered neither fools nor wise men gladly when she encountered anything she didn't like.

"Don't you enjoy the beautiful scenery of trees laden with snow in the courtyard?" Shiyi asked, trying to amuse her as he knew she had never seen snow before. But she was not pacified and longed for the warmer climate in their native village. The second lady was busy taking care of her baby daughter, but not so occupied that she could ignore the complaints of Madam. Even though the maid was in the room unpacking the luggage, she took it upon herself to soothe her husband's wife, "The hot tea may warm you up a little, Madam." She gently passed a cup of tea to the Madam before turning to their husband, "Would you like to have a cup too?"

"No. Thank you." Shiyi sat silently, trying to calm himself. He knew Madam had agreed to come to Beijing for one and only one reason: to be with him and produce a son. She was not interested in anything outside of her living quarters. There was no way to change her mood when she was not in a mood to change. "This," he thought, "may be a very long year."

When Shiyi reported to Hanlin Academy, he was given rotating assignments intended to broaden the experience of new compilers. He first served at Wuying Hall in the palace compound, and then in the National Archives. The dull routine was broken only with periodic outside activities. One such occasion was an invitation to serve as a proctor of the palace examination and to collect the examination papers. Trivial as the title might sound, it was a great honor for prestige-conscious officials in addition to the not-so-insignificant honorarium for a poor Hanlin scholar.

At home, however, it was anything but routine. The year of 1897 was full of excitement for Liang Shiyi and it went by very quickly. Less than six months after their arrival in Beijing, both his wife and his second lady were pregnant. Perhaps competition did increase productivity. It was anybody's guess who would produce a son first to gain the favor of her husband. In March 1898, his wife gave birth to his second son Dingji, and the household was filled with joy. However, Madam had trouble with breastfeeding, and had to feed the baby with rice broth. Cow's milk was not readily available and was considered unsafe. Her maid ventured a suggestion. "Most families with your circumstances would hire a wet nurse to feed the baby. Why don't you do that?"

"Mai San, you don't know your master," Madam replied. "He is firmly against it." She had already brought up the subject with Shiyi when their first son was born, but he objected to it as a matter of principle. Most women who became wet nurses either sold their own babies, if the newborn was a son, or allowed the family to practice infanticide if the newborn was a girl. Shiyi thought the prevalent use of wet nurses by well-to-do families would simply encourage such terrible practices.

Eighteen days later, Liang Shiyi's second lady delivered Shiyi's third son, Dingwu. Losing no time to pacify Madam, the second lady offered to nurse both infants since she was able to do so. Gradually Madam recovered from the depression that she had sunk into after the birth of her son. Shiyi could only count his good fortune; he hated to imagine what might have happened if the circumstance had been the other way around. While he had found both women accommodating in his bed, his second lady was, by far, the most accommodating in his life.

* * *

In April 1898, Liang Qichao dropped by for a visit while another national civil service examination was taking place. "What made you decide against repeating the exam this time?" Shiyi inquired. "I certainly would like to see you receive the Jinshi degree."

"I'm too busy helping Kang Youwei to do something else," Liang Qichao replied. "He's now organizing the National Protection Society and is trying to enlist the Juren degree holders who are now taking the national examination in Beijing. We hope to attract several hundred members from this group, plus other officials as well." Qichao walked around the room, admiring Shiyi's children. When he paused he commented, almost as an afterthought, "We would like to enlist your support of the reform movement."

"Political reform has never been far from my mind since our days studying together in Guangzhou," said Liang Shiyi. "However, I think Kang Youwei is repeating the same mistakes he made when he organized the petition to the throne three years ago. The court officials would not listen to the plea of scholars who tried to undermine their powers. I don't wish to join his effort."

Shiyi was an admirer of Weng Tonghe, the Grand Councillor and long-time tutor to the emperor. Shiyi had known Weng Tonghe since the latter served as one of the examiners for the palace examination in 1894. Liang regarded him as an honest man who had pushed reforms as far as court politics would allow. Liang had waited patiently for the right opportunity to serve under his tutelage.

On the other hand, Kang Youwei had taken the unorthodox approach to effect political reform, first by seizing the intellectual leadership and then trying to win over the emperor. For all his authority, the emperor still had to act within the moral code of Confucianism. The school of Confucianism favored by the emperor would enhance the influence of the supporters of that school. Using the discovery by some scholars that sections of classics and historical documents held dear by the Han and Song Schools were forgery, Kang Youwei justified his own opinion that Confucius was an advocate of radical reforms and discredited the conservatives in the imperial court.

Kang Youwei had also presented, since 1888, a barrage of petitions to the throne. All were blocked by various ministries and the Censorate, except one submitted in May 1895. In that petition, he recommended methods for enriching the country, educating its people and training the military forces. That petition was deemed relatively mild and harmless by the court officials. After 1895, Kang turned his energy to sponsor and participate in "study societies" and newspapers. Within three years, many societies were organized and met frequently to discuss political reform while 30 newspapers promoting reform sprang up throughout the country. Kang Youwei initiated some of the most outspoken forums, later banned by government officials. The National Protection Society was his latest project.

Shiyi shared some of Kang's ideas of reform, those influenced by Western thought. Shiyi had read translations of Western publications and had been exposed to the British-dominated municipal governments in Hong Kong and Shanghai. Still, he detested Kang's means for achieving the end. He thought that Kang's use of a new interpretation of Confucianism to propel his political reform was disingenuous.

"I have not joined the societies espoused by Kang," Shiyi explained to Qichao. "But I have formed a study group with several Hanlin Academicians. We exchange opinions, but we don't sponsor public lectures or invite attention."

Qichao knew better than to argue. Shiyi was a patient man. He would not support a leader he did not trust, even if he did support some of the leader's philosophies.

In one of the discussion "study society" sessions, Shiyi said to Guan Mianjun, "The divisive issues raised by Kang Youwei repelled some sympathizers and hurt the reform movement." He was even more concerned about Kang's attempt to win over the emperor at the expense of the empress dowager. Shiyi disliked disunity and instability, which he regarded twin evils reinforcing each other.

* * *

Kang Youwei was a lowly sixth-ranked secretary in the Ministry of Public Works, and though his ideas of reform were not taken seriously at the imperial court, he was considered a constant irritant and public nuisance. However, after receiving one of his petitions in January 1898, a sympathetic Supervising Censor recommended that Kang be granted an imperial audience. Since Weng Tonghe was seeking ways to buttress his position as a reformer against the opposition, he saw in Kang Youwei a capable young scholar knowledgeable in Western institutions. After some initial hesitation, Weng Tonghe supported the recommendation. Little did he know he had taken a loose cannon into his camp. But Prince Gong was more prudent, and reminded the emperor, as a matter of court etiquette, he could not interview officials below the fourth rank.

However, Emperor Guangxu's curiosity had been piqued. In less than three weeks, he ordered that Youwei be allowed to present petitions to the throne any time without obstruction or delay by court officials. Emperor Guangxu found Yang Youwei's writings intriguing. At the risk of offending the emperor, Kang asserted that if radical reforms were not instituted, the fate of this emperor might be that of the emperor of the previous Ming Dynasty, who hanged himself in the ruins of his empire. Impressed with his courage to face the emperor with such declarations, Emperor Guangxu saw in Kang's reform proposals his own vision of a new China.

On the death of Prince Gong on May 30, 1898, Kang urged Weng Tonghe to forge ahead with reform at once. Weng was both annoyed and frightened by the turn of events forced upon him by Kang. He tried to persuade the emperor that Kang was dangerous and should not be trusted. By this time, however, Kang's writings had totally convinced the emperor of the need for radical changes. On June 11, 1898, Emperor Guangxu issued the first edict to set the stage for comprehensive reforms. Four days later, he dismissed Weng Tonghe from all positions with the consent of Empress Dowager Cixi who was disgusted with Weng's introduction of Kang to the emperor. Emperor Guangxu naively and mistakenly thought that the empress dowager was on his side. In fact she was disturbed by some of the proposed changes that threatened to weaken the prerogatives of Manchu rule. She also had a strong suspicion that the emperor was using political reform to wrest power from her.

The next day, Emperor Guangxu granted Kang Youwei an imperial audience lasting five hours. On the same day, Kang was appointed a secretary in the Foreign Office, a position close to the imperial court but far enough from the throne to allay the fears of the conservatives. Three weeks later, Liang Qichao was appointed a sixth-ranked official in charge of the Translation Bureau where he could fan the ideas of political reform by introducing the latest Western publications.

* * *

Liang Qichao could hardly contain his euphoria as he rushed through the door of the Sanshui Hostel to visit Shiyi. Without even taking a seat, he proclaimed, "Youwei finally broke through the barriers and gained an audience with the emperor. The emperor seems to be sympathetic to his approach and has issued the first edict on political reform."

Shiyi was alarmed. He paced back and forth across the room. Seeing his frustration, both his wife and his second lady left the room. "No one in his right mind would want to put any distance between the emperor and the empress dowager. Both must be of one mind if any political reform movement is to succeed. What you regard as barriers are powerful court officials who have the ears of the empress dowager." He stopped to look at Qichao. "It will be a rude awakening to them when they realize the threat to their interests as Kang Youwei gains access to the emperor. They will not lie down without a nasty fight. If you fail, the harm done to the reform movement will be irreversible."

Beijing Odyssey

"We're quite aware of the possible consequences," Qichao countered. "But sometimes we must be willing to take risks. Besides, bold action at this critical juncture may change the course of history."

"I cannot fault your logic. History might be changed. But are you seizing the right issues? Or the right moment? Qichao, you and Kang Youwei are playing with fire. I hope you will not perish in the flames."

* * *

Shiyi felt sorry for Weng Tonghe, who decided to return to his native Jiangsu Province after his dismissal. Shiyi rode to the outskirts of Beijing with his friend and bid him farewell. When Shiyi arrived at Hanlin Academy the next day, Guan Mianjun noticed that he was disturbed. Asked about his weariness, Shiyi replied, "Ever since our defeat in the war with Japan, court officials point their fingers at each other instead of being united for the interest of the country. It's getting worse every day. China simply cannot survive as a nation in this way."

Learning about Shiyi's trip the day before, Guan asked, "Isn't it dangerous to associate yourself with Weng Tonghe? He's been discredited by the court."

Shiyi sat down on a low bench. "I don't desert true friends when they're met with disappointment." Shiyi replied. "I only regret that I wasn't more assertive in cautioning him about Kang Youwei and in forwarding my ideas to him. Imagine if I had attempted to help him institute his idea of reform through the cooperation of the emperor and the empress dowager!"

* * *

From June 11 to September 20 of 1898, the emperor issued more than 40 reform edicts as if he finally had his chance to vent all the frustrations of his young life. Westerners wrote of this "hundred days of reform." Kang Youwei finally had his time in the sun and Liang Qichao, just as he predicted, was by his side, his chief lieutenant.

Emperor Guangxu called for drastic changes affecting all areas of government and the life of its citizens, including education at all levels, economic development in agriculture, industry and commerce, modernization of army and navy, and reorganization of bureaucracy. He also recommended modernization of the civil service examination system, abolishing the highly-styled format for essays and de-emphasizing calligraphy and poetry. His tinkering of the examination system horrified the conservative scholars. His proposal to abolish sinecure appointments alarmed the eunuchs in the empress dowager's inner circle. Believing these edicts would eventually be overruled by the empress dowager, most court officials and regional leaders were dragging their feet.

In a bold move, Emperor Guangxu appointed four radical reformers as fourth-ranked secretaries in the Grand Council so that they could coordinate important policy decisions. He had also dismissed a number of high-ranking officials, and no court official felt safe to be spared. At the urging of the conservatives, the empress dowager was poised to intervene and alerted General Ronglu, Minister of War and Governor-General of Zhili, to transfer troops from Tianjin to Beijing. The emperor, who had no control over any troops, feared there might be a coup d'etat and urgently requested help from the reformers. Out of desperation, the reformers tried to enlist the support of Yuan Shikai, a young military officer whom they thought was sympathetic to radical reforms. Yuan was now training a new army in Tianjin under General Ronglu's direction. On September 14, the emperor granted Yuan an interview and appointed him Acting Deputy Minister of War, purportedly with a vague promise that he would be promoted to Minister of War in the future. Shortly afterwards, Tan Sitong, one of the new secretaries in the Grand Council, asked Yuan to save the emperor by staging a counter coup. When he found Yuan hesitant to act, he knew the cause of the reformers was doomed.

On September 19, the reformers' scheme was reported to Empress Dowager Cixi. She suddenly returned to the Forbidden City. Two days later, she issued an edict claiming the emperor was ill and had asked *her* to resume power. She put Guangxu under palace detention and arrested six reputedly radical reformers, including the four new secretaries in the Grand Council, a younger brother of Kang Youwei, and the Censor who had recommended Kang Youwei to the emperor. On the order of the empress dowager, they were summarily executed without trial. Tan Sitong, who could have escaped, chose to become a martyr, declaring: "Since time immemorial, no revolution has succeeded without bloodshed." His voice was echoed throughout the country: let this disaster be the dawn of a revolution!

* * *

Liang Boyin rushed to Sanshui Hostel. "Shiyi. Shiyi. Li Duanfen just confided to me privately," Boyin gasped for words. "The Minister of Punishments! Liang Qichao is in imminent danger. Kang Youwei's brother has been executed! Without trial! Qichao has fled to the Japanese Legation for asylum. Li Duanfen, too, is in trouble, not only because he's been identified as a reformist, but because he's related to Qichao by marriage."

"What's happened to Kang Youwei?"

Boyin paced back and forth across the room. "He's not in Beijing. Nobody knows his whereabouts."

"Boyin, there's nothing we can do except wait, wait for new developments," Shiyi concluded. The friends said good-by. It was uncertain if they would ever see Qichao again.

Three weeks later, Shiyi learned that Qichao had managed to escape to Japan and Kang Youwei had gone to Shanghai on business just before the coup. When an order was issued for Kang's arrest, he was on board a British vessel, under the protection of the British authority. They refused to surrender him in Shanghai. The vessel carried him to safety in Hong Kong and from there he went to Japan.

The repercussions of the failure of the reform movement were widespread and severe. Although not involved personally, Shiyi was deprived of two of his most valuable mentors in Beijing. Weng Tonghe was exposed to further humiliation by being barred for life from holding any public office. Li Duanfen, the reform-minded

Minister of Punishments, was exiled to Xinjiang Territory in northwest China. And he had no idea how long Qichao would be safe.

Shiyi put down a letter he was reading when Guan Mianjun arrived unexpectedly. "What a terrible blow to all of us," Mianjun remarked, "to see those good people die or in exile because they wanted to do something to save the country."

"My heart goes to Qichao, and to our country." Shiyi sighed. What a waste of his talents! What a dark time."

Both friends sat quietly for a few moments. Shiyi picked up the letter laying on a small table. "I can only find solace in the good news from my family. Here is a letter from my father. I'll read it. Perhaps it will cheer you, Mianjun." He proceeded to read aloud:

"Since I became the Chairman of Commerce at Beihai County, I was able to negotiate with the magistrate to reduce the tax burden of businessmen. As a result, I was asked recently by the businessmen in two neighboring counties to assume the new post of Chairman of Commerce for them as well.

Shixu has developed a great deal of business skills, and many of my colleagues speak very highly of him. However, I am quite afraid that he has not been able to concentrate on his studies of Confucian classics. At the age of 19, Shixu should think seriously about the county examination, and I have arranged for him to study at Fenggang Academy back home next year. In the meantime, Deng Zishan, a respectable businessman who came here from Sanshui County, proposed to me the marriage of his daughter to Shixu. I just received the blessing of your mother and have informed Mr. Deng of our consent. Since his daughter is four years younger than Shixu, the wedding should be postponed for a couple of years. Hopefully by then Shixu will have completed his preparation for the county examination."

Mianjun nodded and smiled but his interest was clearly drawn to the other events.

The Gathering Storm

"I received a letter yesterday from my brother-in-law in Hong Kong." Liang Boyin leaned toward Shiyi, speaking in a hushed and almost conspiratorial voice. "He told me that Liang Qichao is now publishing a Chinese newspaper in Japan while Kang Youwei has gone to Canada to raise money from the Chinese, there, for the promotion of political reform in China. With the news blackout here, the Hong Kong newspapers are the only source of such information."

"I hope both of them are safe and well," Shiyi replied. "The future of China is gloomier than ever. I just received a new assignment to work in the Government Publishing Bureau. Ironically, the Government Press had been ordered closed. What's the use of editing books when they cannot be published?"

Boyin put his head in his hands, "I'm about to give up my job here and return to Guangzhou."

Shiyi comforted him, "You should wait to see what happens. It's premature to leave now."

"Perhaps I should stay, but not much longer. I need some assurance."

The political situation in the national capital was indeed muddy. After Empress Dowager Cixi officially regained control of power, she shrewdly declared that the reform itself was not in question, only the way it was carried out by Kang Youwei. To lend creditability to her intention, some moderate reforms were left in place, but it was just for show. The Imperial University at Beijing and the colleges at provincial capitals, which were established only a year earlier, were allowed to continue. The schools at provincial and district levels could also operate, if they were deemed suitable for local conditions.

But some of her decisions were damaging. She established a new power structure in the imperial court, restoring most reactionaries, particularly the Manchus, to high offices including the Grand Council. Formation of study societies was prohibited. Newspaper publishers and editors in several big cities were arrested, and private citizens were forbidden to submit petitions on state affairs. In one stroke, these very tools of freedom of expression and of the press that Kang Youwei had used so effectively to influence public opinion and gain access to the emperor, were wiped out.

Beijing Odyssey

* * *

After the coup of 1898, Empress Dowager Cixi had been anxious to depose Emperor Guangxu. The Western powers were concerned about the personal safety of the emperor, partly in sympathy with the reform movement and partly on humanitarian grounds. The Western diplomats issued repeated warnings to imperial court officials that they would be held responsible if anything threatened the life of the emperor. On the other hand, Empress Dowager Cixi and the court officials viewed the actions of the Western powers as a smoke screen for interfering in the internal affairs of China. How dare the Westerners demand that the emperor's health be examined by a French physician—a demand which was ultimately acceded to by the imperial court! And how could they claim to protect human rights of Chinese citizens when criminals like Kang Youwei and Liang Qichao were given political asylum by the British and Japanese authorities!

Empress Dowager Cixi had good reason to suspect the motives of foreign powers which took advantage of China's weakness to seek more territorial concessions. Using various pressures, some related to Chinese attacks on the missionaries, the foreign powers forced the Qing court to yield long-term leases of territories throughout the country, with one-up-manship of one foreign power over another. Jiaozhou Bay in Shandong Province was leased to Germany, Lushun (Port Arthur), was leased as a naval base, and Dalian as a commercial port, to Russia, and a new territory in Kowloon Peninsula, as well as Weihaiwei in Shandong Province, to Britain. Within a year Guangzhou Bay in Guangdong Province was leased to France. New treaties granting exclusive spheres of influence to Western powers and Japan were also forced upon China. Alarmed by this trend, the United States declared an "open door" policy for China, pleading with all countries not to deny others access to their spheres of influence. The declaration might have slowed the slicing up of China, but it lacked power of enforcement.

The tension between the Westerners and the Chinese populace was also exacerbated by the increasing number of foreign missionaries who poured into China after 1890. Their kind motives were largely offset by their lack of tact and understanding. They attacked Confucian values and traditional virtues. They also viewed Chinese politics and institutions through their own perspective. With the exception of some poor and dispossessed who became Christian converts, most Chinese hated the missionaries with a passion, and used every means, including murder, to frustrate their efforts.

* * *

In this atmosphere of hostility and fear, the Boxers United in Righteousness (Yihetuan), as they referred to themselves, began to emerge as a force in Shandong Province during 1898. They drew their name and their practice of martial arts from a variety of secret societies and self-defense units initiated by peasants and spreading across Shandong and Zhili Provinces. As the foreign powers intensified their imperial expansion, the foreigners quickly became the target of the Boxers' resentment and struggle. In 1899, the once secret organization went public and projected a new patri-

73

otic image of pro-government and anti-foreigner.

By the end of 1899, the Qing court, under foreign pressure, had removed the Governor of Shandong who patronized and subsidized the Boxers, and appointed Yuan Shikai as his successor. Yuan stood for the policy of suppression even though the imperial court repeatedly admonished him to refrain from punishing the Boxers. The main forces of Boxers were then shifted to neighboring provinces where they joined forces with local groups. The leaders declared themselves invincible and claimed magic powers. As the movement gathered strength and momentum, it moved toward Tianjin and Beijing. The imperial court had to face the problem the movement posed. Should it oppose the Boxer movement and appear to be the supplicant of the foreign powers? Or should it declare itself the patron of the movement and use this seemingly powerful force to emancipate itself from the domination of the foreign powers?

The reactionaries at the court naturally favored the latter course and openly allied themselves with the Boxers. The most vocal of them was Prince Duan, who became the new confidant and favorite of the empress dowager. On January 24, 1900, Empress Dowager Cixi appointed Prince Duan's eldest son, Pujun, as heir apparent to the throne—not to the reigning Emperor Guangxu, but to his predecessor, the late Emperor Tongzhi who was the empress dowager's own son—with the intention of deposing Emperor Guangxu at the appropriate time.

As the Boxer movement unfolded, Liang Boyin decided that time had come to leave Beijing. "I want to leave here one step before the disaster," Boyin said after coming to Sanshui Hostel to say good-bye. "I hope to come back when the political climate in Beijing is more favorable."

"Perhaps you have made the right decision," Shiyi replied, "but I will hang on to see what's going to happen."

Shiyi realized that his network of mentors and close friends was shattered by the "hundred days of reform" that fizzled. Without staying in Beijing to mend fences and to save whatever connections that were left, it would be difficult for him to ever get back into the center stage. He had the premonition that Liang Boyin had foreclosed any chance of a comeback. With Liang Qichao now in exile in Japan and Boyin back to Guangzhou, Liang Shiyi suddenly felt queasy at the unfulfilled promise of the Three Liangs of Guangdong.

* * *

In May 1900, part of the regular government troops joined the Boxers, and the distinction between the two became blurred. Manchu General Ronglu, now the Grand Councillor and Commander of the Qing Army, was known to have no sympathy for the Boxers. However, he was unwilling to offend the empress dowager and took some half measures so that he could extricate himself if the Boxers should lose.

By the first week of June, the foreign diplomats in Beijing were convinced that the court intended to kill all foreigners, and sent for urgent help from the foreign ships off the harbor near Tianjin. An international force of over two thousand men left Tianjin by train for Beijing on June 10 but was blocked by the Boxers midway between Beijing and Tianjin. The railways and telegraph cables between the two cities were also cut off, leaving the foreigners in the capital in complete isolation.

In the meantime, the Boxers swarmed into Beijing, burned churches, chased out missionaries, and even punished local bullies and corrupt public officials. On June 10, the Boxers burned the British summer legation in Western Hills, a suburb of Beijing. A day later, the chancellor of the Japanese legation was killed by troops under the command of a reactionary general. On June 14, the Boxers made several attacks on the legation guards and on June 20 killed the German minister. In Tianjin, the Boxers were equally uncontrollable. Facing such fanatic disorder, foreign troops on the ship outside the harbor landed at the Port of Dagu on June 16 and occupied the port the next day. On June 21, the Qing court declared war on the allied powers, and plunged China into a major catastrophe.

However, the empress dowager had anticipated that Li Hongzhang was the man eventually needed to deal with foreigners whatever the outcome of the war might be. At that time, Li was Governor-General at Guangzhou, a position intended for his retirement after being eased out of the imperial court. Three days before the declaration of war, Li Hongzhang was summoned to the court in Beijing. When Li hesitated, he was restored to the position of Governor-General of Zhili and Commissioner of the Northern Ports, the posts which he had held from 1870 to 1895. Only then did he sail for Shanghai on July 21. Within a few days, came the news that five high officials who counseled peace had been executed. Sensing that the imperial court was still under the control of the reactionaries, Li refused to go further north.

As the Qing court issued the declaration of war, the regional leaders in the southeast provinces collectively refused to recognize its validity, insisting that it was an illegitimate order issued without proper authorization. Led by Li Hongzhang, these leaders entered into an informal understanding with foreign consuls in Shanghai that they would protect foreign lives and property under their jurisdiction. In return, foreign troops would not invade those regions. Hence the whole southeast of China was exempt from the Boxer disturbance.

* * *

The weakness of the Qing court fueled the momentum of the revolutionary movement overseas. Its leader, Sun Yatsen, was born into a poor rural family in Guangdong Province and later emigrated to Hawaii. He received his education in the mission schools which introduced him to democracy and Christianity before he went to study medicine in Hong Kong. There he was befriended by Dr. James Cantlie, then Dean of the College of Medicine for Chinese, who encouraged him to put his ideas into action. Alarmed by the fate of China, Sun Yatsen had given up his medical practice in 1894 and devoted himself to the cause of overthrowing the Manchus and the establishment of a republican form of government.

In the fall of 1894, Sun Yatsen went back to Honolulu to further his cause by forming the Revive China Society. He sought help from overseas Chinese, secret societies, and Christian converts—men existing on the fringes of Chinese society. He returned to Hong Kong in early 1895 and established headquarters, with secret branches in the provinces. After a failed uprising to capture Guangzhou, Sun fled to Hong Kong only to find the British authorities had complied with a Qing request to ban him there. He escaped to Japan and established a branch of Revive China Society in Yokohama. The revolutionaries began to develop connections with Japanese sympathizers.

Shortly thereafter, Sun Yatsen went to the United States to arouse his supporters in the secret societies. Arriving in London to seek support of the Chinese community there, he was lured into the Chinese Legation and detained there on October 11, 1896. The Chinese minister had secured the approval of the Qing court to send him home secretly in a chartered ship. However, through an English attendant at the Chinese legation, Sun was able to slip a message to Dr. Cantlie who was then in London. Dr. Cantlie brought the case to the attention of the British Foreign Office, and the *London Globe* exposed the illegal kidnapping in bold headlines. The Chinese legation was forced to release Sun the next day and he became a world-wide celebrity overnight.

Sun Yatsen remained in Europe for two years to study political and social thought. He returned to Japan in 1897 only to find that the Chinese there were largely apolitical and conservative. However, after the disaster of the radical reform movement in 1898 and the Boxer disturbance in 1900, the people in China and the overseas Chinese communities became far more receptive to his ideas. Sun Yatsen tried to exploit these disruptions, and his followers began to infiltrate into some southern provinces of China. The Qing court suddenly felt their presence even as it strained to put out the fire caused by the Boxer movement.

* * *

By late June 1900, Beijing was filled with Boxers roaming menacingly in every corner of the city. Liang Shiyi contacted several close friends, mostly Cantonese, and made plans to evacuate their families. Guan Mianjun responded in a desperate voice, "Where can we go?"

"We must get out of this city to avoid the onslaught," Shiyi said. "The railway to Tianjin is out of service, but we can move in that direction and find some way to go south. Please spread the word to our friends so that all of us can be ready to leave tomorrow morning. We'll have to take any means of transportation available."

After Guan left, Liang Shiyi thought of the conditions of Madam and his second lady. Both were pregnant and were in no position to travel on the rugged country roads. But leaving Beijing was the only hope to escape even more unpleasant surprises. He quietly told his second lady, "Ask the servants to do the packing for this trip. We'll take them along, from the cook to the errand boy. We need all the help we can get along the way. Don't alarm the Madam."

"Yes, I'll see to it that Madam has all she needs. But we will travel light in view of the difficulty of getting enough carts for all of us," his second lady replied.

As Shiyi assessed the bleak future, he saw the gathering storm that would engulf the entire nation in chaos.

A Run For Life

The morning was bright. It would be a beautiful summer day, but Liang Shiyi had little appreciation for it. He and his extended family, and eight friends with their families, met in front of Sanshui Hostel. Over one hundred persons, including children and servants, were loaded into a train of carts. Liang Shiyi moved swiftly from one cart to another, directing the entourage to move toward the east gate of the city.

Shiyi had no time for his own family. He was too absorbed in planning the next move. He relied on his servants and his second lady to prepare everything. He and the other men had decided to head for Hexiwu, a town about midway between Beijing and Tianjin, and go south from there by boat. As the carts were pulled away, Shiyi finally moved to a seat next to his wife. Holding the hand of her two-year old son, Madam sobbed, "I don't know what to do when the baby comes." Under normal circumstances, she would have protested loudly for the discomfort she would endure in her seventh month of pregnancy. But she knew this was no ordinary time and her husband could do nothing to alleviate her worry.

"We tried to make our trip on land as short as possible," Shiyi whispered to his wife. "By the time we get on a boat at Hexiwu, I hope you will feel better."

"I hope so too," Madam retorted. "What else can I do?" She was so agitated that she sobbed again.

His second lady sat at the back of another cart with their four-year old daughter and two-year old son. She had the same thought as Madam as she, too, was pregnant, though only four months along. She would never complain to her husband, even if she had the chance. But he understood her condition and told a maid servant to attend to her needs.

On the way, they saw sacrificial altars in every village for people to pray for victory against the foreign devils. Shiyi was anxious. He had heard that many villagers, wearing the badges of the Boxers, would force people passing by an altar to kowtow while they burned silver and gold papers as offering to their gods and to the dead. If the ashes from the burnt papers flew into the air when a person rose after kowtowing, he was considered a righteous person; otherwise he would be regarded as a traitor and put to death.

Just outside the Hexiwu village limits, the carts rumbled to a stop. Shiyi saw several Boxers waving their arms. Shiyi and his friends jumped down from the carts and waited while the Boxers lit the silver and gold papers. He could hear the women softly weeping.

Liang Shiyi offered to be the first one to go through the ritual of kowtowing as he had figured out a way to acquit himself. Since the traditional Chinese gown he wore had long and wide sleeves, he brushed the ground with his sleeves as he got up from the kneeling position, stirring up the air near the ashes. He did it deliberately. The others in his group watched him carefully and understood his message. They followed him, one by one, imitating his technique. When Guan Mianjun's turn came, he panicked and failed to accomplish the feat. The mob cried for his blood and he was terrified. Out of desperation, Liang looked to the sky and yelled, "Master Guan! Don't be afraid." The villagers stopped yelling as suddenly as they had begun.

The leader spoke to the crowd: "If Master Guan appeared in heaven, this man must be a righteous person. Liang Shiyi then realized the leader was referring to a legendary figure named Guan Yu who was revered by the peasants as Master Guan (Guan Lao Ye). The villagers thought Master Guan had revealed himself in answering Liang's prayer. Unexpectedly, Liang had saved his friend's life.

When he climbed back into the cart, Shiyi looked at Madam, A'er and his children. They were white with fear. None looked up to meet his eye.

Shiyi spoke to Madam. "The danger is over. We will search for boats heading south." No sooner had he spoken, than suddenly a gang of 30 bandits came to them and demanded 300 taels of silver for each boat. All his friends were frightened but Liang peacefully said to the bandits, "Our boats are now under your protection and we ought to pay for the protection. However, we haven't got such a huge amount of silver. Should we send someone to Tianjin to bring the silver here?" The bandit chief agreed.

"Saddle a horse," Liang told an errand boy, "I want you to take an urgent message." Then he quickly wrote a note to a friend who was Head of Customs at Tianjin. The wait seemed even longer than it was. Children cried and the women huddled together, afraid of what might come next.

After receiving the note, Shiyi's friend dispatched a team of armed guards to accompany the servant and the silver to Hexiwu. When the bandits saw the guards coming, they fled. The guards wanted to chase the bandits, but Shiyi stopped them. "The nation is now in such chaos," he reminded them, "let's not plant evil seeds of revenge."

Settled in the boat, and sensing that the southern route was too dangerous a place, the entourage changed direction and moved northward along the Chaobar River to Huairou County, located to the northeast of Beijing. They saw several groups of bandits during the trip, but by their wits they avoided them. They could not avoid the last group of bandits who insisted they pay 200 taels of silver before they were allowed to pass. Liang stood beside the mast of his boat and called out to them, "We haven't got that much silver with us. All our belongings are simple. We have nothing to give you."

The chief of the bandits told his followers, "This man speaks without fear or anger. Don't bother talking to him. Just take away his sons and he will see things differently."

Liang Shiyi responded meekly, "Though I have been working hard for more than twenty years, I'm just a poor Hanlin scholar. My children may not get as far as I do when they grow up. If you like my sons, you may take them away." Then he sat down and dozed. His wife and concubine were horrified, but they hid their fear. They gathered their children close to them and remained calm. When Shiyi woke up, the bandits were gone without bothering his sons. His friends admired his calmness in meeting the danger.

After a short ride in the slow boats, they finally reached a small town in Huairou County. During the trip, Liang Shiyi had been too occupied with the fateful events to pay much attention to his wife. Now he saw she moved slowly and with pain. Liang clapped his hands and the servants came running. "Madam," he said, "are you in labor?" She bit her lip and looked into his eyes.

Madam was carried to a small inn. Once in their rooms, Madam was aided by her maid Mai San, but the servant had no experience with childbirth. Shiyi leaned over his unhappy wife. "We have been lucky. We will continue to be lucky. Under such circumstances, the second lady will perform the delivery."

Happily, Madam gave birth to a girl, and Liang Shiyi named his second daughter Huaisheng (Born in Huairou). A few days later, the magistrate of Huairou County heard about the arrival of Liang's party and paid them a courtesy call. He also invited them to move into the city for protection. Only then did they learn that Tianjin had been occupied by foreign troops and that the foreign legations in Beijing were under siege by the Boxers.

* * *

The troops of General Ronglu were assigned to attack the legations. They carried out their duties half-heartedly, sometimes firing noisy but empty guns and withholding the large caliber cannon. The defense of the compound of legations was led by Sir Claude MacDonald, the British Minister Plenipotentiary, and supported by about 450 guards, 475 foreign civilians, and 2,300 Chinese Christians. They put up stiff resistance against the on-and-off onslaughts. George Morrison, the influential Beijing correspondent of *The Times* of London, did not want to miss the chance of his life to witness this heroic event even though he was soon immobilized by a gunshot to the leg. With him was Edmund Backhouse, his interpreter and a brilliant Oriental scholar. Backhouse was inept at helping Morrison nurse the wound or filling his place for the defense of the compound. Since the defenders had been cut off completely from the outside world, it was announced in England that the legations had been captured and the defenders massacred. *The Times* thereupon published an obituary of Morrison so laudatory that, when he emerged alive later, the paper felt compelled to raise his salary and grant him lifelong employment.

Allied reinforcements arrived in the Port of Dagu near Tianjin in late July 1900, and a foreign expeditionary force of about 20,000 troops, mainly from Japan, Russia, Britain, France and the United States, plus small contingents from Germany, Italy and Austria, was organized under a complex joint-command structure. On August 4, the expeditionary force of eight nations left Tianjin for Beijing. Boxer resistance under the command of reactionary officials quickly crumbled as their leaders committed suicide. General Ronglu did not send his troops to rescue the Boxers and was not unhappy to see their demise. The Western troops entered Beijing and relieved the beleaguered legations on August 14.

As the allied troops came into the city from the east, Empress Dowager Cixi and Emperor Guangxu fled in disguise to the west, establishing a temporary capital in Xi'an. The emperor had actually wanted to remain in Beijing to negotiate a peace treaty with the foreign powers, but the empress dowager would not allow him to establish himself at her expense. Blaming his favorite concubine, Pearl Consort, for exerting a bad influence on him, the empress dowager ordered that before their departure this consort be thrown into a well in the Forbidden City.

For three days the allied soldiers pillaged the city. All the treasures, documents, and historical relics in the Imperial Palace and in the Summer Palace were looted or otherwise destroyed. Everyone was in on the hunt for treasures: ministers plenipotentiary, customs staff, journalists, even missionaries. The connoisseurs went straight to houses of rich Manchus and well-known Chinese collectors of porcelain and jade. Others just grabbed anything they could lay their hands on in Chinese mansions and places whose owner had fled. Sir Claude MacDonald even arranged the auction of the loot later, and other foreigners shipped their bounty to Tianjin for export.

Oddly enough, most Japanese soldiers did not join their counterparts of the allied forces in the pillage. The Japanese played safe and stayed out of trouble, partly because they looked like Chinese and could not commandeer the properties of powerful Chinese owners, but partly because they were afraid of being mistaken as Chinese looters and shot at by European soldiers.

Altogether, some 136 foreign Protestants and 44 Catholic missionaries, along with 53 children of missionaries and 30,000 Chinese Christians were killed in the Boxer movement. Angered by the Boxers' atrocity, some American missionaries joined the looting and justified their actions on grounds that Christians, including Chinese converts, deserved to be indemnified for their loss. News of the looting, as well as the demand by home churches for summary vengeance, took the American public aback. Mark Twain expressed that sentiment when he wrote in the *North American Review*, "Sometimes, an ordained minister sets out to be blasphemous. When this happens, the layman is out of the running: he stands no chance." To the missionary who claimed to have only followed local custom, Twain rejoined that the Commandment should be revised to read, "Thou shalt not steal—except when it is the custom of the country." He likened the claim of excess looting as indemnities for destroyed property to the girl who said, "But it is such a little one," when she was reproached for having an illegitimate child.

As the allied expeditionary forces occupied Beijing, the Qing court in exile urged Li Hongzhang to search for a settlement with the foreign powers. The United States had announced the second open door policy on July 3, supporting "Chinese territory and administrative entity" and "permanent safety and peace," but that did not prevent other powers from demanding large sums of indemnity. Li Hongzhang went north under Russian protection, arriving in Tianjin on September 18. To checkmate the reactionaries still at the court in Xi'an, Li petitioned the Court to appoint General Ronglu and Prince Qing to join him in negotiating the peace settlement. However, the Western powers regarded General Ronglu as a major culprit and rejected him as a negotiator. During the negotiations, the allied representatives, working at cross purposes, had a difficult time agreeing on the terms, causing the stalemate to continue without a solution.

* * *

They had been in Huairou County for over a month when Shiyi learned that the Boxers in Beijing had been suppressed even though the peace negotiations were stalled. He and his friends were ready to return to Beijing which was now under foreign occupation. Just at that moment, a large gang of bandits unexpectedly attacked Huairou County, capturing the city and killing the magistrate and his entire family. The bandits were undecided whether to clean out all the spoils in the surrounded city or to hold its residents as hostages in demand for more money. In this tense moment, one of Liang's friends, Ou Pengxiao, attempted to escape and call for outside help. He was caught and brought before the bandit chief. After long interrogation, he was unexpectedly released, to the great relief of his family and friends.

Asked about this terrible experience, Ou Pengxiao told his friends, "When the bandits discovered that I was not only a Hanlin Scholar but also a tutor to the children of royal princes, they feared that any punishment meted out to me might cause eventual revenge. They thought the easiest way out was to forget the entire episode of my escape."

Looking at his friends around him, practically all of whom were Hanlin scholars, Shiyi commented mischievously, "If one Hanlin scholar could cause the bandits to backtrack, this group together should be able to scare them off from the city." Everybody had a good laugh, breaking the tension that had built up during their captivity.

But that optimistic scenario was not going to happen. The bandits held on to the city until they were forced out upon the arrival of the Qing forces and the new magistrate from Beijing. Finally, in late September, Liang and his family and friends left Huairou County by carts for Beijing.

The entourage moved slowly. As it came within reach of Beijing, Liang's second lady went into labor. Looking back at her with anxiety, Shiyi shouted, "We'll move on quickly and hope to arrive home soon." When the carts carrying Liang's family passed Hufangqiao Lane, just a few long blocks from Sanshui Hostel, the second lady began to moan and cry out. If the birth of Liang's second daughter in Huairou seemed ironically lucky, this birth was not. Fortunately his second lady had prepared an emergency kit for just such an occasion. With minimum help from a servant, she instinctively spread out layers of cloth and managed to deliver her third daughter in the most precarious of situations. Liang Shiyi named her Yusheng (Born in a cart).

When Shiyi and his family reached Sanshui Hostel, they found the hostel had been stripped, everything possible had been stolen or destroyed. Madam was beside herself as she found her wardrobe was empty. She yelled at her servant, "Mai San, tell the errand boy to bring my trunk in as soon as possible. I don't want to leave it in the cart and have it stolen too."

Shiyi took notice of her agitation and said, "Of all treasures, only our children are priceless. We are so fortunate that not only our older children have returned safely but we have also gained two daughters in this difficult journey." His second lady was too weak after childbirth to worry about anything. She just wanted to crawl into her bed for a good rest and leave her newborn to the care of her servant.

As Shiyi entered his study, he was met with his own loss. "Who would have taken my manuscripts and papers? They have no value to anyone but me." He sat down on the floor, his head in his hands. "I have labored on them for almost twenty years. Now they are gone forever." His wife and his children stood in the doorway.

Although the outward appearance of Beijing was calm under foreign occupation, the Chinese government was practically nonexistent. Liang Shiyi decided to go back to his native village as soon as transportation could be arranged. A week later, they arrived in Tianjin to wait for the steamship to take them to Hong Kong. After much delay, they eventually reached their native village in Sanshui, where Liang Shiyi once again became the principal lecturer at Fenggang Academy.

Quiet Retreat

"I want the curriculum to emphasize the idea of learning for practical application," Shiyi told his fellow teachers as he resumed the position of principal lecturer at Fenggang Academy in early 1901. After assessing the reaction from his listeners, he added, "I'll add to the curriculum the study of world history, geography and modern political institutions of Western nations." This was a drastic and bold departure from teaching strictly traditional Chinese classics and poetry. The reputation of the academy was greatly enhanced by his innovation and student enrollment increased rapidly.

The academy offered scholarships to encourage the enrollment of outstanding students, and Liang lent his support by making contributions to increase the number of scholarships. The scholarship students were selected by examination each month as a group of new students was enrolled. Liang Shiyi was very pleased when a gentry member brought his two young sons to the academy for the scholarship competition. Liang was astonished when the gentleman sneaked in during the exam and passed some papers to one of his sons. As Liang returned to his seat at the podium, he saw the gentleman hiding behind a large pillar in the hall, but he pretended not to notice. Before returning the examination paper to the boy the next day, he wrote, "Parents love their sons with their hearts and souls. All sons should love their parents as much as their parents love them. If you should become famous in the future, don't ever forget the time when your father suffered the indignity of embracing a pillar in the twilight, all because of his concern for your success."

When the news of this comment leaked out, the students were greatly surprised by his humor as well as his grace in exposing the scandal without inflicting severe punishment on the boy for his father's transgression. One admiring student commented to his friends, "Our teacher is really ingenious in treating this obnoxious act."

A second boy added, "You can expect that from someone who last week gave us unusual homework assignments, including 'A critique of Kaiser Wilhelm II of Prussia' and 'An analysis of the decline of Song Dynasty'."

One day, when Shiyi was alone in his office at the academy, he heard someone reciting familiar lines of blank verse in the courtyard. Looking out from the window, he saw a student and waved to him to come in. "You are reciting the lines I composed when I was 18," Shiyi told him. "My teacher at that time asked the class to use that form for a composition in celebrating the occasion of the Bathing Buddha Festival. He singled out my work for praise, particularly the lines you just recited: 'Today I learn the famous Lotus Sutra to seek the tranquil state of a pure orchid. Next year I shall find the Buddha on the petaled throne in the renowned Temple of Flowers.' Even then I had the ambition of eventually going to Beijing and visiting the Temple of Flowers (Huazhisi) there. My classmates were so impressed by my work that they made copies and passed them out to their friends. That is probably how you got a copy."

"Yes, my father is one of your admirers. I got my copy from him," the student blushed as he spoke. He was greatly surprised by Liang's openness.

Shiyi continued, "Frankly, I now feel guilty to have spent time in writing such prose or poetry. Not that I am against the enjoyment of finer things in life. However, I have set my mind for public service and tried to do the best I can to reverse the misfortune of our country. The emphasis of literary skills in civil service examinations contributes nothing to promote the dire need of competent public officials. I hope the government will soon change the examination system along with instituting other much needed reforms." The student was gratified by Liang's insight and the earnestness with which he expressed his feeling.

Shiyi's brother Shixu, who had returned to the village two years before to study at Fenggang Academy, was now one of his students. Married and worldly, Shixu was more interested in going into business than in studying the classics. Shiyi was eager to prepare him for the county examination as his father wished.

However, he missed his youngest brother Shixin who had gone to study under Jian Chaoliang in Yangshan County. Jian was a Juren degree holder and an accomplished Confucian scholar. He was particularly fond of Shixin, who was barely 15 years old, but was already showing signs of a classics scholar. Shiyi thought about this brother and wrote to him: "My teaching assignments at Fenggang Academy are quite heavy. I've forgotten a lot of the classics I have learned. Your presence here will help me recall suitable materials in the classics for my teaching.

"On the other hand, I can give you some tips from my own experience in Beijing. Nothing is more important than practicing what you preach. As Confucius said, 'A man of noble spirit first practices what he preaches and then preaches what he practices.' I wish to take this opportunity to guide you personally for a few months before I return to Beijing, possibly at the end of this year."

Shixin was delighted and flattered by his brother's message since he was suddenly treated as an adult worthy of serious consideration by an older family member. His father never praised him or his siblings, no matter what they had accomplished. So he interrupted his study under Jian Chaoliang to return home.

* * *

Shiyi was waiting eagerly for the outcome of the negotiations between the Qing court and the allied expeditionary forces in Beijing before reaching a decision to go back. Unfortunately, the process of negotiations was protracted and contentious.

Beijing Odyssey

On August 7, 1901, Li Hongzhang was appointed minister plenipotentiary by the Qing court to negotiate peace with the foreign powers. Upon the urgent plea of Li, the fugitive imperial court formally signed a Boxer Protocol with the allied powers in September. Among the unpleasant terms imposed on the Qing court were agreements that China would expand the Foreign Office (Zongli Yamen) into a fully prestigious Ministry of Foreign Affairs, and execute the leading Boxer supporters in the court. China would also allow permanent foreign guards and the placement of defense weapons to protect the legation quarters in perpetuity. Finally, China agreed to pay an indemnity of 450 million taels (around 67 million pound sterling or $333 million U.S. at the then current exchange rates) for damages to foreign life and property. That was a staggering sum at a time when the total revenue of the government was estimated at around 250 million taels. The Chinese were to pay the indemnity in gold, with 4% interest charged, until December 31, 1940. In November 1901, the allied troops withdrew from Beijing. After completing his last measure of devotion to the Qing court, Li Hongzhang died of illness and disillusionment at the age of seventy-eight.

In January 1902, the empress dowager and the emperor returned to Beijing from Xi'an. Empress Dowager Cixi re-established herself in the Forbidden City, which had been the headquarters for the foreign expeditionary forces for a year. In a gesture to charm the Westerners, the empress dowager promptly received the senior members of the diplomatic corps in person at her palace. In another unprecedented action, she held a reception for their ladies a week later. But Emperor Guangxu was still not allowed to play any political role.

* * *

Eager to re-establish himself in Hanlin Academy, Shiyi also returned to Beijing with his family in January 1902. Life in the city gradually returned to normal, at least for the Mandarin class. Social activities in Shiyi's circle began to pick up, particularly among his Cantonese friends. With the income of a Hanlin scholar, he could hardly afford the lifestyle of court officials. He wrote his brothers Shixu and Shixin about his predicament:

"On cold winter days, most of my colleagues and friends wear fur-lined gowns. I never owned one until recently when I bought a second-hand marten-lined gown at the price of 110 taels of silver. Because I didn't have formal and ceremonial robes in my wardrobe, I didn't go with other members of the Hanlin Academy to pay my respects to the emperor in the palace, either at the Winter Solstice Festival or on the Lunar New Year's Day. On occasions that demand my presence, I borrow formal and ceremonial robes for court appearances from Ou Jinan, a fellow Cantonese from Nanhai County, who has been a court official in Beijing for some time. Last month, when I was on duty at Hanlin Academy, the emperor dropped in unexpectedly on his way back to the palace after worshipping at the Temple of Heaven. He gave those of us present an impromptu audience. He looked healthier than he was before the Boxer disturbance."

A month later, Shiyi wrote to his brothers about a pending proposal for implementing a new educational system by converting major academies in provincial capitals to colleges, those in the prefectures to secondary schools, and those in the counties to primary schools. He strongly argued in favor of modern schools over the traditional examination system, and advised his brothers to enroll in modern schools as soon as they became available.

"I am happy to inform you," his brother Shixu wrote back, "that I have finally passed the county examination. Unlike your success for passing this examination at 17, it took me six more years to accomplish the same." Then he modestly added that because of his advantage of being older, he was able to do well enough to rank first among the successful candidates.

Shiyi was more than gratified to note that his grandfather, father and now younger brother all had passed the county examination with the top rank. He was surprised to hear later that his brother Shixu took the entrance examination at the newly established Guangdong Military Academy and was admitted for its first class beginning in September. Obviously Shixu took the advice of attending a modern school instead of preparing for the higher level examinations, but, thought Shiyi, what an unexpected choice of school.

* * *

In late 1902, Li Duanfen, the former Minister of Punishments, was eligible for parole from exile in Xinjiang Territory if a fine of 20,000 taels of silver could be paid. Out of his loyalty to a former official whom he regarded as a man of high integrity, Liang Shiyi led a fund drive for his release. As the examiner of the provincial examination in Guangdong in 1889, Li had many admirers among the Juren degree holders of that class.

"I wish Liang Boyin were here," Shiyi remarked to Ou Jinan. "He would be delighted at the news and able to help me in the fund drive."

"He probably can help you more in his present capacity," Ou replied. "His business is prosperous in Guangzhou. I know he will respond generously to your request. We trust each other to the extent that we have agreed to the marriage of my youngest daughter to his eldest son, when they come of age."

Indeed, Liang Boyin helped to raise money in Guangdong Province as well as making a major contribution himself. That put the fund drive over the target and Li Duanfen was released several months later.

Through rotating assignments, Shiyi gradually moved in the inner circles of the ruling elite. In early 1903, Liang wrote to his father, who was still the chairman of the Three-county Chamber of Commerce in Beihai, about his observations of the court intrigues: "Empress Dowager Cixi announced her intention to improve state affairs. But most ministers are satisfied with the status quo and are not eager to rock the boat. The Grand Councillors are neither vigorous nor courageous in their actions. General Ronglu is the first among equals but he has a leg ailment and often is unavailable for consultation. Wang Wenshao has hearing problems and, whenever unpleasant situations arise, he pretends to be a deaf mute and avoids involvement. Yet he is far better than two other grand councillors who argue atrociously all the time, and Wang at least tries to be a peacemaker to defuse their heated arguments. The empress dowager is not resolute in eliminating those who always follow the outmoded ways. One may notice the perfunctory tones of recent edicts from the throne. The court has not been strict and fair in meting out rewards and punishments. That is why no capable persons emerge."

Shiyi was very frustrated when he uttered such disparaging remarks about the imperial court and the criticism of the empress dowager. And of all people, he chose to express such feelings to his father whose respect for authority was legendary. Was he trying to justify why he was still languishing in Hanlin Academy without a lucrative appointment? Or was he trying to prepare his father to accept that he would soon abandon the ship of the state?

In February 1903, Liang Shiyi celebrated the sixtieth birthdays of his father and mother by throwing an elaborate party in the social hall of Sanshui Hostel. The Chinese count age by considering a baby one year old (one "sui") when he or she is born, and adding another "sui" each subsequent new year's day. Thus, 60 "sui" was somewhat short of sixty years. This milestone was quite a distinction since at that time life expectancy was about 55 for men and considerably shorter for women. It was considered a double honor that both a man and his wife could reach the age near 60. The birthday party in Beijing was the gesture of a filial son to honor his parents in the company of his friends even though his father was in Beihai County and his mother was in his native village.

Shiyi invited more than 200 guests, mostly Hanlin scholars, to the party. All guests were asked to compose a poem for the happy occasion. It was customary for a formal gathering of scholar-officials to be engaged in such pastime after a gourmet dinner. Some were itchy to flaunt their literary talent on such occasions; others felt an obligation to practice the art for which they had lost interest since passing the last government examination. Very proud of the tributes to his parents by his friends, Liang collected these poems in a bound volume entitled: *Visions of Fortune and Longevity*, and sent it to his father.

* * *

On this happy occasion, Shiyi missed his good friends Boyin and Qichao who would have been the leading contributors to the volume had they been in Beijing. Only a week earlier, he heard from Boyin that since he was not able to make any headway in getting a new job in Beijing, he was content to stay in business in Guangzhou. Of course Liang Shiyi would not dare to communicate with Liang Qichao. He heard, however, about the activities of Liang Qichao and those of Sun Yatsen's revolutionaries in Japan through the rumor mill in Tianjin, where newspapers published in the British settlement could evade the censorship of the Qing government. Under the leadership of Kang Youwei, an Emperor-Protection Society had been formed in Japan to promote the restoration of the power to Emperor Guangxu as a constitutional monarch. Aiding Kang's effort, Liang Qichao, through his newspaper editorials, had become an eloquent proponent of constitutional monarchy. Kang vehemently attacked the idea of revolution and republicanism. Revolutionaries eventually launched a powerful counterattack and advocated forcefully the overthrow of the Qing Dynasty and the establishment of a republic.

The people in China, who read such overseas newspapers surreptitiously, suddenly realized the fate of their nation had reached a deep crisis. Liang Qichao's editorials contributed significantly to the national clamor for reform-minded officials inside China. But the voice of the revolutionaries convinced a younger generation of Chinese that more drastic measures would be necessary to reverse the tide.

The question of war and peace loomed heavily in the mind of Shiyi: Would there be a peaceful transition through political reform, or a civil war to settle the future form of government?

Perilous Crossroads

"Are you going to take this exam in July?" Shiyi asked his friend Guan Mianjun when he heard about the announcement of the Special Examination on Political Economy in late spring of 1903. It was a national examination given rarely by the imperial court to reach young men of unusual administrative talent. Although the empress dowager had no intention of opening up high offices to talented strangers, she was under pressure to proceed with the examination in view of public demand for political reform.

"No, I don't think that I'm up to that," Guan replied in a measured tone. "But I heard that Gui Jian is going to take it."

Gui Jian was another Jinshi degree recipient in the class of 1894 who had become a compiler in Hanlin Academy. He and Liang Shiyi were active in the same social circle of Cantonese scholars in Beijing. Ambitious but cautious, they had languished in Hanlin Academy year after year, waiting for the right patron and the right moment to advance. When Liang asked him about the exam, Gui's reply was direct, "Yes, this is a rare chance to get ahead. With so many changes in the power structure at the top in the last few years, I cannot count on any connection that will lead to a promising career."

"I plan to do the same," Shiyi confided to Gui. "Political economy is my strong suit. I hope to prove myself in this exam. I've already lined up two sponsors in order to qualify for the examination." His sponsors included a minister and a deputy minister who vouched for his character and ability. In this high stakes game, the imperial court did not want to take any chances.

In spite of Empress Dowager Cixi's lukewarm attitude, Emperor Guangxu expressed a keen interest in the special examination and made the unusual announcement that he would be present for supervision. The examination would be held under newly promulgated rules. Shiyi was among 191 qualified candidates.

The special examination took place at a time when anti-reform and anti-revolutionary phobia among reactionary imperial officials reached a peak. In Shanghai, the trial of two popular reporters of a suppressed newspaper received wide national publicity. On July 19, another newspaperman in custody of the police in Beijing was fatally beaten. On the following day came the announcement of the results of the special examination: Shiyi ranked first among 48 successful candidates in the first grade, and Gui Jian ranked first among 79 successful candidates in the second grade.

These results caused a furor at the imperial court because the exiled radical reformers Kang Youwei and Liang Qichao, as well as the revolutionary leader Sun Yatsen and many of his followers were Cantonese. Grand Councillor Qu Hongji allegedly informed the empress dowager that Shiyi was a Cantonese whose surname was the same as Liang Qichao and whose given name contained the character "yi" which was the same as the last character of the given name of Kang Youwei (a.k.a. Kang Zuyi). Qu deduced that, having the "head" of Liang Qichao and the "tail" of Kang Youwei, Liang Shiyi might be an agent of Liang Qichao and Kang Youwei. The fact that Liang Shiyi was well acquainted with these two exiled reformists was sufficient to alarm the empress dowager. She ordered a re-examination on July 22, admitting only candidates whose backgrounds would be more carefully screened. Shiyi denied the charges against him but refused to leave Beijing or to compete in the second examination.

At this critical moment, his friend Ou Jinan came to visit him. A sunny day, they sat in the courtyard while Shiyi's children played nearby. "Shiyi, your life may be in danger if you stay in Beijing. No one in power at the court would dare to recommend you for promotion. I have a brother who is a very successful importer-exporter in Penang, Malaya (Malaysia). I can arrange for you to join him in business there."

"How grateful I am to have a friend like you when I am in trouble," Shiyi replied. "In spite of the current setback, I am not ready to give up public service for which I have prepared all my life. I am not eager to make a fortune even though I see the great opportunity in Malaya."

"In case you change your mind, you know that I am always ready to help out."

"Thank you." Liang was truly appreciative of his friend's concern. "I've done nothing wrong and I want to vindicate myself. I will change my mind only if I am forced to leave Beijing."

Among Shiyi's social circle of Cantonese friends was Tang Shaoyi who was working in Tianjin. He heard about Shiyi's predicament and went to see him in Beijing. Tang was acting on behalf of Yuan Shikai, then the Governor-General of Zhili and the Commissioner of Northern Ports (Beiyang), with offices located in Tianjin. Tang intimated to Liang, "Yuan Shikai heard about your top performance in the special examination and about your misfortune. He will be glad to employ a person of your talent. You don't need to wait in Beijing if you are willing to work for him."

Unlike most of Liang's friends in Beijing, Tang Shaoyi did not go through the civil examination system. At the age of 14, Tang was among a group of young men sent by the Qing government in 1874 to study in the United States. As he enjoyed telling his friends, "As the youngest of four sons, I was wild as a youth and my father would not have minded if I had gotten lost at sea." Tang attended high school in Hartford, Connecticut, and later enrolled at Columbia University. During Yuan

Beijing Odyssey

Shikai's tour as Chinese Resident Commissioner in Korea from 1885 to 1894, Tang was recommended to him as an aid for diplomatic liaison. Now the Head of Customs in Tianjin, Tang was Yuan's chief deputy in charge of fiscal and diplomatic matters. He spoke with authority when he told Liang Shiyi, "Probably no high official except Yuan would dare to risk the displeasure of the imperial court by hiring you. This is your last chance."

Shiyi was confronted with a vital decision. If he chose to go to Penang, his public service career would probably end for good, even though he might gain a fortune. On the other hand, if he decided to work for Yuan Shikai, he would place his allegiance to someone with a blemished reputation who ruthlessly sought to gain influence at Empress Dowager's court.

Noting Liang's hesitation, Tang remarked, "Xu Shichang will soon be Head of the newly established Army Training Center under Yuan Shikai. Your job will be the Chief of the Editorial Bureau." That piece of information was persuasive to Shiyi. If a politician as savvy as Xu decided to serve Yuan's cause, he might as well join the winning team. This was perhaps his only chance to move ahead in public service. In the end, that argument won.

* * *

Shiyi, or even Tang Shaoyi, did not know the private Yuan Shikai whom Xu Shichang knew. A native of Xiangcheng in Henan Province, Yuan was born in 1859 to a well-to-do gentry family which provided him with a private tutor to prepare for civil-service examinations. However, he did not do well in the study of Confucius classics but took great interest in riding and other outdoor activities. A friend of his family, who could not afford to provide his son with tutoring service, sought and received permission to send his son to study with Yuan under the same tutor. The name of this boy was Xu Shichang who would be forever indebted to the Yuan family.

When Yuan Shikai reached 19 years of age, his family arranged his marriage to a local girl who soon bore him a son. By then, Yuan decided that his future would lie in a military career. Although there was a parallel set of military degrees to the civil-service degrees that could be earned by examinations, they did not confer the same social prestige, and most military officers rose through the ranks without taking them. Impatient with step-by-step promotions, Yuan went to Beijing and spent a fortune to purchase a civil-service title that was allowed in the late Qing period under the scheme of "contribution for appointment to public office" by which the government enriched its treasury.

After a stint in Shanghai sowing wild oats along the way, he gambled away his money and could not afford to keep a prostitute he was madly in love with. However, his lover saw in him as an unpolished diamond. She said to him, "Take this meager savings of mine to start your life anew. Don't forget me when you become successful." Yuan finally landed in Shandong Province and served on the staff of the Provincial Military Commissioner. At the age of 22, Yuan already showed his decisiveness and courage under fire. When this commissioner was assigned to a military post in Korea in 1882, he took Yuan with him.

When Yuan was in Shandong, he was befriended by a kind-hearted stranger who was a close friend of the brother of Li Lianying, the notoriously corrupt eunuch who was the favorite of Empress Dowager Cixi. Yuan lost no time to cultivate this new friendship and, through this man, he secured the favor of the eunuch by showering him with gifts. Nobody could know for sure the contribution of Li Lianying to Yuan's career but this connection to the empress dowager certainly did not hurt him. Ambitious and brash, Yuan probably stood out as a rising star in the army on his own merit. However, without the consent of the empress dowager, no one in the imperial court would or could have appointed such a young and untried officer to be the Chinese Resident Commissioner in Korea in 1884.

After Yuan Shikai was entrenched in Korea, he sent for the prostitute in Shanghai and took her as his first concubine. He contemptuously left his wife in the native village, but he brought their son to Korea. When a prominent Korean tried to court his favor by presenting him a young woman of noble birth, Yuan callously took her and her two maids as his concubines. Yuan authorized the first concubine to discipline the three Korean women, invoking a prerogative that only his wife would be allowed to exercise according to the traditional social order. "Teach them the Chinese tradition of submission," Yuan told his first concubine, and she took his word as license to inflict physical wounds on the helpless Korean women.

When Li Hongzhang was eased out of power after the defeat of the war with Japan, his power base in Tianjin was taken over by Wang Wenshao who was later succeeded by Manchu General Ronglu. Yuan Shikai became a military officer in General Ronglu's headquarters and was assigned to train a new army during the "hundred days of reform" in 1898. Whether he betrayed Emperor Guangxu or was just loyal to the Empress Dowager Cixi in that episode was beside the point. Except for the radical reformers, no one in the imperial court thought the emperor had a chance to succeed in the power struggle, and Yuan was simply prudent to side with the winner.

Before the outbreak of the Boxer rebellion, Yuan Shikai became the Governor of Shandong Province. By then, his passionate obsession for his first concubine had cooled off and he decided to allow his wife to join the rest of the family. As if to emphasize his own authority in family affairs, he took a willowy woman to be his fifth concubine who instantly emerged as his new favorite. He later took four more concubines to make a total of nine.

In 1903, Yuan succeeded General Ronglu as Governor-General of Zhili and Commissioner of Northern Ports. Yuan Shikai got his wish to expand the few thousand soldiers he had trained under General Ronglu several years earlier to what was now called the New Army. Ever since Xu Shichang passed the Jinshi degree examination and became a member of Hanlin Academy, Yuan had counted on Xu's talent and influence to support his own career. In return, he was instrumental in placing Xu in strategic positions whenever opportunities arose. It was not surprising that Xu would accept this most recent appointment in Yuan's camp. As the Head of Army Training Center,

Beijing Odyssey

Xu would become the civilian chief of a group of young and ambitious army officers who would someday be generals and commanders in the vast Qing empire.

* * *

Shiyi did not take up his new job in Tianjin until fall because his wife was expecting. His precaution of delaying his departure to Tianjin didn't help. Madam gave birth to a premature baby, his fourth son, who died after a few days. He could only console her with the same refrain, "there would be another son in the future."

Madam was conditioned to accept her fate too, but she wished her son had survived. She did not want to go through the pain of bringing another son into the world, though she wanted two sons to insure her own security in old age.

"I certainly do not want to move to Tianjin," Madam said to her husband. "We have at least some friends here who can help in time of distress."

"You can rest comfortably in my absence," Shiyi told Madam. "A'er can keep you company and look after your needs." In view of the high rents in Tianjin, Liang was glad to leave his family in Beijing. He would commute to visit his family.

In the meantime, Shiyi received a letter from his father in Beihai, bringing up-to-date news from home.

"Shixin has studied under Master Jian Chaoliang for several years and, according to Jian, he is quite an accomplished scholar. Nothing could have pleased me more than to hear this from Master Jian whom I respect tremendously. He even proposed the marriage of his daughter to Shixin. At 18, Shixin has reached the marriageable age. Jian's daughter is quite literate for a woman, and she will be a good companion for him. Naturally your mother and I gave our consent. The wedding will take place when I return home for the family gathering at the end of this year."

Several months later, Shiyi heard from his father again. The letter was full of joy and hope as his brother Shixin had just passed the county examination and had become a Xiucai degree holder. His father was sure that Shixin would follow Shiyi's footsteps in successfully passing higher levels of examinations. Shiyi reflected on the good fortune that both of his younger brothers were now officially recognized scholars. However, Shiyi had lost his faith in the civil service examinations for selecting capable public officials. He thought too much was left to chance and too little substance was included in the examinations.

* * *

As the Chief of the Editorial Bureau, Shiyi became the editor of a series of military textbooks, widely known as *Yuan Shikai's Military Manual* or *Strategies of Beiyang Army*. Shiyi often wondered how Yuan could finance the grandiose operations in his headquarters while the rest of the nation was struggling for financial survival.

On a social occasion, Shiyi met Grand Councillor Wang Wenshao. After dinner and a few drinks, Wang told him, "Yuan Shikai is really lucky to be able to tap a seemingly bottomless coffer. Li Hongzhang raised an enormous sum of money from private sources for his Huai Army. There was an accumulation of eight million taels of silver from the unused funds at the end of the war against Japan. Anyone with less honesty and integrity than Li would have treated such unused funds as private property. However, Li left the entire sum under the control of the Governor-General of Zhili. When I succeeded him, I preserved the sum and passed it on to my successor General Ronglu. Yuan Shikai inherited this money from Ronglu when he became Governor-General."

Shiyi now knew the source of funds that supported his work in the Editorial Bureau. He began to understand Yuan's scheme of empire building and his own role in it. Willingly or not, he had become a part of the Beiyang clique of generals and civilian personnel answerable only to Yuan. As Yuan subtly used his influence to channel funds and personnel into his Tianjin headquarters, he was in control of the most modern military and civil bureaucratic order in China.

Diplomatic Missions

On a gloomy afternoon in the fall of 1904, Tang Shaoyi hurried to the Editorial Bureau to see Shiyi. He dropped a bombshell. "I've been promoted by the imperial court to a third ranked official with the title of Special Envoy Plenipotentiary on a mission to India." After pausing for a minute to catch his breath, Tang confided, "This special mission is an urgent response to a British expedition into Tibet which threatened Chinese sovereignty. As soon as my appointment is made public, I intend to submit your name for appointment as one of the two counselors for the mission. We'll also need a secretary to accompany us on this trip."

"This is so unexpected," Liang said after recovering from his shock. "Can Yuan Shikai spare you for this trip?"

"I think he was behind my appointment," Tang replied. "Since the imperial court desperately looked for some one to undertake this mission, Yuan would surely get the credit and gain greater influence for recommending an English-speaking official with diplomatic experience. The special mission will depart in December. We'll have less than three months to make all necessary preparations."

Shiyi was again caught in an uncomfortable position. His wife was expecting another child. There was no way to delay the trip this time, no matter what happened. Fortunately, in November, Madam delivered a healthy baby girl, and Shiyi named his fourth daughter Zangsheng (Born during the Tibet crisis). He would leave his family in Beijing and enlist several close friends who could help in case of emergency.

As Shiyi left with the official mission for Hong Kong, Madam was concerned. How she wished her new baby had been a boy! If she had two surviving sons, she would not want to have more children. Since that was not her fate, she longed for an early reunion with her husband.

While the delegates of the mission were waiting in Hong Kong for the passage to India, Shiyi took a quick trip to visit his mother in his native village in Sanshui. The trip was made easier with the completion of Guangzhou-Sanshui Railway the previous year. His mother was worried about his trip and gave him advice, "You have to be careful in dealing with foreigners. You don't speak their language and don't know their customs."

"Yes, Mother," Shiyi said, appreciative of her loving concern. "Tang Shaoyi and another counselor speak English. They will keep me in line." Then he turned to his younger brother Shixin to say good-bye.

To his surprise and delight, Shiyi found his youngest brother Shixin deeply interested in state affairs. "Brother Shiyi, the opium trade from India to China has been the greatest menace to our country for decades. I hope you will take the opportunity to find ways to ban the opium trade while you are on this diplomatic mission."

"I will take your thought to heart," Shiyi told Shixin as he left. When he reached Guangzhou, he met his other brother Shixu who was attending the Guangdong Military Academy. After asking Shixu to keep an watching eye for the welfare of their mother, Shiyi departed for Hong Kong.

* * *

The special mission was a desperate effort of China to resist the British imperialist expansion over the Himalayas from its bases in India. Invoking its sovereignty over Tibet, China had signed a treaty with Britain in 1890, establishing the borders with India and Sikkim. Under further pressure from Britain, the treaty was renewed in 1893, granting more special privileges to Britain at the expense of the Tibetans. As the Tibetans refused to enforce the terms of the treaty, border conflicts continued. In 1903, a British expeditionary force headed by Colonel F. E. Younghusband invaded Tibet. After inflicting heavy casualties on the Tibetan army, the British forces reached Lhasa in July 1904. Since the Dalai Lama had fled from the capital with the defeated army, his rival Banchan Lama stayed behind to negotiate the Lhasa Treaty with the British forces.

Sir Ernest Satow, the British Minister Plenipotentiary in Beijing, insisted that the Chinese government should approve the Lhasa Treaty since China could not exercise its power over the Tibetans to protect British interests. The Chinese side refused to recognize the British claim of its exclusive sphere of influence. After fruitless negotiations, both sides agreed that China would send a special mission to meet with a representative from the British Foreign Office in India to continue the discussion.

When the special mission headed by Tang Shaoyi arrived in Calcutta in February 1905, they met first with the Honorable S. M. Frazer, Secretary for India from London, and then with Lord Curzon, the Viceroy of India. The negotiations bogged down almost immediately, and after three months of negotiations, no progress was made. Neither side would yield an inch in its position.

After numerous social whirls in Calcutta, Shiyi sensed a difference of attitudes toward Tibet between Frazer's team from London and Lord Curzon and his staff in India. In one of their nightly discussions, Shiyi said to Tang, "Lord Curzon seems eager to push the British influence into Tibet as far and as fast as possible, at all costs, while Frazer's team appears to take a more cautious approach toward Tibet. I think the team from London is preoccupied with the tense relation between Britain and Russia in other parts of the world. What do you think?"

"You're absolutely right," Tang replied, "although I don't know how you've figured it out without understanding their conversations."

Shiyi was not sure how he had reached that conclusion; he seemed to sense it. He remarked, "Sometimes the facial expression and the movement of the body convey a person's thought. I am particularly impressed by the openness of General Herbert Kitchener, British Army Commander in India, who spoke to me through an interpreter. He asked if he could join us for lunch tomorrow. I told him to meet us in our hotel lobby at noon."

General Kitchener was most friendly in greeting Tang's group at lunch. He was particularly interested in antique Chinese porcelain. Knowing nothing about the subject, Tang turned to his colleagues for an answer. The general confided to them, "I would like to visit China someday as a private citizen. Don't be surprised if I show up and ask you to be my tour guide." As they walked out of the hotel dining room, General Kitchener noted a photo studio in the lobby. "Why don't we take a picture together as a memento for this joyful occasion?" the general proposed. All five of them disappeared into the studio.

After considerable discussions, Liang and Tang concluded that a more favorable treaty might be possible if some understanding could be reached between London and Beijing. Consequently, Tang declined the invitation of Lord Curzon in June to move the negotiations to Simla where Curzon maintained a summer residence. Later Tang cabled the Ministry of Foreign Affairs in Beijing, recommending that no treaty was better than an unfavorable one. Negotiations were hopelessly deadlocked.

Remembering the parting words of his brother Shixin, Liang Shiyi took time to learn about the opium export from India to China while the special mission languished in Calcutta. With the encouragement of Tang, he collected information about the planting, harvesting, and refining of the opium crops, and the system of taxation on opium products. He estimated the annual domestic taxes collected from opium trade by the Indian government. He also found that David Sassoon and Company had a virtual monopoly on opium export at that time. With that information, he wanted to devise a plan to reduce the opium export to China gradually by compensating the injured parties for destroying the opium crops over a ten-year period.

"Nothing would please me more than to find some way to reduce the import of opium to China," Shiyi added, after telling Tang Shaoyi about his plan.

"Yuan Shikai can push your plan at the imperial court if you can convince him of its merit," Tang replied. Through Shiyi's persuasion and persistence, the Chinese government eventually adopted this plan in its negotiation with the British.

In September 1905, the Qing court recalled Tang Shaoyi to Beijing. Shiyi left India with Tang, but Tang's other counselor stayed on in case the British reopened negotiations.

* * *

On their way back to Beijing, Shiyi was anxious to stop by his native village in Sanshui County again. In late summer, he received news from home that his brother Shixu had just graduated from Guangdong Military Academy. However, there was no joy in the family, not even when the wife of his youngest brother Shixin gave birth to a daughter. Shixin had contracted tuberculosis and was now in serious condition. By the time Shiyi arrived home, Shixin had already died a month earlier at the age 20, leaving his widow and a two-month-old daughter. Hearing the news of the death of his beloved son in whom he had such high hopes, Liang Zhijian resigned from his post as Chairman of Chamber of Commerce in Beihai County and returned home. It was a sad occasion for the family and no words could soften the sorrow over the loss of a young and promising life.

Shiyi had a long discussion with Shixu about the affairs of their extended family. "We are our brother's keepers," Shiyi said, "We will see to it that Shixin's daughter will be raised in the family like our own children." Since their youngest sister was closest to Shixin and his wife, she was assigned to take care of the immediate needs of Shixin's widow and daughter. This discussion between the two brothers established a pattern of close consultations when a crisis developed.

Shiyi also told his brother Shixu, "Tang Shaoyi has been asked by Yuan Shikai to handle the status of Japanese interests in Manchuria in the aftermath of the Russo-Japanese war. Tang wants me to be his assistant on this mission and I must return to Beijing soon. However, under the present circumstances I feel uneasy in leaving our parents."

Shixu had already thought about the situation. "The tragic death of Shixin took place less than two months after I graduated from the military academy. Foreseeing the needs in our family, I applied for an instructorship in the academy instead of a military post in another province. I intend to stay close to home to take care of our parents until their lives are back to normal again."

"On my way back from India, I stopped by Penang in Malaya to see Ou Jinan who was visiting his brother there," Shiyi told his brother. "During our conversations, I learned that Ou was looking for a bride for his 19-year-old son. I suggested our youngest sister. I was going to talk to our parents about this possible match. But this is no time to bring up such a matter. I leave the thought with you to ask them at the appropriate time."

"My wife and I will take care of that and many other things. You can go back to Beijing without worry."

Then Shiyi turned his thought to a different subject. He told Shixu, "The Qing court finally decreed that the civil service examination system will soon be abolished. It is time to convert Fenggang Academy into a modern primary school according to official regulations. You should urge the administrator of the academy to take appropriate action according to the plan that I laid out for them several years ago."

After taking care of his business at home, Shiyi caught up with Tang Shaoyi who had some personal business in Hong Kong. Without further delay, they hurried back to Beijing together.

* * *

Beijing Odyssey

When Tang Shaoyi and Shiyi arrived in Beijing in November, a team was already in the midst of negotiating a treaty with Japan resulting from the aftermath of the Russo-Japanese war. The team was led by Yuan Shikai, Prince Qing and Grand Councillor Qu Hongji. By then, Prince Qing had become a close ally of Yuan Shikai in modernizing the Chinese military, but Qu Hongji still represented the arch-conservatives in the imperial court. Working at cross purposes, they did not get very far. Tang and Shiyi joined Yuan's team to handle the details of negotiation.

Russia had started its occupation of Manchuria at the height of the Boxer disturbance in July 1900, when it sent in a large contingent of troops under the pretext of restoring order there. Their troop movement was facilitated by the Chinese Eastern Railway which had been financed and constructed by the Russians under a treaty in 1896, and the lease of Dalian and Lushun to Russia in 1898. Within three months, their troops gained control over all Manchuria. The Qing court refused to accept the terms of settlement dictated by the Russians, and appointed Prince Qing and the venerable Li Hongzhang to negotiate a treaty. However, Russia was determined to continue the occupation of Manchuria and wanted a treaty only to legalize its gain.

The Russian incursion into Manchuria alarmed other powers, especially Japan, whose interests conflicted with those of Russia. The Japanese minister in Beijing warned that any Chinese concession on Russian occupation of Manchuria could lead to the partition of China. Facing powerful international opposition, the Russians promised in 1901 to withdraw their troops from Manchuria in three stages of six-month intervals. When Russia reneged from its agreement six months later, Japan was more determined than ever to checkmate the expansion of Russia.

After the signing of the Anglo-Japanese alliance on January 30, 1902, Japan began to make intensive preparations to exert its power. By 1904, Japan had built up an efficient army and navy to challenge Russia. On the night of February 8, without any declaration of war, the Japanese fleet took the Russian squadron at Lushun (Port Arthur) by surprise, inflicting serious losses and imposing a blockade on the harbor.

Eventually Japan captured Lushun and Shenyang in Manchuria, and destroyed two-thirds of the Russian fleet sent from the Baltic. However, Japan was exhausted and could not hope to pursue the war to a successful conclusion if Russia should mobilize its overwhelming forces in Europe. Instead, Japan took the initiative in proposing peace negotiations, anticipating that war-weary Russia was ready to accept. Through the mediation of President Theodore Roosevelt at the peace conference in Portsmouth, New Hampshire, a peace treaty was signed on September 5, 1905. The skillful diplomacy of Roosevelt, with his famous pronouncement that in this war there was no victor, hence no vanquished, won him the Nobel Peace Prize.

Under the Russo-Japanese treaty, Russia agreed to surrender its lease of Lushun and Dalian, to evacuate from occupied areas including the railway properties in Manchuria, to cede half of Sakhalin annexed in 1875, and to recognize Korea as Japan's sphere of influence. Without paying one-cent indemnity, Russia essentially transferred some of its ill-gotten gains in the Far East to Japan by acknowledging the latter's hegemony in the area. China was left with the task of negotiating a treaty with Japan to accept all terms pertaining to China in the Russo-Japanese treaty.

The Russo-Japanese war was fought by two foreign powers on Chinese territory for one and a half years, devastating the land and impoverishing its people. China received no compensation whatsoever for damages, but was forced to negotiate with Japan to protect its own interests in Manchuria from further encroachment. The treaty was concluded on December 22, 1905.

When Tang Shaoyi and Liang Shiyi arrived in Manchuria to survey the devastation, they were struck by the depth of penetration of the Japanese occupation. Having experienced face-to-face confrontations with both Western and Japanese varieties of imperialism, Tang spoke to Shiyi with undisputed authority, "Drafting this treaty is the easy part because all we can do is to make sure that Japan will not claim more than it has wrested from Russia. The difficulty lies in the implementation. Wait and see how often we will be called upon to settle local disputes resulting from Japan's deliberate misinterpretation of the treaty."

"I understand the danger," Shiyi replied. "I hope that we will not be tested but we must prepare for the worst."

As if to underscore the work that remained to be done on the diplomatic fronts, the imperial court appointed Tang Shaoyi Junior Deputy Minister of Foreign Affairs, concurrently with the position of managing director of two major railways. Shiyi was accorded the title and office of Expectant Counselor in the Ministry of Foreign Affairs and was also appointed as Tang's principal secretary in railway affairs.

In his new capacity, Tang Shaoyi proposed to Sir Ernest Satow a new treaty on Tibet. Allowing Britain to receive favorable treatments, China in return would firmly retain sovereignty over Tibet. When the treaty was finally signed in May 1906, Tang said to Shiyi, "Maybe we can now turn our attention to the railway affairs."

Bitter Fruit

Shiyi and his family began the new year of 1906 with great excitement. After being awarded the new position, Shiyi finally became a fifth ranked official with sufficient income to move his family from the cramped family quarters in Sanshui Hostel to a rented house with a private courtyard.

After inspecting the new house, Shiyi's wife could find nothing new to complain about. As she sank into a comfortable chair in the living room, she said to her husband, "We barely managed to survive last year during your long absence. I hope you don't have to take such a long trip again."

Although, like most Chinese, Shiyi did not usually discuss business with his wife, he told her, "No such trip is on the horizon. My work in the Ministry of Foreign Affairs is winding down. My work will keep me busy in Beijing most of the time."

The second lady came into the living room to report that the children obviously enjoyed playing in their private courtyard. Shiyi suddenly broke in, "Perhaps we should invite Tang Shaoyi's children for a visit. They miss their mother very much. She died after childbirth a year and half ago."

"How old are they?" Liang's second lady asked. "We certainly should do something kind for them."

"His younger son is less than two years old," Liang replied. "But his oldest daughter is at least ten years older. Tang Shaoyi relied on relatives to take care of his children when he was away last year."

"Perhaps we should wait for a little while before we invite them over," Madam suggested. "We are far from being settled. Besides, their whole family just moved to Beijing from Tianjin. They must have other things to do." That settled the discussion. The second lady was sent to visit the Tang family and to offer help if the need should arise.

* * *

When Tang and Shiyi were in India, Yuan Shikai pushed for the appointment of his trusted friend Xu Shichang as Senior Deputy Minister of War with the support of Prince Qing, who was then the most influential advisor to the empress dowager. Sensing popular demand for constitutional monarchy after the Russo-Japanese war,

Yuan Shikai proposed to the empress dowager that the court send Manchu princes and officials abroad to investigate foreign political systems as a prelude to introducing a constitution. In an effort to dampen the momentum of the revolutionaries, the empress dowager assented to Yuan's proposal in July 1905. An investigatory mission of five members was created under the leadership of Prince Zhaize, with Xu Shichang as one of its members.

On August 26, 1905, when the mission members were to depart from Beijing, a revolutionary set off a bomb in the railway station. Falling to ground for cover, Xu Shichang was slightly wounded as was another member next to him. After the two submitted their resignations, a reconstituted delegation took off in December.

"Xu Shichang was lucky in more ways than one," Tang Shaoyi remarked to Shiyi after they visited Xu to comfort him. "I'm glad that not only is he recovering from his injury but he is also removed from the debate about constitutionalism."

"You're right," Shiyi agreed. "The mission simply serves as window dressing for the imperial court which has no real intention of implementing its recommendations."

When the mission returned home the following July, it recommended the adoption of a constitution for China in five years, and the recommendation was approved by a royal commission. On September 1, 1906, the empress dowager shrewdly endorsed the adoption of a constitution without specifying the date of promulgation. However, she ordered an immediate reorganization of the central government, adding several new ministries as well as revamping the old ones. The net effect was an institutional reshuffle that increased Manchu power.

* * *

In order to regain some degree of control of the maritime custom service, the imperial court issued an edict in 1906 to set up a Commission to oversee the service, which had been operated as an independent agency under a British Inspector General. The court appointed the Minister of Revenue, a Manchu official, to serve concurrently as the Controller, and Tang Shaoyi, the Junior Deputy Minister of Foreign Affairs, as Deputy Controller of the commission. As Expectant Counselor in the Foreign Ministry, Shiyi was to assist Tang in this new assignment.

"We're not going to make much headway in gaining control since the revenues from the customs duties have been pledged to pay off foreign debts under various treaty obligations," Tang commented to Shiyi after taking over his new position.

"I'm not familiar with the background of the maritime customs service," Shiyi replied. "Please enlighten me."

"The Chinese customs service has a long history of dominance by Westerners," Tang recalled. "In 1854, a temporary foreign inspectorate of customs was created in Shanghai under the treaty system. Since the money turned over to Beijing far exceeded Chinese expectation, the Qing officials turned to an Englishman to create a model customhouse at the port of Shanghai, which became the foundation of an international civil service with a tradition of honesty and impartiality in the administration of customs dues. By 1863, another Englishman, Robert Hart, had extended the customs service to eight new ports and established a uniform customs procedure. Hart moved his office from Shanghai to Beijing in 1865 at the request of the Chinese Foreign Office. Hart technically became an official in the Chinese civil service even though he retained considerable independence. He appointed a head commissioner of customs at each port, responsible to him alone. He also made a wide search of talents for his staff. The service was cosmopolitan in its general constitution."

Turning to his own involvement in this service, Tang explained, "The staff in the customs service was officially considered to be of mixed Chinese-foreign composition, but we Chinese invariably held low positions—clerks, accountants and secretaries. When I first returned from the United States, it was difficult for me to find suitable employment even though I had been sent by the government to study abroad. I decided to work for the maritime customs service since I would have a better chance than other Chinese to get ahead because of the fluency of my English." Then he added with a cunning smile, "Although Robert Hart emphasized the need for foreigners to acquire fluency in Chinese, he was in no hurry to train the Chinese staff to take over. However, the pay was good and the job was free of politics."

Indeed, by Chinese standards, the salary scale in the customs service was unusually high, particularly for the foreign staff. By 1898, the customs service produced one-third of the entire revenue of the Chinese government. After the imposition of the Boxer Protocol by the Western powers in 1901, the customs service took on even greater responsibilities of controlling inland customs as well as customs in the treaty ports to insure the payments of the indemnities. Robert Hart's unchallenged authority allowed him to retain his post as Inspector General even as he was aging and failing in health. The new commission on which Tang Shaoyi would serve as Deputy Commission was the imperial court's latest effort to oversee Hart's operation and to negotiate quietly with his subordinates to regain some control. Shiyi was assigned by Tang to help him in this effort.

Tang Shaoyi was very excited as he recalled his earlier days in the custom service. He remembered poignantly his assignment by the service to Korea in the 1880's when he met Yuan Shikai, who was then the powerful Chinese Resident Commissioner in Korea. With visible pride, Tang Shaoyi told Shiyi, "When I was stationed in Korea in 1894, I learned about a plot by the Japanese to assassinate Yuan Shikai. I asked my British superior to seek help from John Jordan, who was then the British Consul in Korea. One night under the cover of darkness, Yuan and I rode on horseback with pistols in our hands and raced to the harbor where a British warship was prearranged to take Yuan back to Tianjin. Without giving our action a second thought, I risked my own life to save Yuan's." Now Shiyi understood why these two men with such different backgrounds could become friends and close associates.

* * *

When their official duties were outlined, Tang Shaoyi confided to Shiyi his personal affairs. "When I made a short trip to Korea last month, I met a wealthy businessman for whom I had done a favor years ago when I was stationed there. Learning that I am a widower, he introduced me to his two daughters and offered them as my concubines. I promised him to consider it seriously since I somewhat like his older daughter."

"What a strange offer!" Shiyi was completely surprised. "Wealthy Chinese parents would never offer their daughters as concubines, let alone both daughters to be concubines of the same man."

Then Tang unfolded his own plan and sprang another surprise on Shiyi. "This Korean businessman told me that if only one of his daughters is married to me, she will be very lonely in China. I do not judge people who take concubines. Look around this capital and you find that practically every official, including yourself, has concubines. But my own outlook has been shaped by my youthful years in the United States. I want to take the older daughter of this man as my wife. But I have no desire to take her younger sister as a concubine. The fear raised by the old man can be solved if you can take his younger daughter as your concubine."

Shiyi was shocked by Tang's revelation. In Chinese society, a woman married to a widower was referred to as "successor wife," and was often viewed as a villain, prone to mistreating the children from the previous marriage. Given the opportunity, a woman would choose to be a successor wife instead of a concubine since a successor wife would command more respect. However, a widower with young children often took a concubine instead of a successor wife out of respect for his children's sensibility. In Tang's world, the logic seemed to turn upside down.

Shiyi shrugged. "I must think about this suggestion. I've not been seeking a third lady."

After several more hours of entertaining conversation, Shiyi agreed to do the favor for his friend. And perhaps he could not resist the temptation. The fate of the two daughters of the Zheng family of Korea was sealed. They would soon travel together to China.

* * *

The second lady decided it was time to visit the Tang family to get acquainted with the new Madame Tang as well as to invite the Tang children to come over. Madam found no reason to go with her. After all, the new Madame Tang was only a "successor wife," hardly her equal. When the second lady returned home, she described the beautiful garden and exquisite furniture in Tang's residence, the kind of luxuries she had never dreamed of. Madam cut short her jubilant conversation, "This is the first time you have been to the residence of a second-ranked official. Of course, these officials can afford such life style. Don't be so overwhelmed by it." Although Madam had never been in such a residence either, she was well informed about the astronomical difference of pay scales between the high and low ranking officials. She wondered what stroke of luck the new Madame Tang had received in order to deserve such a reward in life.

Fate was not so kind to Madame Tang's younger sister who was married to Shiyi. Under the best of circumstances, the addition of the third lady to the Liang family was not an event that would upset its family members. Shiyi ruled the family religiously according to the Confucian moral code. The peaceful coexistence of his wife and the second lady was the envy of many of his friends. However, this third lady was quite naive about Chinese culture and customs even though she was of Chinese descent. She came with her own maid servant, a confidant whom Madam considered to be potentially dangerous in leaking the affairs of Liang family to Madame Tang.

The third lady felt intimidated in this new household dominated by Liang's wife, the famous Madam whom everyone feared. Her every move was scrutinized by the watchful eye of Madam, who was not known to mince words and would criticize her on even trivial missteps. "We must not pamper Asan (No. 3)," she told her husband.

"Of course not," Shiyi assured her. "but we should excuse her for not knowing many of our customs. She is young and can learn quickly."

Blushing, Madam vilified the third lady as her husband walked away. Could the presence of this third lady prevent her from monopolizing her husband until she gave birth to another son? Only she knew the answer.

With constant complaints from Madam, even Liang's diplomatic skill could not alleviate the bitter atmosphere in the family.

A Solemn Memorial

Shiyi spent much of his time in the office since becoming Tang Shaoyi's principal secretary in railway affairs in February 1906. He was initiated into the delicate task of taking over the administration of the five railways constructed with foreign loans. The discord in his family, though tenacious, did not disrupt his attention to this new assignment.

In August, Shiyi received a cable via Guangzhou from his younger brother Shixu, informing him that his mother had died from pneumonia. Shiyi grieved over the loss as he reflected on the full measure of her love for him and for the rest of the family. The squabble between his wife and his third lady suddenly seemed trivial. He must now make plans to attend his mother's funeral.

Heaven seemed to have fallen as Shiyi read and re-read the short telegram bringing the unexpected news of his mother's death. Fond memories of his mother filled his mind. She had always brought warmth to the family as a counterweight to his austere father. Shiyi remembered vividly the times when he failed the national examination. His mother understood his pain as no one else did, not even his wife, and provided him with comfort and encouragement so that he could recover from the agony. She had held the family together when the men were away advancing their careers. Shiyi wished he had spent more time with her, but she always insisted that he should pursue his career without worrying about her. "You'll honor your father and mother when you distinguish yourself in public service," she had told him many times.

After recovering from the shock, he immediately made travel arrangements to attend the funeral. The least of his worries was to get a leave of absence from his job since the Qing court encouraged filial piety as the foundation of Confucian ethics and allowed a long mourning period for a parent's death. As he got the family together, he sadly announced, "I am going to take only Dingji and Dingwu with me for this trip. There is no more berth for the rest of the family on the steamship leaving Tianjin for Hong Kong in the next few days."

Madam was pleased with his decision. She disliked travel. "I like this arrangement. Our family has outgrown the size of my father-in-law's house. According to the Cantonese customs, we cannot stay with relatives and friends during the deep mourn-

106

ing period. It is out of the question for us to stay in a hotel because there is none in the village. In any case, members of a family in deep mourning, including sons and daughters-in-law of the deceased, are not supposed to be seen in public, except those on their way home for the funeral. Yes, husband, I agree." It was quite a relief to Madam that she would be spared such inconvenience.

"Can you take care of the two boys by yourself on this trip?" Madam asked after she thought about her husband's decision. She was aware that the presence of his two eight-year-old sons at his mother's funeral was mandatory. She raised the question only to highlight her concern for the safety of her own son. The second lady, without uttering a word, accepted the fate that her son Dingwu would also make the trip.

"There will be no problem for me," Shiyi reassured both Madam and the second lady. "I hope you'll take good care of yourselves when I'm away."

Pointing a finger at the third lady, Madam said to her husband, "You better tell Asan to take orders from me during your absence. Lately, she has not been listening to my instruction."

"I have arranged for her to stay with the Tang family when I'm away." Shiyi replied.

Choking with anger, Madam could hardly put it in words, "It is unbecoming for her to stay with another family while we are in deep mourning. What will the Tang family think?"

"Tang Shaoyi does not believe in the superstition that a visit by someone in deep mourning will bring bad luck to the family," Shiyi said quietly, knowing the reply would further infuriate Madam. "He's quite Westernized in his thinking, you know."

How about Madame Tang?" Madam said, not letting down the pressure. "Hasn't she any sense about our customs?"

"I don't know what the tradition for deep mourning is in Korea, but she apparently has no objection to having Asan stay with her for a while." After that exchange, Shiyi sent his third lady and her maid off to the Tang family.

Waving good-bye, Shiyi and his two sons went to the railway station and headed for Tianjin. During the train ride, he coached his sons on the etiquette of the funeral ceremony and memorial service. The two boys were attentive as they knew their grandfather would be extremely upset if they did not follow the proper etiquette.

During the voyage from Tianjin to Hong Kong, their ship was caught in a typhoon near Taiwan. Next morning, they saw many wrecked fishing boats. The sailors on board their ship tried to rescue the floundering fishermen. Shiyi went back to his stateroom to search for some spare clothes and donated them to the shivering victims when they were brought to safety. "I have very few clothes to spare," he told the fishermen. "Take the money and get yourselves some necessities when you go ashore."

It took the steamship another two days to reach Hong Kong. Shiyi and his sons immediately transferred to a small boat that sailed to Guangzhou. They took the Guangzhou-Sanshui Railway on the last leg of their trip home.

Steven T. Au

* * *

As the train moved slowly toward his native land, Shiyi's thoughts turned to the funeral arrangements. His father was an orthodox, uncompromising Confucian scholar. Confucius stressed reverence and acts of service to one's parents according to the rules of propriety, but he was not a religious leader. Neither he nor his disciples posed as a prophet or established a church with creed and clergy. Confucius never used the word Shangdi (Lord-on-high), but preferred the less personal word Tian (Heaven) in referring to the spiritual beings. He said "Respect ghosts and gods but keep them at a distance." Other Confucian scholars would consider him an agnostic by quoting his other utterances, such as: "We don't know yet about life; how can we know about death?" or "We don't know yet how to serve men; how can we know about serving ghosts?" After Confucianism was elevated to a state doctrine, it took on the trappings of an organized religion. Like many Confucian scholars, Liang Zhijian believed man should take care of his own affairs according to Confucian moral principles, not through supernatural guidance.

Religions such as Daoism and Buddhism could flourish in a society dominated by a state sponsored Confucianism only when their practices did not cause conflict with the Confucian doctrine. Philosophically all three spiritual traditions sought to advance the age old Chinese belief in the orderly universe. In each tradition, there was a dichotomy between a philosophical construct for the educated and a corresponding popular religion for the masses, and the two almost never met. Generally the scholar-officials tended to carry the Confucian ideas of proper human relationships to the extreme in their official capacities, but in their private life, many attempted to escape, to some degree, into the mysteries of nature and to find spiritual meaning in Daoism or Buddhism. Liang Zhijian was not among them.

Understandably, most women were more pious than men, given their sufferings in a male-dominated society. Since they were illiterate, they also tended to practice popular religions which offered them comfort and hope for salvation. Men were generally tolerant towards the religious practices of their wives even though they might be non-believers. Shiyi's mother had not held a strong religious belief, but she was known to have visited Buddhist temples with her neighbors. Although Shiyi adopted his father's orthodox Confucian view, he was not dogmatic and his heart was open to his mother. He wondered: Might his father stop being so rational in time of sorrow and allow his mother's religious practice to be used in the funeral service?

Because the rituals of Confucianism, Daoism and Buddhism influenced each other through the centuries, there were many common elements in their rituals of worship, such as burning of incense and placing food on the altar. But there were also notable differences. As an insurance policy, many people, including some Confucian scholars, accepted funeral rites evoking all three religious traditions simultaneously so the deceased would ascend to heaven or another spiritual destination, no matter which faith turned out to represent the ultimate truth. Shiyi's father had been scornful of such contradictions.

Beijing Odyssey

Shiyi was jolted from his thoughts when the train pulled into the railway terminal. He saw many relatives and friends waiting at the platform to meet him and his two sons. In observance of the etiquette of deep mourning, his brother Shixu was not among them. As soon as Shiyi got off the train, one of his brothers-in-law cornered him, "Your father has already made preliminary arrangements for the funeral." To no one's surprise, he added, "It will be strictly in the orthodox Confucian tradition. He wants to spare no expense and will do the utmost to honor your mother in a dignified way."

* * *

As Shiyi and his sons approached his home, they saw a bamboo frame with a thatched roof erected in front of the gate. The thatched roof structure was a temporary shelter for the staging area of the funeral procession, be it rain or shine. Two large lanterns with blue-colored characters on a white background were hung from the bamboo frame, pronouncing the mourning of the death of a family member. As soon as Shiyi walked through the gate, he knelt down and inched forward on his knees to the hall where his mother's coffin lay in state. His sons were horrified by the sight that as their father moved, he was whipped with a cane by an elderly man who was yelling, "unfilial son, unfilial son," until their father reached the coffin. It all had to be played out according to the rites if a son was not at the deathbed when his mother died. Then Shiyi's sons crawled into the house on their knees amid shouts of "unfilial! unfilial!" but without the threat of whipping.

Liang Zhijian led his family to perform the daily rituals during the seven weeks of deep mourning when members of the family dressed in make-shift white mourning robes. The daily rituals included worship at breakfast, lunch and dinner with food and drinks as well as incense and candles. These offerings were placed on a table in front of a wooden tablet on which the name of the deceased was inscribed. In Confucian tradition, such worship was an expression of one's gratitude according to the same rules of propriety that one would observe with the living. The adult members would remind children not to cut their hair or clip their nails as one should not destroy any part of the body inherited from the deceased. After the deep mourning period, the general mourning would begin, lasting three years for sons and daughters, and one year for spouse and grandchildren. Since no wedding would be permitted for persons affected by the general mourning period, the marriage of Liang Zhijian's youngest daughter to her betrothed would be delayed.

More than two weeks had already elapsed when Shiyi arrived home. Thus the funeral and memorial service was scheduled for the end of the third week. The living room was turned into a hall of worship, in which the coffin was placed at the center in the rear. This arrangement was no accident because only the coffin of a woman who in life had been a wife could be placed at the center; while that of a concubine would have to be placed on the side. The walls of the hall were decorated with words of mourning from friends and relatives. In lieu of flowers, the practical minded would send words of condolence pinned on large sheets of cloth of dull or dark colors which could be used to make garments suitable for the general mourning period afterwards. The gentry friends would send lyrical couplets written in fine calligraphy on white scrolls to express their sympathy. Since both Liang Zhijian and Liang Shiyi had so many friends who were distinguished scholars, no wall was big enough for all the scrolls, and the overflow had to be hung from the temporary bamboo frame outside the house.

On the day of the memorial service, friends and neighbors were received and took turns to pay their respects. No collective ceremony with eulogy and music was offered since the sounds from human or musical instruments were deemed too distracting to silent prayers or thoughts of individual mourners. However, a drummer was stationed at the gate to beat the drum three times to signal the arrival of each mourner. Most mourners knelt down three times, kowtowing thrice to the tablet each time. The elderly mourners would simply bow three times without kneeling. The sons and daughters-in-law of the deceased stayed on their knees on both sides of the mourners all the time to express their thanks.

Tables had been set up at the periphery of the thatched-roof structure outside so that mourners could rest there until all mourners had completed their rituals. The early arrivals would find time to read the scrolls hung on the walls and from the temporary bamboo frame. They also chatted with friends. After reading the lyrics on these scrolls, which were full of lavish praise of the virtue of the deceased, one mourner remarked to another, "I'm surprised there is no marching band nor the Daoist priests or Buddhist monks for the funeral procession. This distinguished family certainly can afford that." He also thought of the popular Daoist and Buddhist ceremonies performed in the deep mourning period which offered an opportunity for the living to affect the well-being of the dead in the spiritual world. Paper money of gold and silver, or even paper worldly possessions such as houses or figures of servants would be burned to ensure an easy life in another world for the dead. Daoist monks and Buddhist nuns might also be engaged to recite their respective scriptures so the dead could journey safely and speedily to their spiritual destination. "Most wealthy families would love to show off such extravagance," the mourner concluded.

"Oh no!" said the second mourner. "The Liang family does not approve popular ceremonies which mix all three spiritual traditions. They would have nothing to do with such irrational practices. They do not regard lavish spending for a funeral as an expression of the filial devotion of the family to the deceased when it promotes superstition and ignorance."

After all the mourners had paid their last respect to the deceased, they were invited to a catered lunch before the funeral procession. Since there was a long walk from the house to the grave, some mourners followed the procession to the graveyard while others left as the procession began to move.

At the start the funeral procession, the coffin was taken to the staging area and placed on a bier which was then carried on the shoulders of sixteen strong men. The immediate family followed the bier closely. As the women in the family were crying loudly, the men were expected to restrain their emotions other than displaying a solemn face. At the staging area, a moving rectangular tent supported by four posters, carried by one person at each corner, was ready to protect the immediate family from exposing their state of pain and sorrow. At the gravesite, a simple ceremony was conducted by the immediate family to put their beloved to rest.

* * *

When the deep mourning period of seven weeks was over, Shiyi intended to stay in his native village for as long as his father wished. He even thought of asking the rest of his family in Beijing to come join him. However, in early November, he received a cable from Tang Shaoyi which read: "Yesterday the imperial court announced the establishment of the Ministry of Posts and Communications, which encompasses all railway operations as well as telegraph and post offices. I have been named Senior Deputy Minister of this new ministry. I urge you to return to Beijing immediately."

In the next two days, Shiyi quietly consulted with his brother Shixu. "I am really worried about father," he told Shixu. "He looks very weak to me."

Shixu who had watched their father's mood replied, "Since father returned home from Beihai last year, he kept himself busy by becoming the principal of a school in the county. Hopefully this volunteer work will help him forget his pain and sorrow. My wife and I can manage the household chores and take care of him. You can go back to your important job in Beijing." Then Shixu told his brother, "My wife is expecting our first child. I hope the commotion of the mourning period has not done anything to hurt her pregnancy."

Shiyi's face brightened with the joyful news. "Tell her to take a good rest."

Without hearing from Shiyi about his reaction to the cable from Beijing, his father sensed his dilemma and broke the silence. "I know your devotion to me exceeds everything else. However, you can make significant contributions to the new field of communications in Beijing. I'm still healthy and Shixu has taken good care of me. You should not hesitate to accept a post in the new ministry. This is a good opportunity to serve your country and I will be very proud if you answer the call." With that encouragement, Shiyi and his two sons departed.

Triumph and Tragedy

As soon as Shiyi returned to Beijing in January 1907, he buried himself in working with Tang Shaoyi on the urgent business of the new Ministry of Posts and Communications. The appointment of Tang as the Senior Deputy Minister of this new ministry allowed Yuan Shikai to expand his influence in railway affairs through his proteges and allies. As Tang's principal secretary in railway affairs, Shiyi got a taste of the raw power.

"The establishment of this ministry is part of an effort by the imperial court to centralize and increase its railway authority," Tang told Shiyi as the two worked side by side to map their strategy for organizing the new ministry. "The feverish pitch at which the foreign powers tried to grab a piece of action in China was not unlike that of the railway expansion in the United States after the American Civil War. I was an eyewitness to that madness when I was a student in the United States."

"As I see it, the current state of railway affairs is the result of the imperial court's wavering policy for railway development pursued over the past three decades," Shiyi thoughtfully observed. "This zigzag course led to a hodgepodge of railways, many still under construction, scattered throughout the country, without a national policy or direction."

Tang Shaoyi added, "We must fully understand the the problems before we can correct them. Ambitions of regional leaders saw the administrative control of railways as a powerful base. The difficulties of central control were exacerbated by the designs of foreign powers. They dangled huge loans for railway construction as a means of expanding their spheres of influence. These factors created a fever of competing interests for the railways."

* * *

As early as 1876, the British-owned Jardine Matheson & Co. constructed a light railway for freight transportation between Shanghai and the Port of Wusong near the entrance from the sea to Yangzi River. One month after its inauguration, a Chinese soldier was killed by the train. In the spirit of Luddites in England, the people in the countryside near the railway demanded its demolition. When the British consul in Shanghai rejected the request of local officials, the imperial court in Beijing took up

112

the case. After full compensation was made in late 1877, the tracks were dug up and sent to Taiwan where the local government had intended to build a railway on the island. When Taiwan could not raise the money, all the tracks and rolling stock, including locomotives and cars, were dumped into the nearby harbor.

Two years later, the government-owned Kaiping Coal Mining Company petitioned the Qing court to build a six-mile railway to facilitate the shipment of bituminous coal. The coal mining company was a government-supervised enterprise under the sponsorship of Li Hongzhang, who received the final approval of the project in 1881. This short line was extended to Tianjin in 1888, and was named Tangshan-Tianjin Railway. After the completion of this first Chinese-owned railway, some regional leaders saw the importance of railways for industrial development. However, most officials in the imperial court were against the idea. After hearing many arguments from regional leaders, the imperial court finally took a more conciliatory attitude toward railway construction.

The first major railway project sponsored by the Chinese government was the extension of the Tangshan-Tianjin Railway eastward from Tangshan to Shanhaiguan, the strategic pass to Manchuria. In April 1891, Li Hongzhang was appointed Managing Director of Beiyang Railway Administration, which was in charge of this extension. After its completion in 1894, Hu Yufen took over as its managing director and began the construction of a section from Beijing to Tianjin, linking the national capital to the border of Manchuria. In 1898, Hu Yufen secured a loan of 2.3 million pounds sterling (11.5 million U.S. dollars) from British and Chinese Corporation for further extension of this railway beyond Shanhaiguan to Shenyang in Manchuria. This railway, which had been started with Chinese government funds, had to surrender its administrative control to a foreign lender when it became the major lifeline of transportation between Beijing and Manchuria.

Using his influence in the imperial court, Yuan Shikai got his hands in the railway business in January 1902, when he succeeded Hu Yufen as Managing Director of Beijing-Shenyang Railway. In August of the same year, he took over the construction of the Tianjin-Zhenjiang Railway which was also the bailiwick of Hu Yufen. After wresting these two major railways from his rival, Yuan exercised direct control of his new power base through his trusted subordinates and close friends.

"We must respect those who pioneered the railway construction before Yuan Shikai," Tang Shaoyi cautioned Shiyi. "We should examine the power structure that led to the present state of affairs."

"Yes," Shiyi responded thoughtfully, "we must deal firmly but gingerly with those who are going to transfer their powers to us."

* * *

After Yuan Shikai got a foothold in the railways in 1902, the most important railways remained in the hands of Sheng Xuanhuai, who had been Commissioner of the Imperial Railway Corporation since its inception in 1896. A former manager of government-sponsored enterprises, Sheng was responsible for opening the door of railway construction in China with foreign loans. Public apathy doomed the possibility of domestic loans. Even new forms of taxation could not provide enough capital. The railways constructed with foreign loans were nominally administered by the Qing government but in reality were in the hands of foreign lenders. Administrative control of these railways became chaotic as each railway followed the dictate of its foreign lender.

The Imperial Railway Corporation under Sheng Xuanhuai secured a series of loans from a Belgian Syndicate for the construction of Beijing-Wuhan Railway, linking the nation's capital to the heartland of China, which was completed in April 1906. It was widely believed that the Belgian syndicate was acting as a front for the French government. The Imperial Railway Corporation was also in charge of constructing a number of shorter lines, all financed by huge foreign loans from British, French, Russian and German banks backed by their respective governments. The Imperial Railway Corporation also borrowed 40 million U.S. dollars from the American China Development Company for the construction of the Guangzhou-Wuhan-Sichuan Railway. When the project faltered and was far behind schedule, most American shares were sold to the Belgian interests. Fearing this railway as well as Beijing-Wuhan Railway would be controlled by the Belgians, the successor of Sheng Huanhuai negotiated a loan from the Hong Kong Government to pay off the balance of the American loan.

The appointment of Tang Shaoyi in 1905 as Managing Director of Beijing-Wuhan and Nanjing-Shanghai Railways was another blow to Sheng Xuanhuai's control of railways. Sheng was completely routed when Tang Shaoyi was appointed to replace him in early 1906 as the Commissioner of the Imperial Railway Corporation. During the transfer, Tang ordered Shiyi to examine the accounts and verify the funds of the corporation. As Shiyi went over the records of the corporation, he found very sloppy bookkeeping that left many unanswered questions. He avoided confrontation with Sheng's former subordinates who were sullen and un-cooperative. Nevertheless he aroused the resentment of Sheng Xuanhuai who would neither forgive nor forget.

Reflecting his experience in these encounters, Shiyi told Tang, "I'm afraid we are making enemies before the job even begins. The incumbent administrators consider your order an affront to Sheng Xuanhuai."

Tang replied, "We are not going to conduct a witchhunt, but we must keep the records clear. You will appreciate that when someone audits our own transactions in the future."

* * *

With the establishment of the Ministry of Posts and Communications, the unfinished business of the Imperial Railway Corporation was transferred to this new ministry under the supervision of Tang Shaoyi. Looking ahead to strengthen the position of the Qing court, Tang Shaoyi told Shiyi, "I'm planning to set up an inspectorate over five railways which are nominally administered by the Qing government but in fact are under foreign control. Two of these railways were financed with Belgian loans, two with British loans, and one with a Russian loan. Since separate foreign loans were negotiated for each railway, the loan agreements with the different countries have different terms. As a result, government authority is not uniform for the administration of these railways. Our job is to regain control of these railways by negotiating new loans with better terms."

"Of the five railways, we should begin with Beijing-Wuhan Railway which has the most unfavorable terms and the most restrictive authority, although it has the greatest economic and strategic importance to the nation." Shiyi suggested.

"I'll leave the details of implementation to you, but we must proceed as soon as possible," Tang warned. "Our minister is not in the best of health and no one knows how long he will last in his position. If we don't act now, the opportunity may be lost forever."

Tang Shaoyi sensed correctly that the power struggle for this new turf was not over. In March 1907, he was appointed Governor of Fengtian Province in Manchuria when the minister resigned on account of ill health. Tang's departure from Beijing meant he would relinquish his positions in both the Foreign Ministry and the Ministry of Posts and Communications. As Tang's principal assistant in both ministries, Shiyi's career was left in limbo except that he had already established a reputation in railway affairs. The acting minister followed through with the appointment of Shiyi as Director of the Inspectorate, allowing him to retain a foothold in the ministry. Shiyi's position was again threatened when an adversary of Yuan Shikai was appointed the new minister in May. Fortunately this minister lasted for less than four weeks and was transferred by the imperial court to be the governor-general in Guangzhou. Finally Chen Bi, an ally of Yuan Shikai, took over as the minister.

"I want to centralize the handling of all foreign loans and the management of railways in one agency within the ministry," Chen Bi told Shiyi. "The Inspectorate will be reorganized as the General Railway Bureau, and you will be the head of this new bureau." Shiyi gained a free hand in reshaping a new railway policy.

In August 1907, the Qing court delivered a coup de grace when it transferred two of the most powerful Governor-Generals, Zhang Zhidong and Yuan Shikai, to Beijing as Grand Councillors, with Yuan serving concurrently as Minister of Foreign Affairs. In one stroke, the court took away the troops of Yuan and Zhang in the provinces so that military authority finally rested with the Manchus in Beijing. Although Yuan's military power and influence in his former Beiyang base had been reduced, his presence in the imperial court would provide protection to his men in railway affairs.

It was also a personal triumph for Shiyi who could now exercise his skills in managing this vast railway empire.

* * *

With his numerous activities in his job since returning to Beijing in January, Shiyi paid scarce attention to his family. However, he immediately sent for his third lady who had stayed with the Tang family during his absence. Torn between the feelings of ecstasy and abandonment, the third lady came home with complaints of some vague pains in the stomach.

"You must not let the pains continue," Shiyi said. "You should see a doctor to find out their cause."

"I'm all right," she replied, "Nothing is serious. I don't need to see a doctor."

Then the news of Tang Shaoyi's appointment as the Governor of Fengtian Province struck her like a thunderbolt. She understood too well that she would soon part with her sister when Madam Tang would move to Manchuria. She became extremely depressed and secluded herself most of the time in her own room.

The second lady noticed her weakened conditions at mealtime and said to her, "You must eat more to keep yourself strong. Can I help you in any way?"

"Thank you for your concern," the third lady replied, "but I really don't have the appetite for anything."

When Madam heard their exchange, she grumbled, "It's a waste of time to urge her to eat."

When the third lady went back to her room, she was all in tears. As her maid tried to undress her, the maid too could not help sobbing.

One morning when Shiyi was away for a short trip on railway business, this maid knocked at the room of the second lady and cried, "I cannot wake up the third lady. Can you come and help?" When they went into her room, they found that Shiyi's third lady had died in her sleep. This mysterious death excited the whole family and Shiyi came home just in time to take charge of her simple funeral. Being a concubine without a son, she was an insignificant element of the family in death as well as in life.

There was no autopsy or inquest as neither was practiced nor required. If Shiyi felt sorry for this tragedy, or even quilt or responsible, he didn't say. Men of good upbringing would never discuss such private matters with family and friends. It was too much even to explain to his friend and mentor Tang Shaoyi.

The family was eager to put aside this most unfortunate incident as well as the family discord before her death. According to the maid of the third lady, who heard the rumor from the servants of the Tang family, Madame Tang suspected that her sister might have committed suicide. But her maid who was her confidant and liaison to Madame Tang insisted there was no clue to that effect. Some thought the maid was protecting the dignity of her mistress, or avoiding any complicity in aiding a suicide. Others thought Madame Tang was suspicious because of the unhappy life her sister had in the Liang family. Such speculation strained the relationship of the ladies in the two families as no one could provide an adequate answer.

The Eminent Railway Administrator

Fortune smiled kindly on Shiyi. His promotion marked the sudden turn of his otherwise lackluster career in Beijing. For the first time he could be his own man in making major decisions instead of living in the shadow of someone else.

The basic structure of the Ministry of Posts and Communications consisted of a Council and a Secretarial Office. Of the five departments in the ministry, the Department of Land Communications oversaw all railway matters. The General Railway Bureau was the branch in that department concerned with those lines which were constructed with foreign loans. The General Railway Bureau had the main administrative responsibility of the ministry and supplied over 95 percent of its annual revenue. The frequent change of leadership at the top provided Shiyi, a mere fifth-ranked official, with opportunities to exercise extraordinary influence within the ministry.

Shiyi immediately assembled a group of young and capable men to be his assistants. They became the pillars of strength in his effort to regain control of railways from foreign concessionaires.

The situation at home also changed for the better shortly after the death of his third lady. He was buoyed by the news that his second lady was expecting another child.

"I trust that you will have the comfort of delivering the baby at home this time," Shiyi mused, alluding to her last delivery in a cart almost seven years before.

In September, his second lady gave birth to a healthy baby, his fifth son, who was named Dingshu. She was glad to have another son.

Madam steeled herself to remain calm when she heard about the birth of Dingshu. Since the birth of her daughter Huaisheng seven years before, she had longed for another son. She tried to dominate the attention of her husband for just that purpose, but she hated every moment of it. She had only her unlucky star to blame, she confessed to herself when she was in a reasonable mood. Two of her three sons did not survive infancy. Now the second lady had two sons, though it was too early to know the fate of the new baby. Madam was exceedingly envious and tried to suppress her feeling.

What irritated Madam most was that she had been outwitted by her husband. He was not supposed to have sexual relations within a year after the death of his mother, if he observed the admonition of his father. Obviously, he had ignored that lesson completely when he returned to Beijing and favored the company of the second lady. I must do something to regain the initiative, Madam thought.

* * *

The most important task in the General Railway Bureau was the recovery of the administrative authority of Beijing-Wuhan Railway. The eight hundred and fourteen mile line from Beijing to Wuhan formally opened in 1905, having been bonded to a Belgian syndicate by virtue of construction loans. Its immediate financial success and the recognition of its strategic military value aroused Chinese public opinion and officials to agitate at the imperial court for redemption of the Belgian loans. For planning this top-priority project, Shiyi recruited Ye Gongchuo from the council of the ministry to work in the new bureau.

Ye Gongchuo had received the Juren degree at the age 17 and had gained a reputation as a poet. Twelve years younger than Shiyi, he joined the ministry in 1906. Perhaps because both were Cantonese, Shiyi and Ye hit it off very well as soon as they met.

"I want you to handle the affairs of Beijing-Wuhan Railway when I attend other urgent business," Shiyi told Ye Gongchuo. "We must restructure the debts by negotiating with the Belgians if possible, or by seeking new capital from other sources."

When the construction of Zhengding-Taiyuan Railway was completed in October 1907, Shiyi went to inspect it with an aide, Guan Genglin. The 160-mile railway was constructed with a Russian loan for linking the coal producing regions in north China to nearby populated areas. After reviewing its operating budget for the first year, Liang remarked to Guan, "There must be ways to improve the revenue or reduce the expenditure or both for this railway. We cannot afford to rely on subsidies in running government business."

Young and uninhibited, Guan responded to the budget with contempt, "I'm surprised the administrator would resort to red ink without trying harder to control cost. There is fat that can be trimmed." Guan Genglin, a Cantonese, had received a Jinshi degree at the age 24. He was just as brilliant as Ye Gongchuo. He'd spent a year studying in Japan before traveling around the world with the Imperial Constitutional Commission. Shiyi recruited him to work in the new bureau while Guan Kenglin continued to hold a concurrent appointment in the council of the ministry.

"You're right," Shiyi said to Guan with a smile. "You can have the job to help trim the budget." They soon developed a close working and personal relationship.

Shiyi also had to interfere when Nanjing-Shanghai Railway in the lower Yangzi River Valley was completed in 1908. According to the loan agreement, the railway was administered by a commission consisting of three British members and two Chinese members. Even though the Chairman of the Commission was Chinese, all decisions were made by the majority British members. The Chinese Chairman complained to the

General Railway Bureau that he had absolutely no power to act. Shiyi suggested changes to Sir John Jordan, the British Minister in Beijing, to resolve the gridlock.

John O. P. Bland, the representative of the British and Chinese Corporation, was assigned to discuss the gridlock issue with the Chinese. Shiyi asked another young aide, Zhao Qinghua, to negotiate with him. "Our goal is to appoint a Chinese Managing Director for the day-to-day operation," Shiyi told Zhao.

"It will take time to get this job done," Zhao replied, "but I think that Mr. Bland is a reasonable person. Eventually he will understand our point of view."

Zhao Qinghua had graduated from the Diocesan Boys School in Hong Kong and had worked briefly in the telegraph office in Guangzhou. He made his way to the ministry in 1906 through the contact with Tang Shaoyi. Because of his English speaking ability, he was invaluable as a member of Shiyi's team.

Another of Shiyi's immediate concerns was the completion of the Beijing-Zhangjiakou Railway, which was started with government funds in 1905. This line linking Inner Mongolia to the nation's capital was the only railway remaining in Chinese hands. It was also the first railway with a Chinese chief engineer, Zhan Tianyou, who had attended Yale University. Shiyi's long-time friend Guan Mianjun had been its Assistant Managing Director since 1906. Shiyi allocated funds in 1908 sufficient to complete the construction of this railway without seeking foreign loans.

By March 1908, the Ministry of Posts and Communications announced Shiyi's plan for the recovery of Beijing-Wuhan Railway: first to adjust the loan agreement with the Belgian syndicate on more liberal terms; or, if this failed, to negotiate new foreign loans for seventy-five percent of the required amount for redemption and raise the remaining twenty five percent from domestic sources.

* * *

After taking care of the urgent tasks in the General Railway Bureau, Shiyi began to implement a new salary policy for its personnel. Shiyi confided his plan to Ye Gongchuo. "In the railway business, large sums of money change hands in various transactions. There is a possibility for corruption if the employees in the ministry are not adequately paid. Moreover, some of our staff members work side by side with foreigners who are much better compensated. I plan to eventually promote our staff members to supervisory positions. It will be demoralizing and demeaning to the supervisors if their salaries are much lower than the foreign employees who report to them."

"I respect your opinion," said Ye. "However, the imperial court's backing of this recommendation from the ministry is necessary for its implementation."

Shiyi knew he could count on Minister Chen Bi to approve the proposal because they had discussed the corrupt practices in the past. They both hoped that their mentor at the imperial court, Yuan Shikai, now a Grand Councillor and the Minister of Foreign Affairs, would lend his support.

Since the Ministry of Posts and Communications had its own sources of income from railways to support the new salary structure, the proposal became a reality. However, Ye's observation proved to be prophetic. As soon as the new salary policy became public, newspapers spread words that the ministry was a "gold mine" and a railway job was a "golden rice bowl"

When such comments got back to Shiyi, he said to Ye Gongchuo, "Yes, I am receiving 1,200 taels monthly salary as head of the General Railway Bureau. But I could have received at least ten times as much from the perquisites for top administrators under the old system, which I refused. The new system will really save money for the ministry as well as improve the morale of employees."

"You don't have to convince me, but you must contend with continuing criticism that will be forthcoming," said Ye.

* * *

Shiyi's achievements in recovering the control of railways impressed Minister Chen Bi. In April 1908, Grand Councillor Yuan Shikai and Minister Chen Bi commended Shiyi for his "exceptional talent as a statesman" to Empress Dowager Cixi. Shiyi soon received formal recognition from the imperial court.

Shortly thereafter Shiyi was in the company of Yang Shizang, the powerful Governor-General of Zhili, to attend the entourage of Empress Dowager Cixi and Emperor Guangxu when they went to visit the Western Tombs in Zhili. After being given a royal treat for lunch, both Yang and Shiyi followed the protocol to thank their royal highnesses for the special food. The empress dowager turned to Shiyi, "You need a full stomach to do good work. Make sure you have eaten enough." Others in the entourage were surprised the dowager spoke only to Shiyi, by then a fourth-ranked official, but made no comment to Yang, a first-ranked official. Shiyi had his own explanation: the empress dowager was generous to the lower-ranking officials because they were not threatening to the imperial court.

After such a favor by the empress dowager, Shiyi received a promotion in rank. He also petitioned the court for an honorific title for his father, a title at the same or several ranks higher than his own. In matters of honoring his father, Liang was never timid in asking for the most, particularly since his father was a Juren degree holder in his own right. With Empress Dowager Cixi's blessing, the imperial court granted the title of a first-ranked official (Guanglu Dafu) to his father. His mother was given, posthumously, a corresponding first-ranked title for the lady.

In August 1908, when Shiyi was rushing to his office for an important appointment, the horse-drawn carriage in which he was riding overturned on a busy street. His forehead bruised and bleeding, he insisted on continuing to his office. After being treated, he met with Minister Chen Bi who praised him for his devotion to duty. He said to Chen, "Ye Gongchuo, the two Guans, and Zhao Qinghua support me so well, as if they were the four legs of a horse on which I rode. They deserve your praise more than I do." Chen Bi understood why Shiyi could command the undying loyalty of his subordinates.

After Shiyi was sent home, he tried to downplay the seriousness of his injury. He didn't want to alarm his wife who was pregnant and could be easily agitated. The second lady dressed his wound daily until he fully recovered.

In October, his wife gave birth to a baby boy. She had finally fulfilled her dream of having more than one son for protection of her old age. Shiyi named his sixth son Dingmin.

* * *

Shiyi could expect rapid promotion to even more important positions when he completed the redemption of the Beijing-Wuhan Railway. However, that was not going to be his fate. On November 13, 1908, Empress Dowager Cixi announced that, in consideration of Emperor Guangxu's illness and of her own old age, provision had been made for a new heir to the throne in the event of the emperor's death. This new heir was the emperor's three-year old nephew, Puyi. His father was the emperor's half brother, Prince Chun, and his mother was the daughter of the late General Ronglu, who for many years had been the most loyal protector of Empress Dowager Cixi. While Prince Chun was named the prince regent of the new heir apparent, Guangxu's wife, Longyu, was designated as the new empress dowager with special powers, if Puyi should ascend the throne before reaching maturity. The next day, Emperor Guangxu's death was announced; and on the day after, Empress Dowager Cixi died.

"Such a remarkable coincidence, too unbelievable to be natural," Ye Gongchuo remarked to Shiyi when they heard the news.

"This dramatic sequence of deaths will cause speculations all over China," Shiyi replied. "The political implications remain to be seen."

Emperor Guangxu was once again denied succession to power at the critical moment. His widow, whom he had despised in his lifetime for her manipulations on behalf of Cixi, now became the powerful Empress Dowager Longyu. Before her death, Empress Dowager Cixi had made sure of the continued domination of her own clan in the ruling house of the Qing Empire. The intriguing question was: could the empire survive the succession arrangements so elaborately dictated by the late Empress Dowager Cixi?

The Incipient Financier

In planning the recovery of the Beijing Wuhan Railway, Liang Shiyi noted that domestic and foreign funds from all transactions in the railways had been handled by foreign banks. Citing the advantage of a modern Chinese bank to capture such transactions, Shiyi recommended to Minister Chen Bi that the Bank of Communications be established by the Ministry of Posts and Communications. The minister agreed with his proposal and petitioned the imperial court for permission to organize such a bank.

"Up to this time, national banking in China has been monopolized by the bank established by the Ministry of Revenue," Ye Gongchuo commented. "When other ministries requested permission from the imperial court to organize a bank, they were refused. Do you think our ministry can get away with it?"

"I believe so," Shiyi replied. "The imperial court recognizes the size and importance of the revenue derived from railways. I have structured the deal in such a way that it costs the government nothing up front. The court cannot afford to refuse it."

For whatever reason, the imperial court promptly granted the permission. The capitalization of the Bank of Communications was immediately oversubscribed, causing the initial investment to be raised from five million to ten million taels. Profits from the Beijing-Shenyang Railway, Beijing-Wuhan Railway and the Imperial Telegraph Administration provided the ministry's share (two-fifths of the initial capital investment in the bank). The remaining amount came from the private sector.

The Governing Board president went to Li Jingqu, a nephew of Li Hongzhang, who had considerable political influence as well as entrepreneurial skill. The vice president was a major stockholder and was responsible for raising a large amount of capital from the private sector. As the head of the General Railway Bureau, Shiyi served as associate vice-president and, by special order of the ministry, he also oversaw the establishment of the bank's branches. The establishment of the Bank of Communications added financial influence to the growing power of the Ministry of Posts and Communications.

Because of the success in raising capital from private sources for the Bank of Communications, the imperial court established a Government Bonds Bureau. Shiyi and Li Jingqu were appointed as its co-directors. Shiyi was quite realistic about the prospect of selling government bonds for public subscription. "The imperial court may be mistaken that the public will subscribe to the government bonds enthusiastically." he told Li Jingqu. It is one thing to raise capital for the Bank of Communications for which the returns are quite tangible; bonds without a dedicated source of revenue to back them up are altogether another thing."

"I'm inclined to agree with you," Li Jingqu replied, "but we cannot refuse to ingratiate ourselves with the court officials after they threw their support to establish the Bank of Communications."

* * *

Shiyi also noted the harmful effects of provincial customs duties. Under an established policy to improve the revenue of local governments, duties were imposed on goods transported by boat or on land across the boundary of a county. It was a deterrent to the expansion of trade and industry, particularly to the development of railway freight transportation. Shiyi was a strong advocate of abolishing the duties and replacing them with subsidies from railway revenue.

In the recovery of Beijing-Wuhan Railway, Shiyi advised the Ministry of Posts and Communications to consult with the governors of Hubei and Zhili Provinces about the cancellation of such duties imposed on railway freight transportation. The ministry sent a deputy minister to assure the two governors that the ministry would compensate their losses from railway revenue if the provincial custom duties were eliminated. Although the governors agreed to the proposal verbally, they reneged on the agreement when asked to sign the written confirmation.

"It is a sign of the weakened authority of the central government and the rise of the power of the regional leaders," Shiyi lamented when he met with Ye Gongchuo afterwards. "After all the ground work, our plan failed in the last minute."

"This failure has very serious consequences," Ye observed. "It will surely plague us in the years to come."

In the meantime, negotiations with the Belgians for redemption of the loans for Beijing-Wuhan Railway were not fruitful. Subsequently, a favorable loan agreement for five million pounds sterling was signed in October 1908 with two foreign banks, the Hong Kong and Shanghai Bank and Banque de L'Indo-Chine. This amount represented about seventy-five percent of the redemption money. An amount of 17 million taels representing the remaining twenty-five percent would be raised from domestic sources. Eventually ten million taels were obtained through additional foreign loans for lack of public interest in government bonds. On December 28 of that year, the Chinese repaid the debt in full to the Belgian syndicate.

On January 11, Minister Chen Bi dispatched Shiyi and Ye Gongchuo to recover the control of Beijing-Wuhan Railway from the Belgian Syndicate. It was a delicate task since the Belgian syndicate was reluctant to relinquish its control.

"The ministry has designated us to recover the railway's records, accounts, funds, and materials from the Belgians," Shiyi told Ye Gongchuo. "We must proceed with care lest the Belgians use any excuse to delay the transfer."

"Naturally." Ye was elated. "We want to do our best without giving them any excuse to upset our goal."

* * *

When Liang Shiyi and Ye Gongchuo were busy with the affairs of Beijing-Wuhan Railway, a political tremor in the imperial court almost knocked them out of existence.

It all started with the dismissal of Yuan Shikai by Prince Chun, the new prince regent and father of Puyi, now enthroned as Emperor Xuantong. Prince Chun had been hostile to Yuan Shikai because of Yuan's alleged betrayal of the late Emperor Guangxu during the abortive "hundred days of reform." In a bold move, Prince Chun forced Yuan to retire on January 2, 1909, on the pretext of Yuan's "leg ailment." Targeting Yuan's proteges in the Ministry of Posts and Communications, the court censors attacked Chen Bi and thirty of his subordinates, including Shiyi and his trusted aides.

"How ironic that we are being accused of corruption!" Shiyi was outraged at the accusation as he complained to Ye Gongchuo. "Chen Bi has been appointed by the imperial court to take charge of the construction of the royal mausoleums for the late Emperor Guangxu and Empress Dowager Cixi precisely because of his success in overseeing the railway construction in our ministry."

"Trumped up charges are never based on reason," Ye Gongchuo sighed. "Otherwise there would be no such charges."

"Chen Bi advised the two grand councillors in charge of the budget that the estimate of the contractor was bloated in anticipation of traditional bribery to officials," Shiyi added. "He felt that the construction budget could be reduced by eliminating such corrupt practices. Now one of these councillors allegedly told Empress Dowager Longyu that the late emperor could not even have a comfortable final resting place because Chen Bi wanted to skimp on the construction cost!"

Whether the allegation was true or not, Empress Dowager Longyu was so eager to exercise her newly gained power that she decreed that Chen Bi must be dismissed. Prince Chun ordered an investigation of the matter by Natong and Sun Jia'nai, two highly respected elder statesman. In their report, they concluded that the charges could not be proven. In an effort to appease the critics, however, they hedged with a statement that lack of evidence did not necessarily clear the charges. Finally, Chen Bi and three others were dismissed, but Liang Shiyi and his aides survived the attack.

Even though Yuan Shikai was out of power, he used his ally Prince Qing to counteract the influence of Prince Chun and to protect his proteges. Xu Shichang, Governor-General of Manchuria, sensed the court's suspicion about his loyalty in controlling the strategic area of Manchuria after Yuan's downfall. With the support of Prince Qing, he was appointed to succeed Chen Bi as Minister of Posts and Communications. It did not hurt Shiyi to have a friend as his boss.

A savvy politician, Xu Shichang recognized Shiyi's strengths as a man of principle. Shiyi and his aides were energetic, open, and resourceful, and set good examples of practicing what they preached. Together they nurtured a relationship of trust with people by exhibiting candor which was in short supply among government officials. Xu concluded that they could survive on their own and did not need his protection. By then, Shiyi and his aides became so valuable to the Ministry of Posts and Communications that the imperial court could get rid of them only at its own peril. That consideration, more than anything else, saved them from prosecution.

In July 1909, Shiyi was appointed senior secretary of Ministry of Posts and Communications in addition to being head of its General Railway Bureau. Except for the minister and deputy ministers, he became the highest ranking railway official in the ministry. Shiyi was increasingly in a position to place men loyal to him in key positions both within the ministry and in the railways themselves. He could now exercise his influence to effect broader and more lasting changes than ever.

* * *

The success of the redemption of Beijing-Wuhan Railway and the furor caused by the investigation of the Ministry of Posts and Communications did not escape the attention of the foreign correspondents in Beijing. In December 1908, *The Times* of London, published two favorable pieces by its part-time correspondent John Bland on the recovery of the Beijing-Wuhan Railway by the Chinese authority. However, two months later, George Morrison, its famous and colorful correspondent in Beijing, commented in *The Times* that the ministry was a "by-word for inefficiency and corruption."

The Chinese press, which often looked to foreign peers for their news sources, followed the sensational reporting of Morrison and ignored the plain-spoken analysis of Bland. Little did they know the backgrounds of Bland and Morrison nor did they try to find out. An avid Chinese scholar, John Bland had direct contact with Shiyi and his aides on behalf of the British and Chinese Corporation. He grudgingly acknowledged the skill of the Chinese negotiators and even cited the patriotism of Cantonese bureaucrats in the Ministry of the Posts and Communications. George Morrison, on the other hand, frankly made no attempt to understand the Chinese view. What interested him was China as a theater of competing imperialism in which the British interest must be protected. His concern with the internal politics of China was entirely subordinated to his imperialism. The flip-flap in *The Times* of London was the result of the difference of their opinions.

Because of the one-sided reporting in the Chinese press, Shiyi became the target of attack. Public opinion, which hailed the recovery of Beijing-Wuhan Railways as a victory for China only a short while before, suddenly denounced the entire ministry as the center of corruption.

When Ye Gongchuo dropped in to visit Shiyi, he was furious at the Chinese newspaper stories about the corruption in the Ministry of Posts and Communications. Shiyi understood the price of fame in public service and said to Ye, "They never singled you out for praise when the censors found you had refused to accept bribes from influence peddlers. Now they lump you together with an unnamed crowd of corrupt officials in the ministry. Remember the old saying, 'Men should be weary of fame just as the hogs are afraid of getting fat,' for both would be ripe as a target for slaughter. You have not seen the worst yet."

"I don't see how you can be so magnanimous towards your political enemies who are out to destroy you," Ye Gongchuo protested.

Shiyi calmly replied, "We cannot escape accusations from our detractors but I do not hold grudges against them. Their acts of desperation will ultimately destroy their credibility. As long as I am sure of my own innocence, I never feel compelled to protest."

Unexpected Diversions

"This will be the last time I will go through this pain," Shiyi's second lady said to her servant when she woke up from a short nap after the birth of a daughter. She was surprised to find her husband by her side, and he was smiling radiantly at her.

Shiyi had just been appointed senior secretary of the Ministry of Posts and Communications, so he named his fifth daughter Yisheng (Born when he became the senior secretary). The birth of Yisheng was a painful reminder to the second lady that she could not escape her duty to satisfy Shiyi's desire.

With his concurrent jobs in the ministry providing extra financial compensation, Shiyi lived comfortably in Beijing with his family, now consisting of his wife, his second lady, four surviving sons, and five daughters. Madam felt secure enough with two surviving sons that she absolutely refused to share the bed with her husband. His second lady, too, had two sons, but she was in no position to dictate to her husband.

Until recently, Shiyi could barely make ends meet and was not in a position to save much money. Even now he had not saved enough to buy a house. However, he made no secret of his zest for life and enjoyment of all the material comfort he could afford. He was quite philosophical about accumulating wealth. "If my children will do as well as I am when they grow up, they do not need my money. If they are not doing well, my money will not help them to get very far." He was amused to read exaggerated newspaper stories about his great wealth. "Let them have fun if writing such stories will make them happy."

* * *

One day in September 1909, Shiyi was surprised by the visit of a Chinese interpreter from the British Legation. This young Englishman invited Shiyi to ride with him to meet General Herbert Kitchener, former British Army Commander in India, who was in Beijing as a tourist. Shiyi was delighted at the opportunity to renew his friendship with Kitchener and to invite him to a tour of Beijing.

"After some sightseeing in Beijing, I plan to visit Manchuria, stopping at Shenyang and Dalian. I'll sail for Japan from Dalian," General Kitchener told Shiyi.

"If you can stay here for several more days, I'll go with you," Shiyi said, "This is the best time of the year to see Beijing. The weather is not too hot or too cold. I have planned to meet Duke Ito Hirobumi next week." Shiyi was referring to the Japanese resident overlord in Korea, who was expected to be in Dalian at that time.

"That will be wonderful," General Kitchener said. "I'll enjoy your hospitality in Beijing for ten days."

Stopping first at Shenyang, Shiyi introduced General Kitchener to Xiliang, Governor-General of Manchuria. Because the officials in the Ministry of Foreign Affairs in Beijing had heard General Kitchener was an avid collector of Chinese porcelain, they had telegraphed Xiliang to select two items of porcelain from the royal storage in Shenyang as a gift to Kitchener in the name of Empress Dowager Longyu. When Xiliang gave him a pair of red vases, General Kitchener commented, "In Chinese tradition, a pair of vases is regarded as one item. Isn't it true'?"

Xiliang was terribly embarrassed and looked to Shiyi for an answer. Shiyi quickly interrupted. "Since this gift is a goodwill gesture, you should telegraph the ministry in Beijing for instructions."

When a favorable reply arrived, Xiliang sent another piece of porcelain to Kitchener. The general was delighted.

As Shiyi bade goodbye at Dalian, Kitchener commented: " I've noticed the training of the New Army of China is not yet completed. Don't try to divert your resources to develop a new navy. Without a strong army to resist an invasion, a new navy will provoke Japan to destroy both before they are ready."

Shiyi stayed in Dalian for another week on business. One night he received a telegram from Governor-General Xiliang urging him to come to Shenyang at once. When Shiyi arrived, he found Xiliang in a state of frenzy. "Ito Hirobumi was assassinated in Harbin. The Japanese will blame me for negligence in handling his safety. I am totally at a loss what to do. Can you give me any advice?"

"You don't have to do anything. There won't be any trouble." Shiyi replied.

"This is a serious matter. It is no time for jokes."

"Of course. I'm not joking about such serious matters. In our treaties with Japan after the Russo-Japanese war, Japan claimed the garrison rights in the territory along the South Manchurian Railway as well as the administration of the railway itself. Harbin in Heilongjiang Province happens to be in the territory under Japanese control. If Japan should put the blame on you, our government could ask for the return of the control of the territory along the railway. I don't think that the Japanese government would want to risk such confrontation."

"Should I ignore this incident then?" Xiliang asked.

"Not entirely. You should telegraph your local representative in Harbin to send condolences. I understand Ito's coffin will be shipped home through Shenyang. You can express your sympathy to his family there, in person."

"Can you stay here for a few days." Xiliang asked. "Your presence comforts me."

Three days later, when Ito's funeral train passed through Shenyang, Xiliang and Shiyi went to the railway station together to pay their respects. After they returned to the governor-general's residence, Xiliang patted Shiyi on the shoulder. "Everything went off as smoothly as you expected. Your talent and power of analysis amaze me. No wonder scholars are so well respected in the Chinese tradition."

Shiyi smiled. This was no small compliment from a Manchu official.

* * *

The excursion to Manchuria also offered Shiyi the opportunity to visit his brother in Changchun, the capital of Jilin Province in northeast China. This was their first reunion in almost three years.

After Shiyi left Sanshui in December 1906, his brother Shixu had stayed in the native village to be with their father. Shortly afterwards, Shixu's wife gave birth to a daughter, their first child, but she died in infancy. A year later, Shixu decided to leave his wife and the widow of his youngest brother, Shixin, to take care of his father while he pursued his military career.

Shixu received a commission as an officer in the New Army. By then, many men embarked on a military career because it was regarded as a swift and sure channel to social and financial success after the abolition of the civil-service examinations. Since Shixu had a Xiucai degree in addition to being a graduate of Guangdong Military Academy, he was rated by the army as the equivalent of a Juren degree holder. He was then assigned to a position in the Military Commissioner's office in Jilin Province. Because of his exceptional administrative and financial skills, he attracted the attention of the local magistrate who appointed him principal assistant to the magistrate of Changchun.

The two brothers exchanged warm greetings after years of separation. They celebrated the occasion in a restaurant that evening.

"As you know, I'm in charge of establishing branch offices for the Bank of Communications," Shiyi reminded Shixu after the dinner. "The time has come to set up a branch in Guangzhou. I've thought about many possible candidates to handle this. But I cannot think of anyone more qualified to do the job than you."

"I'm very pleased," Shixu replied. "but I'm doing quite well here. My appointment in the bank may cause outcries of nepotism. I certainly don't want people to think that I seek your help in getting a job."

Shiyi reached for his tea. "I wouldn't have asked you if I didn't believe my action was right. I will be glad to match my record with anyone else in promoting people on the basis of merit. I'm making this offer to you only after I have given serious consideration to the consequences. You can take this job without worry."

They talked for hours about their wives and Shiyi's children, but the subject eventually returned to the position Shiyi had offered him. "Then it's settled. Come to Guangzhou after the first of the year. Your position will be waiting for you."

When Shiyi left his brother Shixu, he was glad that he had accomplished so much on his trip to Manchuria.

* * *

In August, in another reshuffle of ministers, Tang Shaoyi succeeded Xu Shichang as Minister of Posts and Communications. Shiyi was given another concurrent job as counselor of the ministry. He was also charged with the responsibility to seek a settlement with the British authority in Hong Kong on the long-stalled issue of the Guangzhou-Kowloon Railway, which was slated to open for operation in late 1910.

The British wanted to connect their portion of the Guangzhou-Kowloon Railway directly with Guangzhou-Wuhan Line to avoid transshipment at Guangzhou. That would allow imported goods to be transported directly from Hong Kong up to the Yangzi River valley in central China. The Chinese side wanted to extend Guangzhou-Wuhan Line to Sanshui, a confluence of the main tributary of the Pearl River. Because each side had a high stake, the British demanded a strong hand in the management of Guangzhou-Kowloon Railway to advance the British position.

"I believe you are the only person who can get us out of this bind," Shiyi said to Zhao Qinghua. "I want you to accompany me to Guangzhou to resolve the conflict in the affairs of Guangzhou-Kowloon Railway." He assumed Zhao would have the confidence of the British side because he had attended the Diocesan Boys' School in Hong Kong. To facilitate this negotiation, Shiyi appointed Zhao managing director of the Guangzhou-Kowloon Railway with full power to negotiate the solution with the British authority in Hong Kong.

After arriving in Guangzhou, Shiyi and his party conducted surveys of the locations of the proposed railway connections. The final agreement stipulated that no connection would be made until China could build a spur line from Guangzhou to the nearby deep-sea port of Huangpu. Hong Kong would not be able to monopolize the shipment of imports by rail to the Yangzi River valley at the expense of Guangzhou. The British side also agreed that the construction of yards and terminals for the connection would be handled under Chinese administration. It was a major victory for the Chinese control of railway construction in its own territory.

* * *

In his spare time in Guangzhou, Shiyi spent many hours with his brother Shixu, who by then had established the Guangzhou branch of the Bank of Communications. Shixu was also authorized to set up branch offices in Hong Kong and Singapore. He had just returned from Hong Kong where he was honored by the Chinese business community for being the first Chinese bank manager in the British colony.

Shixu had moved his wife to Guangzhou when he returned from Manchuria. They had a happy marriage but his wife's health was always precarious and deteriorated further after the loss of their daughter. Eager to have a son, Shixu had taken a concubine earlier that year. Urbane and graceful in manner, this second consort had been brought up as a maid in a well-to-do family. It was an old practice in China that destitute families sometimes resorted to selling their children to relieve their financial burdens. While sons could command an enviable price when being put up for adoption, daughters could only be sold to wealthy families as maids. These young girls would perform light household work and the adopting families would promise to marry them off when they reached maturity. Some families treated their young maids well while others abused them. Shixu's second consort was lucky to have been brought up in a good family and was married into a prosperous family.

Very sophisticated for her young age, Shixu's second consort was trained to serve and please people. She made her husband and his wife quite happy in their new home in Guangzhou, and she was now in an advanced stage of pregnancy.

"I asked father to come to Guangzhou to stay with us," Shixu told his brother. "But after a brief visit, he decided to go back to the village. He enjoys volunteer work with an organization for the promotion of education in our village. I'm worried, though, that no one takes care of him at home."

Several months ago, the widow of their youngest brother Shixin took her daughter Wosheng to visit her father, the noted scholar Jian Chaoliang. She now decided to stay with her father instead of returning to the Liang family. Jian wrote to Zhijian to apologize profusely for his daughter's action as both old men were sticklers for protocol in the Confucian tradition. Shiyi and his brother Shixu, too, were saddened by this development, but they did not want to hurt the feelings of their sister-in-law by demanding their brother's child.

"I'm going to visit father as soon as I finish my business in Guangzhou." Shiyi announced. "Perhaps I should persuade him to take a concubine since some personal chores cannot be carried out by servants."

"That's probably a good solution," Shixu agreed. "I'll go with you."

When they arrived in their native village, they sought the help of matchmakers who immediately spread the word that this was a good opportunity for girls in poor families to marry into a family of wealth and respectability. With considerable reluctance, Zhijian, at 66 took a woman one-third his age as his concubine. This "second elder lady," as she was called, not because of her own age but because of the generational status of her husband, became a private nurse and companion to their father.

In other conversations with some village leaders, Shiyi noted the need for a vocational school in his native community. He donated a considerable amount of money to establish such a school before leaving for Guangzhou.

* * *

Having solved the domestic problem for his father, Shiyi thought about his own needs. Since he received repeated signals from his wife and the second lady that they were too old to satisfy his desire, he decided to take a younger woman as concubine. However, he wanted to find a sophisticated woman who could handle the complexity of his family life in Beijing. In a short time, he found a charming and refined woman of barely eighteen from the He family. Without ceremony or fanfare, he took her as his fourth lady.

"Do you have any misgivings about our trip to Beijing?" Shiyi gently asked his new lady.

"No, not at all," his fourth lady replied. "I look forward to meet the rest of your family. I will try to please them and make you happy."

Liang Shiyi knew he had picked a winner.

Derailment

"Madam, I have come back with Asi (No. 4)," Shiyi said to his wife as he returned home in early January 1911. "When will be the best time for her to pay her respect to you."

Madam understood her husband's message and was not a bit surprised. In a way, she had driven him to take this course of action. Madam always thought Shiyi might fall in love with a waitress in one of the clubs frequented by high officials in Beijing. Such waitresses did more than serving food and drinks. They provided entertainment, both open and illicit. Now he brought home someone from Guangzhou who would at least speak Cantonese.

"Where is she now?" Madam inquired.

"In a hotel for the night," Shiyi told her, "until our servants get a room ready for her."

"Tomorrow is as good as any day." Madam spoke with irrefutable logic since it would save hotel expenses. She accepted her husband's new amour as inevitable, but didn't want him lavishing money foolishly on his new concubine.

The next day the fourth lady came to the family living quarters and performed the ritual as directed by her husband. After kowtowing to Madam, the fourth lady offered her a cup of tea as a symbol of submission. She then bowed to the second lady before meeting the children.

Madam wondered about the origin of the fourth lady. Was she an humble girl from a poor family? Not likely, since she seemed to know the etiquette of respectable families. Was she a maid working for a wealthy family? Probably so, but she seemed to be more refined than other young maids. Was she a sing-song girl from the house of disrepute? Quite possibly, judging from the way she charmed her husband. Out of respect for protocol between husband and wife, Madam did not want to quiz her husband for an answer to this puzzle.

Since Shiyi gave Madam a free hand to set the rules for the family, she took full advantage of it. The fourth lady not only knew how to please Madam, but she also offered to take care of Yisheng for the second lady as if the toddler were her own daughter. Consequently, the family enjoyed some degree of harmony.

132

Beijing Odyssey

* * *

During Shiyi's absence from Beijing, seven court censors jointly instituted impeachment proceedings against him. They accused him of monopolizing power in conducting railway affairs, practicing favoritism in staffing, and squandering public funds. It was an effort to force him out of office and subject him to prosecution by his political opponents. The people in power who were engaged in corrupt practices with impunity could denounce similar acts by others with intolerable arrogance. Shiyi was back to Beijing just in time to face the charges.

In late January 1911, Tang Shaoyi resigned under pressure as the Minister of Posts and Communications. His archenemy, Sheng Xuanhuai, was appointed to succeed him. Sheng lost no time in advising the imperial court to dismiss Liang Shiyi from his posts and launch an extensive investigation of his administration. Within one month of Sheng's appointment, Shiyi was stripped of his positions as head of General Railway Bureau and associate vice-president of the Bank of Communications while the investigation was pending.

In his petition to the court, Sheng Xuanhuai concluded, "We are rigorously checking all accounts of General Railway Bureau and the railways in the years under Liang Shiyi's control, and will report to the imperial court any irregularities or corruption. We dare not be partial, nor shall we be prejudiced against him." The last phrase "nor shall we be prejudiced against him" was added at the insistence of Wu Yusheng, the junior deputy minister. Having been a mentor of Liang Shiyi and Guan Mianjun in Hanlin Academy, Wu strongly felt that Shiyi was being framed by his political enemies on fabricated charges.

Shiyi handed over all the accounts of the General Railway Bureau and the railways under his supervision to dozens of men who were assigned to audit them. He was undisturbed by the fuss, even though he knew that his enemies would try to make his life miserable. He left his posts and took his fourth lady to Western Hills, a Beijing suburb, for their belated honeymoon.

"You will enjoy the beauty of the countryside," he told her after they said goodbye to the rest of the family.

"Everything is so new to me in Beijing. I enjoy every minute with you wherever we go," his fourth lady said, enthusiastic about the trip.

After three months of investigation, no evidence of irregularities or corruption was found. Nevertheless, Shiyi was criticized for the lavish pay scale instituted by him and for promoting his own people in the railways. The censors cited his monstrous monthly salary of 1600 taels as head of General Railway Bureau plus 300 taels of additional compensation as the expectant counselor and secretary of the ministry. They also criticized Ye Gongchuo and Guan Genglin, each of whom drew a monthly salary of 240 taels plus 100 taels of compensation for additional titles.

Even George Morrison of *The Times* of London got into the fray. In 1911 he estimated Liang's personal fortune at 15 million pounds sterling (75 million U.S. dollars), which would put Liang in the same league as J. P. Morgan in the United States.

Considering that the projected national budget of the entire Chinese Government in 1911 was 338 million taels (186 million U.S.), Morrison's estimate was sheer fantasy.

Even though he was not proven guilty, Shiyi's brilliant career in railway administration was derailed by the accusations and investigation. He was allowed to keep his nominal title as senior secretary of the ministry while he went on administrative leave. His close associates, Ye Gongchuo and Guan Genglin, lost their positions in the General Railway Bureau but retained their positions in the Secretarial Office of the ministry. Shiyi's friends hailed the result as a vindication, but his enemies were furious that he still had supporters in the imperial court to defend him.

* * *

On May 8, 1911, Prince Chun, the Royal Regent, introduced a responsible cabinet system of government and appointed Prince Qing as Prime Minister, and Natong and Xu Shichang as Deputy Prime Ministers. Of the thirteen ministers, nine were Manchus, including five imperial relatives. The cabinet was immediately dubbed as the "royal cabinet" by the ethnic Han Chinese. When the provincial assemblies protested against the royal domination of the cabinet, they were pointedly reminded by the prince regent that according to the outline of the constitution, the throne had absolute control of all appointments. Prince Chun had removed the fig leaf to expose his genuine intention of strengthening the Manchu rule in the name of constitutionalism.

Although Sheng Xuanhuai was reappointed Minister of Posts and Communications in the new cabinet, Shiyi's friend Xu Shichang remained in power as Deputy Prime Minister. Shiyi did not worry about his own safety in this new alignment, but he was deeply concerned about the state of the nation.

Indeed, the anti-Qing feeling among the Chinese elite gradually swung public opinion toward the revolutionary cause under the leadership of Sun Yatsen. The revolutionaries had quietly moved back to Hong Kong and some had secretly slipped into China since the formation of Sun's Revolutionary Alliance. The revolutionaries staged no less than eight uprisings against the Qing government. The attempt in April 1911 to capture Guangzhou was the boldest and resulted in the loss of 72 of Sun Yatsen's most loyal supporters. However, it created such a sensation that it shook the nerve of the Qing court.

At the same time, Sheng Xuanhuai was unable to dismiss Shiyi and his capable associates without endangering his own position. Zhao Qinghua was allowed to remain Managing Director of Guangzhou-Kowloon Railway at the most delicate stage of negotiations with the British. Guan Mianjun, who had been Assistant Managing Director of Beijing-Zhangjiakou Railway since 1906, was unexpectedly elevated to Managing Director during the purge of Shiyi's friends. Some insiders suspected it was the handiwork of Wu Yusheng, the junior deputy minister.

Though dejected, Shiyi consoled himself with the thought that he had done his best. When Ye Gongchuo traveled to Western Hills for a visit in late spring, he commented, "What a pity that we end up in such a predicament!"

Shiyi soberly replied, "The investigators found that I do not have any investment in various enterprises and do not even own a house. All they can do is to attack the high salaries I received from the ministry. They have even less to complain about with you. The investigation cannot last forever. I believe, in fact, it is near the end."

"Our opponents reflected their own unethical practices in speculating on our motives," Ye Gongchuo added scornfully, "Since we handled so many foreign loans, they expected us to have received commissions as kickbacks or bribes. Some of them did just that when they were in power."

Shiyi was philosophical. "My greatest concern is not what has happened to you or me. When the imperial court so blatantly and unjustly punishes its scrupulous public servants and rewards its flatterers, the glue which has held the dynasty together for so long will soon fall apart."

Shiyi's comments to Ye Gongchuo were not idle speculation. He saw the unraveling of the empire he had supported and helped to preserve. With each passing day, the tide was turning against the once powerful Qing empire. All his relentless efforts to help sustain it might now go down the drain.

Shiyi's success in railway administration would be a lasting testimony to his legacy. Between 1907 and 1911, the Ministry of Posts and Communications had expanded its administrative control from one railway (Beijing-Zhangjiakou) to six railways (Beijing-Wuhan, Beijing-Shenyang, Jilin-Changchun, Guangzhou-Kowloon and Tianjin-Pukou). When Shiyi was finally cleared of any wrong doing, he told his friends who came to cheer him, "I knew how merciless my opponents would be in their investigation. If I had the slightest doubt that I might be implicated in corruption charges, I would not have been so calm as to enjoy myself in Western Hills. Someday the real story of this episode will come out to vindicate my actions."

Explosions

Sheng Xuanhuai was at the height of his influence after being reappointed as Minister of Posts and Communications in the new cabinet in May 1911. Still smarting over the takeover of his power by Tang Shaoyi and Shiyi in 1906, Sheng was delighted when the imperial court adopted a new railway nationalization policy espoused by him. This policy offered Sheng an opportunity for personal triumph and sweet revenge.

The railways under the control of General Railway Bureau headed by Shiyi had turned in a handsome annual profit of 8 to 9 million taels of silver. The court mistakenly thought it could increase its income from railways if the private shares were taken over by the central government. Using patriotism as a rallying cry, the imperial court announced in May 1911 that all trunk-line railways would henceforth be owned by the central government.

The railway affected most severely by this new policy was Sichuan-Guangzhou-Wuhan Railway. Its Guangzhou-Wuhan Line was still under construction and the Sichuan-Wuhan Line was on hold. The private shareholders of these lines had anticipated profits from their investment and refused to settle with the government for redemption. They were furious that their investments were rejected by the imperial court which in turn borrowed heavily from foreigners.

Ten days after the announcement of the new policy, Sheng Xuanhuai signed a loan agreement of 6 million pounds sterling with a consortium of the Hong Kong and Shanghai Banking Corporation, the American Financial Group, the Deutsche-Asiatische Bank, and Banque de L'Indo-Chine. The ghost of foreign control re-ignited the anti-imperialism of the Chinese people. The populace in the four provinces affected by the nationalization protested vigorously. Sensing the popular sentiment, two court censors immediately instituted impeachment proceedings against Sheng with more than 20 offenses, denouncing the selling of railway rights to foreign powers.

The most ominous development was the prominent role played in the protest by the officers and soldiers of the New Army. Many of these troops were deeply nationalistic and felt betrayed by the Qing court. The provincial assemblies which had been

136

established two years earlier under the banner of constitutionalism acted with surprising independence. Although the representatives of various provincial assemblies differed in qualifications, in general they were talented people with distinguished education and careers. When the soldiers helped agitate the public to protest and urged the provincial assemblies to defy the imperial court, the situation became extremely tense.

* * *

During this turmoil, Shiyi stayed in Western Hills near Beijing and watched haplessly the unfolding of the latest railway drama. Even though he still held the nominal title of senior secretary in the ministry, he wanted no part in the new railway policy and decided to continue his administrative leave.

He recognized the change in the political arena. It was not a power struggle between Sheng and himself that mattered any more. The tone of the national debate had changed from constitutional reform to revolution. Many leaders of provincial assemblies were Jinshi or Juren degree holders like himself, but they were now fanning the public with flaming rhetoric against the government. In the long history of China, the gentry-scholars who were major beneficiaries of the imperial ruler would die for the emperor when a dynasty was overthrown. However, the current anti-Qing sentiment among the elite was directed at Manchu rulers as aliens who were bent on dominating the ethnic Han Chinese majority with an antiquated system of government. They justified their actions on patriotic ground to lessen their guilt at biting the hands that fed them.

After taking his daily walk in the hills with his fourth lady, Shiyi pondered the question of loyalty versus the will of the people. He devoted himself to the study of Confucian classics, particularly the *Book of Change*, a pastime he indulged in when his mind was troubled. He wondered what his action should be when confronted with the moment of truth?

His fourth lady was restless in the secluded life. Even the natural beauty of summer colors on the hillside no longer interested her. She could not resist the urge to ask, "When do you plan to return home?"

"Not until the political situation calms down," Shiyi replied. In view of the turn of events in the last few months, that day seemed very far away.

At this bleak moment, Tang Shaoyi visited Shiyi. "You may have heard that a new treaty banning opium was signed by the British and Chinese governments in Beijing on May 8," Tang told him. "I want to be sure you know it since you worked so hard to stamp out opium in China by pushing through the 1907 treaty."

"Yes, the British were to reduce the opium import from India by 10 percent per year for ten years, providing the Chinese government would enforce the reduction of planting and sales of opium in China," Shiyi replied. "Instead, our Chinese peasants increased production and oppose banning opium to protect their profits. The anti-opium drive of the government has antagonized people across a wide social strata, including distributors, transporters, opium-den operators and millions of addicts. The one decent act of the Qing court has unexpectedly caused considerable discontent. One could say the opium war against Britain in 1840 was the beginning of the downfall of the Qing court, and this new British treaty banning opium sales could very well be the final curtain fall on the dynasty."

"Even more surprising is the news from Tibet," Tang said suddenly, changing the subject. "The British have eased the pressure in the region after successful campaigns by the New Army. General Yinchang went into Tibet to thwart the independent claim of several local princes instigated by the British. Chinese troops have unseated the recalcitrant princes and occupied Lhasa, the capital city. They forced the flight of Dalai Lama to India as they advanced to the borders of Nepal, Bhutan and Sikkim."

Shiyi stopped walking and sat down on a small stone bench. "I remember the trip to India with you to negotiate with the British. This victory shows that if we stand firm on our rights and work hard to protect them, China may yet redeem itself from foreign encroachment."

* * *

Throughout the summer, popular anger against the railway nationalization policy remained unabated, especially in Sichuan Province. The shareholders of the Sichuan-Wuhan Line were angered by the unfair treatment against their interest. The leaders of the provincial assembly and prominent stockholders vowed to fight for the retention of their rights by refusing to pay further tax to the government. In August, the Governor-General of Sichuan detained the leaders of the protesters after the court rejected his petition to delay the nationalization of railways. When the people demonstrated in front of the governor-general's office and demanded the release of these leaders, the commander ordered the troops to fire on the crowd. As the news of defiance reached Beijing, the court ordered a massive roundup of the opposition in Sichuan which resulted in indiscriminate killing of local militia men. By the time the court ordered the release of the protest leaders in retreat, it was too late.

As the Qing court faltered, the Revolutionary Alliance under Sun Yatsen gained strength through his energy and persuasion. By the summer of 1911, the number of active Revolutionary Alliance members had grown to 10,000. Some had risen to be members of the new provincial assemblies, and others were soldiers or officers in the New Army. The area in and around the three cities of Wuhan in Hubei Province was a particularly fertile ground for the revolutionaries. To the south of Yangzi River was the city of Wuchang; to the north, separated by the Han River, were the cities of Hankou and Hanyang. This was a powerful industrial base, including an arsenal and ironworks in Hanyang.

Wuhan also had a large foreign community with several foreign consulates in Hankou since it had become a treaty port for commerce. Some radical Chinese students who had joined the Revolutionary Alliance in Japan returned to China and secretly positioned themselves in that area. Their recruitment of new members into their own ranks was carried out through an elaborate network of supposedly literary or fraternal societies. By the fall of 1911, these various anti-Qing secret societies in the Wuhan area had attracted over 5,000 New Army troops, about one third of the total force in Hubei Province.

On October 9, an explosion occurred while a group of revolutionaries were making bombs at their meeting house in the Russian settlement at Hankou. The magnitude of the explosion alarmed the Qing authority, which initiated an investigation. After summarily executing several surprised revolutionaries on the spot, the Qing investigators found a list of revolutionaries who were soldiers in the New Army or in other societies. The revolutionaries realized that unless they could launch an uprising immediately, their lives would be endangered and their movement would be suppressed.

The next day, an armed uprising was organized by members of the Revolutionary Alliance after seizing an ammunition depot in Wuchang. A fierce battle went on throughout the night as the insurgent troops launched a successful attack on Wuchang's main forts. By daybreak, the revolutionaries occupied the city; two days later, they took over Hanyang and Hankou. On October 13, the delegation of foreign consuls in Hankou recognized the Revolutionary Army as an independent organization and proclaimed neutrality. Soon the nearby cities in Hubei Province were captured by the Revolutionary Army. Unable to muster loyal troops to defend the governor-general's offices, both the governor-general and the divisional commander retreated from the Wuhan area.

The revolutionaries desperately needed a public figure with national stature to take over the leadership of the uprising which unexpectedly had mushroomed into a full-fledged revolution. The rebellious troops approached the chairman of the provincial assembly, who cautiously declined. They then found Li Yuanhong, the commander of a brigade of the New Army in Hubei, hiding under his bed in his official residence. They forced him at gunpoint to serve as the revolutionary military governor since he was popular with the troops. In addition, Li had been an activist in agitation against railway nationalization and was well liked by the provincial assembly leaders. He could speak English which would be useful in dealing with the foreign community whose neutrality and sympathy was absolutely essential to their cause. Without following the script, a revolution was suddenly born.

***

The Qing empire was threatened from within as it had never been before. It had to find a scapegoat for the court's own folly. On October 25, Sheng Xuanhuai was denounced in an imperial edict for "deceiving the court and his superiors, infringing upon the people's interests, violating the laws, and practicing bribery." He was further accused of recommending the wrong railway policy which caused the unrest and uprising in Sichuan. He was dismissed immediately and deprived of the right for life to any future appointment. Prime Minister Prince Qing and Deputy Prime Ministers Natong and Xu Shichang were also reprimanded for allowing themselves to be deceived and for putting their signatures of approvals on Sheng's railway rationalization policy.

As if to prove that it could dispense poetic justice, the imperial court immediately appointed Tang Shaoyi to succeed Sheng as Minister of Posts and Communications. In the meantime, Ye Gongchuo and Guan Genglin received court promotion to third-ranked officials. Zhao Qinghua was appointed Assistant Managing Director of Tianjin-Pukou Railway, a north-south 634-mile trunk line which had been completed early that year. Shiyi's younger brother Shixu succeeded Zhao as the Managing Director of Guangzhou-Kowloon Railway. It was quite a change of fortunes for these men.

Ye Gongchuo was jubilant when he came to Western Hills to visit Shiyi. He was surprised to find Shiyi did not share his mood. "The country is sitting on a powder keg. It will take only a few sparks to ignite the fuse to blow up the Qing Empire. The military situation in Wuhan area may just provide that."

"Yes, I understand that," Ye replied, "but with the fall of Sheng Huanhuai, we have been completely vindicated."

"I'm afraid we will encounter even greater challenges," Shiyi warned. "The Qing empire has lost the mandate of heaven to rule. This is the end of an era." His mind again wandered to the question of loyalty versus the will of the people. The general agitation over constitutionalism, Manchu power, opium ban, foreign encroachment, and railway nationalization all combined to convince him the day of reckoning would not be far away.

After Ye Gongchuo left, Shiyi told his fourth lady, "It will not be long before we return to Beijing."

An Uneasy Truce

The fierce battle in the Wuhan region caught the revolutionaries as well as the Qing court by surprise. By installing Li Yuanhong, a brigade commander of the Qing's New Army, as their leader after the initial success, the revolutionary forces were buying time until their own leader could take over. When Huang Xing, a brilliant military strategist in the Revolutionary Alliance, arrived at the scene, he was immediately sworn in as Commander-in-Chief and Li Yuanhong was named Deputy Commander.

On October 14, the Qing court ordered Manchu General Yinchang, Minister of War, to coordinate a counter attack on Wuhan with two divisions of Beiyang army troops. Since Yuan Shikai maintained a loyal following among the troops of the Beiyang army, the court summoned him back from forced retirement and appointed him Governor-General at Wuhan. Manipulative and devious, Yuan needed time to see how the situation might develop. He stalled his acceptance by claiming "a leg ailment" which had been invented by the imperial court to force his retirement. What sweet revenge!

* * *

After his forced retirement three years earlier, Yuan Shikai had slipped out of Beijing to the British settlement in Tianjin. When he was assured of his personal safety, he and his family quietly moved back to his native Henan Province. Now many of his former subordinates had reached positions of power. Prince Chun, the Royal Regent, had no choice but to swallow his pride and take the advice of Prince Qing, the Prime Minister, to invite Yuan back to take charge.

Yuan Shikai was at home in Zhangde of Henan Province when he received the news that he had been appointed Governor-General at Wuhan. His "home" was a large compound surrounded by a high wall with watch towers. Besides the imposing mansion, there were guest houses, large buildings for two battalions of cavalry, and stables for horses, housing for farm hands and gardeners, workshops for making farm implements and other equipment, a telegraph station for instant communication with the outside world, and a man-made lake. It was a self-contained fortress with cannons installed in the watch towers, the nearest thing to a castle of a feudal prince of medieval Europe.

As Yuan pondered his appointment which would rehabilitate him to public office, he felt fate had indeed been kind to him. In his retirement in Zhangde, he had kept in touch with his former military colleagues in the Beiyang army through General Duan Qirui who secretly visited him from time to time. He also relied on a number of political operatives as emissaries, notably Yang Shiqi, the brother of a former Governor-General of Zhili. Yuan could count on Prince Qing, his ally at the court, to do his bidding. He was in no hurry to accept the appointment of Governor-General at Wuhan.

When Manchu General Yinchang was ordered to make a counter attack on the revolutionaries at Wuhan, he went to Zhangde to coordinate with Yuan Shikai. Noting the two divisions under his command were led by Beiyang generals, General Yinchang hoped Yuan would encourage these generals to give their full support to the Qing cause. Humbly, Yuan pleaded, "I'm out of touch with national events. I dare not comment, never mind to interfere with, the military operation at Wuhan."

On the heels of General Yinchang's visit, General Feng Guozhang, a divisional commander at Wuhan, also arrived in Zhangde to consult with Yuan on the battle plan. Suddenly, but predictably, Yuan became his old self and gave his advice to this former Beiyang colleague in the most confident voice, "Go slow and see what happens next."

In the meantime, Yuan Shikai secretly sent an emissary to contact Shiyi who was still on his extended honeymoon in Western Hills near Beijing. While Yuan outwardly maintained his reluctance to return to power, his real intention was betrayed by his message: "It is easy to end the fighting in the south, but the court politics are difficult to fathom. I hope that you'll plan for contingencies. Please contact Tang Shaoyi to make appropriate arrangements."

"Why me? He has many more powerful political allies in Beijing," Shiyi inquired.

"They have their missions too," the emissary replied. "But Yuan wants you and Tang Shaoyi to think about the possibility of negotiating a peace settlement with the revolutionaries that is acceptable to the imperial court. You two are Cantonese and understand the minds of the revolutionaries in the south."

Shiyi was glad to know of Yuan's intention for peace negotiations What he had feared most was a protracted civil war which would destroy the political stability and devastate the whole nation. Now there was a ray of hope that such a war might be averted. Shiyi decided to return to the center of action in Beijing.

* * *

Yuan Shikai's delay in accepting the appointment of Governor-General at Wuhan embarrassed his friend Prince Qing, the Prime Minister of the royal cabinet. Prince Qing secretly sent Xu Shichang, one of the deputy prime ministers and longtime friend of Yuan, to Zhangde to persuade Yuan to assume the post. Xu passed along the message of Prince Qing but did not try to influence Yuan one way or the other. However, Yuan did not hesitate to advise Xu, "You should remain a Manchu loyalist no matter what I do. We need someone inside the imperial court to guide the royal family in seeing clearly the new developments."

Beijing Odyssey

On October 22, the New Army in both Shaanxi and Hunan Provinces had mutinied to express their support for the revolution, killing Manchus and Qing commanders. Three days later, the imperial court increased Yuan's power by appointing him concurrently the Imperial Commissioner in charge of all Qing armies. While Yuan still hesitated at the new appointment, a Qing general stationed in Fengtian Province defied the court order to send his troops south, and joined with a number of field commanders to issue twelve demands to the court, including the establishment of a national assembly and the promulgation of a constitution through the national assembly. Five weeks after the Wuchang uprising, 15 provinces, one after another, elected their own military governors and declared independence.

In reaction to these developments, the leaders of the war faction in the royal family advocated to fight to the bitter end. By then, Tang Shaoyi and Shiyi were active in offering their advice to Prince Qing, the leader of the peace faction. Through the mediation of Tang and Shiyi, calmer heads in the imperial court finally prevailed. Responding to the demands of various protest groups, the court announced a new constitution on November 1.

The national capital plunged into chaos as the people, fearing the worst, sensed the withering of the Qing empire. "We must ask General Duan Qirui to send loyalist troops to maintain law and order in Beijing before a new cabinet is formed under the new constitution," Shiyi urged. Tang agreed. They jointly appealed to General Duan Qirui who quickly ordered his troops to strengthen the garrison of the national capital until the arrival of Yuan Shikai.

Three days after the provisional national assembly elected Yuan prime minister, the imperial court formally appointed him to that position. Only then did Yuan travel to Beijing to accept his new assignment to form a cabinet. Three days later, Yuan submitted the names of his cabinet to the court, naming his partisans to key positions. Yang Shiqi was named Minister of Posts and Communications and Liang Shiyi Deputy Minister. Through the influence of Prince Qing, Xu Shichang was named Grand Councillor and tutor to the boy emperor by the court, since Xu chose to be a loyalist to the Qing ruling house and would not join Yuan's cabinet.

After returning to power, Yuan Shikai and his family stayed in a mansion inside the Ministry of Foreign Affairs at Shidaren Lane, a convenient location for his numerous activities. Throughout November, he delicately used his influence over the Beiyang army to pressure Manchus and revolutionaries alike. To flex his muscles, Yuan directed the Qing forces to recapture both Hankou and Hanyang. However, The revolutionaries had moved on to the Yangzi River Valley where they made the most gains. During the heavy fighting near Zhenjiang, they were surprised to find a Western newspaper man who was deeply interested in advancing their cause.

This man was William Henry Donald, the south China correspondent for the *New York Herald*. A native of Australia, he had served since 1903 as the editor of *China Mail*, a large afternoon paper in Hong Kong. The pages of *China Mail* reflected his efforts to print what Chinese men of merit had to say, and to report news of life and happenings in remote provinces transmitted to him by missionaries. In addition to being editor of *China Mail*, he was correspondent for a string of Australian newspapers. In 1908 he was hired by James Gordon Bennett, owner of the *New York Herald*. William Donald did not fail him. A champion of Chinese causes, he provided firsthand information about the activities of the revolutionaries through his articles in the *Herald*.

At the railway station near Nanjing, Donald met Roy Scott Anderson, an American manager of the Zhenjiang Office of Standard Oil Company. Roy Anderson was born in China and spoke seven or eight Chinese dialects. He became Donald's invaluable interpreter, and Donald had deep respect for his honesty and affable nature. He remarked to Donald, "I want to see China rid of the corrupt Manchus, but the revolutionaries will make a mess of any substitute government."

* * *

The Qing court's position was weakened when Manchu and loyalist troops were defeated at Nanjing in early December. The capture of Nanjing by the Revolutionary Alliance provided a truly national base to consolidate its position and increase its prestige. Nanjing had been the national capital for several previous dynasties. The revolutionaries intended to declare it the capital of a new republic.

Yuan Shikai had left Tang Shaoyi out of his cabinet precisely for this moment when a compromise with the revolutionaries became necessary. In the previous week, Tang Shaoyi and Shiyi had worked behind the scenes to convince the ministers and court officials of the merit of a peaceful settlement, and to neutralize the royal family members. The day after the fall of Nanjing, a three-day cease fire was reached in Wuhan between the Revolutionary Army and the Qing Army. Shortly after the cease-fire went into effect, Prince Chun resigned as prince regent, citing his own failure to protect the throne.

As the revolutionaries in the south clamored for a peaceful solution to overcome the uneasy truce, Yuan Shikai was ready to dispatch Tang Shaoyi to Shanghai to negotiate with them. In the meantime, Shiyi was assigned the task of convincing the imperial court to extend the ceasefire several times over four weeks to allow the negotiations to continue. Tang hailed from the same Xiangshan County as Sun Yatsen. His background of Western education made him uniquely qualified to understand the positions of the revolutionaries. For the same reason, Tang was too independent for Yuan to trust his judgment completely. On December 7, Tang Shaoyi was appointed the chief delegate representing Beijing government, and Yang Shiqi the deputy chief. Yang, who was widely viewed as a political operative acting on behalf of Yuan's personal interest, was there to watch Tang's steps.

Shiyi succeeded Yang Shiqi as Minister of Posts and Communications. With so many ups and downs in his political life, he had finally reached the height of a first-ranked official, the long coveted reward for a scrupulous mandarin. However, this was no time for celebration as the Qing dynasty was on the verge of total collapse. His wife automatically became a first-ranked lady (furen) as she had always wished to be. Since his concubines were not qualified for the honor, Madam was excessively happy.

Beijing Odyssey

* * *

The delegations of North and South met on December 17 in the Town Hall of the International Settlement in Shanghai, a neutral ground protected by the foreign community. Tang Shaoyi's counterpart from the South representing the revolutionaries was Wu Tingfang, a former Qing minister to the United States. Both Cantonese, they were not strangers to each other, and the discussions were held in a frank atmosphere. Four days after the negotiation began in Shanghai, the British, American, French, German, Russian, and Japanese consuls in Shanghai urged the delegations from both sides to settle hostilities at an early date.

Sun Yatsen was fund-raising in the United States when he heard the news of the Wuchang uprising. Sun saw the importance of securing promises of neutrality from European powers in the emerging conflict and decided to travel to London and Paris first before returning to China. He was able to persuade the British government not to advance any major loan payments to the Qing government. He returned to Shanghai from France, arriving on Christmas Day.

For several days, Sun Yatsen was closeted with important members of the Revolutionary Alliance in discussing their future plans. The negotiation for a peace settlement with the North did not go as well as they had hoped for, but they were not in a position to bring down the Qing government militarily. They were forced to continue the uneasy truce and to negotiate further. To gain legitimacy and credibility from the outside world, they decided to form a new government immediately. On December 29, the delegates from sixteen provincial assemblies, meeting in Nanjing, proclaimed a new republic and elected Sun as provisional president.

On the first of January, Sun Yatsen assumed the office of Provisional President of the Republic of China, adopting the solar calendar instead of the traditional Chinese lunar calendar. Acknowledging his weak power base and uncertain military support, Sun sent a conciliatory telegram to Yuan Shikai, asking the latter to come to terms with his new government. Even though he had accepted the presidency, Sun Yatsen told Yuan, "The position is actually waiting for you, and my offer will eventually be made clear to the world. I hope that you will soon decide to accept this offer."

The entire nation waited anxiously for the reactions of Yuan Shikai and the Qing court. Would there be war or peace?

Abdication of the Emperor

"Tang Shaoyi has resigned as the chief delegate from the North," Yuan Shikai announced when Shiyi went to see him about the peace negotiation on January 2, 1912. Shocked beyond belief, Shiyi immediately sensed a serious setback in the negotiation. He pressed Yuan for the reason of Tang's resignation.

"I have no choice but to ask him to resign," Yuan said defensively. "He has exceeded his authority by signing an agreement with the chief delegate from the South, stipulating that the provisional national assembly would meet in Shanghai to discuss the future form of the government. The imperial court will never agree to that."

Shiyi understood Yuan's predicament very well. The original basis of the peace negotiation was predicated on an edict issued by the Qing court on November 9 stating that "the provisional national assembly will be held to resolve the question on the form of government." The edict had opened the door for a debate between constitutional monarchy and absolute monarchy supporters in the court-sanctioned provisional national assembly in Beijing. With the declaration of a new republic in Nanjing on January 1, 1912, the debate on the form of government would clearly be changed to the choice between monarchy and republic. Furthermore, by convening the provisional national assembly in the international settlement in Shanghai instead of Beijing, the court would be subjected to greater pressure from Western Powers. To pacify the Qing court, Yuan Shikai had no choice but to force Tang Shaoyi to resign.

After searching for an adequate answer, Shiyi said hesitantly, "I agree with your assessment of the imperial court's position. However, the court has as much to gain as the South to consult the Western Powers. Their recognition of the new government, whatever the form may be as a result of the peace negotiation, is prized by both sides. Now the negotiation process itself is in jeopardy. What do you plan to do?"

Yuan Shikai smiled cunningly. "Tang Shaoyi has resigned in name only. I'm not going to appoint anyone to succeed him. I have instructed him privately to stay in Shanghai for backstage maneuvering. In the meantime, I will publicly notify Wu Tingfang, the chief delegate of the South, to negotiate directly with me by cable in the future."

Beijing Odyssey

The Qing court's reluctance to accept the agreement signed by Tang Shaoyi with the South actually played into Yuan's hand. Outwardly, Yuan was acting on behalf of Qing's interest, but behind the scenes, he could bargain with the South on terms best suited for himself. One of his prizes was the presidency of the Republic of China, not just the title but the real power he had to wrest from the revolutionaries who controlled the new provisional congress in Nanjing.

By now, Shiyi had bowed to the inevitable as he had detected the popular support for the new republic. The only question in his mind was how to effect a change from monarchy to republic in China without bloodshed. As the court procrastinated for weeks on the question of abdication, Shiyi confided to his close friend Ye Gongchuo, "The Chinese ministers in European capitals may tip the scale in favor of the republic if they urge the emperor to abdicate. I'm planning to ask them to do that. Is it the right thing to do?"

"Yes," Ye replied. "They can do it without endangering their own lives since they're out of reach of the imperial court." Reassured by the opinion of his trusted ally, Shiyi cabled Lu Zhengxiang, the Chinese minister to Russia and the dean of Chinese diplomats in Europe, urging him to line up other ministers to express their preference for a republic. Lu was impressed by the sincerity of Shiyi's argument. On January 3 he initiated a petition to the imperial court for circulation to other Chinese ministers in other European capitals. Citing foreign public opinion, Lu and several Chinese ministers jointly sent a telegram to the Qing court suggesting the abdication of the emperor.

* * *

Tang Shaoyi approached Wu Tingfang privately on January 14 and asked him about the probability that Sun Yatsen would give up the presidency of the republic in favor of Yuan Shikai. Sensing some new development, Wu Tingfang ordered the extension of the cease-fire for two more weeks while he consulted with the Nanjing Government. He received a cable from Sun Yatsen next day, agreeing to resign in favor of Yuan Shikai if the latter could persuade the emperor to abdicate and end the fighting. Sun also approved the principles for generous treatment of the deposed boy emperor.

On January 16, when Yuan Shikai was on his way home from the Forbidden City in a horse-drawn carriage, three grenades were thrown at his carriage from the balcony of the famous Dongxing Restaurant. Two of them exploded, killing one of his horsemen and wounding the other. The two horses ran wild but fortunately were restrained by the wounded horseman. Yuan survived the assassination attempt unharmed. However, he moved to a residence inside the compound of the Department of Army at Iron Lion Lane (Tieshizi Hutong) for better protection. Once inside this fortress-like compound, he stayed in his mansion and refused to go to the imperial court.

Yuan Shikai assigned three cabinet ministers—Hu Weide as Minister of Foreign Affairs, Zhao Bingjun as Minister of Internal Affairs, and Liang Shiyi as Minister of

Posts and Communications—to deal with Empress Dowager Longyu, who took over the imperial court functions after the resignation of Prince Chun as prince regent. Liaisons between the empress dowager and the republicans were carried out by Shiyi, who had to bridge divergent views, even disagreements between Yuan and Tang, who became increasingly irritated by Yuan's manipulations. Under such circumstances, Shiyi asked Ye Gongchuo and Cai Tinggan to help him in handling all communications. Every time Shiyi returned from the imperial court, dozens of reports, documents and cables were waiting for his perusal.

By this time, patience was wearing thin on both sides and the situation had almost reached an impasse. Some revolutionists pressed for quicker actions to overthrow the Qing government, while calmer heads in Nanjing favored the continuation of negotiation in view of their own weakness in military powers. In Beijing, most royal princes and Manchu generals continued to refuse to consider the abdication of the emperor, but others knew the Qing Dynasty was on the verge of collapse.

On January 19, the three cabinet ministers, Hu, Zhao and Shiyi, jointly petitioned the court: "Since the Qing empire has lost the support of the people, the monarchy cannot be saved. We sincerely hope that the imperial court will be in favor of the new republic so as to effect a peaceful settlement." There was no immediate response from the imperial court. As sporadic fighting resumed by Qing generals who were against the abdication of the emperor, some governors in southern provinces supporting the revolution clamored for military response. In the meantime, secret peace negotiations took place fervently in Shanghai between Tang Shaoyi and Wu Tingfang, on behalf of Yuan Shikai and Sun Yatsen respectively. The essential framework of an agreement for the transfer of power was eventually finalized.

Believing the impasse would simply prolong the agony and result in the breakdown of the peace negotiation, Shiyi suggested to General Duan Qirui that it was time for him to line up other generals to urge the emperor to abdicate. On January 26, Duan and 46 other Qing generals jointly sent a petition to the imperial court requesting the emperor's abdication. On the same day the court received Duan's petition, Manchu General Liangbi was assassinated by the revolutionaries. General Liangbi was the Commander of the Imperial Palace Guards and a diehard opponent of the republican form of government.

When Shiyi and the two other cabinet ministers were summoned to the court by the empress dowager immediately after the assassination, the mood in the imperial court was gloomy. Shiyi told Ye Gongchuo after the audience, "Empress Dowager Longyu sobbed and said to us, 'Oh, Liang Shiyi, Zhao Bingjun and Hu Weide! The emperor's destiny and mine are in the hands of you three. Please tell Yuan Shikai to save our lives.' Hearing these words, Zhao Bingjun cried and pledged that he would safeguard the royal family. I also could not hold back my tears."

Empress Dowager Longyu then summoned the royal princes and court officials for a series of emergency meetings. Both Prince Qing and Yuan Shikai refused to attend by pleading illness, and no action was taken by the imperial court.

Beijing Odyssey

Sun Yatsen became increasingly impatient and blamed Yuan Shikai for reneging on his promise of urging the emperor to abdicate. On January 28, a Provisional Senate was proclaimed in Nanjing, with two members each from seventeen provinces and other territories for a total of 38 members. The rapid unfolding of uncontrollable events finally convinced Prince Qing and Prince Chun to recommend to the Empress Dowager that the emperor should announce his abdication in favor of a republican form of government. The empress dowager authorized Yuan Shikai to negotiate with the South on the terms of favorable treatment to the royal family in return for the abdication.

"Yuan Shikai has leaned on me to work out the terms of abdication with the royal house," Shiyi told Ye Gongchuo after Yuan's audience with the empress dowager. "You must help me draft these terms on short notice." The terms and their wording were finalized after several dozen negotiations between the two sides. The task in the North was carried out by Shiyi in Beijing. His counterpart in the South was Wang Jingwei, a revolutionary who had recently been released from jail by the Qing court. Each draft was presented to Empress Dowager Longyu by Liang Shiyi and Zhao Bingjun. She would go over the articles word by word and express her opinion, with particular attention to the section concerning ancestral temples and imperial tombs. Since the strongest objection to the abdication had come from the palace guards, they had to be pacified. Ye Gongchuo suggested the addition of an article to the effect that "the number of palace guards and their salaries shall be continued as before." This statement finally dispelled the anxiety of Empress Dowager Longyu about the protection of the royal family.

During this critical national crisis, Liang Shiyi received word from his father: "The fall of the Qing Empire is the fault of the powerful men in the royal ruling house, not that of the boy emperor and the widow of the late emperor. The nation should be lenient towards the emperor and the empress dowager in setting the terms of abdication." The old man still could not get over the habit of instructing his son on important matters.

* * *

After many proposals and counter proposals on the terms of abdication, the version acceptable to the Qing court and the royal princes was finally approved by Yuan Shikai's cabinet in Beijing and the Provisional Senate of the republican government in Nanjing. The terms of agreement would guarantee the boy emperor and his family the right to continue to live in the Forbidden City, the ownership of the great imperial treasures, an annual stipend of four million taels (to be replaced by four million Chinese dollars pending the coinage of the new republican dollar), and the protection of all Manchu ancestral temples. The imperial court proclaimed the abdication of the emperor on February 12, 1912.

A brief but majestic and gracious edict issued in the name of the emperor had been drafted by Zhang Jian, the valedictorian of the Jinshi Class of 1894, and endorsed by the provisional government in Nanjing. However, to the consternation of the revolutionaries, political operatives of Yuan inserted a sentence to insure his future power before the edict was finalized: "Since Yuan Shikai had been elected by the national assembly in Beijing as prime minister, he shall have full power to organize a provisional republican government and to negotiate concrete measures concerning the unification with the South." As the edict had become a fait accompli before Yuan's machination was discovered, the Nanjing government in the South reluctantly swallowed the statement and could only hope to deal with Yuan on his terms. This edict was co-signed by all cabinet ministers in addition to the emperor's seal.

A second edict listing the terms of abdication in detail was issued simultaneously. Drafted by Shiyi, it stated in part: "Instructed by the imperial court, the cabinet of the Qing Empire has negotiated with the South about the future of the Qing Royal House. After reviewing the articles of favorable treatment, I, Emperor Xuantong, proclaim that the terms for my abdication are comprehensive and acceptable. I sincerely hope that the royal family and the people of five major nationalities would eliminate all racial prejudice, ensure public safety, and enjoy the prosperity and happiness brought forth by the republic."

On the same day the edicts of abdication were proclaimed by the imperial court, Yuan Shikai sent a telegram to the provisional government in Nanjing stating that he favored the republican form of government. The next day, all ministers of foreign powers in Beijing were notified of the abdication of the Qing emperor. Keeping his promise in the bargain, Sun Yatsen immediately resigned as provisional president and recommended to the senate in Nanjing to elect Yuan Shikai as his successor. Acting on his recommendation, the 17 electors representing 17 provinces in the Provincial Senate voted unanimously on February 15 to elect Yuan Shikai as the new President. They also invited him to come to Nanjing to take the oath of office as soon as possible. China was united once again—under the banner of a new republic in Nanjing with a president who was a relic of the deposed monarchy in Beijing.

Because of Liang Shiyi's success in handling the delicate task of the abdication of the emperor, he earned the respect and trust of Yuan Shikai and became an insider in Yuan's circle of closest advisers. Shiyi had contributed to Yuan's telegram to Sun Yatsen with these ringing words: "The monarchy has been transformed into a republic. It is in large measure the outcome of your years of endeavor in the best interest of the Chinese people.....May we strive for a perfect future so that the monarchy will never be revived in China."

Shiyi felt that he had done all he could to effect a peaceful transition. It was now up to Yuan Shikai to keep his word.

The Consummate Insider

Welcome Party at Zhangjiakou Railway Station, September 1912
In the front row, the first four persons from left to right: Guan Mianjun,
Zhu Qichen, Liang Shiyi and Sun Yatsen.

An Ominous Beginning

"They should be here any minute now." Liang Shiyi was looking at the ornate grandfather clock in the dignitaries' room of the railway station in Beijing as he spoke to his assistant. Standing next to a cast-iron stove, they both tried to warm themselves with the steam coming from the kettle.

"I have lined up the coachmen outside of the station," his young assistant replied. "As soon as the guests arrive, the carriages will be ready for them."

It was a cold morning in early 1912, barely two weeks after the abdication of the Qing emperor on February 12. As the official representative of President-elect Yuan Shikai, Liang Shiyi was at the station to greet a nine-member delegation dispatched by the Provisional Senate in Nanjing to escort the President-elect to assume his office there. The delegation was accompanied by Tang Shaoyi who had been the chief negotiator representing Yuan in the North for the Peace Conference between North and South.

As the train pulled into the station, iron wheels squealing against the rails, Liang went out to the platform area reserved for the dignitaries in the special car. When the group stepped down from the train, before a waiting crowd, Shiyi greeted Tang Shaoyi warmly and directed the group to the dignitaries' room. Tang and Shiyi looked at each other in surprise but neither one wanted to comment on the other's attire, clearly reflecting a change in allegiance. Since the fall of the Qing empire, which had imposed the indignity of keeping a pigtail on Chinese men, both of them had cut off their queues They had also left behind the garments of the Manchu court for high officials and now dressed in traditional Chinese gowns. Liang was attired in a dark blue silk gown with fur lining and a classic black jacket, while Tang wore a thick grey woolen gown.

Tang Shaoyi introduced the delegates one by one. Liang Shiyi bowed politely as each name was called. Liang walked past the four delegates in military uniform and approached the delegates in civilian clothes. He noted that all five members in civilian clothes wore Western-style suits and topcoats, surely a symbol of forsaking the old Chinese tradition. When he reached Cai Yuanpei, the chief delegate, he spoke in a firm voice. "President Yuan asked me to extend his greetings to all of you. He

153

appreciates the invitation to assume the Presidency of the Republic in Nanjing."

"We are delighted to be here. We are honored to accompany President Yuan to Nanjing as soon as he is ready to leave."

Rounds of tea were served while hot steamy towels were passed to the delegates. When Liang's assistant signaled that the carriages were ready, the delegates were whisked away to the official guest house.

After the delegates were settled in the new surroundings, Shiyi told the delegates, "President Yuan will meet you briefly this afternoon to receive the official invitation to Nanjing from the Provisional Senate. He hopes to discuss with you his future plans at a reception in your honor the day after tomorrow. If there's anything I can do to make your stay more comfortable, please let me know."

Shiyi knew very well that Yuan Shikai had not yet made plans to go to Nanjing and needed more time to arrange the details. Ever since the attempted assassination on his life in January, Yuan had chosen to live inside the compound of the Department of the Army at Iron Lion Lane (Tieshizi Hutong), a status symbol for the commander-in-chief of the Qing Army. He used the fortress compound as office and residence for protection and seldom ventured out. Only a few days before, Liang Shiyi had been summoned there to set up a temporary office and a small transition team in preparation for Yuan's inauguration.

However, the delegates from the South pressed to get more information about Yuan's travel plan. Liang Shiyi confided, "To be very frank with you, I was totally exhausted after the protracted and intensive negotiation on the terms of abdication with the Qing Royal House, and I took several days off for complete rest. When I returned to work, I barely had time to organize a transition team. It will take President Yuan another week or two to put things in order before leaving for Nanjing. I hope you'll understand."

The delegates from the South were buoyed by the holiday mood of the city which was busy celebrating the lunar new year. Although the new republic had officially adopted the solar calendar, the people continued to celebrate the traditional "Chinese New Year" for several weeks. Most families visited with friends and relatives in their homes or in their favorite restaurants, and the streets were filled with children who were given long vacations from schooling. Adults wore their best shining outfits and the children were dressed in bright-colored clothes. Periodically, the delegates stopped to watch a parade of dragon dancers and other festivities in the street, indulging in delicious foods sold by vendors scattered among the shops.

The next day the delegates from the South took a ride in the busy city streets after fresh snow had cleared the air. When they arrived at a restaurant for lunch, Wang Jingwei, a young and resourceful delegate, remarked to his colleagues, "What a difference two years have made for me and for our new nation since my last trip to Beijing." Two years before, he had sneaked into Beijing to assassinate the prince regent. When the police discovered an unexploded bomb beneath a bridge the prince regent passed by daily, it was traced to Wang and he was quickly thrown in jail. After

20 months of imprisonment, he, along with several other revolutionaries, had been released in November.

"I read a newspaper account saying that Empress Dowager Longyu was so impressed by your handsome looks that she decided to set you free," said Song Jiaoren, another young delegate. Wang and Song had known each other since the days when both of them were in exile in Japan. Song had studied constitutional governments in Western democracies and was a strong proponent of a parliamentary system with a responsible cabinet and loyal opposition for China. After the collapse of the Qing empire, barely two weeks before, the newspapers had a field day exercising their new-found freedom. They all behaved like tabloids pandering to the ignorance of the populace by circulating rumors and innuendos. Responsibility and loyalty would have to wait.

"No. No. You don't believe that, do you?" Wang protested. "What nonsense! Why would the empress dowager want to see a terrorist?"

"Ah, but that's what we've heard, Wang. There must be some bit of truth in it." a delegate teased.

Wang waved his hand in dismissal. "By the time we were released, she was quite worried about her own neck. The Manchu Court held us as bargaining chips. When the revolutionaries gained the upper hand after the uprising in Wuhan last October, the court freed us in a goodwill gesture for a negotiated peace." He looked away, regretting bringing up a subject that allowed him to be the butt of a joke.

* * *

On February 29, Yuan Shikai met the delegates from the South in a noon reception. After dining on the gourmet delicacies, Yuan offered a toast to the good health of the delegates but mentioned nothing about his plans to move to Nanjing. Cai Yuanpei, the chief delegate, responded with a subtle reminder, "We in the South wish Your Excellency to be the George Washington of China whom the world will admire for bringing unity and prosperity to our country." Cai's toast was not exaggerated since Yuan controlled the most effective army in the country and was the only person who could tip the balance of war and peace.

As the delegates returned to their guest house, they passed by the business district. Many lovely paper lanterns had been strung from building to building or were carried on long poles, or had been attached to carts, all in celebration of the lantern festival. In the evening, the moon was almost full, but the lanterns in the courtyard of the guest house outshone the flood of bright moonlight. The delegates were seduced by the beauty of the evening and went outside to enjoy the scenery. They were politely stopped.

Wang Jingwei's watchful eyes saw the menacing faces of soldiers with firearms just outside the gate of the courtyard. Without waiting for explanations, he told the alarmed delegates to go back into the guest house. The presence of soldiers were distressing to the group. They huddled together, debating whether they should seek refuge in the homes of foreign friends, but finally decided not to risk being caught by crossfire in the streets. They slept fitfully, the night air thick with muffled voices and the crack of explosives.

The next morning, Liang Shiyi rushed to the guest house to inform the delegates that a mutiny of several army battalions had taken place the night before. "I have no idea, nor does anyone else, what causes the mutiny," Liang told the surprised delegates from the South. "I'm greatly disturbed that some soldiers even came near this guest house. Please be patient until I find out more about the situation. Army battalions are garrisoned throughout the city." Liang understood too well that any suspicions of the delegates about the intention of the mutiny could cause serious political fallout. Liang immediately went to consult Tang Shaoyi. Together they rushed to see Yuan Shikai.

Tang and Liang were ushered into Yuan's private study. Distraught, Yuan greeted them briefly and pointed to stacks of telegrams littering his desk. "What's the latest news?" Tang inquired.

"Please, sit down. I've just received reports that some army units stationed in Tianjin and Baoding have joined the mutiny. The situation is serious but I've dispatched several loyal generals to order the local commanders to vigorously suppress the mutiny."

"Can they be trusted?" Tang asked.

"They were trained by me when I was the Commissioner of Northern Ports (Beiyang)."

Liang Shiyi offered, "What shall we tell the delegates from the South to calm their fears?"

Yuan was not surprised by the question and ready with a blunt answer, "I don't believe I can leave Beijing when control of the army is so shaken by the mutiny. I need to stay here to restore discipline. You two may inform the delegates from the South that for the sake of peace and security of the nation, I cannot now go to Nanjing."

Shiyi was stunned. Tang Shaoyi demurred at the suggestion and asked, "Would it be advisable to delay your decision for a few days?"

"No," Yuan turned toward the window. "Any delay in my decision will simply encourage speculation. There's no room for an alternative course of action." With a polite nod, Tang and Liang stood and left the room.

Both men were quiet as they rode through the chaotic streets, jostled by the heavy and noisy traffic. The answer had not been one they wanted to hear.

After reaching the privacy of his home, Tang said to Shiyi, "I suspect Yuan knows more than he discloses to us. I can't believe that any general will rise up against a republican president who was his commander-in-chief under the banner of the Qing Empire only a few weeks ago."

"That's my impression," Liang spoke with sadness. "Facts about the mutiny are hard to come by; the motives are even more difficult to determine. Yuan has always prided himself on his ability to enforce orders, his orders, in the army. I'll give him the benefit of doubt."

Beijing Odyssey

"I believe it's all a performance for our benefit." Tang was angry at Yuan's insincerity. "That man—" He said no more.

Shiyi sighed, "The presence of mutinous troops near the guest house will no doubt be interpreted by outside observers as a threat to the life and safety of the delegates from the South. We can't allow that to derail the peace settlement with Nanjing regardless of the culprits of the mutiny."

As soon as Yuan's decision was revealed, speculation spread like wildfire that Yuan had staged the mutiny as an excuse to stay in Beijing where he could influence and intimidate officials in the new government. The foreign communities in Beijing were up in arms about their own safety and were vocal against any moves that would cause chaos in Beijing. When Liang and Tang met the delegates from the South, they pleaded with the delegates to withhold judgment about the mutiny for the sake of national unity. "Do you think the Senate in Nanjing would be willing to move the seat of the new government to Beijing?" Liang Shiyi inquired.

The delegates balked. Throughout the night they discussed the matter, over and over. Sometime during the night, an agreement had been struck. Reluctantly, the delegates from the South agreed that it was not advisable for Yuan to leave for Nanjing at this time. Shiyi congratulated them. "The creation of a coalition government is the only hope to avoid a civil war," he said, stressing the theme once again.

The next day, chief delegate Cai Yuanpei cabled the provisional government in Nanjing, "Under the present circumstances, the top priority is to proceed with the formation of a coalition government under Yuan Shikai even if it means that Yuan will take his oath of office in Beijing. Please act quickly to save the peace settlement." Ultimately, the Provisional Senate in Nanjing approved Cai's recommendation. It also approved a provisional constitution for the new republic. Liang Shiyi's persuasion had prevailed.

***

On March 10, Yuan Shikai cabled his oath of allegiance to the Provisional Senate in Nanjing and assumed the office of Provisional President. Immediately afterwards, Yuan turned to Liang Shiyi and exclaimed, "A new era has dawned in China. Your skills in negotiations both for the abdication of the Qing emperor and for the establishment of the national capital of the republic in Beijing have not gone unnoticed. Now I want you to be the Chief Secretary of the President. You can help me tackle the unfinished tasks."

"I am greatly honored." Liang replied with genuine humility. Although Liang was aware that Yuan could be quite a charmer on occasions, he felt flattered that Yuan had passed over many long-time colleagues and intimate friends and promoted him to the center of power. Liang appreciated this rare opportunity for public service that he had prepared himself for all his life. With proper expression of gratitude, Liang finally added, "I'll do my best to serve you and the new republic. I hope that I can prove deserving of your confidence."

An Uncharted Course

The euphoria of Yuan Shikai in assuming the presidency of the republic was overshadowed by the daunting task of unifying the nation. He had lost his legitimacy to govern except for the consent of the revolutionaries who feared the military power under his control. As Yuan was assembling his transition team, he told Liang Shiyi privately, "I must pay full attention to the military. I'll rely on you to deal with the Provisional Senate. I know nothing about the trappings of a republican form of government and I have no patience for prolonged negotiations."

Liang did not know much about how democracies worked either, but he was more than willing to learn. After abandoning the monarchy he had faithfully served, he wanted very much for a new government supported by all sides would succeed.

Earlier in January, the revolutionaries had modeled *their* provisional government in Nanjing after the Western parliamentary system. Since they had to navigate through an uncharted course, the government structure was determined on an ad hoc basis. Sun Yatsen, then provisional president, appointed all cabinet ministers and some governors from the ranks of revolutionaries and other Qing officials who were perceived to be sympathetic to his cause. With so many shades of opinion about the future of the republic, some appointees declined to serve since they had not even been consulted in advance.

Now it was Yuan's turn to form a new government after being elected Provisional President. Since the revolutionaries suspected Yuan might abuse the presidential power, the Provisional Constitution provided very stringent safeguards for the balance of power. The new government under Yuan could not function until a Premier was appointed by the President and the new cabinet members were approved by the Provisional Senate.

* * *

In his crowded temporary office, Liang Shiyi said to Cai Tinggan, one of his assistants, "Since the collapse of the Qing Empire, generals and politicians of all persuasions run for cover to defend their own interest. The prolonged war between the Qing government and the revolutionaries has left the country in ruin. These people channeled the taxes collected locally to build up their own bargaining power and refuse to send the spoils to the national treasury." Indeed, under the umbrella of provincial assemblies, local officials formed new alliances with regional military commanders to support or denounce the central government in Nanjing or Beijing. They switched their allegiance as quickly as they changed their clothing when they felt their interests were not served.

"How long can this last before the government runs out of money?" Cai Tinggan asked. Cai was among the group of teenagers sent by the Qing government to study in the United States in 1873. He had been an aide to Liang in the last days of the Qing Dynasty. Fluent in English, he now served as an interpreter for President Yuan in addition to other duties in the Office of the President. He was aware of the impasse in the negotiation of a loan by Yuan's transition team with the Four-Nation Consortium representing the banks of Britain, United States, France and Germany.

"The saddest of all is that the government has to depend on foreign loans to survive," Liang replied. "It has exhausted all avenues from domestic sources."

Indeed, the Great Qing Bank which was half owned by the Qing government and half by private sources was essentially defunct. The private shareholders of the bank in Shanghai had petitioned to the provisional government in Nanjing to make this bank the central bank of the republic and rename it Bank of China. But it took some time to terminate the unfinished business of the Great Qing Bank and start new transactions. The Bank of Communications, the other national bank owned jointly by the Qing government and the private sector, was also in terrible financial conditions after Liang Shiyi was forced out as its associate vice president in 1911. Liang had thought about revitalizing this bank by raising money from the private sector, but that idea had to wait until the new government in Beijing was firmly established.

"Is there any new development in the negotiation with foreign banks that I'm not aware of?" Cai asked.

"I'm not involved in the loan negotiation and have no knowledge of it," Shiyi replied. "However, it will be my job to get the approval of the Provisional Senate if the negotiation is successful. I need your suggestion on how to deal with the senate since you are more familiar with the operations in democratic countries."

"I'm all for openness," Cai remarked. "The revolutionaries know the dire situation of the national treasury as we do. They should support any reasonable solution."

"But President Yuan has the tendency to work in secrecy to avoid opposition," Shiyi said. "He doesn't trust the revolutionaries, who in turn are suspicious of his intentions."

Cai nodded. "President Yuan cannot govern effectively without the support of the Provisional Senate. The opposition forces know how to use open telegrams to stir up public opinion in their favor. To that extent, at least, they are exercising their rights in a democracy." Cai had put his finger on one of the new phenomena in the republic. Since newspapers existed only in large cities and each had a very small circulation and limited resources, open telegrams were the most popular form of news release by politicians to a national audience. The newspapers depended on such open telegrams for political news. The politicians could flaunt their literary dexterity in promoting their causes and avoid press conferences or interviews. The newspapers loved to publish their flowery language verbatim, and the educated readers enjoyed the rhetoric. This form of communication worked perfectly for all sides and the practice thrived in the Chinese social and cultural setting.

* * *

Shutting the door behind him, Liang Shiyi confided to Cai Tinggan, "I hope the president will announce a new premier very soon. Our transition team is straining to the limit. Technically, I'm still the caretaker Minister of Posts and Communications until a new cabinet is sworn in. Fortunately, Ye Gongchuo has been able to take over my duties in the ministry and keep it running smoothly."

"Is there any reason for the delay of the appointment of a premier?" Cai asked.

"Not really," Liang replied. "The choice is very limited since the President must appoint someone who is acceptable to both the North and the South."

"Do you have any inkling of the President's choice?" Cai ventured to ask.

"Tang Shaoyi is the most logical choice," Liang replied. "Unfortunately, just before the abdication of the Qing emperor, the Provisional Senate in Nanjing voted to recommend Tang Shaoyi as the Premier of the new republic without his prior knowledge or consent. The fact greatly embarrassed Tang who was at the time a secret emissary of Yuan Shikai in negotiating the terms for a coalition government. It came across Yuan's mind whether Tang had betrayed him behind his back. That may explain President Yuan's hesitancy in naming him the premier."

A few minutes later, there was a knock at the door. An office boy stood in the doorway when Liang Shiyi answered. "The President wants to see you right away, sir."

Liang glanced at Cai.

When Liang reached Yuan Shikai's private office, Yuan announced, his tone crisp, "I've decided to appoint Tang Shaoyi as the Premier since he's the only person acceptable to me and to the South. Send his name to the Provisional Senate for approval immediately." Liang was delighted but he restrained his enthusiasm.

With the approval of the Provisional Senate, it was officially announced on March 13, 1912 that Tang Shaoyi was the first Premier of the coalition government.

The next day, Tang Shaoyi dropped by Liang Shiyi's office after his meeting with the president. After the door was closed, Tang looked around with his eagle eyes to make sure no one else was in the office. "I just came from the President's office," Tang began after sitting down in an armchair close to Liang. "Even before we had a chance to discuss cabinet appointments, President Yuan wanted me to secure an emergency loan to pay off the debts incurred prior to the establishment of this government. He requested that this be done immediately without waiting for the consent of the Provisional Senate since the Senate will not be convened in Beijing until after the approval of the new cabinet."

Shiyi had already learned from Yuan Shikai that half the loan would be used to repay debts for the cash gifts, more properly called bribes, to influential Manchu noblemen for their support of the abdication of the emperor. The other half would be used to pay individuals who supported the Revolutionary Alliance so the operation of the provisional government in Nanjing could be shut down. This sum was above and beyond the compensations allotted legitimately to the concerned parties. Without such payments, however, it would have been impossible to reach the agreement of a coalition government.

The finance experts in Yuan's transition team had quickly negotiated with a Belgian Bank to obtain a bridging loan of one million pounds sterling, using the future profits from the Beijing-Zhangjiakou Railway as the guarantee for repayment.

"I intend to run this government in a democratic way and my action should be accountable to the Provisional Senate," Tang continued. "The Senators are by and large men of honor even though they were appointed by the provincial assemblies which were elected under the auspices of the Qing dynasty. But the disclosure of the purpose of this loan will not only be an embarrassment to all parties concerned but will also rock the foundation of the provisional government." Indeed the names of the recipients were such a well-kept secret that even Liang Shiyi was not privy to them.

"Our major objective must be to strengthen the coalition government," Liang observed. "There are no hard and fast rules. Is it possible to obtain the loan now and have a private session with the Speaker of the Senate later? You may disclose the details only to him in good faith but ask him to refrain from divulging the information to other Senators in public debate."

"That could have been a possible solution if it were acceptable to President Yuan and to the Senate." Tang replied. "However, since the need for cash is so urgent, there's no time to do even that."

Liang looked at his friend. "Then what can you do?"

"I'm not sure. Whatever it is, no one will be pleased."

When Tang announced the Belgian loan three days later, the Four-Nation Consortium was furious at being undercut by the Belgians. It denounced the terms of the agreement and demanded the Chinese government cancel the loan. But the Chinese treasury was so empty that the government had to ignore the protest even as it tried to cultivate the good will of the consortium.

*　*　*

"Sun Yatsen envisions the revolution as a social as well as political renewal," Tang Shaoyi told Liang Shiyi as he pondered the appointments of cabinet members. "Many of his supporters are far more conservative on social issues than he is. I must strike a balance in the selection of cabinet members."

Agreeing with Tang's assessment, Liang Shiyi observed, "Sun Yatsen has issued proclamations almost weekly to change the traditions and customs affecting the daily life of ordinary people—from the way citizens should address government officials and each other to the policies of land ownership and capital formation." On the surface, the changes were sweeping as men cut off their queues and women loosened their bound feet. But deep in their hearts, old habits died hard and most people continued to carry on business as usual.

"Of course, I must also consider the demands of various factions in President Yuan's camp," Tang Shaoyi added. "I will consult with the president for his recommendations."

After receiving instructions from President Yuan, Tang Shaoyi decided to go to Nanjing to discuss the cabinet appointments with Sun Yatsen. When he arrived in Nanjing on March 25, he was met by Huang Xing, a brilliant military strategist and close political advisor to Sun Yatsen, who joined in the discussion. After intense negotiations, a compromise was tentatively reached. Of the ten ministers, four would be supporters of the Revolutionary Alliance. Yuan's men would control the portfolios of Army, Navy, Interior and Foreign Affairs. The Finance Minister would be selected from the budding Unification Party, and Tang himself would become the Communications Minister in addition to Premier.

Four days later, Sun Yatsen accompanied Tang Shaoyi to the Provisional Senate and requested the approval of the portfolios of the cabinet as well as the candidates to head various ministries. To show his sympathy with the revolutionaries, Tang Shaoyi outlined his future vision for the nation. Realizing the Provisional Senate was dominated by members of the Revolutionary Alliance, he joined the Alliance in a gesture to assume the leadership of the majority party. After Yuan Shikai announced the cabinet appointments in Beijing, the Provisional Senate in Nanjing formally accepted Sun Yatsen's resignation as Provisional President and voted to move the provisional government to Beijing.

* * *

"Tang Shaoyi has walked the extra mile to please the revolutionaries in order to get a cabinet acceptable to the South," Yuan commented to Liang Shiyi. "I'm not thrilled about working with some of his ministers as I hardly know them." Yuan was not exactly complaining. He knew the price he had to pay in order to succeed in forming a coalition government. In fact, he had offered the post of Army chief-of-staff to Huang Xing, but Huang declined. Instead Huang accepted the post of Coordinator of Southern Armies in Nanjing. But after hostility ceased, the scarce resources must be spent in rebuilding the nation instead of keeping the various armies. When soldiers did not succeed in getting back pay or severance pay, mutinies occurred in Southern as well as Northern armies. Huang's appointment was an important step in organizing a national army with a single allegiance.

"We must develop trust between those of us who used to serve the Qing Dynasty and the revolutionaries," Liang said thoughtfully. "We are all republicans now. We must work toward the common goal of a constitutional government." He hoped to provide a voice of compromise in the turbulent time.

"The clamor by the revolutionaries for a new constitution worries me," Yuan interrupted. "I'm constantly reminded that this is a provisional government. What we need now is a strong and stable government that can tackle so many serious problems confronting the nation." Yuan's concern was not unjustified, Liang thought, since the populace wanted stability more than anything else. The foreign powers were withholding the recognition of the new government until they were satisfied that it could meet all foreign obligations. After a pause, possibly for for emphasis, Yuan continued, "Their latest request is that a new Parliament be elected by the end of this year. This new Parliament will study and eventually finalize a Constitution. Only then an election will be held to fill the posts of President and Vice President according to this Constitution. I'm not interested in being the Provisional President forever." The tone of his last statement had a sharp edge to it.

Although Liang Shiyi was hesitant to express his opinion which would contradict his president, he braced himself to sound a warning, "If you ask the other side to lay down their arms, you must meet them half way and consider their suggestions seriously. If they perceive your actions as arbitrary and contrary to their interests, the republican government will not last. Not even the army under your control can save it." He watched Yuan turn to him. Shiyi had gone as far as he could.

"You believe that too, I see." Yuan was far from pleased, but he understood. Among his many subordinates and operatives, Tang Shaoyi and Shiyi were most attuned to the sensibilities of the revolutionaries in the South. Yuan needed them now more than ever to bide his time in consolidating his power. Perhaps that was the reason why he had entrusted them with tremendous responsibilities in the new republican government.

Four week later, the Provisional Senate met in Beijing for the first time and President Yuan went before the chamber to deliver his first state of the nation address. Liang was particularly happy that his own vision of China was now clearly laid out in the President's speech. Li Yuanhong, who had been elected Vice President by the provisional government in Nanjing, remained Vice President under Yuan. The Provisional Senate elected a supporter of the Revolutionary Alliance as its new speaker; it also voted to adopt the bicameral system of Parliament, authorizing the creation of a new House of Representatives in the next Parliamentary election.

"Unlike the Vice President of the United States, Li Yuanhong is not the presiding official of the Senate," Cai Tinggan observed. "What is he going to do to kill time?"

"You don't need to worry about that," Shiyi replied. "Since Li is popular with the Provincial Assembly of Hubei, the president may offer him a concurrent appointment as the governor of Hubei Province. At least, I certainly hope President Yuan will follow such course of action."

Even Best Friends Must Part

"You'll be happy to know the Zhongnanhai compound will soon be ready for occupancy," Liang Shiyi told President Yuan Shikai after receiving word from the staff of the Manchu Royal House that they had vacated the former Winter Palace near the Forbidden City.

Yuan Shikai was elated. "There are plenty of buildings in the compound to house the expanded functions of government as well as my family. I intend to live in the compound and have my office inside my residence. You and your staff can set up an office in a separate building next to my residence. I want to be close to your office and make all major decisions of the government."

Yuan Shikai's family took up several large buildings in the compound. By now, his family consisted of a wife and seven concubines, two others having died. His wife was left in his native village but his eldest son by this marriage lived in the Zhongnanhai compound. With wife and concubines of his own, this son was a malefactor in national politics as well as in domestic affairs. His undisguised ambition gave rise to the rumor, though unconfirmed, that he conspired with General Cao Kun to instigate the mutiny of the soldiers near Beijing in late February.

Yuan's office was located on the first floor of Guren Hall, which included many rooms of various sizes for receptions and meetings. All these rooms were decorated with vintage porcelain and paintings of exquisite taste. Some conveyed the atmosphere of intimacy; others radiated power and grandeur. Yuan's own living quarters were in the east wing of the second floor. His concubines and children were scattered in various buildings. Yuan would summon different concubines to his living quarter on different occasions. Within this self-contained arrangement, Yuan lived a secluded life, like an emperor, and made contacts with the outside world only through intermediaries.

At the same time, the Office of the President was organized with a more formal structure, including a Secretariat and a National Military Council. Shiyi became the chief of staff in the Secretariat. To fend off office seekers and influence peddlers whom he did not want to see, Yuan wanted to give an impression to visitors that Liang was the official gatekeeper who could act on his behalf in all important matters. In reality, Yuan had many operatives who would report to him secretly on polit-

164

ical and military affairs. Aware of the jealousy of Yuan's operatives, Liang Shiyi avoided even the appearance of building up his own power base. He pointedly said to Yuan, "I'll handle official business that is addressed to the Office of the President. Tell me if there are those you prefer to see privately."

"That's not a problem," Yuan replied. He had already told the guards of the presidential compound to direct such persons to his own residence. Then Yuan added, "Your most important responsibility is to make the coalition government work."

After an extended stay in Nanjing and Shanghai to discuss various aspects of the new government with the representatives of the Revolutionary Alliance, Tang Shaoyi returned to Beijing with two cabinet ministers, Cai Yuanpei and Song Jiaoren, on April 20, 1912. Immediately he organized the cabinet as a State Council. Dropping by to say hello to Liang Shiyi in his new office, Tang was in a good mood and his tone was ecstatic.

Liang Shiyi was eager to seek the service of people who understood the operation of democracies and could help modernize China. When he heard that Tang Shaoyi had recruited Wellington Koo (aka Gu Weijun), a recent graduate of the law school at Columbia University, as counselor of the State Council, Liang offered Koo the concurrent position of counselor in the Office of the President. "I desperately need your knowledge of Western governments and their policies toward China," Liang told the young man. Self-assured and diplomatic, Koo accepted both jobs with pleasure.

Koo was the epitome of the social changes of the time when East met West. Several years before, his parents had arranged his marriage to a young girl in his native village while he was home for a summer vacation. When he returned to Columbia with his bride, she was unable to cope with the life of her ambitious husband. The marriage ended in divorce, a new social phenomenon of the republic. It was not yet institutionalized nor sanctioned by the society at large. Yet the desire was strong among those educated in the West to seek a wife with compatible outlook and interests, and the divorced wife could only suffer in silence without any recourse. Koo charmed the social circles of the wealthy and powerful, and before long he married the second daughter of Tang Shaoyi.

* * *

While Tang and Liang rejoiced in the progress of cooperation in the coalition government, President Yuan was upset by the turn of events. Yuan had regarded the Provisional Senate as an obstacle to decisive actions that would consolidate the authority of the new government. He was too used to exercising unrestrained power backed by an army under the control of Beiyang generals who were answerable only to him. He simply could not stomach anyone who would second-guess his decisions or disobey his decrees.

Even more alarming to Yuan was the influence of the Revolutionary Alliance which began to draw many non-revolutionary regional leaders to their cause. Adding to Yuan's frustration was the insistence of the Four-Nation Consortium of foreign banks on imposing harsh terms for a loan the government desperately needed to survive. Tang Shaoyi and his Finance Minister, Xiong Xiling, negotiated repeatedly with the Consortium but at best they could get only a bridging loan of less than half a million pounds sterling. In the meantime, the consortium decided to include Japan and Russia to form a Six-Nation Consortium.

Soon a rift developed between Tang and Yuan regarding the important appointment of the Governor of Zhili Province. Before Yuan was elected Provisional President, the Provincial Assembly in Zhili Province had jumped the gun and voted to recommend General Wang Zhixiang as its governor. At that time, General Wang was stationed in Nanjing and was sympathetic to the Revolutionary Alliance. After Yuan became President, the local leaders in Zhili again pressed him to accept Wang as its governor. Confronted with this fait accompli, Tang asked for and received the consent of President Yuan to appoint Wang the Governor of Zhili in a compromise that he worked out with the Provisional Senate.

"Tang Shaoyi sometimes goes overboard with wild ideas," Yuan told Liang after giving his grudging approval of the compromise. "Zhili is such a pivotal province which embraces Beijing. Throughout Chinese history, whoever controlled Beijing eventually ruled the rest of the country. How can he be so naive as to entertain a compromise that allows someone other than one of my most trusted Beiyang colleagues to be the governor of Zhili? After he proposed the deal, I could not reverse the course without being criticized by the Senate. You should watch his actions in the future and remind him of the practical consequence if he gets too far out on a limb."

Liang cautiously injected his opinion. "With rising popular sentiment, it is difficult to ignore the candidates recommended by the provincial assemblies. In return, Tang Shaoyi has convinced the Provisional Senate to give you the undisputed power to appoint the governors under the Provisional Constitution." After the demise of the Qing empire, regional leaders immediately moved in to fill the vacuum. Some of them allied with the revolutionaries; others took over the control of local militia and organized independent armies. All of them wanted to share power with the central government even as they exercised autocratic control within their own borders. Liang was quite aware of the limit of the power of the central government.

To placate the wrath of Yuan, Tang invited Wang Zhixiang to meet the President in person before the appointment was to be announced. Within days the news of the meeting had spread throughout Beijing. All of a sudden, military leaders in Zhili cabled Yuan and the Senate expressing their opposition to Wang. Yuan responded by reneging on his promise to appoint Wang on the grounds of military opposition. To add insult to injury, Yuan then appointed Wang to the job of disbanding the army personnel under the control of the revolutionaries in Nanjing, a deliberate affront to the revolutionaries. When Tang refused to countersign the appointment, as required by the provisional constitution for the appointment to take effect, Yuan issued it anyway without Tang's signature. Outraged, Tang tendered his resignation and left for Tianjin where, in the safety of the French Concession, he was beyond Yuan's reach.

Tang's abrupt resignation and departure caught Yuan by surprise. Highly agitated, he told Liang, "Tang Shaoyi must be out of his mind. I have given him fame and power in the republic only second to myself. How can he walk out on me like this and endanger my presidency, let alone his own future? You must talk sense to him and ask him to withdraw his resignation."

Liang reached Tang in Tianjin and conveyed Yuan's message. He suggested Tang change his mind for the sake of the coalition government if not for Yuan. "I know, I know," Tang said in frustration. "I understand that no one except Yuan can hold the nation together because of his enormous influence in the military. And yet—without the cooperation of the revolutionaries, he cannot rule because the Revolutionary Alliance clearly has the support of many regional leaders." After a pause to calm his anger, Tang continued, "In the last three months, I've tried to reconcile the views and interests of both sides in intense negotiations. However, Yuan can never shake off his outworn ideas. The entire episode of military opposition to the appointment of Wang Zhixiang must have been engineered by him."

Liang nodded in agreement. He looked around the room and lowered his voice. "You know that Yuan always uses parallel tracks of operation to insure his interests are served. He has direct control of the military through the National Military Council, which is off limits to me. I don't know much of what is going on behind my back." Catching his breath, he added, "President Yuan and his political operatives are hostile to the revolutionaries. Each time you or I accept a compromise to win support from the Revolutionary Alliance, they question whether we are advocates of the cause of revolutionaries."

"What a distortion of our good intentions!" Tang retorted angrily, getting up on his feet and pacing the room. "I have worked with Yuan for many years and tolerated some of his infractions. I don't need to apologize for my compromising attitude in dealing with the revolutionaries in order to win them over. I had high hopes that he would cooperate with the Revolutionary Alliance and act in the best interest of the nation. Even the revolutionaries hoped he would be the George Washington of China." Then he added contemptuously, "Yuan's ambition knows no bounds. Obviously he's no Washington. Instead, he is acting more like Napoleon."

Tang might remember Yuan as a dashing young military officer when both of them were in Korea years ago, Liang thought. Standing at just five-feet tall, Yuan certainly resembled Napoleon. But Liang's current image of Yuan was of a political infighter, not a military genius, who schemed behind his desk all the time and was not interested even in getting out of his official residence. When he thought of Tang's comparing this fifty-something rotund figure to Napoleon, Liang could not keep himself from smiling. Realizing the seriousness of Tang's remark, however, Liang immediately dismissed the pictures from his mind.

"I find myself in a very difficult position," Liang said to Tang in total frankness. "I owe Yuan my present position which allows me to make significant contributions to our country as I have always wanted. I know too well that I am putting my personal reputation at risk by supporting Yuan. But realistically I don't see a better alternative if we want to give peace and unity a chance."

Tang was stirred with emotion. "My friendship with Yuan dates back almost twenty years, Shiyi, but he will not let our friendship or anything else stand in the way of his ambition."

Liang tried a different approach. "Unfortunately, peace is built of compromise, which is painted in shades of gray. There are many powerful actors in the political arena, all of whom are ambitious and unyielding. Seeking a perfect political system may be satisfying in principle, but it does not lead to the road for peace under the present circumstances. You and I are among the few persons close to Yuan who still can moderate his views. We should take the opportunity to play a constructive role."

"Oh, I'm not so sure of that," Tang sighed, more in sorrow than in anger. "Evil is a constant factor in human affairs, but I don't have to tolerate it."

Running out of argument, Liang Shiyi simply pleaded with Tang, "Can you give President Yuan one more chance?"

Tang was resolute. "I'm just too independent for Yuan's liking. Sooner or later even best friends must part. I regret that I have to resign my premiership after only three months in office, but I will not change my mind." After hearing Tang's words, Liang sadly said goodbye.

Two days after officially accepting the resignation of Tang Shaoyi, President Yuan appointed Lu Zhengxiang as Premier. Lu, who had attended a Jesuit operated school in his youth, was the most senior diplomat to a European capital in the Qing Dynasty. As the Foreign Minister in Tang's cabinet, he was considered a moderate with a good reputation as a diplomat. Yuan regarded him as loyal but not forceful—a suitable compromise candidate. The Provisional Senate quickly gave its consent. But the four ministers affiliated with the Revolutionary Alliance and the Finance Minister supported by the Unification Party resigned and refused to join Lu's cabinet.

By July 12, 1912, Yuan completed the appointments of all 22 governors. In a move to pacify local discontent, most governors were regional leaders supported by their respective provincial assemblies at the outbreak of the revolution. Even Vice President Li Yuanhong, who was a military commander in Hubei Province before the revolution, was appointed to serve concurrently as governor of Hubei. On August 10, the structure of the new parliament and the procedures for electing its members in upper and lower houses were announced. Three weeks later, the procedures of electing assemblymen for the new provincial assemblies were announced.

Shiyi was cautiously optimistic when he said to Cai Tinggan, "The impact of these new institutions and their operating procedures remain to be tested. However, the provisional government has at least conferred upon itself the legitimacy of its rule over the vast republic."

Nights to Remember

Shiyi breathed a sigh of relief when he received a telegram from Sun Yatsen in the summer of 1912. Without any rancor, Sun gracefully accepted the invitation of President Yuan to come to Beijing to exchange ideas about the future of the new nation. After stepping down as the Provisional President of China in favor of Yuan, Sun had traveled all over the country to deliver the message of transforming China into a modern nation. Liang felt that cooperation with the Revolutionary Alliance was extremely important because they enjoyed the support of a large number of regional leaders. Their consent of Yuan's policies was needed. They controlled the Provisional Senate. The resignation of Tang Shaoyi as Premier had convinced Liang that it was now more urgent than ever to find a new channel to transmit the aspirations of the revolutionaries to Yuan.

Some weeks earlier, when Liang caught Yuan in a receptive mood, he had brought up the subject of inviting Sun to Beijing.

"Sun Yatsen is a dreamer beyond belief," Yuan said to Liang. "I don't see how he could implement his ideas even if he were in my position."

"But he believes in his dreams," Liang countered. "Twenty years ago, no one except him believed China would be a republic."

"I'll grant that's true. Perhaps he is worth listening to." Yuan finally softened his position enough for Liang to send the invitation. Yuan also invited Huang Xing to come along since Huang was a trusted and savvy advisor to Sun. Both responded positively, but Sun would make the trip first.

On August 24, 1912, Dr. Sun Yatsen and Madame Sun arrived in Beijing with a sizable staff. Liang Shiyi was at the railway station to greet them and directed them to the guest house in the compound of the Department of Foreign Affairs. It was another first, Liang thought, that a prominent political leader would take his wife along on an official trip. However, he was hardly surprised, knowing Sun had lived in many foreign countries over the years. Even Liang himself now wore Western-styled business suits when he met foreigners, and donned a tuxedo for state functions. Times certainly had changed.

While Liang was deferential to Sun, he would not allow that to interfere with the heavy schedule he had planned for the private meetings between Sun and Yuan. After dispensing with the formalities of welcoming ceremonies, Sun and Yuan agreed to meet daily from four o'clock in the afternoon to ten in the evening for as many days as they would like to continue. It turned out that the talks often lasted until midnight and on three or four occasions, they lasted until two o'clock next morning. The atmosphere of the talks was informal, with wide ranging topics concerning the future of China. Liang was the only other person present.

In the opening session, Sun stated plainly what was dear and near to his heart, "China needs a million-man modern army for national defense. She also needs a railway network for transportation. This will be the backbone for the unity of China." Then he looked Yuan in the eyes, "With your extensive military experience, you can build that modern army. I will concentrate my own efforts to promote the construction of the railway network. What do you think?"

"I'm not at all confident that I can build such an army from the ruins of the ragtag Qing armies with divided loyalties." Yuan replied. As an afterthought, he added, "You may have better luck with the construction of the railway network."

Then Sun turned to Liang, "I think it's possible to have a railway network of 200,000 li—almost 70,000 miles—for China. Am I too ambitious?"

"No, if it's a long-term goal," Liang replied. "Twice as many miles of railways were built in the United States between 1880 and 1890. A network of 200,000 li is not out of question. China has a comparable size. Although China is too poor to undertake the construction on its own, I believe many foreign investors are poised to provide loans for the endeavor. However, we must first have a stable government which is in a position to negotiate favorable terms for foreign loans. We cannot allow foreign interests to dictate terms which are detrimental to our national interest. We have learned some valuable lessons from the history of railway development in the last five decades."

Sun smiled. He was quite encouraged by the first round of talks and was eager to have more.

* * *

One night, as Liang Shiyi accompanied Sun back to the guest house, Sun said to him, "In my conversations with President Yuan, I find him a willing listener to my views on the future of China. I have no reason to doubt his sincerity when he agrees with me on many issues, except one. I'm puzzled by his ready acquiescence to my idea on a particular subject."

"What's that?" Liang asked.

"China is a country of peasants," Sun replied. "There is no way to bring China into the modern world if we do not introduce meaningful agrarian reform. I have long advocated the policy of redistribution of agricultural lands to the tillers. Even some of my supporters in the Revolutionary Alliance would be uncomfortable with this proposal since many of them come from land-owning families. President Yuan did not seem to be perturbed by my proposal. On the contrary, he agreed with me readily and completely. That's why I'm puzzled."

Shiyi was not sure what Yuan was up to, but he saw some logic in Yuan's acquiescence. He told Sun, "You have traveled far and wide, and are familiar with the pain of tenant farmers in many lands. You don't have to go very far in south China to find absentee landlords who own huge plots of farmland. It is natural for you to come up with the idea for tillers to own their plots. However, you will find many small parcels of farmland that are owned by the peasants in north China. President Yuan was raised in north China and hardly set foot south of Yangzi River. Based on his own observation of the conditions in north China, he might not see the explosive nature of your proposal. That's probably why he could agree with you."

Sun was satisfied with Liang's answer and turned to a different subject. "Two nights ago, I heard your wonderful exposition on economics and monetary reform. I always thought paper money just as good as silver coins, if it is backed by the government. But you insisted the government must earn the confidence of the people before issuing paper money. Why?"

Liang was surprised by Sun's naivete. He patiently explained. "Throughout the long history of China, coins were used as the medium for business transactions. If we change from coins to paper money overnight, the population will be skeptical. We must first have a healthy central bank and then redeem all types of coins issued by local governments as well as the central government in the past. When new bank notes are issued for nationwide circulation, they must be backed by more than the government's word." Then he added lightheartedly, "Suppose the government wants to issue 50 million yuan of bank notes and places at least 15 million yuan's worth of silver as reserve. We can melt this amount of silver coins and cast it into a mountain for public display at Tiananmen in Beijing. When the people see this silver mountain growing as the government issues more bank notes, they will gradually gain confidence in the paper money." Both Sun and Liang laughed as they bade each other good night.

* * *

Sun Yatsen spent most of his mornings in the guest house receiving a stream of Chinese and foreign visitors. A frequent caller was William Donald, the Australian correspondent of the *New York Herald* who had become a self-appointed unpaid advisor to Sun. Although he had penetrated into Sun's inner circle through sheer tenacity, Donald was very protective of Sun against the daily rush of other visitors, particularly foreigners. He had the notion that Sun could not fend off those who might try to take advantage of him.

One day, during his visit to Sun, Donald was accompanied by his friend Roy Anderson, the manager of Beijing Office of Standard Oil. On their way he told Anderson, "Your transfer to the Beijing Office is most timely. I need your help as an interpreter when I meet Liang Shiyi this afternoon."

"Has Doc Sun agreed to introduce you to him?" Anderson asked.

"Yes. When Liang comes to pick him up for the meeting with President Yuan, we will get a chance to talk to him for a few minutes."

"I thought you have taken up the thankless task of playing Dutch uncle to old Doc Sun to prevent him from being exploited. And you are now asking him this favor?"

Donald was very sure of himself. "My action will cost him nothing, in either money or reputation. I may even help China in the process. If I give up what you call playing Dutch uncle, China might be hurt. Doc Sun is known as the Father of the Revolution. We can't let him do anything to arouse unfavorable attention."

Shortly after three o'clock, Liang Shiyi arrived. Sun invited Liang to step in and introduced Donald and Anderson to Liang as friends of China who had helped the cause of the Revolutionary Alliance. Liang looked at Roy Anderson, a burly man with a boyish face, blue eyes and slightly gray hair, who spoke in impeccable mandarin, "My friend William Donald is a correspondent for the *New York Herald*. He wishes to ask your good office to arrange an interview with President Yuan."

Liang had been tipped off by Dr. Sun to this unusual request. He was quite aware that Yuan would not want to be questioned by a foreign correspondent. On the other hand, Yuan was very much aware that his provisional government had not yet been recognized officially by Western powers. A controlled interview with a correspondent representing an American newspaper could be helpful. So Liang laid down the rules in his reply. "President Yuan is not accustomed to giving interviews to newspaper reporters, domestic or foreign. However, knowing that you are a friend of China, he is interested in your views of helping China to become a member of the international community. If you are satisfied with a brief visit of this nature, I shall arrange for you to meet President Yuan."

Getting a nod from Donald, Anderson replied, "My friend will be greatly honored and very delighted." With a few words of pleasantry, Sun and Liang excused themselves.

After thirteen memorable evenings together, Sun and Yuan had exhausted all topics that were relevant, or even not so relevant, for discussion. When the last session was over, Liang suggested to Yuan, "Sun is very interested in the construction of a railway network throughout the country. Why don't you ask him to spend some time to study its feasibility?"

Yuan calculated his answer, "At least that will keep him out of mischief for a while. Be generous on his salary and expenses. That should make him happy."

Two days later, it was announced by the Office of the President that Sun Yatsen was appointed the Director of National Railway Planning and Construction. "I want to assure you that I intend to support your plan fully," Liang told Sun. "I have arranged for you to meet my former colleague Ye Gongchuo in the Ministry of Communications tomorrow. He is the Chief of Railway Bureau and he can coordinate your effort with the current activities in the ministry." After Sun expressed his deep appreciation of such support, Liang continued, "I'm going to sponsor a Chinese Railway Association which will encourage the promotion of a sound railroad plan for the nation. I will lend my support to your goals publicly at the meetings of the association. All I ask you in return is to examine very carefully any loans offered to you by foreign banks so that national interests will not be sacrificed."

* * *

Yuan also honored the request of William Donald for a meeting which was indeed brief. Donald did most of the talking and selling. "You should rely on more people who have a good understanding of the Western world." Donald advised him.

"We have Wellington Koo working for us," Yuan said defensively. Was this a man trying to be a self-appointed advisor to Yuan as well as to Sun? In any case, Yuan had already invited George Morrison, another Australian correspondent, to be his political advisor a few weeks earlier and had no intention of bestowing the same honor on Donald.

The appointment of George Morrison was a political move to win the formal recognition of the new government by foreign powers. Although Sir John Jordan, the powerful British Minister in Beijing, was sympathetic to Yuan, he was holding the formal recognition as a club to gain further guarantee to protect British interests in China. Other powers were watching for clues on the sideline. Since George Morrison, the influential Australian correspondent for *The Times* of London, was a close friend of Sir John, Yuan hoped he could use his influence to speed up the recognition.

For his part, George Morrison had some soul-searching to do before accepting the position. In the twilight of Qing Dynasty, Morrison had argued that a constitutional government after the British model could cure most of the problems of the monarchy and there was no need for a revolution. Later, he did an about face and become sympathetic to the revolutionaries because some of them were educated in the West and advocated Western-style democracy. His opinion had strong influence on the British government in favor of the abdication of the emperor at the crucial moment of negotiation between the revolutionaries and Yuan's forces. Now he had to swallow his pride to become a political advisor of Yuan whom he had dismissed with contempt not long ago. But then, like many Chinese politicians, Morrison could adapt his views to every change of circumstances. He was not called "Chinese Morrison" by his Western contemporaries for nothing. They even nicknamed the thoroughfare Wangfujing Avenue in Beijing the "Morrison Street" in honor of its most famous foreign resident.

William Donald was disappointed to find Yuan was not the easiest man to talk to. He feared he had offended Yuan by being too argumentative, so his interview with Yuan came to an abrupt end.

***

Sun Yatsen and his party stayed in Beijing for another ten days for other business and some pleasure. Before returning to Shanghai, where he would set up his office for railway planning, Sun wanted to take a railway tour of the rugged and impoverished land in the northern provinces. A long train with elegant decor was placed at his disposal. The reception room was the ornate and comfortably furnished saloon car of the late Empress Dowager Cixi. There were two dining cars, several other saloon cars and many sleeping cars.

The traveling party included an assortment of people. Donald was there, and so was Sun's wife, his bodyguard and his staff. To show support for Sun Yatsen's railway development plan, Liang Shiyi went with him on the first leg of the journey along with Zhu Qichen, Minister of Communications; Ye Gongchuo, Chief of Railway Bureau; and others. They were greeted at Zhangjiakou (aka Kalgan) by Guan Mianjun, Managing Director of Beijing-Zhangiakou Railway and other local officials. Liang was proud to show off the first railway designed by a Chinese engineer and financed by the Chinese government under his watch as Chief of the General Railway Bureau.

Liang Shiyi and Ye Gongchuo were at the railway station to see Sun off. Liang noticed that Madame Sun was shy and did not seem to enjoy the attention lavished on her husband and his party. Sun's pretty secretary, Soong Ailing (aka Song Ailing), the daughter of his major financial supporter, Charlie Soong, stood out with grace and poise. A female secretary was an oddity in those day, but rarest of all was the fact that she had graduated from Wesleyan College in Macon, Georgia. Ye Gongchuo remarked to Liang, "Sun's secretary is an unusually intelligent woman. When she was sixteen, she got the chance to meet then-President Theodore Roosevelt in the United States."

It was a triumphant tour for Sun Yatsen. At large cities, he got off to meet the dignitaries, and occasionally had lunch and made a speech. At each stop, Donald elbowed his way into the crowd to stand or sit next to him. Did Donald think the presence of a Westerner might discourage any potential assassin in the territories dominated by Yuan's army? Donald was not sure, but the thought did cross his mind. On board the train, Sun intermittently pulled out a pencil and drew railway lines on maps of China with the excitement of a child playing with a train set. Occasionally he showed those maps to Donald who grinned cynically at the lines criss-crossing the length and breadth of China without discriminating between high mountains or deep gorges. Donald thought: This man is a dreamer beyond belief. But Sun believed in his dreams!

A Tumultuous Year

On the heels of Dr. Sun Yatsen's four-week visit in August 1912, his close adviser Huang Xing arrived in Beijing for further discussion on the operation of the constitutional government. While Sun was an idealist searching for far-reaching goals, Huang was a practical strategist seeking workable solutions to pressing problems. After Sun Yatsen had concluded his talks with Yuan Shikai, he urged Huang to travel to Beijing without delay, before he would take off for the railway tour of north China.

The urgency of the discussion was caused by the sudden emergence of political parties which sprang up like flowers after spring showers. The members of each party were often strange bedfellows with different dreams, and they did not hesitate to split or regroup at the slightest excuse. The Revolutionary Alliance was no exception. There were even rumors of discord between Sun Yatsen and Huang Xing which both found necessary to deny publicly. They also decided to reorganize the Revolutionary Alliance to form a new political party, called the Nationalist Party, in order to exercise its influence more effectively in the Parliament. The task of strengthening this new party fell on the shoulders of Song Jiaoren, a young and energetic organizer who was an expert in modern political systems and was impatient with the slow progress toward a constitutional government. Sun Yatsen wanted Huang Xing to go to Beijing to show their solidarity.

Shiyi was asked by President Yuan to work with Huang Xing in developing a set of principles to make the constitutional government a reality. Liang was quite at ease with Huang as they saw eye to eye on many critical issues even though they were on opposite ends of the political spectrum. The two agreed first to promote civility in parliamentary debates on advise and consent, and then to develop trust in government in order to achieve the unification of armed forces and to revamp the national tax system. Finally they worked out an agreement containing the basic principles for gradual implementation, which was signed by President Yuan and Dr. Sun.

In the following weeks, Liang was too busy dealing with another cabinet crisis to worry about anything else. The Provisional Senate had repeatedly requested information on the use of the Belgian loan negotiated by Tang Shaoyi. But President Yuan had repeatedly denied any information to the senate. Premier Lu Zhengxiang was

175

weak and ineffective and irritated many senators. Finally the Provisional Senate gave his cabinet a vote of no confidence and Lu was forced to resign on September 22.

Noting that Liang Shiyi was on good terms with the Nationalists, President Yuan turned to Liang for help. "I would like you to be the next Premier. I cannot let this impasse last forever."

Liang had anticipated this crisis as he followed the parliamentary maneuver on the sideline. He had heard Yuan's derogatory comments about Tang's handling of this matter even though he knew too well that Tang had acted on Yuan's order. But he did not expect Yuan to ask him to be the Premier to defuse the crisis. For his part, Liang had no intention of ruining his hard-earned cordial relations with the Nationalists. With some hesitation, Liang replied, "I appreciate your confidence in me. However, I think that I can contribute more to the republic by staying in the Office of the President than becoming the premier."

Yuan appreciated this logic since he relied more and more on Liang's skills in the survival of his presidency. To settle the thorny issue of foreign loans, Yuan appointed a hardliner, Zhao Bingjun, the Interior Minister in the previous two cabinets, as the new premier.

Mindful of the agreement he had worked out with Huang Xing to promote civility in parliamentary debate, Liang suggested to Yuan what he had previously suggested to Tang in handling the loan crisis. Yuan was more willing to listen after he had failed to silence the Senate with his obstructionist tactic. Liang saw in Wu Jinglian, the Speaker of the Provisional Senate, a young firebrand who could swing the sentiment of its members. Wu had attended the new school system in late Qing and then had gone to Japan to study education. After joining the revolutionary cause, he rose quickly from the rank to become an effective leader in the Provisional Senate. Thus Yuan invited Wu Jinglian to a private dinner which was also attended by Premier Zhao Bingjun.

Yuan was blunt in his opening remark, "After receiving ten requests from the Senate, I have come to the conclusion that we must settle the question on the use of the Belgian loan. The truth is, this is a very delicate matter. I trust that even some Nationalists want to maintain confidentiality. Can you believe that?" Without waiting for an answer, he pulled out a list of names and laid it on the table. "A half million pounds from the loan were paid to the Manchu princes and noblemen whose names and respective sums of payments are shown on this list. You may note that in one case it was marked unpaid because that particular prince refused to support the republic to the very end. There was no point to pay him off." With an air of triumph, he continued, "The other half million pounds were paid to some members of the Revolutionary Alliance through Tang Shaoyi. You can check with your colleagues whether the money was delivered." Wu Jinglian was surprised but he promised to check.

After discussing this with the leaders of the Nationalist Party, Wu Jinglian concluded that all the money passed on by Tang was accounted for. Indeed some Nationalists might well be embarrassed by the disclosure. So Wu made it known to all Senators privately that he had received confidential information from the president about the use of this loan and was satisfied with the explanation.

* * *

After several hectic weeks of almost non-stop activities, Shiyi was glad to get a break from work when his family moved into their new home at Ganshiqiao Lane. It was a lovely compound of large courtyards and scattered dwellings, a far cry from the modest rented house his family had occupied during the last five years. This compound was also a residence they could call their own.

The acquisition of the residence at Ganshiqiao Lane was Liang's reward for revitalizing the Bank of Communications. This bank was in terrible financial condition after Liang was forced out as its associate vice president in 1911. As soon as the republic was established, Liang lost no time in raising money from private sources to revitalize the bank. In May 1912, the new government approved the reorganization of the bank as a public-private joint venture. Following the precedent set in the Qing Dynasty, the three principal officers were: a president who had access to the highest level of government, a vice president who represented the private shareholders, and an associate vice president who represented the Ministry of Communications. The Board of Directors elected Liang Shiyi as president, Ren Fongbao as vice president, and Ye Gongchuo as associate vice president.

Ren Fongbao was a wealthy man who owned many businesses including real estate. He thought Liang should have a spacious official residence to entertain the bank's clients. He persuaded the shareholders of the bank to buy a compound at Ganshiqiao Lane from a Manchu owner and deed it to Liang as a part of his compensation. At a bargain price negotiated with the hard-pressed owner, the bank paid 50,000 taels for the compound including the antique furniture inside the buildings. Since the bank was a public-private joint venture, a government official was expected to be in charge. No one inside or outside of the government ever raised the question of conflict of interest when the chief secretary of the republic's president served concurrently as the chief executive officer of the bank!

An early visitor to this new home was Liang's old friend Guan Mianjun who was then the managing director of Beijing-Zhangjiakou Railway. He was one of Liang's former associates in the Ministry of Posts and Communications who had kept the railways running when the country was in political turmoil. Liang's friends and subordinates in the Bank of Communications also helped to restore at least some sense of financial stability to the struggling new nation.

Guan Mianjun was a connoisseur of antiques and at the moment was absorbed in examining a well sculptured teak wood table when Liang called him back to reality, "Mianjun, what is the future outlook of the revenues in your railway?" Surprised by the suddenness of the question, Guan muttered, "So far, so good. The revenue is holding up in spite of occasional interruption of commercial services caused by troop movements."

That was music to Liang's ears. Under the charter of the Bank of

Communications, all revenue from government-operated railways, posts, shipping and telegraph would be deposited in the Bank of Communications. "I'm glad to hear that," Liang said. "With the chaotic conditions throughout the country, not only tax revenues from normal channels have gone down, but the provincial governments have also asked for subsidies from the central government to keep them going."

After deciding it was the right moment, Guan Mianjun changed the conversation to the purpose of his visit. "I intend to send my son Zuzhang to study railway engineering in America," he began. "I don't want him to get any idea of marrying a foreigner, or even a stranger. Ever since your oldest daughter was born, I thought to myself: wouldn't it be wonderful if my son and your daughter could unite our families some day?"

Liang was not surprised since the rich and powerful often wanted to consolidate and expand their influence through intermarriage. After a long pause, he said, "I personally think it's a good idea, but I must not make the decision until I get a chance to talk to my daughter and her mother." That was the end of the initial round of Guan's delicate mission.

* * *

Shiyi had good reasons to be happy with Guan's proposal. His eldest daughter Haoyin was now sixteen years old, too young to get married but not too soon to be engaged to a promising young man who needed a few more years to complete his education. Pretty, but petite for her age, Haoyin was sent to the best known modern finishing school for girls in Beijing. She was well prepared to assist a husband of the modern breed who would expect his wife to play an important part in his life and career. She knew the Guan family and their children and had probably formed her opinion about them. What arrangement could be better than this?

Liang promptly gathered his wife and second lady to break the news. According to the Confucius-inspired tradition, the marriage of a child of his concubine was the business of his wife. Sure enough, Madam took over center stage to make an opening remark, "Thank goodness, Zuzhang is the oldest living son of Master Guan's wife, not an issue from one of his concubines. That is certainly a plus. But Haoyin must still contend with several future mothers-in-law."

Trying to find a way out of such awkward discussions, Liang turned to his second lady and asked, "What do you think?"

Her reply was deferential. She was so used to the bluntness of Madam that she tried to avoid the appearance of irritation. "Haoyin will be lucky to find a family as close to us as the Guans," she said. "I really do not have any opinion."

"Why don't you ask Haoyin herself," Liang finally instructed the second lady. That took the issue out of the hands of Madam who was not really interested in the matter beyond exercising her authority. Liang was sure the second lady would somehow deal with Houyin in their best interests.

As he reflected on the rest of the family, Liang was very pleased with the progress of his two teenage sons. Although he did not find time to participate in the daily life of his children, he set firm directions for their education. Tall and hand-some, Dingji was now attending Qinghua Preparatory School in the west suburb of Beijing. This school was established by using the U. S. share of the Boxer Rebellion Indemnity Fund expatiated by the United States to the Chinese government. This fund was designated for the purpose of preparing Chinese students to study in the United States. The entry to Qinghua Preparatory School was the first step to gain a scholarship to study in the United States through competitive examination. Only 18 days younger than his half brother, Dingwu was not so tall or handsome, but he was very bright and highly motivated. Liang was more aware of the rivalry between Madam and his second lady than that between the siblings. To avoid comparison of his sons' performance in the same school, Liang sent Dingwu to an exclusive board-ing school for boys.

* * *

Soon after the Belgian loan controversy was defused, another loomed even larg-er and more ominous. While the senate was still protesting against the Belgian loan, President Yuan had asked Finance Minister, Zhou Xuexi, to negotiate secretly with the Six-Nation Consortium of foreign banks for a "reorganization loan" of 25 million pounds sterling. Now serving under Premier Zhao, Finance Minister Zhou Xuexi brought the negotiation close to a successful conclusion, thus Yuan sent a feeler to the Provisional Senate for approval of this loan. The Senate was in no mood to comply.

In the meantime, Song Jiaoren, the Nationalist Party organizer, realized the Nationalists could not possibly stop the abuse of power by President Yuan toward the Provisional Senate. He decided the hope of his party would lie in winning the nation-al election for the bicameral Parliament scheduled to take place in December 1912. If the Nationalists could win a majority in both Houses, then according to the Provisional Constitution, the President must appoint their candidate for Premier. With that goal in mind, Song travelled throughout the country to solicit votes for the Nationalist Party.

The Provisional Constitution gave the vote to Chinese males over twenty-one years old who held property or paid taxes over certain levels and held an elementary school graduation certificate or equivalent. At most, ten percent of the population would qualify, but far less participated in the voting for lack of a democratic tradi-tion. Some feminists protested the exclusion of women in the electoral process but to no avail. The 274 Senate seats were taken by 10 Senators from each province plus a number representing overseas Chinese; the 596 seats in the House of Representatives were allocated in proportion to the size of the population. There were hundreds of small political groups or parties which contested in one or more seats in the election. It seemed that everyone was for himself in the contest!

But Song Jiaoren was undaunted. Under his effective guidance, the Nationalists had absorbed most splinter parties by urging those in smaller parties to run under multiple party tickets, one of which would be the Nationalist label. It was a brilliant idea to swell the ranks of the Nationalists but it also sowed seeds of divided loyalty.

When the results of the parliamentary election were announced in January 1913, the Nationalists gained a plurality of 123 seats in the Senate and 269 seats in the House of Representatives.

Against the Nationalists in the new Parliament were several smaller parties, among which were the Republican Party and the Democratic Party. The Unification Party, which had supported Xiong Xiling as Finance Minister in the first cabinet, had by now joined forces with the Republican Party headed by Vice President Li Yuanhong. The Democratic Party was chaired by Liang Qichao whose "one hundred days of reform" under Emperor Guangxu had made him famous. The members of these parties were by no means completely supportive of President Yuan. However, by education and cultural heritage, they were closer to Yuan than to the revolutionaries and were opposed to the idea of drastic social revolution.

* * *

Unpleasant as the news of the national election might be to Yuan, it was at least one step closer to a permanent government that he preferred. Sensing a brief period of relief after the recess of the Provisional Senate, Liang Shiyi told Yuan about his plan to go back to his native village for a short visit. "My brother Shixu asked me to go home for the celebration of my father's 70th birthday," Liang began. He knew Yuan could not refuse his request in fulfilling his filial obligation. "I believe this is a good time for me to make such a journey."

Nodding his approval, Yuan asked casually, "What is your brother doing?" Liang did not expect such a question.

"He's the managing director of the Guangzhou-Kowloon Railway," Liang replied. "Under his administration, the construction was completed last year." Then he told Yuan about his brother's military background.

"You have never asked any favor for him. Someone might think he is a good-for-nothing guy." Yuan was in good humor.

Liang had some inkling what Yuan was up to. Many officials close to Yuan had asked him to dispense jobs or honors for their relatives and friends, but Liang was not about to do that. "My brother is doing well on his own, and he does not want me to interfere with his business," Liang told Yuan politely but firmly.

Liang was greatly surprised when Yuan said, "I will make him a colonel on reserve in the infantry. When the annual promotion time comes next August, he will automatically become a major general." Liang did not know what to think. Was Yuan trying to please him by giving this honor to his brother Shixu? Or did Yuan have a future assignment in mind for his brother. But in the next breath, Yuan provided the answer, "Some day I may want to make use of his connections to the generals in Guangdong Province in settling their infighting there." Liang Shiyi did not know what to say and let the matter rest.

On February 12, 1913, the first anniversary of the abdication of the Qing emperor, President Yuan conferred honors on many who had contributed to the peaceful transition from the monarchy to the republic. Liang Shiyi received a Second Rank

Merit Award. He looked back to a tumultuous year with some satisfaction. He had played a constructive role in averting the disaster of civil war and famine to the country. In assessing the difficulties in years ahead, he wondered how long Xu Shichang, Yuan's close friend and long-time political ally, would stay away from the center stage of political action.

Indeed, Xu Shichang pondered the same question quietly in the city of Qingdao in Shandong Province. When Yuan was out of power in early 1911, he saw to it that Xu remained in the service of the Manchu Royal House through the influence of several princes who were loyal to him. Sure enough, Xu was not only a Grand Councillor at the court but was also appointed a royal tutor for the boy emperor. These same princes were later bribed to insure their support of the abdication of the emperor in exchange for their comfortable retirement. Now these princes lived peacefully in the beautiful seaport of Qingdao, thanks to the protection of the German Settlement. Publicly Xu was a Qing loyalist who served the Manchu Royal House to the end. Privately, he was assigned by Yuan to keep a close watch on the activities of the royal princes and to learn through them about any intrigues inside the Forbidden City.

Shiyi got his chance to see the action inside the Forbidden City himself on February 15 when he was sent by President Yuan to congratulate Empress Dowager Longyu on her birthday. Presenting his credential as the representative of the President Yuan, he bowed three times according to the protocol of the republic. Gone were the ceremonies of kowtowing and the inhibitions at the court. Liang conveyed in a solemn voice the best wishes of the republican president to the health of her imperial highness. Liang felt great pride, as John Adams must have felt when presented to King George III as the American ambassador to the Court of St. James after the American revolution. Yet the Manchu Royal House was so helpless inside the Forbidden City that few people had any illusion that it deserved such generous treatment. Exactly one week later, the empress dowager died of illness, and perhaps the dream that the Manchus would ever rule the empire again died with her.

Liang Zhijian and His Family on His Seventieth Birthday in 1913

Home

"Madam, I plan to take the whole family home next week," Shiyi told his wife. For him, home was the humble grey brick house beside the rice field in his native village where his father still lived. His immediate family now consisted of his wife, two concubines, four sons and five daughters, not counting their two faithful maid servants Mai San and Liang San who were very much a part of the family. In late 1912, Shiyi had heard repeatedly from his brother Shixu, urging him to come home for the celebration of their father's 70th birthday in the coming year. He had discussed his plan on and off with his family but pressing affairs of state had prevented him from finalizing such a long trip. He now saw an opening in his calendar after attending the celebration of Empress Dowager Longyu's birthday.

His wife was not surprised by his decision, only the abruptness of its timing. She calmly replied, "The family is quite ready. The children are all very excited about the trip." Not that Madam needed to do anything herself to prepare for the trip; everything was taken care of by others—servants, concubines and friends. But her husband always wanted her to feel her opinion would count. After hearing Madam's enthusiastic reaction, he cabled Shixu in Guangzhou that his family would be on its way.

At dinnertime that day, Liang Shiyi announced to the family that his two oldest sons, Dingji and Dingwu, would go to study in the United States immediately after the celebration of their grandfather's birthday. Both his wife and second lady were stunned. With the instinct of a doting mother, Madam protested, "I thought they would go to America later. They are not even fifteen and cannot take care of themselves."

Shiyi was ready for resistance. "They will be fifteen next month. A friend of mine has arranged for them to stay with an American family in Boston so they can get used to the American way of life before enrolling in a private boarding school next fall."

But Madam insisted, "They will forget our family values and culture when they go to live in a foreign land at such a young age."

Shiyi interrupted her. "Look, Tang Shaoyi went to America when he was twelve. He experienced no unsurmountable problems either in dealing with foreigners nor in preserving our own culture." When he calmed down, he said, "I want my sons to have the best of both cultures. I have ingrained them with Confucius classics since

183

they were three years old. Now I want them to learn what makes other societies tick when their minds are not yet clogged with prejudices. When they grow up, they will live in a world very different from our own and must be able to adapt to survive."

On the issue of educating his children, Liang Shiyi was unyielding. While he was at it, he thought he might as well bring up a related subject. Suddenly he announced, "Since Haoyin is engaged to Guan Zuzhang, she too will soon go to America to study and to be near Zuzhang, when proper arrangements are made." Everybody was surprised.

Madam did not like the idea for various reasons, not the least of which was the expenses lavished on a daughter, particularly not her own daughter. But she had already protested too much. So she shrewdly turned to the second lady and said, "A'er, what do you think of this plan? After all, Haoyin is your daughter." Without such an invitation, the second lady would not dare to volunteer her opinion. With this invitation, she could now join in to dampen her husband's enthusiasm.

The second lady did not disappoint Madam as she said to her husband, "Does a girl need that much education in a faraway land?"

Liang had no pretense when he said to his second lady, "I think you are mistaken. Do you remember our discussion about footbinding many years ago? When Houyin was three years old, you thought that she should be subjected to such cruel practice lest she could not be married to a good family. Only I prevented that from happening. Can you imagine now that Zuzhang will marry a girl with bound feet? Many years from now, you will find that her education in America will serve her well in coping with her American-educated husband." Naturally, the second lady deferred to such an opinion whether she fully understood or agreed with it. As if he could read the mind of Madam, Liang added, "When it comes to the education of our children, I spare no effort or expense. Education is the most precious thing we can give to a child because no one can take it away." His statements ended the discussion.

* * *

Brother Shixu had overseen the needs of his aging father since his return to Guangzhou from Manchuria in late 1910. Taking a short train ride from Guangzhou to Sanshui, he visited his father often in his native village. Although Shixu was quite satisfied with the life in Guangzhou, a tragic event had struck his family. The health of his wife had not been robust for some time but she was eager to have another child ever since the death of their infant daughter. In the fall of 1912, there were some signs that her hope might come true. Then one evening after supper, she had a sudden burst of pain and fainted. By the time a doctor arrived for the house call, she was unconscious and was soon pronounced dead. The cause of her death was later diagnosed as an ectopic pregnancy. The tragic death had happened a day before Shixu's own birthday, and the memory was still fresh. The planning of his father's birthday celebration was a painful reminder even though it was a duty that he could not escape.

After learning the itinerary of his brother, Shixu immediately set the date for celebration to accommodate his brother's busy schedule. His father was delighted with the forthcoming family reunion even though the date was far in advance of his birthday. Many last minute preparations for the big occasion awaited Shixu's attention.

While his brother Shiyi was blessed with nine children, Shixu had only a two-year old son from his second consort. In his introspective moments, he inevitably compared his sparse line of offspring with that of his late younger brother Shixin, who had only a daughter, Wosheng. Now seven years old, this girl had followed her widowed mother who left the Liang family and subsequently remarried. Shixu never forgot that he and brother Shiyi had vowed to take care of Wosheng like their own daughter. But then they did not want to hurt the feeling and wishes of Wosheng's mother to raise the child herself. With the forthcoming celebration for his father's birthday, would it be appropriate for Wosheng to be reunited with the family?

Shixu had pondered this question for some time. With the celebration date approaching, more relatives arrived from all parts of the country, among them his youngest sister Fugui who had the most contact with Shixin's widow. Now Shixu assigned this sister the delicate task of asking Shixin's widow to permit Wosheng to join the celebration in the Liang Family.

Sister Fugui had tracked down the most recent information about Shixin's widow who was now remarried to Mr. Lou, a business man of modest means, living in Guangzhou. Shixin's widow had acquired literacy through studying under her father as a child and went to a school for herbal medicine after she left the Liang family. Joining the rank of the rare species of "new woman" in the new republic, she had not only taken up the practice of herbal medicine but also kept her maiden name in her profession. She was a brave soul and trailblazer in her time.

Fugui decided to send a note in advance, explaining the purpose of the upcoming visit. She was debating whether to address the letter to "my dear sister-in-law" or "Mrs. Lou." The former salutation was no longer appropriate even though it still reflected her sentiment while the latter was too painful for her to acknowledge. So she put down Dr. Jian, as if she were one of the patients addressing the herbal doctor.

When Fugui arrived at the appointed date, she was directed into the private consulting room of the doctor. When she saw the doctor, they embraced silently and in tears. They understood each other's feeling that no words could express. After a moment, Fugui apologized for the intrusion. Then Dr. Jian spoke, "I don't have a busy schedule since I started my practice only recently. Please tell me, how are you? How is everything?"

"I'm now married and live in Beijing. After mother died, my fiance's family decided to send him to college in Japan for several years. So we were married upon his return only a few months ago." Fugui replied.

"Then you don't know the aches and pains of being a mother yet." Dr. Jian was getting close to the point. "You will find the joy of having children around. Wosheng is a joy and comfort to me. I understand that you want to take her back to your native village for the celebration of your father's birthday."

"Yes, if you give me your permission. That will make father very happy." Fugui knew they had reached the critical stage of negotiation.

"I don't want to deny your father the pleasure of seeing his granddaughter. However, I'm realistic in assessing the situation. The Liang family has now reached the zenith of power and fortune. If your father decides to keep Wosheng after the celebration, I have no recourse to get her back." Then Dr. Jian's tone suddenly changed. "But I have prepared myself to embrace that possibility. I shall let you take Wosheng to see the Liang family."

Fugui could not let the conversation end on such a sharp note even though Dr. Jian's fear was quite real. She proceeded with great caution. "I have been instructed to 'borrow' Wosheng only for the occasion of my father's celebration. I cannot speculate if my father may wish to have her stay a little longer afterward. You probably don't know that my father took a concubine a couple of years ago. My stepmother is a kind woman in her twenties and will be able to take good care of Wosheng during her stay in the village."

"I'm sure Wosheng would be in good hands if she stays in the Liang family, but she would be very lonely. I'm also thinking about my own life without her." The words came naturally from a loving mother.

"You needn't be so pessimistic. You're so young and may start a new happy family. And if Wosheng does stay in the Liang family, she would have a better future." Fugui was quite aware of the prevalent prejudice against a girl whose mother was remarried.

"Material comfort, no doubt. Respectability, too. Who can argue with that? I don't want to be selfish. But will she be happy without me?" The tone of the conversation certainly had taken a strange turn.

"She would easily blend into my brother's family. He has nine children. They could grow up like brothers and sisters. She would have the best education money can buy." After a pause, Fugui added, "My brother plans to send his oldest daughter to study in America. He believes in a good education for his daughters as well as his sons."

Dr. Jian was impressed. "Perhaps that's all for the best. You convince me that it will not be a calamity if Wosheng does not come back to me. However, I reserve the right to change my mind. I'll arrange for Wosheng to meet you here at five this afternoon." With that cordial exchange, Fugui's mission was accomplished.

* * *

After all the excitement of anticipation, the 70th birthday of the patriarch of the Liang family was a simple affair. Only relatives and close friends from the village were invited to the ceremony and banquet. But even without an invitation, Liang Shiyi's friends and colleagues in Beijing who heard of the celebration sent gifts for Shiyi's father. President Yuan led the parade of generous givers, and their gifts were shipped to the village in time for display.

On the day of the celebration, the whole family went to the Ancestral Hall early in the morning. The patriarch, Liang Zhijian, led all his descendants in kowtowing to the tablets of ancestors to express their gratitude. Then his children and grand-children kowtowed to Liang Zhijian. Later friends and other relatives showed up to express their congratulations and were treated to a dinner in the Ancestral Hall. No other place in the village would be large enough to seat over two hundred guests, including children. Liang Shiyi and his brother Shixu became the center of attention at the dinner as their Western-style tuxedos were a strange sight amidst a crowd who wore traditional Chinese gowns and dresses. Liang Zhijian was very proud of his sons, even though he was not eager to accept their new attire.

Shiyi had introduced more changes in the family than just his appearance. Sending his sons to study in America at an early age was not his father's idea of a good education. Nevertheless, the decision was irreversible. Shiyi had asked a friend in Hong Kong to arrange their passage to America as soon as the celebration was over. His whole family, except Liang Shiyi, would go to Hong Kong and sail for Shanghai on the *S.S. President Jackson*. His two sons would continue to go to the United States while the rest of family would return to Beijing from Shanghai by train.

Liang's sister Fugui also left for Beijing with his family and Wosheng after sending a note to Dr. Jian: "The members of Liang family appreciate your generosity for allowing Wosheng to stay with them. You will understand they act in the best interest of the child. We will get in touch in the future."

It was confusion at the dock as members of Liang family were lining up to get on board *S.S. President Jackson*. A servant was holding the hand of Liang Shiyi's youngest daughter as they walked up the gangway.

"Be careful, Miss No. 6. Don't dance around on the plank," the servant told the four-year-old girl.

"Don't call me Miss No. 6," the little girl replied. "I am Miss No. 5."

The servant looked at the innocent girl who was oblivious of the order of her father to add Wosheng into the ranking of his daughters. She kindly told the little girl with a wink, "From now on, you will be Miss No. 6."

* * *

Shiyi always felt invigorated when he talked to the people in his native village and got the sense of goodness in the grass roots. However, he did not have time to stay long and soon departed on a train to Guangzhou. As the train moved slowly across patches of rice paddy, Liang Shiyi looked out of the window at the oxen in the rural landscape, reminding him of his boyhood. Because the people in his native village were predominantly peasants, some wealthy "cousins" in the next village would call them oxen. He recalled that on the traditional memorial day of Qingming Festival on April 5 each year, his father would take him to the graveyards of their ancestors and perform the solemn rites of worship. He remembered particularly that when he was six, he saw many oxen working in the rice paddy and remarked to his father, "What is wrong with the oxen? They are the ones who do all the hard work without complaining. When I grow up, I want to be as tough as an ox." Was that a premonition that he would need the toughness of an ox to confront the crises in his life? He suddenly felt a surge of inner strength to carry on the burden of state affairs.

At Guangzhou, Liang Shiyi paid a visit to Hu Hanmin, the Governor of Guangdong, a strong supporter of Sun Yatsen. Liang wanted to discuss with him the urgency of strengthening the value of the local currency and a proposal for constructing a new harbor near Guangzhou for ocean-going ships. While he was a guest in the Governor's Mansion, a servant ran in with news that would compound his duties. To the dismay of all present, the servant carried news of Song Jiaoren's assassination. Song had been the minister of agriculture in Tang Shaoyi's cabinet and was expected to become the new premier if the Nationalists could get enough votes in the new parliament. On March 20, 1913, just as he was leaving the railway station in Shanghai to take up his duty in the new parliament in Beijing, he had been shot by an assassin and was rushed to hospital where he died two days later. Liang Shiyi understood how this incident would undermine the relations between the Nationalists and President Yuan. He spoke, half to himself. "There will be serious repercussions."

Liang immediately cabled a friend in Hong Kong to book a berth for him on a ship sailing for Shanghai. Three days later, he arrived in Hong Kong in time to board the *S.S. Mongolia* to return to Beijing.

Upon arrival in Beijing on April 1, Liang received the following telegram from Huang Xing who had been on friendly terms with him since their meeting in Beijing:

"The assassination of Song Jiaoren was swiftly investigated by the Police Department of the International Municipal Government in Shanghai. The confession of the captured assassin and the discovery of incriminating documents seem to confirm widespread rumors of politically motivated conspiracy. Even though Song was my most valued colleague, I do not wish to allow this unfortunate incident to jeopardize the shaky foundation of the republic, particularly at a time when the recognition of the new government by the United States appears to be imminent. As I mourn the death of my dear friend and help comfort his family, I cannot find words to express my deep grief and concern about the future of our country. If you can shed some light on any action that may ease my pain, please advise me confidentially."

Never a man running out of ideas, Liang Shiyi was genuinely touched by the sincere expression of Huang Xing. However, since people in high places in the government might be suspect of conspiracy in the assassination, he could not think of any reply that could soothe Huang's skepticism about the future of the republic.

Bitter Tears

"I'm glad that you dropped by tonight," Shiyi said to Guan Mianjun as they settled into the comfortable chairs to enjoy a cup of tea. "I have been so busy since my return to Beijing that I haven't had a chance to call on you."

Guan had come to make a courtesy call since their two families were now linked by the engagement of Liang's eldest daughter to Guan's eldest son. Politely, Guan asked, "Have you heard from you sons yet?"

"Yes, but only a very brief telegram telling me of their safe arrival in Boston," Liang replied. "The mail from America takes a long time. Both Dingji and Dingwu are expected to stay with an American family in Boston until they are ready to enroll in Phillips Academy next fall."

"Zuzhang is doing well at Stanton Academy in Virginia. He should be ready to attend college next year." Guan was making a progress report about his own son.

"You know," Liang said in a deliberately measured tone, "I have decided to send Houyin to the United States so that she can be near Zuzhang. As soon as she gets an admission to a finishing school for girls, she will be on the way."

Guan was speechless. He thought Liang was way ahead of him, both in outlook and in planning their children's future. After a short pause, he realized that he should say something to express his appreciation. "It's a splendid idea," Guan said before hurrying home to tell his wife.

* * *

On behalf of President Yuan Shikai, Liang Shiyi welcomed the members of the new Parliament to its opening session on April 8, 1913. He tried to strike a conciliatory tone even though the assassination of Song Jiaoren had poisoned the atmosphere of the political arena.

In a cynical move, Yuan Shikai appealed to American Protestants to pray for China in their churches as the new parliament met, although Yuan was no Christian. The request made headlines in the American press. The *Christian Herald* compared Yuan's appeal to Constantine's and Charlemagne's decisions "in subjecting pagan nations to the yoke of Christ." President Woodrow Wilson and his Secretary of State William Jennings Bryant were duly impressed.

The Nationalist Party which had gained a plurality in both houses in the parliament felt the loss of Song Jiaoren, their most effective organizer and dynamic leader. Without Song to hold the coalition together, those members whose allegiance to the Nationalist Party were based on self interest rather than on democratic principles could easily be swung by other considerations.

The Progressive Party, which was a new alliance of the Unification Party, Republican Party and Democratic Party, now provided a strong opposition to the Nationalists. While the leaders of the party professed to be independent, their conservative social view was more in tune with the traditional culture since most of their members were former Qing officials. The Nationalists viewed them with strong suspicion and thought of this party as a Trojan horse that would eventually serve Yuan's interest.

Sensing the weakness of the Nationalists, President Yuan Shikai lost no time in wooing their dissenting members, with his purse when necessary, to deny the Nationalists an absolute majority in both houses and avoiding an unacceptable Premier. In a meeting with his hold-over premier, Zhao Bingjun, Yuan said, "I have no desire to name a new Premier until I'm forced to do so by the Parliament. Go ahead and submit my plan for a reorganization loan to the Parliament for approval."

Yuan was referring to the secret negotiations with the Six-Nation Consortium of foreign banks for the reorganization loan of 25 million pounds sterling. The negotiation was initiated by Zhou Xuexi, the finance minister, but the approval of this loan had met with resistance from the Provisional Senate before its recess. After many twists and turns, American interests withdrew from the consortium in March 1913, claiming the terms imposed on the Chinese government were exploitative and were interfering with the internal affairs of China. On April 26, Zhou Xuexi finally brought the negotiation to a successful conclusion with the consortium of the remaining five nations. The secret broke wide open when Yuan submitted a request to Parliament for approval of the loan. The request was like a bombshell for the newly-constituted Parliament which had not yet set its feet firmly on the ground.

After the Senate and the House of Representatives elected their respective Speakers, Zhou requested secret sessions to discuss this matter. During the discussions, he presented the terms of the loan agreement but refused to disclose the plan for using the loan, except for the portion designated for refinancing current debts. The Nationalists in the Parliament suspected the remaining fund would be used to wage a civil war against them. Frightened by the possibility, the members did not even want to examine the terms of the loan as long as the real purpose for it was not fully disclosed. A stalemate was unavoidable.

When Liang Shiyi was summoned to the President's Office the following day, Yuan Shikai said to him, "I think our damage control after the national election has been moderately successful. At least I don't have to deal with a Nationalist Premier. The Nationalist Party will eventually come to its senses and support a compromise candidate outside its own rank. It's now time to push my agenda for the approval of the reorganization loan."

Shiyi was not against the foreign loan since he knew that several bridging loans and large sums of indemnities to foreign countries incurred under the Qing rule would be due in June. However, he was dismayed by the unfavorable terms of the consortium which could bind the hands of the government and the nation for years to come. He had been aware of the general outline of the terms negotiated by the finance minister, but he'd had no opportunity to inject his opinion. He decided to break his silence. "The terms of this loan are unusually harsh. Perhaps it's better to improve our tax collection before asking the parliament to approve a new loan."

"We need the money now, Shiyi. We have no time for further delay." Irritated by Shiyi's lukewarm response, Yuan stopped listening and said, "The Parliament is dead set against this loan regardless of the terms. The Nationalists questioned my intention for securing foreign loans in the Provisional Senate last year. They will no doubt do the same in this Parliament. They want to create a gridlock and destroy my presidency. I will not let them do it."

Yuan Shikai took the offensive by appealing to Sir John Jordan, the British Minister to Beijing. Jordan had known Yuan since the 1880's when both served their respective countries in Korea. He was a major influence behind the consortium's decision to withhold the loan until the Chinese government gave formal guarantees on the preservation of foreign rights and investments. Furthermore, Britain insisted on the autonomy of Tibet, while Russia wanted the autonomy of Mongolia, as conditions for recognition of Yuan's Government. On the other hand, Britain understood that the reorganization loan would provide funds to repay previous foreign loans and would also guarantee the new loan. Playing to Jordan's fear that Britain would have more to lose if the reorganization loan failed to materialize, Yuan secured a secret pledge from him that the contract would be honored by the consortium whether or not it was approved by the parliament.

Emboldened by the secret pledge of Jordan, Yuan said to Zhao Bingjun, "I have my way of obtaining this loan regardless of the action of the Parliament. Be prepared to stand firm." Yuan was not bluffing.

As opposition and protests mounted, Premier Zhao resigned on May 1 under the pretext of illness, which would also allow him to evade the subpoena from the Municipal Court in Shanghai in connection with the assassination of Song Jiaoren. President Yuan immediately appointed Duan Qirui, Minister of Army, as Acting Premier. He sent the loan contract to Parliament for approval on May 2. The parliament demanded an open debate on the contents of the contract. Autocratic and brash, Duan secretly organized a group of noisy protesters to picket the Parliament, demanding immediate approval of the loan. Duan told the Parliament in no uncertain terms, "You are not going to go home until this contract is approved." When members of the Parliament walked out without giving their approval, the hecklers yelled insults to them. Some even tried to rough them up.

Although the price tag of the reorganization loan was 25 million pounds sterling, the actual proceeds to the Chinese treasury were 21 million, deducting a 10 percent discount for the origination fee, commissions and other expenses. The designated use of the funds fell into two major categories: The first was the obligatory payments to foreigners, including 6 million to repay the bridging loans coming due, 2.87 million to clear debts owed by provincial governments to the five banks in the consortium, and 2 million to pay the claims of foreigners for destruction of properties during the revolution. The subtotal was 10.87 million pounds. The second category which would consume the remaining 10.13 million pounds included 3 million for disarming and rehabilitating the military remnants in various provinces, and 5.5 million for government expenditures from April to September in 1913. The remaining funds would allow upgrading the administration of salt tax collection.

To guarantee the repayment of this loan, the consortium would gain more control of duties from Chinese Customs, and would have full access to the collection from a salt tax, a major source of income for the Chinese government. The loan would last 47 years at an interest rate of 5 percent per annum, with interest payments beginning immediately and partial repayments of the principal beginning ten years later. The estimated interest payments over the 47 years totaled 42.85 million pounds.

The Parliament was in no mood to approve such a loan contract in spite of the threat expressed by the Acting Premier. The terms of the loan were perceived as a enormous sellout to foreign interests. The government gained 10.13 million pounds in discretionary funds which the Nationalists were sure would enrich the war chest of President Yuan to wage a civil war against all opponents.

* * *

During this impasse in the Parliament, President Yuan Shikai got an unexpected lift from the United States. President Woodrow Wilson, who had urged the recognition of the Chinese Republic during the 1912 presidential election campaign, primarily to embarrass the Taft Administration, now decided to fulfill his promise. In May, the American minister in Beijing called on President Yuan to inform him that the United States extended full diplomatic recognition to his government. Mexico, Cuba, Peru and Brazil quickly followed.

Sir John Jordan, the British minister to Beijing, called the American action "outrageous." Dismissing the altruism of the United States, he emphasized that Britain had a much greater claim on the preservation of foreign rights and investments. Of course, the consortium would seek the formal acknowledgement of the Chinese government to that effect, he said.

As President Yuan became more obstinate and arrogant in pushing the approval of the reorganization loan, the news of Britain's secret backing leaked out. The Parliament suddenly realized it could do nothing to stop the consummation of the contract and was outraged. Since the premier had already resigned, the Parliament could only heap its wrath on Finance Minister Zhou Xuexi, who asked for and was granted a leave of absence by President Yuan on May 16.

Beijing Odyssey

Yuan Shikai once again turned to Liang Shiyi for help. "I don't think anyone but you can get us out of this financial crisis," Yuan began. "You can provide the leadership for the Finance Ministry."

Liang demurred as he replied, "I can't do any better than others in handling the approval of the reorganization loan. Not only the parliament but also the provincial governors are denouncing this loan."

"I'm not asking you to defend the reorganization loan," Yuan said firmly. "What do I care about all the protests as long as I have the money? That tempest is now reduced to a whisper. Anyway, I cannot spare you from the Office of the President. Would you accept a concurrent position as finance minister to build an efficient system for tax collection?"

Shiyi was of two minds even about this specific mission. He finally said, "It is difficult for me to say no when my service is badly needed. However, I do not want to be in the way of the future Premier who should name his own Finance Minister. It will be better if you appoint me as Acting Finance Minister until the next Premier is named." Yuan was satisfied with Shiyi's suggestion while he searched for someone to replace the Acting Premier.

Amid calls for cancellation of the reorganization loan, newspaper headlines periodically carried the investigations on the assassination of Song Jiaoren as the case was vigorously pursued by the International Municipal Government in Shanghai. After a hearing before the court during which the assassin named his conspirator, he died suddenly in prison. Searching the home of the conspirator, the police found documents linking him to a secretary in the Interior Ministry and a secret code for sending telegrams to Premier Zhao. Although this secretary had disappeared, the evidence pointed to Zhao as a suspect since Zhao had been Interior Minister prior to assuming the premiership. Under the protection of the President, Zhao refused to be subpoenaed to the court on the pretext of illness. The trial in Shanghai dragged on without reaching a verdict.

However, Zhao Bingjun was not too ill to become the Governor of Zhili when the post was offered to him by President Yuan. After the assassination of Song Jiaoren, the psyche of the Nationalists had changed from hope to desperation. The protection of Zhao Bingjun was the latest indication that President Yuan was probably implicated in the crime. The Nationalists saw their effort to gain power through democratic means had not succeeded. The constitutional government was on the verge of shattering into pieces.

* * *

Liang Shiyi was now busy with his new job in the Finance Ministry. He had little time for his family, but he was happy when he had finally received letters from his sons Dingji and Dingwu in Boston. Then on May 22, 1913, Shiyi was shocked to receive a telegram from Dingji informing him that Dingwu had drowned while swimming in the seashore. Although the account from the telegram was sketchy, it appeared that Dingwu, who had just learned to swim, answered the call for help from a drowning woman. After a brief struggle, both perished.

When Shiyi took the news to Madam, she was understandably silent. This was no time to crow about her earlier misgivings. She could only feel relief that her own son, Dingji, was safe. But the second lady was devastated. Like all concubines, she had placed all hopes on the success of her sons to raise her own status in the family. Her silence and restraint over the years suddenly ended. She released her anguish in bitter tears.

As the news of Dingwu's death reached Guan Mianjun, he rushed to comfort the Liang family. There was not much that could be said to drown Liang's sorrow but Guan tried. "It was a tragedy that the great promise of a young life was prematurely and cruelly cut off. You may be comforted by the fact that he died because he was trying to save the life of someone, even in a foreign land."

Shiyi soberly answered, "Dingwu didn't know his own limitations and couldn't survive just from his good intention. Even his heroic act cannot alleviate my pain. I will miss him forever."

A House Divided

Earlier in February 1913, President Yuan Shikai had appointed a Finance Policy Commission to study and propose solutions to improve the public finance. Liang Shiyi and Liang Qichao were among the commission members. That gave the two Liangs a chance to renew their association since their forced separation after the "one hundred days of reform" in 1898. In fact, Liang Qichao did not dare return from exile in Japan until General Cai, one of his former students, had obtained an assurance from President Yuan that all would be forgiven.

After Liang Shiyi assumed the post as acting finance minister, he asked Liang Qichao to review his new proposal for rectifying the serious financial problems confronting the nation. Qichao was quick to respond.

"This setting is superior to the ones I remember, Shiyi." Quichao said as he stepped into Shiyi's office.

Shiyi smiled. "Sit down friend. The light is superior by this window."

"Does that mean I will have to read your proposal? Can't we just talk about the issues, as we did in the old days?"

"Of Course." Shiyi sat down across from him. "I want to go over my proposal with you before presenting it to the Finance Policy Commission. In order to raise revenue and reduce expenditures, I will propose several measures: First, reducing military expenditures through demobilization; second, streamlining the government structure to cut waste; third, levying new taxes on income, property, tobacco and liquor; and fourth, strengthening the tax collection system. What do you think?"

"You've outlined some very important objectives. But how are you going to implement them, Shiyi?"

"That is the most difficult part," Liang Shiyi replied. "I intend to publish my proposal for public scrutiny after it's approved by the Commission. I hope people of good will throughout the nation will respond and urge their leaders to act for the good of the nation. I will appeal to the governors not to intercept tax revenue and customs duty that rightfully belong to the central government."

"I appreciate your sincerity, Shiyi, but is that enough?"

"The Finance Ministry will set up procedures to monitor the progress."

"Then it's worth trying," Liang Qichao concluded. "I can't think of a better alternative, even though I remain skeptical."

When they parted, Liang Shiyi said to Liang Qichao, "I really appreciate the frank discussion with you. We should get together more often. Why don't you drop by my home some evening?" That was enough of an invitation for Liang Qichao.

Liang Shiyi decided to call a meeting of the Commission the very next day. After his passionate speech detailing his proposal, the Commission voted unanimously to follow his recommendations. His full speech was published as a pamphlet *A Letter to My Fellow Citizens*.

* * *

A week later, Liang Qichao sat comfortably in the living room of Liang Shiyi's residence at Ganshiqiao Lane. After exchanging news about their families, they turned their attention to the issues that had recently made the headlines. For days, the governors in the Yangzi Valley, who were Nationalists supporters, continually bombarded the newspapers with open letters and telegrams, attacking the reorganization loan contract signed by the government without the approval of the parliament. In a preemptive move, President Yuan dismissed the Governor of Jiangxi Province on June 9 and asked Vice President Li Yuanhong to take over as acting governor.

"Did you get any warning about the governor's dismissal?" asked Qichao.

Liang Shiyi looked grave, "I wasn't consulted. I don't know what remedy would undo this harm."

"I'm afraid it's already too late," Liang Qichao replied. "Even with your good intention, this conflict is irreconcilable. The two sides are at cross purposes which were papered over during the peaceful transition. The Nationalists agreed to the coalition government because they believed they could take control in a hurry by democratic means. President Yuan, on the other hand, had no intention to relinquish power and the coalition government is a means to his own end."

"Our country is tottering toward a civil war which nobody wants, least of all the people in whose name the conflict is waged," Liang Shiyi said in desperation. "A house divided will eventually fall."

Liang Qichao was philosophical. "Nothing is black and white. There are idealists as well as opportunists in both camps. Even if you ignore the ambitions of individuals, you still have a serious problem of conflicting values. The society is ripe for change, but we can't agree on how far and how fast." Then he added reflectively, "More than ten years ago, both the revolutionaries and the reformers in exile in Japan argued this very point. In our publications, Kang Youwei and I insisted on reforming the existing system because the people in China were not ready for wholesale political and social upheaval. In the newspapers published by the revolutionaries, Song Jiaoren and Wang Jingwei denounced my stand at every turn. The basic argument has not changed even though we now have a republican form of government."

"You know more about the working of democratic governments in the world, Qichao. I'm in favor of rapid change within reason, and I am ready to compromise.

But I don't accept the idea of destroying all existing social institutions, and I don't believe people in this country are ready for it either."

"Many people are still wistfully harking back to things past," Liang Qichao observed. We don't have a functioning and institutionalized democracy.That requires a tradition of negotiation and compromise. The politics in China have always been a winner-take-all game. Those who advocate drastic change of the social structure are, by and large, young men who have been exposed to modern ideas in the United States and Japan. They constitute a small minority, even among the educated, and they have no patience for foot dragging. The rest of us have been deeply ingrained with the teachings of Confucianism and cannot shake it off quickly, even if we try. Besides the hardcore followers of Sun Yatsen, many Nationalist supporters do not believe in social revolution and they will melt away at the first sign of the collapse of the Nationalist armies. We're confronted with a situation more like the French revolution rather than the American Revolution. Only through the actions of the moderates of both sides has a full-scale civil war or brutal repression been avoided."

"Yes. That's our only hope. Didn't I tell you two decades ago that the arduous quest for a prosperous and stable China requires patience? This is no time to give up hope. I've worked too hard for a peaceful transition from a monarchy to a republic to allow my efforts to fail."

"You deserve credit," Liang Qichao conceded. "I don't belittle the value of seeking a truce so people can work out differences. But given the deep suspicions in both camps, it's difficult to achieve lasting peace. The revolutionaries aren't going to sit back and accept the dismissal of the Governor of Jiangxi without protest. What's President Yuan planning to do?"

"I have no knowledge of his plan," Liang Shiyi replied. "I only know there's plenty of activity in the National Military Commission headed by General Feng Guozhang. I think President Yuan is consulting with General Feng. I think he's prepared for a fight."

"Like it or not, Shiyi, both of us will be forced to take sides in this irreconcilable conflict, once it begins. Having been in the wilderness for so many years, I'd hate to be on the losing side this time. I hope to play a constructive role. I can't be a dissident forever."

"We'll all be losers, my friend." Shiyi's eyes grew sad. "The people of our beloved country will suffer even more."

* * *

The trust between President Yuan and the Nationalists had deteriorated since the assassination of Song Jiaoren. After the reorganization loan debacle, some Nationalists decided to get rid of Yuan by force. In order to stop the Nationalist revolt before it could expand, Yuan sent emissaries to various provinces to defuse the movement; at the same time he moved his army to the south.

Vice President Li Yuanhong, who owed his ascendency from obscurity to the revolutionaries, unexpectedly sided with Yuan. As Governor of Hubei, in addition to his post as Vice President, Li crushed the Nationalists revolt in the Hubei area by arresting its leaders in late June, opening the way for the Beiyang Army under Yuan to make a decisive thrust southward. By then Yuan had dismissed all governors in the Yangzi Valley and in Guangdong and Fujian Provinces who had voiced strong protest to his reorganization loan.

Within two weeks, the dismissed Governor of Jiangxi announced the independence of Jiangxi Province and appointed himself the commander-in-chief of a newly organized revolutionary army. Sun Yatsen decided it was time to launch a "second revolution" and urged the Nationalists in the Yangzi Valley to support him against Yuan. He sent a cable to the Parliament in Beijing and the to the governors in revolt, expressing his firm conviction in these fighting words, "For the sake of the nation, I had resigned from the post of Provisional President in favor of Yuan Shikai. Now that all the people in the south are against Yuan's current measures, he would be wise to resign instead of causing bloodshed between our compatriots. If he ignores the national interest and clings obstinately to his present course of action, I am determined to fight against him as I did against the monarchy before 1912."

Outraged by the personal attack, Yuan publically stripped Sun of his post of Director of Railway Planning. Liang Shiyi was disheartened that the railway development plan he'd worked out with Sun Yatsen was the latest victim of the conflict. He called Ye Gongchuo, who had just been promoted to Deputy Minister of Communications, to discuss its implications to the future of railways. "This is not my most pressing concern," Ye commented. "I'm on alert to protect the existing railways which are threatened by military maneuvers."

However, the contest was an uneven match as Yuan had ample supply of ammunition after the reorganization loan was approved. When the Nationalist army under Huang Xing was routed in Nanjing, the revolutionaries lost their major stronghold. By late July, the defense of the Nationalists collapsed for lack of money and supplies. The people in the nation were exhausted, and were resigned to accept peace at any price.

On August 2, Sun Yatsen left Shanghai by boat to Fuzhou. He had planned to go to Guangzhou to rally his supporters, but he had to change plans when he heard his supporters there had defected. Unwelcomed by the British colonial government in Hong Kong, he took a Japanese steamship to Taiwan and then on to Osaka, Japan. He later moved on to Tokyo under a cloak of secrecy and did not appear in public until his Japanese friends successfully obtained permission for him to stay in Japan. Some of his supporters joined him in exile in Japan while others left China for Southeast Asia or Europe to plan their next move.

Although Yuan Shikai had suppressed the revolutionary armies and consolidated his power by the end of July, it was not until early September that the revolutionaries in Jiangsu and Sichuan Provinces gave up the last resistance. The second revolution of the Nationalists had come to an abrupt end.

* * *

Beijing Odyssey

Since the Progressive Party, supported by Vice President Li Yuanhong, also sided with Yuan in the suppression of this conflict, it was rewarded with the premiership of the new government. One of its leaders, Xiong Xiling, was named the new Premier in late July and his cabinet appointments were approved on September 11. Liang Qichao had the first taste of power and became the Minister of Justice. Zhang Jian, the famous valedictorian of the Jinshi Class of 1894 and a successful industrialist, was persuaded to become the Minister of Agriculture and Industry. As Xiong Xiling took over concurrently as Finance Minister, Liang Shiyi resigned his post in the Finance Ministry.

As Chief of Staff to the President, Liang Shiyi now turned his attention to the two most pressing problems which would inevitably surface. The first was the adoption of a constitution of the republic which would enable the establishment of a permanent government; the second was seeking the formal recognition of the new republican government by foreign powers.

Earlier in March, President Yuan had appointed an American, Dr. Frank J. Goodnow, Professor of Political Science and Government at Columbia University, to be his advisor on the constitution. In June, the Senate had nominated 30 of its members to form a Constitution Drafting Committee. By August, the committee completed a draft outline of the constitution. The point of contention in committee deliberation was whether a permanent constitution should be adopted before the election of the president and vice president. In August, Vice President Li Yuanhong advised the members of the committee that he supported the position of electing the president first. His opinion ultimately prevailed.

A Joint Session of the Parliament met on September 12 to discuss the outline of the constitution. During deliberation, the atmosphere in the Parliament was tense as President Yuan threatened and harassed its members, arresting several. The Parliament finally adopted the election procedures for the President and Vice President for a five-year term, but left the question of the constitution unsettled. On October 6, Yuan Shikai was elected President on the third ballot amid both fanfare and threats by thousands of Yuan supporters and spectators outside of the Parliament. Li Yuanhong was voted Vice President the next day. Yuan had finally got rid of the provisional status which he detested so much.

Immediately afterwards, Japan and thirteen European nations in succession recognized Yuan's government. Even President Woodrow Wilson of the United States, which had recognized Yuan's government in May, sent a telegram of congratulation. On Oct 10, 1913, the second anniversary of the Wuhan uprising of the revolutionaries, the President and the Vice President, who had wrested the fruit of victory from the revolutionaries, took the oath of office in the presence of their supporters and foreign dignitaries.

Steven T. Au

President Yuan Shikai and Foreign Dignitaries at His Inauguration on October 10, 1913
Liang Shiyi was standing at right in the third row

Little Brother's Dilemma

"How's father adjusting to his new environment?" Liang Shiyi asked his brother Shixu as the two sat alone in front of the fireplace. It was a wintry night in late 1913 when Shixu arrived in Beijing for a visit. After a gourmet dinner with the entire family, the two brothers had closeted themselves in the living room to discuss the serious business of their extended family. Although ten years apart in age, they shared a cultural heritage that commanded strong ties between brothers.

Gazing into the fire, Shixu replied, "He's finally over his initial reluctance to stay in Hong Kong for an extended period of time. But he's still concerned about the welfare of the clansmen in our native village."

As the managing director of the Guangzhou-Kowloon Railway, Shixu and his family stayed in Guangzhou to be close to his aging father who lived with Shixu's young stepmother. A sensational kidnapping for ransom had taken place in Sanshui County just two months earlier. Shixu, worried that his father might be a future target, persuaded his father and stepmother to stay with his family when he moved with his second consort and two-year-old son to Hong Kong.

"I've rented a spacious European style two-story duplex near Caine Road," Shixu continued. "Father occupies one unit on the first floor, which has a large library in addition to the living room and dining room. He prefers to use the library as a combination bedroom and study in order to avoid the stairs, and essentially leaves the second floor vacant. My own family occupies the other unit. There's plenty of room for your family when you come to Hong Kong."

"What does father do most of the time?" Liang Shiyi asked.

"He seldom ventures out of the house and spends most of the time at his desk," Shixu replied. "He's working on the 'Daily Lessons' from Confucian's Four Books. It is an annotation of the work of Confucius according to his interpretation."

The deterioration of the conditions in his native village alarmed Liang Shiyi. Ever since the crumbling of the Qing Empire, the rural gentry class, who had maintained law and order in the name of the emperor, had fallen apart. Some former gentry members joined unsavory elements in engaging in profiteering and extortion while others sought refuge in nearby cities and towns. Now, this unfortunate situation had struck close to home.

Many magistrates and governors in the Republic, who had formerly belonged to the high gentry class, felt the need to revive Confucianism as a moral force to stem the tide of anarchy. They looked back with nostalgia to the days of their youth, and conveniently forgot how squalid the life of the peasants had been.

"As you know, the preservation of Confucian moral precepts is a volatile topic in Beijing right now," Liang Shiyi observed. "Father can certainly teach those advocates a thing or two."

"Father keeps saying his work is not good enough for anyone except his former students and his own children and grandchildren because they will accept his imperfection. He has no intention of ever publishing the manuscript for fear critics will find fault with his work."

"He's a modest man."

The next evening, Shixu spoke to his brother about his own career. Gauging Shiyi's reaction, he said, "I've had my share of public service. I plan to quit my railway job soon after the new-year celebration. I intend to go into real estate business in Hong Kong."

"You must have given a lot of thought to this course of action. What makes you decide to make the move at this time?"

"I don't like the ups and downs in politics. You're a public man and have devoted your life to public service, regardless of the consequences. I can take care of father and free you from any worry, if I establish a solid financial base in Hong Kong."

Liang Shiyi understood very well his brother's predicament. In July, when Yuan Shikai made the preemptive move to suppress the spread of the "second revolution," Yuan asked Shixu to convince the generals in Guangzhou area not to take part in the anti-Yuan movement. Shixu knew that not only his political skill would be tested but also Shiyi's loyalty to Yuan would be called to question. However, by the time he got the message, the local generals had already forced the pro-Nationalist Governor of Guangdong into exile. All Shixu did was to persuade these generals not to grab power by fighting against each other and to wait for the appointment of a new governor from Beijing. For his effort, Shixu was scheduled for promotion to lieutenant general and to receive a Fifth-Rank Merit Award on New Year's Day.

"Shiyi, I'm uncomfortable with all the backstage political maneuvering for which I will be given an award. In deference to President Yuan, I'm here to receive it. Being a private citizen living in Hong Kong, I hope to be able to escape any future obligations or honors in the service of the government in Beijing."

The celebration in the Presidential Palace on Jan 1, 1914 was indeed joyous for the Liang brothers. Many honors and awards were announced as the recipients paraded to the front of the reception line and bowed to President Yuan. Wearing a blue hat with a raised white tassel to match his blue uniform with braided trimming, Shixu stood tall in the crowd amid well wishers and admirers.

Shortly afterwards, Shixu bid farewell to Shiyi's family and rushed back to

Beijing Odyssey

Guangzhou for an event which was more important to him than even the ceremony in the Presidential Palace.

* * *

Ever since the death of his wife more than a year before, Liang Shixu was often pensive and sometimes moody. Adding to his worry was the delicate health of his second consort and their two-year-old son. Some of his close friends in Guangzhou tried to cheer him up and urged him to marry again. At the age of 34 and in robust health, Shixu was eager to expand his nuclear family. Just before he moved his family to Hong Kong, he found an attractive young girl as his intended. Having refined tastes and small bound feet, this girl had been brought up in a respectable family with declining fortune, a family eager to marry her off as a "successor wife" to Shixu. However, Shixu did not want a successor wife to obliterate his memory of his first wife and insisted taking her as his third consort. While her father was ready to give in, the girl from the Chen family obstinately resisted. With his impending trip to Beijing, Shixu had left the problem with the father of the girl, to see if she could be persuaded.

Back in Guangzhou, Shixu again visited the Chen family. He reiterated his view to the girl's father, "I have no intention of humiliating your family or your daughter, but my deceased wife will always have a place in my heart as long as I live. I will be fair to my consorts as if each were a successor wife." After listening to Shixu, the girl's father came up with a scheme to resolve their dilemma. He promised his daughter that she would have a ceremony at home befitting her marriage as a successor wife. He also compromised her future by allowing Shixu to take her as the third consort in the Liang family. That arrangement called for an unusual "half-way wedding."

On the wedding day, the bride dressed in a black silk jacket with embroidered flowers and a crimson skirt. A sedan chair decorated in red silk with a front screen to hide the bride's face was ready for the bride. Both were proper symbols for the marriage of the daughter in the Chen family to be the wife in the groom's family. However, instead of waiting for the groom to arrive to pay respect to the bride's parents and welcome the bride, the red sedan chair with the bride in it was carried off unceremoniously to a large riverboat rented by Shixu.

It was a long haul from the bride's home to the riverboat moored in the Lizhi Bay in the southwest end of Guangzhou. Such riverboats in the bay were floating restaurants noted for their fine food and entertainment. Each boat had a small back room and a large open space in front. Shixu chose one with bright decor for the occasion. As the red sedan chair arrived, it was not met by the groom but was carried into the private room at the back of the riverboat. Two female attendants helped Shixu's third consort put on new make-up and change dresses. They took off the crimson skirt and put a pink skirt on her. Then they slowly ushered her to the front of the riverboat where Shixu and a dozen of close friends were waiting.

The absence of the groom to greet the bride at the arrival of the red sedan chair was highly symbolic, and the meaning was not lost on the bride. If she needed more proof that she was not recognized by her husband as a successor wife, the pink skirt she was wearing would remove any doubt. It announced to the world that she was a concubine. Such thought provoked sadness in her. She could not recover as the evening wore on. Fine food and good company did not cheer her up. She never blamed her husband for his forthright stance, but she deeply resented her father for deceiving her.

Liang Shixu and his third consort soon left for Hong Kong to join the rest of the family. As they got on the train, Shixu realized this would be his last ride on Guangzhou-Kowloon Railway as its Managing Director. He had already submitted his resignation and was waiting for the formal approval.

Shixu's third consort found Hong Kong immensely pleasing. Approaching the city from Kowloon on a ferry, the scenery was magnificent. Shixu pointed out to her a white dot at mid-height from the peak which was their house on Caine Road. Two more rows of white dots were houses above Caine Road, occupied primarily by British settlers, he explained to her. When they got off the Star Ferry, a few taxicabs and a large number of sedan chairs were waiting to pick up customers. Instead of taking a taxi, Shixu hired two sedan chairs to carry them uphill to their home. Perhaps it was another subtle reminder, that the third consort came to the Liang Family in a plain sedan chair instead of a red sedan chair reserved for a successor wife.

Shixu's father was delighted to greet his new daughter-in-law who kowtowed to him and reverently served him a cup of tea. Liang Zhijian always relished the prospect of having many grandsons around him in his old age and this new daughter-in-law offered hope. The third consort then tried to kowtow to Shixu's stepmother who blocked her move by yelling "I don't deserve it." Although the protocol demanded the third consort's respect to elders in the family, the "second elder lady," as Shixu's stepmother was called, must also display modesty because of her own humble position in the family. True to his words that his consorts would be treated equally, Shixu did not ask his new consort to kowtow to his second consort.

When the brief ceremony was over, Shixu dispatched the good news to Shiyi in Beijing.

* * *

A few days later, when Shixu offered his usual "good morning" to his father, the old man said, "I have just read in this newspaper the translation of an editorial from the English daily *North-China Herald*. Although the article seems to praise the abilities and achievements of Shiyi, its undertone implies that he often acts independently of President Yuan. I don't like that speculation." He knew the opinion of the paper, published in Shanghai, was influential and well respected by the foreign community.

Shixu picked up the paper and read the translated article himself. The importance of the article was not lost on him. "What can be done?" he asked.

"I intend to write to Shiyi to warn him," his father replied. Walking slowly to his desk, Liang Zhijian sat down and composed his thoughts. He finally wrote:

"I am enclosing the translation of an editorial from the English daily *North-China Herald*. Although the article seems to praise your abilities and achievements in recent years, the people who fed the information to the newspaper might have an ulterior motive. Since the article states that you are the logical person to succeed President Yuan Shikai in the future, I suspect that some one in the inner circle of President Yuan tries to create doubts about your loyalty to the President. Many such palace intrigues can be found in Chinese history. I hardly need to remind you that in the period of Three Kingdoms, Cao Cao, the King of Wei, killed one of his most capable staff, Yang Xiu, who proved to be more intelligent than the king. Many wise officials through the centuries retired quietly after achieving monumental successes. These people not only tried to avoid suspicion by others but also acted to avert tragic consequences for themselves. I advise you to review you situation carefully and take the appropriate action."

The Capricious Drift

As Liang Shiyi stood in front of his residence to bid farewell to Shixu, the chill of the morning wet his quilt jacket. But his heart was warmed by Shixu's visit in the past few days. The memory of the new-year celebration at the Presidential Palace was still fresh. What a good way to start a new year!

Liang Shiyi's sweet thought soon turned into a nightmare. When he arrived at his office, he learned of President Yuan's decision to dissolve the Parliament. Liang Shiyi had always counseled compromise and patience in building a stable government. But his repeated advice of moderation and caution to Yuan had fallen on deaf ears. His heart sank when President Yuan formally announced the dissolution of the Parliament on January 10, 1914.

It had begun in the fall after Yuan successfully suppressed the second revolution of the Nationalists. By then the Progressive Party was the ruling party with the blessing of Yuan, and he was bent on revenge to silence his oppositions. Realizing some Nationalists in the Parliament were not radical revolutionaries and needed a home to shield them, in September Liang Shiyi contacted several splinter groups in the Nationalist camp and announced the formation of a Citizen's Party. It was not an opposition party, loyal or otherwise, which would not have been tolerated by Yuan, but it would provide a channel for consultation and keep alive a flicker of hope for reconciliation. Hope was short-lived. Other events moved so swiftly, the Citizen's Party was soon swept out of existence.

Four days after Yuan's inauguration as President on October 10, the Constitution Drafting Committee announced the completion of a draft constitution. Within two days, Yuan asked the House of Representatives to revise the draft because he did not like the provisions limiting the power of the President. Quite unexpectedly, Vice President Li Yuanhong supported Yuan's position and asked the committee to shelve the draft constitution. It was a shock to members of the Parliament to learn that this reluctant revolutionary soldier had turned into an ally of reactionary forces.

Ignoring the protests of the President and Vice President, the Constitution Drafting Committee submitted the original draft to the Parliament for approval on November 3. Outraged by the independence of the Parliament, Yuan criticized the draft once again, in blistering terms. The next day President Yuan ordered the disbanding of the Beijing Branch of the Nationalist Party, and declared null and void the parliamentary credentials of all 438 Nationalist members on charges of sedition. Three days later he ordered the disbanding of other branches of the Nationalist Party in other cities. A week after that, he ordered the expulsion of Nationalist members in all provincial assemblies.

This sequence of events caused great turmoil throughout the country. The most serious problem was the safety of the Senators and House members after they were stripped of their credentials. The speaker of the Senate and some other Nationalist leaders had already slipped out of Beijing in July to join the revolutionists in Shanghai. By mid-November, C. T. Wang (aka Wang Zhengting), the deputy speaker of the Senate, found himself targeted for arrest. Wang, who had befriended the Australian journalist William Donald, made an urgent call to Donald for help. As the Beijing police were casting their net for Wang, he was disguised as a charwoman and was wisked away from his office by Donald. They first went to the Methodist Mission and then slipped out from its back door to the Legation Quarters Lane where Donald kept a combination office and private apartment. Before sunrise, Donald accompanied Wang abroad a train to Tianjin.

In the safety of the British settlement there, Wang thanked Donald for his rescue effort. Donald could not help but lament the sorrowful state of affairs. "I have implored Doc Sun Yatsen to be patient and let democracy have a chance to work," Donald said. "Rome was not built in one day, as people say. Doc Sun simply thinks that because China has been declared a republic, the government must function as a working democracy overnight. The second revolution was premature and ended with such disastrous consequences."

* * *

As a result of the expulsion of its Nationalist members, the Parliament lacked the quorum to convene and ceased to function. Then President Yuan ordered the formation of a Political Congress to replace the Parliament. Eight of its members were appointed by the President, two by the Premier, two by the Chief Justice of the Supreme Court, one by each cabinet minister, and several others by the Bureau of National Minorities. The Chairman, who was appointed by the President, expeditiously convened the group for action. After he formally dissolved the Parliament. Yuan Shikai urged the Political Congress to work on a new constitution.

On January 26, President Yuan announced the guidelines for establishing a Constitution Conference to draft a new constitution, forfeiting the draft previously prepared by a committee with representation from the Nationalists. As recommended by the Political Congress, Yuan appointed 57 members representing different provinces for this Constitution Conference. Liang Shiyi was among them. Liang was confronted with a great moral dilemma. He knew politicians often had to trade their differences in a very untidy world, but he knew the worthy ones had to keep a sense of common good. As long as he sought solutions based on compromise with restraints, he was bound to cut corners periodically. But did he go too far in the light of this nightmarish scenario? He wondered.

The Constitution Conference did not convene until a month and half later because Yuan received conflicting advice from his trusted aides. Yang Shiqi, Yuan's confidant and political operative behind the scenes during the previous two years, suddenly emerged in the open as a leading member of the Political Congress. He had some very definite ideas of expanding the power of the President in the new constitution. Liang Shiyi, on the other hand, preferred to change as little as possible from the draft constitution prepared by the now defunct Constitution Drafting Committee. Since the new constitution would eventually be approved by the Political Congress, Yang Shiqi had the upper hand in the final control. In fact, Yang Shiqi was secretly working on a new "constitutional covenant" under the direction of President Yuan. Before long, a rough outline of this covenant emerged, calling for a Secretary of State answerable to the President instead of a Premier answerable to the Parliament.

"I would like to adopt the American Presidential system for our new constitution," President Yuan said one morning to Liang. "What do you think?"

Liang was frank in his reply. "In the American system, the Secretary of State is the first among equals, not the chief cabinet officer above all ministers including the Foreign Minister, as in your proposed system. While the Secretary of State in the American system is answerable only to the President, the President himself must govern with the advice and consent of the Congress elected by the people."

"You don't seem to be enthusiastic about the proposed system," Yuan continued. "But the existing system is worse. We have had four premiers in the last two years. We cannot do anything without a stable government. The members of Parliament could not agree even with each other to produce a majority on many issues, let alone with me."

Liang Shiyi had to concede his point as Premier Xiong Xiling had just tendered his resignation in protest of Yuan's high-handed treatment of him. Liang Qichao had also resigned as Justice Minister, but was appointed head of the National Mint. Yuan wanted to cultivate the friendship and support of General Cai, a former student of Liang Qichao, who as a regional leader of Yunnan Province had successfully held off the revolutionaries. President Yuan had summoned General Cai to Beijing and appointed him the chief of National Cadastral Survey.

On February 12, President Yuan accepted the resignation of Xiong Xiling and fashioned a caretaker government. Foreign Minister, Sun Baoqi, was appointed to serve concurrently as Premier. Zhou Zhiqi, the Minister of the Army, was to serve concurrently as Finance Minister. Zhu Qiqian, the Interior Minister, was to serve concurrently as Minister of Communications. All three had worked closely with Liang Shiyi and could be counted on to hold the nation together during the crisis.

As if to assure Liang Shiyi that his service was still appreciated, President awarded him two First-Rank Broad Ribbon Medals on the second anniversary of the abdication of the Qing emperor.

Beijing Odyssey

Two weeks later, President Yuan issued an order to suspend all provincial assemblies. After ingratiating himself with more power, Yuan received a confidential report that Zhao Bingjun, Governor of Zhili, had died of poison in the Governor's residence. The Office of the President fell silent as Yuan issued a terse announcement of the death of the former Premier and Interior Minister. No cause of death was given in the statement.

But the people outside of the Presidential Palace did not need a reminder. Zhao Bingjun was linked to the assassin of Song Jiaoren through several layers of intermediaries and conspirators, as documented in detail by the Shanghai Municipal Court. But the link between Zhao and President Yuan could not be proven since Zhao refused to honor the subpoena to testify. Now he was dead.

Because of the secrecy surrounding the police investigation, rumors were rampant about the cause of Zhao Bingjun's death. No suspect was arrested for foul play. Was it a suicide to avoid the prosecution doggedly pursued by the Municipal Court in Shanghai? Or was he poisoned by Yuan's agent to avoid any trace that might link Song's assassination to the President? The truth might never be known since the principal suspects in the case either died or disappeared mysteriously eleven months after Song's assassination. But the public was not willing to give Yuan the benefit of doubt in this political melodrama.

Although political assassinations had been a weapon of the revolutionaries out of power, President Yuan had now developed its use in power. Liang Shiyi was a consistent advocate of benevolent governance against violence. He hated the adoption of assassinations or executions by powerful rulers even more than he deplored the use of these same tactics by the revolutionaries. He had never associated himself with any of Yuan's secret operations. He was very disturbed by Zhao's death. It implied that even Yuan's friends, as well as his enemies, might become the target for elimination.

Several days later, Liang Shiyi received his father's letter enclosing a copy of the translation of the editorial of the English daily *North-China Herald*. The editorial not only praised his performance but considered him a logical future candidate to succeed Yuan as the President of the Republic. Although Liang never had any ambition to become Premier, let alone President, the article could easily give his political enemies ammunition to destroy him. No wonder his father was worried. He agreed with his father that he had better watch out for himself.

* * *

Even noisier than this political melodrama was the sudden appearance of a social and cultural morality play. It was caused by the heated public debate on the adoption of Confucianism as a state religion.

The idea was first proposed by some conservative governors who supported Yuan in suppressing the second revolution of the Nationalists. The momentum reached a high point when Kang Youwei of the "one hundred days of reform" fame was invited by the Society of Confucian Religion to be its president. However, his one-time disciple, Liang Qichao, was unimpressed. As he visited Liang Shiyi in

December, Qichao lamented, "Listen to the sudden cries for reviving Confucianism as a state religion. I concede to no one of my deep belief in the goodness of Confucianism, but we don't need another issue to divide the people."

Liang Shiyi shrugged. "Personally I believe our country can be a better place if we all practice the humanistic values of Confucianism. I admit we do not always practice faithfully what we preach. Confucianism has lost its influence in our society. The advocates of Confucianism as a state religion simply use the dogma to resist change. There must be a middle ground that all of us can accept."

To placate those who advocated the separation of church and state, the Interior Ministry announced the protection of religious practices, but only those religions with systematic organization, traceable history and established tradition. Ironically, on the same day, President Yuan urged the Political Congress to take up legislation adopting Confucianism as a state religion and outlining the rites of worship "in respecting Heaven and honoring Confucius." The Political Congress dutifully approved the proposal and President Yuan immediately ordered its implementation.

Yuan Shikai welcomed the opportunity to lead the public prayer in the Temple of Heaven in Beijing, where all emperors in the Qing Dynasty had periodically performed such rituals. However, he would delegate someone to lead the ceremony in the Confucian Temple which was a function traditionally assigned to scholars close to the Imperial Court. On March 12, Liang Shiyi was selected to represent President Yuan at the ceremony in Beijing. The ceremony was an annual ritual performed to honor the teacher when the school year began in early spring, a tradition dating back to the time of Confucius. In a public lecture after the ceremony, Liang extolled the virtues and moral values of Confucius. He stressed not only that political leaders should set examples of high moral standards, but that the elite in society, including school masters, elders of towns and cities, and people of the press, should also exert moral influence on the masses. How ironic the speech must have sounded in the Presidential Palace!

In the meantime, Liang Shiyi's frequent contacts with foreigners had earned him international recognition. When the new American Minister, Dr. Paul S. Reinsch, arrived in Beijing in March of 1914, he presented his credentials to President Yuan and then made a point to visit Liang Shiyi. Shiyi was glad to learn from him the rationale of U.S. withdrawal from the Six-Nation Consortium and the backstage maneuvering of Russia and Japan to join the consortium. Dr. Reinsch also expressed the interest of U.S. banks in financing future developments in China without demanding exploitative terms.

In April, the King of Belgium presented Liang Shiyi the Order of Leopold's Grand Cross Medal, and the Czar of Russia presented him the Second-Rank Precious Star Medal.

* * *

At the instigation of Yang Shiqi, President Yuan's eldest son, Yuan Keding, began to circulate false accusations against Liang Shiyi in the Presidential Palace. One version leaked to Liang was that Yuan Keding accused Shiyi of collusion with some army generals in order to become the president of the Republic. As evidence, he pointed to the fact that governors and generals of various provinces, who came to pay respect to President Yuan, usually dropped by Liang Shiyi's office. That much was true. Liang was often regarded as the "assistant president" by outsiders. This rumor gained currency when Liang heard these words from Yuan's own mouth, "You have a great future in the political arena. Don't try to make any promise to the generals when they visit you. You can never satisfy them." Because of the rumors, Liang Shiyi knew his days as the Chief of Staff in the Secretariat were numbered. Reflecting on his father's earlier warning, he felt relieved without any regret.

All the conjecture on palace rumors became moot when a new "constitutional covenant" was announced on May 1. The term of the President was extended to ten years, with no term limit for re-election. Moreover, the President had the right to nominate his own successor. Instead of the premier heading a responsible cabinet, a Secretary of State would function in the same capacity, but he would be answerable only to the President. A Privy Council would replace the Secretariat in the Office of the President. On the same day, Xu Shichang was named Secretary of State, and Yang Shiqi was appointed Senior Councillor of the Privy Council.

Before the announcement, former Premier Xiong Xiling, who had heard about the pending constitutional covenant from the grapevine, phoned Liang Shiyi. He was curious and asked who would be the new Secretary of State.

"Xu Shichang," Liang told him.

Xiong was greatly surprised. "I thought you would get that post." Since Xu was supposed to be a loyal supporter of the Manchu Royal House to the end, he had lived quietly in the seaport of Qingdao to check on the activities of the Royal princes living in retirement there. Yuan obviously decided he no longer needed to worry about the resurrection of the Qing Dynasty, and his trusted friend Xu could now serve him better in this new capacity.

Then Xiong asked who would be the new Senior Councillor of the Privy Council. "Yang Shiqi," Liang replied.

"Good heavens," Xiong expressed alarm. "You will be out of a job!"

Out, But Not Down

As Liang Shiyi was vacating his office at the Secretariat, Yuan Shikai summoned him to the Office of the President. "There is no hard feeling between us, and I want you to know that," Yuan began. "I will appoint you to be the Controller of Maritime Customs Service. Your appointment will be effective the day after the Secretariat is replaced by the Privy Council according to the provision of the new Constitutional Covenant. I wish you the best."

"I appreciate your generous offer," Liang replied. "This new job will give me an opportunity to review the policies regarding tariff collection." With polite exchanges, Liang Shiyi found his way out of the Presidential Palace.

Yuan Shikai had a way of saying "don't leave angry" to those whom he wanted to put "on reserve." Maritime Customs Service was an independent agency established by Sir Robert Hart on behalf of the Qing Court. As Inspector General, Hart built a team of competent and efficient international civil servants in the agency. In 1906, the Qing Court set up a commission and appointed a controller and a deputy controller to oversee the agency with the intention of eventually taking over the operation. However, Hart retained his title and power of Inspector General until his official retirement in 1911. He was succeeded by Sir Francis A. Aglen.

After the revolution, the Maritime Customs Service officially became one of the bureaus in the Finance Ministry, but continued to operate as an independent agency. The Chinese controller of the service had very little power. He could not dismiss the inspector general or appoint one without the concurrence of foreign debt holders. Because of unrest and threat of civil war, Sir Francis Aglen deposited all customs revenues in foreign banks so they could be used to pay off the interest of the rapidly accumulating foreign debts. He could do almost anything he wished without consulting the controller as long as he could satisfy the foreign debt holders. However, the job of controller was lucrative because the pay scale was pegged to the salaries of foreign employees in the service. As the nominal supervisor of Sir Francis, Liang Shiyi would receive substantial remuneration.

Liang Shiyi was familiar with the operation of the Maritime Customs Service as he was a counselor in the Ministry of Foreign Affairs under Tang Shaoyi when Tang was appointed concurrently deputy controller of this service in 1906. With characteristic deftness, Liang did what was within his power to improve the service. He streamlined existing procedures that allowed loopholes for evasion of customs duties, drug smuggling by sailors abroad foreign ships, and other undesirable practices. When he noted the drastic decline in exporting of tea in recent years, he went beyond his jurisdiction to find ways to reverse the trend. He recommended to President Yuan that domestic taxes on tea earmarked for export should be reduced by as much as twenty-five percent and taxes on other Chinese products for export should also be reduced. After reviewing his report, the President approved his recommendations and ordered the Finance Ministry to take appropriate actions.

* * *

With a more leisurely pace in his current position, Liang Shiyi could devote more time to other activities in banking and industrial development.

Since he had revived the public-private joint venture of the Bank of Communications in May 1912, Liang was elected its chief executive officer. Under his leadership, the bank expanded its commercial banking, taking advantage of the deposits of revenues from government-controlled railways, shipping, telegraph and post office as required by law. The Bank of Communications and the Bank of China jointly purchased silver nuggets and impure silver coins of various origins, and established strict regulations for the coinage of a new silver yuan, the Chinese dollar. Because of the purity of the new silver coin, it gained wide circulation in a short time.

In early 1913, the Bank of Communications had been authorized to issue banknotes shortly after the Bank of China received authorization from the government. A year later the activities of these two banks also included the handling of foreign accounts and gold reserves of the government. Both banks essentially took over the treasury function of the government and formed a twin central-bank system.

The profit of the Bank of Communications in 1914 was the highest among all banks in China. This was not lost to the shareholders as well as the banking community as they flocked to do business with the bank with the most political protection. On the other hand, the Chinese government, under Yuan, borrowed money from the bank often without sufficient collateral. Many people even suspected that Yuan had channeled some of the money for personal and political use. Whether he realized it or not, Liang Shiyi had struck a Faustian bargain, doing what he thought was good for the shareholders and the country only to discover later the devil wanted his soul.

In the same year, Liang founded the Tonghui Industrial and Commercial Corporation for the development of new industries. Relishing his new role as an entrepreneur, he also became a shareholder of a mining company. He was on his way to opening new paths outside national politics. That was, however, not to be his fate.

On May 24, 1914, President Yuan established a Consultative Senate to replace the Political Congress as the Legislative body. Its 73 members were appointed by President Yuan. Vice President Li Yuanhong was appointed its Speaker. Liang Shiyi was appointed by the President as one of its members. By now, Yuan felt increasingly isolated and missed Liang's valuable service though not his periodic unsolicited advice for moderation. For his part, Liang Shiyi justified his own participation by rationalizing that even as Yuan subverted the constitution, he brought a strong and stable government for China. Gratitude obliged him to acknowledge Yuan's past favors, and prudence would require him to cultivate his continued friendship.

Indeed as Yuan sought to develop modern institutions and limited reforms, he relied on a team of foreign advisors that included a French military attache, a Belgian judge and a Japanese railway expert, in addition to Dr. Morrison and Dr. Goodnow. By their own admission, these advisors were over paid and under utilized. While Yuan's intention of doing good was suspect, some of the reforms, nevertheless, produced fruitful results.

Even William Donald now came to know Yuan Shikai well. As usual, Donald knew how to charm his way to Yuan's attention. They had many a long and friendly talks together. Despite Yuan's flagrant reactionary qualities, Donald respected him for a certain magnetic power, and both men shared the quality. He was particularly impressed by Yuan's incisive action in aiming his targets with battlefield precision. Donald would hammer at him on the urgency of placing more foreign-educated Chinese in positions of responsibility, a constant theme that Yuan found amusing rather than annoying. One day Yuan countered with a smile, "Wasn't my first Premier, Tang Shaoyi, American educated? How about my first Justice Minister, Wang Chonghui? He was a brilliant lawyer who graduated from Yale University. They went 'over the hill' when I needed them."

* * *

"Better one hundred years in authoritarian rule than one day of instability! That is what President Yuan was saying to the people when he trampled on the constitution." Liang Shiyi was startled by Liang Qichao's outburst as the two sat in the living room of his home in Ganshiqiao Lane. Qichao had lost none of his sharpness as a pamphleteer even though he was now the head of the National Mint. As Justice Minister in the last cabinet, he continued the work of his one-time predecessor, Wang Chonghui, and pushed for the development of an independent judiciary for China. He believed the establishment of an impartial system of courts and a modern penal system was the best way to end the special privileges granted to foreigner powers and to try their nationals suspected of committing crimes in China. President Yuan seemed to agree although he had no concept of equal justice under law. The Supreme Court, which was established under the Qing Dynasty in 1906, vigorously took up issues such as commercial laws and married women's rights. Yuan also authorized the improvement of the penal system, including the construction of new prison facilities, improvement of sanitary conditions, provision of work training and attempts at moral reform of criminals.

Qichao realized such utterance in public would not only cost him his job but would also endanger his life. But in the private company of his good friend, he felt safe to speak his mind out. "I have to give him credit for approving the reform of the court system," Liang Qichao admitted.

Wanting to vary the focus of their conversation, Shiyi asked, "How's Tang Hualong doing in the Education Ministry?"

Tang Hualong was a member of the Progressive Party and a political ally of Liang Qichao. Because Tang's brother was a strong supporter of the President, Tang was appointed as Education Minister in the current cabinet even though other members of the Progressive Party were left in the cold after the resignation of their leader from the premiership. Tang continued nationwide expansion of primary schools for males, which would be compulsory and free. However, Tang was lately under increasing pressure to decree that Confucius be revered as a sage in all public schools. To the consternation of conservative elements in the government, he obstinately resisted.

Liang Qichao replied, "I understand he received limited backing from President Yuan who insisted the study of Confucianism must be included in primary curriculum, though Confucius need not be worshiped as a saint. That was sufficient to get Tang off the hook." A few days after their talk, the Education Ministry announced the compromise which has finally put the outcries from advocates of traditional Confucian values to rest.

* * *

The outbreak of the European War in July 1914 caused more than a ripple in China. Liang Shiyi saw this as a great opportunity for China to join the winning side and to gain a place in shaping the post-war world. He now wanted to participate actively in realizing this goal regardless of domestic politics. His reservations about continuing his service under Yuan were overcome by his desire to exert his influence over China's foreign policy. He eagerly answered Yuan's call to attend an emergency meeting of cabinet ministers. To Liang, it was almost like old times when he attended the meetings as President Yuan's chief of staff; for Yuan, it was a reunion that happened none too soon.

On August 6, China declared its neutrality in the European conflict. President Yuan also appointed Liang to assist Foreign Minister Sun Baoqi to draft a Neutrality Act and set up an office to enforce neutrality. Almost overnight Liang threw his hat in the ring of quiet personal diplomacy.

Several days later, Yuan telephoned Liang and asked him to come to the Presidential Palace for a discussion concerning the European conflict. Upon arrival in the late evening, Liang was ushered into the President's private study where Yuan was eagerly waiting. Jolted by Liang's entry, Yuan blurted out his concern, "I would like to hear your views on the effects of the European war on Asia and on the most urgent tasks confronting China as a result of this conflict." Noticing that Liang remained standing, Yuan motioned for him to sit. "Please. We have much to talk about."

Liang handed his hat to a waiting servant and took a seat. "As I see it, the most serious problems are our impending financial crisis and the lurking Japanese aggression as a result of this war.

"Can you expand your comments?" Yuan asked. "I'm eager to know details."

"As most European countries are now engaged in this war, further loans from them will be unavailable," Liang replied. "By now the reorganization loan of 25 million pounds sterling is almost exhausted. To the best of my estimate, the treasury will be depleted in two or three months. Since we have declared neutrality, we can suspend our payments of annual indemnities to all belligerent countries. The customs duty and salt tax, which are used to guarantee such payments, can be deposited in our own banks to collect interest. That's only a brief reprieve. We need to raise money by issuing domestic bonds to finance government operations in order to avoid a major crisis."

Yuan leaned back in his chair, "Your suggestions to solve our financial problems make sense. However, we've had quite a few disappointments with previous domestic bonds. I shall entrust you in planning for the new bonds and will give you full power to implement your plan."

Over tea, the conversation drifted to the lurking Japanese aggression. "Since the outbreak of the European War, British Minister Jordan, Russian Minister Kroupensk, French Minister Conty and Japanese Minister Hioki Eki separately visited me on different occasions," Liang Shiyi told President Yuan. "Sir John Jordan told me that since Britain and Japan are allies, Japan would soon try to take over German interests in China. If China does not reclaim German occupied territory around Qingdao in Shandong Province, someone else would come and get it."

"You paint a dark picture," Yuan remarked with alarm. "But I suspect Jordan would support Japan instead of China in claiming the Qingdao area since Japan is an ally of Britain while China has declared neutrality."

"That's enough reason for us to change our position of neutrality if necessary," Liang replied. "I think we should act before Japan makes the move. Since Britain is eager to stop the German influence in China, we can persuade Britain to accept a secret deal which will allow us to act in Shandong Province on her behalf. We shall negotiate with the German Minister on the peaceful return of Qingdao to us. In the meantime, we shall send Chinese troops to surround Qingdao and, if necessary, take the German settlement by force. After the Germans give up Qingdao, one way or the other, there will be no reason for Japan to send troops to Shandong Province."

"Not yet. not yet." Yuan was cautious. "Such actions will violate our neutrality and cause a firestorm in the diplomatic circle. Japan will no doubt protest."

Liang thoughtfully laid down his own reasoning. "Sooner or later, China will be drawn into this war. In my opinion, it's difficult for Germany and Austria to win because of their limited resources. By declaring war on Germany and reclaiming the Qingdao area by surprise, we may in fact avoid conflict with Japan. If China becomes an ally of Britain, there's no excuse for Japan to send its troops to China."

Yuan responded wearily, "This is too much of a gamble. Let me think it over."

It was almost dawn when Liang Shiyi left the Presidential Palace. He had done his duty. Would President Yuan accept his advice?

God of Fortune

"I'm calling you about the domestic bonds," the voice on the other end of the line was that of Finance Minister Zhou Ziqi. As Liang Shiyi was about to respond, the voice continued with a stutter. "Can y-y-you stop by m-my-y office to dis-s-s cuss the d-d-details?"

Zhou Ziqi was one of the rising stars in Yuan's inner circle. Having served as Minister of the Army as well as Finance Minister, he was a powerful figure. A former Chinese consul in New York, he spoke English fluently. As former Governor of Shandong Province, Zhou had a commanding presence—but he stuttered when excited. And like Liang Shiyi, he had a good sense of humor. In the company of his close friends, Zhou was a charming conversationalist and a sympathetic listener. Unwittingly he often served as a depositor of the political gossip of the day.

In spite of his own accomplishments, Zhou respected Liang Shiyi, respect which grew into admiration. He, too, had thought about the necessity of floating domestic bonds to finance government operations ever since the outbreak of the European War. When he spoke to President Yuan about such a prospect, he had been reminded of previous failures in raising substantial amounts of money from the domestic bond market. Since the President had now been convinced by Liang Shiyi that a workable solution could be reached, Zhou wanted to work with Liang to make it a success.

"In our estimate, we need to raise 16 million yuan (approximately 6.5 million U.S. dollars) for this year alone," Zhou Ziqi suggested to Liang Shiyi as they discussed the domestic bond issue. "How should we proceed to get that desired result?"

"You have to offer an annual interest of 6% to attract buyers," Liang replied. "The principal of the bond should be repaid from the fourth year until the twelfth year."

"I'll get the approval of the President as soon as possible," Zhou spoke approvingly. "I will also recommend the President set up a Domestic Bond Bureau to handle this transaction."

Within days, President Yuan announced the establishment of the Domestic Bond Bureau with a 16-member board which included the president of the Bank of China, the president of the Bank of Communications, the Inspector General of Maritime Customs Service, the president of the Sino-French Bank, and a representative of the business community. Liang Shiyi was appointed director of the bureau along with four assistant directors. Because of his reputation in the foreign business community, Sir Francis Aglen, Inspector General of Maritime Customs Service, was designated as Assistant Director for Accounting. Up to six more members would be added to the board, among those were members representing organizations subscribing 500,000 yuan or more.

Liang immediately launched a national promotion for the sale of these bonds. The Bank of China and the Bank of Communications jointly subscribed to the first issue worth two million yuan. The Hong Kong and Shanghai Banks became subscribers of Chinese domestic bonds for the first time. Liang personally contacted various governors and military leaders to advertise the favorable terms of these bonds. The planned target of 16 million yuan for the bonds was fulfilled in two months. The bureau decided to expand sales by 50% and ultimately exceeded even that goal. It was the first time that such success occurred in China's domestic bond issues. Apparently the smart money in the market expressed implicit confidence of the government although the people on main street might not agree.

* * *

As Deputy Minister of Communications, Ye Gongchuo was also appointed to the board of the Domestic Bond Bureau. Liang Shiyi could count on his help on the board as in many other occasions. One day, when they were leaving a board meeting at the Bureau, Liang asked Ye to come to his office at the end of the hall.

"I have waited for President Yuan to ponder the merit of declaring war on Germany, and he apparently has decided against it," Liang confided to Ye. "I think that is a mistake. We must do something to insure that China's voice will be heard in the postwar world."

"Given President Yuan's position, what can you do as a private citizen?" Ye asked.

"I've thought about this frequently," Liang replied. "Since China has declared neutrality, my option is very limited. Although China is very poor, we have an excess of unskilled labor which is now in short supply in Europe. I'm thinking of organizing a private company to recruit Chinese laborers for non-combatant work in Europe under a contract with the British or French government."

Ye seemed sympathetic but cautious. "It will take a well coordinated plan to pull this off."

Liang was warming to the subject, "It will take quite some time to organize the private company. It should be located in Hong Kong to avoid the issue of neutrality. I'll contact the British and French Ministers to see if this idea will work."

"That is a reasonable approach," Ye replied. Knowing Liang often bounced untested ideas on him, Ye carefully considered his reply lest it might be misinterpreted. Shiyi waited patiently. Ye Gongchuo, their friends would say, was the soul of Liang Shiyi.

In the last two years Ye Gongchuo had moved up the ladder from Head of

Bureau of Railways to Deputy Minister under Zhu Qiqian, the Minister of Communications. Zhu had inherited many of Liang's former colleagues in the ministry and depended on them to operate the railways at a time of political turmoil. He also valued their connections to Liang whose advice he often sought.

Zhu Qiqian was another rising star in Yuan's inner circle. In the latest cabinet reshuffle, he became the Interior Minister, a sensitive position which would not have been given to anyone but Yuan's most trusted aide. Orphaned at an early age, he was brought up by his uncle, a Grand Councillor in the Qing Court. Zhu Qiqian was a self-reliant and fast learner who became successful on his own merit. He had been, and was still, on friendly terms with Liang Shiyi.

One of the most controversial railway policies in the early Republic was the nationalization of railways under construction. It was this issue that sparked the revolution in 1911. No one wanted to see a repetition. However, by the summer of 1913, it was clear that private investors were unable to raise enough funds for the completion of these railways in various provinces. In order to secure and guarantee the repayment of foreign loans, the government had to redeem the railway shares still in private hands. As Zhu Qiqian pondered this problem, he consulted Liang Shiyi, who counseled patience. Liang said to him, "You must negotiate with these provinces separately and sequentially in order to avoid collective opposition." Zhu then ordered Ye Gongchuo to follow this suggestion in negotiation. Starting with the railway in Hupei Province, Ye approached each province one at a time. By the end of 1914, he had signed agreements with private shareholders in all eight provinces, calling for the government to compensate private shareholders in stages. The crisis had been averted.

* * *

Since the inception of the Finance Policy Commission in 1913, Liang Shiyi was recognized by his colleagues on the commission as a maverick. Liang Qichao was most appreciative of Liang Shiyi's lucid interpretations of economic and financial affairs in the periodic meetings. He was particularly grateful to Liang Shiyi for proposing a set of detailed guidelines for the silver coinage at a meeting of the commission the previous year.

"Your proposal on the trial operations of silver coinage has been successful." Qichao said to Shiyi. "You have made my job at the National Mint much easier."

"I had no idea, nor did anyone else, if the public would react favorably to my proposal of giving up the old Mexican silver coins which were in wide circulation," Liang Shiyi replied. "I suggested the trial approach by minting a small batch of new Chinese coins at a time to gauge the willingness of the public to exchange the old Mexican coins for these new coins. As the public gradually gained confidence in the value of the new coins, another batch could be minted for exchange until the Mexican silver coins were no longer used for daily transactions."

Qichao spoke approvingly. "You have patience."

"I've learned it from bitter experience," Liang Shiyi said with unaffected modesty and courtesy. "Remember the nationalization of the railways which triggered the revolution against the Qing Dynasty? It could have happened again last year if the Ministry of Communications had not chosen to settle the dispute one province at a time."

Qichao admired his friend's balance and perception, and his ability to separate political predilection from his judgment. He asked Liang Shiyi's opinion about the redemption of local currencies issued by provincial governments, an issue which would come up in the next commission meeting. Liang Shiyi replied, "Chinese currencies cannot go unpunished if the bank notes are not supported by adequate reserves in the central bank system. I'm going to propose to the commission take steps to redeem such currencies and to strengthen the central bank." His proposal received favorable consideration by the commission.

At the same meeting, Liang Shiyi urged the removal of restrictions on grain trade imposed by provincial and central governments. Since grains were staple food for the population, restrictions of trades between provinces and on export to foreign countries were traditionally considered a protection for the local population against famine. Liang was ahead of his time in arguing that a free market on grains would boost farm income and benefit the national economy. He explained patiently, "As the farmers receive higher profits, they have the incentive to grow more crops. The competition in the marketplace will eventually drive down the price of grains." Although he was unable to convince the majority of the commission, he kept a notably strong conviction against the conventional wisdom. His respect for others went far beyond good manners.

Liang Qichao was appreciative of Liang Shiyi's effort. "Your contributions to the Finance Policy Commission may be unglamorous, but they are important and long lasting."

"In politics, you win some and lose some," Liang Shiyi sighed. "As you well know, I have made many compromises in the belief that it is all for the best. Since the powerful are so obstinate and the ordinary people simply want to be left alone without protest, what else can I do beyond exerting some benign influences?" His remark reflected an experienced and intensely practical man.

* * *

Liang Shiyi was glad to see Liang Boyin who showed up one day in his residence at Ganzhiqiao. The oldest of the "Three Liangs of Guangdong," Boyin was on one of his infrequent business trips to Beijing since leaving government service fifteen years earlier.

"I've heard that you are doing very well," Boyin said. "The newspapers have a propensity in reporting your new triumph day after day."

"It depends on whether you read about me from my friends or my detractors," Shiyi replied. "I don't trust my own senses when I read reports which are too favorable."

Indeed, the success of the domestic bond sales during 1914 had attracted public attention to Liang Shiyi's reputation as a financier. He was invited by wealthy friends to join them in new ventures. In quick succession, he became the co-founder of the New China Savings Bank and the Salt Industry Bank. Other commercial banks founded by his former colleagues were modeled after the Bank of Communications. Among the most notable were the Golden City Bank, the Continental Bank, and the Central South Bank. With his connection and influence, Liang Shiyi was invited to serve on the board of directors of several banks.

Soon Liang Shiyi was depicted in the popular press as fabulously rich and, by Chinese standards, he certainly was. It did not take a mathematical genius to add up his high salaries as the president of Bank of Communications and as the controller of Maritime Customs Service, the generous stipends for his service on the board of directors of commercial banks, and the lucrative dividends from his investments in various enterprises. Because of his prowess in raising huge sums of money, he was acknowledged as a financial genius and was nicknamed Liang Caishen. In Chinese vernacular, the name "Caishen" meant "god of fortune," a god whom many Chinese worshiped in the hope of bringing great wealth for their families and businesses. Even the foreign press noted Liang's celebrity status and dubbed him the "god of wealth" or the "god of gold."

When Liang Boyin got a chance to visit Liang Qichao, he could not help but bring up the never-ending newspaper accounts of Liang Shiyi. Qichao said to him, "Liang Shiyi's public reputation is not built on his ability to amass a personal fortune. He's able to win support of a group of capable men with diversified backgrounds and, through his network, leads this group to maintain the economic lifelines of the government amid chaos."

The concerted efforts of this group of officials in public affairs and in business were noticed by perceptive observers. The group was collectively called the "Communication Clique" and Liang Shiyi was identified as its leader. He earned the loyalty of his supporters by holding himself to exceptionally high standards of performance. To the envy of Liang's political enemies, this clique included new converts. Zhou Zhiqi and Zhu Qiqian were two cabinet ministers who seemed to align themselves willingly with him. Liang Shiyi's independent power base did not please President Yuan, who was a master of power game and kept a score card all the time.

"And yet," Liang Qichao continued, "Liang Shiyi's secret of success is that he knows himself and never seeks a position beyond his capacity. He's very good at backstage maneuvering to make incremental improvements and letting others take credit for the successes."

Liang Boyin looked into Qichao's eyes. "He has no faults, then?"

"Oh, yes. He's not good at confrontation with adversaries to force an issue. He tends to compromise at all cost. To his admirers, he is the symbol of a class of devoted public men who struggle to hold the country together during years of painful adjustment to resist foreign domination and economic corrosion. His critics decry his conservative instincts which, they contend, inevitably lead him to accommodate Yuan's authoritarian rule."

"But even his critics concede that it would be difficult to imagine Chinese politics without him," Liang Boyin injected. "They say he has an instinctive understanding of the Chinese people. That's quite a compliment."

A Date of Infamy

The year of 1915 began with a happy occasion in the Presidential Palace as President Yuan presented honorary awards to deserving friends. When his turn came, Liang Shiyi received the title of Honorary Counselor. As he sat down in the large auditorium, Liang's mind was not on this honorific title but on the foreign policy issues confronting China as a result of the European War. He wanted to be an active participant in shaping such policies. In fact, he relied on networking with high officials in government, including the President, instead of his title, honorary or otherwise.

For his part, President Yuan needed Liang Shiyi's counsel on diplomatic and financial matters more than ever. On the other hand, he had no regret in forcing Liang out as his chief of staff. Liang's successor, Yang Shiqi, the Senior Counselor of the Privy Council, was more compliant. Unlike Liang, he would not give unsolicited advice and certainly would not inject any objection on moral grounds. Yuan could trust him with all palace intrigues, some of which would have offended Liang.

Liang Shiyi reviewed China's position since the outbreak of the European war. He was unhappy with Japanese military actions in Shandong Province. Citing its alliance with Great Britain, dating back to 1902, Japan declared war on Germany in August 1914 and began to attack German settlements in Shandong Province. China argued that Chinese troops should be used to retake the German Concession in Chinese territory, but the British government was too busy in Europe to challenge the Japanese expansion.

The unfortunate combination of Chinese neutrality and British indifference resulted in the landing of Japanese troops in Shandong Province on September 2, 1914. They took over the railway station of Jinan on October 6 and occupied Qingdao on November 7. The Chinese people were outraged by the savage assault by the Japanese Army on a neutral nation. The Chinese government summoned the Japanese Minister to lodge a strong protest, but the Japanese government simply ignored the complaint.

While the Republic was confronted with the most serious foreign crisis since its birth, the pot of palace intrigue was boiling and spilled out its odious brew. On December 29, 1914, President Yuan announced the decision upon the recommenda-

223

tion of the Constitution Conference, the section of the constitutional covenant concerning the term of the presidency had been revised. Henceforth the presidential term would be extended from five to ten years; the President could succeed himself with no term limit and he would name his successor. In short, Yuan Shikai became the President for Life and beyond. It had been a curious chant to ring out the old year.

* * *

Liang Shiyi did not have to wait long before receiving a call from the President. On January 18, 1915, the Japanese Minister Hioki Eki delivered the "Twenty-One Demands of Japan" to Yuan Shikai, binding him in absolute secrecy. President Yuan immediately summoned Xu Shichang, the Secretary of State; Sun Baoqi, the Foreign Minister; Cao Yulin, the Deputy Foreign Minister; and a few trusted advisers, including Liang Shiyi, to an emergency meeting. These demands exposed, as never before, the Japanese ambition of reducing China to a Japanese colony. All those attending the meeting were shocked beyond belief. The President jotted down his comments item by item in red, noting the last seven demands represented blatant interference of Chinese internal affairs. Before the all-night meeting broke up, Liang Shiyi made a poignant remark, "It's a bad precedent for the envoy of a foreign power to deal directly with the President, particularly on an issue of life and death to China. You should remind Hioki that he should go through the regular diplomatic channels."

In response, on January 20, the Japanese government sent the Twenty-One Demands to the Chinese Foreign Ministry. Divided into five groups, the first consisted of four demands to legitimize the transfer of all former German interests in Shandong to Japan; the second consisted of seven demands dealing with exclusive economic rights for Japan, including railways and mining in south Manchuria and east Mongolia; the third group listed two demands concerning joint Sino-Japanese administration of the huge iron and coal works, including the arsenals in Wuhan area; the fourth group listed a sole demand that China would not lease any ports or islands along the Chinese coast to other foreign powers. The most ominous was the fifth group with seven demands including employment of Japanese advisers in all Chinese political, financial and political administrations; stationing of Japanese police in north China; and allowing Japan a free hand in propagating its religious doctrines in China.

The Chinese government was warned that it would suffer severe consequences if it did not maintain absolute secrecy regarding these demands. In late January, the Japanese government notified other foreign powers with interests in China of only eleven of the demands in the first two groups. The Japanese embassies in Western capitals also stuck to this falsified information in answering questions from Western governments and reporters. With absolute secrecy, neither the Western powers nor the ordinary Chinese could mount an effective protest. The Chinese government was too weak to resist and the Western powers were too preoccupied in Europe to care.

Noting China was no match for Japan in an armed conflict, President Yuan felt he had to yield to Japanese demands if they could be moderated. The Chinese government initiated intense negotiations with the Japanese Minister in Beijing to pare down the severity of the demands. In order to strengthen the Chinese team, President Yuan asked a veteran diplomat and former premier, Lu Zhengxiang, to take over as Foreign Minister. Reacting to Chinese protests, Hioki Eki scornfully and shamelessly told one of the Chinese officials in private that when there is a fire in a jewel shop, neighbors cannot be expected to refrain from helping themselves. Very little progress was made in the negotiations even though the two sides had met 25 times in 1915, from February 9 to April 24. To increase pressure on the Chinese government, Japan had sent 30,000 troops to China in March. Through Wellington Koo, a counselor in the Foreign Ministry, Liang Shiyi tried in vain to stiffen the Chinese negotiation position. The Japanese knew it had China cornered.

* * *

Frustrated and alarmed, Liang Shiyi felt he had to exercise personal diplomacy and risk the wrath of the Japanese government. When the British and American Ministers in Beijing visited him to inquire about the details of the Japanese demands, Liang gave them the full contents on the condition that the source be kept absolutely confidential. Liang Shiyi also communicated privately with two Japanese senior statesmen, Duke Yamagata Aritomo and Marquis Matsukata Seigi, and prevailed upon them to urge the Japanese government not to seek domination of China.

After learning of the secret Japanese demands, Liang Shiyi also approached Zhou Ziqi, the Finance Minister, to find methods of getting the news out to the Western powers whose support China desperately needed. He found Zhou in full agreement. "Those damned Japanese not only want China to be its colony but want to do this without a trace of blood," Zhou remarked. "We must try to stop it."

Liang made a suggestion. "You have many foreign friends. Can you appeal to their self interest to rally against Japan?"

Zhou Ziqi thought of William Donald who had often used him as a news source in the past. Donald regarded Zhou as an intimate friend whom he called "old Joe." Although Donald was stationed in Beijing, he had gone to Shanghai on one of his monthly trips in connection with his editorship of the *Far Eastern Review*, a prestigious English magazine. By then Donald had resigned as the correspondent for the *New York Herald* and a string of Australian newspapers. Instead he had accepted a similar position with *The Times* of London. Zhou sent him a telegram and urged him to return to Beijing immediately.

Arriving at Zhou's home in Beijing, Donald immediately sensed something of grave concern to China. As they sat near the fish pond in the garden, Zhou stammered, "We are in a b-b-b-bloody mess. Now I c-c-cannot tell you exactly w-w-what it is. All I can say is that the insatiable Japanese are making d-d-d-amnable d-d-demands on China."

Although Zhou explained the intrigues of unfolding events to Donald, he stopped short of divulging state secrets. Finally Donald said to him, "I'll write down all the demands I believe Japan is capable of making, Joe. You strike out anything that is not correct. If I omit any details, perhaps you may be able to suggest something that will make me think of them." In the process, Donald got the gist of the demands. In the next few days, he repeated the same technique on several other cabinet ministers until he was able to fine tune a long list. By February 11, Donald was confident he had the essence of the Japanese demands and wanted the whole world to know it.

William Donald went to see Sir John Jordan who was extremely cautious and almost imperturbable. "I've heard about this from another source," Jordan said. "It's all unconfirmed rumors. I've already advised the Foreign Office in London." When Donald cabled the news to *The Times* of London, the foreign editor of the newspaper checked with the Foreign Office. Sure enough, the story was nothing but pure rumors, he was told, so he decided to kill it. Although Donald was used to the British official attitude as a stickler of orthodoxy, he was fuming at the editor for not publishing his scoop.

Then Donald went to see Dr. Reinsch, the American Minister. Dr Reinsch told him he had also received similar information from another source and had reported it to Washington. In fact, he told Donald, he had just received instructions from President Wilson to avoid any direct intervention in the negotiations lest it might provoke the hostility of Japan. While Donald appreciated the frankness and sensitivity of Dr. Reinsch, he didn't want to give up his crusade to get the news out. That evening Donald met Frederick Moore, the manager of the Associated Press. He gave Moore a copy of the Japanese demands for dispatch to Washington, providing Moore would not divulge its source. Next morning the first reaction came back from Melville Stone, head of the Associated Press, saying the Japanese Ambassador in Washington had categorically denied the information in the dispatch—and Stone requested the source of information in order to take further action. Again, the publication of the secret demands was routed.

Donald devised a simple but brazen plan and asked Zhou Ziqi to deliver a message to George Morrison, President Yuan's political adviser. The next day, Donald called on Morrison in his office.

"George," he said, "I've come to tell you about a plan—"

"I know," Morrison interrupted, "I have been talking to Mr. Zhou."

"Well?" Donald asked with an amused smile.

"It's risky business," Morrison said flatly. He rose and looked strangely at Donald. "Would you excuse me? I have to go into the library for a moment."

While Donald watched, Morrison straightened a number of papers at the center of his desk before walking out of the office.

That was Donald's chance! He stepped toward the desk and quickly snatched up the papers and stuffed them inside his coat before Morrison returned.

"Sorry to keep you waiting," Morrison said.

"That's all right, George. I'll be running along anyway," Donald replied and left.

When Donald reached his office, he opened the document. Before him was the official translation of the Twenty-One Demands. Morrison had played the game. Donald quickly dispatched a telegram to *The Times* of London and gave a copy to

John Jordan who grudgingly thanked him. He also took a copy to Dr. Reinsch who gripped his hand and praised him. "It took a fellow like you to do it."

* * *

On April 26, Japan sent an amended Twenty-One Demands to the Chinese Foreign Ministry which responded on May 1, requesting further amendments on the fifth group of demands. Impatient with the Chinese foot dragging, on May 7 Japan delivered an ultimatum to China, stating that the fifth group could be reserved for future consideration, but that the Chinese government must give a satisfactory response before 6 p.m. on May 9, 1915.

On the morning of May 8, Sir John Jordan sought an interview with Foreign Minister Lu Zhengxiang. The British minister said to Lu, "I know your President has called a meeting of the cabinet ministers and other advisers to discuss the Japanese demands this afternoon. I come here to give you my advice and I hope you will assist the President to make the right decision." After a long pause, he continued, "Since the European powers cannot come to the aid of China, it is in the best interest of China to accept the Japanese demands. Hopefully, when peace is restored in Europe, the fifth group of Japanese demands will become moot. I have been in China for almost 40 years and a friend of President Yuan for 30 years. I would not like to see China be destroyed in a war with Japan. Please forward my advice to President Yuan and other attendees at the meeting." Sir John was most earnest and solemn as he concluded his visit.

The atmosphere of the meeting that afternoon was tense. After Lu Zhengxiang reported his interview with Sir John Jordan, President Yuan addressed the group in front of him, "Although the amended demands have eliminated some of the most obnoxious terms, this treaty is still humiliating to us. At present we are not strong enough to wage a war against Japan. On balance the advice of Sir John Jordan is correct. I must now accept the ultimatum from Japan. Out of the ashes of this distressing experience, we must redouble our efforts to strengthen our armed forces, financial affairs and diplomatic relations. We should all work hard in the next ten years to wipe out this national disgrace and uphold the independence of our nation." Yuan could hardly hold back tears after the speech. All attendees succumbed to silence and tears.

In the afternoon of May 9, the staff at the Foreign Ministry worked frantically to put the final touch on the document to answer the Japanese ultimatum. At six o'clock, there was still confusion in completing the final draft. It was not until eleven p.m. the reply was delivered to the Japanese Legation in Beijing.

Immediately after the announcement of the Chinese acceptance, strong protests broke out throughout the nation. Nevertheless the treaty was officially signed on May 25. The Twenty-One Demands earned Japan nothing but bitter hatred from generations of Chinese people. May 9, 1915 went down in Chinese history as a date of infamy.

Personal Diplomacy

"This is a surprise of all surprises," Liang Shiyi said to Guan Mianjun who dropped by for a visit shortly after the crisis created by the Japanese demands. They were sipping tea in the courtyard of Liang's home in Ganshiqiao Lane on a bright spring day. After folding the letter he had just finished reading, Liang continued, "You can never guess it. My father's second elderly lady gave birth to a baby girl." He was referring to his father's young concubine, so-called because of her generational status.

"Congratulations!" Guan was shocked beyond words. He could not imagine Liang Shiyi's father would sire an offspring beyond seventy years of age. It was unusual enough for any man of that age to have a child, but especially for this elderly scholar who counseled moderation on everything, including sex. Was his home in Hong Kong such a cozy place that he accomplished what he didn't when he lived in his native village? Did he keep this secret until he was sure of a live birth? For if a stillbirth had occurred, he certainly would not have disclosed to the world his private relations with the second elderly lady. Guan privately mused about his future relatives. His son would marry Liang Shiyi's daughter, soon, after a long engagement.

"My father sounds very happy in the letter," Liang said. "He can count on me and my brother to take care of our sister if anything happens to him." Liang was thinking about this half sister, 46 years his junior, whom his father probably would not live to see grow into adulthood. In the Chinese family structure, to take care meant not only to support but also to control her, smothering her young life with overprotection.

Guan changed the subject. "I came to check a persistent rumor with you. I hear something is afoot in the Presidential Palace to make the President an emperor. Is there any truth in the story?"

"I've heard as much," Liang replied. "Yang Shiqi, the Senior Councillor of the Privy Council, along with the President's eldest son, Yuan Keding, are busy behind the scenes. I don't know if the President approves what they are doing, but it adds fuel to the speculation that Yuan accepted the Twenty-One Demands from Japan in exchange for Japanese support of his plan to become an emperor. It was difficult enough to deal with the Japanese government without having injected Yuan's selfish motive into the equation." Guan Mianjun was satisfied with the answer, but Liang uncharacteristically continued, "I'm no longer privy to the inner working at the Presidential Palace, and I am dead set against the idea of monarchy. Having worked so hard to facilitate the abdication of one emperor, I'm the last person to want another emperor to roll back the progress and modernization in the last few years."

A month later, Liang was pleased, but not surprised, to receive news from his brother Shixu whose third consort had given birth to a baby boy. Ever since they were married the year before, Shixu had hoped his new consort would bring many sons to his family. He was not to be disappointed. The news of the birth of her first son, and Shixu's second, was a big occasion.

* * *

In early June, Sir John Jordan also heard the rumor of a movement to make Yuan an emperor. He thought he would sound out President Yuan, very diplomatically, when he was invited to lunch with the President. Two days before the lunch appointment, however, he was distracted by a telegram from the Foreign Office in London asking him to seek clarification from President Yuan on a more urgent matter. With his usual deference to his authorities, he complied.

It all began in March when Jordan received a feeler from the Foreign Office in London about the purchase of arms in China. The inquiry was based on rumors that Russian rifles captured in Manchuria in the Russo-Japanese War in 1905 had later shown up in the Chinese black market during the revolution. Since hostilities had now ceased in the Far East, could such arms be purchased for the European War? Based on his informed judgment, Jordan expressed a strong negative view to this feeler from London. In his estimate, the quantity of arms available could not be more than 30,000 rifles and some ammunition. Besides, the Chinese government had declared neutrality and would forbid the export of even such small quantity of arms.

However, the Foreign Office in London was not so easily silenced. The War Office and the Army Council pressed for action. At the request of Lord Kitchener, the Field Marshall and Secretary of War, the Foreign Office sent a "private and secret" telegram to Jordan on March 17. The Foreign Office acknowledged the delicate position of Chinese neutrality, but wrote that Jordan might "be able to find a means of effecting a deal through an intermediary from whom the sale to us would not be open to the same objection." Copies of this telegram were sent to the King, the Prime Minister, the Secretary of War, the Foreign Secretary, the Munition Minister and the Ambassador to France. On receipt of this telegram, Jordan felt he had no choice but to yield to the request.

Jordan consulted with Sidney Barton, the Chinese Secretary at his Legation, and came up with a plan for action. The plan called for the use of a secret agent to purchase the arms in a private capacity to avoid any suspicion of complicity of the British government, which would ultimately pay for the purchase. Assurance would be given to the Chinese that the British government would cover President Yuan if the transaction should be found out. By now even the Foreign Office questioned the wisdom of purchasing this quantity of arms at such a high risk of exposure. But the need for arms and ammunition was so great in Europe that Lord Kitchener could not escape the wishful thinking: perhaps more arms, say 100,000 rifles, might be available to justify the risk. Or perhaps the arms could be sent through Vladivostok to the Russians who were less squeamish about breaches of neutrality.

Jordan had to select a secret agent in a hurry and found Edmund Backhouse, an Oriental scholar well known to the British Legation in Beijing. He would act in his capacity as the representative of a private firm, John Brown & Co, which was given a formal letter of indemnity by the Foreign Office, taking full responsibility for anything the secret agent might do in the company's name in the purchase of arms in China. It took over two months to complete all the preliminary arrangements. Now Jordan was asked to clear the last hurdle by informing President Yuan of this plan and giving him the British assurance to China's neutrality. Jordan thought that he could tactfully bring up this subject during his lunch with President Yuan.

* * *

A day after his lunch with President Yuan, Jordan received an unexpected call from Liang Shiyi requesting a private interview. Jordan knew Liang Shiyi well and had regarded him a confidant and alter ego of Yuan Shikai. As the Controller of the Maritime Customs Service and, more importantly, the president of the Bank of Communications, Liang must have come to see him on behalf of President Yuan.

"I meant to come to see you sooner except for the hectic diplomatic activities on Japanese demands last month," Liang began. But his remark was interrupted by Jordan.

"I have spoken to President Yuan about our needs for arms in the European war," Jordan said to Liang, "Perhaps you can help us in locating arms through official or private sources." Jordan soon found out that Liang knew nothing about his conversation with President Yuan on the purchase of arms in China.

"I know Lord Kitchener and I can imagine his need of men and ammunition," Liang said quietly. "It has come to my mind that China can help solve the manpower problem of the allies without violating the letter of its Neutrality Act. It can supply 300,000 men through a private firm under contract with your government. The men will be shipped as laborers for non-combat duties under the 1904 emigration convention and will serve under British officers wherever required. Since this is my own idea, I act as a private citizen to solicit your opinion without the knowledge of the President."

Jordan could not believe his ears as he listened to this offer. "Our greatest concern is not non-combat laborers on the European front. On the other hand, we urgently need arms and ammunition. Can you help us locate them in China?"

"Perhaps 20,000 to 30,000 rifles and some ammunition can be obtained through private channels," Liang suggested.

"How about 100,000 rifles and heavy arms?" Jordan boldly upped the ante.

Liang Shiyi hesitated and then made a counter offer, "It is difficult to find such a large supply of arms through either official or private channels. I cannot speak for the Chinese government. However, I shall try my best to accommodate your wish through private channels if your government is willing to consider my proposal of Chinese laborers for Europe." Liang was insistent and Jordan knew he had to compromise, but he wanted to clarify Liang's position on other issues before forwarding Liang's proposal to the Foreign Office.

"Would you be willing to find private sources to supply arms to Russia?" Jordan asked.

Liang's reply was direct and terse, "No, the Chinese government will not approve the supply of arms to Russia, only to Britain."

"Are you concerned with the risk of possible exposure of this arrangement?" Jordan tested Liang's attitude toward risk.

"Of course I want assurance that the arms are designated for use by Britain only and that the British government will indemnify the Chinese government for any unpleasant consequences if the secret should leak out."

Jordan was satisfied with his grilling. It did not dawn on him that Liang was not partial to Britain over Russian but that the British connection would help China participate on the side of the Allies by sending Chinese laborers to the European front. Finally Jordan told Liang, "In spite of my own misgivings, I'll forward your proposal to London and get back to you when I receive a reply."

After Liang Shiyi left his office, Jordan immediately sent a telegram to Beilby Alston, who handled the purchase of Chinese arms at the Foreign Office in London. Alston was the charge d'affaires in the British Legation in Beijing during Jordan's absence in 1913. When Alston received Liang Shiyi's "extraordinary fantastic suggestion," he read it with contempt. He noted for the record, "It is a typical example of the working of Liang Shiyi's mind. (He is the Machiavelli of China.)" He added that it was no doubt intended as a hint to Japan and a device to extricate China from her present diplomatic isolation and to obtain a seat at the settlement of peace conditions at the end of the war. He absolutely wanted to have nothing to do with the offer of 300,000 Chinese laborers, but he could not overlook the vague promise of help to obtain 100,000 rifles which would make it "more worthwhile giving the assurance required." The Army Council agreed.

* * *

Immediately after his interview with John Jordan, Liang Shiyi called on Ye Gongchuo in Ye's private office in the Ministry of Communications to discuss his proposal to the British government. After reviewing all possibilities, they concluded that if the entire proposal was accepted, it would be necessary to set up a private company for large-scale purchase of arms for the British agent. Another private company would have to be set up to recruit Chinese laborers for non-combat duties in the European War. The risk to take up the former task was worthwhile only if the latter was accepted by the British government.

As they were about to end the meeting, Ye Gongchuo's trusted aide, Zheng Hongnian, rushed in with great excitement. He had just received an official notice which dismissed Ye from his post while pending further investigation for corruption charges.

"I'll leave for Tianjin by the first train tomorrow morning, taking advantage of the darkness of the dawn," Ye told his aide. "You have to decide if you want to go with me to protect yourself. But there's no time to lose. We must act quickly."

"I think I'm low ranking enough to avoid any involvement," Zheng replied. "Besides, the business of the ministry must go on. I'll wait out the storm."

"In that case, please report to the ministry tomorrow that I'm taking a leave of absence," Ye said to his aide. "I shall check in a hotel incognito for the night."

Then Ye turned to Liang. "The charges are false, but I don't want to take any chances."

"I know," Liang replied, trying to comfort him. "The prosecutor was actually sending me a warning by charging you of wrongdoing. You are wise to go to Tianjin and see what will happen next."

Liang Shiyi knew too well what was happening. In the past month, Yang Shiqi, Yuan Shikai's new right-hand man, and his eldest son, Yuan Keding, could no long conceal their secret plan to make Yuan the new emperor of China. Yuan's paranoiac suspicions deepened as he was isolated from the outside world by a small group of flatterers in the Presidential Palace. Yuan Keding saw to it that his father was screened from unfavorable news by publishing a private palace newspaper which was calculated to excite his father to accept the crown of an emperor.

Yuan Shikai began to sound out his friends and associate about their views on constitutional monarchy. Yuan always started the conversation by claiming he had no intention of ever becoming an emperor, but that he must weigh the merit of this possibility since it was so strongly urged on him by others. He was irked by the negative reactions from three of his long-time friends who had built up their own strong power bases. To trim their feathers and to show them who was the boss, Yuan decided to send them a strong warning. His intended targets were General Duan Qirui, Secretary of Army; Xiong Xiling, a former Premier; and Liang Shiyi, the acknowledged leader of the "Communication Clique." The method he chose to express his displeasure was the dismissal of three deputy ministers: the Deputy Minister of the Army, a protege of General Duan Qirui; the Deputy Finance Minister, a close associate of Xiong Xiling; and the Deputy Minister of Communications, the "soul" of Liang Shiyi.

Two days later, it became clear that the purge of Liang's friends in the Ministry of Communications went much deeper. Besides Ye Gongchuo, various charges were made against Zhao Qinghua, the managing director of Tianjin-Pukou Railway and Guan Kanglin, the managing director of Beijing-Hankou Railway. Ye had the foresight of having left for Tianjin in the safety of the French Concession. Guan Mianjun, the managing director of the Beijing-Zhangjiakou Railway was also charged, but he happened to be on an inspection tour of the railway and remained free in Zhangjiakou. Both Zhao Qinghua and Guan Kanglin were arrested in Beijing.

On the same night, after the latest announcement, Yuan Shikai summoned Liang Shiyi to the Presidential Palace for his advice about John Jordan's proposal on arms purchase. Liang found the President's mind wandered. Assessing Yuan's mood, Liang decided not to inform the President about his proposal to Jordan offering a supply of 300,000 Chinese laborers. The British government had already given the assurance of confidentiality to the President for its arms purchase. What advice was Yuan seeking?

Liang soon discovered the consultation on arms purchase was only a pretext when Yuan turned to a different subject. With an expression of sympathy, Yuan told him, "Your name was originally in the indictment of corruption of government officials. I have ordered it removed." It was an unmistakable warning to Liang if he hadn't got the message so far. Liang said to himself: how strange indeed that the President would know what was in the "secret" proceedings of the prosecutor.

In a way, the purge of the Communication Clique reminded Liang Shiyi of the high-profile accusation of him and his associates in 1910. However, in the earlier accusation he had been the target of investigation because he was a supporter of Yuan, who had lost power. This time he himself was spared, but his friends became the pawns in the war of nerves because he did not approve Yuan's ambition to become an emperor.

Liang Shiyi took a sick leave from his job as Controller of Maritime Customs Service to assess his own situation. He took the same tack as he did in 1910. No one in the outside world should know that he had fallen from Yuan's favor. They needed only to know he was spending his summer vacation in the Western Hills. He was determined to carry out his personal diplomacy to win China a place in the conference table after the European war.

* * *

The foreign diplomats did not disappoint Liang Shiyi. They came to visit him in the Western Hills. First to stop by was Dr. Paul Reinsch, the American Minister. They discussed in detail a Chinese-American joint venture to form a Sino-American steamship company. Liang was very pleased with results of their discussion and pledged his assistance in implementing the plan.

However, the most awaited visitor was Sir John Jordan who showed up unexpectedly one day in a torrential rain. After dispensing the formalities, Jordan explained, "Since secrecy and discretion are of utmost importance, I decided to come in person as soon as I got the words from London. His Majesty's government has authorized the purchase of 100,000 rifles and other available arms in China through a British private firm. An agent of this firm will act independently with full authority and will not associate himself with the British Legation in Beijing or the British government. Just give him as much assistance as you can if he should contact you. Officially we maintain silence on this matter and want to know as little as possible."

As to the supply of Chinese laborers to Europe, the British government declined the offer. Even though Beilby Alston in the Foreign Office was so perceptive in reading Liang Shiyi's intention of trying to gain a seat for China in the post-war peace settlement, he did not understand the importance of the linkage of Chinese laborers and arms purchase in Liang's proposal. Jordan was too absorbed in the arms purchase to note Liang's coolness after hearing of the refusal for Chinese laborers.

Finally, the visit of Mr. Conty, the French Minister, was music to Liang's ear. After hearing Liang's plan to supply Chinese laborers for non-combat duties in Europe, Conty exclaimed, "Why, this is the most exciting idea I've heard for a long time. We certainly can use them in our factories. I'll report your proposal to my government immediately."

Liang Shiyi uttered a sigh of relief. This was a sweet personal diplomatic triumph.

The Plot Thickens

Foreign diplomats were not the only visitors to Liang Shiyi's abode in the Western Hills. Yuan Shikai sent an emissary to persuade Liang to support the monarchical movement. Liang told the unwelcome visitor, "I was unfortunately born thirty years too early and was bred in the Mandarin tradition. I could not shake off my ambition of public service and became an official under the Qing emperors. In the new Republic, I owe my meteoric ascendency in my career to President Yuan. However, I cannot let our friendship blind my judgment on the critical issue of national importance. I have no more to add to what I have told him repeatedly." His firm reply left an unmistakable impression on the emissary.

Liang Shiyi could not avoid Yuan's long arms in the Western Hills. By the end of June, he decided to return to Beijing. His decision was also influenced by the pending arrival in July of Philip Manson, a representative of Metherns & Sons Co. of Maryland who, at the request of Dr. Reinsch, came to Beijing to discuss a contract for the proposed joint venture of the Eastern Pacific Steamship Company.

Liang Shiyi had hardly cleared the correspondence of his desk at the Maritime Customs Service, when his secretary reminded him, "You have an appointment with Mr. Edmund Backhouse on June 30. He's with John Brown & Company of England. He did not disclose the purpose of his visit."

"I've never met him," Liang replied. "but I've some idea what he's up to. Just bring him in when he arrives."

As the secretary ushered in a mild-mannered Englishman, Backhouse spoke softly in impeccable Mandarin, "I have a business proposal of a confidential nature. Can we discuss it privately without an interpreter?" Liang Shiyi waved his hand to dismiss the secretary.

"Our company would like to purchase 200,000 rifles that may be available in China," Backhouse began. "It must be quite clear to you where the rifles will end up eventually. Since my government wants to respect China's neutrality, my company treats this deal strictly as private business. I ask you not to make inquiries at the British Legation." Liang keenly noted that Backhouse had upped the ante from 100,000 in Jordan's proposal to 200,000.

"I understand your situation and I'm eager to help," Liang replied. "However, your expectation is very unrealistic. In my own estimation, it will be lucky if we can find 20,000 rifles and a supply of ammunition."

Backhouse was undeterred and said, "I can proceed on my own if you can tell me the possible sources of available arms."

Liang Shiyi was now so uncertain of his own fate, he could not over commit himself. He had squashed the idea of setting up a private company to actively solicit arms in large scale. He cautiously said to Backhouse, "The major battles of the revolutionary war were fought in the Yangzi Valley, particularly in the Wuhan area. That's where the left-over arms may be found. But I'm not in a position to contact the officials or military leaders in those provinces. I do know some officials in Guangdong Province who can help. If your shipment of arms should go through Guangdong to Hong Kong, I can ask them to facilitate your transshipment."

That was encouragement enough for Backhouse to start his arms hunt. He thanked Liang Shiyi profusely and left.

* * *

The summer of 1915 was simmering hot in Beijing, but hotter still were the tempers of those involved in the monarchical movement. Things did not go as they had planned. Earlier in April, Yuan had reinstated Zhou Xuexi as the Finance Minister in order to bolster the sagging national economy. The Domestic Bond Bureau had to raise 24 million yuan to balance the budget. By now the smart money in the market had lost confidence in the government because of rumors about Yuan's ambition to become an emperor. The sale of the 1915 domestic bonds was at first sluggish but the goal was finally reached through Liang Shiyi's frantic persuasion of potential buyers. It was difficult to reproduce the spectacular success of the 1914 drive.

On July 3, the Consultative Senate appointed a group of ten to draft a new constitution as a forerunner to change the "national polity" from republic to monarchy. Liang Qichao, appointed one of the members because of his previous role in drafting the constitution under the auspices of the lawfully elected Parliament, was in the minority. The group was stacked with supporters of the monarchical movement. Liang Qichao found out soon enough that he was there primarily for window dressing. Within a few months, he would resign.

One sizzling summer evening in August, Liang Shiyi was invited to a dinner at the home of Zhou Ziqi, also attended by several cabinet ministers. Zhou, who had become the Minister of Agriculture and Commerce in April, was eager to find ways to improve the performance of his new ministry. Also invited was his good friend William Donald who was accompanied by his interpreter Scott Anderson. At the dinner table, Donald sat next to Zhou Ziqi and across from Liang Shiyi. The delicious courses were interspersed by pewter pots of warm Shaoxing wine. After each serving of wine, steaming towels were passed out for sticky hands and faces before the next course. An overhead electric fan helped cool the crowd.

Aggressive in his manner, William Donald dominated the dinner conversation by championing more and reliable statistical data in agriculture and commerce. Then he suddenly broke off to remark that, in his opinion, the Republic under Yuan was a bloody failure. Anderson grunted and said in a clear, loud voice, "Gentlemen, Mr. Donald and I were engaged this afternoon in an argument on whether a republic or a monarchy is better for China."

Everyone stopped and looked intently at Anderson and then at Donald. "That's so," Donald said. "I contend the Republic must be upheld. Mr. Anderson says a monarchy will be better in the long run."

The table burst into talk, as if the guests were no longer afraid to air their views. After all, this sensitive subject had been broached by two foreigners. One by one they agreed with Anderson that China would be better off under a monarchy. But Donald observed one exception. Across the table, Liang Shiyi sat quietly scowling into an empty tea cup. He nodded his head approvingly as Donald, alone, defended the Republic and warned of a major civil war.

While looking at the expression of Liang Shiyi, Donald was startled by the voice of Zhou Ziqi, "The South, I mean the revolutionaries, are beaten and broken."

"Gentlemen," Donald said, "you cannot restore the monarchy. The South will revolt. You can take my word for it." Donald always tried to have the last word. There was a moment of dead silence. Liang Shiyi looked earnestly at Donald and admired his political acumen.

Soon the dinner broke up in a babel of voices. After other guests dispersed, Liang Shiyi stayed on, alone, with Zhou Ziqi. Liang said to him, "Your friend Donald is right. There will be civil war if President Yuan proclaims the monarchy. I want to warn you privately that your view on monarchy is quite dangerous."

Zhou was puzzled and replied, "Sun Yatsen's in exile in Japan. His supporters have staged annoying raids now and then in various parts of the country, but they were squashed quickly. I don't see how they can start a revolt now."

Indeed, Sun Yatsen had encountered numerous obstacles in his long struggle to fulfill his dream of revolutionizing China. After fleeing to Japan in 1913, he had divorced his wife and married the second daughter of Charlie Soong, his ardent supporter and financial backer. A devoted Christian, Charles Soong had objected strenuously to Sun's marriage proposal to his eldest daughter, Soong Ailing, Sun's one-time secretary. A more traditional daughter, she acquiesced to her father's wishes. But his second daughter, Soong Chingling (aka Song Qingling), fresh out of Wesleyan College in Macon, Georgia, was very headstrong. She ignored her father's warning and married Sun, a man of destiny in his late forties. Sun rationalized that he needed a constant companion with a modern outlook to support his revolutionary cause.

Sun Yatsen also reorganized the Nationalist Party in the summer of 1914 into a tighter structure under the name Chinese Revolutionary Party. Members were required to pledge personal allegiance to him and to fingerprint their written pledges. Sun retained strict control of the central and branch organizations as well as the power of appointment at all levels. After being declared the generalissimo of a Chinese

Revolutionary Army, Sun and his supporters vowed to fight Yuan Shikai for his abject betrayal of the Republic. However, except for a few unsuccessful uprisings staged by his supporters in China, Sun was by and large ignored by the government in Beijing.

"But the revolt will come from some other unexpected sources," Liang said, surprising Zhou with his answer. "Most governors and generals who now tolerate the Beijing government will find the monarchy unacceptable. Anyone of them can start a revolt and others will soon respond."

"Do you seriously believe that?" Zhou asked.

"Yes, I do," Liang responded. "That's why the monarchical movement is so detrimental to the nation."

* * *

The news of the resolution of the charges against his friend Guan Mianjun caught Liang Shiyi by surprise. By the order of the President, the prosecutor dismissed Guan from his job as Managing Director of Beijing-Zhangjiakou Railway on August 12, but imposed no other penalty. Why was the action so swift and the penalty so lenient for a political crime? Liang Shiyi pondered the question at home.

Soon he got his answer from a visit by Yuan Keding, the eldest son of President Yuan. The younger Yuan came to solicit his support of the monarchical movement. After the exchange of pleasantries, Liang's answer was polite but firm. Yuan Keding countered. Did Liang Shiyi not realize Guan Mianjun could have received a long jail sentence except that the President wanted to help Shiyi's friend? What a pity if his other friends, still under custody, would receive a harsher fate? Did he ever think about the safety of his friends in the Bank of Communications who, so far, had not been touched by the prosecutor? Liang Shiyi remained silent after listening to the veiled threats.

"Don't make life miserable for yourself and your friends," Yuan Keding said, altering his tone. "Let's be reasonable. We're not asking you to play an active role. All we expect is that you remain silent in public. If we do anything in your name, don't repudiate us. Don't get smart and try to slip to the opposition camp. Stay with us and you will be all right. I know it's difficult for you to make the decision in a hurry. Why don't you think it over?" Yuan's tone was more pleasant, but the message was the same. He left hurriedly, leaving Shiyi with his thoughts.

Although he had remained calm, Liang was in the grips of terror after Yuan Keding left. He never dreamed he would end up in such a terrible position. He always thought of himself as a voice of compromise in times of turbulence. He had stayed on as a free-lance adviser and trouble shooter for President Yuan in good faith. If the President no longer wanted to listen to him, they could always part company with no ill feeling. Why would an old friend resort to intimidation to silence him?

Yuan Keding's words were frightful and pervasive. Shiyi thought about the questions Keding had asked. One stood out: "Did he ever think about the safety of his friends in the Bank of Communications who, so far, had not been touched by the prosecutor?" That must be it, Shiyi thought. President Yuan could not let him escape because Yuan needed the money in the bank—which was still under Shiyi's control. He was overwhelmed by the thought of having been trapped. He would have to take desperate measures.

In the next few days, Liang Shiyi gathered with his close friends in the Bank of Communications and consulted about his next move. "I cannot slip away and let you suffer the consequence," he said. "However, if I should hurt myself in an accident, the President may allow me to resign out of mercy. Perhaps there would be less harm to you." Of course it was wishful thinking, but Liang could think of no better way to extricate himself.

"This scheme will not work," came a loud voice from the group. "The President is a person whose sympathy I will not count on. Look, even some people in the second echelon of the Ministry of Communications have now been arrested as accessories to trumped-up charges. Why should he spare anyone in the Bank of Communications?" Liang sensed their helplessness in addition to his own. Among those arrested recently was Lin Zhenyao, a young man in the Ministry of Communications who was married to Shiyi's favorite niece, the only child of his oldest sister. The threats were getting closer to home.

In desperation Liang Shiyi sought the opinion of Zhou Ziqi who was still well entrenched in Yuan's camp. Could he throw some light on Yuan's inner thought? Zhou was philosophical, "Resistance is useless. President Yuan is going to follow through with his plan no matter what happens. You might as well brace yourself for the hurricane and not be swept away." Liang Shiyi knew he would be severely tested in days ahead.

Shortly afterward, the commander of the infantry battalion in Beijing paid a surprise visit to Liang Shiyi. After introducing himself, he told Liang, "The streets of Beijing are no longer safe. Rabblerousers are staging all sorts of protests. At the request of my superior, I'm providing you with armed guards for your protection. You have no more worries." After the commander left, Liang discovered he now had a new chauffeur and several unfamiliar doormen.

Suddenly the monarchical movement broke wide open in public and quickly gained momentum. After testing the water for a week, six sponsors of the movement headed by Yang Du organized the Peace Planning Society on August 23 to draft Yuan for emperor. Yuan himself remained conspicuously aloof, denying continually any imperial aspiration. Nevertheless, the monarchical movement grew more pronounced as numerous petitions favoring the monarchy reached the government almost daily.

All doubts were removed when Yang Shiqi spoke on behalf of the President to the Consultative Senate on September 6. He requested the Senate create an acting legislature to consider the change of the "national polity" from republic to monarchy.

On September 19, an organization called "National Citizens Union to Petition for Monarchy" was formed and it circulated a petition entreating President Yuan to become an emperor. The head of the organization was Shen Yunpei, a former Deputy Minister of Posts and Communications in the late Qing dynasty. One of the two associate heads was Zhang Zhenfang, a cousin of Yuan Shikai. Inexplicable to Liang Shiyi, *his* signature was on the petition. How strange, Liang thought. If someone forged his signature on a public petition, how many signatures might appear in secret communications? Whether he liked it or not, someone had made him an accomplice in silence.

Not content with limiting the propaganda for domestic consumption, Yuan's lackeys found an avenue to influence foreign opinion through one of Yuan's foreign advisers. Dr. Frank J. Goodnow, a professor from Columbia University and a former President of the American Political Science Association, published an article in which he stated that China was yearning for a symbol of central authority transcending the president and that the restoration of the monarchy would be good for the country if it met no opposition. A Japanese adviser to Yuan also extolled constitutional monarchy as the source of national strength in Japan as well as in Britain.

As Yuan approached the Temple of Heaven in one of his visits as the chief official to perform the public prayer to heaven, he must confront the question: Would his monarchical movement deserve to receive the Mandate of Heaven?

Moment of Truth

Sir John Jordan was reviewing the case of the arms purchase in China before meeting President Yuan on October 2, 1915. He had requested this interview reluctantly because it would mean blowing open the cover for the British government which he had worked so hard to maintain. But the situation was so desperate, he had to take this step in spite of the risk of exposure.

Jordan had taken all precautions before giving the go-ahead signal on June 25 to Edmund Backhouse to purchase arms on behalf of the British government. Backhouse was to act independently as a representative of John Brown & Co. except that he would report, only on important developments, to Jordan personally and confidentially. Backhouse seemed to be the right man for the job since he spoke Mandarin like a native and had a vast knowledge of Chinese personalities and events.

Within a week of the assignment, Backhouse reported to Jordan that he had located in various places over 150,000 Austrian and German-made rifles, complete with exact details of the type, caliber and year of production. The War Office was delighted with this news and urged him to proceed with utmost speed. Unfortunately Backhouse reported delays and further delays due to political intrigues. For reason of profound secrecy, pervading in all these deals, Backhouse could not divulge the names of the Chinese authorities with whom he had been in contact. Just when Jordan became impatient and suggested he would discuss the obstacles with President Yuan, Backhouse announced that the difficulties had disappeared and all seemed smooth sailing. By early August, Backhouse had secured over 100,000 rifles and about 350 Krupp machine guns. The War Office suggested the machine guns should probably be shipped through Vladivostok for the Russian front.

While the pace of negotiations with the mysterious Chinese officials quickened, the indefatigable Backhouse was discovering more and more arms. The War Office jumped at most of these new offers and sent instructions to the Governor of Hong Kong to be ready to inspect the arms on arrival. On August 27, Jordan was able to report that negotiations were complete and shipment to Hong Kong would soon begin.

On September 15, Backhouse reported the cargo ready to be on its way. A week later Jordan was able to send the good news to the Foreign Office that the flotilla carrying the cargo to Hong Kong left Shanghai for Fuzhou the night before. The information was obtained by Backhouse from the Chinese authorities who insisted on managing the whole business in their own way. Then on September 25, Backhouse announced a sudden hitch. Jordan was obliged to report to the Foreign Office, "Owing to strong protests from German and Austrian Legations, there is grave doubt whether the flotilla which has reached Fuchow (Fuzhou) will be allowed to proceed from there to Hong Kong." Jordan told Backhouse to warn the Chinese authorities that any further delay would necessitate his personal intervention with the President. That seemed to have scared the Chinese more than protests from the Germans and Austrians. The flotilla was reported to continue on its way.

After four days of anxious waiting, Backhouse reported another hitch which held up the arrival of the flotilla. The Chinese authorities attributed the delay to the Governor of Guangdong who was not a party to the transaction and had stopped the flotilla outside of Huizhou Bay. A helplessness overcame the experts in the Far Eastern Department of the Foreign Office. They could not even find Huizhou Bay in their vast collection of maps, and could only conclude the wily Governor of Guangdong had outsmarted his enemies in their internal squabble. The Under Secretary therefore gave Jordan full discretion to present "the argument which would appeal most strongly to the Canton Viceroy."

Jordan did not take that route. Instead, he went to see President Yuan in the afternoon of October 2. The President professed to know nothing about Backhouse's grandiose operation, although he was sympathetic to the British predicament. The Foreign Office in London was highly indignant at President Yuan's disclaimer, but Jordan did not lose patience. Four days later, he called on Liang Shiyi and received some encouraging news. Liang had met with Backhouse and was aware of his intention, Jordan reported. Although Liang had alerted some officials to help Backhouse if requested, he had no up-to-date information about Backhouse's activities. If Backhouse's report on the movement of ships was correct, the delay probably arose from the necessity of picking up different consignments on the way. Liang suggested that if the ships were now in Guangdong, the easiest solution would be to sail to Guangzhou. The ammunition could then be conveyed to Hong Kong by rail. With Liang's explanation, Jordan felt more hopeful of success.

After receiving an appeal from the Foreign Secretary to expedite the transaction on October 10, Jordan resolved to get to the bottom of the problem. He promptly obtained an interview with Liang Shiyi the next day and took Backhouse with him for a confrontation. Once he arrived at Liang's house, Jordan made Backhouse tell his whole story. Liang was very skeptical and said his statement to Jordan several days earlier was misunderstood. He did not participate directly or indirectly in Backhouse's transactions with other Chinese. He never expected Backhouse to have collected such a large quantity of arms which was far beyond what China could spare. Ships containing them could not possibly have moved without his knowledge since he was the Controller of Maritime Customs Service. He assured Jordan that he was quite willing to supply Britain with a moderate quantity of rifles, but not machine guns. He would send them by Chinese gunboat to Hong Kong. All in all, Liang professed to think Backhouse had been duped.

The Foreign Office expressed disappointment and amazement at the latest news. Could nothing be saved from the wreck? Fortunately, the two million pounds credited to the British Legation in Beijing had not actually been paid out. Sir Edward Grey, the Foreign Secretary, added a final memorandum in his own hand, "Liang Shiyi can hardly refuse after what he has said."

* * *

Liang Shiyi was really too preoccupied with his own security to worry about the British interest in purchasing arms in China. Several days after Jordan took Backhouse to visit him, Liang was surprised by another pronouncement from the prosecutor's office. On October 19, by the order of the President, Shiyi's friend, Zhao Qinghua, was censored and dismissed as the managing director of Tianjin-Pukou Railway, but he was free. Ye Gongchuo was found innocent in the case and was ordered reinstated as Deputy Minister of Communications, but he was not out of the woods yet. Ye was a defendant in another case since he was also the nominal supervisor of Guan Kenglin who was still in detention. Liang was horrified to see his friends twisting in the wind. Why was Ye reinstated at this time while the other case was still pending? Was that a bait to induce him to come back to Beijing? Liang wondered. Ye Gongchuo knew better and stayed in Tianjin.

In the morning of October 25, Sir John Jordan visited Liang Shiyi again. For a change, instead of the arms purchase, the topic of discussion was Yuan's plan to become emperor. "Can President Yuan at least delay if not forego the acceptance of a monarchy?" Sir John was probing. Liang Shiyi was apologetic. He could not, he said, influence such a decision. In the afternoon, Obata Yukichi, the Acting Japanese Minister in Beijing, came to Liang Shiyi's office to ask the same question and got the same answer. Three days later, the British, Japanese and Russian Ministers jointly requested an interview with the President during which they advised Yuan to postpone the implementation of monarchy. Yuan brushed off their advice by pleading ignorance of a specific plan.

By now not only Yuan's enemies but also some of his close friends began to desert him. On the pretext of illness, Xu Shichang resigned as Secretary of State, and Lu Zhengxiang was appointed to succeed him. Lu was the workhorse that Yuan could count on, particularly to deal with foreigners, at this difficult time. Yuan had to use strong-arm tactics to keep his cabinet in line.

On October 31, President Yuan decreed that the Bank of China and the Bank of Communications would henceforth be the official twin central-bank system. Actually, these two banks had become de facto central-bank system since March 1914 when they adopted by-laws to that effect. However, the decree had the effect of legitimizing government borrowing from these two banks without collateral. The President needed money for crowning himself. No wonder Ye Gongchuo was ordered reinstated to his position in the Ministry of Communications. He could represent the ministry in exercising his power as associate vice president in the Bank of Communications.

* * *

John Jordan had allowed Backhouse to continue his negotiations with his mysterious Chinese authorities in the forlorn hope of salvaging something from the deal. After a while, though, Jordan felt enough was enough, and decided to deal openly and directly with Liang Shiyi. On November 7, Jordan was accompanied by M. B. Kroupensk, the Russian Minister in Beijing, when he visited Liang Shiyi to discuss the arms purchase in China. Jordan expressed hope that President Yuan would facilitate such a transaction that would help both Britain and Russia in the European War. Liang promised Jordan a quick answer after talking to President Yuan.

When Liang went to see Yuan next day, Yuan smiled cunningly. "You have been meeting with foreign diplomats quite frequently in the last few months. Rumors circulating outside indicate you want to desert me. I have therefore ordered Zhu Qiqian to dispatch a telegram to provincial governors, in his name along with your name and that of Zhou Ziqi, urging them to support the monarchical movement before the foreign diplomats can organize any interference."

Liang was silent while Yuan continued. "Zhu Qiqian has finally come to his senses, and Zhou Ziqi should know better than wavering. After all, they are cabinet ministers. But why are you so stubborn, Shiyi? Why do you want to be on the outside?"

When Liang Shiyi remained silent, Yuan suddenly darkened, issuing a warning, "Don't get any idea that your defection from me will be welcomed by the generals revolting against me. After they learn about the telegram to the provincial governors, all three of you will be the target of their scorn."

Liang ignored Yuan's threat and went on to report Jordan's pleading for assistance in purchasing arms and ammunition in China. After some hesitation, Yuan gave his approval of a limited supply for transfer to the British government.

Within days, Liang informed Jordan that President Yuan had given orders to appropriate military authorities to collect 20,000 rifles and an adequate supply of ammunition to the British government. Such arms would be shipped through inland routes to Guangzhou, avoiding attacks by German submarines or surface ships on the Chinese coast. The President only insisted the British government receive the arms in Hong Kong to minimize the chance for detection by the German government. Zhao Qinghua, the English-speaking former managing director of Guangzhou-Kowloon Railways, recently released from detention, was assigned to contact the British officials in Hong Kong. He would supervise the shipment of arms in the last leg from Guangzhou to Hong Kong. "The quantity of arms will be modest and the process of collecting them will be slow," Jordan warned the Foreign Office in London, which replied cryptically, "We must be thankful for small mercies."

It would not be until January 1916 that some 24,000 rifles and a few canons were shipped to Hong Kong. Zhao Qinghua had arranged, with the cooperation of

Beijing Odyssey

Sir Henry May, Governor of Hong Kong, to ship these arms by Chinese gunboats through Pearl River and transfer them to a British cruiser in Hong Kong. Sidney Barton, the Chinese Secretary in the British Legation in Beijing, was on hand to inspect the delivery. The entire episode finally came to an end.

Like his colleagues in the Foreign Office, Jordan at first accepted the charitable view that Backhouse had been duped. As he reflected the sequence of events, Jordan gradually discovered many holes in Backhouse's story. How could Backhouse have found such a large quantity of arms in a short week? How could he single-handedly command the officials to arrange the shipment of the cargo? Indeed, how could he convince the Chinese authorities of his private firm's ability to pay without touching the two million pounds credited to the British Legation and designated for this purchase? Ultimately Jordan was forced to conclude that Backhouse's story, from beginning to end, was pure fabrication. Jordan was horrified to realize, in fact, he had been duped.

As Jordan realized he had been lied to by Backhouse, he felt totally humiliated. He was terrified by the thought that many of his colleagues in Beijing had used Backhouse as the source of information on Chinese politics. Much of such information were passed on, unfiltered, to the Foreign Office in London! However, he could not expose Backhouse's fabrications to his compatriots without acknowledging his own misjudgment. He decided to remain silent beyond suggesting to the Foreign Office that Backhouse should not be used for future missions. Jordan was fearful of ruining his distinguished career of almost four decades in China and Korea.

* * *

The news of the monarchical movement and the negative editorial comments about Liang Shiyi's role eventually caught the attention of his father in Hong Kong. An extremely cautious man, Shiyi's father was deeply concerned about the safety and reputation of his son. He sent his younger son, Shixu, to see Shiyi in Beijing. The meeting of the two brothers in Beijing was emotional. They both realized how little could be done to change the situation. Liang Shiyi was now trapped and was entirely at the mercy of Yuan unless he cooperated in the monarchical movement. He asked Shixu not to tell their father about the tight securities and other worrisome surveillance against him.

For his part, Shixu had become a very successful businessman in Hong Kong. He was not as naive as his father about Chinese politics even though he despised them. When his father told him to visit his brother in Beijing, Shixu agreed. He had another incentive to go there. A month earlier, Liang Shiyi had persuaded a friend to set up the Huimin Company in Hong Kong in preparation of sending Chinese laborers for non-combat duties in France. Although the company was secretly backed by Liang Shiyi, the new manager, Liang Rucheng, was supposed to act independently. While waiting to establish an office, the manager drafted a detailed contract for negotiation with the French government. Learning Shixu was going to Beijing, he asked Shixu to deliver the draft to his brother for review.

"Of all people, you've picked someone with a family name of Liang to be the manager of Huimin Company," Shixu said as he gave the package containing the draft contract to his brother. "Someone may think he's our relative."

"I've been accused of so many things, I've ceased to count them,' Liang Shiyi replied. "All I care about is whether my action can make a difference for the better. Liang Rucheng is a man of vision and he will look after the interest of the Chinese laborers."

Liang Shiyi kept the draft contract for several days and made some comments on the margins of several pages. When it was time for his brother to leave Beijing, Liang Shiyi gave the draft back to Shixu and said, "Show it to Ye Gongchuo in Tianjin on your way home." The brothers embraced in sadness before parting.

* * *

In November 1915, a special "National People's Representatives Assembly" was convened to deliberate the issue of monarchy. Noting this was a proof of Yuan's serious intention to become emperor, the British, Japanese, Russian and French governments *officially* asked President Yuan whether the implementation of monarchy could be postponed. Yuan's answer was provided November 20 when, by the action of the assembly, the monarchy was approved by an overwhelming majority. A monarchy was a step closer.

After deflecting the interference from foreign powers, Yuan was confident of the success of the monarchical movement. He also believed Liang Shiyi was now under his full control and he could let go of the last of Liang's friends still under detention. By the order of the President, the prosecutor resolved the case against Guan Kenglin on December 5. Ye Gongchuo and Lin Zhenyao, husband of Shiyi's niece, charged as accomplices to Guan Kenglin, were found innocent and restored to their positions in the Ministry of Communications.

On December 11, representatives of various provinces petitioned in the name of the people that Yuan consent to become emperor of China. After a polite declination on grounds he lacked virtues, he acceded when a second petition was received the next day. He decreed that 1916 would mark the beginning of his new reign which, ironically, would be named the Glorious Constitution (Hongxian).

To commemorate the solemn occasion of a new reign, Zhu Qiqian was appointed Director of Coronation Ceremony on December 19. Although Zhu was asked to handle the sticky legal formality, the lavish celebration was placed in the hands of Yang Shiqi. Yang had been in the shadow in the past year, conspiring with Yuan's eldest son, Yuan Keding, to form what was known as the "crown prince clique" to push for the monarchy. He could now reap his rewards and Yuan Keding would no doubt become the crown prince. Yuan Shikai placed an order at the former imperial potteries for a 40,000-piece porcelain dinner set costing 1.4 million yuan. He also ordered a large jade seal befitting an emperor and two imperial robes at 400,000 yuan each for the ceremony.

* * *

During all these maneuvers, General Cai E, who had been shadowed by Yuan's secret operatives since October, quietly slipped out of Beijing and headed back to his native Yunnan Province via Tokyo, Japan. His political mentor, Liang Qichao, also reached Tianjin safely in early December. According to a prearranged plan, as General Cai E reached Yunnan Province, he would start a revolt against Yuan's monarchy movement. Liang Qichao would then go to Shanghai to arouse public opinion to support the revolt. While Liang Qichao waited for news in Tianjin, he visited Ye Gongchuo.

"I would like to send a personal message to Liang Shiyi and urge him to come to Tianjin," Liang Qichao said. "Do you have any way to pass the note to him safely?"

"I've not been in contact with him for quite some time," Ye replied. "If he could come to Tianjin, he would have come and stayed long ago. He has been overconfident. He thought he could part with Yuan amicably whenever he wanted. But under Yuan's devious and subtle maneuver, he had only the choice of defecting and letting his friends be executed, or staying and ruining his own reputation. 1 was lucky enough to have left before Yuan's long arms could reach me. No one can induce me back to Beijing right now."

Liang Qichao wrote a short note to Liang Shiyi anyway. "In this hour of crisis, I would like very much to meet you in Tianjin. If you can spare the time, please do come." He looked at the calendar and dated the note December 4. He asked a mutual friend to take it to Liang Shiyi in person, but he did not receive a response. Two weeks later, Liang Qichao sailed for Shanghai and joined in a new quest to save the Republic.

Sudden Retreat

The New Year celebration of 1916 was muted in the Presidential Palace, now the Imperial Palace, on the first day of the reign of the Glorious Constitution. The President, now the new Emperor, encircled himself with his closest advisers to discuss the postponement of his coronation. Yang Shiqi, the Senior Councillor of the Privy Council, in charge of the elaborate celebration for coronation, was fuming at the suggestion of the delay by some cabinet members. "There's no end to the timidity of the faint hearted," Yang barked at his colleagues. "Let's stop this talk of defeatists." Yuan Shikai overruled him, suggesting a compromise. "For the time being, all government business with the outside world will still be conducted in the name of the Republic but the reign of the Glorious Constitution will be adopted inside the palace." Yang stormed out of the room. It was all very confusing.

The delay of the coronation was not a change of heart on Yuan's part. It was forced upon him by a sequence of unexpected events. As General Cai E arrived in Yunnan Province from Japan via Vietnam on December 19, 1915, he and several other generals immediately staged a revolt against Yuan Shikai's monarchy. On December 25, they jointly announced the independence of Yunnan Province. Within days, the revolt in Yunnan suddenly spread like wildfire throughout the nation. In the meantime, Liang Qichao turned on his considerable skills in fanning the flame of public opinion against the monarchical movement in Shanghai. Yuan Shikai became greatly alarmed.

By now, Liang Shiyi was more worried about the aftermath of Yuan's demise than his ascension to the throne. He believed Yuan could never succeed in rallying the country behind the monarchy, and would damage the fragile unity of the nation permanently. He decided to take an active role to convince Yuan that his monarchical movement was futile. He hoped to enlist the help of Zhou Ziqi and Zhu Qiqian who were still close to the President.

On January 4, 1916, Liang Shiyi went to the Palace for the customary New Year's greeting. Liang caught Yuan Shikai in a depressed state. With his eyes looking blankly toward the ceiling, Yuan was unresponsive to Liang's suggestion that China should declare war against Germany in order to strengthen China's position in the post-war peace conference. Yuan's thoughts seemed to wander aimlessly when Liang told him the monarchical movement had damaged China's reputation abroad. Suddenly Yuan pulled out two documents from his drawer and showed them to Liang. The first was a letter from the Prime Minister of Japan which vaguely praised his achievements without a word about the monarchy. The second was a verbatim transcript of his recent conversations with Sir John Jordan in which Jordan seemed to endorse constitutional monarchy for China.

After Liang finished reading the documents, he placed them on the desk. Yuan looked at him. "These documents don't seem to bear out your fear about the damage to our international reputation. If you get a chance to see Jordan, try to find out for yourself whether his expression of support to me is sincere."

On hearing this remark, Liang knew he had not succeeded in diminishing Yuan's determination to hold on to the monarchy. He took a different tack. "It may seem the throne is within your grasp when your dubious friends give you the impression of endorsement. But wait until they are no longer interested in placating you. I've already heard ominous rumblings. How many emperors in Chinese history who abdicated their thrones could save their heads? It's better to change your mind before it is too late." Yuan stared again at the ceiling. He had not been moved by Liang's pleading.

Two days later, Zhou Ziqi came to see Liang Shiyi. "I must discuss with you privately on this important matter," Zhou began. "I've been asked by President Yuan to be his special envoy to Japan for the purpose of delivering a highest Presidential Award to the Emperor Taisho. The Chinese Minister in Japan had been instructed to notify the Japanese government."

"What did President Yuan instruct you to say in Japan?" Liang asked.

"Simply put," Zhou replied, "he wants to gain the support of Japanese government for his ascension to the throne."

Liang then told Zhou of the two documents Yuan had shown him in the Presidential Palace.

"My goodness." Zhou sighed, "How could Yuan be so blind? He will be at their mercy. He will be the laughingstock of the world if the Japanese turn from him. What should I do?"

You should stall your departure as long as possible and see what happens," Liang advised him.

A few days later, Lu Zhongyu, the Chinese Minister in Japan, reported to Yuan that Zhou's visit to Japan had been approved by the Japanese government. On January 14, Hioki Eki, the Japanese Minister in Beijing, invited Zhou to a farewell dinner on the eve of his departure. The next morning, Zhou received an urgent message from the Japanese Minister that the Japanese government had second thoughts and asked Zhou to cancel his trip to Japan. But Zhou's plan had already been leaked to the Japanese press. One editorial commented that since Yuan Shikai would soon be an emperor, the Presidential Award would be worthless and, in fact, quite an insult to Emperor Taisho. Four days later, the Japanese government sent Yuan a warning of military intervention if he did not delay the monarchy. When Liang Shiyi heard about the news, he could only echo Zhou's comment, "How could Yuan be so blind?"

Liang Shiyi had no intention of checking with Sir John Jordan about his true feeling toward the monarchy as Yuan had suggested. It was humiliating enough to suffer in silence. Why should anyone be so foolish as to invite more insult? Liang could only console himself with the thought that he had received Yuan's approval to collect arms for the British before the revolt against the monarchy broke out. As a result, at least some rifles and a few cannons were delivered to British authorities in late January. It was not the large quantity that he had hoped to provide, but given the current condition in China, it was the best that he could manage.

For his tenacity in personal diplomacy, Liang Shiyi at least succeeded in convincing the French government of the merit of using Chinese laborers for non-combat duties in Europe. Upon the recommendation of Conty, the French Minister to Beijing, the French Army sent Colonel Truptil in the guise as an "agricultural expert" to Beijing in January 1916 to negotiate a labor contract with the Huimin Company. Liang Shiyi outlined his plan to Colonel Truptil and emphasized that Chinese laborers must be given the same rights as French laborers in the labor contract. After taking initial steps of seeking tacit approval of the Foreign Ministry and obtaining credits from the Bank of Communications, Liang turned over the detailed negotiation to Liang Rucheng, Manager of the Huimin Company of Hong Kong.

Since the agreement included specific terms about qualifications, payment, medical care, travel expenses, interpreters and other considerations for the benefit of the laborers, it took months to finalize the document. Liang Rucheng was particularly careful in reviewing all provisions to eliminate unequal treatment that had characterized previous contracts with foreigners when sending Chinese laborers abroad. On May 14, 1916, the agreement was signed by Colonel Truptil, representing the French government, and Liang Rucheng of Huimin Company. Colonel Truptil also agreed to station one of his assistants in Beijing for settling any future problems arising from the agreement.

* * *

At the instigation of General Cai E, on New Year's Day, the regional leaders in Yunnan Province had named General Tang Jiyao the Military Governor. They declared the formation of a Republic Protection Army to fight against Yuan Shikai and their troops moved toward the neighboring Guizhou, Sichuan and Hunan Provinces. President Yuan ordered his generals to resist, but Guizhou Province declared its independence on January 27 and Guangxi Province followed on March 15. During this period, many of Yuan's Beiyang generals had no interest in fighting for Yuan's monarchy. Two of his leading generals, Duan Qirui and Feng Guozhang, declined in tandem the appointment as the commander of the expedition army on the pretext of illness. Even the most loyal supporter of the Qing monarchy, the reactionary General Zhang Xun, did not follow Yuan's order to move his troop to launch an attack on the Republic Protection Army.

Beijing Odyssey

On March 17, Liang Shiyi received a phone call from Yuan Shikai, asking him to come to the Presidential Palace. Upon his arrival, Liang sensed Yuan had completely lost touch with reality. Pointing ruefully to a stack of telegrams and letters, Yuan asked Liang to read them. Liang quickly sorted through the pile of reports about the losses in raging battles and personal messages urging the cancellation of the monarchy. He was particularly impressed by a telegram sent by five Beiyang generals stationed in the coastal provinces, including General Zhang Xun. They urged Yuan to cancel the monarchy to avoid total military disaster. Even Yuan's old crony, Xu Shichang, sent him a letter, pleading, "Don't lose your last chance to return to the right track." But most alarming was a telegram from Lu Zhongyu, the Chinese Minister in Japan, stating that a Palace Conference had been called by the Emperor of Japan to study the possibility of sending troops to China to maintain peace.

When Liang finished reading, Yuan said to him, "I've made up my mind to cancel the monarchy. I intend to ask Xu Shichang and General Duan Qirui to take charge of the government and General Feng Guozhang to handle the military affairs on the war front. I need your help now more than ever. Can you move into one of the guest houses in the palace compound and help me in this transition period?"

Liang Shiyi was reluctant. Was this another plot to tighten the noose around his neck? Or had Yuan lost confidence of those around him who would resist his order for cancelling the monarchy? Then Liang thought of the consequences of not responding to Yuan at this critical moment. Given Yuan's unstable mental condition, Liang felt he could at least buttress Yuan's professed desire to cancel the monarchy and avert a bloody civil war. Testing Yuan's real intention, he said cautiously, "If you issue an order to stop the fighting, I shall move in to help you until Xu Shichang arrives from Tianjin."

"I want you to stay here right now," Yuan sounded desperate. "Your chauffeur can pick up your daily necessities if you call home to get things ready." Liang went to the phone and asked his fourth lady to pack a suitcase. He also asked her to come along to spend a few days in the presidential palace. After making the arrangements, Liang returned to his chair.

"Please draft a telegram for me to General Chen Huan of Sichuan, asking him to negotiate a cease fire with General Cai E," Yuan said. "General Chen has been my most loyal general in suppressing the revolt." Then he looked straight in the eyes of Liang Shiyi and mumbled, "Have you read the long letter from Kang Youwei? I guess this is his way of getting back at me."

"Yes, I have," Liang replied. He was surprised Yuan would bring up the subject. There was no love lost between the two men since the failure of the "one hundred days of reform" in 1898. Kang's letter was a most penetrating analysis of Yuan's predicament, with some well-reasoned advice interspersed with highly critical and sarcastic remarks. Liang remembered Kang's ringing statement in summing up Yuan's place in history, "For ordinary mortals, there is a time to retire after fulfilling one's wish of attaining the most prestigious status of commanding general or prime minister. If you had died of illness four years ago, you would have been honored for your achievements far beyond the wildest dreams in the life time of any man—from an unknown plebeian to the Commanding General and Prime Minister of the Qing Empire and the President of the Chinese Republic! Granted that you may be greedier than most people, you should still be satisfied for having ingratiated yourself with the grandeur of an emperor for a few months. But if you continue to occupy the public office any longer, you will be remembered as a traitor who has betrayed the trust of the Republic."

"Please draft a response to Kang Youwei for me, asking him to persuade his friend Liang Qichao to stop agitating the whole nation against me." Yuan was almost in tears but Liang was silent. How could Kang's letter, which contained such gems of wisdom, be answered?

After a long pause, Yuan continued. "Since Liang Qichao is your old friend, can you send him a personal letter advising him to mediate between the Beijing government and the leaders of the revolt? Tell him I'll sacrifice to any extent if peace and stability can be restored to the nation." Liang Shiyi was now convinced Yuan's intention of canceling the monarchy was sincere.

* * *

Early the next morning, Liang Shiyi and his fourth lady looked out from the window of their building in the palace compound at Zhongnanhai which served as their temporary home. A few ripples played on the smooth surface of the lake stirred by a sudden breeze. The willows beside the lake waved as if to welcome them to their new abode. The azalea and rhododendron near the building competed with each other in their full glory. A place so pleasant, it would be ideal for long vacation.

But Liang Shiyi was not here for a vacation. His fourth lady had been his constant companion in the last five years, serving as his valet as well as his lover. He chose to bring her along even though he left the rest of the family at home. He was certain his wife would not be interested in the beautiful palace compound. She and his second lady were too occupied in taking care of their children.

On March 20, Yuan Shikai called an emergency meeting of important government officials: the Secretary of State, the cabinet ministers, the members of the Consultative Senate, members of the judiciaries including the Chief of the Supreme Court. During the meeting, Yuan announced his reluctant decision to give up the throne. He also agreed to issue an edict abolishing the reign of the Glorious Constitution immediately. With his resolve, the dream of crowning himself in the long-anticipated coronation vanished.

Liang Shiyi waited throughout the day in the guest house. No word came from the Presidential Palace. In the evening Liang got a call from Zhu Qiqian, the Interior Minister, with an urgent message, "President's Yuan's eldest son, Yuan Keding, has blocked a formal announcement. What can be done?"

"We must shore up President Yuan's resolve before he changes his mind." Liang was frantic. "Come to the palace immediately. We'll go see him and convince him of the seriousness of the delay. This is a most critical moment. Don't miss this chance."

The meeting lasted late into the night. Yuan agonized over his decision. In the end, however, he agreed to reprove his son and issue the announcement on March 22. It was pointed out that he would need to act immediately to stabilize the government. President Yuan took heed, reactivating the Acting Legislative Council, and appointed Xu Shichang as the new Secretary of State and General Duan Qirui as the new Army Chief of Staff.

Three days later, March 25, Zhu Qiqian confided to Liang Shiyi, "President Yuan has just ordered me to return to the Consultative Senate the document authorizing him to accept the monarchy. He wants the Acting Legislative Council to vote for the restoration of all laws prior to his acceptance of the monarchy. Why such elaborate formality?"

Liang Shiyi shuddered. "This is ominous. It could mean he wants to establish himself firmly as the legitimate President of the Republic under the constitutional covenant. It could also signal other desires. I thought, after reading the letter from Kang Youwei, he might consider retiring from public life once a cease fire can be arranged."

"That's not how I read his mind," Zhu remarked. "He's struggling to hold onto his power. He has just appointed Zhou Ziqi to take charge of the affairs of the Bank of China. With you at the helm of the Bank of Communications, he probably feels secure, that he can tap the resources of both banks to wage war.

"That's an illusion. He could bankrupt both banks quickly," Liang said. "I hope Xu Shichang will arrive to take charge soon. He has his job cut out for him."

In fact Liang Shiyi himself had a job to do. As Director of the Domestic Bond Bureau, he had to initiate the 1916 bond drive in response to the request of the Finance Ministry. Not only was his heart not in this work, no one in his right mind would purchase bonds issued by such a shaky government. Out of a target of 20 million yuan, the drive netted only 7 million, and only from sources obligated to comply. No one should be surprised at the difference between this drive and the successful one of 1914 or even the moderately successful one of 1915!

Xu Shichang finally arrived to assume the office of the Secretary of State. He immediately sought ways to make peace with the Republic Protection Army. He ordered General Chen Huan in Sichuan to discuss a ceasefire with General Cai E who was directing the offensive drive in Sichuan. But could Yuan's new administration survive the rising tide of opposition?

Unwept, Unhonored and Unsung

"We will move out of Zhongnanhai as soon as possible," Liang Shiyi told his fourth lady after President Yuan agreed to let him go home. With the help of their chauffeur, they were soon on their way.

Liang knew the task of reconciliation with those revolting against Yuan Shikai was far from over. Already, Tang Shaoyi and Wu Tingfang had sent an open telegram from Shanghai to challenge Yuan's legal status as president of the Republic. Their telegram stated in part, "Although the monarchy was cancelled, Yuan Shikai's credentials for president was voided when he made himself an emperor. It is unlawful now for him to transform himself from emperor to president. For the sake of the nation, it is best for him to retire from public life." The generals of the Republic Protection Army also requested that Yuan resign immediately. Even Yuan's closest Beiyang generals echoed this sentiment and privately urged Yuan to retire. Only the reactionary General Zhang Xun insisted he would fight to the end to keep Yuan in power.

Liang called Zhou Ziqi on the telephone, "The current situation is as dangerous as the period before President Yuan gave up his monarchical dream. We must find ways to persuade him to retire from public life."

"William Donald visited me yesterday and said the same thing," Zhou replied. "Perhaps we should get together to discuss this matter." So it was settled that the three would meet in Liang's residence at Ganshiqiao Lane.

Donald was impatient the minute he arrived and rushed to express his opinion, "I told you two last month that the cancellation of the monarchy alone won't do. You must try to get Yuan out of his office."

"We must do one thing at a time, and the first thing first," Liang answered calmly. "Kang Youwei suggested to Yuan that one possible course of action was for him to retire to a foreign country where he cannot plot a return to power. In fact, Yuan once told Kang he had longed to be a sojourner in London. Perhaps a trip to England is the best solution for him."

"I can contact Sir John Jordan to make the necessary arrangements," Donald said. "In the meantime, you both work on Yuan. Calm him down for the time being."

The next few days, Donald called Liang Shiyi almost incessantly. Serving as

Donald's interpreter, Roy Anderson told Liang that Sir John was unwilling to arrange Yuan's retirement in England because he still thought Yuan was the only man who could hold the country together. Donald had also contacted Dr. Reinsch, the American Minister, who was willing to transmit Donald's request to Washington.

* * *

In the meantime, Liang Shiyi received a cable from Liang Qichao, a reply to his plea for understanding after Yuan had cancelled the Monarchy. A month earlier, Liang Qichao secretly left the safety of the International Settlement in Shanghai on board a Japanese steamship for south China. After arriving in Guangxi Province, he joined the Republic Protection Army against Yuan. Liang Shiyi's message to Liang Qichao finally reached him in Guangxi on April 16. Liang Qichao's reply was a lecture to both Yuan and Liang. It stated in earnest his thought:

"Your message touches a cord of resonance in my heart! My hope for peace and love of justice has long been known to you. But contemptuous politics have cruelly made the situation so hopeless, and I have no choice but to part company with you in tears. You are a wise judge of men and events. Based on the record of palace intrigues and manipulations in the past four years, can you in good conscience project a future with a ray of bright light? The proclamation and cancellation of the monarchy have become almost trivial, considering that they can be changed back and forth at will. The greatest pain inflicted on the people of this nation is Yuan's travesty and skillful distortion of the political system to fool the people. Once he has lost the trust of the people, whatever he now proclaims is nothing but a piece of paper not even worthy of the ink on it. I too am concerned about foreign interference if the battles continue unabated for a long time. We all know that such a course of action is not good for the nation. But if we do not get rid of the root of all evils, how can the people find peace and justice? Even if I try to shrink from my duty to fight these transgressions, how can I convince the generals in the Southwest to do the same? If I can persuade them, how can they answer the call of the people throughout the nation? Yuan Shikai so loves his power and position that he is trigger happy to slaughter the people. If I had to wait for someone else to do the job of getting rid of him, I should be ashamed of myself and rightfully be blamed for inaction. As an erstwhile friend of Yuan, I do not want to see him end up as a traitor. Since Guangdong Province has just declared its independence, the situation becomes even more urgent. You should also think about your own future."

For the first time, Liang Shiyi sensed the anger of Liang Qichao toward him. He realized a peaceful settlement would be impossible unless Yuan retired from public life. The difficulty was to convince Yuan that such an action would be for his best interest as well as the nation's. Liang Shiyi showed the letter to Xu Shichang and Duan Qirui who agreed with his assessment. Then Liang Shiyi went to Yuan's office. Yuan was sitting behind his desk, absorbed in thought. Cautiously Liang Shiyi gave Yuan the reply from Liang Qichao. Without uttering a word, Yuan read carefully, stopping from time to time to write comments in the margin regarding specific statements.

Beside one statement, "Yuan's travesty and skillful distortion of the political system to fool the people," Yuan wrote, "cabinet, senate," meaning they were the responsible parties. Next to the statement, "Yuan Shikai so loves his power and position that he is trigger happy to slaughter the people," he noted, "They attacked Sichuan and Hunan Provinces first." In answering the claim, "If I had to wait for someone else to do the job of getting rid of him, I should be ashamed of myself and rightfully be blamed for inaction," Yuan added, "Does destroying the government make him a hero?" Finally at the end of telegram, he wrote, "End all fighting," his way of saying that ending the fighting would be the only solution.

Quietly Liang Shiyi walked out of Yuan's office with the telegram. It was clear to him that Yuan was not willing to give up the presidency. Shiyi could see no end to confrontation between the two sides.

As bad news continued to pour in from all battle fronts, Xu Shichang resigned as the Secretary of State on April 23. Duan Qirui was appointed to succeed him.

* * *

On May 1, a joint command of armies in Guangdong and Guangxi was established. These generals represented a wide spectrum of political persuasions, but they were united in fighting against Yuan's forces. Within a week, their troops captured cities in Fujian and Hunan Provinces.

In separate moves, the opponents of Yuan urged Vice President Li Yuanhong to force Yuan's resignation and take over the government under the provisional constitution of 1912. They also cabled Duan Qirui, urging him to resign as Secretary of State.

In a move indicating a tacit concession to at least the resemblance of a responsible cabinet system, Yuan abolished the Privy Council and changed the title of Duan Qirui from Secretary of State to Premier. However, the Consultative Senate appointed by Yuan remained intact.

By then people had completely lost faith in the Beijing government, including the banknotes issued by the Bank of China and the Bank of Communications. Yuan had dipped his hands into these two banks to finance government operations and to finance his extravagant preparations for crowning himself. The people struck back. They demanded silver coins instead of banknotes for ordinary business transactions. As a result, the values of the banknotes depreciated considerably in the black market. In order to forestall a run on government banks, Duan Qirui discussed the problem with various financial experts, including Liang Shiyi. The government was unable to obtain foreign loans to finance its huge budget deficit resulting from military expenditure, but it had to print more banknotes to avoid bankruptcy, in spite of the threat of inflation. Between a rock and a hard place, the government ordered the Bank of China and the Bank of Communications to stop the exchange of banknotes for silver coins on May 12. The order also restricted the amount of cash withdrawals from deposits in these two banks. When the news was announced, the values of the banknotes dropped precipitously overnight to only two thirds of their face value. In light of the debacle, the finance minister resigned and Zhou Ziqi was appointed as his successor on May 20. But even Zhou Ziqi's magic could not save the day.

When William Donald received word from the American Minister that Yuan could relocate to the United States, Donald, in the company of Zhou Ziqi, went again to Liang Shiyi's home at Ganshiqiao Lane. By then, Yuan had told Liang he would not accept exile abroad as a condition for his retirement.

"What are his conditions then?" Donald inquired.

"He wants to retire to his native Zhangde," Liang replied. "He needs guaranteed safety for himself and his family. But who will or can provide such a guarantee?"

"Let me see if I can persuade the revolutionary leaders to accept such a condition," Donald said. "I'll leave for Shanghai tomorrow."

* * *

Sun Yatsen, in exile in Tokyo since August 1913, had returned to China in late April to join the fight against Yuan. In his hideout in the French Concession in Shanghai, he issued a declaration asking all opponents of Yuan, in all political parties, to unite and demand the restoration of the provisional constitution of 1912. His close friend, Huang Xing, in exile in the United States, left San Francisco for China in late April. On his stop at Tokyo on June 1, he lent his support to Sun's declaration in an open telegram. The voices of Yuan's opponents grew louder each day.

On May 22, Yuan Shikai received a copy of an open telegram sent by General Chen Huan, Yuan's point man in Sichuan. The telegram explained to the nation how painful it was for Chen to declare independence of Sichuan Province against Yuan's rule. Gripping the telegram in his hand, Yuan shook with anger, muttering, "He was a trusted friend, a confidant. He has betrayed me!" From then on, Yuan fell into a state of depression, showing little interest in state affairs. Even then, although he became an irrelevant figure, no one could push him over the brink. He would not resign from the presidency.

As if Heaven was repudiating his mandate, Yuan was removed from office by a power higher than his own. On June 6, 1916, Yuan Shikai died of uremia after a brief illness. He was 56.

Shortly after Yuan Shikai's death, many provinces cancelled their declaration of independence. Vice President Li Yuanhong took over the rein and announced a state funeral to honor Yuan's distinguished public service. He authorized a generous sum, a quarter of a million yuan, to pay for the event. Yuan's close friend, Xu Shichang, was appointed the chairman of the funeral committee, with several cabinet ministers as committee members.

Yuan's coffin was placed in state in Beijing for two weeks before it was taken for burial to his native Zhangde in Henan Province on board a special train equipped with private cars for distinguished guests. The members of the funeral committee, other high government officials and the governors of many provinces took this train to Zhangde. Since Yuan had initiated a grandiose plan for his final resting place, including a gigantic mausoleum surrounded by trees on a twenty-acre plot next to his mansion, even the generous amount allotted by the government was insufficient to cover the expenses. The funeral committee had to appeal to Yuan's influential friends for contributions to double the government's allotment. The entire group stayed in Yuan's mansion at Zhangde for seven days until after the burial on June 28. Liang Shiyi was among those, paying his last respect to his one-time mentor, benefactor and tormentor.

Among many couplets mourning Yuan's death, the one composed by Yang Du, the leader of the Peace Planning Society, posed the most intriguing questions: "Has republicanism hurt China? Or has China given a bad name to republicanism? Let this debate be renewed a hundred years later. / Has constitutional monarchy done injustice to you? Or have you betrayed constitutional monarchy? Think it over when you journey to eternity."

Many of Yuan's friends attending the funeral wondered.

To the people of China, there was no disagreement about Yuan's betrayal of the Republic and his shameless drive to become emperor. His action went beyond reasonable ambition, intolerable not only to his critics but even to his own followers. In spite of the fanfare created by his funeral committee, Yuan was unwept, unhonored and unsung by his countrymen.

The Fugitive

Upon the death of Yuan Shikai, Vice President Li Yuanhong took over the reign of the government. A modest and decent man, Li did not have a power base of his own. He had to deal gingerly with the Beiyang generals who urged him to follow the Constitutional Covenant of 1914. On the other hand, he was being pressured by the leaders of the revolting generals in south China to respect the Provisional Constitution of 1912. Those in the south also wanted him to punish those behind Yuan's monarchical movement. Trying to please both sides, Li was indecisive and ineffective. Those critical of him began to refer to him as the "clay Buddha," a patient and merciful god who could not even protect himself from destruction.

One of the first acts of President Li Yuanhong was to send word to Liang Shiyi through an emissary, "I need you to handle the financial crisis. Please feel at ease to stay on and help me." But Liang knew he would be the easy target if President Li acceded to the demands of the leaders in south China. He also knew the looming infighting of the Beiyang generals could cause him to be sacrificed as a scapegoat. In anticipation of these troubles, Liang Shiyi tendered his resignation as Controller of Maritime Customs Service and Director of Domestic Bonds Bureau.

Liang also went to see Ye Gongchuo who had just returned to Beijing to resume his duties in the Ministry of Communications. Liang confided to him, "I have decided to leave Beijing with my family until the dust settles here."

"How about the business of the Bank of Communications during your absence?" Ye inquired.

"Since the private shares of the bank outnumber the public shares," Liang replied, "I don't think there will be any change in my position as president of the bank until the next meeting of the board of directors. That's several months down the road. The board's decision will depend, of course, on my own fate in the hands of the government. In the meantime, as associate vice president and representative of the Ministry of Communications in the bank, you will have to shoulder a lot more responsibilities. I'll be available for consultation in Hong Kong."

On June 29, the day after Yuan's burial in Zhangde, Li Yuanhong gave in to the demands of the leaders in south China and adopted the 1912 Provisional Constitution until a new constitution could be approved. He also abolished the Consultative Senate and reconvened the old Parliament. President Li tried to build a coalition government by appointing General Duan Qirui as Premier and Minister of Army, and Tang Shaoyi as Foreign Minister.

Liang Shiyi and his family left for Tianjin on July 10, where they would wait for passage to Hong Kong. Four days later, the government announced the names of the conspirators of the monarchical movement and issued an arrest warrant for eight persons. Liang Shiyi was not surprised his name was on the list in spite of his protestation of innocence. What did surprise him was that, of the six sponsors of the Peace Planning Society, only two were included, but the names of the head and associate heads of the National Citizens Union to Petition for Monarchy were nowhere to be found. Yang Shiqi, who conspired with the "crown prince" to promote the monarchy from its inception, did not make the list, while other names on the list included a curious assortment of people: the chief of the Bureau for Organizing the Legislature; a secretary in the President's Office; the editor of Asian Daily in Shanghai; and Liang Shiyi and his two close friends Zhu Qiqian and Zhou Ziqi. The arrest warrant concluded by stating that "all other persons who participated in the monarchical movement will be pardoned."

* * *

After learning about the issuance of the arrest warrant of Liang Shiyi, Ye Gongchuo rushed to Tianjin. "This is the most outrageous act," Ye stormed into Liang's hotel in the French Concession with his aide Zheng Hongnian. "You don't deserve this insult. You should give your side of the story to the public."

Liang was philosophical. "After my name was forged on documents supporting the monarchical movement, no outsiders would believe I was not involved in the conspiracy."

Ye was not convinced., "Your name was forged on the documents only because they needed to ride on the coattails of someone who could inspire trust. Many people who were active and vocal in supporting the monarchical movement are escaping punishment. It's totally unfair to you."

"People also blamed me for allowing Yuan's government to borrow heavily from the Bank of Communications," Liang said in introspection, "Some of the money, no doubt, went to his monarchical movement."

"You were a captive under Yuan's surveillance," Ye argued. "My own head was almost on the block and was saved by your quick thinking. Your other friends were not so lucky. If you had refused to cooperate, at least passively, their heads would have rolled! You should not be responsible for any action under duress."

"In the old Chinese tradition, I should have been courageous enough to ignore his threats and be willing to die for principle. Since I did not take that action, what can I now say?"

"But you were only trying to save the necks of your colleagues. That was noble enough for me."

"Don't you see, this is precisely the reason for the arrest warrant for me." Liang was resigned to his fate. "Of all the cabinet ministers, only Zhu Qiqian and Zhou Ziqi are included in the arrest warrant. The three of us are viewed as the leading members of the so called Communication Clique who can rally the support of a group of competent civil servants and others in business. Those who want to take over the government in the current power struggle want to capture this useful base to serve their own purpose."

Under normal circumstances, Ye was levelheaded, but he was enraged. Finally, he sat down and rested his head in his hands. "I see that I will be a pawn in another power struggle after having been spared only so recently from the previous one. I can only admire your magnanimity, Shiyi."

"Look, Gongchuo," Liang was touched by Ye's sincere concern. "Yuan Shikai is dead. Whatever epitaph the people may have for him, he can no longer defend himself. I don't want to join the chorus of detractors. If I can redeem myself through my service to the cause of peace and unity of the nation in the future, all will be forgiven. If I fail to do that, any denial of my responsibility in the monarchical movement will not clear my name in the harsh judgment of history."

With a bow to acknowledge his respect, Ye Gongchuo left with his aide. On the train back to Beijing, Zheng Hongnian commented to Ye, "I have never seen someone who can be so calm in the face of adversity. Liang Shiyi does not attempt to defend himself at all."

Ye remarked sadly, "The impact of the arrest warrant has not sunk in his mind, yet. He's now a fugitive and cannot return to public service if he doesn't try to convince the public of his innocence."

"I have learned a lesson from the misfortune of Liang Shiyi," Zheng said, "Never brood upon the past. Always think of the future. Ambitious and undisciplined demigods will rush to destroy others for their own gain. If we really want to serve our country in these difficult times, we are bound to meet criticisms. We must let our conscience dictate our actions and do our best. No one can change the verdict of history by manipulating public opinion. All politicians should be reminded of this plain and humble truth."

* * *

On July 22, Liang Shiyi and his family left Tianjin for Hong Kong on board a British steamship. He was overjoyed to find his father in excellent health and to see other members of the extended family upon their arrival in Hong Kong. His brother Shixu's two consorts immediately ordered the servants to rearrange their living quarters to make room for Liang Shiyi's entire family: his wife and two concubines, two boys and five girls including his niece Wosheng.

His son Dingji had been in the United States for three years, attending Phillips Academy in Andover, Massachusetts. His oldest daughter Haoyin had gone to the United States a year earlier, and was now attending Vassar College in Poughkeepsie, New York. Her fiance, Guan Zuzhang, was an engineering student at Rensselaer

Polytechnic Institute in Troy, New York.

Now eighteen years old, Dingji had been dating a girl in Boston whose father was Chinese and whose mother was American. When he deliberately leaked the news and the background of this girl to his mother through a friend who returned to Hong Kong, Madam was very upset. She would be upstaged by someone who probably wouldn't subscribe to the Confucian code of filial devotion. She would miss the chance to become a traditional Chinese mother-in-law with all the authorities she could exercise over her poor daughter-in-law. She told her husband to squash their son's idea of marrying the girl in Boston.

In spite of his high position in public life, Liang Shiyi always paid attention to his wife's authority in family affairs. He tried to meet her demands more than halfway, maintaining a harmonious atmosphere in his family—at least on the surface. Now that he had plenty of time on hand, he wrote a long letter to Dingji about the Madam's, and his own, expectation of a daughter-in-law. Toward the end of the missive, he added, "In anticipation of your return for summer vacation, your mother and I had planned to introduce you to a few very refined girls from respectable families in Hong Kong. Since you have now decided to stay in the United States this summer, we have told these families and their daughters not to wait any longer. If you find any Chinese girl who can meet the expectation of our family, please inform your mother and myself so that we can guide your decision." Being the oldest surviving son of Liang Shiyi, Dingji was expected to fulfill not just his own destiny, nor just the expectations of his parents. Instead, it was assumed that he would fulfill the expectations of his grandfather and the entire extended family. As a respectful son, Dingji must heed his father's words. The letter settled the problem of Dingji's marriage—at least for awhile.

In his leisure time, Liang Shiyi often spent his evenings at Wuben Club, a gentlemen's club at the west end of Hong Kong Harbor. There, he and the other members of this private club of the wealthy and powerful mingled in a district studded with houses of disrepute. Some of Liang's friends in Wuben Club were accomplished literary men. They enjoyed each other's company as well as the good food and fine wine. They often played mahjong late into the night. Occasionally they inspired each other with their latest poems. When in the right mood, there were always sing-song girls next door who could provide entertainment.

* * *

In the fall of 1916, activities in the Hong Kong Office of Huimin Company were at a hectic pace. Immediately after signing a contract with the French government in May, the first group of Chinese laborers, numbering 5,000, had been recruited in Tianjin. These laborers left the port city by French steamship in the summer and were warmly welcomed by the French people when they landed in Marseilles. The Chinese laborers were placed in ammunition factories or worked in the transportation of ammunition. The French authorities were impressed by the dedication of these laborers and asked for more of them. The Chinese complied. Recruiting stations were set up in Pukou, Qingdao and Hong Kong as ports of embarkation. When thousands of laborers enlisted from distant places and gathered at these port cities, the Huimin Company provided shelters and food for them before the French ocean-liners arrived. Since Liang Shiyi was now in Hong Kong, he often lent a hand to this effort in south China while Ye Gougchuo did the same in the north.

Because of the success of the French experience, Britain started its own recruitment of Chinese laborers for non-combat duties in the Western Front. Its recruits in the port cities of Qingdao and Weihaiwei in Shandong Province soon reached 75,000 men. The Russian government soon followed on a smaller scale. How ironic that the British recruitment was handled by Beilby Alston who had replaced Sir John Jordan as the British Minister to Beijing. Not very long before, he had laughed off this idea as an "extraordinarily fantastic suggestion" of Liang Shiyi, the "Machiavelli of China." By the end of 1917, over 200,000 Chinese laborers were sent to Europe. The participation of Chinese laborers in supporting the war in Europe received praises from Allied officials, but their contributions were not acknowledged by the Chinese government since China had declared neutrality.

* * *

In Beijing, members of the old Parliament, who had been elected in 1913 but disqualified by Yuan Shikai, reconvened on August 1, 1916. Three weeks later, the Parliament confirmed the appointment of Premier Duan Qirui as recommended by President Li. However, Duan refused to accept Tang Shaoyi as Foreign Minister in the coalition government fashioned by the President. To Duan, Tang Shaoyi was the black sheep of the Beiyang Clique who had betrayed his former colleagues by join-ing the enemy camp. They considered him worse than the enemies. In view of the prolonged deadlock, Tang Shaoyi resigned without ever assuming the post.

In the meantime, the Parliament had to elect a Vice President to fill the vacan-cy. Duan saw that as an opportunity to advance his power base. However, Feng Guozhang, another senior Beiyang general, posed a serious challenge. Duan's ambi-tion was thwarted by the maneuver of Wu Jinglian, a Nationalist member of the House of Representatives. Wu remembered Duan as the autocratic Acting Premier who had hired men to rough up members of the Parliament in 1913. He was deter-mined to deprive Duan of his aspiration and led a coalition in the Parliament to elect Feng Guozhang as Vice President on October 30.

After losing his bid for Vice President, Duan completed the appointments in his cabinet. Giving in to President Li Yuanhong's insistence for a coalition government, Duan finally appointed Wu Tingfang, a supporter of Sun Yatsen, as Foreign Minister. The appointment was approved by the Parliament.

Enjoying his leisure life style in Hong Kong, Liang Shiyi was not interested in the infighting of various groups in Beijing. However, he was periodically informed of the situation by some of his friends. By October 1916, German agents learned that Chinese laborers had been sent to France, and the German Legation in Beijing lodged a strong protest with the Chinese Foreign Ministry. Since the Huimin

Company of Hong Kong, supported by Liang Shiyi, was privately owned, the Chinese government simply denied any involvement.

One news item of great interest to Liang Shiyi was the resumption of the open exchange of silver coins and banknotes of the Bank of Communications. Another was the decision of the board of directors of the Bank of Communications, in January 1917, to elect Cao Yulin as president of the bank. Cao was the logical choice to succeed Liang since he had been an auditor general of the bank several years previously and was a close political ally of Premier Duan Qirui.

In early February 1917, the German Minister Schintz, in Beijing, notified the Chinese Foreign Ministry in a diplomatic note that Germany would blockade the Chinese coast in accordance with Germany's new aggressive policy on submarine warfare. The State Council in Beijing sent an urgent cable to Liang Shiyi, soliciting his opinion on the policy toward Germany. It was a strange twist that the government should consult a fugitive about an important national policy. Nevertheless, Liang did not want to miss the chance to express his long-held opinion that China should declare war against Germany and advised the State Council accordingly.

Liang Shiyi received additional cables from the Chinese Foreign Ministry. The German Minister had protested against the use of Chinese laborers in France as an act of war against Germany. By then, another group of Chinese workers sponsored by the Sino-French Friendship Association was also helping the war effort in France under a work-study program. It was rumored that some Chinese laborers, possibly those recruited by the British government, were digging ditches in the Western Front. Liang calmly advised the Foreign Ministry to reply to the German protest by citing the contract of Huimin Company which clearly stated that Chinese laborers under its sponsorship would not be engaged in military action.

Sir Henry May, the Governor of Hong Kong, occasionally invited Liang Shiyi to meet with him to exchange views on the European War and its effect on China. At a meeting during which Liang Shiyi told Sir Henry about the German protest, Liang smiled mischievously. "Sir Henry, Lord Kitchener has finally got his wish to have more men on the Western Front after all."

On March 14, 1917, under pressure from Premier Duan Qirui, President Li Yuanhong announced that China would break off diplomatic relations with Germany. Ten days later, the German Minister left Beijing after notifying the Chinese Foreign Ministry that German interests in China would be handled by the Dutch Legation. Liang Shiyi was elated that his earlier opinion finally prevailed. For a person who had never been a foreign minister, and had limited experience in government, Liang Shiyi's influence in diplomacy, finance and communications was far beyond the titles or the positions he held. He would be the first to admit that without proximity to power under Yuan Shikai, he wouldn't have been able to accomplish so much. For him, it was more important to accomplish something positive than to hesitate in fear of criticism. Regrettably, he was now a fugitive, but what a strange political life for a fugitive.

Theater of the Absurd

On April 11, 1917, Dr. Reinsch, the American Minister in Beijing, notified the Chinese Government that the United States had declared war against Germany. As the Chinese newspapers in the capital reported this event, the European War suddenly became the World War. The Associated Press carried part of President Wilson's speech advising Congress to declare war against Germany. The translation of the text appearing under flashy newspaper headlines read:

"It is a war against all nations. American ships have been sunk and American lives taken. . . .But the ships of other friendly and neutral nations had been sunk in the same way. There is no discrimination. The challenge is to all mankind. . . ."

As Premier Duan Qirui picked up a newspaper the next morning, he was greatly inspired by Woodrow Wilson's fighting words. Earlier in March, he had delivered to the Parliament a request for breaking off diplomatic relations with Germany. The resolution had been passed by both Houses with a comfortable majority even though Sun Yatsen, Tang Shaoyi and several southern governors cabled members of the Parliament to oppose it. Subsequently President Li Yuanhong signed the resolution. Duan could not understand that when he sent a follow-up request for declaration of war against Germany, members of the Parliament were reluctant to consider his request. Wasn't it about time they, too, should listen to Wilson's call to meet the challenge?

To the dismay of Premier Duan, the cables from Sun Yatsen and Tang Shaoyi had delayed effects, not only on members of the Parliament, but also on the Nationalist members of his coalition government. When Premier Duan sought a unanimous consent of his cabinet to pass a motion to declare war on Germany on May 1, Foreign Minister Wu Tingfang and three other ministers resigned in protest. As Duan pressed on for a resolution to declare war against Germany, the House of Representatives voted to table his request indefinitely. Duan was furious and complained to President Li, "No risk is involved in this declaration. Germany cannot send troops to China and will not cause more harm than it has already done through the blockade of Chinese coast with submarines. Can't the members of Parliament see the advantage at the peace conference if we declare war against Germany?"

But his opposition did not see it that way. They thought Duan was using the war against Germany as a excuse to raise money to launch a civil war against his opponents in south China. President Li Yuanhong was unsympathetic to Duan's call. He felt that to press the issue of declaring war against Germany would divide the nation and nullify his effort for reconciliation. When Premier Duan asked the President to dissolve the Parliament, President Li refused on constitutional grounds. As a precaution to guard against Yuan Shikai's abuse of power, the Provisional Constitution of 1912 had specifically prohibited the dissolution of Parliament by the President or the Premier. President Li was not nitpicking, only setting an example of government by laws. Never a true believer of democracy, Duan saw nothing but paralysis and deadlock in government. He invited the Beiyang generals to cable the President, demanding the dissolution of the Parliament. The Parliament, in return, asked the President to dismiss Duan as Premier.

Normally a reasonable man, President Li could be very stubborn when he was bullied and cornered. All peacemaking efforts by their mutual friends, working behind the scenes, failed to produce a compromise. Tired of Duan's pressure tactics, President Li dismissed him as Premier on May 23 and appointed Wu Tingfang as Acting Premier. Outraged at being outmaneuvered, Duan abruptly left for Tianjin. He immediately challenged the legality of his own dismissal since, according to the Provisional Constitution, all important Presidential appointments and dismissals must be approved by the Parliament and co-signed by the President and the Premier.

Disgusted with the shenanigans, Tang Hualong resigned as the Speaker of the House of Representatives. The defiant House immediately elected Wu Jinglian, who was not afraid of confronting Duan Qirui.

* * *

"I wish you had been here in the last few months," Ye Gongchuo wrote to Liang Shiyi from Beijing. "With your strong position in favor of the declaration of war against Germany, you are perhaps the only person who might have had a chance to persuade Duan Qirui that he must not use differences on this issue to threaten the President."

Before Liang could reply to Ye's letter, events in Beijing had taken a turn for the worse. Duan Qirui understood, too well, that many Beiyang generals had been unhappy with President Li for his compromise with the southern leaders. When he appealed to them to challenge the President, they readily complied. Within a few days after Duan's dismissal, nine northern governors announced their independence. The commanding generals in these provinces met in Tianjin and set up a headquarters for the joint chiefs of staff in preparation to form a new provisional government. The leader of this group was the reactionary General Zhang Xun who threatened to take military action against the government unless President Li dissolved the Parliament and discarded the constitution.

President Li was at the end of his rope. One person after another turned down his offer of premiership. Even Vice President Feng Guozhang offered his resignation. The President refused to accept. Instead, President Li asked him to take over the presidency and Li, himself, would resign. Vice President Feng declined. All of a sudden, it seemed no one was interested in the highest office in the land except, of course, the Beiyang generals waiting in the wings. Watching this desperate situation from Shanghai, Sun Yatsen called on the southern governors and generals to send troops to support President Li and protect the constitution, but they were too far away from Beijing to exert any influence.

Out of desperation, President Li appealed to General Zhang Xun to mediate his dispute with Duan Qirui. On June 8, General Zhang arrived in Beijing with 5,000 troops and demanded the dissolution of the Parliament within three days as the condition of his mediation. The next day, Admiral Cheng Biguang, the Minister of Navy and a supporter of Sun Yatsen, went to see President Li and said to him, "You do not need to suffer the indignity of Zhang Xun. I can smuggle you to Tianjin. From there you can sail for Shanghai with me on the First Fleet under my command."

"It's too risky," President Li replied. "And my escape to Shanghai will not solve the pressing problems of the government in Beijing. But I appreciate your thoughtfulness, and I wish you a safe journey." After these parting words, Admiral Cheng left Beijing and sailed to Shanghai with the First Fleet.

Frightened by the prospect of a coup by General Zhang Xun, President Li capitulated to Zhang's ultimatum to dissolve the Parliament, but Acting Premier Wu Tingfang refused to co-sign the decree. By now, even Xu Shichang, who had lived quietly in Tianjin after his resignation as Secretary of State a year earlier, chimed in to ask President Li to dissolve the Parliament. Fearing further delay would only deepen the crisis, President Li dismissed Wu Tingfang and appointed Zhang's man as Acting Premier to co-sign the decree. Only then did Zhang Xun asked the northern provinces to cancel their declaration of independence and close their headquarters in Tianjin.

Some members of the Parliament who were able to slip out of Beijing to Shanghai openly challenged President Li's decision in an open telegram on June 19. The next day, the governors of Guangdong and Guangxi declared temporary independence from the Beijing government. With his erratic decisions, President Li placed himself in a desperate position.

Unbeknownst to President Li, his worst fate was yet to come. General Zhang Xun had the support of the Beiyang generals to put down the remnants of resistance in southwest China, by any means, in order to advance his secret agenda to restore the Qing monarchy. Zhang had received encouragement, or at least acquiesce, of some former officials of the Qing Dynasty, including Xu Shichang. After getting an upper hand over President Li, Zhang took advantage of the presence of his troops near Beijing to carry out his plan for the restoration of the Qing Emperor on July 1, 1917.

On the eve of his action, Zhang called the new Minister of the Army, the Inspector General of Police and the Head of the Beijing Garrison to inform them of his intention. He ordered them to open the gates of Beijing city and let his troops enter. Under heavy pressure from Zhang, they reluctantly gave in and followed his order. By dawn Zhang and a small group of his followers entered the Forbidden City and petitioned the former emperor Puyi, by then a boy of eleven years old, to restore his reign. The petition was accepted by the Qing Royal House and an imperial edict was issued to restore the Qing Empire.

In the afternoon, several delegates were dispatched by General Zhang to the Presidential Palace and asked to see President Li. They demanded the resignation of the President who refused to acquiesce. Since the Beijing Telegraph Service was already under the control of Zhang's troops, President Li had to send someone to take his open telegrams calling for help to Tianjin for transmission. At this critical juncture, President Li reappointed Duan Qirui as Premier. He also sent a telegram to Vice-President Feng Guozhang in Nanjing, asking him to accept the position of Acting President. When the news reached other parts of the country, four provinces denounced the restoration on July 3 and several other provinces followed suit a few days later.

Just before the guards of the Presidential Palace were replaced by Zhang's troops, President Li fled with his secretary and aide-de-camp. They had planned to seek asylum at the French Hospital, but on their way they changed their mind and entered the Japanese Legation. In the meantime, General Zhang and his civilian followers, including Kang Youwei, were propping up the boy emperor inside the Forbidden City.

* * *

Liang Shiyi watched this farce in the comfort of his home in Hong Kong. He joined the chorus of leaders condemning the restoration of the Qing emperor. Now that Duan Qirui was once again the Premier, he could command other Beiyang generals to defeat their erstwhile comrade Zhang Xun. But military campaigns required money and Duan turned to his close friend, Cao Yulin, president of the Bank of Communications. As a founder and shareholder of the bank, Liang Shiyi wanted to assure Cao of his support for lending money for the cause of defeating General Zhang. He immediately dispatched a telegram to Ye Gongchuo via the Tianjin Office of the Bank of Communications since direct-cable communications with Beijing had been cut. By July 11, General Zhang's troops were routed. He sought refuge in the Dutch Legation. Kang Youwei went to the American Legation for protection. The curtain finally fell in the theater of the absurd.

During this high drama, Tang Shaoyi and a group of Sun Yatsen supporters were waiting in Shanghai for their next move. When Liang Shiyi heard that Vice President Feng Guozhang had assumed the position of Acting President in Nanjing, he cabled Tang Shaoyi, "Since President Li Yuanhong is now under the protection of the Japanese Legation, it may create a delicate diplomatic problem. With your experience in foreign affairs, please go to Nanjing immediately to advise Vice-President Feng how to handle this situation." Liang also cabled Feng to offer his support.

When the stage was cleared after the restoration of the emperor failed, Duan Qirui returned to Beijing on July 14 and resumed his post as Premier. He also sent a representative to the Japanese Legation and welcomed President Li back to his office. Ashamed of what he had done, President Li sent an open telegram to the people of the nation and tendered his resignation. Vice President Feng Guozhang arrived in Beijing to take over the reign of government on August 1. Since the Parliament which had been dissolved by President Li was not able to convene to approve the President's resignation, Feng Guozhang assumed the title of Acting President.

As the Parliament had been dissolved earlier, Acting President Feng succumbed to Premier Duan's pressure and declared war against Germany and Austria on August 15, 1917—without the approval of the Parliament. The German Minister in Beijing had already left his post in March when the two countries broke off diplomatic relations. The Austrian Minister followed in his footsteps.

* * *

Looking at the chaotic political landscape in Beijing, Liang Shiyi realized he might stay in Hong Kong for a long, long time. In the summer of 1917, he and his brother decided they needed a bigger house for their families. They jointly bought two adjoining properties which they had admired for some time. An exclusive residential area, facing the harbor, which had been primarily occupied by colonial officers and other foreigners, had recently been opened to Chinese. They settled on an old English mansion on Robinson Road which was back to back to a new twin townhouse on Conduit Road. They bought both properties and linked them together by constructing a steep stair inside as well as sloping concrete steps outside.

The extended family of the Liang clan soon moved into this new residence. The first consideration was the comfort of the patriarch. The mansion on Robinson road consisted of two floors with very large rooms. On the first floor were a living room, a dinner room, a library and a balcony overlooking a tennis court and a small garden. On the second floor, a large drawing room and three bedrooms took up the same floor space. At the back of the mansion was a courtyard abutted on one side by an annex housing the kitchen and servant's quarters and on the other side by a two-story guest house. The patriarch modestly chose to occupy the guest house with his young concubine and small daughter. The first floor of the mansion was reserved for formal activities of the family. The second floor was occupied by Liang Shiyi's wife, her two daughters and youngest son. She, of course, was the acknowledged first lady of the house.

The twin townhouse on Conduit Road had a symmetrical floor plan with a small common courtyard. In addition to the basement for the kitchen and servants' quarters, each of the twin townhouses had two full stories with three large rooms on each floor, plus an extra room at the roof level adjoining a roof garden. Liang Shiyi and his remaining family occupied one side of the twin townhouse while his brother Shixu's family took up the other side. Liang Shiyi and his fourth lady occupied a suite on one floor while his second lady and her two daughters and a son took up another floor. His brother Shixu shared his side with two consorts and three young sons, plus their niece Wosheng.

Liang Shiyi's father was an early riser and enjoyed seeing his grandchildren every morning. So all the grandchildren would line up in his living quarters to say good morning before leaving for school. Shixu's two younger sons, a toddler and a baby, would be brought there by their mother. Of course, all other daughters-in-law would come to pay their respects each morning. However, Liang Shiyi and his brother would show up only at times convenient to them, usually late in the day. In more than a few occasions, when Liang Shiyi played mahjong at his club until dawn, he found it convenient to say hello to his father in the early morning, pretending he had just gotten up. That was the life with the patriarch.

A rock garden was created near the living quarters of the patriarch so he could enjoy the beauty of the outdoors. The clay tennis court located in front of the mansion was converted into a Japanese garden with an artificial pond. At one corner of the garden a small hut was added to house a pair of deer kept in a fenced area. At another corner, a bower with spreading grapevine provided a shaded playground for children. The patriarch often spent his day sitting in a small pavilion at the center of the pond to contemplate and occasionally watched the fish swimming in the pond.

As the family got together to celebrate the completion of the new construction, the patriarch said to his two sons approvingly, "Through your accomplishments and filial love, I'm able to enjoy a comfortable life that few people can afford. I have attained the pinnacle of personal fulfillment of a Chinese classic scholar."

Beauty of the Season

"Aren't these deer adorable?" said Liang Shiyi's fourth lady as she finished feeding them cooked soybeans. She looked up at her husband. They were alone in the garden and were walking toward the narrow bridge leading to the pavilion at the center of the pond. Appearing outwardly serene, the fourth lady was anxiously waiting for the right moment to speak her mind.

After they sat down inside the pavilion, she carefully brought up the subject. "My dear husband," she began, "I sometimes feel I no longer have enough energy. I'm afraid I cannot keep up with your many activities."

Liang Shiyi sat quietly, pondering her meaning. His fourth lady could be quite devious when she wanted something. At the age of forty-eight, he viewed her not only as a lover but also as a personal attendant. He sighed. Still in her late twenties, she could not possibly find life so burdensome. True, in the seven years of their marriage, she had enjoyed the happy times, but she had also endured times that proved to be some of the most difficult of his life. She had been beside him during political exile, first in the Western Hills near Beijing, and then in the thick of a political crisis in the Presidential Palace. She had been so close to her husband and yet so far from the reality of his political activities as she had always been excluded from her husband's public appearances.

Not wishing to misjudge her intention, Liang Shiyi asked directly but tenderly, "What has been troubling you?"

"I heard you telling your brother at dinner last night," she replied, "that you are going to tour Japan for three months. I don't think I can survive such a long trip."

"That's only in the talking stage," her husband said. "You don't need to worry about it for at least a couple of months."

"But I do worry," the fourth lady was insistent. "When you attend your business with the other men of the world, I will be alone in the hotel with strangers who have different customs. I don't know their language and I don't like their food."

"We'll have some leisure hours," her husband assured her. "We can go sightseeing together on the days when there's no scheduled business."

"You will be better off to have a younger consort when you travel to Japan," she

271

suggested. It was a statement of faith in her own ability to hold her husband against competition as well as an opening to relieve herself from the demands she had been trying to avoid.

"You worry too much," her husband comforted her. "I'll think about that when the time comes. I have no definite plan to make the trip to Japan. The political situation in Beijing is so complex that any plan of mine can be undone by new developments there. For this precious moment, why don't we just enjoy the beautiful roses blooming in this balmy summer day?"

* * *

Sun Yatsen was also watching the developments in Beijing in the French Concession in Shanghai as he had been doing since his return from exile in Japan more than a year before. When Duan Qirui resumed his premiership after defeating the short-lived restoration of the Qing emperor, Sun Yatsen asked him in an open telegram to uphold the 1912 Provisional Constitution and to restore the Parliament. Duan refused. Buoyed by the arrival of Admiral Cheng Biguang and the First Fleet in Shanghai, Sun declared that the Beijing government was illegitimate, and urged the generals and governors in the southwestern provinces to support his effort. His long-waited moment arrived when he received word that he would be welcome by Zhu Qinglan, the Governor of Guangdong, to set up a new national government there. On July 21, 1917, Sun and Admiral Cheng sailed for Guangzhou with the First Fleet. A number of former members of the Parliament went with them.

On board the First Fleet, Sun Yatsen reflected on the difficulties he had encountered in his years of exile. Even after his return to Shanghai in April 1916, his Chinese Revolutionary Party could do little to influence the politics in China. With the death of Huang Xing in Shanghai in late 1916, Sun was deprived of a capable strategist. His fortune finally took a turn for the better when he saw the welcome signs displayed on the wharf as the First Fleet sailed into the harbor near Guangzhou.

In late July 1917, Sun Yatsen immediately began organizing a new national government in Guangzhou and cabled to Li Yuanhong, urging him to come to Guangzhou to assume the presidency of the republic under the 1912 Provisional Constitution. Living in Tianjin after being driven out of office in June, Li refused to join Sun's new government in Guangzhou. However, Sun received the crucial support of the Governor of Yunnan in an open telegram on August 11, forming a solid block of opposition in southwest China. A week later, more than 130 members of the Parliament, who had arrived in Guangzhou, were invited by Sun to join him in setting up a military government. Under the leadership of Wu Jinglian, who had become the Speaker of the House of Representatives in May, this resurrected Parliament declared the formation of a "Constitution Protection Government" to wage war against the Beijing government. Sun Yatsen was elected the field marshall and head of the military government on September 1 and was sworn in with his cabinet ministers ten days later. The nation was divided into North and South once again.

* * *

Beijing Odyssey

"A letter for you from Ye Gongchuo just arrived today," Shixu said to his brother one afternoon as he saw Liang Shiyi walk into his office at Queen's Road Central. The suite also served as a temporary office for Liang Shiyi when he returned to Hong Kong.

"Qichao is back in Beijing and is very active in Duan's cabinet," Liang Shiyi commented briefly after reading Ye's letter. He thought about his old friend Liang Qichao who had joined the southern generals in their campaign against Yuan's monarchical movement in the previous year. After Yuan's death, the revolt stopped almost spontaneously. Shortly afterwards, General Cai E quietly went to Japan for treatment of an undisclosed illness and died in a Tokyo hospital in November 1916 at the age of 35. Since Liang Qichao had lost his brilliant and trusted former student, as well as his insider connection to the southern generals, he decided to return to the familiar political arena in Beijing.

As a first step for his return to power, Liang Qichao had lined up some former members of the Progressive Party to form a Constitution Research Society, dubbed the "Research Clique." When Premier Duan Qirui looked to the Research Clique as the backbone of his administration, Liang Qichao was named Finance Minister. Although Liang Qichao's strong suit was his knowledge of political systems in the Western world, he was ambitious in tackling the financial woes of China. Shiyi was aware of Qichao's inexperience and limitations in financial affairs and expressed his concern, "I hope Qichao knows what is in store for him when he assumes responsibility in the Finance Ministry."

"It seems incredible that Liang Qichao would accept the post of Finance Minister," his brother Shixu echoed.

"You must give Qichao credit for modesty," Shiyi told Shixu. "He has appointed someone who is very knowledgeable in financial affairs as Deputy Finance Minister." Noting that Cao Yulin, president of the Bank of Communications had been appointed to serve currently as Minister of Communications, Shiyi remarked, "Gongchuo should be safe in his positions as the Deputy Minister and Associate Vice-president in the Bank of Communications." The fate of Ye Gongchuo was of utmost concern to Liang Shiyi.

After the brief talk with his brother, Shiyi left and headed for his club on the west side of the town.

* * *

"You're in good company today," a friend at the Wuben Club greeted Liang Shiyi upon his arrival.

"I'll be glad to join you in a game of mahjong," Liang replied as he sat down to enjoy a cup of tea.

"Oh, I don't mean that," his friend said. "I'm referring to the latest news that the Beijing government has issued arrest warrants for Sun Yatsen and Wu Jinglian. They have now joined you as fugitives if the Beijing government can find them."

"They're safe in Guangzhou as long as their military government survives,"

273

Liang replied. "Guangzhou is so close, yet seems so far. I have no desire to set foot in Chinese territory."

"Tang Shaoyi is now Finance Minister and Wu Tingfang is Foreign Minister in Sun's cabinet. They're your good friends." His friend casually reminded him. "Aren't you interested in joining the military government in Guangzhou?"

"No," Liang replied. "Their base of support is very thin and may not last long." Liang looked around. "Let's not talk politics, but treat ourselves with some good wine while enjoying the beauty of the season."

Accompanied by his friend, Liang Shiyi walked to the balcony to see the beautiful flowers in the garden below. The water in a small fountain reflected brilliantly the mellowing autumn sunset. The fragrance of the jasmine floated on a light breeze.

In the evening, a group of young women joined the men in the club for after-dinner entertainment. One was Cai Shaoxiang (little fragrance from the Cai family). She was indeed the beauty of the season. Liang Shiyi had noticed her on previous occasions. Tonight he would ask her to become his fifth lady. When the music hushed and the women began to leave, he invited Cai to a join him in a private room. Before the night was over, he had proposed to her.

It was an awkward moment. She seemed both frightened and delighted by the prospect. She explained that she was not free to leave the house and could not give an immediate answer. Shiyi assured her it could all be arranged. With little fanfare, Awu (number 5) was soon brought into the Liang family as his fifth lady. A wealthy businessman who lived across the street from Liang's residence had also acquired a young and beautiful concubine recently. Their neighbors dubbed these two young ladies the "two beauties of Conduit Road."

All members of Liang's family adjusted to the addition of the fifth lady, but none felt more uncertain about the adjustment than the fourth lady—even though she had triggered the whole episode. With a feeling mixed of relief and regret, she yielded to reality and invited the fifth lady to share the chores for their husband.

To ease the fear of his fourth lady, Liang Shiyi said to her privately, "Some women expect their husbands to give them jewelry or ornaments for security. I have never done that because my father frowns on display of jewelry by women in our household. To provide for your security, I have purchased one hundred shares of stocks of Hong Kong Power Company under your name. You will soon receive dividends which you should save for rainy days." His fourth lady was greatly relieved to know she had not been forgotten.

By now Liang Shiyi's trip to Japan was finalized after months of planning. His fourth lady almost wished she had never revealed her reservations about the trip. Liang sensed her feeling. "I would like you to go to Japan with me," Liang said, offering his invitation. "Awu (No. 5) is new and does not know my habits and routines as well as you do. Since Japanese conduct business very much like the Chinese, women will not be invited. You two can keep each other's company when I go about my business, and no one will be wiser."

Beijing Odyssey

His fourth lady liked the idea. Liang's novel suggestion removed her fear and envy. She was now on the way to a new journey in her life.

* * *

Liang Shiyi encountered bitter disappointments involving several business ventures because of political turmoil in China. The contract for the Eastern Pacific Steamship Company he had so carefully worked out with an American company went up in smoke after he left Beijing. Other plans for helping budding domestic industries did not pan out as expected. Distressed, when several friends in Tianjin asked him to join them establishing a new company for promoting the export of native products, he gladly accepted the opportunity. With initial capital of 500,000 yuan, the Wuda Company would develop warehousing and ocean shipping business.

When two prominent Japanese industrialists, Baron Shibuzawa Eiichi and Baron Okura Kihachiro, sent word to invite Liang to visit Japan, Liang jumped at the chance. An admirer of Liang's knowledge in economics and finances, Baron Shibuzawa hoped to discuss with him the future development of Chinese industries. Already in an advanced age, Baron Okura, who had enormous investments in China, planned to turn over his business to his son when he reached eighty years old. He saw in Liang a valuable partner for his son.

For his part, Liang wanted to learn more about the Japanese experience in industrial revolution and to attract Japanese capital for the development of Chinese industries. He was aware of foreign competition for China's market once the World War ended. Overzealous competition would impair the budding domestic industries of China. Japan could help China develop new industries at a quicker pace under the principle of respecting the sovereignty of China.

Liang Shiyi assembled a group of Japanese experts in Hong Kong, Tianjin and Beijing to facilitate this trip. Liang Shiyi asked Liu Tiecheng, his private secretary and Japanese interpreter, to negotiate the itinerary with his Japanese hosts. Three Japanese businessmen in different parts of China were added to the entourage at the suggestion of the Japanese hosts who also appointed Baron Okura's son to be the Chairman of the Reception Committee. Joining the entourage were Liang's fourth and fifth ladies. Accompanied by Japanese Vice-Consul Karai in Hong Kong, Liang and his group left Hong Kong on October 27, 1917 on a Japanese ocean liner *S.S. Tenshin Maru* for Shanghai where they were joined by the remaining members from other parts of China.

As the ship steamed out the Hong Kong Harbor, Liang wondered how he would be received by the Japanese business and industrial leaders. His fourth and fifth ladies leaned on the rails outside their cabin, looking toward their home on the island and pondering their uncertain future.

A Grand Tour

The ocean liner *S.S. Tenshin Maru* sailed into the harbor of Nagasaki, Japan on November 1, 1917. Waiting for Liang Shiyi's party at the port was Baron Okura's son, the head of the Reception Committee, and Liu Tiecheng, Liang's private secretary and interpreter, who had been the advance man to make all necessary arrangements. This was no ordinary tour. Liang Shiyi was scheduled to meet practically all important members of Japanese financial and political circles. After stopping by the Mitsubishi Shipyard, Liang's group attended a reception sponsored by the Nagasaki Overseas Chinese Association.

Two days later, Liang's party arrived in Kobe and attended a reception sponsored jointly by four banks. The next day, Liang met with Baron Okura Kihachiro who had just returned from a business trip to Beijing. After a whirlwind tour of the scenic Nara, Liang attended a reception sponsored by the Kobe Overseas Chinese Association and a banquet at the Chinese Consulate in Kobe. It was a strange occasion since Liang was a fugitive and should never have been invited as a guest of honor by the Chinese Consul. On the other hand, Liang could be arrested by the host and shipped back to China as a prisoner. However, neither side had any qualms about the matter. When Liang returned to his hotel with his private secretary afterwards, he said to Liu, "What an astonishing evening! I enjoyed it thoroughly."

The opportunity finally came for Liang's two ladies to join in when the group traveled to Kyoto on November 10 for four wonderful days. They visited temples, shrines and canals. In Arashiyama Hot Springs, Liang's two ladies were shy about the unusual experience of bathing, Japanese style. Liang said to them mischievously, "Half the fun of an adventure is the surprise. You might as well enjoy it." To the delight of the ladies, they also toured a textile mill and an embroidery shop.

Then the delegation traveled eastward to Baron Okura's resort home in Kokufutsu. It was intended to be a week of rest before a five-week visit to Tokyo. As a precursor of the hectic days ahead, the baron invited Honta, a representative of Japanese newspapers, to meet Liang Shiyi. Two delegates of the Yokahoma Overseas Chinese Association at Yokahoma also came to Kokufutsu to welcome Liang. They were followed by the Chinese Consul at Yokahoma. At the end of the week, the host invited Liang's party to tour Ashino Lake. A caravan of twenty four rickshaws, each pulled and pushed by three men, attracted many bystanders in the village who had never seen so many visitors at one time.

In the afternoon of November 21, a special train arranged by the Japanese Railway Administration brought Liang Shiyi and his delegation to Tokyo. As Liang looked out the window of his railway car, he saw a crowd waiting for him at the Tokyo Railway Station. To his amazement, his secretary and interpreter told him the crowd was comprised of twelve hundred people, from all walks of life, who came to welcome him. After thanking the people, Liang and his party settled in the Tokyo Station Grand Hotel.

* * *

The visit began with Liang and his party embarking on an inspection tour of the battleship Yamashiro, accompanied by Vice-Admiral Otsuno. They also visited the naval shipyard, weapon factory and a nearby aircraft factory. However, his major mission was to meet the Japanese industrial and business leaders during his first two weeks in Tokyo.

At a private dinner with Marquis Omura Shigenobu, attended only by Liang and his interpreter, the marquis told him that, because of significant expansion of Japanese industries during the war against Germany, the political power of Japan had been shifted from the warlords to the industrialists. Then Baron Shibuzawa Eiichi invited Liang to his resort home outside Tokyo. A devoted Confucian, he believed laws should be supplemented by social order based on Confucian ethics. Shibuzawa encouraged Liang to become an industrialist first and a politician second. "There is a dire need for more industrialists serving in our Parliament since the government policies should facilitate the operations of industry and commerce," the baron told him. Liang got the unmistakable message that the Japanese would like to help him become a major partner in developing Chinese industries.

In the evening of December 6, Baron Mitsui hosted a formal banquet in honor of Liang attended by many industrial leaders. After the dinner, Liang delivered a speech about cooperation between Japanese and Chinese industries, using Japanese advanced technology and capital to harness Chinese natural resources and abundant labor. After outlining the types of industries most suitable for joint ventures, he stated emphatically, "Japanese businesses must respect Chinese sovereignty and obey Chinese laws. Business contracts between Japanese industrialists and their Chinese counterparts should be mutually beneficial and not be exploitative of the Chinese people. Finally, the Japanese businesses must support the Chinese aspiration to regain control of its maritime customs from foreigners." Shiyi sat down to the loud applause of the audience.

* * *

When Shiyi returned to his hotel, he tried to catch up with the latest news from China as he was scheduled to meet Tanaka Giichi, the Japanese Army Deputy Chief of Staff, the following morning. Tanaka, a strong supporter of Duan Qirui's policy of unifying China by force, had approached Baron Okura and requested the opportunity to meet Liang Shiyi in private. The baron appreciated the sensitive nature of the discussion and asked both of them to meet in his own residence. Liang wanted to be well prepared for such a meeting.

Ever since returning to power in the summer of 1917, Premier Duan Qirui wanted to unify China through military conquest. On the other hand, Acting President Feng Guozhang had sent secret emissaries to the South to search for a negotiated peace with the military government in Guangzhou. Their differences were exacerbated by the presidential election scheduled for October 1918 in which both were strong contenders. Then on November 14, 1917, the army of the military government in the South won a decisive battle in Hunan Province and took its capital, Changsha, by surprise. Shaken by the failure of the Beiyang generals to protect the first line of defense, Premier Duan Qirui took the blame and resigned the next day. However, Duan's resignation was only a tactical retreat. He anticipated that Feng could not handle the situation any better.

Duan Qirui's confidence had been boosted by the support of Japanese militarists, of which Tanaka was a powerful representative. In the past four months, Duan had secretly obtained several loans from Japan. The loans amounted to 152 million Japanese yen and were used for weapons, telegraph equipment, railway construction, mining and "war against Germany." With the Bolshevik Revolution in Russia on the horizon, Japan was deeply concerned about its interest in Manchuria which had been ceded to Japan by Russia in a series of treaties. By gaining military alliance with China, Japan could send troops to Manchuria to protect its interest there. For his part, Duan welcomed the idea of making war against Germany the central focus of the loans, which would give him a cover for financing his expedition against the military government in Guangzhou.

The meeting was simple and direct. Shiyi listened carefully. Unaware of Duan's secret dealings with the Japanese militarists, Liang Shiyi nevertheless sensed Tanaka's unusual attention to Duan's political future. In addition, Liang felt Tanaka was using him to get another reading of Chinese politics from an insider. Liang understood that and tried carefully not to take sides between Feng and Duan. After listening to Liang's cautious analysis, Tanaka commented, "I have received reports from other sources that Duan Qirui is expected to return to power soon. I hope you will support his plan to unite China by force. China cannot afford to stay divided without an effective central government."

"I beg to disagree," Liang said politely. "Duan Qirui is my friend and I agree with him on the issue of declaring war against Germany. But I disagree with him on unifying China by force. Military action will be harmful to both sides of the conflict. China needs a breathing spell to develop its industries in order to achieve stability and prosperity. An effective central government can be achieved only through painstaking compromise"

Realizing his views were not well received, Tanaka politely concluded his interview. They walked out of the meeting room to thank Baron Okura who invited them to have lunch in an amicable setting in his garden.

After meeting with Tanaka, Liang's visits to Rear Admiral Moriyama and Army Minister Oshima Ken'ichi over the next two days were brief and anticlimactic.

* * *

Liang's itinerary included visits with many government officials, among them, Interior Minister Goto Shimpei, Foreign Minister Honno Ichiro, Deputy Foreign Minister Heihara Kijiro, Finance Minister Katsuda, Post and Telegraph Minister Denken, and Prime Minister Terauchi. The Prime Minister offered his good office to settle the military conflicts between North and South in China if his service was needed. Not wishing any interference of Chinese internal affairs by foreigners, Liang politely thanked him for his goodwill toward peaceful unification in China.

Making his rounds to see the elder statesmen, Liang visited Viscount Ito of the Highest Privy Council. In his visit to Marquis Matsukata Seigi, Liang enjoyed a discussion of the financial reform in the early reign of Emperor Meiji. During his visit with Duke Yamagata Aritomo, the duke hinted that he could plead with the Beijing government to dismiss Liang's arrest warrant. Liang declined his offer. "It's certainly my wish to be free of the arrest warrant, but I must tell you in all candor that I should earn my freedom without any plea that might cause a scandal."

On December 17, Liang Shiyi attended a dinner party hosted by Zhang Zhongxiang, the Chinese Minister in Tokyo. After dinner, the minister handed him a telegram addressed to Liang, personally. It was a coded message from Ye Gongchuo in Beijing concerning the latest developments in China. Earlier that month, fifteen provincial military commanders had gathered in Tianjin to review the war efforts against the South. They came to the conclusion that the power struggle between Acting President Feng and the deposed Premier Duan would only be intensified unless someone mediated their differences. They also concluded that only Xu Shichang and Liang Shiyi had enough prestige to influence both Feng and Duan. They first approached Xu Shichang, then living in Tianjin. But Xu, who was nurturing the ambition of running for President himself, artfully refused. They turned to Liang Shiyi, suggesting the cancellation of arrest warrants for Liang and his allies Zhu Qiqian and Zhou Ziqi. They asked Ye Gongchuo to verify Liang's willingness to mediate before proceeding any further. The result was Ye's telegram to Liang, care of the Chinese Minister in Tokyo.

Liang Shiyi was more than willing to mediate the conflict between Feng and Duan. In fact, he had a vision of a peaceful settlement with the South after these two powerful leaders reconciled their differences. He asked Zhang to send a coded reply to Ye.

Liang and his party had been entertained by many official receptions, sightseeing tours, dinners, luncheons and tea parties, far more than he felt necessary. On December 21, before leaving Tokyo, he hosted a dinner party to express his appreciation to his Japanese friends.

* * *

Liang's party spent three additional days at Nikko for sightseeing and rest. They toured a copper refinery and a hydroelectric power station. Liang's two ladies joined the group to visit the Buddhist temples on the hillside. Then the group returned to Tokyo one more time for Liang to attend the opening session of the House of Lords where he was presented as an honor guest. The next day, they toured the Royal Palace at Singyoku. Liang was surprised by the simplicity of the decor and furnishings at the Palace. He remarked to Liu Tiecheng, his private secretary, "When I compare the frugal practice of the Japanese royalty with the lavish life style of the former Qing emperors, I cannot help but realize why Japan could surge ahead while China failed in their respective attempts for modernization since the Meiji Restoration."

Liang's party left Tokyo and continued their excursion. On New Year's eve, they were in Kyoto to attend a banquet hosted by Hamaoka, the Chairman of the Chamber of Commerce. Among those at the dinner were professors of Kyoto Imperial University who were eager to talk to Liang about monetary policies. They were invited to Liang's hotel for further discussion two days later. These professors suggested China should adopt the gold standard as a part of currency reform. Liang explained to them that because of its weak economy, China had to stay with the silver standard until such time when its economy was strong enough to join the international monetary markets.

After a week in Kyoto, Liang's party went to Yamada and visited the inner and outer palaces at Yamada. Two days later, they left Yamada for Osaka where they toured many factories, including Sumitomo Copper Refinery, Osaka Electric Bulb Factory, Osaka Weapon Factory, Osaka Zinc Company, Nippon Paint Manufacturer, a textile factory, an oil refinery, and a synthetic ivory company. After inspecting the construction site of the Osaka harbor aboard a municipal steamboat, they attended a banquet hosted by Baron Sumitomo, Chairman of Osaka Chamber of Commerce. As Liang's party arrived in Kobe from Osaka, they were welcome at a reception sponsored by the Kobe Chamber of Commerce.

Liang's party then traveled from Kobe to Hiroshima on a special train for distinguished guests arranged by the Western Japan Railway Administration. Accompanied by Vice-Admiral Ito, the Base Commander, they visited the Kure Naval Base. After all these visits, his private secretary asked Liang Shiyi if he was impressed by the Japanese industrial and military might. "Oh, yes," Liang replied, "I'm awed by the Japanese accomplishments which also make me uneasy. The Japanese can do a lot of good if they use their power to promote mutual benefits for Japan and China. But they can cause tremendous damage to both countries if their leaders choose to take a short-sighted view of exploiting China."

On January 17, Liang's party left Hiroshima for Shimonoseki. When their train passed the Okura Steel Plant owned by Baron Okura, Liang was startled by employees standing along the railway waving Chinese flags and hailing, "Long live Liang Shiyi!" After watching this demonstration of admiration, everything else paled in contrast. Even the huge Haciman Iron and Steel Plant where Liang's party had to travel by cars from workshop to workshop did not seem to be as impressive.

Leaving Shimonoseki for Omuda, Liang's party toured the Menda Coal mine owned by the Mitsui Corporation. They also visited an Instrument Factory of the Mitsui Technical School and a coke production line. They left Omuda for Nagasaki on the last leg of their journey. On January 24, Feng Mian, Chinese Consul at Nagasaki, hosted a farewell luncheon for Liang's party at the Chinese Consulate. That evening, they embarked on the S. S. Harunami for Shanghai. Some in Liang's party would return to their stations in north China while Liang and a small group continued their trip to Hong Kong.

As the steamship sailed into Hong Kong harbor on January 29, 1918, Liang's two ladies were relieved to view the familiar landscape once again. Both had enjoyed the trip. The fourth lady felt secure in knowing she could influence and control the newcomer according to her will. For her part, the fifth lady felt she had gained a sister and found her place in a good family with a new start in her life.

Wedding of Liang Shiyi's Eldest Daughter, 1918

Father of the Bride

When Liang Shiyi returned to Hong Kong from Japan, a terse telegram from Ye Gongchuo was waiting for him in his office. Dated January 24, 1918, Ye informed him of the good news that Acting President Feng would soon cancel the arrest warrant against him. A few days later, he received a letter in which Ye elaborated on the substance of the telegram.

Ye's letter stated in part, "At the suggestion of the provincial military commanders who had met earlier in Tianjin, President Feng summoned me to the Presidential Palace this morning. He spoke warmly of you as a personal friend and hoped that you could be available for the service of our country. He also expressed his high regard for Zhou Ziqi and Zhu Qiqian. He said that these three men are indispensable in time of crisis and the arrest warrants against them will be cancelled as soon as he returns from his tour to the battle front. He asked me to convey the news to you first. Since you were scheduled to leave Nagasaki yesterday, I am sending you a cable as well as this letter to Hong Kong."

By now, Liang was deluged with news of military victory of the South. Although President Feng had gone to the front line to rally the Northern troops on January 25, the Southern forces captured the strategic town of Yueyang in Hunan Province two days later. President Feng returned to Beijing in desperation.

On February 4, President Feng announced that arrest warrants for Liang Shiyi, Zhou Ziqi and Zhu Qiqian had been canceled. A free man, Liang Shiyi decided to leave Hong Kong for Beijing in early March.

* * *

When Liang arrived in Beijing, he went to see Guan Mianjun to discuss the wedding plans for his daughter and Guan's son. They had made some preliminary arrangements through correspondence. Until now, Liang had not been free to travel to Beijing, and Guan had offered to have the wedding in Hong Kong. Liang deeply appreciated Guan's thoughtfulness since, by Chinese tradition, the groom's family usually dictated the wedding plan.

"I'm glad to be here," Liang told Guan. "Perhaps you want to reconsider the wedding plan for Zuzhang and Haoyin."

"Zuzhang is expected to graduate from Rensselaer Polytechnic Institute with a bachelor degree in civil engineering in June," Guan proudly told Liang. "Everything is on schedule. I don't see any need for changing the wedding plan."

Although Haoyin had enrolled at Vassar College, Liang realized she would have to give up her studies and return home. "I'm not thinking of changing the date of wedding," Liang said. "I just wonder if you may have second thoughts about having the wedding in Hong Kong. After all, it's quite inconvenient for your family to travel that far to accommodate me."

"That's not a problem at all," Guan told Liang. "My father lives in my native district of Cangwu. He certainly wants to attend the wedding of his first grandson. It's more convenient for him to travel from Guangxi Province to Hong Kong than to Beijing."

"My father will also find it more convenient and desirable if the wedding is held in Hong Kong," echoed Liang. "He's not traveled outside of Hong Kong for more than five years. I doubt very much that he would want to travel to Beijing."

"That settles it. The wedding will take place in Hong Kong in July in the presence of the grandfathers of both families."

"Then I shall instruct my son Dingji to escort Haoyin to Hong Kong as soon as the school year is over. He will be delighted to be home in time to attend his sister's wedding."

"Perhaps Dingji can meet some eligible girls from prominent families in Hong Kong when he comes home this summer," Guan allowed.

"You can be sure his mother would work overtime to make the necessary arrangements," Liang said. "However, sometimes parents, too eager to interfere, are quickly disappointed.

* * *

To fulfill his mission of mediation between Acting President Feng and Premier Duan, Liang Shiyi went to see President Feng on March 18. Feng was obviously pained by the news from the battlefield. "I know my limitations and I cannot produce a peaceful settlement with the South as I desire," the President began. "I blame myself rather than the generals for the military defeats. Last November I had no choice but to accept Duan Qirui's resignation when he refused to reconsider his decision. I really wish he would change his mind."

Liang Shiyi knew too well the dilemma confronting President Feng. Duan Qirui had used his resignation as Premier as a threat to block Feng's peace overture to the South. Since his resignation, Duan had agitated for the establishment of a World War Mobilization Headquarters in order to expand his own influence in the military. To seek the cooperation of Duan, President Feng finally caved in, and on March 1 he appointed Duan as the Director General of a newly-created World War Mobilization Headquarters.

"You've done all you can to allow Duan to pursue his policies in the war against Germany and Austria," Liang assured President Feng. Shiyi agreed with Feng in advocating war against Germany.

"But Duan tries to undermine my effort to find an honorable way to end the conflict with the South. I don't know what else I can do." President Feng said in frustration.

As they spoke, reports poured in indicating the Northern troops had recaptured the strategic town of Yueyang in Hunan the day before. Liang thought this was a stroke of luck. Something positive could come from this. Duan could claim his policy of aggressive pursuit had finally won. "Since the political and military situations have changed in the last three months, Duan may accept the premiership if you offer it to him now." Liang tried to be a peacemaker between the two stubborn old soldiers.

"It's my wish, certainly, but—" Feng suddenly felt it prudent to stop giving his conditions. Instead, he asked, "Have you seen Duan lately?"

"No," Liang replied. "I'll go see him right away if you want me to convey an encouraging message."

Feng studied Shiyi's face. "I will offer Duan the premiership if he agrees to be more cooperative." Feng said unenthusiastically. "I hope you will make that point clear to him."

With that information, Liang went to see Duan Qirui at the World War Mobilization Headquarters. Duan anticipated the purpose of Liang's visit since most of the provincial military commanders who had proposed Liang's mediation were his supporters. However, Duan pretended to be ignorant and waited for Liang to break the news. Liang started the conversation with a polite note. "Three months ago, I met in Japan with Tanaka, the Japanese Army Deputy Chief of Staff. He spoke very highly of you."

Duan did not know what to make of this comment and hoped Tanaka had not told Liang too much about their secret negotiations. His concern was unnecessary. Liang still did not know General Duan had obtained loans from the Japanese for a military build-up. He was now using the World War Mobilization Headquarters as a cover to justify military alliances with Japan. Probing, Duan asked, "What else did he tell you?"

Liang felt Duan's uneasiness and changed the tone, "Oh, we just had a polite exchange. He thought that you will not be out of the premiership for long. And with recent encouraging news from the front line, you must have second thoughts about the premiership."

Duan was reassured. "The provincial military commanders think I should not shrink from my duty at the time of crisis." Duan opened the door a little carefully, and then shut it grudgingly. "But I'm not going to beg for the job."

"What if the job is offered to you again?" Liang asked, pressing the point before the opportunity slipped away.

"Oh, I suppose I would accept it," Duan said, reaching for a pear. That was a good enough answer to break the impasse between Duan and Feng. Shiyi returned to Feng with Duan's comments. Immediately afterwards, President Feng appointed Duan

Qirui the Premier who in turn announced his slate of cabinet ministers on March 23.

At least in public, the dispute between the two had been tempered, but Liang knew full well their conflict was far from over. According to the 1912 Provisional Constitution, Feng was serving as Acting President for the unexpired five-year term. With his incumbency, Feng expected he would be elected by the Parliament as President for a full term in the coming election. Duan, on the other hand, had the support of most army commanders who had nothing but contempt for the Constitution. Duan and his supporters would do anything, short of open revolt, to dislodge the President before the election so that he would not have the advantage of incumbency.

Shortly afterwards, Liang went to Tianjin to see Xu Shichang, the elder statesman of the Beiyang Clique. Liang asked him to mediate the explosive situation lest President Feng might be driven out of office by force and Duan would take over the government without legitimacy. Xu sighed. "I have mediated their difference before without any result. The only way out is to change course completely." Liang understood Xu's reluctance and did not press. Did Xu mean the election of himself as the next President would represent a complete change of course? Liang wondered.

* * *

Returning to Beijing, Liang Shiyi met with his old friend Liang Qichao. Since Qichao had joined Duan Qirui's cabinet as Finance Minister the previous year, he saw the need for streamlining the 1912 Provisional Constitution and making it work more efficiently. After resigning from his post as Finance Minister the previous November, he spent even more time in refining his idea. Adopting the recommendation of Liang Qichao, President Feng had announced in February the revision of the membership structure of the Parliament and the laws for the election of its members. Liang Qichao was excited about his own handiwork, but Liang Shiyi cautioned him, "With due respect to your great effort and honorable intention, the South might regard it as a sabotage of the 1912 Provisional Constitution. It's important to convince the military government in Guangzhou to accept your revision and to participate in the election. I'll try to discern the reaction of the generals in the South when I go back to Hong Kong."

Before he could get away, Liang attended a reception in his honor sponsored by the Chinese Railway Association. Ye Gongchuo, Chairman of the Association, asked Liang to speak on his vision of future railway developments. Liang was also invited to speak to the National Association on Finances. He stressed the importance of tax reform, increased liquidity for the financial market, promotion of industry, and expansion of transportation infrastructure. He later expanded this theme in a pamphlet and printed one hundred thousand copies for general distribution.

On April 2, the Northern troops recaptured Changsha, the capital of Hunan Province. The news from this and other battle fronts encouraged Duan Qirui who decided to go to the front line to boost the morale of his generals and troops on April 20. Viewing this show of arrogance with alarm, Liang Shiyi hoped to calm the reaction of the South as he headed for Hong Kong.

Soon after Liang Shiyi arrived in Hong Kong in May, the events in Guangzhou took an ominous turn. Members of Parliament under the banner of a "Constitution Protection Campaign" suddenly wavered in their support of Sun Yatsen and threw their weight on the side of the Southern generals. Deserted by his political allies and devoid of a mass base of support, Field Marshall Sun Yatsen tendered his resignation to the parliament on May 4 and left Guangzhou for Japan. Subsequently, the Parliament in Guangzhou, responding to the machination of its leader, Wu Jinglian, adopted a Directorate of seven members to take charge of the military government. Although Sun Yatsen was elected as one of its members, he declined to take part in such an awkward scheme of power sharing.

Tang Shaoyi was also elected as one of the seven members of the Directorate but he too declined. Lu Rongting, a general from Guangxi Province, became the most powerful member among equals in the military government. Liang Shiyi dispatched a mutual friend to see Lu and express his interest in negotiating a peaceful settlement between the South and the North. Lu Rongting quickly responded, "If the Beijing government follows the Provisional Constitution of 1912 and elects a new Parliament, all disputes can be settled smoothly. I shall cancel the independence of the South in a few days when the Beijing government announces the acceptance of this proposal." Amicable as this response might seem, Liang knew he had hit a brick wall. The Beijing government had already adopted a *revised* version of the 1912 Provisional Constitution and would not back off.

Worse than the attitude of the Southern generals, was the news from Beijing that Premier Duan Qirui had signed a Sino-Japanese Joint Army Defense Pact on May 15 and a Sino-Japanese Joint Navy Defense Pact four days later. As public opinion was aroused against these pacts, students of Beijing University and other institutions of higher learning in Beijing, marched to the Presidential Palace, requesting the government to abolish the military pacts. But Premier Duan was unyielding, citing the uncertainty of the Russian Bolshevik's Revolution. On May 22, Russians invaded Outer Mongolia, and ten days later, Russians intruded on the border of Xinjiang Province in the northwest. These developments further strengthened the argument of Premier Duan.

In the meantime, Premier Duan Qirui continued to expand his military influence. His trusted aide was busy recruiting for an army under the auspices of the World War Mobilization Headquarters. It would be financed with Japanese loans, presumably for the defense of the northern borders. This new army was stationed in the northern province of Shaanxi where some of Sun Yatsen's supporters were active. Duan's scheme fooled nobody and his militancy caused alarm throughout the country.

The only encouraging news from Beijing was about Liang himself. At a shareholders' meeting of the Bank of Communications in June, Liang Shiyi had been elected chairman of its board of directors and chief executive officer. It was a clear indication of the board's recognition that Liang's political influence was rising again.

* * *

In early July, Haoyin and Dingji arrived in Hong Kong. Guan Zuzhang, Haoyin's fiance, was with them since his family had already assembled in Hong Kong.

After paying respect to their grandfather in his quarters, Haoyin and Dingji went to Madam's drawing room. Liang Shiyi and his second lady were there waiting to discuss the details of Haoyin's wedding plan. As usual, Liang Shiyi was courteous and the second lady deferential when they approached Madam. "The Guan family is unfamiliar with the customs, here" Liang Shiyi informed his wife. "They have entrusted me to make all the arrangements. Do you have any suggestions?"

"The wedding will be a big day for A'er," Madam referred to the second lady in her customary way. "I'll leave everything to her." Madam knew a concubine must wear a pink skirt in the wedding ceremony, but she, the wife, would display her status by wearing a crimson skirt. She was sure the second lady would observe this custom scrupulously, even without her reminder.

Liang Shiyi had to admire her quick thinking and the grace of her words. His second lady wanted to be sure what Madam really meant. She said without any pretense, "You are so kind and considerate to me. But I can assure you that we will do everything according to your wishes."

Although Haoyin had become a Christian at Vassar College, her fiance was a non-believer. Besides, the elders of both the Liang and Guan families held strong traditional Confucian views. A church wedding was out of the question. Liang Shiyi rented a social hall in a public building for the occasion. The wedding ceremony would leave many traditional customs behind, seeming contradictory, if not chaotic, to Shiyi's generation. In response to the modern trend, the bride would dress in white satin with a train and a head piece. The groom would dress in Western attire. However, the wedding would be officiated by a prominent Confucian scholar.

Liang Shiyi made a precedent-setting decision. In Chinese society, the family fortune stayed within the family and passed on to the sons. The daughters would not receive an inheritance, even if the extended family separated from one another. With his father still living, Shiyi and his brother always shared the burden of supporting the extended family, a burden that would pass to the next generation. He could not break away from the old tradition of preserving the family properties through the male line. Instead, he decided to give Haoyin a substantial dowry, which he hoped to offer to his other daughters when they married. After consulting with his brother, he wrote her a check for twenty thousand Hong Kong dollars, a substantial sum, even for his family.

Houyin looked radiant on her wedding day. Liang Shiyi spoke softly to her mother, "Second lady, you've done wonders." Liang had never addressed her as second lady. It was a recognition she deserved, to be elevated to the rank of elders as her daughter was about to be married. Shiyi's fourth and fifth ladies were impressed, but they would not receive such honor unless they bore Liang Shiyi's children.

The Kingmaker

"We're leaving for Beijing in a couple of days," Liang Shiyi told his fourth and fifth ladies after Haoyin's wedding. "I'm expected to be there before August 1. "The Guan family will travel together with us. You'll have a lot of company."

"I don't think I'm in a very good shape for travel," his fourth lady replied. "I was overwhelmed by the excitement of the wedding." In fact, both ladies had complained of being tired and a loss of appetite, but they felt it was their duty to attend to the personal needs of their husband. They were obliged to go along.

When they arrived in Beijing, Liang Shiyi was immediately immersed in Parliamentary and Presidential politics. He had no time to pay attention to his two young concubines, even though both of them looked pale and had frequent spells of coughing. Their trip to Beijing probably contributed to the deterioration of their health. The doctor suspected they had contracted tuberculosis which had not been detected. They waited for laboratory tests to confirm the diagnosis.

When the bad news finally came, Liang Shiyi was shocked beyond belief. The two ladies were ordered to take complete bed rest in an isolated wing of their residence at Ganshiqiao Lane. At that time, there was no miracle drug to cure the disease. The fifth lady, particularly, seemed to be in a very weak condition. A shadow of gloom hovered over Shiyi's family.

This tragic event in the family could not have occurred at a worse time for Liang Shiyi. The new Parliament, to which he had been elected as a Senator, had convened for the first time a few days earlier. Many Senators turned to him for consultation in the election of a Speaker of the Senate.

* * *

Several months earlier, the Beijing government had gone ahead with the election of the members of Parliament under the revised membership structure and election laws. The total membership in the two houses of Parliament was reduced from nearly 900 to approximately 500. Of the 19 provinces and the Mongolia Autonomy Region in the nation, only five provinces in the South refused to participate on the ground that the revision of election laws was illegal. However, the Beijing government had found ways to create representation for those provinces. Whatever rules pre-

289

vailed, the election results were announced on July 12, 1918. The members of both houses were advised to be in Beijing for a joint session of the Parliament in August.

There were no formal political parties at the time. However, three loosely organized political groups shared most of the votes in the election. The Anfu Clique, consisting primarily of Beiyang generals loyal to Duan Qirui, received the most votes. The second largest block went to the Communications Clique, of which Liang Shiyi was the acknowledged leader. The third block was the Research Clique under the joint stewardship of Liang Qichao and Tang Hualong. On August 20, the House of Representatives elected its Speaker and Deputy Speaker, who were from the Anfu Clique. With the support of the Research Clique, the Senate elected Liang Shiyi the Speaker and, two days later, Zhu Qiqian as the Deputy Speaker. The Senate was in the control of the Communications Clique.

While the Parliament in Beijing was busy organizing, the fighting between North and South broke out again in Hunan Province. On August 31, the military government in Guangzhou issued an open telegram challenging the legality of the Beijing government and vowed not to recognize the Presidential election scheduled by the Parliament for September.

According to the election laws, the President and the Vice President of the Republic were to be elected by members of both houses of the Parliament under the one-man-one-vote rule. As the Speaker of the Senate, Liang Shiyi would chair a joint session of both houses for the election. Feng Guozhang, the incumbent Acting President, had the respect of many Beiyang generals and politicians even though he did not have a hard core of followers. On the other hand, Duan Qirui might have had enough votes to win the Presidency if his supporters had not overplayed their hands and angered those who respected Feng Guozhang. In late July, the provincial military commanders who were supporters of Duan floated the name of Xu Shichang, the elder statesman of Beiyang Clique, as a compromise candidate. This strategy worked as a smoke screen to thwart the momentum of Feng's candidacy for a while, but it did not advance their man.

Sensing a deadlock, Liang Shiyi urged the provincial governors and other national leaders of all political persuasions to support the candidacy of Xu Shichang. Except for the leaders of the military government in Guangzhou who strenuously opposed the choice, most replies were positive or neutral.

Liang Shiyi was particularly buoyed by the reaction of Sun Yatsen who had just returned to China from Japan. He received a reply from Wang Jingwei, the right-hand man of Sun Yatsen, which stated, "Dr. Sun returned to Shanghai on August 25. The telegrams and letters sent to him by you and by Zhou Ziqi were transmitted to him immediately. Dr. Sun concluded that since this is not the appropriate time for him to re-enter the political arena as an active player, he intends to devote his energy to political writing and to educate the masses on democracy and social justice. He only hopes that the current problems in China can be solved by other capable statesmen. If Xu Shichang is elected president, he will raise no objection."

Beijing Odyssey

At a joint session of the Senate and the House on September 4, Xu Shichang was elected the President with 425 votes out of 436 ballots cast by members of both houses. The election of the Vice President was supposed to be held the next day. In view of the fact that two former Vice Presidents had successively served as President for the unexpired term of the first and only elected President, the contest for the Vice President was no less contentious. Four candidates, including Duan Qirui and Feng Guozhang, expressed interest. However, because of his role in initiating the Japanese loans and defense treaties, Duan had no chance in winning in a four-way contest. After he withdrew his candidacy, Feng Guozhang also withdrew in the interest of harmony. When Cao Kun, another Beiyang general and the commander of the Northern armies against the South, surged ahead as the leading candidate, General Zhang Zuolin, Military Commander of Fengtian Province, also withdrew from the race. Cao Kun suddenly appeared to be the leading candidate for Vice President.

Liang Shiyi was alarmed by the prospect of Cao Kun's possible election because of his militant position against the South. Xu Shichang had indicated to Liang privately that he would favor peace negotiations after he was sworn in, but the election of Cao Kun as his vice president would spell the end of the peace effort between North and South. As the Speaker of the Senate who chaired the joint session, Liang insisted in delaying the election of the Vice President until a later date. Surprisingly, many members of the Parliament agreed and boycotted the joint session on September 5. For lack of a quorum, the election of the Vice President had to be postponed.

When negotiations behind the scene by various cliques did not produce an acceptable compromise, Liang Shiyi boldly suggested the post of Vice President be left vacant for a member from the South as an inducement for a peaceful settlement. That radical idea was well received by many members of the Parliament. Since the inauguration date was scheduled for October 10, a last ditch effort was made to call another joint session of the Parliament on October 9 to discuss the election of the Vice President. However, because of lack of a quorum, the election had to be postponed again. The next day, Xu Shichang was sworn in as President, leaving the position of the Vice President vacant indefinitely.

* * *

"Feng Guozhang deserves a lot of credit for the peaceful transfer of power even though it is not generally acknowledged," Liang Shiyi commented to Liang Qichao after the inauguration. "For a former Beiyang general, he has overcome his military background and personal ambition to allow this to happen. Having lost a bitter struggle for power with Duan Qirui, he has gracefully bowed out and supports the effort for a peaceful settlement with the South. He can now go back to his native village for retirement with a good conscience."

"The joint effort of the Communications Clique and the Research Clique has been essential in providing the necessary number for the boycott," Liang Qichao replied with some satisfaction. "Without the cooperation of the members in these two cliques, Cao Kun would have been Vice President today."

After Xu Shichang became President, Duan Qirui resigned as Premier. President Xu appointed the Interior Minister in Duan's cabinet, Qian Nengxun, to serve concurrently as Acting Premier for the transition.

Liang Shiyi was determined to make a peaceful settlement with the South his first priority even though the military government in Guangzhou had denounced the election of Xu Shichang as President. He persuaded President Xu and Acting Premier Qian to authorize him to make an overture to the South.

However, Shiyi could not get away from Beijing at the moment because of pressing business in Parliament and the poor health of his fourth and fifth ladies. He turned, instead, to Guan Mianjun for this delicate mission. Guan had given up his government post three years earlier and pursued his hobby as a ardent collector and dealer of Chinese antiques. A native of Guangxi Province, he had some influential friends who could speak frankly with Lu Rongting, the Guangxi general who was the most powerful man in the Guangdong Military Government. Guan took up this mission and went south to meet the Governor of Guangxi. Together they approached General Lu and presented a plan for peace negotiation from Liang Shiyi. A week later, Liang received a reply by telegram from General Lu, indicating his willingness to discuss this matter further. Liang decided to take an active part in the negotiation as soon as he could go south.

By the end of October, Shiyi's fourth lady seemed to respond to complete bed rest and was getting better. However, his fifth lady's health had deteriorated rapidly. Her case was so virulent that she was placed in an isolation ward. Her doctor warned that she might not live much longer. When Liang went to see his fifth lady in the hospital on a brisk autumn morning, they both sensed that this was their last meeting.

In the past two months, his fifth lady had reflected on the misfortunes of her own life. Born in a poor family, she was sold at the age of seven by her parents to a woman who operated a brothel. Because of her exceptional beauty, she was taught to sing and dance before being forced to become a prostitute at fifteen. After several years of misery, she finally became Liang's fifth lady. She was overjoyed to find a loving husband and a family which treated her with understanding. The year of her marriage, she told him, was dream-like, almost too good to be true. Even in her current state of failing health, she was thankful for the good care she had received. Without self pity, she was at peace with herself in death as in life.

When she saw her husband sitting at her bed side, she struggled to express herself slowly, "You have rescued me from misery and have given me everything I could hope for in life. I only regret that I cannot live longer to repay your kindness. My illness has caused you great pain. You deserve someone who is healthy and can serve you well as my life is coming to an end."

Liang Shiyi, choked with emotion, whispered, "When your life ends, you will be buried among my ancestors in my native village." The fifth lady was relieved by the assurance that, in death as in life, she would be accepted by his family. As he walked away, he turned back to look at her once more. He sadly saw the beauty of the season withering away.

After the funeral for his fifth lady, Liang Shiyi's time was dominated by the debate on foreign policies in the Parliament. In late summer, he had received a letter from Wellington Koo, the Chinese Minister to the United States, appraising him of the possible outcome of the war in Europe. Koo regarded Liang as one of his early mentors and, periodically, kept in touch with him. Koo sent word that victory by the Allied Powers was imminent. "China must move swiftly if it wants to claim a seat at the peace conference," Koo cautioned. With Koo's letter in hand, Liang Shiyi urged President Xu to take decisive actions to assert China's position in supporting the Allied Powers.

President Xu was also pressured by the Ministers of the Allied Powers in Beijing. They jointly complained to him on October 31 that China had not seriously come to the aid of the Allied cause. Although a declaration of war against Germany and Austria had been issued by then Acting President Feng Guozhang on August 14, 1917, it had not received approval of the Parliament. President Xu now took the lead in advising the Parliament to rectify this mistake. On November 2, 1918, both houses of Parliament voted to approve the declaration of war retroactively. It was a necessary action to formalize China's participation on the side of the Allied Powers before the armistice took effect on November 11. Three days after the armistice in Europe, Liang left for Hong Kong.

Before his departure, Liang Shiyi saw to it that the Beijing government announced a ceasefire to demonstrate its good faith for a peaceful settlement. The Guangdong Military Government responded by announcing a ceasefire a week later.

* * *

As soon as Liang Shiyi arrived in Hong Kong, he sent an emissary to Guangzhou to see Tang Shaoyi who was then active in the military government in Guangzhou. Liang proposed a peace conference between North and South without preconditions. Could Tang check with the authority in the South whether such a proposal would be acceptable? Tang promised to give him an answer within ten days.

While waiting for Tang's reply in Hong Kong, Liang Rucheng, the manager of Huimin Company came to see him with a message from Beijing. "The government is concerned about China's future in the Peace Conference at Versailles. To boost China's claim of contributing to the cause of the Allied Powers, the State Council has asked me to report to the government the activities of this company in recruiting Chinese laborers for non-combat duties in Europe. This is the first time our secret operation will become public knowledge."

"I trust you will handle it expeditiously," Liang Shiyi replied. "As I planned all along, we would allow the government to claim the credit if our mission is seen as successful, but we would take the blame as a private enterprise if it is seen as a failure. I certainly hope China can argue its way into the peace conference, one way or the other."

Although planned as a self-supporting operation with initial loans backed by Liang Shiyi, to be reimbursed by France, the company suffered losses due to the depreciation of the Franc. Liang Rucheng was uneasy that the company was left with a debt of 160,000 yuan. However, Liang Shiyi agreed to donate an amount equal to the deficit so the company could close its books.

Tang Shaoyi's reply was generally encouraging and moderate in tone. The South would no longer contest the presidency but would not accept the new Parliament. If some way could be found to reconstitute the Parliament with representation from the South, the Guangdong Military Government would send a delegation to a peace conference to be held in Shanghai, a neutral ground under the protection of the International Settlement. The South would also send Tang Shaoyi as its chief delegate and would have no objection to Zhu Qiqian as the proposed chief delegate from the North. The sticking point appeared to be the re-organization of the Parliament which could undo the promising start.

With the detailed proposal, Liang Shiyi felt he could persuade President Xu to start the negotiation process with the South. If he had to give up his post as Speaker of the Senate in order to facilitate the re-organization of the Parliament, he would gladly do so.

* * *

In his leisure in Hong Kong, Liang Shiyi thought of his fourth lady who was still convalescing at home in Beijing. He realized she would not be able to lead a normal life for some time. To fill the void of a personal attendant and lover, Liang hurriedly took another young woman from the Zheng family as his sixth lady before leaving Hong Kong.

The trip to Beijing had become almost routine for Liang Shiyi but his sixth lady was excited as they boarded a steamship in Hong Kong. In the past few weeks, everything happened so suddenly that her life was like a dream. Beijing was so far away, she had no idea what to expect. Her husband noticed her trepidation and tried to comfort her. "Everything will be all right," he gently told her.

When Liang arrived in Beijing, he found the condition of his fourth lady improving but her spirit broken.

"Your doctor thinks you have improved a great deal," Liang Shiyi said, trying to comfort her. "With continued rest, you should be back to normal very soon."

"I hope the doctor is right," she replied, "but I don't know if I can ever serve you again in the same way as before."

Liang Shiyi thought this was the right moment to introduce the addition of the sixth lady in the family. Liang hoped she could be as helpful to this newcomer as she had been to the fifth lady. "I have brought Aliu (No. 6) with me from Hong Kong. I trust she will be helpful to you as she has been to me."

The fourth lady looked at the newcomer with cold eyes and said nothing. She seemed to have lost her usual confidence. Liang changed the subject.

* * *

For the moment, Liang Shiyi was most concerned about the proposed North-South Peace Conference which he had personally brokered. Noting that Parliament remained the obstacle to the negotiation, he felt he could not continue to be the Speaker of the Senate and, at the same time, an honest broker for the conference. With Liang's persistent persuasion, President Xu finally gave his consent to send a delegation from the North to the peace conference with the condition that the re-organization of the Parliament would be an agenda item. Liang Shiyi then tendered his resignation as the Speaker of the Senate. In accordance with custom, so did the Deputy Speaker, Zhu Ququian.

After he announced his resignation, Liang found Zhu in his Senate office. "I trust you don't regret having resigned your leadership position in the Parliament in order not to diminish your value as a negotiator with the South. My desire for peace is so great that no obstacle should stay in its way. The President has agreed to appoint you as the chief delegate to the peace conference. I assume you will accept it."

"I cannot think of anything more important than the proposed conference," Zhu Qiqian thoughtfully replied. "Seven years ago, you worked so hard behind the scenes to negotiate the abdication of the Qing Emperor to avert a civil war. Now you find yourself working earnestly on another peace mission of no less historical significance. Whether or not I succeed in the negotiation with the South, you have made the ultimate sacrifice in the arduous quest for peace."

Steven T. Au

Liang Shiyi leaving Beijing Cathedral
after the Victory Celebration on November 13, 1918

The Ultimate Conciliator

Liang Zhijian and His Family on His Eightieth Birthday in 1923

Three Fervent Wishes

"Have you given any thought to serving in some significant capacity in the new cabinet?" President Xu Shichang asked Liang Shiyi when they were finally alone in the President's office. Liang had come to the Palace for the 1919 New Year greeting and was invited to stay for a chat. Liang Shiyi looked around. The setting was far more subdued than when the office was occupied by Yuan Shikai.

"No, but I don't think it's such a good idea," Liang replied. Although his resignation as the Speaker of the Senate the month before had confounded his political enemies, his altruistic motive was questioned. The supporters of General Duan Qirui blamed him for their own failure to advance their candidate for President; and the supporters of General Cao Kun saw him as the instigator who denied their candidate the Vice Presidency. If he joined the present administration, it would be interpreted as a quid pro quo for his support of Xu.

"I'm planning to reshuffle the cabinet," the President spoke with a knowing smile. "You're wasting your talent by staying on the sideline."

"Oh, I'm not so sure of that," Liang replied. "Perhaps I can make greater contributions to the cause of peace as a private citizen." He thought it would be easier for him to maintain his role as an honest broker between North and South if he was not a part of the administration. He could not allow any speculation of his intention to ruin the peace negotiation he had labored so hard to initiate.

President Xu stroked his mustache. "What is your future plan, then?" he asked.

"Ever since my return from the tour of Japan last year, I have had three fervent wishes for China," Liang replied. "First, North and South will be united as one China to meet external threats. Second, China will fight for a place at the peace conference in Europe in order to renegotiate the unequal treaties imposed by foreign powers. Third, China will develop its industries to improve the living conditions of its people." After a pause, he added, "As a private citizen, I will do my best to support the government in pushing the first two objectives. I hope the government will set enlightened policies to encourage private investment and unleash the energy of its people to pursue the third objective."

"I understand." President Xu nodded. "Your wishes are my wishes. In spite of so many obstacles ahead, I hope you can achieve what you want."

President Xu knew Liang had made up his mind and did not press him further about a cabinet appointment. Instead, he changed the subject, "I missed your wise counsel since you stepped down as the Speaker of the Senate. I trust you won't mind serving in an advisory capacity to the government. As you know, I have set up two government commissions to study the urgent problems arising from the World War. You are preeminently qualified to serve on the Foreign Relations Commission and the Post World War Economic Commission. I want to appoint you a member of both."

Liang Shiyi had indeed a deep interest in such forums for national policy debate. It did not take much persuasion for him to accept the membership on these commissions. He thanked the President and took another look at his office before leaving.

* * *

President Xu Shichang's reshuffled cabinet continued to be dominated by friends and supporters of Duan Qirui. Xu appointed Qian Nengxun, a holdover in Duan's cabinet, as the new Premier. Duan was content for the time being to hold the military power as Director General of the World War Mobilization Headquarters. Even though the World War was over, Duan used his position as Commander of the Mobilization Army to station his troops along the Mongolian border from northeast to northwest China. When a rebellious group in Shaanxi Province declared its independence and invited a military leader loyal to the South to take over its defense, only Duan's armies could stop the spread of the rebellion. Duan found himself in a good position to exert pressure on President Xu and to sabotage the peace negotiations Xu had initiated with the South.

General Cao Kun, the Commander of the Northern armies in the frontline against the South, had, at least, followed the cease-fire order. Encouraged by the cessation of hostility, the Military Government in the South announced on January 9 that it would send a team of ten delegates headed by Tang Shaoyi to attend the North-South Peace Conference in Shanghai. However, on the same day, Duan's army, stationed in Shaanxi Province, launched an attack on the pocket of supporters of the South. In desperation, President Xu wanted to exclude Shaanxi Province as a cease-fire zone but his scheme was denounced by the South.

Although alarmed by the deterioration of the cease-fire agreement, the Military Government in the South ordered its delegates to proceed with their trip to Shanghai in the hope of salvaging the tenuous truce. This move was a welcome respite to President Xu since he desperately needed more time to resolve conflicting advice on the negotiation strategy for the Northern delegates headed by Zhu Qiqian.

Terribly upset, Zhu Qiqian called on Liang Shiyi at his home in Ganshiqiao Lane. Zhu told him, "In conversation with some of the delegates, I got the impression they have a hidden agenda. I have the suspicion they were appointed to appease Duan Qirui and would hinder my ability to negotiate. I feel betrayed by men I saw as friends."

"You must be patient," Liang advised him. "Try to put them on a leash. Just remember that you have something to offer to the South. The office of Vice President is still open and the President is receptive to accept someone from the South to fill that post in a gesture of reconciliation."

"I wish you had taken this job instead of recommending me to President Xu," Zhu commented. "You have the wisdom and patience I lack."

"Are you serious?' Liang laughed. "Can you imagine Tang Shaoyi and I sitting across the table in negotiation? We used to be on the same side and planned strategies together. Could anyone trust an agreement produced by the two of us?"

"I guess you're right." Zhu suddenly appreciated the irony that friends and foes could change sides so easily. "If the negotiation is successful, Tang Shaoyi may very well be nominated by the South as the candidate for the next Vice President. With the present make-up of the Parliament, his candidacy will probably be blocked by the supporters of Duan Qirui under the best of circumstances. If you are perceived to have a hand in his nomination, his chance of being elected will be further damaged."

Liang Shiyi was deep in thought. He finally said, "I hope you will convince the South that both sides must compromise in order to succeed. The election of President Xu was only the second presidential election of the Republic. If both the South and the North accept the result of the election of the President and Vice President, it would legitimize the political process for the future."

"Yes, the stakes are high and all will be losers if we fail." Zhu Qiqian concluded his visit with a renewed sense of resolve.

* * *

The next day, Liang Shiyi was in his office at the Bank of Communications when he received a phone call from Premier Qian Nengxun. After reshuffling his cabinet, Qian had turned his attention to the peace conference in Versailles, scheduled to begin on January 18, 1919. He asked Liang to come to his office for consultation.

Earlier in December when Liang Shiyi was still Speaker of the Senate, he had prepared a position paper for the Chinese delegation to the Versailles conference. He had also helped to assemble a delegation of five seasoned diplomats, including the Foreign Minister, the Minister to the United States, the Minister to Great Britain, and two others knowledgeable in international laws. Under the instruction of the Premier, these diplomats had immediately sailed for France. They were followed by a large entourage of advisors and observers. However, at the insistence of the Japanese government, on the grounds that China had contributed nothing in winning the war, the allies denied China its right at the conference table.

The outline of Liang Shiyi's position paper emphasized four major points. First, use of the good offices of the United States, Britain and France, to force Japan to forfeit its Twenty-One Demands on China. Second, reclamation of China's sovereignty of all former German possessions in Shandong Province which had been taken over by Japan. Third, the elimination of the unequal treaties in the economic sphere which restricted the Chinese government, such as the limitation on import duties and the exemption of foreign companies from alcohol and tobacco taxes. Finally, demand of the publication of all secret treaties among nations affecting innocent parties. It was an echo of Woodrow Wilson's advocacy of "open covenant openly arrived at."

As soon as Liang sat down, the Premier began, "The peace conference in Europe is only a week away. The Chinese delegation is now in Paris, waiting to attend this conference. But so far China has not been invited."

Liang Shiyi noted the Premier's nervous gestures. He replied calmly, "This is a most unfortunate development. What's the latest news from our Foreign Minister?"

"I have already instructed the Foreign Ministry to incorporate the ideas in your position paper as our negotiation position," Premier Qian replied. "Furthermore, Foreign Minister Lu Zhengxiang has fought hard to forward China's contribution to the war effort through the Chinese laborers in Europe. So far he has not succeeded."

As the Premier spoke, his face grew red and angry. He hoped Liang Shiyi could provide him more information about the Chinese laborers in France, for whom Liang had played an important role.

"You have to push the issue of Chinese contribution as hard as you can," Liang advised the Premier. "After that, you can only wait to see the result." In his heart, Liang felt equally frustrated. He offered as much help as he could before leaving the Premier's office.

At this same time, the Chinese laborers in Europe suddenly became very visible. Almost 200,000 men in France alone, they were no longer shielded in ammunition factories or railroad cars. Many of them were waiting to be shipped home at French ports. Others wanted to stay in France. Under the sponsorship of the Chinese Y.M.C.A., Yan Yangchu (aka Jimmy Yen), who had started a self-study program in the Chinese labor camps during the war, now tried to help those who wanted to get a foothold in France. With shortage of manpower immediately after the World War, France allowed some Chinese laborers to continue to work there.

As the peace conference began in Versailles, the Chinese delegation was still left out in the cold. Three days later, however, the Chinese delegation received welcome news. The perseverance of the Chinese diplomats had worked! The five diplomats appointed by the Chinese government were officially accredited for the conference.

As the good news reached Beijing, Premier Qian called Liang Shiyi to thank him. "We wouldn't even know how to begin the argument with the Western Powers if it were not for your foresight in recruiting Chinese laborers for non-combat duties in Europe."

Liang was sober in his reply. "The people of China have spoken. The Western Powers can no longer ignore their cries. But the difficult tasks still lie ahead. I cannot take credit or comfort in advancing just one small step to shake off the bondage of the unequal treaties imposed on China."

* * *

The World War had adversely affected European industries and trade with Asia. Between 1913 and 1918, British exports to China fell by one half, French to less than a third, and German to zero. It was a golden opportunity for China to develop its industries relatively unhindered by foreign competition. Chinese industries and commerce grew by leaps and bounds. As a result, the Chinese foreign-trade deficit was cut by ninety percent.

These new industries and enterprises gave rise to new merchant and labor classes who were sensitive to China's predicament under imperialism. At least ten million from these classes had received some sort of modern education. Most of them lived in the cities where they contributed to the expansion of urban centers and their economy. They were determined to defend Chinese national interests and eagerly watched their government's performance at Versailles. Many private citizen groups sent observers to Paris to rub shoulders with the official delegates in order to influence their action.

Liang Shiyi shared their hopes and fears about the fate of China. He understood the window of opportunity for economic development in China might be short-lived. If uncompetitive industries were left to perish, foreign imports would again rise to threaten China's young industries. He recognized that a successful transformation of the state-dominated economy was impossible without deeper political change. He appealed to industrialists to join forces in improving their products for export.

An efficient national transportation system was a high priority for economic development. Foreign bankers were practically knocking at the doors to offer financing for railway construction in China. In fact, at the preliminary gatherings of the delegates at the Versailles peace conference, several major foreign powers had floated the idea of a multi-nation consortium of bankers as an umbrella organization for providing development loans to China. Under a railway unification plan which would consolidate existing loans for railway construction, the consortium would control all revenues from all railways in China to repay the existing and new loans. Liang Shiyi was leery of the plan. He strongly opposed the multi-nation consortium because of its monopolistic power in dictating the terms of foreign loans.

When Liang Shiyi took his seat on the Foreign Relations Commission, it was dominated by the Research Clique, including Xiong Xiling, Zhang Qian and Liang Qichao. Another member of the clique was the chairman and executive secretary of the commission. The commission had been in operation only since late December, but had already passed a resolution in favor of the railway unification plan. They had also voted on January 8 to send the resolution by telegram to the Chinese delegates waiting to attend the peace conference at Versailles. In the name of the State Council, it instructed the Chinese delegates to present the resolution to Western powers. Given the prominence of the Research Clique members, the telegram received the full attention of the Chinese delegates in Paris, even though the Ministry of Communications and the Cabinet had no prior knowledge of the independent action of the Commission.

That Chinese foreign policy could be so influenced by individuals reflects a time when many prominent citizens felt it was their patriotic duty to take matters into their own hands. They realized the fate of China was hanging in the balance at the peace conference and that their government was not doing enough to enhance the position of China toward Western Powers. In a break with the government on various policies, Xiong Xiling and Zhang Jian founded the People's Foreign Policy Association to further their own agenda. Their political allies, Liang Qichao and several Research Clique members, were already in Paris to champion their cause.

Not to be outmaneuvered, Liang Shiyi cabled Ye Gongchuo, who was also in Paris in his capacity as the Deputy Minister of Communications, and asked him to forestall any action taken by the Chinese official delegates on this critical issue. In the absence of Ye, who was also the President of the Chinese Railway Association, Liang used his prestige as an elder statesman to urge its members to voice their opposition to the consolidation of foreign loans for railway construction. Finally, Minister of Communications Cao Rulin, added his voice opposing the resolution of the Foreign Relations Commission. Consequently, at a meeting of the State Council, the Cabinet voted to instruct the official Chinese delegates in Paris to sidetrack this issue.

The events of early 1919 highlighted, vividly, the weakness and indecision of the Chinese government. President Xu Shichang had to contend himself with military commanders of questionable loyalty, high civilian officials nurturing their own agenda, and rising expectations from an increasingly vocal populace. No wonder Liang Shiyi thought he could accomplish more outside rather than inside of the government. His fervent wishes were tenuous at best, but without them he would have nothing to hope for.

Signature Not Forthcoming

After initial posturing and maneuvering on both sides, the North-South Conference brokered by Liang Shiyi finally began to take shape. The delegation from the South, headed by Tang Shaoyi, arrived in Shanghai in late January 1919. They met with the Southern supporters to map a coherent strategy. The delegation from the North, headed by Zhu Qiqian, arrived three weeks later. The North-South Peace Conference met for the first time in the former German Chamber of Commerce Building in Shanghai on February 20.

From the beginning, Tang Shaoyi insisted on two preconditions for negotiating a permanent settlement. First, the cease-fire must include the contested area in Shaanxi, and second, the Beijing government must curb the military power of Duan Qirui. This included the elimination of the World War Mobilization Army and the cancellation of the Japanese loans and Sino-Japanese military alliance negotiated by Duan Qirui. Unable to persuade Duan to accept the terms of the South, President Xu was hesitant in conceding to Tang's preconditions. Outraged at Xu's indecision, the South sent the Beijing government an ultimatum on February 28, requesting a reply within forty-eight hours.

Lacking satisfaction from the North after two days, Tang announced that the Southern delegates would stop further negotiation. Caught in an untenable position, the Northern delegates proclaimed they were not responsible for Duan's action and sent in their resignations to the Beijing government. The peace conference was in peril.

In the meantime, there was a flurry of activity among foreign diplomats who wanted to save the cease-fire. In succession, the ministers of Britain and France went to see President Xu, expressing their concerns about renewal of fighting in Shaanxi. To apply additional pressure on the Beijing government, the ministers of Britain, France, United States and Italy requested that Duan's army not be used for fighting a civil war. The minister of Japan declined to join in their effort.

Liang Shiyi, who had remained in the background all this time, also went to see President Xu in order to salvage the peace conference which he had so painstakingly arranged. He offered to intercede with General Lu Rongting, a powerful member

305

of the Military Government in the South, on the condition that the Beijing government would curb Duan's military action. Caving in to the inevitable, President Xu ordered Duan to stop fighting and sent a personal representative to Shaanxi to supervise the cease-fire. Still working behind the scenes, Liang Shiyi pleaded with his friends in the South to reconsider. It was not until the end of March that fighting in Shaanxi came to a halt. President Xu was confident enough to plead with the South to resume the peace negotiation. There was every hope that the North-South conference would be resumed in early April.

* * *

In Versailles, China faced other obstacles. The five seasoned diplomats, including Foreign Minister Lu Zhengxiang, Minister to Great Britain Alfred Saokee Sze (aka Si Shaoji), and Minister to the United States Wellington Koo (aka Gu Weijun) had met a persistent foe. Despite their gallant efforts, the Chinese delegates were outwitted by the Japanese.

In late January, the special committee of the Versailles Conference, which consisted of two delegates each from Great Britain, France, Italy, Japan and the United States, invited two Chinese delegates to attend its meeting. At the outset, Japan demanded that China unconditionally recognize the transfer to Japan all the privileges previously ceded by China to Germany in Shandong Province. Wellington Koo, one of the Chinese delegates, countered that China should be given the opportunity to present its side of the argument before the committee took any action.

Koo made a passionate and eloquent plea for a just solution of the "Shandong Problem." Noting Woodrow Wilson's principle of "open covenant openly arrived at," he declared that the secret treaty signed by former Chinese Premier Duan Qirui with Japan in early 1917 would not survive the scrutiny of the Allied Powers. In return for Japanese naval assistance against Germany, a common enemy, Japan had forced Duan to accept Japan's claims to the disposal of Germany's rights in Shandong Province when the war ended. Koo thought the disclosure of this secret treaty would win the sympathy of the Western Powers, and his strategy seemed to gain some ground.

Infuriated by Koo's assertion, the chief Japanese delegate took the floor to disclose other secret agreements made by Duan Qirui in 1918 while he was still the Premier. To their complete astonishment, the Chinese delegates learned for the first time that Duan Qirui had also entered into secret agreements with Japan in securing huge Japanese loans to enhance his military power. These agreements granted the Japanese the rights to station police and establish military garrisons in Jinan and Qingdao in Shandong Province. Duan had also mortgaged to Japan the total income from two proposed Shandong railways as partial payment for its loans to China. The hope of the Chinese delegates was totally shattered by these humiliating secret agreements. President Woodrow Wilson, who had earlier been sympathetic to China's desire to recover its Shandong rights, now felt Japan had staked out a firm claim to them on the basis of international law. In April 1919, he agreed with David Lloyd George of Britain and Georges Clemenceau of France to transfer all of

Germany's Shandong rights to Japan.

As the Chinese delegates at Versailles realized they had not been fully briefed of the situation by their own government, urgent telegrams were dispatched between Paris and Beijing. Not even the Foreign Ministry in Beijing had any record of Duan's secret agreements with Japan but the State Council finally admitted that a copy had been found in the Premier's office. The Chinese delegates acknowledged their case as hopeless because of the prior secret agreements. This admission by the Chinese government on May 1 shook the Chinese public like an earthquake.

Three days later, students from universities and colleges in Beijing staged a mass protest in front of the Legation Quarters but were denied access to the ministers of foreign powers in Beijing. The student demonstrators then went to the home of Cao Yulin, Minister of Communications, who along with Lu Zhongyu, a former Chinese Minister to Japan, were blamed for helping Duan in the negotiation of the Japanese loans. Unable to locate Cao, who was in hiding, they found Zhang Zhongxiang, the Chinese minister to Japan who had just completed his tour of duty and happened to be in Cao's home. Without losing a moment, the students struck blow after blow on Zhang, who was finally rescued by the police and sent to a hospital.

* * *

The disclosure of Duan Qirui's secret agreements with Japan did not help negotiations in the North-South peace conference which had resumed on April 8. It confirmed the South's long-held suspicions that Duan had been using the Japanese loans to fight an all-out civil war against the South. Since the Beijing Parliament was dominated by Duan's Anfu Clique, the South insisted on the abolishment of the current Beijing Parliament as the precondition for recognizing Xu Shichang as the legitimate President of a united China. However, the Parliament would not accept the South's condition regardless of the desire of President Xu. The negotiation, which had raised such high expectations, broke off and the peace conference ended on May 13.

Zhu Qiqian went to see Liang Shiyi in his home at Ganshiqiao Lane shortly after he returned to Beijing. He was quite demoralized by the outcome of the negotiations with the South. Zhu complained bitterly. "Tang Shaoyi has taken the moral high ground even if it makes no strategic sense. But the stakes are too high for him to play such a dangerous game."

Liang defended his one-time mentor. "Don't forget that Tang acted on behalf of the revolutionaries even though he himself has come from the upper echelon of Chinese politics. I have never doubted his profession of democracy but I'm not so sure of the ruling members of the military government in the South. They are a mixed bag of politicians, from visionaries to power grabbers, who use Tang's prestige to advance their own causes."

"I must have disappointed you who have put so much faith in me," Zhu said in apology. "In any case, I will not be a member of the delegation even if the talk is resumed."

"It's not your fault," Liang consoled. "Bad as the situation is between North and

South, the news from Paris is even worse. I hope President Xu takes a strong position against the Versailles Treaty as it now stands. There's no point in dithering while the nation is on fire."

Indeed, the Beijing government was bombarded with angry protests from all directions. Following the student protests in Beijing on May 4, demonstrations by students, merchants and workers sprang up in cities all over the country. The Chinese public was aroused as never before by the betrayal of Chinese sovereignty to Japan in Shandong. China's delegates at Versailles were bombarded by petitions and protests from political and business groups from overseas Chinese communities, and from Chinese students abroad. The government in Beijing was under unrelenting pressure from the public to instruct the Chinese delegates in Paris not to sign the Versailles Treaty.

At first President Xu tried to restore calm by ordering the police in Beijing not to interfere with orderly student demonstrations. However, after hearing the report of violence against government officials, he ordered a crackdown on demonstrators. When the situation worsened by mid-May, the Minister of Education resigned. Several days later, Cai Yuanpei, the President of Beijing University, left town after turning in his letter of resignation. There was no credible leadership that could defuse the tense situation when high-school students in Beijing joined with the university students to call for a strike of classes. On June 3, the government took the offense and arrested one thousand student activists gathering at Beijing University. Almost immediately, the merchants in Shanghai went on strike in sympathy and demanded the release of the arrested students and the dismissal of Cao Rulin, Lu Zhongyu and Zhang Zhongxiang, who became the target of the fury. Soon the government gave in to the demands by releasing the students in custody and accepting the resignation of the three officials.

On June 11, President Xu announced his resignation to both Houses of the Parliament. It was a tactical move to force out the Premier who was in sympathy with Duan Qirui. After the resignations of the Premier and his cabinet were accepted, the State Council advised the nation that the President decided to cancel his resignation. President Xu was so preoccupied with the fight for his political life, he simply ignored the urgent pleading of the Chinese delegates in Paris for his instruction on the signing of the Versailles Treaty.

As the date for the treaty signing ceremony on June 28 drew near, the Chinese delegates in Paris became desperate. They huddled among themselves and decided against signing the treaty in the absence of any instruction from Beijing. However, the Chinese students and demonstrators in Paris were unaware of their decision. They organized a group of demonstrators, surrounded the hotel where the Chinese delegates stayed and forcibly prevented the delegates from attending the signing ceremony. Belatedly President Xu telegraphed an instruction not to sign, but the telegram was sent too late to reach Versailles before the June 28 deadline. The Versailles Treaty, nontheless was concluded without China's acceptance or signature.

Cupid Gone Astray

Amid the political fallout of the Versailles Treaty on the government in Beijing, Liang Shiyi stayed home at Ganshiqiao Lane most of the time in the spring of 1919. Since his return to Beijing with his sixth lady the previous December, Liang Shiyi had tried to cheer his fourth lady who was recovering from her illness. When her doctor informed the family that her condition was no longer contagious, Liang encouraged her to get back to her normal activities. To fill in for the rest of his family, who were in Hong Kong, he invited his eldest daughter Haoyin and her husband to make the east wing of the house their home.

Liang Shiyi was delighted when his niece and her husband Lin Zhenyao came with their children from Tianjin for a short stay in early April. After dinner on the night following their arrival, Liang told them his son Dingji, a sophomore at Boston University, would return home for summer vacation. Liang Shiyi intimated that Dingji, at 21, should think seriously about marriage.

"Do you want to find a suitable girl for him when he comes back from the United States in July?" Lin asked.

"That's crossed my mind," Liang replied. "Do you have suggestions?"

"As you know, the daughters of Zhao Qinghua, our former colleague in the Ministry of Communications, are the toast of the town. They are beautiful, intelligent and modern, although I'm not sure of their ages."

"I have heard as much," Liang said, "but I think they are too Westernized and sophisticated for our family."

Lin suddenly thought of the family of a fellow native of Fujian Province. "Perhaps you may consider the daughters of Zheng Lequan?" Zheng managed an American-style five-and-ten-cent store in Beijing. A person of modest means, he was best known for being a grandson of Lin Zexu, the famous Imperial Commissioner who precipitated the opium war against Great Britain in 1839. Although China lost the war and suffered terrible consequences, most Chinese still respected Lin Zexu as a great patriot who'd had the courage to resist the British at all cost.

"I don't know the family well," Liang Shiyi replied. "However, our family would be honored to be related to someone descended from Lin Zexu."

"I heard their eldest daughter is unassuming and wise beyond her years," Lin added.

"That's what I like to hear," Liang said, clapping his hands together. "I trust you can convey my intention and extend an invitation to them to visit us when Dingji is in town."

It was so arranged. Liang Shiyi immediately informed his wife in Hong Kong about the prospect and asked her to come to Beijing. He knew Madam would be very happy to receive the news, even though she was not very keen on traveling.

Just as he anticipated, Madam sent words to her husband that she would come to Beijing with her daughter Huaisheng as soon as the girl finished the spring semester in school. By the end of June, both mother and the daughter were on their way. Liang's household was excitedly making preparations for the arrival of Madam.

* * *

Liang Shiyi insisted his wife must retain the undisputed authority in running the household. He had tried to create the impression that his concubines were ladies-in-waiting for her, too. For her part, Madam had long given up her prerogative of sharing a bedroom with her husband. Although she wouldn't believe for a moment the fact or fancy of her husband's smooth comforting words, she had tolerated his new amours as men's folly. But she was not happy that her husband had spent lavishly to buy the favor of younger women, and was particularly concerned that some of them might produce more sons and heirs to his fortune.

Since each concubine would kowtow to Madam when they joined the family, she used the occasion to establish her dominance with each newcomer. And beginning with the fourth lady, Madam dictated that the concubine must come to her living quarters to say good morning and offer her a cup of tea for a period of one month. However, Madam barely knew the sixth lady since this new concubine left Hong Kong with her husband for Beijing almost immediately after she joined the Liang family. That had irked Madam and worried the sixth lady.

The arrival of Shiyi's wife, the famous Madam to the rest of the household, was a big event. His fourth lady, who had lived with Madam under the same roof for much of the past ten years, knew what to expect. She acted discreetly in the family and in public, exhibiting a trait which endeared her to her husband. On the other hand, the sixth lady was a gentle and timid woman who was obedient but was easily frightened. Her husband knew her anxiety and was sympathetic. He tried to sooth her fear and coached her on how to please Madam.

"Madam places a premium on her being served tea in the morning," Liang Shiyi told his sixth lady. "She will expect you to do that for a month since she was deprived of such pleasure when we left Hong Kong in a hurry last December."

"That is easy enough to do," his sixth lady replied. "What else will she expect of me? I will be most happy to comply."

"You can observe Asi for the rest," Liang said, referring to his fourth lady. "She knows the likes and dislikes of Madam."

Beijing Odyssey

Indeed the fourth lady had ordered the servants to clean up the large bedroom in the central living quarter reserved for Madam. The cook was also reminded of Madam's favorite dishes. When Madam finally stepped into the gate of her home, she found no reason to complain, and she was given a wide berth, even by her children. Her daughter Huaisheng preferred to stay in the east wing where her sister Haoyin and her husband lived.

Within days, Dingji also arrived in Beijing for a reunion with his parents. A handsome young man with a bright future, he immediately became the most eligible bachelor among the social circle of his family friends. However, his parents had already set their minds on the oldest daughter of the Zheng family and tried to steer him away from the modern and rebellious girls who defied traditional family values.

* * *

The visit of the Zheng family to Ganshiqiao Lane was a big social event. Zheng Lequan and his wife were accompanied by their two daughters and two sons. The older girl, Shungu, was 19, her younger sister barely 16, and their brothers were also teenagers. It appeared natural for the elders to chitchat in the living room while the young people of both families went out to the courtyard to pursue their own interests. In reality, it was all a planned event so that after a comfortable period with the group of young people, Dingji and Shungu would be left alone in the garden. When all members of both families rejoined in the dining room in the evening, it was a foregone conclusion that everything would have gone as expected.

When the Zheng family returned home, the older boy asked his younger sister privately, "Did you notice that Dingji seemed to pay undue attention to you before walking toward the corner of the garden with Shungu?"

"No. I don't believe so," his sister replied defensively. "Since I was not the intended target for matrimony, I probably acted more freely and was more playful."

"I think it was more than that," he continued. "You might be more attractive to him than our sister. You have a happy-go-lucky and mischievous disposition."

It had occurred to her that what her brother said might be true. She knew her older sister had a very serious demeanor. She remembered when their mother divided the dishes on the table onto the plates of her children, she always ate the most delicious food first while Shungu always did the opposite. Very often, Shungu could not finish the food and she would get the leftover which was really the best on the plate. With girlish instinct, she tried to deflect her brother's comments, "Oh, we are very different. But that has nothing to do with the proposed marriage."

"I'm not so sure about that," he persisted. "We'll wait and see."

"There's nothing to wait for," she protested spiritedly. "Shungu may have a strong will but she always accepts her fate through rationalization. She wants respectability and security which she will get from the Liang family. In return, she will be obedient to her in-laws and get along well with all members." After a brief pause, she added, "Besides, I will not trade my freedom for security. You might as well purge any evil dream from your mind."

But her brother regarded this "evil dream" seriously enough to alert his parents. He was soon relieved of his worry as his parents insisted their older daughter must be married off first. Any other action would doom their older daughter to spinsterhood. There was no room for compromise.

In the living room of Liang family at Ganshiqiao Lane, a similar scene was played out. Dingji told his parents that he preferred the younger of the two sisters of the Zheng family. His mother was the first to express an opinion that raised the eyebrows. She liked the older sister who was plump and healthy, a good sign that she would have many children, and she had been unassuming and very attentive to the conversations of the elders. The younger sister was an immature girl who was, in her view, too clever for her own good, to put it charitably. For all practical purposes, her comment settled the issue once and for all.

Liang Shiyi tried to be more sympathetic. "You must have your own reason to express your preference. However, whatever we may think, the Zheng family will never allow the younger sister to be married first. Why don't you try to go out with the older sister a few times while you are in Beijing? You may learn to like her much more than you realize."

That seemed to be a reasonable approach. Dingji had no real choice unless he wanted to start a family revolution. Some of his contemporaries had made that choice and most had lost out in the skirmishes. After a month of supervised dating, the engagement of Shungu to Dingji was announced.

* * *

Among many visitors to Ganshiqiao Lane in the hectic months of that summer was an American accountant from Boston who worked as an auditor for an international accounting firm. He had befriended Haoyin and her husband who had some business dealings with him. When he heard Dingji was home from Boston, he wanted to meet him and find out the latest hometown news. Since Dingji's sister Huaisheng was also in town, she was often in the company of her sister and brother-in-law and had met Edward Thomas, the American.

Huaisheng had recently graduated from St. Stephen's Girls School in Hong Kong and could speak English reasonably well. At nineteen, she was interested in boys, much to the displeasure of her mother. Tall by Chinese standards, she was very conscious that she was taller than most Chinese men, at least among those that her family considered eligible for marriage. When she first met the red-haired, light-skinned American, she was intrigued by his openness. Before long he asked her for a date which she politely declined, even though she was falling in love with this stranger. She discreetly consulted her brother Dingji who could sympathize but not encourage her to accept the invitation. Knowing their mother, he too would place probity above sentimentality.

After Dingji returned to the United States, Huaisheng met another young man named Ou Shao'an to whom she had expressed more than a casual interest. Tall and handsome, he was the son of Ou Pengxiao, a Hanlin scholar whose family had fled to Huairou with the Liang family during the Boxer Rebellion in 1900. Six years her senior, he might have remembered the time when Huaisheng was born in Huairou. He had recently graduated from Cornell University and was looking for a job after returning from the United States. Recalling the friendship of Liang Shiyi and his father, who was now dead, he came to Ganshiqiao to seek help from "Uncle" Liang. It was only a coincidence that he ran into Huaisheng. He was not in a position financially to consider marriage.

But Huaisheng was intrigued by this young man, who was eventually offered a job at the Tianjin Office of the Bank of Communications by her father. Surely her mother would not object to a well-educated man from a distinguished family, Huaisheng thought. When she took her mother into confidence, she was shocked to learn that her mother was not pleased.

"You know that his family fortune had deteriorated precipitously even before his father died," her mother said calmly. "He has to take care of his mother and a younger brother. I don't want you to suffer. He cannot support you adequately with his salary." Then she added, as if it was an afterthought, "Besides, his mother is a concubine. I don't want my daughter to degrade herself by marrying the son of a concubine."

And there was more! Madam seemed to know all about him. Had she investigated this prospect even before her daughter approached her? Possibly, although she might have known these facts through mutual friends. However, one piece of information had to be extracted from someone who knew this young man well. It was rumored that he had decided to major in agricultural economics instead of economics at Cornell University because the Agriculture College was supported by the Land Grant and charged lower tuition. This was proof enough to her that he was not the ideal son-in-law she was looking for.

Huaisheng confided her grief to her sister Haoyin who brought the matter to the attention of their father. Always the diplomat when he approached Madam, Liang Shiyi said to her, "Huaisheng has reached the age of marriage. Do you notice that she has shown interest in screening eligible young men of our acquaintances?"

Madam replied without hesitation, "Yes, she has indicated her interest in Ou Shao'an, but I don't think it's a good match."

"Why? He's a young man with a bright future and he's descended from a very honorable family."

"I don't think that he's able to support a family yet." Madam was unyielding. "I don't mind having a daughter-in-law from a family of modest means since it's our responsibility to provide for her. But we should look for a well-to-do family for our daughter to free her of financial worries."

"I have never denied the blessings of money," Her husband said, taking on a didactic tone. "I'm aware of the freedom it allows, the achievements it nourishes, and the sense of honor it inspires. But we must also understand the darker side of money that corrodes human spirit if we let money overwhelm every other consideration."

Madam knew how to retreat when she could not have her way. Quiet for a few moments, and finally said, "Huaisheng is still very young. She has plenty of time to think it over when she returns to Hong Kong with me. If she still thinks highly of Ou Shao'an after a period of separation, we can approach the Ou family about marriage." That seemed to be a sensible solution that no one could object to. As usual, Madam prevailed.

* * *

In spite of repeated urging of foreign diplomats, the renewed negotiation for peace between the North and South had reached a stalemate in the summer of 1919. In June, the Premier and his cabinet resigned amid criticism of his failure to return Japanese special privileges in Shandong Province to China. When the Acting Premier in Beijing appointed a protege of Duan Qirui as the new chief delegate for negotiation with the South, the peace process was doomed. The only good news to the Beijing government was that the newly formed All-China Student Union in Shanghai declared the boycott of classes over and urged the students to return to their classes.

In the meantime, there was a power struggle within the ranks of the Military Government in Guangzhou. Sun Yatsen announced his resignation as a member of the Directorate, and the remaining members were not able to establish a united position for the South. Liang Shiyi realized the desperate situation but was hoping against hope that the something might still be salvaged. The South might still soften its stand. In August, he decided to make a last ditch effort to communicate with his contacts in the South as he left for Hong Kong to visit his father.

No Seventh Lady

"I'm so glad all of you returned safely," Liang Zhijian said, greeting his son Shiyi and the entourage who returned home with him from Beijing in the summer of 1919. The clan members were used to these soothing words since they were a part of the ritual after each of them paid respect to the patriarch when they returned from a journey. But this was a special occasion for celebration because Liang Shiyi brought home the most welcome news about Dingji's engagement. His father had never kept it a secret that he wished to see a great grandson in his lifetime.

Receiving the news with great joy, the patriarch could not help but ask, "How soon will the wedding take place?"

"Some time next summer," Liang Shiyi replied. "but we have not set the date yet. We plan to have the wedding in Hong Kong since it will not be convenient for you to travel to Beijing."

The patriarch noted the preliminary arrangement with satisfaction. "What will the bride's family think of this plan?"

"We intend to invite the bride's family, all six of them, to come to Hong Kong with expenses paid. Since they have never been in Hong Kong, they will enjoy the trip." Liang Shiyi invoked the privilege of the groom's family who usually dictated the wedding plan.

"Can the bride speak Cantonese?" his father asked.

"Hardly. But she can pick up the dialect soon enough as she is young and educated." The bride's inability to speak Cantonese did not bother the patriarch since he himself had learned to speak broken Mandarin in his younger days when he prepared for the national civil service examinations.

Left unsaid by Liang Zhijian was the news of the sudden death of his four-year-old daughter, borne by his concubine, the second elderly lady. The girl was a weakling in her short life, but she was the darling in the eyes of her parents. She had contracted diphtheria in late spring and died. Her death, nearly two months earlier, had been a blow to the second elderly lady who had counted on her for security in the Liang family. However, the death of a child was typically hushed in the family and the event was put to rest without much sentimentality. Liang Shiyi had received the bad news from his brother Shixu earlier but he did not bring up the subject to avoid evoking pain to his father.

As he passed out of earshot of his father, Liang Shiyi caught the second elderly lady and could not refrain from saying to her, "It must be very hard on you for such a loss. But you must take good care of yourself and father."

* * *

After fulfilling his duty to report to his father, Liang Shiyi and his entourage went to Madam's living quarters where his second lady and his third daughter, Yusheng, were waiting to greet them. His other children were ushered into see him as soon as they arrived home from school. It was a warm reunion for the children with their father who had been absent for many months. Liang Shiyi looked at his children with great pride and joy. Yusheng, who was only a few months younger than Huaisheng, had graduated from St. Stephen's Girls School in June. His fourth daughter Zangsheng, almost fifteen, was beautiful and lively. His youngest daughter Yisheng, at ten, tried to imitate her sisters in greeting their father. His son Dingshu, at twelve, was quiet and unassuming, while Dingmin, at eleven, was bright but very boisterous.

On their trip home from Beijing, Madam had asked her husband to do something to deflect Huaisheng's fixation on Ou Shao'an. She thought a trip to study abroad might give her a new perspective. After all, Haoyin went to study in the United States. Why not give Huaisheng the same opportunity? Once again her logic was irrefutable, and her suggestion was accepted by her husband. Liang Shiyi would use this family gathering to ask Huaisheng if she would like to study for a year or two in the United States.

Huaisheng was horrified at the proposal and murmured, "I'm quite content to stay home and be close to mother." For a young girl who had graduated from St. Stephen's and admired almost everything Western, the answer appeared to be out of character. Both her father and mother understood her message: she had no intention of giving up her boyfriend. For once, Madam's scheme had backfired.

But Madam was quick to salvage the wreck and said to Huaisheng, "As you know, your brother will come home next summer to get married. After the wedding, he and his wife will go back to the United States to continue his study. You can live with them and you will not feel lonely or homesick."

Huaisheng was almost in tears. She understood the meaning of her mother's message. She was always conscious that her height would make it difficult for her to find a suitable husband. Now she had found a respectable young man whom she loved— tall and handsome beyond her dreams. She would not let her mother turn him away. So she stalled to find an adequate answer.

Fortunately her father came to her rescue. "You don't have to make up your mind now. I just want to let you know that you have the same opportunity as your older sister if you choose to study abroad."

"Thank you, father," Huaisheng said, greatly relieved. "I'll give some thought to your generosity."

Beijing Odyssey

Liang Shiyi might not have known or cared that he had opened a floodgate of requests from his other children. Yusheng saw the opportunity and asked timidly if she could go abroad to study. That was reasonable enough, her father thought, since she had just completed high school. "Well," Liang Shiyi said to her, "That can be arranged if you want to wait until next summer and go to the United States with Dingji after his wedding."

"Of course." Yusheng was thrilled by her father's reply. "I need to prepare myself for the trip anyway."

Suddenly, Madam sprang a surprise, "Why don't you send Zangsheng to study abroad, also. She will be almost sixteen by this time next year."

Liang Shiyi was unprepared for this outburst. Did Madam think this proposal would increase the chance of Huaisheng's willingness to go abroad, or was she trying to make sure Zangsheng would not miss her chance? Whatever her motive, her husband did not want to question. After hesitating for a moment, he replied in a soft voice, "Why not?"

It was Madam's turn to be surprised. She asked, "Do you think the girls can stay with Dingji in Boston?"

"I don't think so," Liang Shiyi said. "Yusheng should attend a finishing school for a year before attempting to apply for admission to college. Both she and Zangsheng can attend the same private school near Boston so that they can keep each other company. Dingji can take care of them in case of emergency and can invite them to Boston during the holidays."

Madam was satisfied with the arrangement. Then Liang Shiyi turned his attention to the younger children and their less expensive requests.

In late afternoon, the children were shepherded like a herd to the library where their grandfather would teach them Confucius classics. The patriarch had lost neither the zeal of his mission nor the fire to discipline his rowdy heirs. No grandchildren older than three years would be spared from this daily routine. The children of Shiyi were joined in the library by the three sons of Shixu, aged eight, four and three. The patriarch used the old techniques he had acquired from years of tutoring adults and children in the same classroom to teach moral values and enforce conformity. His grandchildren had to suffer through his stern lectures each day, even during the regular school year. Only Shixu's one-month-old son was young enough to escape.

* * *

As soon as Liang Shiyi was freed from his family obligations, he sent an emissary to contact the leaders of the Military Government in Guangzhou in order to revive the North-South Peace Conference. However, after the resignation of Sun Yatsen, the Military Government was in limbo and no one could speak with authority for the South. Discouraged by the development, Tang Shaoyi resigned as the chief delegate of negotiation team for the South on October 4, 1919. Liang Shiyi's hope for a unified China was totally dashed.

While Liang Shiyi was waiting for the return of his emissary to Guangzhou, he frequently went to Wuben Club to meet friends and play majong. One evening after dinner, they were entertained by a song-and-dance girl who recited an enchanting classical Chinese poem. A bright woman at eighteen, she had mastered the songs and poems favored by the gentry even though she was barely literate. Endowed with only moderate beauty, she had considerable charm and wit which won the heart of Liang Shiyi. They spent many nights together for carnal pleasure.

Liang Shiyi was intrigued by her unusual candor about her predicament. Her name was Tan Yuying. She had been sold by her parents when she was a child. Her story was a familiar one for girls from poor families who shared her fate, but she struggled to become literate. She confronted her unfortunate situation with character and good judgment. She did not hop at the first opportunity to become someone's concubine, she explained, because that step would be her last opportunity. She had passed over a few men who were willing to pay the price and take her as concubine because she found their character wanting. She was not eager to accept Liang Shiyi's offer, either, until she found out more about him and his family.

She was not upset when Liang Shiyi told her about his strict Confucius upbringing and his respect for his wife in setting rules for his family. She understood Liang's interest in politics which often took precedence over family affairs. Liang Shiyi found her a sympathetic and compatible lover, a quality he did not find in his sixth lady. After a fortnight of courtship, she finally succumbed to his desire to have her as his new concubine. However, since Liang's mother was the seventh child in her family and was addressed by her parents as Aqi (No. 7), he would avoid calling the new concubine Aqi out of respect for his mother. He would call her, instead, Aba (No. 8), and the servants would address her as the eighth lady.

As Liang Shiyi planned to leave for Beijing in late October, he had the delicate task of breaking the news of his new amour to his family. He decided not to repeat the mistake of rushing through the family ritual as he had done with the sixth lady. Besides, it would be awkward to make room for the eighth lady in his living quarters in such short notice. He informed the family that he would postpone the ceremony of accepting the eighth lady into the family until he and the eighth lady returned home from Beijing the following year. In the meantime, he found suitable quarters for her in King's Hotel which was conveniently located in the central part of the city.

Then he asked which members of the family would like to go to Beijing with him. Of course Madam and the second lady wanted to stay in Hong Kong with their children who had just started another school year. The sixth lady wished to stay in Hong Kong to help the second lady rear her children since she did not feel comfortable in the new situation. But the fourth lady preferred to go back to live at Ganshiqiao Lane where she could dominate the household with no need to defer to Madam or the second lady. Huaisheng clearly wanted to go to Beijing to be near her boy friend and Yusheng wanted to travel once more to the north before going abroad. It was so arranged. They would leave by boat to Shanghai.

In the meantime, Liang Shiyi visited his eighth lady nightly at King's Hotel after finishing his business in his office at Queen's Road Central. On the fourth day after his eighth lady moved into the hotel, he arrived early only to find that she was out. He waited patiently and, after a while, composed a poem to express his feeling of despair. Before leaving, he left on the desk the poem entitled "Waiting for My Eighth Lady in the Hotel."

> I remember when we parted, you leaned against the left door
> and eagerly asked me when and where we would meet again.
> My heart leaps as I suddenly hear quick steps in the corridor
> but from afar the clock tower chimes anew while I wait in vain.
> Failing to reach you by phone, I can only sense your presence
> through traces of rouge and faded scent from the previous night.
> Recalling our laughter in the jaded chamber, I love the resonance
> of the happy moment when the music stopped in the cool moonlight.

The eighth lady returned to the hotel just in time to catch him in the lobby. She was carrying bags of goods from her shopping trip. She apologized for her delay. The seamstress had held her up while fitting her for a new winter coat which she would need in Beijing. They happily disappeared together into the elevator.

It was all business before pleasure when they got into their room. Liang Shiyi told her that his father disliked glamorous women who wore jewelry because they unduly exposed themselves to temptation. He would not buy any jewelry for her. However, as soon as they arrived in Beijing, he would purchase one thousand yuan worth of government bonds under her name. Then he explained that he could get some bonds with five years remaining to maturity at a discount and that she could collect interest from the coupons. Surprisingly, his eighth lady grasped the complexity of the transaction in a short time.

"You are much younger than I am," Liang said to her. "You should save the interest, as well as the bond, for security. Like all women married into our extended family, you will receive a monthly allowance of fifty dollars in Hong Kong currency. It is a substantial sum which exceeds the monthly salary of some grade-school teachers. I don't encourage you to be extravagant, but you need this pocket money on various occasions because we have many relatives and friends. For birthday and baby gifts, you should spend no more than two or three dollars each time. Your monthly allowance will be deposited in your account in Hong Kong when you travel with me to Beijing. You should learn how to save money."

It was an unexpected disclosure for which the eighth lady was grateful. She surprised her husband by asking, "Do you mind if I use part of the money to hire a tutor to study Chinese classics and learn the basics of calligraphy?"

"I'm delighted to know you have such ambition," Liang replied. "There are times when my personal secretaries are not too busy and they can arrange your study on both." Liang suddenly realized he had found a woman who could communicate with him beyond sensual desire.

Two days later, when Liang Shiyi and his eighth lady reached their staterooms in the S.S. *Empress of Asia*, his fourth lady and daughter, Huaisheng and Yusheng, were already on board. After introducing his eighth lady to his fourth lady, Liang Shiyi walked out to the deck with them. As the two ladies satisfied their curiosity about one another, he pointed to the expanse of water and said to the eighth lady, "It is time you leave the past in the deep blue sea and breathe new life from the fresh air."

The fourth lady was unusually quiet as she stared at the sea. Although she had willingly given up her role as a constant companion to her husband, she did not want to lose her power and influence in the family. She had cultivated the fifth lady as her protege, and regarded the appearance of the gentle sixth lady as a harmless interlude. Now she sensed that she had met her equal and had not figured out how to deal with the newcomer. Her husband seemed to be able to read her mind. "All of you who have served me faithfully will have a warm spot in my heart as well as a comfortable place in my family."

Upon their arrival in Shanghai, they went to nearby scenic towns and villages for sightseeing. After reaching Nanjing, they took a boat ride along the Yangzi River to Wuhan before returning to Beijing by the Beijing-Wuhan Railway. It was a memorable trip for all, but to the eighth lady it was also an unchartered journey to a new life.

An Unwavering Voice

Beijing was cold and windy when Liang Shiyi and his entourage arrived in late November 1919. Since Liang Shiyi was preoccupied with the serious business of state, his fourth lady soon took charge of the household affairs. His eighth lady was impressed by the spacious rooms for public receptions, but was surprised by the simple furnishing in the private living quarters. Even the bedroom of the fourth lady was adorned by no more than a bed, a dresser and a cabinet of modest quality. Shiyi's daughters, Huaisheng and Yusheng, were eager to join their older sister in her living quarters in the east wing.

The first visitor to Ganshiqiao Lane upon Shiyi's return was Ye Gongchuo who had been in Paris for the Versailles Conference. Liang was eager to find out from Ye the status of the railway unification plan proposed by the British and Chinese Corporation to the delegates of Britain, France, the United States and Japan at Versailles. However, before tackling this serious subject, Ye told Liang about the latest news of Wellington Koo whose wife had died the previous year.

The Chinese delegates to the Versailles Conference stayed on for the unfinished business after they had refused to sign the treaty. They spent the humdrum summer in Paris while most Parisians deserted the city for seashore or countryside. The Chinese delegates had been excited by a whirl of social events brought about by the arrival of the wife and two daughters of the wealthiest Chinese businessman in Indonesia. Wellington Koo took unusual pains to court the younger daughter until she finally agreed to be engaged to him. Koo's previous marriage to the daughter of Tang Shaoyi had propelled him into the inner circle of Chinese politics. The fabulous wealth of his fiancee's family could enrich the life of a young diplomat beyond his wildest dreams.

Liang listened and smiled, but he was too absorbed in the railway unification plan for China to comment on Koo's latest good fortune. He said to Ye, "I have no illusion about the railway plan which is supposed to consolidate all the foreign loans to Chinese railways. Left unsaid is the proposed appointment of a foreign chief railway administrator to control the finance of these railways under the direction of a Four-Nation Consortium. It's patterned after the foreign administration of Chinese

321

maritime customs in the late Qing Dynasty and the foreign control of salt tax for the repayment of the reorganization loan to the Republic. Under the proposed plan, all revenue from Chinese railways must be deposited in foreign banks. It would suffocate China in the international financial market."

Ye understood and agreed. "With our experience as railway administrators, we know what can be done to improve the efficiency of railway operation without submitting ourselves to the manipulation of foreigners."

Liang recalled the British effort to control the railways in China. As early as 1913, Sir John Jordan, the British Minister in Beijing, argued that a British chief railway administrator should be appointed to oversee the finance of all railways in China. His argument was that British investment banks had provided loans for the construction of most of the Chinese railways. But the Chinese government under President Yuan Shikai rejected the suggestion. Again in 1917, Jordan raised the same argument to President Li Yuanhong and his suggestion was again rejected by the Chinese government. The British banks did not get their way primarily because other Western powers sided with China to protect their spheres of influence. But since railway ventures in China had gone sour in the past decade, some American businessmen had become inclined to support a multi-nation consortium for the development of Chinese railways after the World War.

"The plan for China was the brainchild of S. F. Mayers, the Beijing representative of British and Chinese Corporation," Liang reminded Ye who was in Paris when the plan first surfaced in Beijing in January 1919. "To implement this plan, a new Four-Nation Consortium consisting of Britain, the United States, France and Japan would be established to administer the Chinese railways. His idea was supported by other British and American businessmen in Beijing."

"I understand that Earl Baker, an American accounting consultant to our Ministry of Communications, also lent his support to the idea," Ye added. "He should have known better. In fact, the Ministry has been working toward railway unification for some time. With the assistance of an American accountant, Dr. Adams, the standardization of the accounting system and languages has produced excellent results. The unification of rail the transportation system, including main and branch lines, yards and passenger and freight cars, is already under way. There are problems. The use of standard materials has been hampered by suppliers from different countries which provided the construction loans."

"That's precisely the point," Liang spoke knowingly. "The plan for China advanced by Mayers is nothing but a smoke screen to control the finance of Chinese railways. I will continue to fight against this plan."

Indeed Liang Shiyi spoke with an unequivocal voice on this issue to almost anyone who would listen. He was instrumental in reversing the decision of the Foreign Relation Commission to support the plan in January 1919. He argued vigorously that the lack of unification of railway standards was caused by the desire of foreign powers to protect their spheres of influence under the unequal treaties. The Commission finally had adopted his recommendations to maintain the status quo of foreign debts for railways already completed and in operation, but had also adopted a new standard contract approved by the Ministry of Communications for railways under construction and in the planning stage.

Liang's vehement opposition to the railway unification plan had also attracted the attention of foreign diplomats in Beijing. In early 1919, Dr. Reinsch, the American Minister in Beijing, wrote him of the American desire to help China in post-war industrial development through private investments. He suggested The Four-Nation Consortium was the proper vehicle for providing collateral on future loans. Liang replied that he understood America's good intentions and sought a personal interview with Dr. Reinsch to discuss the issue.

"American investors shouldn't need to worry about the returns of investment in profitable railways," Liang told the American Minister, "as long as they sign legally-binding contracts with the Ministry of Communications on a case-by-case basis." After listening to Dr. Reinsch's counter arguments, Liang added, "The Four-Nation Consortium will not benefit the United States since the British and French investors are financially strapped and their government simply want the United States to join them in restraining Japan's dominant influence which grew by leaps and bounds during the World War." Unconvinced, Dr. Reinsch agreed to disagree and nothing was settled.

In April, Liang Shiyi received a letter from Sir John Jordan complaining about Liang's unfair attack on S. F. Mayers in a newspaper interview. Liang replied that he had nothing against Mayers personally but was very much against the railway unification plan espoused by Mayers. "The newspaper reporter must be mistaken," Liang stated, "if my attack on an issue is construed as an attack on the person who espouses it." Why did Jordan write such a letter in the twilight of his diplomatic career? Liang wondered. Was he trying to defend the honor of his friend or did he want to blunt Liang's antagonistic voice? In any case, Jordan soon found out that Liang could not be silenced.

In June 1919, Lu Zhengxiang, China's Foreign Minister and Chief Delegate at Versailles, reported that the railway unification plan of China initiated by the British and Chinese Corporation had made its way to the delegates at the Versailles Conference. The argument for the proposal was that since the railways in Shandong Province in China were under the control of Germany before the war, the post-war development of railways in China would belong to the jurisdiction of the fledgling League of Nations. The proposed Four-Nation Consortium consisting of Britain, France, United States and Japan would enforce the plan. Dr. Reinsch again communicated with Liang to explain the American position. Liang replied that by lumping China with other former colonies of Germany, the proposal was a threat to China's independence. "I thought it was your opinion, too," Liang reminded him. There was still no meeting of minds.

"I'm groping for action," Liang Shiyi finally said to Ye Gongchuo after reviewing various options. "It's not enough to plead with foreign diplomats. This railway unification plan must not succeed. Otherwise another source of China's shrinking revenue will be mortgaged to foreigners."

* * *

For almost a year, Liang Shiyi's mind seldom strayed far from his concern for national economic development. He observed that the World War had caused the collapse of the gold standard to which major currencies had been pegged. In all major powers, the governments were left with the task of managing production, currencies and price levels. As government consumption shot up for the war effort, these governments were saddled with huge debts and asserted unprecedented power to control international capital flows. The social unrest after the war also created pressure for a better, more open society and forced extensive social reforms on many countries.

Liang Shiyi noted that China could not escape a similar fate and the traditional network of families and clans would be swept away by the social changes. He reached the conclusion that ordinary people would not participate in the economic growth unless a national administration was established to promote and safeguard the welfare of its citizens. He proposed to the government a plan to establish a national welfare administration. The detailed plan consisted of five major elements: first, to set up employment referral agencies; second, to organize worker cooperatives for mutual assistance; third, to introduce vocational education and job training programs; fourth, to provide safety nets for unemployment; and fifth, to establish institutions to help orphans, elderly and handicapped persons. The plan was very much ahead of its time, not only for China, but even for some industrialized countries.

When Liang Shiyi went to the Presidential Palace in January 1920, he discussed his welfare plan with President Xu Shichang who expressed mild interest but was noncommittal. Instead, Xu surprised Liang with his own proposal, "As you know, the Domestic Bonds Bureau was eliminated in 1917 and its tasks were assigned to the Finance Ministry. I'm not satisfied with the results and intend to revive the bureau with its own independent board of directors. As soon as the State Council approves my proposal, I plan to appoint you as the head of the new Domestic Bonds Bureau."

"I'm indebted to your confidence in me," Liang replied with expected modesty, "but I have already made too many commitments to various commercial and industrial enterprises."

President Xu was unmoved. "I understand your busy schedule, but I cannot think of anyone else who can take over this critical job. It will be April by the time the bureau is re-established. That should give you some breathing time." Liang Shiyi accepted his offer without further protest.

* * *

On January 19, 1920, Obata Yukichi, the Japanese Minister in Beijing, delivered to the Chinese Foreign Ministry a request to formalize Japan's rights over the former German interests in Shandong according to the Versailles Treaty. Since the Chinese government was not a signatory of that treaty, it refused too concede such rights to

Japan. As the Japanese request became public, student and worker demonstrations appeared spontaneously in many Chinese cities. Politicians of different persuasions all over China urged the government to reject the Japanese request. The government in Beijing had to appeal to local authorities to temper the outbursts while stalling for time until Foreign Minister Lu Zhengxiang returned from Paris. Ten days later, Lu arrived in Beijing and took the position of no direct negotiation with Japan on the Shandong problem. The tension between China and Japan remained high.

Lu also met with Liang concerning the railway unification plan. After the meeting, Liang Shiyi decided to make a last-ditch effort to reiterate his opposition to this plan. Acting as a private citizen, Liang sent a telegram of protest to the delegates of Britain, the United States, France and Japan in Versailles. He also sent a similar message to the heads of the Hong Kong and Shanghai Bank in London, Banque de L'Indo Chine in Paris, the Seikin Bank in Tokyo and the House of Morgan in New York. He sounded a warning that the impending formation of the Four-Nation Consortium of foreign bankers in China would enhance neither Chinese industrial development nor investment opportunities of foreign banks because no Chinese government could cooperate with the consortium and survive.

On March 2, the Japanese government notified the United States that it would exclude Japanese railway interests in southern Manchuria and eastern Mongolia from the jurisdiction of the Four-Nation Consortium. Japan would protect its ill-gotten gains from scrutiny while sharing future benefits accorded to Western powers. Japan had finally laid bare the terms on which the United States, Britain and France had to accommodate Japan in order to salvage the Four-Nation Consortium.

Liang Shiyi was now ready with a plan to form a Chinese investment trust corporation. Hopefully, it would strengthen China's self-reliance in promoting its industrial development. Lacking the resources of foreign banks, Liang realized he had to pool all Chinese bankers for the common cause. By then, his view was widely known to the Chinese bankers and their response was overwhelming.

One evening in March 1920, flashy automobiles, still an oddity in Beijing, were lined up outside Liang's residence at Ganshiqiao Lane. Inside the residence, high-ranking officers of Chinese banks gathered for a conference.

One banker said to another, "All of Beijing that matters is under this roof tonight!" Liang reminded them of the need for a Chinese corporation with sufficient capital to supplement, if not compete, with foreigners in the investment-banking business. When the evening was over, a sum of ten million Chinese silver dollars was committed by the thirteen banks represented at the conference. Within a month, the Zhonghua Banking Corporation was brought into existence and Liang Shiyi was elected chairman of the board.

The establishment of Zhonghua Banking Corporation on April 20, 1920, was followed by the announcement of the formation of the Four-Nation Consortium three weeks later. Liang Shiyi hoped his David would eventually slay Goliath.

By coincidence, the ministers of the major Western powers in Beijing were replaced in rapid succession by their respective governments. Beilby Alston became the British Minister in April; Charles R. Crane, the American Minister arrived in May; and A. Boppe, the French Minister, presented his credentials in June. Liang was ready for a fresh round of debates with these newcomers. He would have been more careful if he had known Alston had once contemptuously dubbed him as the "Machiavelli of China."

Paul Painleve, a former premier of France and now Director of the Institute of Chinese Studies at the University of Paris, visited Beijing in June. Liang gave him a warm welcome at the Chinese Railroad Association. The honored guest hardly needed a reminder of Liang's powerful base in Chinese railways.

* * *

In early July 1920, Liang and his family members in Beijing returned to Hong Kong. When their steamship sailed into the pier at Kowloon Harbor, his eldest son Dingji was on hand to greet them. Dingji had returned from the United States a few days earlier to prepare for his wedding scheduled for August 1. After noting the addition of the eighth lady to the family, he directed the servant to take care of the luggage. The group took the ferry to Hong Kong and sped to their home on Robinson Road in several taxicabs.

As the homecoming crowd finally reached the living quarters of the patriarch, they took turns paying their respects. When the eighth lady was presented to the old man for the first time, she performed the ritual of kowtowing and presenting him with a cup of tea. Then they moved on to the living quarters of Madam who was waiting to receive the group.

Madam was more annoyed than ever by her husband's expensive habit of keeping several concubines. She could not say much to him but she could make his latest favorite pay the price. It was her prerogative to instruct the concubine on the rules of the household as the new concubine knelt after kowtowing to her. She took the occasion to lecture her for more than forty-five minutes without any sign of letup. Either by accident or by design, Dingji burst into the room and wanted to talk to his mother about his wedding plans. His action rescued the eighth lady from her ordeal.

Another sticky point to Madam was her inability to shake off Huaisheng's boyfriend. After more opportunities for the lovers to meet while Huangsheng was in Beijing during last year, Huangsheng was more determined than ever to marry Ou Shao'an. She tearfully told her mother that she would be driven to suicide if no consent was given. Fortunately Dingji intervened on her behalf and her mother finally gave in. Her father was delighted and promised to contact her intended as soon as he returned to Beijing after Dingji's wedding.

The Zheng family happily arrived in Hong Kong for the marriage of their daughter Shungu to Dingji. The wedding was a Western-styled ceremony except that it was held in a large social hall without the benefit of a clergy. Since both families were steeped in Confucius tradition, the wedding was officiated by a prominent scholar in the presence of family members and close friends. It was a private affair staged to please the patriarch more than anyone else. Liang Shiyi deliberately tried to avoid inviting his political and business associates who might lavish expensive gifts on the young couple.

Shortly after the wedding, the newlyweds left for Boston where Dingji would continue his college education. His two sisters, Yusheng and Zangsheng, went with them. It was a voyage they all anticipated with great expectations.

Friends or Foes

"I hope that you will stay longer and find time to do some sightseeing here," Liang Shiyi said to Zheng Lequan, whose family had come to Hong Kong for his daughter's union with the Liang family. Before and after the wedding, they were wined and dined for a whole week in the company of other guests and friends. Now that the newlyweds had departed for the United States, the family was ready to go back to Beijing.

"Thank you," Zheng replied. "We have already imposed too much on you and your family. We deeply appreciate your hospitality but we will leave tomorrow as originally scheduled. We booked passage quite some time ago and it's difficult to make changes."

"If you do not have any plan for this afternoon," Liang insisted, "I can at least find someone to show you Repulse Bay. It's a very pleasant place to be on a hot summer day."

Zheng's two teenage boys and their sister were delighted. They hoped their father would say yes to the offer. Looking at their faces, Zheng Lequan slowly nodded his head, "If it's not too much trouble, my children will probably enjoy the beach." He knew his children would be terribly disappointed if he followed the customary courtesy to say no.

Mrs. Zheng decided to stay in the company of Madam. Liang Shiyi was busy and asked his brother Shixu to accompany Mr. Zheng and his children for the outing. Shixu enjoyed outdoor activities and liked the clean beach and crystalline water in Repulse Bay. It was located at the back of the island from Victoria harbor and was accessible by a narrow winding road from the race course in Happy Valley. They went by car and did some sightseeing through the fishing village at Aberdeen before arriving at their destination. The bay was in almost pristine condition and there were not many swimmers since few could afford the luxury of coming here often. They all enjoyed seeing the soft waves edging toward the beach and feeling the gentle breeze on their faces.

The next day Liang Shiyi and his family said goodbye to the Zhengs. "I shall be back to Beijing in less than a month, after finishing my business, here," Liang said.

Beijing Odyssey

Liang Shiyi was still waiting for a last-minute opportunity to broker a peace settlement between the North and South. However, the political landscape of the country had changed dramatically. In the South, members of the Directorate of the Military Government in Guangzhou were embroiled in fierce squabbles. In the North, the balance of power of various factions of the Beiyang generals had been upset. North or South, it was difficult to tell friends from foes as the major figures changed roles almost overnight without warning. Liang Shiyi was left with a profound sense of frustration.

* * *

In Guangzhou, the Military Government had been dominated first by Lu Rongting and then Cen Chunxuan, both of whom were identified as leaders of the Guangxi Clique. Those who were still loyal to Sun Yatsen and opposed to the Guangxi Clique were loosely referred to as the Guangdong Clique, even though several generals supporting this group were from Yunnan and some politicians were from other provinces. By the spring of 1920, the line had been clearly drawn between the Guangdong Clique and the Guangxi Clique in the South.

In late March, Wu Tingfang, a member of the Directorate, and the Speaker of both houses of Parliament in the South openly defied Cen Chunxuan, the strong man of the Military Government in Guangzhou. They joined Sun Yatsen in the safety of the International Settlement in Shanghai to plot strategies for regaining power. Outraged by their action, Cen Chunxuan ordered a search of the offices of both houses of Parliament and denounced the supporters of their Speakers. On June 3, Sun Yatsen and Tang Shaoyi declared the legitimate Military Government of the South would be re-established in Yunnan Province, while an office of that government would operate in Shanghai.

In August, the Parliament of the South met in Yunnan and elected new members of the Directorate for the reconstituted government. The Parliament pointedly stripped Cen Chunxuan as a member of the Directorate, and declared this new government in Yunnan as the only legitimate government of the South. Sun Yatsen then ordered his loyal supporters in Guangdong to attack the troops supporting Cen Chunxuan. The war between the Guangdong Clique and the Guangxi Clique began in earnest on August 12, 1920.

* * *

In Beijing, President Xu Shichang was walking a tight rope. Weakened by the Japanese request for the resolution of the Shandong problem, he had to placate the two major competing Beiyang factions, known respectively as the Anfu Clique under the control of General Duan Qirui, and the Zhili Clique under the leadership of General Cao Kun. To appease his generals, President Xu had appointed Zhan Yunpeng, an unkempt military man well connected to both cliques, as the Premier.

The front line of the Northern army in Hunan Province was defended by General Wu Peifu, a division commander under General Cao. Earlier in January, General Wu had requested permission to withdraw the Northern army from Hunan in support of a negotiated peace with the South. President Xu was reluctant to grant permission to Wu for fear of offending other Beiyang generals who were dismayed by Wu's request. But General Wu Peifu was a very resourceful man who prided himself in being a literate and thinking soldier. After receiving a substantial subsidy or bribe from the South in mid-March to help defray the expenses of his withdrawal, General Wu declared he would return to the North with or without permission from the government in Beijing. He was welcomed by the people along the way as most local authorities and ordinary people were sick of the civil war. Encouraged, General Wu implored the government not to negotiate directly with Japan on the Shandong problem. His moves stirred up the political pot which was already boiling.

On the other hand, the Anfu Clique under general Duan Qirui pressured the Premier to accept the Japanese request in spite of public opinion to the contrary, but President Xu did not give in to the Anfu Clique. On May 8, the Chinese Foreign Ministry finally informed the Japanese Minister in Beijing that the Chinese government would not negotiate directly with Japan on the basis of an international treaty that China had refused to sign. Anticipating the battle cry raised by the Anfu Clique, the Premier announced his resignation as soon as he had approved the reply to Japan.

No sooner than one crisis was dampened, another one loomed on the horizon. By the end of May, General Wu's division arrived in Wuhan, and within days headed north without resistance. With his hands strengthened by Wu's troops, General Cao declared, on July 1, that the Anfu Clique had betrayed the trust of the people and should be driven out of the government. Faced with an impossible choice, President Xu sided with Duan and dismissed Cao and Wu from their military posts for insubordination. Emboldened, Duan started to attack the Zhili army on July 14, and the battle between the Anfu Clique and the Zilli Clique raged.

However, the Fengtian army under General Zhang Zuolin had already moved from Manchuria toward Tianjin to support the Zhili army under General Cao. Although Duan's army was better equipped and had more men and fire power, its morale was low. Sandwiched between the Zhili army on the west and the Fengtian army in the east, Duan's mighty army collapsed within three days. On July 19, Duan Qirui ordered his army to stop fighting. He then relinquished his military command post, rank and medals of honor to save his own life. In an about face, President Xu restored Generals Cao and Wu to their posts a week later. Responding to public clamor for revenge, President Xu declared punishments for ten of Duan's proteges and supporters who had the foresight to seek refuge in the Japanese Legation. The president also ordered the closing of the Anfu Club in Beijing which had served as the nerve center for Duan's plotters and conspirators.

With the support of the Zhili Clique, Zhan Yunpeng was restored as Premier in August. He was eager to dismiss several cabinet ministers who were members of the Anfu Clique. In the reshuffle of the cabinet, Liang Shiyi's friend, Zhou Ziqi, was appointed Minister of Finance and his confidant, Ye Gongchuo, was named Minister of Communications.

Beijing Odyssey

* * *

When Liang Shiyi saw the hopelessness of his peace initiatives, he decided to return to Beijing in September. He could at least concentrate his efforts to strengthen the public finance in his capacity as the head of the Domestic Bonds Bureau. He had instituted a plan to redeem existing debts before he went to Hong Kong. Upon his arrival in Beijing, he went to see his friend Zhou Ziqi, the new Finance Minister. He wanted to get an opinion from Zhou on the merit of issuing a special short-term note for the expressed purpose of redeeming the now defunct banknotes of the Bank of China and the Bank of Communications, still held by some merchants and money exchangers. Liang was direct in his remark to Zhou. "Several years ago, the government abruptly declared these banknotes were in default when it could not repay its loans from the two banks to redeem them. I believe this is the first step to build public confidence in government bonds. What do you think?"

"I agree with you completely," Zhou replied. "I will provide whatever help you need from the Finance Ministry.

"I'm glad to hear that." Liang was encouraged by Zhou's concurrence. "The detailed plan for this special note has been completed, and I don't expect any difficulty in pulling it off in a short while. However, I have something far more important for which I desperately need your help."

"What's that?" Zhou was curious.

"I'm planning to issue a series of new bonds next year," Liang stated gravely, "not for the purpose of financing current government operations, but for consolidating all previous domestic bonds by paying overdue interests and principals over the years. Do you think my proposal has any chance of receiving approval from the State Council and the President?"

"That's a very ambitious proposal," Zhou said. "If we can pull this off, it will be the best thing we can do for our country's finance. I will certainly give it a try."

Liang was satisfied with this answer and went away feeling relieved. He could trust Zhou's words to push his idea in the Finance Ministry.

During that summer, the farm crops in at least six provinces in north China, stretching from Zhili to Gansu, were destroyed by drought. By September it became obvious that many farmers would face famine. With the help of Ye Gongchuo, Zhou Ziqi and Chen Zhensan, a former Minister of Agriculture, Liang Shiyi called on other officials and businessmen to donate funds to the relief effort. Liang proposed creating a North China Relief Organization, and he was elected its President. In the next two months, Liang formulated short-term and long-term relief policies and recruited volunteers to carry out his plan. He emphasized that while distribution of food to the farmers was the most urgent task in the emergency, it must be followed by rehabilitation through a work-relief program so farmers could earn their living again, with aid from the relief organization.

* * *

Steven T. Au

After the Four-Nation Consortium announced its official existence, Mr. Stephen, an American representing the consortium, visited Beijing in January 1921 with high hopes of making business deals. Stephen and Liang met several times, Liang always reiterating his position. He told Stephen that American good intentions were overshadowed by Japanese insistence on excluding its sphere of influence from the jurisdiction of the consortium, and that the Chinese government would not touch the consortium with a ten-foot pole. At the end of their last meeting, Stephen reluctantly came to the same conclusion. He left Beijing a disappointed man.

As a diversion from his regular activities, Liang Shiyi had collected information about tobacco planting and cigarette manufacturing worldwide. He noted the mood altering and recurrent craving characteristics of nicotine in tobacco and the harmful effect of cigarette smoking to health. The annual consumption of cigarettes also represented a huge drain on China's national economy, particularly since most cigarettes on sale in China were imported. In February he founded the Association for Prohibition of Cigarette Smoking and appealed to the public to refrain from smoking cigarettes. Unfortunately, his effort made no lasting impact on his fellow citizens.

On March 3, 1921, President Xu ordered the Finance Ministry and the Domestic Bonds Bureau to act jointly to consolidate all domestic bonds. In April, Xu approved the plan submitted by Zhou Ziqi and Liang Shiyi to redeem all previous domestic bonds in default through the issuing a series of new bonds. When it was all said and done, Zhou Ziqi commented to Liang Shiyi, "Your foresight has strengthened the financial prospect of the Republic as this act will no doubt make it much easier to float any domestic bonds in the future."

"It is as much your contribution as mine," Liang said, always remembering to give credit to others when he succeeded in accomplishing something important. In this case, his praise of Zhou came none too soon. A month later Zhou Ziqi and Ye Gongchuo lost their ministerial posts in a reshuffle of the cabinet. Obviously the Premier gave in to more demands from General Cao to put his men in these important posts.

In the meantime, news from the South was quite disturbing. The Guangxi Clique had essentially lost control of the Military Government in Guangzhou in October 1920 but some in the clique continued to fight as they were driven back into Guangxi territory. The effective resistance of Guangxi Clique collapsed in early 1921. The Parliament of the South was able to reconvene in Guangzhou in April and elected Sun Yatsen as the "Extraordinary President." He was sworn in on May 5.

The existence of an "Extraordinary President" in the South worried the government in Beijing. President Xu tried to provide support for the Guangxi Clique to fight on, but the Guangdong army was unstoppable.

* * *

After successfully consolidating the domestic bonds in April, Liang Shiyi became busy at home preparing for the marriage of his second daughter Huaisheng to Ou Shao'an. His wife arrived with his brother Shixu in time for the occasion.

332

Beijing Odyssey

Madam was her usual self and gave orders as she pleased. Liang's young concubines who were in Beijing with him all along, catered to her wishes. She might have overstepped her limit when she told her future son-in-law, "We don't mind if your family does not follow the Cantonese custom of sending a large number of wedding cakes to us for distribution to our relatives and friends. You might as well save the money for other purposes. However, I want to be sure that your mother will wear a pink skirt as Cantonese custom dictates." Madam wanted to make sure she was the only one in the wedding party to wear a crimson skirt. Did she ever think of her daughter as she risked insulting her future mother-in-law? That consideration seemed not to enter her mind as she felt righteously that a concubine must know her place.

After the wedding, Liang Shiyi suggested to Madam that she could spend a few days enjoying the beautiful spring in Beijing. Of course, his concubines could serve as her ladies-in-waiting, a theme Madam was accustomed to by now. Then Liang Shiyi, his brother Shixu and his friend Guan Mianjun went to Mount Tai (Taishan) near the hometown of Confucius in Shandong Province. It was said that Confucius reached the summit of Mount Tai and proclaimed that the world seemed insignificant by comparison with this magnificent view. Such a trip was regarded by Confucius scholars as the ultimate homage to the sage.

As they arrived in the town of Tai'an at the foot of Mount Tai, they visited Dai Temple, a large walled fortress of halls and pavilions housing ancient relics. The temple grounds were filled with carved stone tablets. At the north edge of the town, a stone arch known as the First Gate of Heaven pointed to the Pilgrim's Road, a broad walk with spacious ramps and massive granite steps. They passed the First Gate and walked for several miles to the Middle Gate of Heaven. They stopped by the temples and monuments of historical interest as they moved along. Beyond the Middle Gate, the next two miles leading to the Southern Gate of Heaven was far steeper. Slowly they walked through the Eighteen Bends, a gigantic stone ladder and finally climbed steeper stairs before reaching the Southern Gate. Along the way, many porters carried heavy bundles from poles on their shoulders. The porters had to stop to catch their breath as they ascended. Passing through a pavilion at the Southern Gate, they walked another half mile amid rock carvings, temples and then more stone stairs. Finally, an inn at the summit was in sight.

They took time to survey the historical treasures, including the Tang Dynasty Rock Inscription (Mo Ya Bei), the Pillar Without Words (Wu Zi Bei) and the Temple of Purple Dawn (Bi Xia Ci). When they returned to the inn, where they planned to stay overnight, the innkeeper told them that the porters who had just unloaded their goods to the inn were for hire to carry visitors on stretchers to see the sunrise next morning if they did not want to walk the distance. Liang and his party declined the offer. The innkeeper advised them that the morning air at the summit was extremely damp and cold. If Liang did not engage a stretcher, which included a padded cover for protection, they should at least rent a padded coat for the same purpose. Liang's party accepted his advice.

At four o'clock the next morning, Liang's party was up and ready to join the crowd to see the sunrise, the ultimate spectacle of visiting Mount Tai. It was windy and dark as they followed a stream of sightseers across the summit. They settled into the rock ledges at the eastern edge and waited in silence. At five o'clock, the sun pierced through the cloud with a feeble yellow light. The crowd gasped. An hour later, the rising sun shone through the purple dawn to reveal its full glory. Echoing an old saying, Shixu exclaimed, "One view is better than one hundred descriptions!"

When they returned to the inn, one of the porters gathered some visitors in front to entertain them with local stories. When he was a child, he said, his grandfather had told him that tigers still appeared occasionally in the vicinity of Tai'an. After hunting down a tiger with his friends, his grandfather declared, "we have killed the evil creature once and for all." After the visitors gave him a round of applause, Liang said to him, "Tigers are violent but not evil. They cannot differentiate good from evil." The porter was puzzled but sensed that Liang must be trying to enunciate some profound truth.

Liang Shiyi was indeed deep in thought about a Confucian legend. One day when Confucius visited Mount Tai, he heard the voice of a woman crying bitterly. He stopped and asked the woman why she was so sad. She replied, "My father-in-law was devoured by the tiger; so was my husband. Now, my son has met the same fate." Confucius gently asked, "Why don't you move away?" Her reply was crisp, "because there is no oppressive ruler here." Confucius could not help but comment, "An oppressive ruler is more terrifying than a tiger." That was the lesson of the day for Liang.

After returning to Beijing, Liang Shiyi found Madam was more than eager to leave the chaotic city, notwithstanding the courtesy of her ladies-in-waiting to go shopping with her. Two days later she went back to Hong Kong in the company of her brother-in-law Shixu.

Brave New World

It was a bright sunny morning in May 1921 when Liang Qichao arrived at Ganshiqiao Lane at the invitation of Liang Shiyi. Qichao had returned from Paris the previous year and had gradually shed his political activities on behalf of his colleagues of the Research Clique. He became a professor of literature at Beijing University. Liang Shiyi had not seen him for awhile and was eager to get his perspective as a vanguard of Chinese cultural heritage. He was particularly impressed by Qichao's calm voice at the height of the recent debate of the Shandong Problem on the campus. He had asked Qichao to spend a few leisurely hours with him to discuss a wide range of current events.

After a brief lunch, the two sat at a comfortable corner of the living room. They began to warm up to the hottest topic of the day. "From the press reports, you had quite a good time lecturing the university students about patriotism the other day," Liang Shiyi teased.

"It was nothing significant." Qichao's modestly replied. "I simply stated the simple truth—that it was futile to put all the blame on politicians when China suffered at the hands of the Japanese. I reminded them that the politicians they are blaming were once young patriots, like you and me, who protested the inaction of the government toward foreign aggressions. Many of them have now become corrupted officials and are the targets of student protests. I asked the students what they would be twenty years from now if they did not take some positive steps to avoid the same mistakes. I was met with a long silence. Then I asked the students to reflect on the emptiness of their slogans and to explain to me how they could save China with their negative statements. There was more silence. And that was the end of that meeting."

Liang Shiyi admired the eloquence of Qichao, which echoed his own sentiment. Then they turned to discuss the more profound developments that had begun to transform the traditional Chinese society into a brave new world.

* * *

When the citizens and students of Beijing protested against the Versailles Treaty on May 4, 1919, they had no idea they were propelling a new cultural movement, widely known as the May Fourth Movement. This intellectual ferment had its origin in dramatic developments during and after the World War. Many scholars returning home from foreign lands learned from their bitter experience of betrayal at home and abroad. Dissatisfied with the superficial political modernization through the adoption of republican institutions, many thoughtful persons were looking for something far deeper to breathe new life into the nation.

A new generation of activists, individually and collectively, began to question China's cultural heritage based on Confucianism. These intellectuals were products of a transitional period, men thoroughly grounded in Chinese classical studies and yet reasonably well acquainted with Western civilization. They provided the impetus to transform the literary and intellectual life of China. Western thought and ideologies, especially liberalism, socialism, pragmatism, science and democracy, suddenly became a part of the national debate.

Among the most prominent and influential returned scholars were Chen Duxiu, Cai Yunpei and Hu Shi (aka Hu Shih). They rode the wave of nationalism to seek national salvation through the creation of a new China—thoroughly Westernized, yet distinctly Chinese. In their own way, they rapidly became the guiding spirit of the intellectual revolution, calling on a younger generation to begin anew without the hindrance of the past.

A firebrand writer, Chen Duxiu had returned from France in 1915 and soon founded a monthly magazine, *New Youth*, in Shanghai. It was written in the semi-classical and semi-colloquial journalistic style which Liang Qichao had pioneered while he was in political exile in Japan. This periodical urged the destruction of stagnant, conservative traditions and encouraged the struggle against the old and rotten elements of society. He called on the youth of the nation to reform their thought and behavior to form a new social culture and to spearhead a national awakening. Chen's bold attack on the establishment quickly struck a chord of resonance among the educated youth.

When Cai Yuanpei returned from France in 1916, he was appointed the President of the National Beijing University. Cai admonished the students that the university was a place of higher learning, and ought not be viewed as a short cut to position and wealth. To expose students to competing ideas for national salvation, he appointed professors from a wide range of political persuasions. In 1917, Chen Duxiu was appointed dean of the university, and Hu Shi a professor of literature. The following year, he appointed Li Dazhao, a radical thinker, as the university librarian.

Hu Shi had returned to China from the United States in 1917 and, using his prestigious position at Beijing University, became an energetic proponent of scientific thinking, pragmatism and the vernacular style of writing. Perhaps his most important single contribution was the introduction of Baihua, the plain language style of writing. Up to this time, the Chinese language had used the same linguistic forms for over two thousand years. The old literary style of writing, which was so different from the spoken language and took almost a lifetime to perfect, trapping the culture and people in ways of the past. It also created a permanent elite class with no escape from the past since only gentlemen of leisure could provide their sons such an education.

The students at Beijing University responded to the calls of their professors and sprang into action. In 1918, they organized a magazine, *New Tide* (Xinchao), launching an all-out attack on the bastions of traditional Confucianism—old literature, old ethics and old human relations. The forum of debate at Beijing University excited the entire nation as never before. This intellectual outburst dealt a shattering blow to traditional customs, moral values and social conventions.

* * *

The student protest against the government on May 4, 1919 fueled the wildfire of nationalism which was already burning in the heartland of China. In spite of the absence of Cai Yunpei for a short period to avoid cooperation with the government in prosecuting the students, the cultural activities in Beijing University went on unabated. Hu Shi became the high priest of Westernization, championing science and democracy. His Baihua style of writing invaded the domain of poetry and prose, overshadowing the more restrictive journalist style developed by Liang Qichao.

However, actions came far slower than firey rhetoric of revolution. It was not until February 1920 that two female students were admitted to Beijing University, a first for a national university. Outside of intellectual circles, the cultural movement as an expression of nationalism was less a symbol and more a curiosity. The competing ideas of national salvation seemed remote to ordinary people. Many felt a loss of familiar social structures and were confused about the goals. While the cultural movement excited the young, it did not convince the skeptics to take up the burden that had been thrust upon them by destiny.

The government in Beijing tolerated the new cultural movement as long as it did not dominate student protests. In fact, the Ministry of education decreed in 1920 that the Baihua style of writing would be taught in grade schools throughout the country. It also established a commission to standardize the national common spoken language (Mandarin), and to adopt a new set of symbols for punctuation, absent in classical writing. Millions of Chinese who craved stability were not interested in politics of confrontation. They accepted the fruits of the new cultural movement that made life easier for them, but they were not thrilled by a social revolution which might disrupt their own personal and family relations.

The Beijing government did not practice what it preached. Government communications and documents still used the classical writing style instead of the Baihua style. On the other hand, the advocates of the Baihua style of writing had to adjust their style to the cadences of ordinary speech, and at the same time absorb a bewildering mass of new foreign concepts and terminology. It would take some time before the Baihua style becoming widespread in the literary world.

* * *

Liang Qichao was amused that Liang Shiyi was surprised with the news his old friend had practiced the use of the Baihua style of writing since he joined the faculty of Beijing University earlier in the year.

337

"Is this what people mean when they say, 'if you cannot beat them, join them'?" Liang Shiyi chuckled.

"Not really," Liang Qichao was defensive. "I find it very convenient to use Baihua when I prepare a speech. You can literally read the speech when you make the delivery. You don't need to improvise an oral version as you have to when the speech is written in the classical style. But I don't use the Baihua style for posterity, not yet anyway."

"What else is new on the campus?" Liang Shiyi asked.

"Speaking of beating your opponent, the current debate on the cultural issues is getting quite serious. I'm in the minority in defending the traditional Chinese culture. The slogan of the majority is, "Go West!" My answer is, "Go East!"

"You didn't always take such a position," Liang Shiyi interjected, "although I'm not surprised to find you in the present predicament. What made you change your mind?"

"I'm disillusioned by the vast destruction in Europe wrought by the World War. Western statesmen may speak of moral obligations, but they're capable of carrying out unbridled imperialism. The blind worship of science gives them the confidence to win a conflict but the result is devastating to both the winner and the loser. I believe Chinese traditional values, when applied in moderation and modified to accommodate the developments of the twentieth century, might redress the imbalance. But my view has few supporters, except Professor Liang Shuming."

"That's all very interesting," Liang Shiyi sighed. "I'm glad someone can see through the duplicity of some of the claims of foreigners. Bad apples can be found both at home and abroad. I can't understand why so many educated Western persons don't see the danger of total Westernization without examining what is good and what is bad in Western culture."

"Western thought and ideologies are eagerly pursued by Chinese intellectuals," Liang Qichao added. "There is a gradual shift from Anglo-American to German-Russian sources, though. The French influence is also strong, given that many faculty members studied in France."

Liang Shiyi recalled Paul Painleve, the former Premier of France, whom he had met the previous June. As the Director of the Institute of Chinese Studies at the University of Paris, Painleve was awarded an honorary doctorate from Beijing University in August; so was Dr. Joubin, President of the University of Lyon in France. It was a first for a national university to confer a degree to foreigners.

However, the most prominent and influential foreign academic visitors to China were John Dewey and Bertrand Russell. They gave a series of public lectures which contributed to the substance of public debate. John Dewey and his wife had been in China in May 1919. With his former student Hu Shi as interpreter, Dewey gave many lectures on his social and political philosophy of pragmatism, on his own idea about education and methods of thought and on his view of leading contemporary philosophers. Bertrand Russell had been in China since October 1920. Using a noted Linguist as an interpreter, he also gave a number of lectures. His main message was that the West should learn from China the humane conception of life while China should acquire Western knowledge without acquiring its mechanistic outlook.

"Both John Dewey and Bertrand Russell will leave China for home in July," Liang Qichao said. "Obviously, Dewey fired the imagination of the audience when he said China could not be changed without a social transformation of ideas. But the audience was not very responsive to Russell's message which sounded much like 'Chinese learning for foundation; Western learning for application' advocated by Zhang Zhidong during the Qing Dynasty."

Indeed, the current new cultural movement resembled the One Hundred Days of Reform of 1898 during which Liang Qichao was a major player. Then, as now, the young scholars were the prime movers of the reform. Even though the movement fizzled, the mild reform afterwards led to the revolution in 1912 and the acceptance of Western political institutions for the Republic. The present movement advocated a further shift away from the traditional Chinese culture toward complete Westernization. In Liang Qichao's mind, nothing would change unless there was a spiritual renewal compatible with the traditional culture. Otherwise foreign ideas would not take root in China. Contrary to the majority of Chinese intellectuals, he was much more in tune with Bertrand Russell.

"I don't see a commitment from most students to break up the traditional kinship, personal loyalty and influential connections in their own behavior," Qichao explained. "Sooner or later, they will be drawn back to old habits if they don't make a clean break. But they can't because of the burden of the past. Their interest in politics is an elitist approach, very much like our own twenty years ago. How can the leaders ask the people to make sacrifices required by modernization if the intellectual elite is not willing to follow the rules? In a democracy, they have to submit to the law."

That explained the motive of his speech to the students of Beijing University a couple of weeks ago. Liang Qichao was asking them to search their own souls.

* * *

Li Dazhao and Chen Duxiu agreed that society could not be transformed without thorough soul searching. But they argued for an immediate social and political transformation, by force if necessary, patterned after Soviet-style revolution. They understood that citizens, as well as corrupt government officials, would never accept any change that might upset their natural tendency to practice old habits. The radicals spoke characteristically in the name of the people, but they were afraid of leaders who preached philanthropy and humaneness. They suggested that bourgeois morals were far more dangerous than bloody self-sacrificing for revolution. Their fear was probably justified, but the possibilities of civil war horrified the average citizens—perhaps because grim death had so completely shaped their life.

By 1920, the radicals also had disagreements as they tried to put their theories into practice. Chen Duxiu left Beijing University and became an active political organizer in Shanghai. His distrust of the inert peasants led him to place his hope in urban workers as the bulwark in an uprising. Li Dazhao, on the other hand, stressed the importance of the peasantry, which constituted ninety percent of the population. He argued powerfully that intellectuals needed to go to the countryside to work side by side with the peasants in order to escape the corruptive influence of urban life. Following Li's spiritual guidance, some students in Beijing University organized a Mass Education Propaganda Corps to promote the revolutionary ideas among villagers, but their rhetoric was not matched by a willingness to share the pain and labor of the peasants.

The student leaders who rose to fame soon found themselves recreating in miniature the real-life problems of attaining power. They were torn by arguments of the evolutionary versus revolutionary route to national salvation, but they no longer had the luxury of sitting on the sidelines. They had to take sides to boost their own positions. This created confusion and disagreement within student ranks about the nature of democracy in a land that had never known it. The new cultural movement had stirred a series of debates and polemics without creating a new social order.

The critical evaluation of Chinese and Western civilizations left many people in a situation like a man who missed his train, too late for the last one but too early for the next. The debate raged on.

* * *

Liang Shiyi led Qichao to a bench in the fragrant garden. "We can learn a humble lesson from the students' predicament. Government is not simply a matter of pure principle or political philosophies in collision. It's also a matter of practice of collaboration, compromise and patience."

"Yes," Liang Qichao replied, "Friends can make different judgments on important decisions confronting the country, but still respect each other's motives and remain friends."

As Liang Qichao was ready to leave, Liang Shiyi told him, "I have learned so much this afternoon. We must get together more often. I always value your wise counsel." It was quite an education for Liang Shiyi on that spring day in May.

An Unexpected Call

"I'm pleased to learn Shungu is doing well," Liang Shiyi said to his eighth lady as he put down a letter from Dingji. "Her baby will reach full term soon. Dingji says he will telegraph us as soon as the baby is born." Liang anticipated the joy of being a grandfather.

His fourth lady and sixth lady overheard this conversation from the other end of the sitting room hurried to congratulate him.

"I can see you are excited," his eighth lady said. "Aren't you worried about her delivery in a foreign country?"

"Not at all," Liang replied. "The delivery will be done in the best hospital in Boston. Both Yusheng and Zangsheng are by her side. They should be able to help take care of the baby."

Liang Shiyi's mind wandered. When his two daughters left with Dingji and his wife, Shungu, for Boston last year, there was a slight change in the plans for their education. Yusheng was then almost twenty and had completed her high school education in Hong Kong a year earlier. She wanted to attend a finishing school for only one year before considering marriage. Zangsheng was almost sixteen and would be a junior at the same school. However, their sister-in-law, Shungu, did not speak English well and wanted to study at home under a private tutor. It was decided that Yusheng, who also needed help speaking English, would defer her admission to school for one year and would study English at home with Shungu.

A lively and daredevil kind of girl, Zangsheng was as bright and witty as she was beautiful. She didn't hesitate to attend the House in the Pines, the small boarding school for girls at Norton, Massachusetts, without the company of her sister. Their father approved the idea as both girls would graduate at the same time and return home together with Dingji, who by then would have completed his bachelor's degree. Their father never thought of the prospect of rivalry when the two sisters, four years apart in age, would enroll in the same class.

After spending a year at Norton, Zangsheng returned to her brother's house for summer vacation. She and Yusheng provided all the help Shungu needed. The good news came on the Fourth of July when Shungu gave birth to a boy. What a way to

341

celebrate the happy family event on American Independence Day!

Shiyi got the news by telegram within a day. Although he proclaimed it would make no difference whether the baby was a boy or a girl, Shiyi knew a boy would mean more to his father. He immediately transmitted the good news to Hong Kong.

Shiyi's brother, Shixu, wrote back that their father couldn't be happier. However, Shixu intimated that other events in the family had made the patriarch rather unhappy, and urged Shiyi to come home when he could get away from Beijing.

* * *

Liang Shiyi went to see Ye Gongchuo after President Warren Harding announced on July 13 that China would be invited to attend the Washington Conference scheduled for November 12, 1921. Since the United States had refused to join the League of Nations, it proposed to convene the conference to settle, with other powers, the post-war issues in the Pacific The major items on the agenda included: the settlement of the possessions and dominions of mandated islands in the Pacific Ocean by the four powers, (the United States, Britain, France and Japan); the limitation of naval armament and use of submarine and noxious gases by the five powers, (the four powers and Italy); and the principles and policies to be followed in matters concerning China by the nine powers, (the five powers plus Belgium, the Netherlands, Portugal and China). The Chinese government was invited to participate in the discussion of the last item on the agenda.

"This invitation is extremely vital to the survival of China," Liang was direct about the purpose of his visit. "We must help the government make a strong case for China. Unfortunately, I have to leave for Hong Kong to take care of some family business soon. I trust you will provide the leadership to awaken the people to the challenge."

"Don't worry," Ye replied matter-of factly. "This is precisely my own feeling. I would have done this even if you hadn't asked me."

Liang was relieved that Ye was now in charge of this important task. After spending a month lining up other supporters, Liang was on his way.

* * *

Ye Gongchuo wasted no time in organizing the Association for Pacific Conference Studies with the supporters of the Communication clique. In its first meeting on August 4, the association decided to send a representative to the United States to coordinate activities with Alfred Saokee Sze, the Chinese Minister in the United States. Ye Gongchuo and Chen Zhensan were asked to speak to the Foreign Minister and to suggest names for the Chinese delegates to the Washington Conference.

The action of Ye spurred the formation of similar associations by other political cliques and community groups in rapid succession. Among them were associations sponsored by Zhang Jian and supporters of the Research Clique who took action on August 17. On August 19, Cai Yunpei, representing the faculties of eight national universities and colleges in Beijing formed their base, and on August 21, a group of former premiers of various political persuasions, including Qian Nengxun, Sun Baoqi, and Xiong Xiling met to form another group. These were organizations representing the movers and shakers outside the government. Not to be outdone, some close friends of President Xu also established an association on August 28 and some members of the Parliament inaugurated one on September 1. Why the latter two groups needed such associations was anyone's guess since they had full access to the official channels in decision making. Some suspected they wanted to garner attention and others thought they were trying to sabotage other groups.

On September 1, Ye Gongchuo invited a large number of reporters to a news conference, among them twelve Japanese reporters and ten Westerners. Speaking in his capacity of a grassroot organization engaged in "people's diplomacy," he implored the foreign reporters to understand the importance of the Washington Conference to China's future and urged them to appeal for international justice in solving the Shandong problem.

Several days later, Obata Yukichi, the Japanese Minister in Beijing, sent a diplomatic note to the Chinese Foreign Ministry, requesting China's direct negotiation with Japan on the Shandong Problem. It was a ploy to settle the problem on terms favorable to Japan so the matter would be off the agenda in the forthcoming Washington Conference. It was a hot issue to which the Chinese government did not wish to respond. With the approval of the State Council, Foreign Minister Yan Weiqing publicly sought the opinions of various grassroot organizations. In response, Ye Gongchuo called an emergency meeting of his Association for Pacific Conference on September 24. He declared a public position that the only acceptable solution to the Shandong problem was for Japan to return to China all special privileges formerly ceded to Germany and taken over by Japan during the World War.

In late September, all grassroot organizations in Beijing formed a "Union of Associations for the Advancement of the Chinese Position at the Washington Conference" to demonstrate their solidity. They decided to send a delegation to Shanghai to attend a proposed meeting of the National Association of People's Diplomacy, sponsored jointly by Shanghai's Merchant Association, Education Association and Agriculture Association.

Responding to public pressure, on October 5, the Foreign Ministry informed the Japanese Minister in Beijing that China would not enter into direct negotiation with Japan. The next day the Chinese government announced the appointment of three delegates to the Washington Conference: Alfred Saokee Sze, Chinese Minister to the United States; Wellington Koo, Chinese Minister to Great Britain; and Wang Chonghui, a former Foreign Minister.

On the eve of the opening session of the Washington Conference, the Union of Associations staged a noisy public demonstration in the streets of Beijing in concert with the meeting of the National Association of People's Diplomacy in Shanghai. Both organizations demanded the government take a strong position at the Washington Conference, particularly with respect to the Shandong Problem and the tariffs. Under intense pressure, the Chinese government instructed its delegates to propose ten basic principles concerning matters related to China and a request for international recognition of Chinese tariff autonomy at the Washington Conference.

* * *

Liang Shiyi was delighted to see a rare smile on his father's face when they met in Hong Kong. The patriarch couldn't wait to see a picture of his first great grandson. As it happened, the extended family got together on that evening for another celebration—for one-month-old celebration of Shixu's infant son, born on July 20. One month was an important milestone for infant survival during the times when childbirth trauma and postnatal diseases often cost the lives of infants within the first thirty days. After the dinner, the patriarch commented, "I now have so many grandsons who will probably look forward to studying abroad. I hope at least one of them will devote himself to Chinese classical studies and to continuing the Confucian tradition." Liang Shiyi did not volunteer a response since he realized he had less and less control of his own children. Shixu also remained silent. He usually deferred to his brother in taking the lead in matters affecting the extended family.

The next day, Shixu brought to the attention of his brother an unpleasant situation which he had tried for sometime to resolve. Since the death of her young daughter two years before, their stepmother had gradually developed a mental disorder. It had reached the point where she was a hindrance rather than a help to their father.

"It's our responsibility to take care of her," Liang Shiyi said to his brother. "I'll leave everything in your hands. You know the situation better than I do."

"I have made some preliminary arrangements," Shixu replied, "but if you agree, you must speak to father about this." Shixu already knew Shiyi would agree, but their father was so stern that even though Shixu was over forty, he still dreaded approaching the patriarch on an issue so important. Even Shiyi bent over backward to agree with his father, who was proud of Shiyi's worldly success, but frowned on his extravagances. Their father had a code for expressing his approval or disapproval, so subtle the two sons did not notice its existence, but both of them could sense it with infallible instinct.

Shiyi had no choice in the matter. It was his obligation to confront his father. "Whatever your plan may be, I'll speak to father when we see him together tomorrow morning."

"The best solution is to take the second elderly lady back to our native village for a rest," Shixu suggested, "She can live in our father's house which has been kept in good condition. She has an unmarried sister whom we can employ to take care of her daily needs."

"Who's going to take care of father?" Liang Shiyi asked, broaching the inevitable.

"Given father's frail condition, he can't live alone without a constant companion. There are some families in our native village who keep young maid servants until they are eligible for marriage. We can find such a maiden for father as a concubine."

It was so arranged, and their father grudgingly gave his consent. Shixu took a trip with the second elderly lady back to his native village. Within days, he was able to find a maid servant of good temper and mild manner whose master was more than eager to marry her off to such a well-to-do family. Of course, no one asked her opinion. In all her life she would never make an independent decision. In the same trip, Shixu accomplished both missions and brought the young woman from the Chen family to Hong Kong. She became the concubine of his father and "the third elderly lady" to the rest of the family.

Liang Shiyi planned to stay in Hong Kong for a long period of time to observe his father's adjustment to the new arrangement.

* * *

The public outcry against direct negotiation of the Shandong problem had once again destabilized the Chinese government. But, in unexpected ways, the internal politics forced President Xu Shichang to exert leadership to calm the nation.

Ever since President Xu had humbly accepted the reinstatement of Generals Wu Peifu and Cao Kun, the Zhili Clique continued to grow in influence. To squash the independence movement in Hunan Province, Wu Peifu had been sent to Hupei to reinforce the troops under its inefficient governor in fighting the rebels. Wu's troops scored a major victory against the Hunan army in late August and defused the independence movement. He became so indispensable to the government in Beijing that he was rewarded with a higher military command.

On the other hand, the Military Government in the South had regained the effective control of Guangdong and Guangxi Provinces. By September, the last resistance of the Guangxi Clique had crumbled and General Lu Rongting fled to Vietnam for refuge. The good news for Sun Yatsen and his supporters posed a menace to the government in Beijing.

Under such circumstances, General Zhang Zuolin of the Fengtian Clique joined forces with General Cao Kun of the Zhili Clique to persuade President Xu that the present cabinet was too weak to survive the national crisis. "Who can do better under extremely difficult times?" President Xu asked.

General Zhang was ready with an answer, "Only Liang Shiyi can raise enough money to support the troops upon which this government depends so heavily. And Liang is perhaps the only person capable of holding together a fractious coalition at this time." General Cao readily agreed.

But Liang Shiyi was in Hong Kong and had no immediate plan to return to Beijing. As an enticement, President Xu awarded Liang a first-class civilian Medal of Honor in September. Then he followed up with a telegram inviting Liang to return to Beijing to discuss the possibility of joining the government. Generals Zhang and Cao telegraphed Liang separately, assuring him of their support. But Liang was not impressed and made no move. More telegrams arrived in Liang's office in Hong Kong and he could not ignore their pleas.

"I'll return to Beijing soon," Liang Shiyi told Shixu. "Although I have no ambition to become the Premier, I cannot ignore the repeated invitations of President Xu to discuss the national crisis. I must give him whatever help I can. You can take care of father without me as you have done all these years."

"Father seems to be quite settled with our new stepmother," Shixu replied. "It will not be a problem."

With that encouragement, Liang Shiyi left Hong Kong by steamship on November 10, arriving in Shanghai two days later. He was in no hurry to plunge into the chaotic political arena in Beijing and watched the situation daily for new developments. Taking a leisurely tour of Hangzhou and other scenic cities on his way to Nanjing, he finally took the Tianjin-Pukou Railway, and then the Beijing-Tianjin Railway, to Beijing. It was the end of November when he stepped into his residence at Ganshiqiao Lane.

The first sign of trouble came when he heard rumors that General Cao had second thoughts about Liang's pending appointment as Premier. Without consulting General Wu Peifu, a deputy commander under him, Cao did not know Wu had another plan for reshuffling the government. He also underestimated the new military power that Wu had wielded right under his nose. He found himself unable to convince Wu to wait and watch.

Liang Shiyi told President Xu he did not need the political hassle associated with the premiership, but would help solve the banking crisis looming on the horizon. With the approaching New Year, the citizens of Beijing almost toppled the Bank of China and the Bank of Communications by demanding withdrawal of their deposits. Liang and other bankers worked overtime behind the scenes to avert the run on the banks.

President Xu was desperate when Premier Zhan Yunpeng tendered his resignation on December 18, forcing him to appoint Yan Weiqing as Acting Premier. He summoned Liang Shiyi to the Presidential Palace. "You understand so well that people of widely different views can work together. We need such a constructive force at the time of national crisis. I hope you will not refuse my offer of the premiership."

Liang Shiyi replied with equal earnestness, "We can have differences, but it doesn't mean we have to differ all the time. I would be less than human if I were not touched by your offer. My head tells me to turn it down, but my heart tells me otherwise. I will answer your call." Liang's unaffected modesty went beyond good manners. Beneath the surface he had a conviction that he was the man of the hour.

On December 24, 1921, President Xu appointed Liang Shiyi the Premier, succeeding Yan Weiqing.

* * *

Liang Shiyi's elevation to premiership was not headline news in the United States. Yusheng and Zangsheng, both now enrolled at the House in the Pines, had gone to Boston to join their brother Dingji for the Christmas holiday. After dinner on Christmas Day, Dingji received a phone call from a friend asking him if he had read the news buried deep inside the *Boston Globe*. He hadn't, but he said he would search for it. He read the short, terse account that his father had become the Premier of China. The news brought cheers to their Christmas celebration.

When the two sisters went back to their boarding school at Norton after the Christmas holiday, a local reporter discovered their identities and asked for an interview. The girls suddenly became celebrities on campus and were led to the office of the headmistress to meet him. Cautious and reserved in nature, Yusheng felt terribly awkward and was completely speechless. Fortunately, Zangsheng was able to field many questions and deflect others. They knew very well how fickle the tenure of premiership in China was. They had no idea what would happen to them if their father should falter in his new position.

Precarious Premiership

"I must move quickly," Liang Shiyi said to Ye Gongchuo who had been summoned to Gangshiqiao Lane. "I need all the help I can get from you." It was the evening of December 24, 1921. The two sat in front of the fireplace in the spacious living room, discussing politics.

"Have you given any thought to cabinet appointments?" Ye asked.

"Yes, I have," Liang replied. "The President pressed the premiership on me for days. As soon as I decided to accept his offer earlier today, I discussed with him a slate of appointees representing various political factions. They should promote national unity. I plan to call prospective appointees tonight, and tomorrow I'll announce the appointments."

"You really lose no time," Ye commented.

"I cannot afford to delay," Liang replied. "My tenure may be short-lived, given the many outside forces acting against my appointment."

"I understand," Ye Gongchuo said sympathetically. "Your appointment to the premiership depends on a tacit agreement between Zhang Zuolin of the Fengtian Clique and Cao Kun of the Zhili Clique. Although their personal relationship is amicable because their families are joined by the marriage of their children, the political goals of the two cliques are divergent and in conflict. Wu Peifu has shown signs of challenging Cao Kun for the leadership of the Zhili Clique. The situation can become unpleasant if the conflict between the two cliques becomes serious."

Since Christmas was not a day of significance on the Chinese calendar, Liang did not anticipate much difficulty in contacting most candidates to confirm their acceptance. The only exception was Wang Chonghui, who was attending the Washington Conference in the United States and could only be reached by telegram.

"I want to appoint Wang Chonghui as Justice Minister and Huang Yanpei as Education Minister," Liang explained. "They have impeccable credentials and enjoy wide support from all segments of the society, including the Nationalists. But my hands are tied in other appointments. I must accommodate various political factions. The portfolios of Army, Navy, Interior and Foreign Affairs, and even the Minister of Agriculture and Commence, are either holdovers or compromise candidates. I plan to

348

appoint Zhang Hu as Finance Minister. He's a capable man with strong links to the Research Clique."

"And for Minister of Communications?" Ye asked.

"My original intention was to appoint you to be the secretary of the State Council because I need your help there. However, that will leave the portfolio of Communications wide open as a battle ground for candidates supported by different political factions. I must turn to you for this job, even if it means you may become the target of the opposition."

"I fully appreciate the difficulty," Ye replied. "I have no intention of seeking this post. But if my presence will help you, I'm willing to serve."

"Thank you," Liang said with relief. "You are most gracious as usual." Then he turned to the serious business of governing. "My immediate objectives are threefold: to establish a strong foreign policy; to provide liquidity to the financial world; and third, to stop the civil war. These objectives seem so simple and yet are so elusive."

"If these objectives can be accomplished at all, you are more likely than others to carry them out," Ye said, giving his friend the encouragement he needed.

When Liang Shiyi was alone, he made phone calls to various candidates. After announcing his appointments the next day, he wrote to his friend Liang Qichao who had withdrawn from politics, "I'm not asking you to jump into this snake pit with me. But I need your wise counsel for the difficult tasks ahead. Please come for a visit within the next few days."

* * *

Liang Shiyi's first order of business was to send a telegram to the three Chinese delegates attending the Washington Conference on Pacific Affairs. He assured Alfred Sze, Wellington Koo and Wang Chonghui that Chinese policy pertaining to all items on the conference agenda would continue under his administration. He also sent a separate telegram to Wang Chonghui informing him of his appointment as Justice Minister, pending his return to Beijing after the Washington Conference.

No issue at the Washington Conference attracted more public attention in China than the Chinese demand for the resolution of the Shandong Problem through an international treaty instead of direct negotiation with Japan. The second major issue was the Chinese demand for tariff autonomy. The nine powers at the Washington Conference promised to establish an international commission to study the issue later that year. While the expectation of the Chinese people might be unrealistic, these issues were so sensitive that politicians could ignore them only at their own peril.

On December 29, 1921, Obata Yukichi, the Japanese Minister to Beijing, made a courtesy call to congratulate Liang Shiyi. During their conversation, Obata brought up the subject of the redemption of the Qingdao-Jinan Railway in Shandong. Japan had bought this railway from German interests. Liang Shiyi told him that as a part of the settlement of the Shandong Problem, China would secure loans to redeem control of this railway from Japan but that the issue should be discussed with the Chinese delegates at the Washington Conference.

Two days later, the Foreign Ministry cabled the Chinese delegates in Washington with the following instruction: "Obata visited the premier on December 29, and asked about the redemption of the Qingdao-Jinan Railway. The Premier suggested that China intends to secure loans to redeem the railway and to regain the control of its administration. The detail must be worked out as a part of the settlement of the Shandong Problem in Washington." The Ministry of Communications also initiated plans to raise money from private Chinese sources for its redemption.

Wu Peifu, an ambitious commander under Cao Kun, was not satisfied with the deal between the Zhili Clique and the Fengtian Clique. He had sent word to Liang Shiyi in late December demanding a huge sum for the army under his command at Luoyang in Henan Province. It was, for all intents and purposes, blackmail. Nevertheless, Liang dispatched an emissary to Luoyang to explain to Wu the difficulties of raising such a sum of money for his army. Outraged, Wu opened his first salvo aimed at Liang on January 5, 1922. Using unusually tough language, he publicly accused Liang of betraying the country by seeking a Japanese loan to redeem the Qingdao-Jinan Railway. It was a malicious plot to fan the hatred of the public toward Liang through rumor and innuendo.

To control the damage, the State Council immediately issued a rebuttal, listing the facts surrounding the redemption of the Qingdao-Jinan Railway. Liang Shiyi also issued a statement stating he favored the redemption of the railway by raising money through domestic or foreign sources, but not through a Japanese loan. The Ministry of Communications also added its voice to deny any consideration of a Japanese loan to redeem the Qingdao-Jinan Railway. But all these efforts to put forth the official version of this issue fell on deaf ears.

* * *

Liang Shiyi understood the fundamental problem underlying the request of Wu Peifu for expenditures for his army. The warlords had built up their own armies far beyond what the national treasury could afford to support. This was the time of the year that ordinary people, as well as the business community, needed financial liquidity to tidy up their debts before the Chinese Lunar New Year. The army commanders were especially desperate for funds to pay off wages what they owed the soldiers.

As Wu was flexing his muscles, a fleet of Chinese naval vessels intercepted a merchant ship carrying the tax receipts from the Salt Administration from Shanghai to Tianjin and confiscated the cash for the navy. Since the salt tax receipts were pledged as collateral for foreign loans, the ministers of foreign powers in Beijing protested to the Chinese government. Such losses in revenue had to be recovered or made up in some other way.

No wonder Liang Shiyi was drafted to be the premier at the insistence of Cao Kun and Zhang Zuolin. He had the reputation of being the god of fortune. But Wu Peifu felt the Zhili Clique was given the short end of the deal and that the Fengtian Clique would benefit and expand its influence. He moved decisively to preempt any attempt at compromise negotiated by Cao Kun, the nominal leader of the Zhili Clique.

Under such difficult circumstances, Liang Shiyi struggled to find ways to stabilize the financial market and avert an immediate crisis. Using his influence as its chief executive officer, he announced that the Bank of Communications would honor unlimited withdrawals from all accounts. That had the desired effect of preventing a run on the banks by the skeptical public. He also ordered the Finance Ministry to make plans for issuing a new domestic bond of ninety-six million yuan. The proceeds would be used to pay off short-term government notes which would soon come due. Hopefully, these measures might ease the financial crunch of the government in the near future.

But Wu Peifu was an impatient man. By January 11, he had lined up the military commanders in six provinces under the control of the Zhili Clique to support his effort to get rid of Liang Shiyi. He cabled Liang with vilifying insults and demanded his resignation. Several days later, he publicly threatened to use force by asking the commanding generals of Zhili Clique in various provinces to move their troops toward Beijing. On January 19, these commanding generals cabled President Xu and asked him to dismiss Liang. The crisis had reached the point of no return.

* * *

President Xu Shichang had operated on the assumption that none of his backers could trust one another. He needed time and space to maneuver, but was never shy about seeking power or using it. He learned from Yuan Shikai how to manage and retain his power simply by forging a complicated set of factions whose leaders were destined to spend half their time looking over their shoulders for treacherous opponents, real or imagined. It was the tradition of Chinese rulers. This bizarre political ploy would guarantee that he retained the real power, and everyone else could be cut off with ease.

When the President received the cable from the generals of Zhili Clique, he was more frightened by their troop movements than by their words. He summoned Liang Shiyi to the Presidential Palace and showed him the cable. This was the sure sign that he wanted Liang Shiyi to resign.

Taking the cue from the President, Liang stated, "I never wanted this job when it was offered to me. I can resign immediately to save you any agony. However, I wish you would use this opportunity to send a message to the generals. You should advise them that you will accept my resignation, but that they will be disciplined for interfering with the rule of the civilian government."

"I'll think about that," President Xu replied. "For now, I grant you a leave of absence to see what happens next."

"This is an easy way out," Liang said bluntly. "since you don't have to confront the generals immediately. But their lawlessness will come back to haunt you. Not only will your presidency be in danger, but the legitimacy of the government will be called to question if the generals can drive you out of office."

After the interview, Liang left for Tianjin. Two days later, January 25, 1922, President Xu announced Liang Shiyi's request for a leave of absence, and named

Steven T. Au

Foreign Minister Yan Weiqing as Acting Premier.

At the same time, the Finance Ministry announced the issuance of a new bond which had been underwritten by banks and other financial institutions. However, because the proceeds were earmarked for the redemption of short-term government notes and unavailable for military expenses, the regional military commanders in the Yangzi River valley opposed the new bond issues. The banks, which had underwritten the bonds, lost confidence in the government's financial solvency after the resignation of Liang Shiyi. As a result, the underwriters of the bond issue requested a full refund and pushed the government into an even greater crisis.

Zhang Zuolin of the Fengtian Clique, who sat on the sidelines during the crisis, saw the dwindling of his own fortune as the Zhili Clique captured the attention of the president. In the name of fairness, Zhang sent an open letter to President Xu on January 30, asking him to disclose the full text of the agreement with Japan on the Shandong Problem. Defending Liang Shiyi obliquely, he asserted, "If Liang Shiyi is guilty of treason by agreeing to secure a Japanese loan to redeem the Qingdao-Jinan Railway, I will be second to none in condemning his action. But if all the wild accusations about Liang are untrue, then his accusers are doing as much harm to our nation as the worst of traitors, no matter how noble their intention may be." Then he asked rhetorically, "At this time of crisis, can we be sure that we can find a new premier who is more capable of handling our national affairs than Liang Shiyi?"

Xu Shichang did not reply publicly to Zhang's letter. But the next day the Foreign Ministry disclosed the settlement of the Shandong Problem with Japan, pending official signatures on February 4. It was negotiated by the Chinese delegates to the Washington Conference, with the mediation of Great Britain and United States as a sidebar to the conference. Essentially, Japan would give up the special privileges previously ceded to Germany before the World War in return for compensations for property improvements undertaken by the Japanese. China would raise funds to redeem the Qingdao-Jinan Railways, but until such time, the Japanese would retain certain power in its administration. The accusation against Liang Shiyi proved to be groundless but the harm was done. There was no hope that he could again serve as Premier.

* * *

Among China's unfulfilled expectations at the Washington Conference was the termination of the Twenty-One demands imposed on China by Japan in 1915. Under heavy pressure from the United States, Japan agreed to give up only the seven demands in Group Five which had been reserved for future consideration and had never been enforced anyway. China gained nothing in this negotiation except the right to place the declarations of China, Japan and United States in the minutes.

At the closing of the Conference on February 6, 1922, the members announced the approval of the nine-powers treaty, a kind of bill of rights for China. The other eight powers jointly agreed to respect China's sovereignty, independence and territory; to aid China in developing and maintaining an effective and stable government; to use their influence in promoting the principle of equal opportunity for commerce and industry of all nations throughout China; and to refrain from taking advantage of conditions in China to seek special rights or privileges in that country.

To many Chinese, the treaties and declarations of the Washington Conference were nothing but empty words. The anti-imperialism sentiment continued to arouse the heart and soul of the Chinese people. They could only curse the impotence of their government to win over the foreigners.

Irrepressible Conflict

When he arrived in Tinajin, Liang Shiyi moved into the guest house of the Bank of Communications in the French Concession. Pondering his own fate in the safety of foreign protection, he was cautiously optimistic. He tended his business in the bank in anticipation of transferring his power to someone else to minimize the political fall-out. He was also making plans to preserve the bank's assets from interference by the government if Wu Peifu should gain an upper hand in his struggle for power.

Although President Xu was not eager to publicly soothe Zhang Zuolin's anger toward Wu Peifu, he did just that in private. When Zhang went back to Shenyang, Cao Kun sent an emissary to ask him for understanding of the brash action of Wu Peifu, his own deputy and comrade-in-arm. President Xu added his weight by sending an emissary to tell Zhang to keep some of his troops inside the Great Wall to balance Wu's influence. So far President Xu could not find a candidate for Premier who would be acceptable to both the Zhili Clique and the Fengtian Clique. A civil war between the two cliques appeared imminent if Wu Peifu's militant view prevailed.

President Xu had made his own calculation. If Zhang Zuolin sent several army divisions to the south of the Great Wall in a show of force, Cao Kun might get the message and somehow put a tight rein on Wu Peifu. If a war between the two cliques became unavoidable, the fighting would drain both sides. President Xu could then step in and appear as a peacemaker. As an elder statesman in the old Beiyang Clique, he could then win back the support of most generals in both cliques. It was a winning situation for him.

By the end of March, Zhang moved some of his army divisions to north China, almost according to Xu's script. Yan Weiqing, the Acting Premier, who did not share the president's optimism, hurriedly resigned. When Yan's resignation was followed by that of the Minister of Agriculture and Commerce, a man supported by Zhang Zuolin, it was a sure sign that Zhang would pursue the course of war rather than peace.

However, President Xu had not exhausted his political tricks for compromise. On April 8, he appointed Zhou Ziqi as Acting Premier, a man identified prominently with the Communications Clique. Zhou was dangled as a consolation prize for Zhang who had strongly favored Liang Shiyi. Since both Zhou and Wu were natives of Shandong Province, Xu hoped the situation would soften Wu's antagonism. Unfortunately, events suddenly altered the situation.

The very next day, Zhang Zuolin ordered the mobilization of all his forces in Manchuria. He announced that he wanted to unite China by wiping out the obstacles to peace. Wu Peifu replied in kind by asking, "Who is the obstacle to unification of China? Did Zhang learn the lesson of Duan Qirui, the last general who tried to unify China by force?" That kind of rhetoric was a prelude to fighting and President Xu recognized it. When some governors offered to mediate the conflict, Xu ordered the army on both sides to return to their bases. But their troops in the front line had already made contact. Zhang Zuolin declared war on the Zhili clique on April 16, 1922.

Wu Peifu was waiting for the first wave of offense from Zhang's troops before sending his men to attack their flanks. The fighting was most critical on April 28 when the unit led by one of Zhang's top lieutenants faltered and other units had to come to its rescue. Advancing under this momentum, Wu Peifu claimed victory while Zhang Zuolin ordered a retreat for regrouping in the Tianjin area on May 5. Neither side sought a truce.

* * *

President Xu knew that although Wu Peifu had won a decisive battle, the power base of Zhang Zuolin was undisturbed. He had to find a scapegoat to appease Wu Peifu. On May 5, he singled out Liang Shiyi, Ye Gongchuo and Zhang Hu as the culprits, and issued arrest warrants for these defenseless civilians. Since they had already gone to Tianjin and were staying in the French Concession, they were beyond the long arm of the government, at least for the time being.

That evening, a long-distance phone call came from Beijing to the guest house of the Bank of Communications where Liang Shiyi was staying. The caller insisted he must talk to Liang Shiyi in person. When Liang picked up the phone, he heard the familiar voice of Zhou Ziqi. "As the A-a-a-acting Premier, I -I I'm obligated to co-sign the a a arrest warrant on you. To my friend of more than two d-d-decades, I send my apology."

"Ziqi," Liang replied in a calm voice, "Please tell President Xu that when this unfortunate episode is over, we may see each other again. As to you, I don't have a trace of complaint. Your action of co-signing my arrest warrant will no doubt provide an interesting anecdote for future historians."

After hanging up the phone, Liang said to Ye Gongchuo, who was also staying in the guest house, "The last time an arrest warrant was issued against me, at least you were spared. I'm sorry that my fate befalls you this time."

"I have expected this," Ye replied. "Wu Peifu is vicious and unpredictable. He may even force President Xu to ask the Western diplomats to kick us out of the foreign concessions in Tianjin."

"In that case, I'd better send all members of my family in Beijing back to Hong Kong," Liang said. "What about you and Zhang Hu?"

"My family will be safe in Tianjin," Ye told him. "And Zhang Hu has his own connections. He may even find his own way back to their good graces, but we had better get out of Tianjin before anything unpleasant happens to us."

"I need a good rest after this ordeal," Liang said to Ye. Why don't we ask a few friends to join us for a vacation in Japan?" That would also allow them to wait out the storm in a foreign country. Two days later, they sailed together for Japan.

After arriving at Nagasaki, Liang rented a cottage in a nearby fishing village graced by the natural beauty of the bay. He spent most of the time watching the life of the fishermen and composing light verses in the company of his literary friends. On one lonely evening, he thought of his eighth lady who was still in Hong Kong. He composed a poem full of love and tenderness which ended with the following lines:

> The clear moonlight over the bay this night
> must also be in Hong Kong shining bright.
> I feel the soft touch of your dark wavy hair,
> like the spray of pounding waves in the air.

After a night of sweet dreams, he posted the poem to her in the early morning.

Liang Shiyi also thought of his son and two daughters in the United States. They were scheduled to return home as soon as Dingji graduated from Boston University. He must now advise them to stay in the United States until his own plans became certain.

* * *

Quite suddenly, the drama in Beijing unfolded with sound and fury. Under heavy pressure from the victorious Wu Peifu, President Xu issued an order on May 10 to relieve Zhang Zuolin of his military assignments, pending further investigation of his misdeeds. Zhang was outraged by this unexpected insult from Xu who had been wooing him only days before when he appeared to be winning. Since Zhang's power lay in his control of the large army in Manchuria, not the nominal titles conferred upon him by the President, Zhang essentially asserted his independence from the Beijing government and continued the state of belligerence against the Zhili Clique. In the meantime, he sent an open telegram to expose Xu's many secret double dealings in his long career as a politician which embarrassed Xu greatly. President Xu had good reason to regret his shabby treatment of Zhang.

Wu Peifu, in the meantime, had planned far beyond what President Xu could ever imagine. The public assault on Xu's character by Zhang was exactly what he needed to discredit Xu's presidency. Wu sent an open telegram to the governors on May 14, seeking their opinion on reviving the Parliament based on the 1912 Constitution. As Wu Peifu well knew, the last time the old Parliament had been in session was in 1917 before Li Yuanhong was forced out as the President of the Republic. Many members of that Parliament had gone South to support Sun Yatsen's cause. However, Speaker of the Senate Wang Jiaxiang, and Speaker of the House Wu Jinglian, had not, and were now in Tianjin. Wu Peifu had contacted them while they tried to convene the members of that earlier Parliament in Tianjin. When some governors responded favorably to his call for reviving the old Parliament, Wu Peifu lost no time in putting his plan into action.

Only then, did Xu Shichang realize the seriousness of Wu Peifu's plan. Xu had been elected President in 1918 by the Parliament organized under a revised constitution, referred to as the new Parliament. If the 1912 Constitution was still in effect, then his presidency was illegitimate. For all his cunning in political infighting, Xu never expected this trick pulled by Wu Peifu. As the old Parliament convened in Tianjin on June 1, the one hundred and fifty members in attendance declared the 1918 revised constitution null and void, and agreed that the Beijing government, as well as Sun Yatsen's government, should be abolished to make room for a new unified government.

Xu Shichang could challenge the legitimacy of the old parliament meeting in Tianjin, particularly since it did not even have a quorum to pass a resolution, but he had lost his will to fight for his political life and was afraid to be trapped in Beijing as a political prisoner. The next day, without any warning, Xu Shichang announced he was resigning, effective immediately. Since the vice presidency was vacant, Xu turned over the seal of the President to the State Council. Zhou Ziqi, the Acting Premier, was caught by surprise. He immediately called members of the cabinet to say farewell to the President at the railway station as Xu left for Tianjin in the late afternoon.

Liang Shiyi's warning to Xu Shichang in January had been prophetic. Xu had dug his own grave when he gave in to Wu Peifu's blackmail while he still could have used his authority to discipline the military leaders. How ironic that in less than one month after he issued the arrest warrant for Liang Shiyi, Xu was now joining other retired politicians under foreign protection in Tianjin!

* * *

Zhou Ziqi, the Acting Premier, announced he would return the power of the presidency to the Parliament. He knew very well that by holding the seal of the President, he would soon be the target of contesting parties. But which parliament would stand up to claim the seal? The new Parliament was not in session. The old Parliament was meeting in Tianjin. He would wait for instructions from the first responder to rid himself of the problem.

Wu Peifu had a ready answer for Zhou. On the same day, he and a number of regional commanding generals recommended that Li Yuanhong, the President disposed in 1917, be returned as Transition President under the advice and consent of the old Parliament. Aware of the unstoppable power of Wu Peifu, members of the new Parliament did not even voice a protest.

Although some generals objected to Li Yuanhong's return to the presidency, their voices were soon drowned out. When Li first received the invitation in Tianjin, he hesitated. Remembering the humiliation he had suffered five years before, he said to his aides, "I have been out of touch with politics for so long. If a man as capable as Liang Shiyi with a reputation as the god of fortune cannot last, how can I find a Premier who can get us out of the current crisis?" However, his aides were eager to return to power and persuaded him to change his mind. On June 6, Li Yuanhong informed Cao Kun and Wu Peifu that he would accept the presidency if all sides in the civil war agreed to disarmament. When his request was granted, Li Yuanhong went to Beijing to assume the presidency and appointed Yan Weiqing as Transition Premier. Two days later, the President rescinded the order of June 12, 1917 for shutting down the old Parliament.

Now that Cao Kun and Wu Peifu had gotten their spoils, they could let their adversaries in Fengtian get off easily. They treated their adversaries as if they had gone through an elaborate set of parade-ground maneuvers that would engage in limited operations under controlled conditions. They could declare victory, surrender or compromise in order to collaborate on the real business—sharing the spoils. The two cliques signed a truce agreement on June 17.

* * *

While the civil war between the Zhili Clique and the Fengtian Clique had raged in north China, Sun Yatsen's government in south China also suffered a severe setback. In 1921, under the protection of Chen Jiongming, the warlord of Guangdong, Sun was named President of a newly-organized Nationalist government by the surviving members of the old Parliament in Beijing who had moved south. Sun appointed Chiang Kaishek as a field officer in Chen Jiongming's army. But Chen disapproved of Sun's plans for using Guangdong as a base for a national unification drive and revolted against him in the summer of 1922. With the help of Chiang Kaishek, Sun narrowly escaped to Hong Kong on August 9. The two left Hong Kong for Shanghai the next day on board the *S.S. Empress of Russia*.

As Li Yuanhong tried to fulfill his promise of promoting national unification through peaceful means, he invited Sun Yatsen to Beijing. Sun declined. He suspected Li Yuanhong was only being used by Cao Kun and Wu Peifu as a front man while they secretly prepared for war. However, without a base of operation, many members of the old Parliament who had supported Sun in Guangzhou were eager to return to Beijing to reclaim their seats.

On August 5, President Li Yuanhong announced the appointment of Tang Shaoyi as the new Premier, a good will gesture toward the Nationalists. He also announced a cabinet with broad representation, and designated Wang Chonghui, the Education Minister, as Acting Premier, pending the arrival of Tang Shaoyi. However, it soon became clear that Li's idea of promoting national unity was not shared by the leaders of the old Parliament. Speaker of the House Wu Jinglian was a one-time supporter of Sun Yatsen who later became a turncoat. Wu had been the prime mover behind the revival of the old Parliament in Tianjin for his own selfish motive. But Tang Shaoyi was no fool. He knew he was persona non grata to the Beiyang generals and did not want to risk his life, nor his reputation, to assume premiership in Beijing. Using the Acting Premier as his proxy, Tang asked the Cabinet to submit an ambitious agenda to Parliament. It was promptly rejected. In his attempt to break the deadlock, President Li dismissed Tang Shaoyi and appointed Wang Chonghui as Premier.

For his part, Wu Peifu had exacted from the new Cabinet what he had long wanted. As the national treasury was practically empty, all government workers, including teachers and police, had not been paid for months. The only steady source of revenue not pledged to foreign lenders as collateral was the revenue from railways under Chinese administration. Under the charter of the Bank of Communications, such revenue would be deposited in the treasury until its use was authorized by the State Council. With Liang Shiyi as Premier and Ye Gongchuo as Communications Minister, Wu Peifu had not been able to lay his hands on the funds. After the Cabinet of Wang Chonghui was sworn in, Wu Peifu forced the new Communications Minister to agree that his army expenditures would be paid directly from the revenue of railways before any funds were deposited in the Bank of Communications. His soldiers would receive pay while other public employees would suffer even more.

Wu Jinglian was not far behind in exacting his pound of flesh from the government. He continued to use his strong-arm tactics to block actions of the Cabinet in every conceivable way. It was a challenge, not only to the Premier, but also to the President. Although the term of a new President would not begin until October 10, 1923, a full year away, Wu Jinglian was flexing his muscle to remind the President that he could be removed at any time if he did not behave himself.

* * *

From his bayside abode in Nagasaki, Japan, Liang Shiyi received the news that stockholders of the Bank of Communications had voted to elect Zhang Jian as the chief executive officer of the bank on June 18. Zhang Jian, the valedictorian of his Jinshi class of 1894, was a successful industrialist whom Liang Shiyi greatly admired. It was no small comfort that the bank was in good hands while Shiyi was unable to play an active role.

Liang Shiyi watched the deterioration of the situation in China with disgust. He chose to ignore what he read in the newspapers, but he could not forget that both he and Ye Gongchuo were still under arrest warrants in China. He invited Ye to stay with him in Hong Kong when they left Japan at the end of September.

Liang Shiyi's homecoming was brightened by the birth of a daughter to his brother Shixu who now had five sons. It was a warm reunion with the extended family after three months of lonely life in Japan.

* * *

"Father should be back in Hong Kong by now," Dingji said to his wife as he looked out the window from their breakfast nook. It was a typical frosty October morning in Boston where they had lived for more than two years. Their toddler son was playfully opening and shutting the doors of the lower kitchen cabinets while they relaxed after breakfast. They were wondering what their next move would be. Dingji said hopefully, "I expect to receive instructions from father soon."

Dingji's sisters were still in bed after a night out with friends. They had been with their brother in Boston since their graduation from the House in the Pines the previous June.

"Zangsheng is barely eighteen," Dingji's wife Shungu commented disapprovingly. "She should not have gone out so late."

"That's why I asked Yusheng to go with her," Dingji replied. "After all, it was a Friday evening and they needed some outlet for their pent-up energy."

"But I don't like the boy from the Chen family," Shungu replied. "He seems to be so immature and yet he sets his eyes on Zangsheng whenever he shows up."

"I've noticed that too," Dingji said calmly. "Zangsheng is usually the life of the party, but I don't think she reciprocates Chen's attention."

Shungu was always proper and cautious in the best Chinese tradition; so was her sister-in-law Yusheng. The two got along extremely well and shared many private thoughts. When Yusheng went out with a group of young people, she often stayed in the background and watched the behavior of the boys at a distance. But Zangsheng was thoroughly Americanized and regarded dating as a natural process of growing up. In any case, Shungu did not want something harmful to happen to Zangsheng, and she often warned her about the Chen boy—to no avail. She even wrote to her mother-in-law, the powerful Madam, and asked her to advise Zangsheng to be more cautious in her dating. Her good intentions got her into trouble at both ends. Zangsheng thought Shungu was too old fashioned and completely out of touch with the modern world; her mother-in-law thought Shungu was defaming the good reputation of her daughter.

Dingji finally heard from his father. Liang Shiyi had contacted a banker friend in Shanghai concerning a job for his son. Although Dingji was in an enviable position as a graduate of an American University, Liang Shiyi wanted his friend to start Dingji at the bottom of the ladder. He truly believed a solid foundation was important for Dingji's future success, and he did not want his friend to place Dingji in a privileged position and deprive his son of that valuable experience. Then he added in his letter to Dingji, "Your grandfather will be eighty years old next year. We plan to have a big celebration to honor him in Hong Kong. Of course, you and your sisters are expected to return home in time for the occasion. You need not begin your job in Shanghai until after this joyous event."

Shortly after New Year Day of 1923, Dingji and his family, along with his two sisters, took a trans-continental train ride to San Francisco. After staying briefly to visit friends, they booked passage on a slow boat back to Hong Kong.

When they arrived in Hong Kong, their extended family was already in high gear, preparing for the patriarch's eightieth birthday. The milestone of "eighty sui" was so rare in China that it called for a celebration. For a man of Liang Zhijian's accomplishment, as a Confucian scholar with two successful and filial sons, the celebration was bound to be spectacular. Liang Shiyi had asked Liang Boyin and Liang Qichao, his two close friends of thirty-five years standing, to write an article to honor his father. In addition to writing about their sentimental recollection of the good deeds of the patriarch, the two appealed to other friends to express their congratulatory messages in poetry or prose. Numerous literary contributions from distinguished friends were received by the Liang family. Their works were collected in a bound volume dedicated to the patriarch.

The patriarch also wrote an autobiographical article to remind his descendants of his humble origin and his moral upbringing under the tutelage of his parents. He urged them to follow the teachings of Confucius which he regarded as the ultimate foundation of family values. With a rare outburst of immodesty, he composed a short poem to express his satisfaction of the life he had led.

On April 24, Liang Zhijian's two sons, all his grandchildren, his only great-grandson, and the women folk of the Liang clan were on hand for the occasion. His daughters and their families also came from afar for the celebration. The first business of the big day was the ceremony of worshipping their ancestors, an important gesture to give credit to the ancestors for the good fortune of the family. Then the entire group went to the reception hall of Taiping Theater to greet friends who had assembled there for the occasion. After posing for a family portrait, the patriarch sat at the center of the lobby, flanked by his two sons standing next to him, and spoke to hundreds of guests in the receiving line. Other family members circulated among their friends for socialization and then attended a banquet in the reception hall and entertainments in the theater.

* * *

Far away in Beijing, the government, under the premiership of Wang Chonghui, had resigned the previous November to protest the meddling of Wu Jinglian, the militant Speaker of the House. After rejecting three successive premiers appointed by the President in six weeks, the Parliament finally approved Zhang Shaozheng as the new Premier. Zhang had served as Minister of the Army in previous administrations, which highlighted his credentials with the military. It didn't hurt at all that his family and the family of Wu Peifu were related by the marriage of their children.

When Zhang Shaozheng took office in January 1923, he followed the policy of President Li Yuanhong, calling for peaceful settlement toward national unity. Elsewhere, Wu Peifu quietly prepared for war. Sun Yatsen, still in Shanghai, responded by securing his base in Guangzhou and announcing his official title would henceforth be Grand Marshall, instead of President, of the Chinese National Government. It was a gesture meant to reduce the level of hostility while negotiating a peaceful settlement with the government in Beijing. However, Cao Kun and Wu Peifu ignored the peace overture by forcing the Premier to appoint new governors for Guangdong and Fujian, the two provinces providing the base of Sun's forces. Within months, the peace initiative from Beijing had collapsed.

As Sun Yatsen regrouped his forces to oppose the government in Beijing, he contacted the Fengtian Clique and other Beiyang politicians who were at odds with Wu Peifu. Sun needed financial help more than anything else, and sent his brother-in-law T. V. Soong (aka Song Ziwen) to see Liang Shiyi in Hong Kong. Since Liang's close associates, Ye Gongchuo and Zheng Hongnian, were also in Hong

Kong for the celebration for Liang's father, they joined in the discussion to find ways to help Sun's cause. It was decided that Ye and Zheng would go to Guangzhou to serve in Sun's government while Liang stayed in Hong Kong to raise money through his connections.

After T. V. Soong left, Liang spoke to Ye, "You'll be safe to work in Guangzhou under the protection of Sun Yatsen."

"I have no fear at all," Ye replied. "The long arm of Beijing cannot reach that far to arrest me."

"That's because the Zhili Clique does not control Guangzhou, but not for lack of trying," Liang Shiyi said. "Wu Peifu certainly wants to nail us to the wall if he gets the chance."

Sun Yatsen must have been satisfied with the negotiation worked out by T. V. Soong. On May 7, 1923, he announced the appointment of Ye Gongchuo as Finance Minister and Zheng Hongnian as Deputy Finance Minister of the government in Guangzhou.

* * *

Just when Liang Shiyi was rejoicing in his latest political rebound in exile, a train robbery occurred on May 6 on Tianjin-Pukou Railway in the vicinity of Lincheng in Shandong Province. Three hundred persons on board, including many foreigners, were taken hostage by the bandits. It was an event furthest from Liang Shiyi's thought. Within hours after the news reached Beijing, Cao Kun and Wu Peifu tried to use this incident to discredit Liang once and for all. Without a thread of evidence, and in an open telegram, they accused Liang Shiyi as the mastermind behind the train robbery. They also sent a similar telegram to Beilby Alston, the British Minister to Beijing, and asked him to notify the Governor of Hong Kong to deport Liang Shiyi as a criminal. Although Alton had once characterized Liang Shiyi as the Machiavelli of China, he knew Liang could not have performed the act of robbing a train. Alston sent the telegram to Liang with an amusing note.

Liang Shiyi's supposed role in the train robbery was widely publicized by newspapers in major cities including Hong Kong. Some editorial writers noted the coincidence of Zhili Clique's accusation and the appointments of Liang's two proteges, Ye and Zheng, by the government in Guangzhou. The three felt it necessary to fire back an open telegram to clear themselves in the forum of public opinion.

Three weeks later, the bandits allowed Mr. Powell, an American hostage, to come out of their hiding place to present the grievances of the captors to the Minister of Communications from Beijing and the Commanding General of Shandong Province. It turned out the bandits were poor peasants who were driven to the act of robbery by desperation. They were more interested in publicizing their plight to the outside world than in demanding a specific ransom. It was difficult to negotiate with them when they offered no unified conditions for releasing the captives. Finally the Commanding General in Shandong suggested the bandits be put on the government payroll as soldiers in order to alleviate their desperate condition. These peasant bandits would be organized as a battalion, under the General's command, in return for the immediate release of the foreigners and the eventual release of the Chinese hostages when the new battalion became a reality. The settlement spoke volumes of how the warlords recruited their troops.

After the foreigners were released, the Portugal Minister to Beijing, who was also the dean of the Diplomatic Corps, delivered a request to the Foreign Ministry on August 10 on behalf of sixteen nations, demanding compensation to the hostages, punishment of the Commanding General of Shandong Province and a guarantee that such incident would not happen again. On behalf of the State Council, Foreign Minister Wellington Koo notified the Portugal Minister that the request was denied.

* * *

The train robbery, which had attracted so much attention from foreign diplomats, overshadowed far more serious troubles in the Beijing government. The Zhili Clique was impatient with Premier Zhang Shaozheng who tried to walk a tight rope between the President and the Zhili Clique. Under heavy pressure from Cao Kun and Wu Peifu, Zhang got a reprieve by offering his resignation, giving Wu Peifu a pretext to force the resignation of Li Yuanhong. Since Li could not possibly find another candidate for Premier who would be approved by the Parliament, Li asked Zhang to rescind his resignation. Zhang refused.

Ten days later, the troops in the garrison units in Beijing, whose commander Feng Yuxiang, was a protege of Wu Peifu, staged a demonstration in front of the Presidential Palace. Feng Yuxiang sent an ultimatum to the President demanding payment of wages for his troops. Li Yuanhong understood Feng's intention and on June 13, slipped out with his entourage to a special train heading for Tianjin. Just before his train reached Tianjin station, it was stopped by the Governor of Zhili Province who went on board to force Li Yuanhong to hand over the seal of the President. He also asked Li to sign a statement that he had resigned and asked several cabinet members to take over the power of the presidency. Li refused at first, but after being imprisoned on the train for several days, he finally gave in.

In the meantime, the Interior Minister in Zhang's Cabinet announced that he and several members would serve as a Regency to exercise presidential power. After Li Yuanhong was free and reached the foreign concessions in Tianjin, he immediately issued an open telegram to the news organizations saying the statement he had signed on the train was not valid because it was done under duress. The Parliament in Beijing countered his action by passing a resolution that any statement by Li Yuanhong after June 13 was no longer valid as a presidential order.

However, over one hundred members of Parliament who were unhappy with the action of the Zhili Clique left for Tianjin. Li Yuanhong encouraged them to go to Shanghai to reconvene the Parliament there. In the meantime, Sun Yatsen sent his senior aide, Wang Jingwei, to Tianjin to welcome the members of Parliament to Shanghai. By July, almost three hundred members of the Parliament had left Beijing and assembled in Shanghai. Knowing Liang's opposition to the Zhili Clique, Li

Yuanhong also sent an emissary to ask Liang Shiyi to support his return to power, but Liang was emphatic in declining to join Li's cause. "I must tell you in all candor that it's a dead issue as far as I'm concerned," he reiterated.

On September 11, Li Yuanhong arrived in Shanghai to plead his case and solicit for support. He was ignored, not only by the supporters of Sun Yatsen, but also by the power brokers in that area who did not want to be involved in a civil war. For the second time in his life, Li left the presidency a broken man.

The Zhili Clique was not discouraged by the public outcry and protest. Under the leadership of Wu Jinglian, Speaker of the House, the Parliament prepared for a new presidential election. Under the Constitution, the President would be elected by a joint session of the Parliament. Of the total membership of 870 persons in both houses, two thirds had to be present to vote, and a presidential candidate must receive three-quarters of these votes in order to be elected. Wu Jinglian knew he had the minimum of 436 votes to elect Cao Kun as President if he could only get 580 members to form the quorum.

Wu Jinglian decided to buy off members of the Parliament: diehard supporters and doubters alike, to insure their loyalty. Through intermediaries, he urged members who had gone to Shanghai or were lingering in Tianjin to come back to vote. Each delegate received a check of five thousand yuan, issued under a bogus name, but guaranteed by the bank, redeemable only if the holder was present to vote. This wholesale vote buying effort soon became an open secret and the Beijing press had a field day. The members of Parliament were dubbed as pigs foolish enough to be bought for slaughter. "Is the price too high?" mused one newspaper editorial. "It is all money nowadays, and nothing is too high," replied another the next day.

On October 5, members of Parliament were ushered into the building to vote, like pigs approaching the feeding trough. When the number of members present reached 590, a respectable figure, Wu Jinglian ordered voting to begin. Within an hour, Wu triumphantly announced the result: Cao Kun was elected President by 480 votes. The swearing-in of Cao Kun as President on October 10 would be an anti-climax.

Five days later, Cao Kun announced the acceptance of the demands made by the Portugal Minister on behalf of the sixteen nations for settling the claims resulting from the train robbery. In the same afternoon, the foreign diplomats from these nations went to the Presidential Palace to congratulate the new President. Cao Kun could now boast triumphantly that he had silenced his critics on the legitimacy of his presidency.

Far away in Hong Kong, Liang Shiyi received the news of Cao Kun's election with a grin. He said to his brother Shixu, "Father taught us to avoid the deadly sin of self-righteousness. But I can't help thinking that anyone who gains the presidency through a stolen election will lose his mandate to govern. As certain as I can be of anything, mark my word that Cao Kun will not be in power for very long."

The European Experience

It was mild and sunny on New Year's Day of 1924 when Liang Shiyi went to the Official Mansion of the Governor of Hong Kong to extend his holiday greetings. Sir Reginald Stubbs, the Governor, was busy talking to a group of Chinese guests in the reception hall. As he was led to Sir Reginald, the governor turned to greet him and then continued to talk about the British Empire Exhibition scheduled for opening in Wembley, England in April. "This is the most significant exhibition in England since 1862. You must not miss the chance to see it," Sir Reginald Stubbs spoke with the persuasion of a slick salesman.

After staying in Hong Kong for more than a year as a fugitive from the arrest warrant issued by the Beijing government, Liang Shiyi was quite restless. In spite of his cooperation with Sun Yatsen behind the scenes, in the last few months twists and turns of the Nationalists had dampened his enthusiasm. He realized he could exercise very little influence in Chinese politics. The British Empire Exhibition provided an incentive for him to travel abroad and learn more about the new world order dominated by the European powers. He also desired to do some sightseeing along the way.

* * *

On January 20, 1924, Sun Yatsen summoned the Nationalist delegates from all over China to attend the First All-China Nationalist Conference in Guangzhou. The manifesto of this conference marked a new radical direction of the party.

Ever since Sun restored the Nationalist Party in 1919, he had selected two of his long-time supporters, Hu Hanmin and Wang Jingwei, to draft new principles for the party. Over several years, Sun Yatsen refined and consolidated his political thought into the Three Principles of the People—Nationalism, Democracy and Social Welfare. Because of his disagreement with the warlord in Guangdong, on whose protection Sun depended, he'd had no opportunity to put his ideas into practice.

When Soviet diplomat, Adolf Joffe, arrived in China to discuss the resumption of diplomatic relations with the Beijing government in January 1923, he held extended meetings with Sun Yatsen in Shanghai. Soviet observers felt the Chinese Communists, only 300 members at that time, were not in a position to lead the country. They toyed with the idea of making Wu Peifu a "bourgeois nationalist" but felt the Beijing government was not strong enough to reunite the country. Although Sun Yatsen was even weaker, he had the national prestige among the younger generation that no other politician could match. Sun Yatsen needed assistance to stabilize the military government in Guangzhou. The Soviet Union was happy to provide it.

By the time the Soviet Union won diplomatic recognition by the Beijing government in early 1924, the Comintern (Communist Third International) had already decided to work with the existing Nationalist organization in China. For their part, some senior Nationalists felt Lenin's anti-imperialist argument formed an admirable basis for Nationalist strategy. When the Comintern agent, Michael Borodin, reached Guangzhou on October 6, 1923, the Nationalists were ready to listen. A week later, Borodin was named a "special adviser" to the Nationalists by Sun Yatsen. Borodin worked hard to convince both the Nationalists and the Communists that it was in their best interest to cooperate with each other. The Communists were allowed to join the Nationalist Party as individuals while maintaining their membership in the Chinese Communist Party.

Of the 165 delegates attending the First All-China Nationalist Conference in January 1924, twenty-five were Communists. After the conference, Borodin proceeded to strengthen Sun's position and the general structure of the Nationalist Party. Sun himself was named party leader for life, and his Three Principles of the People were declared the official ideology. The Nationalist Party's organization was expanded into major cities, and the party actively recruited new members.

The new strategy of the Nationalist Party was to strengthen its military forces. A new military academy was set up in Huangpu (aka Whampoa), an island ten miles down the river from Guangzhou. Chiang Kaishek, who had just spent several months in Moscow studying military organization, was appointed its first commandant. To keep a balance between Nationalist and Communist influences in the academy, Zhou Enlai, a Communist who had just returned from France, was named director of the political department. The students, required to have at least a middle school education, received rigorous military training and were given thorough political indoctrination in the Three Principles of the People.

* * *

Noting the developments in Guangzhou, Liang Shiyi was glad he had decided to go ahead with his European and American tour. He consulted Zhou Shouchen, a well-known Hong Kong businessman who had been knighted by the British government for his philanthropy and charity work in the colony. Zhou was eager to go with him on the tour. So were two other Hong Kong businessmen who were his long time friends.

Liang immediately contacted his friend Chen Guangfu, Dingji's employer in Shanghai, and asked for a leave of absence of six months for Dingji so that his son could accompany him for the trip. He needed Dingji as an interpreter as well as a personal attendant. Dingji's wife and their son would move back to Hong Kong and stay under the same roof as Madam for half a year or longer.

"In some ways, this trip is reminiscent of my tour to Japan in 1917," Liang told his travel companions before departure. "In other ways, though, it is very different." In spite of his fugitive status, Liang had made contact with Chinese Legations and Consulates overseas, which turned a blind eye to the arrest warrant issued by Beijing. Arrangements were made to meet with foreign officials and dignitaries through diplomatic channels. On the other hand, there would be no Reception Committee in the host country, nor a large entourage to accompany him everywhere. The group took off on board a Japanese steamship on March 5.

As the ship sailed from Hong Kong Harbor, Liang told his friends, "Our itinerary has been influenced by the responses of foreign government officials. Our visit to England is most extensive since Governor Reginald Stubbs has helped pave the way."

"That suits me fine. I have more connections in England and can speak the language," Sir Zhou Shouchen happily responded.

"The French government seems to be very cool to my request for meeting with their officials," Liang continued. "The Italian government appears to be the same way. On the other hand, Germany, Czechoslovakia and Austria have expressed interest in having high officials meet with me." Liang looked upon the responses from these governments as a measure of his own political standing in these countries. Then he added, "Of course, I have allowed a lot of time in Switzerland, both for sightseeing and for resting in light of our hectic pace." His travel companions agreed.

In the first leg of their trip, the ship sailed to Malaya, arriving in Singapore on March 10. After attending a reception given by Sir Lawrence Guillemard, the Governor of Singapore, Liang's party moved on to Penang and to Colombo in Malaya. They left Colombo on the same ship and arrived at the Suez canal on March 30. Like most tourists, Liang's party got off at Port Twefik to visit the sites of pyramids and the sphinx near Cairo. As they re-boarded the ship at Port Said for their voyage to the Mediterranean Sea, Liang spoke to his son Dingji, "The pyramid is truly awe inspiring. If we can acquire a knowledge base as broad as its base, and an understanding of humanity as deep as its height, we may begin to solve the problems in the world."

They landed at Marseilles, France and took a train through Paris to Calais where they crossed the channel to England.

* * *

Liang Shiyi and his friends stayed in the Hotel Cecil upon their arrival in London on April 5 until their departure on May 11, except for a few days in Scotland and elsewhere. They all looked forward with excitement to the itinerary that lay ahead.

A day after his arrival in London, Liang Shiyi had a long interview with the head of the Reuters News Service and reporters from major newspapers. He was flattered by the attention he got from reporters who asked for separate interviews. Among them were reporters from the *Evening Standard*, *Daily Mail*, *Financial Times*, *The Times of London*, and *North China Herald*. Their discussions were often substantive, covering topics from Chinese politics and economics to Anglo-Chinese relations. Liang did most of the talking.

Accompanied by the Acting Chinese Minister to the court of St. James, Liang

Shiyi was presented to King George V in an audience at Buckingham Palace on April 10. Subsequently, he met with Sir Edward Crowe of the Overseas Trade Office, Sydney P. Waterlow of the Foreign Office, and J. H. Thomas of the Colonial Office. On separate occasions, he also met with Sir Alfred Mond, former Secretary of Commerce and Sir Robert Home, former Secretary of the Exchequer to discuss trade and foreign loan issues of China.

Prime Minister James Ramsey MacDonald was unavailable to meet with Liang until May 7, but when Liang arrived, he sent a member of his Labor Party to meet with Liang in the Chinese Legation. Liang answered the many questions about labor conditions in China. Afterwards, Liang was invited to visit the gallery in the House of Commons.

Liang Shiyi also took time to meet many old acquaintances in London. Among them were Sir James Jamison, Consul General of Guangzhou, and H. R. Boyd, a former consultant at the Ministry of Communications in China. Liang also met with S. F. Mayers and E. R. Morris of the British and Chinese Corporation which had financed some of China's railways. Liang was asked to speak at a dinner hosted by the company. He also met with Sir John Jordan, former British Minister in Beijing. They spent considerable time discussing the Anglo-Chinese relations. Both S. F. Mayers and John Jordan had been his nemesis while they were in Beijing. Time had mellowed their views and they had friendly visits with Liang.

After these meetings, Liang told his friends, "I have dealt with many of these people in China. If I had done anything dishonest, or even accepted a commission for various financial transactions, I would not have had the nerve to confront them today." His travel companions were impressed by his sincerity and integrity.

Of course, Liang and his party were invited to numerous receptions, lunches and banquets. They grew tired of rounds of theater parties which went on almost every other night. Liang also had his share of speeches and interviews. In their leisure hours, they chose to visit the well-known institutions and landmarks, among them the zoo, Kew Garden, Madame Tussaud's Wax Museum, the Victoria and Albert Museum, the Tower of London, Westminster Abbey, Hyde Park and Windsor Castle.

On April 23, Liang Shiyi attended the opening ceremony of the British Empire Exhibition in Wembley. The Exhibition was indeed unparallel in its grandiose scale, but the crowd was not as large as he expected. Liang heard the organizers were afraid of losing money because the event was held at a time of deep recession in England. Several days later, he hosted a lunch for Chinese and British friends in a Chinese restaurant at the Exhibition. Between the rounds of social events, Liang took a train to Cambridge to attend a lunch reception at King's College. He also went to Oxford University for a lunch reception two days later. He enjoyed the academic atmosphere and lively discussions with faculty members at both universities.

On May 1, Liang and his friends left London for Glasgow. They were invited to a lunch with Sir Thomas Bell, the General Manager of John Brown Shipping Co, which had done business in China. After sightseeing in Glasgow, Liang's party went to Edinburgh. On their return trip, they visited the manufacturing plants in Manchester, Bradford and Birmingham. Then Liang returned to London to keep his appointment with Prime Minister MacDonald on May 7. After fulfilling his last social obligations in London, Liang and his friends left London for Paris on May 11.

* * *

Arriving in Paris in late afternoon, Liang's party attended a dinner at the Chinese Legation. Liang had only two official appointments in Paris, one with the Finance Minister and the other with the Minister of Communications. After making courtesy calls to some French officials the following day, Liang met with the representatives of the Chinese workers in France. It was a sentimental meeting as Liang Shiyi had initiated the program of sending Chinese workers to France during the World War. In the evening, Henry Mazot, a former advisor in the Finance Ministry in China, came to the hotel for a visit.

Liang's party had planned to stay in France for about ten days. However, even this brief period was cut short by a reception on May 15, given by the Rumanian Legation in London honoring the visiting King and Queen of Rumania, followed by a dinner-dance hosted by King George in Buckingham Palace. Liang did not want to miss this opportunity to see the grandeur of European royalty. He went back to London the night before the gala and returned to Paris the day after.

In Paris, he visited the Sino-French industrial Bank and the Bank of France, in addition to keeping his official appointments. He also attended the dinner given by the Chinese Minister who had invited many diplomats, members of parliament, and military officers to meet Liang Shiyi. That left only enough time to visit the Eiffel Tower, the tomb of Napoleon Bonaparte and Versailles. As they left the Palace in Versailles, Liang Shiyi looked back and sighed, "This is the place where, after the World War, the hopes of China were buried."

Liang's party went to Brussels by train on May 18. They visited the Securities Exchange and went to a reception hosted by the bankers in Brussels. After brief sightseeing trips in the countryside in Flanders, they left for Netherlands.

After a brief stop in Antwerp, Liang's party went to the Hague to visit the Palace of the Queen of the Netherlands. They were guests at a lunch hosted by the Chinese Legation in the Hague. Finally, they traveled by car to see the construction of the dikes and other reclamation projects before leaving.

* * *

Liang Shiyi's party moved on to central Europe, including Germany, Czechoslovakia, Austria and Switzerland. As they arrived in Cologne on May 25, Liang said to his travel companions, "These countries in central Europe really want to re-establish their pre-war relations with China. We should not disappoint them."

After Cologne, Liang's party went to Frankfort for more sightseeing and then moved to Berlin. They visited Potsdam Palace and the Krupp Corporation, the famous weapon manufacturer, before Liang was occupied with his appointments. Liang later met with Dr. Schacht, the Chancellor of the German Central Bank. He also met other bankers at a dinner hosted by the Chinese Minister in Germany. Liang was intrigued by the hyperinflation in Germany after the World War and raised many questions about its solution. After attending a dinner hosted by Mr. Maltzan, the Deputy Foreign Minister, Liang's party left Berlin on June 3.

In Prague, Liang was met by Charles Halla, the newly appointed Czech Minister to China, who accompanied him to see Foreign Minister Edward Benes. Liang also met with the Finance Minister before leaving for Vienna.

In a tight schedule, Liang visited Dr. Michael Hainisch, President of Austria, Dr. Alfred Grunberges, Foreign Minister, and Dr. Victor Kienbock, Finance Minister. After visiting Kobenzl Castle and the National Park, Liang's party left for Zurich.

Arriving on June 8, Liang's party enjoyed the natural beauty of Switzerland's countryside. At Berne, they attended a lunch in the Chinese Legation where he met the Ministers to Switzerland from Belgium, Italy and Austria and a representative from the Vatican.

On June 14, Liang's party went to Interlaken. After visiting Harder Kuhn and Trum Melback, they left for Geneva where Liang had an extended visit with Sir Eric Drummond, the Secretary General of the League of Nations. They discussed numerous international problems and the Chinese interest in the organization.

Liang's party left Geneva for Milan on June 18. From Milan they went to Florence, Rome, Naples and Pompei. The only business was a lunch at the Chinese Legation in Rome where Liang met several Italian cabinet members.

Heading back north to Lucern on June 26, Liang's party went to the lake area in Switzerland. After reaching Rigi Kuhn, they left Lucern for Lanterhrun, and then revisited Interlaken to unwind.

Liang Shiyi reviewed the receptions he had received from foreign government officials and Chinese diplomats in Europe. He was taken seriously by those in positions of power. He also learned a great deal about the people and places in Europe that would be valuable for his future transactions with foreigners in China.

"We will stay here until I hear from Minister Sze," Liang told his travel companions. "It's better to stay here longer than to rush back to London."

Alfred Saokee Sze, Chinese Minister to the United States, was expected to arrive in London before Liang's party sailed for the United States.

"Do you have any important business with him?" Zhou Shouchen asked.

"No," Liang replied. "But it's a good idea to check with him about any last minute changes of our itinerary in the United States."

On July 5, they left Interlaken by train, and traveled to Calais, France and crossed the channel to England.

Alfred Saokee Sze arrived in London just in time to see Liang on July 7. After attending a farewell dinner hosted by their British friends at the British Empire Exhibition next day, Liang's party left London for Southampton where they boarded the *S.S. Majestic* for the United States.

Home From America

Liang and his party waved goodbye to their friends at the pier at Southampton as the 60,000-ton *S.S. Majestic* slowly moved out to the Atlantic on July 9, 1924. Liang was in a good mood after the triumphant tour of Europe. He quietly assessed his own political fortune on board as his friends occupied themselves with parlor games and other pastimes.

The receptions in his honor by the Chinese Ministers in various national capitals and by the Consuls in all major cities in Europe had been warm and sincere. No one was afraid that he was a fugitive; all seemed to expect he would return to power in some way after this trip. That was a comfort to him in his quest for rehabilitation.

He was still troubled by the briefing of Alfred Saokee Sze, Chinese Minister to the United States. The U. S. Congress had just passed a new immigration act, placing severe restrictions on Chinese immigration. To enforce the spirit and letter of restricting the number of Chinese who could enter the United States, only fourteen universities throughout the United States would accept Chinese students beginning in the fall of 1924.

Liang Shiyi spoke of his concerns. "If the Chinese government had been stronger and the Chinese people had distinguished themselves by greater achievements, this might not have happened. However, it's foolish for the United States to restrict enrollment of Chinese students in American universities. The students would simply go to Europe for advanced study and dilute the influence of the United States in China."

"You cannot expect the same treatment in the United States as in Europe," Dingji warned his father. "The American people are friendly, but although they admire the rich and famous, they are not deferential to them. Generally they have very little interest in Chinese politics, and they cannot differentiate a good Chinese politician from a bad one."

"I understand," Liang replied. "And there's no telling whether they would classify me as good or bad if they know more."

When Liang's party arrived in New York City on July 15, they headed for the Vanderbilt Hotel. The next day a group of reporters showed up and asked Liang for an interview. Liang thanked them for their interest and talked briefly. This was, he explained, primarily a sightseeing tour.

Since the end of the World War, the United States had settled into an isolationist mood and had little interest in China after the Washington Conference in 1922. The atmosphere toward Chinese became hostile after the passage of the new immigration act. However, Liang would take this opportunity to meet with various Chinese government officials in the Legation and Consulates in the United States.

Liang's most important task in New York was a meeting with J. P. Morgan Jr. over a private lunch. Liang had heard so much about Morgan's famous father and wanted to meet the son who took over the financial powerhouse. Liang also met with other bankers to broaden his knowledge about American financial institutions. After staying in New York for four days, his party moved on to Washington, DC.

Liang's party was met by a ranking official from the Chinese Legation at the railway station. This official happened to be a good friend of Sun Yatsen who had notified him about Liang's visit. In the absence of the Chinese Minister, who was in Europe, the official offered his help to facilitate Liang's visit in every way. He informed not only the consulates, but also the branch offices of the Nationalist Party in the cities Liang would visit.

On the morning of July 21, Liang had a brief meeting with President Calvin Coolidge in the White House. It was a formality for the man with few words. Not much came out of that meeting. Liang would have liked to meet some Congressional leaders to discuss various problems related to American presence in the Pacific and in China. However, these leaders were in no mood to meet a Chinese politician after they had just passed legislation hostile to the Chinese immigrants.

Liang's party went to visit Arlington Cemetery and Mount Vernon that afternoon. The only other officials who met with Liang were the Head of the Far East Section in the State Department, and the Deputy Secretary of Commerce.

Four days later, Liang's party took a sightseeing tour to Niagara Falls. From there, they continued on to Chicago, Denver and Salt Lake city. Still later they went to Yellowstone Park and the Grand Canyon to see the natural grandeur of the West. They arrived in Portland Oregon on August 11. After stopping in Seattle for a day, the party went to Vancouver, Canada.

Liang's party boarded the *S.S. Empress Canada* heading for home on August 14. As the ship left the port, he thought of the kaleidoscopic scenes he had seen in North America. He was impressed by the conservation movement that had preserved the national parks.

Through the courtesy of Sun Yatsen's friend in the Chinese Legation in Washington, D.C., arrangements had been made for Liang Shiyi to visit various branch offices of the Nationalist Party in several cities. Liang was struck by the warm receptions in Chicago, Salt Lake City, Portland, Seattle and Vancouver. For a politician with Beiyang roots, this was a totally new experience. He now appreciated the faith Chinese communities in North America had in Sun Yatsen, and the support they had given him for the revolutionary cause since the 1890's, despite the twists and turns of Sun's fate in China.

For the rest of the trip, Liang spent considerable time discussing financial matters with a Japanese expert whom he met on board. Their conversations continued until the expert departed at Yokohama. Liang's party went ashore, too, at Yokohama to see the damage of the 1923 earthquake. When the ship arrived in Nagasaki the next day, his thoughts turned sentimental about his previous visit there and he composed some lyrical poems for the occasion. He remained in a literary mood on board until his party landed in Hong Kong.

* * *

Returning home from America on September 1, Liang Shiyi was greeted warmly by his family. All wanted to hear about his trip and they wanted to tell him what had happened at home. After the routine of paying his respect to the patriarch, he went to the living quarters of the Madam where his family was waiting.

Soon, Dingji would have to return to Shanghai with his wife and son. Shiyi knew very well how hard it had been for Dingji's wife for the last few months. Chinese mothers-in-law were noted for abusing their power, and Madam was no ordinary mother-in-law. On the other hand, he'd heard raving praises from his concubines about Dingji's wife, who was so kind to them. She was cited as the model of a gentle and kind-hearted woman by all except Madam, who considered herself the best model.

Liang Shiyi also had his daughters, Yusheng and Zangsheng, in mind. They had reached the age of marriage. He felt it necessary to say to his family: "Human relationships must be carefully nurtured, for they not only bring happiness to life, but can also create conflict. It's up to everyone in the family to work hard at it." Everyone got the message.

Returning to his own living quarters, Liang Shiyi asked his eighth lady if she had received a post card he sent to her from Prague.

"Yes," she replied, "I have studied hard in your absence as you suggested in the postcard." The eighth lady had done well in the study of Chinese classics. She was far more ambitious than most women in her station of life.

"It takes a long time to be proficient in reading and writing," Liang Shiyi added. "It requires patience. I think you have made some progress." Then he turned to chat with his fourth lady and sixth lady.

The second lady had been concerned about Yusheng's marriage and wanted to talk to her husband about it. At 24, Yusheng was very eligible for matrimony but she did not have a steady boy friend. However, she liked a boy from the Guo family whom she had met in Boston. The boy was now back in Hong Kong with his family which was prosperous and respectable. Liang Shiyi immediately sent an intermediary to sound out the boy's father. Word got back that the Guo family was flattered by the consideration. However, the father suggested that it would be unfair to his older unmarried son if he gave consent to the marriage of his younger son first. Would the Liang family consider his older son whom he regarded the most capable of all his sons, instead? Of course, it wouldn't hurt if Yusheng would meet and get to know the older brother better. Both families agreed and it was so arranged.

Madam did not have the same problem with Zangsheng, four years younger than Yusheng. However, she hoped Yusheng would be married soon because the delay of an older sister's marriage would affect that of the younger sister. There was no urgency. Zangsheng had turned down repeated proposals from the boy from the Chen family whom she had met in Boston. Back in Hong Kong, the boy was as persistent in his pursuit as ever. After being rejected repeatedly by Zangsheng, he vowed to disrupt her wedding if she should marry someone else. She had concluded he was totally unworthy, but he was such a nuisance that his presence in Hong Kong sometimes discouraged her to go out with other boys.

After reviewing the progress of other children, Liang Shiyi beamed with satisfaction that his children had generally lived up to his expectations. The only sour note in his homecoming came from Guangzhou where Ye Gongzhou and Zheng Hongnian had just resigned as Finance Minister and Deputy Finance Minister, respectively, in the military government.

* * *

Sun Yatsen surveyed the situation in north and central China. He noted the only leaders who could counter the military power of the Zhili Clique were Zhang Zuolin of the Fengtian Clique and Lu Yongxiang, the military commander of Zhejiang Province. Lu represented the remnant of the Anfu Clique formerly headed by Duan Qirui. Both Zhang and Lu were against the presidency of Cao Kun and the militancy of Wu Peifu. Sun decided to ally himself with these two to resist the Zhili Clique.

To limit this alliance, the Zhili Clique started a war in Zhejiang Province against Lu Yongxiang on September 3, 1924. Sun was too preoccupied with the internal problems in Guangzhou to come to Lu's rescue. As Lu faltered, Zhang's army swept into north China through the Shanhaiguan Pass to put pressure on the Zhili Clique. Wu Peifu mobilized his army for a counter-offensive at the Pass. Other generals under Wu, including Feng Yuxiang, were assigned to defend the west flank. Feng Yuxiang, who had grumbled about his shabby treatment by President Cao Kun, was waiting for the opportunity to defect. Wu Peifu was perceptive enough to suspect Feng's disloyalty and had assigned other generals to keep a watchful eye on him. However, after Wu Peifu's main column was decisively defeated by the Fengtian army, Feng Yuxiang was able to persuade others to turn back and race toward Beijing.

As Feng Yuxiang's troops entered Beijing without any resistance from local garrisons, he went directly to the Presidential Palace and demanded the cessation of fighting on all fronts and the unification of China through peaceful means. On October 24, President Cao Kun decreed a truce which stripped Wu of military power. Cao was a virtual prisoner in the Presidential Palace and was forced to resign on November 3. A man who had played with political fire, Cao Kun finally perished in a fire of his own making.

After Cao Kun was dispatched, rumors spread in Beijing that the last Qing emperor, Puyi, might be restored to the throne. To quash the rumor and to prevent any scheme of restoration, Feng Yuxiang dictated new terms of settlement to the Qing Royal House. Puyi would have to move out of the Forbidden City by November 5. Feng Yuxiang also invited Sun Yatsen to come to Beijing to discuss the peaceful solution for national unification. Sun Yatsen responded favorably to Feng's invitation a week later. Turning over the duty of Grand Marshall of the Nationalist Government in Guangzhou to Hu Hanmin, Sun Yatsen decided to go to Beijing with Wang Jingwei and other trusted advisors. He cabled Ye Gongchuo, who was then in Tianjin, and asked Ye to make preliminary arrangements for his arrival.

In the meantime, Feng Yuxiang had reorganized the army under his command as the National Army and asked Duan Qirui to take over as the new Commander-in-Chief. To Duan, who was forced to live in retirement in Tianjin after the Anfu Clique lost the war to the Zhili Clique five years earlier, this invitation was a surprise as well as a challenge to re-unify the old Beiyang Clique. At the urging of Zhang Zuolin, Lu Yongxiang and former Beiyang generals, Duan Qirui accepted the invitation to become the Temporary Chief Executive of the Beijing government on November 24, 1924. It was a new life as well as a new title for Duan, who proved to be adept in the art of survival.

In Hong Kong, Liang Shiyi reflected on this sudden change in Beijing. He marveled at the peaceful presidential succession in the United States as he learned that President Calvin Coleridge had recently won a new term for the Whitehouse.

Liang Shiyi in Washington D. C., July 1924

Rising From Ashes

As the Temporary Chief Executive, Duan Qirui was now in the precarious situation of preventing the government in Beijing from falling apart. Although Cao Kun's presidency had been totally discredited and Cao himself was under house arrest, Wu Peifu still retained considerable power in many provinces, and Duan's own alliance with Feng Yuxiang was tenuous at best. Duan needed to solicit support from all political factions.

In performing one of the most difficult acts of his career, Duan Qirui swallowed his pride and appointed his archenemy, Tang Shaoyi, as Foreign Minister to placate Sun Yatsen. But Tang was not eager to join his administration. Realizing the resourcefulness of the Communications Clique, Duan not only rescinded the arrest warrants against Liang Shiyi and Ye Gongchuo, but also appointed Ye as Minister of Communications and Zheng Hongnian as Deputy Minister.

In December 1924, Duan Qirui proposed to convene a National Reconstruction Conference in Beijing in January 1925. To be invited to the Conference were government officials who had made major contributions to the Republic, military leaders who had played a role in derailing Cao Kun's presidency, provincial governors, and citizens distinguished by their education, experience and reputation. Duan's proposed representation of the conference dominated by warlords and conservative politicians was at odd with Sun's idea. When Sun Yatsen received the invitation, he cabled Duan on January 17, objecting to the narrow representation and to propose the inclusion of business, industrial, labor, farmer and student organizations. He also recommended that ultimate power for the solution of disarmament and finance issues should be vested in a National People's Congress to be convened at a later date. Duan replied to Sun's request twelve days later, offering only a token compromise.

After stopping in Shanghai to meet with his loyal supporters, Sun Yatsen arrived in Beijing in late January with his wife Soong Chingling and a large entourage, including Wang Jingwei and Michael Borodin. By then Sun had been diagnosed as having cancer of the liver, but he insisted in meeting with Ye Gongchuo and Zheng Hongnian to discuss the future plan of railways for China. Obviously he wanted to leave his legacy to these two officials whom he knew well and who were now in charge of the Ministry of Communications.

Liang Shiyi, too, received an invitation to attend the National Reconstruction Conference. He was not thrilled at the prospect because of Sun's reservations. As Sun Yatsen and his entourage traveled north, Liang Shiyi watched carefully their every move and their response to Duan's statements. He wanted to gauge the prospect of success of the conference before making his own plans.

"Why don't you jump at this opportunity?" A friend in Hong Kong asked Liang Shiyi. "You can play a prominent role in the new government, like a fire rising from dead ashes."

"I have no interest in getting into the new government which is transitional at best," Liang replied. 'The only area where I can make a contribution is tariff autonomy which will soon loom large when foreign powers begin to follow through with their promise at the Washington Conference in 1922."

Shiyi also had a personal reason to delay his trip. His home at Ganshiqiao Lane in Beijing badly needed repairs after several years of neglect in his absence. His son Dingji had been promoted recently by the Shanghai Commercial and Savings Bank to Assistant Vice President of its Beijing Branch Office. He would let Dingji go first to take care of the repair work, particularly in the main section where he would live.

Liang Shiyi's son, Dingshu, had graduated from St. Stephen's School for Boys in Hong Kong the previous summer. One of his teachers had arranged admission for him to Wadham College of Oxford University. As this teacher had retired and would return to England in January, he offered to take Dingshu and three other graduates with him. They could live in a private home in England for a few months before enrolling at Oxford in the fall. Liang Shiyi wanted to stay in Hong Kong until Dingshu took off for England in late January.

Then there was the pending marriage of Liang's daughter Yusheng to Guo Jinkun, whose courtship had conquered her initial shyness. The two families agreed on the wedding date of May 4 in Beijing while Liang Shiyi was still expected to be there. It was decided that the second lady and Yusheng would go to Beijing shortly after Dingshu's departure to make preparations. His fourth lady offered to go with them to help.

Liang Shiyi's daughter Zangsheng had found friendship and love with Rong Xianxun, a fine young man from a prosperous family in Hong Kong. With the full blessing of Madam, an engagement was hastily arranged before Liang's departure for Beijing. Since both the Rong family and Madam wanted to have the wedding in Hong Kong, the wedding date was left open to fit into Liang's schedule when he returned to Hong Kong.

Madam also brought up a problem about her son Dingmin, who would graduate from high school in the coming summer. Madam knew Dingmin had shown great interest in a girl whose father was a former Minister of Agriculture and Commerce and a political ally of Liang Shiyi's. Although the girl was a little too modern for her taste, Madam was a doting mother who wished to cater to the desire of his youngest son. She also knew it was premature to discuss marriage. "I don't know what to say about Dingmin's interest in the girl of the Chen family," Madam said to her husband. This was an unusual admission. She always seemed to have full control of all situations. She hoped her husband would say something positive about the match.

"Dingmin told me only a few days ago that he wants to go to college in England after finishing high school," Liang replied. "I don't know what he will think about this girl after he's seen the world."

"I am not so sure about that either," Madam replied. "But if they are engaged before Dingmin goes abroad, they can wait for a while before getting married."

"Dingmin is only sixteen. There will be plenty of time for him to think it over." Her husband was unconvinced. "We shouldn't push them to make a decision now."

"He will be seventeen when he goes to England next fall," Madam still did not want to give up. "Haoyin and Zuzhang were engaged for some time before they were married," Madam reminded her husband that he had given consent to the engagement of his eldest daughter before her finance went to college in the United States.

With such insistence on the part of Madam, Liang suspected she was trying to plead the case on behalf of Dingmin who did not want to bring up the subject directly to his father. Shiyi softened his position enough to leave the door open until next summer.

Liang Shiyi left Hong Kong in late February with his sixth lady and eighth lady. Two of his nephews and their mother also went with them.

Arriving in Shanghai, Liang was invited to speak to various organizations on his impressions of Europe and America. He also met with the Head of the *China Evening Post* who asked Liang about his view on improving the Chinese economy. As it turned out, this editor had just acquired the equipment and skill to record speeches on the phonograph and was looking for guinea pigs for experiments. After talking to Liang, he wanted to record Liang's economic policy for China.

* * *

At a deliberately slow pace, Liang Shiyi arrived in Beijing on March 3. He got the bad news that Sun Yatsen was terminally ill. Sun died in Beijing on March 12, leaving a brief last will and testament full of patriotic and revolutionary sentiments. His death left the Nationalist party no single leader who could command Sun's prestige. It was a great loss, not only to the Nationalist party and to the Chinese people, but even to the warlords who had now lost an effective negotiating partner. The hope of reaching national unification at the National Reconstruction Conference appeared to be doomed.

The Conference had started on February 1 and ended on April 21. Liang's participation in the conference was guarded as he realized the limitations of the conference in solving national problems. At the end of the conference, Duan Qirui declared both houses of Parliament, elected through fraud and bribery in 1923, would henceforth be dissolved.

Since the main section of his residence in Ganshiqiao was still under repair,

379

Liang was invited by his old friend Guan Mianjun to stay in his home in Beijing. Within weeks, Liang rented a house to allow more space for the wedding of his daughter Yusheng. The groom arrived with his older brother from Hong Kong for the occasion, which was celebrated by many friends and relatives of both families.

The National Reconstruction Conference had recommended the establishment of three study commissions—for foreign policy, political structure, and national finance. On May 16, Liang Shiyi was appointed the chairman of the Finance Commission. Upon his appointment, Liang lost no time in outlining the mission of his commission. He also wrote a long article reviewing the history of public finance in the Republic since its inception in 1912.

At a shareholders' meeting of the Bank of Communications, Liang Shiyi was elected to replace Zhang Jian as chief executive officer. Zhang had been supported by the shareholders when Liang was in trouble politically in 1922. Now that Liang was back in power, the shareholders wanted to sail with the wind again. This action of the bank's shareholders infuriated Zhang Jian who thought that he had been ill used.

An old friend came to visit Liang soon after he and his family moved back to Ganshiqiao Lane. This friend told Liang he had visited Zhou Ziqi just before Zhou died. At his death bed, Zhou told him, "Of all the d-d-dumb things I have done in my life, nothing was w-w-worse than co-signing the arrest warrant of Liang Shiyi. You must tell him that for me."

"I have never held any grudges against Ziqi." Liang said. "I'm extremely touched by his sincerity toward our friendship. I appreciate, also, that you have gone out of your way to convey the message."

* * *

The Nationalist Party was confronted with the task of pulling together all elements supporting the revolutionary cause after Sun Yatsen's death. At least the new army trained by Chiang Kaishek and supplied with Soviet rifles, machine guns and artillery won a series of victories over the Guangdong warlord Chen Jiongming and routed two other warlords who had tried to seize Guangzhou. The new army performed well enough to be able to challenge the northern warlords in a national contest. However, it was not clear who could inherit Sun Yatsen's mantle of political leadership. Sun's prestige had been a personal kind without peer. The Nationalists could not move too far to the left politically or it would lose its main supporters. Many of them were landlords or industrialists, and were not sympathetic to peasant demands for lower rents, nor to urban strikes for higher wages. A right-wing group had formed, wanting to expel the Communists from the party. They looked to Hu Hanmin as their leader. The left wing element, who supported Wang Jingwei, was only slightly more tolerant of cooperating with the Communists.

In the meantime, Chinese Communists were restrained by Comintern advisers lest their zeal in social reform would upset the cooperation between the Communists and the Nationalists, essential to launching a national revolution. The Communists could only bide their time by focusing their work on organizing labor unions among urban workers and farmer unions in rural areas.

A test of the coalition between the revolutionaries and urban workers was sparked by a group of Chinese workers in Shanghai who had been locked out of a Japanese-owned textile mill during a strike in May 1925. Angry at the lockout, some workers broke into the mill and were fired on by Japanese guards. When the outraged public learned one worker had been killed and seven wounded by the guards, there were waves of student demonstrations and worker strikes, leading to a number of arrests by police in the British-dominated International Settlement. On May 30, thousands of students and workers assembled outside the police station to demand the release of the six Chinese students. Fearing the angry crowd might get out of control, the British inspector ordered his men to fire, killing eleven demonstrators and wounding twenty more. The crisis was temporarily smothered by enforcement of a city-wide curfew and closing all local universities.

The outrage at the massacre in Shanghai spread swiftly to other cities all over China. On June 23, a huge rally consisting of contingents of college students and soldiers, industrial workers and farmers, school children and boy scouts, assembled in Guangzhou to protest the Shanghai killings. As the demonstrators passed close to the foreign concession area on Shameen Island, the rally was fired at indiscriminately by British troops, killing 52 Chinese and wounding over 100. One foreigner was killed when some of the Chinese fired back. The next day, inspired by the Communists, the labor leaders in Guangzhou launched a major strike directed at isolating Shameen and Hong Kong through economic blockade.

On July 1, 1925, the Nationalists formally established a National Government in Guangzhou according to the principles listed in the manifesto of the First All-Chinese Nationalist Conference. Wang Jingwei was elected Chairman of the Executive Committee and Hu Hanmin the Foreign Minister of the new government. Although Liang Shiyi knew both of them quite well, the death of Sun Yatsen severed the bridge Liang had built to reach out to the Nationalists.

The Vexed Tariff Problem

"It seems your father will not be able to come back in August," Madam told her daughter Zangsheng. "I prefer not to change the date for your wedding even though he will not make it."

Liang Shiyi's brother Shixu had just informed Madam that her husband would be tied up in Beijing indefinitely. Shixu had stopped by to discuss the wedding plans for Zangsheng, including the possibility of changing the wedding date.

"I'll miss Father at the wedding," Zangsheng replied, "but I agree with you. It's too much to ask the Rong family to change their plans to accommodate Father."

When the big day came, Zangsheng was as radiant as ever. Her wedding was attended by her extended family including the patriarch who was very much admired by other guests for his longevity. The groom's family and their relatives also came out in large force. It was a gala social occasion.

For the whole summer, Madam had debated with herself about an important decision that would affect Dingmin's future. Plans had already been made for Dingmin to go to England and stay with an English family for a year before attending the University of London where he intended to enroll in the engineering program. Left unsettled was the engagement of Dingmin to his girl friend. Should he or shouldn't he do that before his departure?

Fortunately, Liang Shiyi knew the tenacity of Madam if she wanted something. He proposed a plan to solve her dilemma. His niece Wosheng, who was in Beijing to attend Yusheng's wedding, had indicated to him she would like to study abroad. Liang decided that if Dingmin wanted to be engaged to Miss Chen, it would be better for both of them to go to England under the supervision of Wosheng who was several years older.

"You need not worry about Dingmin after their engagement," Liang Shiyi advised Madam. "Just send them to Beijing. I've arranged for them to go to London via the Siberia Railway. With Wosheng as the chaperone, there should be no problem on their trip or their stay in London. They will have the opportunity to know each other better before the marriage."

Madam couldn't have been happier. Her son would have the best of both worlds.

Beijing Odyssey

* * *

As a follow-up of the nine-power treaty at the Washington Conference in 1922, the Chinese government in Beijing invited the other eight powers, plus four other European nations, to a Special International Conference on Tariff Autonomy for China to be convened on October 26, 1925. The eight powers were the United States, Britain, France, Italy, Japan, Portugal, Belgium and Netherlands. The four additional European nations were Spain, Denmark, Sweden and Norway. The convening of this conference had been delayed for three years because of the international monetary problems and China's internal politics.

To China, this was a rare opportunity to gain autonomy from the yoke of low tariff rates imposed by interlocking, unequal treaties with foreign powers since the end of the Opium War in 1842. Such rates had been modified only once through bilateral agreements with some foreign powers after the Boxer Rebellion in the 1900's. The Chinese government was extremely cautious in trying to make a successful bid for tariff autonomy in this Special International Conference. On September 5, the Chinese government appointed a twelve-member delegation which would form a Chinese Tariff Commission to develop the Chinese position in advance of the Special Conference. Liang Shiyi and Ye Gongchuo were among those appointed to the commission and were active in shaping the agenda of the Special Conference in accordance with the mandate of the nine-power treaty.

Liang Shiyi noted some topics for discussion at the Conference were tied to the reform of the provincial customs duties imposed on goods when they were transported across county lines. The foreign powers had always argued that tariff rates should be kept low because provincial customs duties for transshipment raised the effective rates of imported goods. On the other hands, provincial governors did not want to give up a lucrative source of revenue without adequate compensation from the central government. These arguments became a vicious cycle in stalling past negotiations for tariff autonomy.

As the Chairman of the Finance Commission for Reconstruction, Liang asked his commission to support a sweeping reform of the provincial customs duties. He wrote to the governors to assure them that such duties would not be eliminated without compensating them, and that the source of funds for compensation could come from increases in tariffs. Liang also actively solicited the support of the representatives of the All-China Chamber of Commerce for such reform. Finally, the Finance Commission for Reconstruction submitted a report to Duan Qirui, the Temporary Chief Executive.

On October 26, the Special International Conference on Tariff Autonomy for China convened in Beijing. In attendance of the opening session were the Ministers to China of the sixteen nations invited to the conference, plus the Chinese delegates, cabinet members and special consultants. The outline of the Chinese proposal was presented by C. T. Wang, a noted diplomat and legal expert, who summarized the Chinese request for tariff autonomy.

After lengthy discussions, the foreign powers agreed to China's tariff autonomy on the conditions that provincial customs duties would be satisfactorily reformed and China would negotiate new bilateral customs agreements with all nations involved in the conference. The existing practice would continue to prevail until January 1, 1929 when the new agreements were expected to take effect. The Special International Conference approved, in principle, the Chinese request on November 19, 1926.

It was easy to adopt the principle, but the implementation was a different matter. Several subcommittees were formed by the Special International Conference to continue the discussion on bilateral customs agreements. Numerous meetings were expected to follow in the future. However, Liang was satisfied that it was a good beginning and looked forward to tariff autonomy in 1929.

* * *

Duan Qirui had acted increasingly as an autocrat subject only to the balance of powers of various regional military commanders. After dissolving the defunct Parliament, Duan appointed a Constitution Drafting Committee to write a new constitution. Liang was appointed one of its members. However, the task of producing a new constitution would take time if it was to be accepted by all political factions, including the Nationalists. There was little hope the Nationalists were even willing to come to the negotiation table. Angry with Duan's dictatorial power, educators and workers in Beijing staged a demonstration on November 28, requesting Duan's resignation. Consequently, on December 26, 1925, Duan announced he would revive the State Council and delegate some of his powers to the cabinet. A week later, Duan announced the new cabinet members who would report to him directly as no premier was named.

In the meantime, Duan Qirui's government was undermined by the recent realignment of northern warlords. Wu Peifu, who began to rebuild his base and influence after his debacle two years earlier, was back in contention to challenge him. In October 1925, a general under Zhang Zuolin attempted to rebel against Zhang, and Feng Yuxiang was foolish enough to support the rebels and demand Zhang's retirement. When Zhang Zuolin regained the upper hand and executed the rebellious general, he was unforgiving toward Feng Yuxiang. Trying to salvage the strength of the National Army he created, Feng Yuxiang resigned as its commander on January 1, 1926.

Unimpressed by Feng's maneuver, Zhang Zuolin announced on January 11 that the he would no longer recognize the Beijing government headed by Duan Qirui. Emboldened by Zhang's move, Wu Peifu and his allies announced on March 4 that they would soon remove Duan Qirui and his ally Feng Yuxiang from power, by force if necessary. The situation in Beijing was extremely tense.

Liang left Beijing for Tianjin before the collapse of Feng Yuxiang's resistance. He had no illusion about Duan's government, but deeply regretted that its fall might jeopardize the promising start of the tariff autonomy for China, which had just been agreed to by the Special International Conference.

* * *

Beijing Odyssey

In Guangzhou, the Nationalists gained a strong leftist flavor after many former Nationalist backers left the party to re-establish themselves in Shanghai or Beijing. Of the 278 delegates attending the Second All-China Nationalist Conference held in Guangzhou on January 4, 1926, 168 were leftists or Communists, with only 65 at the center and 45 to the right. The conference elected Wang Jingwei and other left-leaning members to the Executive Committee and continued to hire Michael Borodin as special advisor. It voted to punish the dissenting members who vowed to get the Communists out of the party. Borodin was confident enough to placate the centralists by imposing limits of the number of Communists who could serve on the committees of the Nationalist party.

On March 20, 1926, a gunboat commanded by a Communist officer mysteriously appeared before dawn off Huangpu Island near Guangzhou. Suspecting treachery to kidnap him, Chiang Kaishek at once invoked his power as garrison commander to arrest the captain and put Guangzhou under martial law. In the absence of Borodin, who was in Beijing to confer with other Soviet agents, Chiang arrested more than thirty Soviet advisers in Guangzhou. When Borodin returned from Beijing in April, Chiang professed he still believed in the alliance with the Soviet Union. Borodin knew a setback when he saw one, and he tried to make the most of it by reaching a compromise with Chiang Kaishek to rein in the influence of Communists in the Nationalist Party.

Staking a centralist position politically, Chiang and other Nationalist leaders developed plans for a Northern Expedition to unify China. The strategy for the military campaign called for three major thrusts: one up Guangzhou-Wuhan Railway to reach Changsha, the capital of Hunan Province; one up the Gan River into Nanchang in Jiangxi Province; and one up the east coast to Fujian Province. If all went well, the armies would have the option to push north to Wuhan or to move eastward to Nanjing and Shanghai. A series of alliance would be worked out with various warlords along the way, and where feasible, incorporated their troops into the Nationalist Revolutionary Army.

Communist and Nationalist party members would move ahead of the troops to organize local peasants and urban workers. They would disrupt hostile forces on the path of the march, but would avoid alienating potential allies. Chiang estimated that at least 85,000 men under arms were loyal to the Nationalists. They would be led by over 7,500 officers, trained in both logistics and tactics in Huangpu Military Academy. The financing of the military endeavors would be delegated to T. V. Soong who had been promoted to Finance Minister the previous year. So far he was able to increase revenues in the Nationalist controlled areas.

Of all the warlords who would confront the Nationalist Revolutionary Army, Wu Peifu and his allies stood out as most formidable. It would be a test of will, as well as strength, when the two sides met in the forthcoming struggle.

* * *

After staying in Tianjin for a month, Liang Shiyi left for Hong Kong with his eighth lady in January 1926. They arrived there just in time to celebrate the Chinese Lunar New Year with his extended family.

Word from Dingmin in England somewhat dampened the holiday spirit. The good news was that Dingmin had been admitted to the electrical engineering program at the University of London in the coming academic year, while Wosheng had decided to study in Germany and had been admitted to the chemistry department in the University of Munich. The bad news was that Dingmin and his fiancee had broken their engagement. She was on her way back to Hong Kong, alone.

Since the story of the broken engagement was told by Dingmin, it might have been one-sided. In animated detail, Dingmin told of his interest in radio, then a new invention. As he tried to assemble a small set from purchased parts to test his own knowledge and skill, his fiancee dropped by and, for whatever reason, ruined his home-made radio set. He told her harshly, "The person I love most is my mother for whom you have never had a good word. My next love is my radio set which you have now destroyed. Our engagement is over and each of us will go our own way." When Madam heard the story, she had a severe headache for days.

On March 9, 1926, Dingji's second son was born in Beijing. Since Liang Shiyi was ready to go to Shenyang in response to an invitation from Zhang Zuolin, he tried to get Madam out of her melancholic mood by asking her to go to Beijing with him to see their new grandson. Madam was uncharacteristically responsive. So she and the eighth lady went with Liang to Shanghai. To please Madam, Liang planned for a tour of scenic places near Shanghai and Nanjing. Accompanied by his friends in local offices of the Bank of Communications, who were familiar with the landscapes in the vicinity, they went to see the famous temples in Zhenjiang and the Ming Tomb in Nanjing. After visiting Yangzhou, they traveled to Lake Tai. Then they went to see the historical gardens in Suzhou and the Grand Canal near Wuxi, before returning to Shanghai. After their sojourn in the area for a month, Liang, his wife and eighth lady continued their trip to Tianjin by boat. Madam enjoyed the trip so thoroughly she allowed herself to forget all her pain.

The Bugle Sounds

Shortly after Liang Shiyi and his wife and eighth lady left Shanghai for Tianjin, the National Army of Feng Yuxiang, the backbone of Duan Qirui's government in Beijing, was under heavy pressure from joint attacks by the armies of the Zhili and Fengtian Cliques. In an attempt to preserve his own power, Feng withdrew his support of Duan Qirui and released Cao Kun from house arrest. He then invited Wu Peifu to come to Beijing to take over the government, but Wu Peifu refused to cooperate with Feng. After Feng's army retreated from Beijing to a more defensible position on April 15, 1926, Duan's government was on the brink of collapse. The Chamber of Commerce in Beijing organized a "Law and Order Committee" and asked several prominent citizens to lend their support in protecting the lives and properties in the city. When the joint forces of the Zhili and Fengtian Cliques reached Beijing on April 19, Duan Qirui was forced to resign and his supporters in the Anfu Clique were detained.

Liang Shiyi arrived in Tianjin the day after Duan's resignation. Dingji and his family had come to Tianjin a week earlier to avoid the chaotic conditions in Beijing. Madam was pleased to see Dingji and his family, particularly their new baby. Dingji was expected to return to his job in Beijing as soon as order was restored in the city. However, his family could stay in Tianjin longer, to the delight of Madam who was no longer eager to go to Beijing.

"Stay here to enjoy your grandchildren," Liang Shiyi told Madam. "When you're ready to return to Hong Kong, I'll arrange to have someone to go with you."

"Thank you," Madam replied. "When are you going to leave Tianjin?"

"Soon," Liang told her. "I have accepted an invitation from General Zhang Zuolin to meet him in Shenyang in early May. But that should not affect your stay in Tianjin. As long as you are here, Dingji's family will stay with you."

* * *

On April 24, a general allied with Wu Peifu arrived in Beijing to take charge of the garrison and police. At first, Wu Peifu wanted to resurrect the old Constitution and the presidency of Cao Kun, but Zhang Zuolin balked at the suggestion. After a hard bargain, the Zhili Clique modified its position to ask Cao Kun to resign formally as

387

President and to appoint Yan Weiqing as the Interim Premier who would act as Regency to exercise the power of the presidency. On May 1, Cao Kun announced his formal resignation as President, a position he had been forced to relinquish at gunpoint a year and half earlier. When Yan Weiqing completed the appointments in his new cabinet, he assumed the position of Interim Premier.

Zhang Zuolin admired Liang Shiyi's unusual skill in financial management and thought of him as the best choice for Premier, if he could wrest the control of the Beijing government from Wu Peifu. Earlier in the year, Zhang had invited Ye Gongchuo to Shenyang and had sounded him out about Liang Shiyi's availability. When Ye wrote to Liang about his conversation with Zhang, Liang replied firmly, "It was a disaster when I was supported by Zhang to be Premier the last time. The political climate is getting worse, not better, so Wu Peifu will have even less reason to tolerate me. I definitely do not want to be considered for the premiership if Zhang should regain his influence. However, in view of Zhang's confidence in me, I'm willing to advise him on financial matters." Zhang Zuolin responded to Liang's determination by inviting him to advise him on the public finance of Manchuria. When Liang arrived in Shenyang, he spent over a month examining all pertinent issues and made detailed recommendations for action.

In the meantime, Zhang Zuolin invited Wu Peifu to meet with him to settle their differences in reorganizing the government in Beijing. As a concession to Zhang's request, Yan Weiqing was dismissed as Interim Premier, and the Minister of the Navy was appointed Acting Premier on June 22. Within a week, both Wu Peifu and Zhang Zuolin arrived in Beijing to discuss strategies of fighting Feng Yuxiang's National Army, still a viable force in threatening Beijing.

* * *

Because the warlords in north China were so busy trying to destroy one another, they were blindsided by the new strength of the Nationalist Revolutionary Army in Guangzhou. They were complacent in strengthening their defense perimeter even when Chiang Kaishek was named the commander-in-chief of this new army by the Nationalists in June. As the bugle sound signaled the mobilization for the Northern Expedition on July 1, 1926, the vanguard of the Nationalist Revolutionary Army at the northern Guangdong border moved swiftly into Hunan Province.

The avowed purpose of the Northern Expedition was to realize the unification of China as called for by Sun Yatsen. The Nationalists singled out Wu Peifu as their target since the warlords in Hunan and Hubei were, by and large, loyal to him. They deliberately omitted Zhang Zuolin's name as an adversary in the hope Zhang would attack Wu Peifu from the north while the Nationalists advanced from the south. The Communists in the Nationalist camp were not happy over the timing of the Northern Expedition for their own reasons, but it was impossible to reduce Chiang's forward momentum. On the advice of the Comintern, the Communists muted their criticism and actively participated in the military campaign.

Profiting from dissension among northern generals who controlled Hunan, the

Beijing Odyssey

Nationalist Revolutionary Army quickly took the offensive and marched toward Changsha, the capital of Hunan Province. The Nationalists took a big gamble, moving northward before Wu Peifu could send heavy reinforcement south to bolster his allies in Hunan. They raced toward Yuezhou where the surprised northern troops either fled by boat or were trapped. Their supplies and weapons fell into the Nationalists' hands. Then the Nationalists pushed their thrust toward Wuhan as Wu Peifu reached the front to rally his troops.

In September, Nationalist forces began the siege of the three cities of Wuhan—Hankou, Hanyang and Wuchang. Betrayed by its own commander who joined the Nationalists, Hanyang, with its huge arsenal, fell first. It was followed by Hankou, prosperous in business and large foreign concessions because Chiang had pledged to protect all foreigners in the city. The commander in Wuchang opened the city gates to the Nationalists on October 10 when the civilian population was on the verge of starvation. Fifteen years, to the day, after the original Wuhan mutiny against the Qing Dynasty, the three-city area had ousted its reactionary overlords and once again welcomed revolutionary forces.

As the Nationalists began to consolidate their holds over Wuhan, Chiang Kaishek shifted his attention to the campaign in Jiangxi Province. Chiang anchored his new base in Nanchang, but many senior members of the Nationalist Party, especially those on the left who were sympathetic to the Communists, remained in Wuhan. The Nationalists now had effective control of seven provinces.

Shortly after Feng Yuxiang retreated from Beijing, he took a quick trip to the Soviet Union. Upon his return, he declared that he and other officers in his National Army would join the Nationalist Party. By mid-October, his forces merged with the Nationalist Revolutionary Army to fight against Wu Peifu.

The outside world began to pay attention to the success of the Nationalists. Up to this time, the British government appeared to be firmly committed to Wu Peifu's government in Beijing. Now the British Foreign Office began to consider extending diplomatic recognition to the Nationalist government and to hold talks with the Nationalist Foreign Minister in mid-December.

* * *

Back in Beijing, a sense of doom fell upon the city. In October, Wellington Koo was appointed Foreign Minister and Acting Premier to shore up the deteriorating situation, but his attempt to increase revenue for the Beijing government failed to materialize.

Liang Shiyi had stayed on the sidelines in Tianjin since his return from Shenyang in late June. Bored with the waiting game, he decided to take a quick trip to Hong Kong to see his father in late September.

"Get ready to leave for Hong Kong in a few days," Liang told his eighth lady.

"How long are we going to stay?" she asked.

"Only a couple of weeks—to see father," he replied. "I need diversion."

"Then let's stay longer in Hong Kong," his eighth lady naively suggested.

389

"No. I must be here when the call comes."

His eighth lady understood immediately and asked no more questions. She knew Liang was waiting for a new assignment from Zhang Zuolin. They went to Hong Kong and returned in late October. Liang continued to stay away from Beijing, except for a short trip to see Dingji and his family.

"I've been elected Director of Beijing Securities Exchange for a three-year term," Dingji told his father during Liang's latest visit.

"That's a good experience for you," Liang said, beaming with approval. "I am so glad you have done well."

"How was mother when you saw her in Hong Kong?" Dingji inquired.

"She was doing fine," Liang replied. "Dingmin has started his freshman year at the University of London and has settled down to his studies. That makes your mother happy."

* * *

On November 15, Zhang Zuolin arrived in Tianjin and called a meeting of regional military commanders still loyal to the Beijing government. They unanimously requested Zhang Zuolin take over the joint command of their forces to fight the Nationalists. Zhang was named the commander-in-chief of the joint forces under the name of the Pacification Army. They also supported Zhang's bid to take over the government in Beijing.

In December, Liang Shiyi was approached by an intermediary from T. V. Soong, the Finance Minister of the Nationalists, inviting Liang to go to Wuhan for consultation on finances. Liang signaled his willingness to cooperate with the Nationalists, but declined the invitation. He left unsaid his prior commitment to Zhang Zuolin on financial matters.

On December 27, Zhang Zuolin arrived in Beijing from Tianjin to take over the reins of government. A day later, Liang Shiyi followed in Zhang's footsteps and left Tianjin for Beijing.

Painful Transition

After Zhang Zuolin arrived in Beijing, he asked Premier Wellington Koo to assemble a new cabinet which would continue to act as regency for the vacant presidency. Zhang wanted to maintain the facade of being the Commander-in-Chief of the Pacification Army while pulling the strings behind the scene.

At the recommendation of Premier Koo, the Chinese Tariff Commission met on January 12, 1927 and approved a surcharge of 2.5% on the tariff rate, effective February 1. This decision was not without controversy or repercussion from foreign governments. After numerous discussions in the subcommittees of the Special International Conference on Tariff Autonomy for China the previous year, most foreign powers came to the conclusion that a surtax of 2.5% on the tariff was necessary prior to 1929 to provide sufficient funds to pay off tariff-backed foreign debts. But Japan opposed the increase vigorously because its trade with China was far greater than other powers. Japan had more to lose. The Chinese government proposed, in June 1926, to reconvene the Special International Conference to vote on this issue. However, because of the unstable political situation, the foreign powers refused to attend. The new government under Zhang Zuolin was determined to push through this surtax even without the blessing of the Special International Conference.

Liang Shiyi was an active advocate for the adoption of the surtax at the China Tariff Commission. After the meeting, he tried to mend fences with the American and British diplomats.

On January 16, Liang went to see John MacMurray, United States Minister to China who was about to leave the country. Liang expressed his appreciation to the United States for being sympathetic to the surtax on tariff. Liang also emphasized the new militant mood of the Chinese people who demanded the elimination of unequal treaties with foreign powers. He hoped MacMurray would take the message of the Chinese people back to the people of the United States.

On the same day, Liang went to visit Sir Miles Lampson, British Minister to China, who had only recently succeeded Sir Ronald Maclay. In his discussion with Lampson, Liang emphasized the importance of the elimination of the unequal treaties with foreign powers. He praised the British support of the 2.5% surtax on tariffs even though the issue was never put to a vote in the Special International Conference on Tariff Autonomy.

Then Liang Shiyi turned to a delicate subject. "Sir Francis Arthur Aglen, Inspector General of our Maritime Customs Service, seems to be reluctant to implement this surtax. Do you think you might help enlighten him?"

"Sir Francis is an employee of the Chinese government," Lampson replied in the most diplomatic manner. "As a person responsible to foreign debtholders, he has to examine the issue from the legal point of view rather than the merit of the issue itself. I can speak to him as a friend, but I cannot influence his decision."

The Chinese government was unyielding on the issue of a surtax on tariffs, and on February 1, Aglen was dismissed as the Inspector General of the Maritime Customs Service, and A. H. Edwards was appointed as Acting Inspector General.

In the meantime, Liang Shiyi reminded the cabinet of its obligation to initiate the reform on provincial customs duties and recommended a detailed plan. The Cabinet also set up a new commission to safeguard the revenue from the surtax for use in repaying tariff-backed foreign debts. Even so, the surtax freed the government from diverting other revenue for this purpose.

After putting his financial house in order, Zhang Zuolin turned his attention to legitimizing his autocratic rule. In his headquarters at the Pacification Army, he set up three discussion groups on foreign policy, political structure and national finance. Liang Shiyi was appointed the chairman of the political structure discussion group and quickly made use of the ineffectual group to embark on an ambitious mission to bring peace and reconciliation with the Nationalists.

* * *

After the Nationalists moved the government from Guangzhou to Wuhan on January 1, 1927, the government was dominated by Borodin and the left wing of the Nationalist Party, while two important ministries of workers and farmers were put under the charge of the Communists. However, T. V. Soong was still the Minister of Finance and President of the Central Bank established by the Nationalists. In responding to T. V. Soong's invitation the previous December, Liang Shiyi secretly sent Zhao Qinghua, his friend and former associate, to see T. V. Soong in Wuhan. Since Soong was most anxious to secure loans from bankers to finance the Northern Expedition, he had also contacted the head of the Bank of China whose power base was in Shanghai. Because most private shareholders of the Bank of Communications were conservative businessmen and politicians in north China, Liang was not in a position to promise Soong a loan from his bank. However, Liang suggested his bank could provide a loan of five hundred thousand yuan to the Bank of China, from which Soong could withdraw and spend in the Yangzi River valley. Liang would consider an additional loan to the Nationalists if they and Zhang Zoulin could settle their differences peacefully.

In a bold move, Liang Shiyi offered to broker a peace settlement between the Nationalists and Zhang Zuolin to form a coalition government. To emphasize his point of reconciliation, Liang proposed future cooperation between the Nationalist Central Bank and the twin central banks of the Beiyang government—the Bank of China and the Bank of Communications. Liang hoped Soong would consider his proposal seriously and would arrange a meeting between the Nationalists and the Beijing government in Shanghai when the time was ripe.

* * *

The victory of the Nationalists in the first phase of the Northern Expedition brought to a head the debate over the next phase of Nationalist strategy. At his Nanchang base, Chiang Kaishek had decided on a drive to Shanghai to seize the industrial and agricultural heartland of China. The Nationalist leaders in Wuhan supported, instead, a northern drive up the Wuhan-Beijing Railway. They believed they could effect an alliance with several sympathetic warlords, including Feng Yuxiang, to make a final assault on Beijing. Chiang traveled to Wuhan in January 1927 to state his case, but he was publicly insulted by Borodin and other leftists. He returned angrily to Nanchang.

Chiang Kaishek was confident of his northeast advance from Nanchang to Shanghai because of his familiarity with the Zhejiang and Jiangsu territories. The head of the Shanghai Chamber of Commerce had secretly offered Chiang the chamber's financial support. Chiang also had the assurance of cooperation from the chief of detectives in the French Concession, a major underworld figure in Shanghai. On March 21, the General Labor Union in Shanghai, under the direction of the Communists, launched a general strike and an armed insurrection against the warlords in support of the approaching Nationalist army. The next day, the first division of the Nationalist troops entered the city.

Following the momentum, Nationalist troops seized Nanjing from retreating northern warlords on March 24. Some of these troops looted the British, Japanese and American Consulates and several foreigners were killed. American destroyers and a British cruiser, in return, shelled the city to allow an evacuation route for foreign nationals. The shelling lead to several Chinese deaths.

When Chiang Kaishek arrived in Shanghai in late March, he issued reassuring statements to the foreign community and praised the labor unions for their constructive achievements. Chiang arranged for generous loans from Shanghai bankers to finance the next phase of his Northern Expedition. He also secured his base in Shanghai by transferring those army units known to be sympathetic to the workers out of the city.

Then suddenly, without warning, a force of one thousand armed men, secret agents of the chief detective in the French Concession, launched a series of attacks against the headquarters of all the large labor unions in Shanghai on April 12. They were assisted by troops from the Nationalist Revolutionary Army in their action. Many union members were killed, hundreds arrested and pickets disarmed. Arrests and executions continued over the next few weeks, and the organizations of the General Labor Union were declared illegal.

On April 18, 1927, Chiang established the Nationalist government in Nanjing and adopted a policy of driving the Communists out of the Nationalist Party. The news of events in Shanghai and Nanjing caused anguished self-examination in Wuhan. Wang Jingwei, who had just returned to Shanghai from abroad in April, vowed to continue the Nationalists' cooperation with the Communists and went to Wuhan immediately to take charge. He was joined by Sun Ko, son of Sun Yatsen by his first marriage, and Eugene Chen, a Trinidad-born Chinese who had been a confidant of Sun Yatsen. Soong Chingling, Sun Yatsen's widow, had dramatically flown to Wuhan from Nanchang to show her support of the Wuhan government. According to the Soviet line, the Communists must work closely with the Wuhan faction of the Nationalists, the true inheritor of the Chinese revolution.

* * *

Zhang Zuolin liked what happened when the Nationalist Party split into factions. A staunch anti-communist, he thought he could cooperate with the right wing of the Nationalists. As if to underscore that he was no longer an ally of Wu Peifu, Zhang ordered his Fengtian army to attack Wu's base in Zhili and Henan in late March and April, forcing Wu Peifu to flee to the west of Zhengzhou. In the meantime, Zhang allowed the news to leak about Zhao Qinghua's secret mission on behalf of Liang Shiyi. Rumors abound in Beijing that Liang would soon be Premier of a coalition government with the Nationalists. Nothing could have been further from the truth.

In fact, after Chiang Kaishek secured his base in Shanghai and Nanjing, he launched a reign of intimidation against the wealthiest inhabitants of Shanghai. He pressed the Chairman of the Chamber of Commerce, who had promised to support his North Expeditions a few months earlier, to honor his pledge with a huge loan. When the man refused, his property was confiscated, driving him to exile. Businessmen were coerced into buying 30 million yuan of short-term government bonds, while the big corporations were each assigned 500,000 yuan or more.

The Nationalists also played hardball dealing with peace feelers from northern warlords. Liang's proposal of reconciliation never received serious consideration. Under such atmosphere of distrust, Liang was unable to convince the conservative shareholders of the Bank of Communications in Beijing to support the Nationalist cause with a huge loan. He even had to reimburse the bank through private fund raising for the advance of five hundred thousand yuan to the Nationalists through the Bank of China earlier in the year. The reluctance of the Bank of Communications to honor the request of the Nationalists for more loans did not endear Liang to the Nanjing government.

Learning that Sir Miles Lampson, British Minister to Beijing, would soon go to Shanghai to meet with Nationalist officials, Liang visited him on May 15 and asked him to use his good offices to bring about a peaceful solution between the Beijing and Nanjing governments. While Liang got a sympathetic hearing, Lampson indicated he would refrain from making any suggestion to the Nanjing government for fear of being accused of interfering with the internal affairs of China.

Beijing Odyssey

As the Soviet advisors in Wuhan debated the future course of action, a general in the Hubei-Hunan area, allied with the Nationalists, mutinied against the Wuhan government in May. Although the general was defeated, he freed other mutinied generals to raid major leftist organizations, arresting and killing students and peasant leaders inspired by the Communists. Wang Jingwei tried desperately to dampen local revolutions and curb the power of the Communists. The Comintern agents saw the writing on the wall. Their mission in China was a failure. Borodin and others were called home, traveling across the Gobi desert to the Soviet Union.

* * *

Failing to reach a reconciliation with the Nationalists, Zhang Zuolin showed his true colors as an autocrat, making himself the Grand Marshall of a new Military Government On June 16, the Cabinet of Wellington Koo resigned, and Zhang appointed a new Cabinet with members catering to his wishes. Zhang himself also showed his grandiose side, given to lavish parties and elaborate ceremonial affairs. He even tried to revive the ceremonial tradition reserved for the Qing emperors. Liang did not like the turn of events and refused to join Zhang's Cabinet.

Liang Shiyi wanted to leave Beijing but his fourth lady, whose tuberculosis had recurred, was too sick to travel. Instead, Liang made several short trips to Tianjin to conduct business for the Bank of Communications. When the condition of his fourth lady worsened, he stayed at her bedside to comfort her. They talked with nostalgia about the happy moments when they were together during the past eighteen years. Quietly, his fourth lady died on July 23, 1927 at the age of 37.

Three days later, Liang Shiyi left Beijing with his eighth lady on their way back to Hong Kong via Dalian in Fengtian Province, Pusan in Korea and Osaka in Japan. On the eve of their departure, Liang received a telegram from his brother informing him that their father was ill. Unable to book an early berth to Hong Kong directly, Liang and his eighth lady proceeded as planned and reached Osaka on August 1. There, Liang received another telegram informing him that his father had recovered from his illness. He could enjoy a few days in Osaka before taking the last leg of the trip to Hong Kong.

* * *

In mid-August, Chiang Kaishek urged the Wuhan and Nanjing governments to unite into one and announced his resignation as Commander-in-Chief to facilitate the unification process. Later, Chiang traveled to see the widow of Charlie Soong, now living in Japan. The purpose of his visit was to propose marriage with Soong Meiling (aka Song Meiling), her youngest daughter. Because Mrs. Soong was a devoted Christian and Chiang was still married to his first wife at the time, the meeting was delicate. After protracted discussions concerning his pending divorce and Christian conversion, Chiang received the permission.

It was not until November that the Wuhan government went out of existence. On December 10, The Executive Committee of the Nationalist Party voted to ask Chiang Kaishek to resume the post of Commander-in-Chief. Chiang returned from Japan for his wedding in December, and resumed command of the Northern Expedition in the following month under a new unified Nationalist Party.

After Liang Shiyi returned to Hong Kong, he wrote an article on the reconstruction of China and sent it to his friends in both the Beijing and Nanjing governments. It expressed his non-partisan approach to the solution of the conflict and to reconstructing the shattered nation. In view of the tense military situation confronting both sides, Liang's article sounded like a voice from the wilderness.

The Lost Cause

"I'll let your travel service arrange my trip to Beijing this time," Liang Shiyi said to his son Dingji in late November of 1927.

"We'll take care of it to your satisfaction," Dingji replied, knowing his father would keep an watchful eye on his new enterprise.

Several months before, Chen Guangfu, Dingji's boss at the Shanghai Commercial and Savings Bank, came up with the idea of setting up a China Travel Service in Hong Kong. Until then, travelers in China made their reservations by contacting separate sources. If they could afford servants, they usually brought them along to handle the luggage. They also asked friends and relatives to meet them at the destinations to help out. Chen Guangfu saw the advantage of providing a single stop for travelers to book their tickets for transportation and reservations for hotels and to take care of their luggage along the way. He also believed the people in Hong Kong, who had more contact with Westerners, would be most receptive to his idea. Noting that Dingji had traveled extensively in Europe and America with his father several years earlier, Chen transferred Dingji from the Beijing Branch of the bank to this new enterprise. Dingji became the founder and general manager of the China Travel Service in Hong Kong in late 1927.

The start-up of the China Travel Service was made easy by sharing the resources of the Hong Kong Branch of the Shanghai Commercial and Savings Bank. Dingji rented an office space next to the bank on Queen's Road Central, and made use of the expertise of the staff in the bank whenever possible. The new enterprise was in business in a short time.

With a father's pride, Shiyi said to Dingji, "There are too few service-oriented enterprises in Hong Kong and China. Too many owners of corporations view themselves as masters and not as servants to the public. I hope you will set a new trend."

"This enterprise intends to fill the unmet needs of travelers in China," Dingji said. "We will match the travel agents who handled our travel in Europe and America."

"You've learned well," Liang Shiyi said to Dingji approvingly. "I hope you will find time to take good care of your mother. I will be leaving in a few days."

Although Liang Shiyi had a premonition that the government in Beijing was a lost cause, he wanted to take up the unfinished business of tariff autonomy which would affect China's finances far beyond the life of the Beijing government. With that in mind, he planned to attend the meeting of the Chinese Tariff Commission scheduled for February 6, 1928. He left Hong Kong in early December with his sixth lady and eighth lady, traveling first to Osaka and Kyoto in Japan for sightseeing before arriving in Tianjin on December 23.

* * *

In January 1928, Liang Shiyi commuted frequently between government business in Beijing and contacts with the Nationalists in Tianjin. He wrote an article on budget planning, lamenting the inability of the government to adhere to the sound principle of budgeting. His discussions with the Nationalists concentrated on the distribution of future revenue from Maritime Customs Service. He provided the Nationalists with a complete list of all foreign debts and maturity dates for which the tariff had been pledged as collateral. Their contacts were amicable.

On February 1, Acting Inspector General A. H. Edwards of the Maritime Customs Service went to Nanjing to discuss with Nationalist officials the transitional tariff increase and urged them to send observers to the Chinese Tariff Commission in Beijing. The Nationalists refused his request.

At the meeting of the Commission, held on February 6, Liang explained the need for a transitional tariff increase of 1.25% beyond the surtax of 2.5% introduced the previous year. This latest increase had been approved by Acting Inspector General Edwards of the Maritime Customs Service since it would not only provide additional funds to pay off tariff-backed foreign debts, if needed, but the residue could also be used to pay off domestic bonds. The Commission was receptive to the adoption of the increase which would be beneficial to the treasury, but decided to defer further action until the return of Edwards from Nanjing on March 1.

In the meantime, Liang Shiyi was appointed the Controller of the Maritime Customs Service, a position he had held years before. His appointment now took on a new significance. He had to negotiate with the government in Nanjing on all issues which might affect both the Beijing and Nanjing governments. Upon his return from Nanjing, Acting Inspector General Edwards reported to Liang about his discussion with T. V. Soong. With the concurrence of Edwards, the Government in Beijing appointed a new commission which would draft the rules for implementing the transitional tariff increase, effective July 1, 1928. Liang was a major contributor in this new commission, examining issues beyond the implementation of the tariff increase.

* * *

The Nationalists in Nanjing had reorganized their party and government structures after the Wuhan government was dissolved in February. They also decided to initiate the final military attack toward Beijing as expeditiously as possible. Chiang Kaishek ordered his troops to move north in late March, and they soon reached Shandong Province.

The Japanese had 2,000 civilians residing in Jinan, a key city in Shandong province, and the Japanese government had decided to send 5,000 regular army troops to Shandong Province to protect Japanese nationals. Five hundred of these troops were already in position as the Nationalists entered Jinan on May 1. Chiang was counting on a peaceful withdrawal of Japanese troops as the Chinese army secured the city. But in a skirmish on May 3, the Japanese troops murdered the Chinese liaison person and fighting grew into a devastating clash with appalling atrocities. After the Chinese troops were driven from the city, Chiang chose to re-route his troops along the north bank and moved northward.

By then Feng Yuxiang was well entrenched in Henan and was ready to join forces with Chiang. Their plan called for an immediate joint attack on Tianjin to cut off the escape route of Zhang Zuolin's troops stationed in Beijing. But Tianjin was the site of five key foreign concessions and the foreigners were determined to protect their own interests. The Nationalists halted their troop movement to allow the foreign powers and Zhang Zuolin to negotiate a peaceful solution. Accordingly, the Japanese took the lead in assuring Zhang that if he abandoned Beijing and retreated peacefully to Manchuria, they would prevent the Nationalists from passing beyond the Great Wall or through the Shanhaiguan pass.

* * *

In late spring, Liang Shiyi gave a lavish party for his friends and relatives to celebrate jointly his and his wife's sixtieth birthdays. A couple of months earlier, Ye Gongchuo had called on his circle of literati friends to contribute poems and prose for the happy occasion. Most of them complied. A collected volume was to be presented to Liang on his birthday.

Liang Shiyi had had some misgivings about the timing of his birthday party since the attendance of this party by members of his family was problematic. Disliking travel, even under the best circumstances, Madam declined to come to Beijing during this chaotic time despite the fact the celebration was also honoring her. As a result, the second lady decided not to go. She wanted to avoid being viewed as having taken over Madam's place in the celebration. With a new job in Hong Kong and his wife expecting, Dingji could not make the trip to honor his father, either. Liang Shiyi's two others sons were studying in England and could only send their best wishes.

Fortunately, Liang's oldest daughter Houyin lived with her family in Beijing, and his second daughter Huaisheng and her family were in Tianjin and his youngest daughter, Yisheng, was attending Yenching University nearby. Several of his nephews and nieces were also students in Beijing. All of them could be counted on to brighten the occasion.

His two other daughters, Yusheng and Zangsheng, were in Hong Kong. Yusheng had two young children, aged two and one, but she wanted to go to Beijing with the older boy for the occasion in spite of the hassle. Zangsheng also had two young children and was expecting the third. She sent her husband to represent her. When Yusheng arrived in Beijing, the sixth lady offered to take care of her son so she could do some shopping. "It must be difficult for you to travel with such an active boy," the sixth lady said to Yusheng. "I'll go back to Hong Kong with you after the celebration."

Amid the boisterous spirit of the guests, Liang's birthday party evoked a surrealistic scene. Nearby, intense negotiation was going on by the Beijing government to surrender the city to the Nationalists. It resembled the act of rearranging deck chairs in the sinking Titanic. When it was all over, Liang said to his eighth lady, "This party was probably my last fling in Beijing. It gave me a chance to say farewell to my friends, many of whom I may not see for a long time."

On June 1, Liang went to Tianjin with his eighth lady. As they were waiting for the train to pull out of the station in Beijing, Liang sat back to read a newspaper. A bullet from a rifle suddenly hit the window next to him and penetrated the glass without shattering it. After raising his head to see what happened, Liang returned to his reading. His eighth lady was alarmed as she saw someone at the platform outside running away. The conductor rushed to Liang but was surprised by his tranquility in the face of danger. Liang said to the amazed conductor, "In times like these, anything can happen. I have no personal enemy and I don't believe that bullet was directed at me. I have encountered so many personal dangers that nothing will disturb me any more."

Liang Shiyi was in Tianjin for the business of the Bank of Communications. In anticipation of a reorganization of this bank by the triumphant Nationalists, Liang wanted to put everything in good order. Up to this point, the private share of the bank was sixty percent against forty percent of government share. The Nationalist government intended to increase its share to a majority so that major decisions would not be left in the hands of private stockholders. Liang was paving the way for transfer of his power as chief executive officer to someone else who would be appointed by the Nationalists after the reorganization.

Liang's departure from Beijing was most timely. Zhang Zuolin was on the verge of accepting the suggestions of foreign powers to resign. Liang said to his eighth lady as they arrived in Tianjin, "This may be the last time that we will see Tianjin. Make the most of your stay here."

"Do you have any regrets?" his eighth lady asked.

"My only regret is my departure from the Bank of Communications which I have spent the best years of my life building. From now on, I will only be a minor stockholder watching from the sidelines."

"You won't miss other actions in Beijing?"

"No," Liang was certain of that. "If my contribution to national affairs is needed, I'll answer the call; otherwise my time is up and I should retire peacefully. Someone else will try to succeed where I have failed."

* * *

The reign of Zhang Zuolin finally cracked in the face of reality. For fear of treachery, he dared not risk his army to fight further. As the Nationalist troops advanced toward Beijing, Zhang reluctantly withdrew his troops to Manchuria where he still could rule supreme. Angered at the collapse of all available options for retaining his power, he resigned from the government in Beijing on June 2.

Zhang Zuolin left Beijing with his entourage in his private train. He had taken the precaution of riding with his friends in an ordinary coach, coupled behind his showy private car. When the train stopped at Tianjin, Liang Shiyi and several of Zhang's close associates went to see him at the station. On June 4, the news from wire services indicated the train was blown to pieces by a bomb placed beneath a railroad bridge not far from Shenyang. There was no report on the casualties in the incident, but Liang Shiyi realized the government in Beijing, as he knew it, no longer existed.

A Haven

A news blackout was imposed by the close associates of Marshall Zhang Zuolin following the explosion of the train on which he returned to Shenyang on June 4, 1928. No one knew for days whether Zhang was dead or alive. The public was told he was gravely wounded. Suspicion of the assassination attempt pointed to the work of the Japanese who controlled the right of way where the explosion had occurred. The Japanese also had the motive of disposing of Zhang for fear Manchuria might become a battle ground between Zhang and the Nationalists.

Hearing the news of Zhang's attempted assassination in Tianjin, Liang Shiyi sent an emissary to Beijing and urged his son, Zhang Xueliang, to return to Shenyang immediately to take charge of the precarious situation in Manchuria. In the meantime, Beijing was in a state of siege as the Nationalist army poised to take the city. Zhang Xueliang left Beijing in disguise and made his way circuitously to Shenyang two weeks later. Thirty years old, Zhang Xueliang inherited a large army and a fabulous fortune, and was hailed as the young marshal by his father's former associates. After the succession arrangement was completed, it was announced on June 19 that Zhang Zuolin had died.

The Nationalist army entered Beijing and took over effective control of the city on June 11. The city wall, once a glorious red, was painted blue by the Nationalists. The new foreign minister, C. T. Wang, appointed by the Nationalists in Nanjing, tried to calm the fears of foreigners in the Beijing area. The city was quiet and subdued under its new ruler.

The new foreign minister was also given the daunting task of negotiating with foreign powers to abolish, or at least revise, the unequal treaties imposed on China. Since the Nationalists made the abolishment of unequal treaties a cornerstone of the party in appealing for mass support, they could not afford to wait to challenge the foreigners. On the other hand, the foreign powers were in no mood to give up their privileges and applied counter pressure on the Nationalists by withholding official recognition of the new government. The Nationalists had an easier time in securing the allegiance of the Chinese envoys in foreign capitals who were eager to continue their service to the new government. Obediently, they showed their allegiance by displaying

402

the new Nationalist flags in legations and consulates.

To remove the last visage of the Beiyang government, the Nationalists renamed Zhili (the direct dominion) as Hebei Province, and Beijing (the northern capital) as Beiping City. As remnants of Beiyang generals continued to fight in north China, Chiang Kaishek promised the warlords considerable independent latitude if they would only pledge their support to the Nationalist cause of unifying China through peaceful means. The greatest prize to the Nationalist government came when Zhang Xueliang announced on July 1 his willingness to accept Chiang's offer of peaceful unification. In exchange, Zhang retained his power base in Manchuria while throwing his weight in support of the Nationalists against all competing claims.

* * *

On June 7, Liang Shiyi left Tianjin amid rumors of Zhang Zuolin's death. Since sporadic fighting south of Tianjin had paralyzed railway transportation, Liang could only book passage on a ship to Hong Kong via Dalian. After a frenzy of saying good-bye to his friends, whom he did not expect to see for a long while, he and his eighth lady boarded the steamboat heading home.

Liang Shiyi left Beijing none too soon. On July 10 the Nationalist government issued arrest warrants for more than a dozen politicians associated with the last Beiyang government. Liang's name, along with Wellington Koo, the last Premier, was on the list. Liang's dream as a peacemaker came abruptly to an end.

Liang Shiyi could always count on the support from his family to renew his strength. As soon as he arrived home and took off his traveling attire, he and his eighth lady went to his father's living quarters to pay their respect. The patriarch looked pale and depended on his cane to move around the room, but he had lost none of his authoritative air.

As usual, Liang Shiyi next went to Madam's living quarters, shared by their eldest son Dingji and his family. This was no routine courtesy call to please Madam. Dingji's wife had given birth to a daughter only a few days earlier. Liang Shiyi was pleased when his daughter-in-law asked him to name the baby. Holding the baby in his hands and looking at his two grandsons, he was a very proud grandfather.

He told Madam how much he and his friends missed her at the birthday party in Beijing. Madam was unmoved by such sentiment. "I preferred to stay home to help out when Dingji's new baby arrived. In any case, I prefer the comfort of this home over long-distance travel. I had my last trip to Beijing two years ago. Nothing will induce me to take another trip."

"We might as well get used to the new name, Beiping, since we may never be able to see the old Beijing again in our life time," her husband said to her.

When he got back to his own living quarters, Shiyi's second lady and sixth lady were waiting for him. He always had a soft spot in his heart for the second lady who was the mother of his son Dingshu and three of his daughters. He could not raise her status to the level of Madam's, but he never placed her in the same category as the other concubines who had no children. He knew what was foremost in her mind and said to her, "Dingshu has graduated from Oxford University in England. He will be home in August." It was quite a relief to the second lady who had placed all her hope and future on her son.

With her gentle disposition, the sixth lady was silent until she was spoken to. Her husband understood her well and said, "You have been a great help to the second lady as she struggled to raise her children while I was away. Both of us appreciate your efforts." His sixth lady was grateful for his comment, but she still could not master enough courage to tell her husband about her failing health. For quite some time she had been feeling severe breast pains. Generally, most women would not want to disclose their illness, particularly if the illness was related to sex or reproductive organs. At age 29, she did not expect serious illness and had confided her symptom only recently to the second lady.

When they were alone, his second lady told him, "Aliu (No. 6) should consult a doctor about her health. I don't know what troubles her, but she has lost a lot of weight and complains of pains in her breast. It can be serious even though she may not want you to know."

"I'm glad you've told me," her husband replied. "I'll see to it that she goes to see a Western-educated doctor. I don't believe herbal medicine will do much good in her case." He stopped talking when the sixth lady returned to the room.

Liang Shiyi derived great satisfaction from his family. His youngest son Dingmin, attending the University of London, had only one more year to complete his studies. His youngest daughter, Yisheng, was still enrolled at Yenching University in Beiping. His niece, Wosheng, the only daughter of his deceased brother, was pursuing her studies in Germany. He had high hopes for all of them.

When Shiyi's younger brother, Shixu, came home from his office, the two brothers greeted each other warmly. They had been partners in their family affairs and contributed to the support of the extended family. Since his resignation as the chief executive officer of the Bank of Communications, Liang Shiyi had lost not only the control of the bank but also his influence in his investments in north China. Confronted with the prospect of forced retirement from politics as well, he was uncertain of his future. Fortunately, Shixu prospered in real estate and other businesses in Hong Kong and Guangzhou. Perhaps he would join his brother in the real estate business.

Most of all, Liang Shiyi wanted to forget the nightmarish months in Beijing when the government he had worked so hard to save collapsed like a deck of cards. Shiyi frequented the Wuben Club at the west end of the city to meet friends and play mahjong. His friends were glad to see him back and wanted to stage a belated birthday celebration for him and Madam. Orchestrated by the president of the Chinese Chamber of Commerce in Hong Kong, the occasion highlighted the contributions of the Liang family to the Hong Kong business community. Several hundred friends and family members attended the banquet to pay tribute to the couple. Madam got her chance to participate in the celebration after all.

In his leisure hours, Liang Shiyi stayed in the garden with his eighth lady. His oldest grandson and a nephew of the same age often kept their company. Sitting in the pavilion, he enjoyed watching the fish in the pond and the children playing. One day when two of the children went to the garden to play alone, his grandson slipped from a rock on the edge of the pond. His playmate went to his rescue, only to be dragged into the pond. Since neither one knew how to swim, they yelled at the top of their lungs. Fortunately a gardener, passing by in the nick of time, saved the youngsters.

* * *

After Dingshu returned home, his first priority was job hunting in China. Having concentrated his studies in Agricultural Economics in Wadham College at Oxford, he hoped to help solve the agrarian problems in China. He had some Chinese friends in England who were children of high officials in the new government in Nanjing. Perhaps they could help him land a job at one of the ministries.

However, the patriarch had his own priority. He let it be known that his health was failing and he would like to see his grandson getting married soon. At 21, Dingshu became a highly eligible bachelor in Hong Kong society. He met a gentle and quiet girl from a respectable family through her brother. The girl, Margarita Huang, had graduated from a parochial school for girls operated by the French Convent.

"I respect your freedom of religious worship," Dingshu told the girl when he was on the verge of proposing, "but my family is very dedicated to Confucianism. I don't know how you will react to their demand of kowtowing to ancestors and elders; nor do I know their reaction to your Catholicism."

"I attended a parochial school where religious education was mandatory," she replied. "After my conversion, I found conflicts of value with my own family, which is less traditional than yours. It will be difficult for me to find a family to marry into without confronting the same problem. As long as we understand each other, we can solve these conflicts without hurting the feelings of the rest of the family."

That answer sounded promising to Dingshu. He pressed further, "Although I expect to raise a family, I'm not ready to have children until my career is more established. I don't want to accept any financial help from my father."

She calmly replied, "You have at least seen the world, but I have not. I don't want to tie myself down any more than you do until both of us are ready."

After this exchange, Dingshu proposed to her and she gracefully accepted. The daughter of the Huang family was now engaged to the son of the Liang family.

The joy of the engagement announcement was marred by the news that Liang Shiyi's sixth lady was diagnosed as having breast cancer which had already metastasized. She felt excruciating pains with increasing frequency. The doctor could do nothing except ease her pains with morphine.

More alarming was the growing senility of the patriarch which had worsened in recent months. He could no longer spend his morning hours studying Confucian classics. It would be unfortunate if he couldn't live to see Dingshu's wedding.

The wedding of Dingshu and Miss Huang was hastily scheduled for January 24,

1929. After years of waiting patiently, the second lady finally had her day in the sun. After the wedding, the newlyweds left by boat to Shanghai as Dingshu had been offered a job as technical specialist in the Agriculture and Mining Ministry in Nanjing.

* * *

Although the Nationalists were plagued with factional strife, the Central Executive Committee of the party adopted a provisional constitution called "An Outline of Political Tutelage" on October 3, 1928. It legalized its guidance of the government by the party. With the formal establishment of the new government in Nanjing, Chiang Kaishek was sworn in as its Chairman on October 10.

Under the new government structure, the Agriculture and Mining Ministry was one of the ten ministries in the executive branch. Dingshu would walk into a vacuum where he was expected to define his own job.

Many difficult tasks awaited the new government, but none was more urgent than consolidation of effective control of the many areas of periodic pockets of resistance. Warlords who paid lip service to supporting the Nationalist government often quietly sabotaged its avowed objective of national unification behind the scenes. Perhaps the most delicate political task was to steer Manchuria into the Nationalist fold and away from Japanese influence.

Ever since Zhang Xueliang expressed his desire to support the unification of China on July 1, 1928, he was under tremendous pressure from Japanese emissaries who warned him of the dire consequences if he took further steps to cooperate with the Nationalists. Fully aware of Japanese influence through the control of major railways and their surroundings in Manchuria, Zhang proceeded cautiously in following through with his commitment to the Nationalists. Delegates were sent back and forth from both sides to reach a compromise. Ultimately he was told that he must subscribe to Sun Yatsen's "Three Principles of the People" and to raise the flag of the Nationalist government over Manchuria.

To Zhang Xueliang, the first condition was a matter of personal conscience and presented no problem. Many warlords, who had absolutely no knowledge or understanding of the Three Principles of the People, had perfunctorily sworn to uphold such principles when they wanted to court favor from the Nationalists. However, the second condition of raising the flag of the Nationalist government could have serious consequences. It was this very issue the Japanese objected most strongly. After stalling for six months, he finally took the advice of those who favored unification with the Nationalist government in spite of Japanese warnings. It was an act of courage on the part of Zhang Xueliang, and a sad commitment as he had to execute two of his father's most trusted generals who opposed him.

Having secured the nominal support of Zhang Xueliang, the Government in Nanjing removed the last visage of an independent Manchuria. Symbolically, Fengtian Province was given a new name Liaoning on February 5, 1929.

In Hong Kong, Liang Shiyi breathed a sigh of relief that the nation was united once again even though he was no longer a player in the new political arena.

Grieving in Silence

"We missed you tonight at the celebration of Dingshu's wedding," Liang Shiyi said to his sixth lady after he returned home with members of his family from a lavish banquet. The night was cold but he found that his sixth lady was calm under a dose of sedative. He sat at her bedside and looked at her emaciated body. Her breast cancer had reached the terminal stage and both of them knew it.

"I have struggled to survive," she quietly whispered, "so that I would not spoil the merriment of the wedding. I know how important it is to you and the family." She recalled how she herself had rushed into marriage ten years ago, before traveling to Beijing.

"You have always been very thoughtful," Liang replied softly. "We all appreciate that." Liang also reflected on their relationship which was at times awkward except for her patience. His sixth lady had devoted herself to him like a chamber maid who took care of all his personal needs. However, she knew she was not his soul mate. Her limited intelligence would not allow her to enter his world of politics and public life. Not that he expected his concubines to take part in public affairs, but he wanted them to understand enough of the political currents to avoid embarrassment or danger. His fourth lady was a master of that; so was his eighth lady who inherited that role after his fourth lady's health faltered.

Like many Chinese women from a humble origin, his sixth lady did not complain when Liang took the eighth lady. How could she when so much of her life was at stake. Instead, she avoided any potential confrontation by staying in Hong Kong to help the second lady rear her children while the eighth lady went to Beijing with her husband. But she had been richly rewarded. When her husband took her to Beijing two years later, she became, she knew, his favorite. She was amazed how her husband could balance his focus on various concubines to create a harmonious atmosphere at home. Holding her pain in check, she told her husband one more time, "I have had a wonderful life in your family. I can now rest in peace."

"Have a good rest,. Liang could not say much more to comfort her. "Is there anything else that I can do?"

"May I see the second lady?" she asked.

"Of course, I'll get her."

Liang went next door and told his second lady, "Aliu is in a good mood tonight. She wants to see you—to say goodbye."

Even Liang's warning did not prepare his second lady for the emotional outburst. The sixth lady struggled to embrace her as the second lady sat on the bed to comfort her. "I'm so happy your son is now married. You have treated me like a sister and showered me with kindness for which I am very grateful. Now that your son is married, I can now go in peace."

The second lady held her close. "I'm the one who should thank you for helping me raise my children. You can rest assured that they will have fond memories of you." The second lady tried to find a way to make her exit and changed the subject, "You look very tired. Why don't you rest?"

"I will," the sixth lady murmured, "now that I have unburdened myself of the deep feeling in my heart."

With that note, the second lady left the room. Three days later, the sixth lady died. She was buried in the crowded Chinese Eternal Cemetery.

* * *

The patriarch fulfilled his wishes to attend Dingshu's wedding even though he had to be assisted into the restaurant for the celebration. The inclement weather had made this rare venture outside of his residence even more difficult. Three weeks later, he came down with a cold and became seriously ill. Liang Shiyi and his brother Shixu were home day and night to be with him when he did not respond to the doctor's treatment. Everyone in the family, including the patriarch himself, knew his end was near.

On the morning March 19, the patriarch insisted on walking toward his desk to leave a last testament. He started to scribble with a weak hand, "I know the days of my life are numbered. I am at peace in death as I have been content with my lot in life. Sima Guang, the famous Confucian and statesman in Song Dynasty, once said, 'There is no action in my life that cannot be opened to public scrutiny.' Searching my soul in a quiet moment, I am afraid that I have not lived up to his standard. I regret that my work on Daily Lessons from Confucian Four Books has not been completed. Ten more sections of the Analects still require annotation—" Suddenly his writing was no longer legible. Waving of his hand as a signal, he wanted help getting back to bed. Within hours, he died.

Outwardly a modest man, the patriarch was anything but modest to his sons and grandchildren. He was very generous in overlooking shortcomings of other people, but he demanded strict self-discipline which was extended to the discipline of his descendants. He said repeatedly that his manuscript was not good enough for publication and should not be published for fear of being seen as immodest. And yet he never hesitated to recommend it to his descendants and disciples as a guiding post to moral behavior. Was this the ultimate demonstration of double standards, or was it the golden rule that led to his humility?

In any case, the patriarch had lived a long and productive life. Born only a few years after the Opium War which opened China to the West, he saw the world as he knew it tumble in front of his eyes. He taught his sons to work hard and to serve their country honorably. But in the end he could not even trust his native village to protect him from kidnappers and he accepted foreign protection in Hong Kong. At the age of 84, he had outlived his contemporaries, but not their values. In his old age, he was treated like a king by his two sons who pampered him and catered to his every whim. It was the height of a fulfilling life by Chinese standards. To close the circle, he wanted to be buried next to his wife in his native land.

Since it would take time to make elaborate arrangements to ship the coffin back to their native village, Liang Shiyi and his brother had to make a quick decision. They negotiated for a temporary burial in the Chinese Eternal Cemetery in Hong Kong. The funeral evoked the solemn rites befitting a Confucian scholar and the funeral procession from Robinson Road to the cemetery was most impressive. Among the mourners was Sir Cecil Clementi, Governor of Hong Kong, who knew Liang Shiyi well through their shared interest in Chinese literary classics and international politics.

Not long after the funeral, the two brothers got together to discuss their own future. Liang Shiyi made it known that he would like to continue the present arrangement of joint effort to keep the extended family together.

"My children have all grown up and one by one have left home," Liang Shiyi said to his brother. "But your children are still young and are in grade school or high school. I want them to feel they will always have a home to come back to wherever they may go in the future."

Shixu agreed. "My family will stay in Hong Kong, but I may travel back and forth between Hong Kong and Guangzhou. As a major stockholder of the Guangzhou Power and Light Company, I've been asked repeatedly by its Board of Directors to become its president. However, I have so far declined in order to be near father. After the extended period of mourning, I intend to accept that position in Guangzhou."

"You have sacrificed your own career long enough to take care of father and the family," Liang Shiyi replied. "You should take advantage of this opportunity in Guangzhou. I'll look after our real estate business in Hong Kong." With that encouragement, Shixu accepted the offer from the company in Guangzhou.

* * *

Dingshu and his wife arrived in Shanghai in late January and were immediately attracted by the excitement of the city. Since the Nationalists decided to move the national capital to Nanjing the previous year, Shanghai had gained added importance in more ways than one. Because of a shortage of adequate housing for government officials and diplomats in Nanjing, the majority of diplomats left their wives in Beijing while they lived in hotels or in temporary offices in Nanjing or Shanghai. The wealthy Chinese, including the wives of many high government officials, lived in the International Settlement in Shanghai. The low-ranking officials had no choice but to stay in shabby dormitories provided by the ministries.

The European and American influence on the rising generation of Chinese in Shanghai was unmistakable. Large billboards advertising American cars and other products were everywhere; Europeans hairdressers introduced "permanent waves" to attract sophisticated women. The avant-garde Chinese artists and writers took the lead in Westernizing the social code of the young to a startling degree—an alarming situation to the older generation. Boys and girls whose parents had met each other for the first time on their wedding day no longer thought twice about going out to nightclubs together. Divorces were casually accepted. The city of Shanghai had become an island of Western culture in a sea of Chinese traditionalism.

"I wish I could get a place in Nanjing for the two of us," Dingshu told his wife. "but it's impossible to find decent housing there. The public transportation is so poor that it takes forever to go to work, if I were willing to rent a rundown house on the outskirts of the city."

"I understand," his wife replied. "It's tough enough to find a decent place to live in Shanghai. In any case, your job comes first."

After reviewing his options, Dingshu decided to rent a small European-style apartment in Shanghai for his wife, and he moved into the dormitory of his ministry in Nanjing. His sister Yusheng, and her family, lived in Shanghai and could look after his wife if she needed help. Every weekend, he joined the exodus of government officials who rushed by train to join their families in Shanghai. Things seemed to be working out well for the newlyweds.

In a short time, Dingshu and his wife had developed a circle of friends in Shanghai. The weekend commuting had become routine for him while she adjusted to her own activities during his absence. After three months, she discovered she was probably pregnant. The unexpected pregnancy horrified her. She had practiced the birth control method that she thought was sanctioned by her religious faith. She suddenly felt the inadequacy of her knowledge in human reproduction and birth control. She immediately consulted a doctor only to confirm that her suspicion was correct. The news left her in a depressed state.

When her husband returned home from Nanjing the following weekend, he could sense something was missing in her usually cheerful spirit. She wanted to tell him and yet she could not, for fear of upsetting him. She was tormented by the conflict of her desire to please her husband and to practice her religious faith. She had made up her mind to take a drastic action.

"You looked very tired today," her husband spoke gently, "Is there anything bothering you?"

"No," she said, mustering her energy to give a spirited reply. "Nothing that can't be cured by a good hairdresser. I'm going to get a permanent wave tomorrow. It's now a fashionable hairstyle, you know. Let's go visit your sister's family tonight."

As they lay in bed that night, she hardly closed her eyes as her husband fell into a sound sleep. She was struggling to convince herself what she was about to do was for the best. She must carry out her plan.

Beijing Odyssey

The next morning, she put on a radiant face and said to her husband, "It may take a long time for my permanent. Please be sure to stay home for my phone call."

"Of course," he replied readily, and watched her hurry out the door.

Instead of going to see a hairdresser, she quickly went to an alley of row houses. She held up a slip of paper to verify the address and ran the bell. A middle-aged woman answered the door, and within minutes, she stepped into the house.

She had hoped, when everything was over, she could call her husband to pick her up. But something went wrong. She continued bleeding after the procedure to terminate the pregnancy. In a hurry, the middle-aged woman helped her get into a taxicab and ordered the driver to go to a nearby hospital. Still conscious when she reached the emergency room, she told the nurse to call her husband. A doctor was immediately summoned to see her but he could not stop the bleeding. When her husband arrived, she was almost unconscious.

Dingshu was shocked beyond belief. He sat by her bedside, calling her name. But there was no response. Suddenly guilt overshadowed his sadness. Did his desire to postpone raising a family cause her death? Was she the victim of their defiance to the laws of nature? His mind could think of nothing but regret and remorse.

After making arrangement for the funeral, he went back to their apartment. Only then did the finality of his wife's death overwhelm him. How could he explain to his sister whom they had seen only the night before? How could he break the news, as he must, to his parents and to his wife's family? There were no words to describe his agony. He could only grieve in silence.

Dingshu held the receiver to his ear. He could hear his sister crying, asking over and over, why she had not suspected her sister-in-law's suffering. Most of all, she feared this would be a serious blow to their mother. It was almost sixteen years since their older brother, Dingwu, had drowned in the United States. After the loss of her older son, their mother had became a devoted Buddhist, seeking comfort for her own suffering and blessings for her family. Why must misfortune visit her again in such a cruel way?

Dingshu finally mustered enough courage to send two telegrams to Hong Kong, one to his father and the other to his father-in-law. He could not think of words that would comfort them, so he was concise. Perhaps he could express his feeling better when he saw them.

When the sad news reached Hong Kong, Liang Shiyi was stunned. He tried to comfort his second lady who had suffered much in her life. Now, they both must endure this pain in silence. What could they say to the family of their daughter-in-law for their tragic loss?

Social Protest

The summer of 1929 was melancholy to Liang Shiyi as he reflected on the losses in his family and his own misfortune in public life. Staying home most of the time, he didn't even venture into the garden to see the roses in full bloom. The withering petals of the blossoms would only remind him of the transitory nature of life and human affairs. His only pastime was the reading of Confucian classics, particularly the *Book of Change*. Occasionally his eighth lady would gently interrupt. "Don't you think you have read enough?" Then he knew it was time for dinner.

Fortunately, since his son Dingji worked in Hong Kong, Shiyi's grandchildren provided much comfort in his darkest hours. His mood brightened when his youngest son Dingmin arrived in Hong Kong from England in August. He had just completed a bachelor's degree in electrical engineering from the University of London. Dingmin soon became the chief engineer of the newly organized Radio Broadcasting Station of Guangzhou. Liang Shiyi felt great satisfaction that all three of his sons had found their own calling.

In the next few months, his activities were again slowed by a severe case of rheumatism which forced him to stay off his feet. Through the loving care of his eighth lady, his life gradually returned to normal by the spring of 1930. His brother Shixu was working in Guangzhou. Shiyi spent more time tending the family business and lavishing his attention on Shixu's children.

In July, his youngest daughter Yisheng returned home from Beijing, now officially known as Beiping. After completing her sophomore year at Yenching University, an institution supported by American missionaries, she was home for summer vacation. She told her father the latest happening at the university that would affect her personally.

"On June 22, the Ministry of Education ordered Yenching University to drop religion courses in its required courses in order to be accredited as a private Chinese institution of higher learning," she told her father.

"Will the university comply?" He was curious.

"I don't think the university has any choice if it wants its graduates to be fully accepted for civil-service jobs," she replied. "Dr. John Leighton Stuart, our American president, will become the Dean of the University while a Chinese will be appointed to succeed him as president."

Because of the anti-imperialism theme of the Nationalist government, Chinese control of higher education became an important political issue. The missionaries were viewed by unsympathetic officials as an adjunct to Western colonization of China. Ever since the opening of China to the West, the Chinese did not like having foreigners denounce the traditional Chinese beliefs. Voltaire captured the mood of many Chinese in his humorous story of the Chinese who, after listening to a theological dispute among a Catholic, a Protestant, a Quaker, a Jansenist, a Jew and a Muslim, finally clapped each of them into separate cells for the insane. Most Chinese were totally confused by different denominations and sects of Christianity. Many early converts were "Rice Christians" who simply appreciated the charities of missionary organizations. As radical reformers, the Nationalists also regarded Buddhism, Daoism and other traditional religions as superstition. Consequently, its education policy had an anti-religious tone.

Instead of relying on religions to link human endeavor to divine wisdom or design, the Nationalists adopted the Chinese tradition of appealing to the legacy of wise men who were dead. Sun Yatsen, founder of the Nationalist Party, was interned in the Western Hills near Beiping after his death in 1925, but his remains were brought to Nanjing for reburial on June 1, 1929 in a solemn ceremony attended by government officials and diplomats. The mausoleum of Sun Yatsen became the Mecca for the faithfuls to seek spiritual guidance.

* * *

"I hope you will come to our school play," his oldest nephew pleaded with Liang Shiyi. "Our high school will stage a play this summer for the benefit of flood victims in China."

"I will buy the tickets from you," Liang replied. The plea was irresistible even though he had no idea what the play was or whether he would actually attend.

Liang Shiyi's daughter Yisheng was sitting next to him and browsing through a newspaper. She stopped reading and asked her cousin the name of the play.

"*A Doll's House*. Do you want to see it, too?"

"I think we should go to see it together," she said. "Why don't we buy enough tickets so your younger brothers can also attend."

Yisheng had a good reason to promote the play besides helping her cousin sell more tickets for the charity. She knew neither her father nor her cousins had been exposed to the central character in the play with whom she was in total sympathy. But for the moment, she put down the newspaper and turned to her father.

"Lingnan University in Guangzhou was accredited as a private university by the Ministry of Education on July 21, according to the newspaper," she said. "Perhaps my cousins will some day attend that university."

"Has Lingnan University satisfied all the requirements for accreditation with the Ministry of Education?" Liang asked.

"Yes," Yisheng replied. "It has a Chinese Board of Directors and has had a Chinese president since 1927. Americans continue to send faculty members and exchange students, but no longer dominate the day-to-day administration. They are way ahead of other universities established by foreign missionaries in north China. Peking Union Medical College, supported by the Rockefeller Foundation, is an exception since it has no undergraduate program."

Yisheng was intrigued by what her father might say after seeing *A Doll's House*. The play, by Norwegian playwright Henrik Ibsen, had been translated into Chinese in 1918. That year, a special issue of *New Youth* was devoted to Ibsen, with laudatory comments on his plays which made a generation of Chinese aware of his fundamental criticism of bourgeois hypocrisy and his powerful advocacy of women's emancipation. His plays were widely performed and admired at the height of the new cultural movement. But the social changes inspired by the movement did not take place until a decade later—when the new generation grew up.

Nora, the central character of *A Doll's House*, decides to leave her husband and go out into the world to find her own destiny. The character became a cultural and personal symbol to young Chinese women. Many of them attempted to live out a vision of romantic freedom as teachers, writers, journalists, artists and political activists. Lu Xun, who emerged as one of the most brilliant writers of the new cultural movement, observed what he called "the Nora phenomenon," with sympathy, but also some anxiety. In addressing a woman's college on the theme "What happens after Nora Leaves Home," Xun warned his listeners not to forget the realities of the society in which they were still living. Until the women gained a level of economic independence and equality, their sense of freedom would be a sham. He added as an afterthought, "I have assumed Nora to be an ordinary woman. If she is someone exceptional who prefers to dash off to sacrifice herself, that's a different matter."

In taking him to the play, Yisheng wanted to send a message to her father. When the curtain fell in the high-school auditorium, Liang Shiyi seemed pensive. Not knowing what Lu Xun had said to the students in the woman's college, he came to the same conclusion. When they reached home, he spoke to Yisheng, "It's very fashionable, in these days, for an ambitious man with a family to get a divorce and marry a younger woman on the grounds that his wife is in the way of his career. However, very few people consider the point of view of the wife. Is she better off because she is free from a man who no longer loves her? Can she remarry a respectable man and live a normal life? Can she be financially independent if she chooses to remain single after the divorce? Indeed, how many women, divorced and abandoned by their husbands, can find happiness? I wonder."

These remarks hit very close to home, Yisheng thought. She and her sisters often wondered why their father's concubines were so devoted to him. Now she understood. Being the daughter of his second lady, Yisheng could sympathize with the concubines since her own mother was one. But when would women wake up and revolt against such an unfair social system which enslaved them?

Beijing Odyssey

* * *

Lu Xun had an answer for women and men who were trapped in an unfair system. He came to the unpleasant conclusion that these people did not know they were trapped and therefore would not try to escape. In his greatest stories published at the height of the new cultural movement, he expressed hope that the oppressed would at least be conscious of their fate and die thinking, even if they could not escape.

In 1930, Lu Xun became the spokesman of a powerful literary organization called "The League of Chinese Left-Wing Writers" founded under the auspices of the Chinese Communist Party. Lu Xun had not lost his glitter in the literary scene. His words almost guaranteed an attentive audience. Two other groups stood out adamantly in opposition. The first was led by Lin Yutang whose humorous, satirical and somewhat playful publications received tremendous public acclaim. The second group was centered around the professors of universities and colleges in Beiping whose articles in literary journals enjoyed wide circulation because of their avantgarde, critical attitude and the use of the advanced techniques of Western writers. The cross-current of these three major groups contributed to an unusually lively literary atmosphere, but more importantly their messages of social protest stirred up the fire of a younger generation.

The works of these writers reflected social realism through satire, sarcasm and pity, condemning the decadence and backwardness of the old society and existing order. Some young writers had bitter experiences as members of large families who struggled to break away from their elders, only to court stubborn opposition with tragic outcomes. These writers explored popular themes such as good versus evil, heroes versus weaklings, and bravery versus cowardice in their characters. Novels with such themes fanned the flame of family revolution in the minds of young readers.

As Yisheng could testify, many of her friends had taken seriously the dictum that life imitates art and rebelled against their families. They were "someone exceptional who prefers to dash off to sacrifice herself," in the words of Lu Xun, and they bore the brunt of family revolution. Yisheng was glad her father understood such conflict. She witnessed his changing attitude toward the marriages of his older brothers and sisters. With the passage of time, he interfered progressively less in each successive marriage. She would not have to worry about any interference in her own.

During her summer vacation, Yisheng developed a rapport with her father she had never known before. They discussed politics, education and a wide variety of topics. Yisheng viewed her father as a gentle authoritarian, a great improvement over her late grandfather who had been an oppressive authoritarian. Occasionally Liang Shiyi lamented the negative aspects of the changing society, "People are no longer rooted in their world and lose their orientation. They just drift in our restless and chaotic time. The quest for a meaningful life demands concentrated attention, and above all, patience."

"Speaking of patience," Yisheng told her father, "college students are the most impatient group. Their trust in government vanished completely when the

Nationalist government suspended the operation of Beijing University two years ago and tried to reorganize all public-supported colleges in Beiping area into a single university. Of course the idea didn't work and was soon abandoned. Now the students will not listen when they're told to be patient. In fact, students in several national universities throughout the country refuse to allow government-appointed presidents to assume their posts if they dislike them for any reason."

"It's a sad commentary on education," Liang Shiyi replied. "I was brought up when teachers were respected, right or wrong. Of course I don't expect that relationship to continue, but I hate to see such a complete reversal."

"I'm glad I'm attending a private university," Yisheng observed.

As Yisheng got ready to return to Beiping to continue her study in late August, her brother Dingshu arrived in Hong Kong on his way to Guangzhou. After the death of his wife, he had tried desperately to leave Nanjing and Shanghai to start a new life. Through his uncle in Guangzhou, he found a job as Senior Technical Specialist in the Agricultural Bureau of Guangdong Province.

In September, Liang Shiyi and his brother Shixu went back to their native village for the burial of their father. All the women of the extended family and the grandchildren of the patriarch, from Hong Hong and Guangzhou, joined them for the trip. Liang Shiyi handled the logistics from Hong Kong to Guangzhou while his brother Shixu coordinated the activities from Guangzhou onward. A 550-word epitaph in memory of the patriarch was composed by Ye Gongchuo, a family friend and literary giant, and was written in fine calligraphy by Liang Shiyi for inscription on a granite slab. This slab and two engraved stone pillars honoring the patriarch were placed next to the tombstone.

After a prolonged stay overseeing the completion of his father's tomb, Liang Shiyi reluctantly left his native village. He felt relieved to have performed his last duty in honoring his father. Spending his leisure moments with Dingji's family in Hong Kong, he rejoiced in the birth of Dingji's second daughter.

* * *

Liang Shiyi went to say farewell to Governor Cecil Clementi who was returning to England after retirement. After the usual polite exchange, the governor glibly observed, "I cannot get over your adroit explanation about the couplet you composed for the Qingshan Temple. The guests at the dedication ceremony obviously appreciated your wit."

"Hardly. They were there to honor you," Liang replied. "They marveled at your knowledge of Chinese culture and admired your fine calligraphy."

"I can make a modest claim that people in Hong Kong enjoy unprecedented peace and prosperity under British rule," Governor Clementi said. "Why should the Chinese government officials fan hatred against my government?"

"You serve your country admirably," Liang retorted. "But the Opium War is a scar on the Chinese conscience. They simply want to address their grievance. None of their hatred is directed toward you personally. I wish you a happy retirement." With that cordial note, Liang left.

Learning of the jousting between the retired governor and Liang Shiyi, the admiring Chinese faculty of Hong Kong University invited Liang to give a lecture at its College of Chinese Studies in December. It was a personal triumph for Liang Shiyi as he took the podium once again to reaffirm the faith of a Confucian scholar.

A Call to Arms

On New Year's Day, 1931, the government in Nanjing announced a general pardon for all political prisoners except communists and traitors to the Republic. The pardon was prompted by the complaints of human-rights violation by various political groups and well known individuals, including Soong Chingling, the widow of Sun Yatsen. But the pronouncement had little practical effect since major oppositions to the government were armed insurgencies led by communists and by the warlords who had formed alliances with dissident Nationalist politicians

In its military action against the communists in late 1930, the government had been unsuccessful in suppressing their uprisings in Hunan, Hubei and Jiangxi. Although the government had finally gotten an upper hand in defeating the warlords in north and central China, other warlords in south China were still active in opposing Chiang Kaishek's authority. The New Year pronouncement was as much a warning to those in opposition as a gesture of goodwill and forgiveness.

In his campaign in the fall of 1930 to defeat an alliance of dissident politicians and warlords now occupying Beiping, Chiang Kaishek received a big boost from Zhang Xueliang, the young marshall in Manchuria. Zhang not only refused to accept the bait from the group in Beiping to join them, he also declared his support of the government in Nanjing. He quickly sent his troops in Manchuria to Beiping and Tianjin, driving the rebellious generals out of that region, and accepting the surrender of their troops. As a reward for his loyalty, Zhang Xueliang was appointed by the Nationalists as the Deputy Commander of all the armed forces of China. Zhang Xueliang arrived in Nanjing in November 1930 to meet with the Commander, Chiang Kaishek. For the first time, the three northeastern provinces in Manchuria were under the de facto, as well as de jure, control of the government in Nanjing.

Liang Shiyi had no interest in the politics of the Nationalists since his forced retirement more than two years earlier. However, the news of a general pardon of political prisoners caught the eyes of his eighth lady who had developed a keen sense of the effects of political issues and events on Liang. Realizing Liang was still haunted by an arrest warrant issued by the government in Nanjing, she asked whether this pronouncement would apply to him.

"No, it applied only to those who were detained," Liang explained.

"That's unfortunate," she lamented.

"It makes very little difference since I can still travel where I want to in south China," Liang replied. "But I will stay away from the area near Nanjing and Shanghai to avoid trouble." Indeed, the arrest warrants issued by the Nanjing government were usually ignored by local politicians, even those who professed to be loyal to Nanjing. With rapid changes in loyalties and allegiances, an ally today might become an "enemy of the Republic" tomorrow. Why bother to make enemies of potential allies by enforcing arrest warrants? Because of the prevailing attitude, Liang Shiyi had been assured of his personal safety before going back to his native village via Guangzhou for the burial of his father. He also received word that Wellington Koo, who was still under a similar arrest warrant, was now in Shenyang as the guest of Zhang Xueliang.

* * *

In April 1931, Liang Shiyi went back to his native village with his eighth lady for the Qingming Festival. This was the traditional time for people to visit the cemetery to honor their ancestors. Liang wanted to honor his father's memory at the grave site and spend his quiet moments contemplating the future. He also wanted to introduce his heritage to his eighth lady who had never been to the village except for the few days during his father's burial.

"You can sense the goodness of the people in our village," Liang Shiyi told his eighth lady. "They have not lost their innocence and are uncontaminated by the cynicism of modern society."

"It is a simpler life, to be sure," his eighth lady replied. "But how long can the people keep it that way?" She sensed the village people were on the threshold of change.

Before returning to Hong Kong, Liang went to Wuzhou in Guangxi Province to meet Guan Mianjun. A close friend in their youth and even closer in recent years through the marriage of their children, Guan was a native of Wuzhou but had made his home in Beiping for a long time. Even though he seldom returned to Wuzhou, he was not forgotten and was welcomed back by his clansmen as a favorite son whose scholastic honors and professional achievements had brought honor to his native land. When he introduced Liang at a village festival, the crowd went wild for the Former Premier of China. However, Guan had another purpose for making this trip home. He wanted to find a scenic spot in his native village for his final resting place. He, too, had not forgotten his roots.

When he returned to Hong Kong through Guangzhou, Liang Shiyi met with his son Dingmin who would soon leave for Suzhou in Jiangsu Province.

"I'll miss your wedding," Liang told his son Dingmin. "Suzhou is too close to Nanjing for me to take the risk of being arrested."

"I understand," Dingmin replied. "We'll come back to Guangzhou soon after the wedding. With my new responsibilities, I have decided to accept a more lucrative position as an electric engineer in the Power and Light Company when I return."

"It's too bad your mother does not want to go to Suzhou for the wedding," Liang Shiyi said. "My best wishes to you."

Dingmin's fiancee, Zhong Huilian, was the second daughter of Zhong Wenyao, who was among the earliest group of teenagers sent by the Qing government to study in the United States. Although Zhong Wenyao was Cantonese, he chose to live in Suzhou after his retirement from an active life. Liang Shiyi knew him and his family well, and gladly gave his blessings to Dingmin's marriage. But Madam had reservations. As a dashing young man, Zhong Wenyao had married a girl whose mother was Caucasian. Madam thought Mrs. Zhong was less than a Chinese because she did not teach her daughters to be submissive to their mothers-in-law.

"We will have a celebration when Dingmin and his bride returned to Hong Kong," Madam told her husband. "I want them to go through the traditional Chinese ritual, here, even though they will follow the Western-style wedding in Suzhou. I want to teach his wife the duties of a daughter-in-law in our family."

"You can tell Dingmin as you wish," Liang told his wife. He never wanted to argue with Madam, particularly when she was not in a good mood. Dingmin was her youngest child and most beloved son, but Madam never minced words when she tried to make a point. She never thought about her children's happiness when she belittled their spouses. While her sons and grandchildren were precious to her, daughters-in-law were expendable. Dingmin knew his mother well and always tried to work around her. Wisely, he stayed in Suzhou for a prolonged honeymoon before bringing his bride back to Hong Kong to face his mother.

Liang Shiyi's fourth daughter, Zangsheng, lived in Hong Kong with her husband after they were married. A happy family with two sons and two daughters, her life suddenly took a tragic turn. Her younger son and baby daughter fell ill and died of tuberculosis. Not long after, her husband died of the same dreadful disease. On hearing about the death of his son-in-law, Liang Shiyi invited Zangsheng home for a rest after her husband's funeral. Madam was surprised.

"According to Cantonese custom, a person can visit a bereaved family to convey his condolence," she told her husband, "but a family member in mourning should not visit relatives and friends for fear of bringing bad luck to them."

Of course, since their marriage, Zangsheng was regarded as a member of her husband's family rather than the Liang family. Shiyi knew that, but for a change, he begged to differ with Madam,. "Zangsheng is our daughter. We share her happiness and her sorrow. We must set an example of defying irrational and superstitious customs."

Madam knew when she should retreat. After all, Zangsheng was her own daughter, not the daughter of a concubine. She remained silent as Liang extended the invitation. But Zangsheng declined to move back to her father's home for an extended stay, although she cherished the opportunity to visit from time to time.

Although Liang Shiyi enjoyed playing mahjong with his friends in the gentlemen's club, he seldom played it at home, least of all with his own children. Knowing Zangsheng liked mahjong, he made it almost a daily affair to play when she came for a visit. When he could not find four members for the game, he invited their old servant Maisan to join in. Zangsheng was grateful that her father would spend so much time helping her endure her sorrow. Maisan only could add, "I have played mahjong with my master, an honor even Madam does not enjoy since she refuses to participate."

* * *

While Liang Shiyi was busy with his family affairs, a new development in the political arena presented an opportunity to cancel his arrest warrant.

Ever since the establishment of the Nationalist government in Nanjing, the Nationalist Party was plagued with factional strife. The right wing, led by party elder Hu Hanmin, was in constant conflict with the left wing, headed by Wang Jingwei. Junior to both Hu and Wang, Chiang Kaishek charted his course, alternately favoring each with support according to the dictates of political expediency. In his new government, Chiang collaborated with Hu while Wang and his left wing followers were left out in the cold.

Then in March 1931, the Central Committee of the Nationalist Party passed a resolution to introduce a Provisional Constitution in a Tutelage Period, a device to justify the delay of popular elections for several years. Hu Hanmin split with Chiang on the issue and was soon placed under house arrest. Wang Jingwei, now in Hong Kong, persuaded Chen Jitong, the military strong man in Guangdong, to oppose Chiang's government. Both the right wing and left wing of the Nationalist Party were in opposition to Chiang Kaishek.

Wang Jingwei and his supporters protested the Tutelage Period as a form of dictatorship and demanded Chiang Kaishek's resignation. Sun Ko, son of Sun Yatsen, and sympathetic dissidents, including Tang Shaoyi, left Nanjing and went to Guangzhou to join Wang Jingwei's opposition group. In May the dissidents established a Military Government in Guangzhou headed by Wang Jingwei. The Military Government in Guangzhou received support from former subordinates of some northern warlords who provoked a civil war and threatened the government in Nanjing. It was Zhang Xueliang who once again came to Chiang's aid, and their combined forces dealt a crushing blow to the rebels. That further endeared Zhang to Chiang.

On the second anniversary of the entombment of Sun Yatsen in Nanjing, Chiang Kaishek went to the shrine on June 1 to announce the Provisional Constitution for the Tutelage Period. He invoked the memory of Sun Yatsen in defying his opponents.

At the same time, Zhang Xueliang became the garrison commander of Beiping as a part of his duty as deputy commander of all armed forces. He used the third anniversary of his father's death to stage a memorial service. Liang Shiyi sent a message to Zhang Xueliang, expressing his regret of the tragic death of Zhang Zuolin, reminding him of Liang's friendship with his father. In return, Zhang Xueliang used his influence to ask the government in Nanjing to cancel the arrest warrant against

Liang Shiyi. Liang became a free man again.

* * *

Chiang Kaishek gave top priority to eliminating the communists through military action. In July 1931, he sent 130,000 troops to start another campaign against the communists. He directed the battle himself at Nanchang in Jiangxi Province. It was partially successful, but was cut short by the Japanese invasion of Manchuria in September.

Zhang Xueliang's contribution in Chiang's showdown with warlords had been crucial. Yet in transferring his troops to North China, Zhang left Manchuria in a vulnerable position. The Japanese were quick to take advantage. During the summer of 1931, two incidents occurring in Manchuria played into the hands of the Japanese. In July, a clash between Chinese farmers and Korean settlers near Changchun, the capital city of Jilin Province, resulted in the killing of hundreds of Chinese by Japanese police. The second incident was the murder in August of Captain Nakamura Sintaro and three companions while traveling in disguise to plot in Inner Mongolia against the Chinese government. These incidents brought the already over-charged atmosphere of Manchuria to a new pitch.

Anticipating a Japanese attack, Chiang Kaishek warned Zhang Xueliang, on September 15, not to engage the Japanese. Deeply embroiled in civil strife, Chiang could not afford a foreign war. As a result, the bulk of Chinese forces at Shenyang were transferred elsewhere. In the evening of September 18, at about ten o'clock, a bomb exploded on the Southern Manchurian Railway track outside Shenyang. The damage was so minimal, it didn't even disrupt the railway service, but the Japanese claimed it was an act of terrorists aimed at the Japanese. After the explosion, a contingent from the Japanese army stationed in Manchuria raced to the nearby barracks housing the crack troops under the command of Zhang Xueliang. The Japanese claimed that Chinese soldiers opened fire and the Japanese fought back in self defense. By three-thirty the following morning, the city wall of Shenyang had been ruptured and the city occupied. A new mayor of Shenyang was appointed by the Japanese occupying forces on the following day. Orders were given by the Japanese authority to attack and advance. Changchun was taken on September 21.

When hostilities broke out on September 18, Zhang Xueliang lay sick in Beiping. He again asked Chiang for instruction and was told once more not to resist. On September 21, Chiang Kaishek returned to Nanjing from Jiangxi where he had been directing the fight against communists. The government in Nanjing cabled the Guangzhou Military Government and urged it to unite behind Nanjing to fight the Japanese. When the government in Guangzhou replied favorably, Chiang sent a delegation headed by Cai Yuanpei to start the process of discussing terms of reconciliation.

Running out of options, Chiang Kaishek decided to appeal to the League of Nations with full knowledge that it was powerless to intervene. The Western powers declined to help. By appealing to the international organization for justice, he hoped to gain time to organize his defenses and await a favorable turnaround in Japanese domestic politics. But he did not want direct negotiation with the Japanese because he was afraid of being forced into compromise in the negotiation.

On September 23, the League of Nations asked both China and Japan to limit hostility, and a day later, the United States urged the two countries to suspend military operations in honor of the Nine-Power Treaty. To these warnings, the Japanese turned a deaf ear. Without international sanction or Chinese resistance, the Japanese army attacked Heilongjiang Province in November and overran Manchuria in five months. The only flicker of Chinese heroism came from a local general, Ma Zhanshan, Acting Governor of Heilongjiang, who stubbornly resisted the enemy in spite of all odds against him. But these sporadic resistance movements from "righteous volunteers" failed to stop the enemy.

At the meeting of the Executive Council of the League of Nations on September 21, the Chinese Delegate, Alfred Saokee Sze, asked the League to order both sides to return to their original positions. The Japan delegate objected and wanted bilateral discussion only between China and Japan. On December 10, the League decided to dispatch an investigative mission to Manchuria.

* * *

Liang Shiyi learned about the Japanese invasion of Manchuria at Longci near his native village in Sanshui. He was there at the invitation of a former student of Fenggang Academy to open a new ancestral hall in Longci Village. Liang Shiyi was the guest of honor who would add his literary touch to glorify this hall of worship. He gladly composed several couplets for the entrances of public buildings in the village. His brother Shixu and several old friends joined him there for the celebration. As he was ready to leave for Hong Kong, he solemnly told them, "This terrible news reminds me that I am out-of-date. I have advocated peace and reconciliation all my life. But this is a turning point. Japan clearly wants to subjugate China by force. If we want peace, we must prepare for war." He ended his trip to Longci on a note of regret for lost youth and promise.

There was a congruence of Liang's personal downfall and China's slide into dominance by Japan. In his youth, Liang's patriotism against Japan was fueled by the humiliation of China after the Sino-Japanese War in 1894. At the height of his career, he had tried to channel the Japanese ambitions to constructive ends by encouraging them to invest in industrial developments of China for the benefit of both countries. In the twilight of his life, his hopes were dashed by the Japanese militarism which once again aroused his anti-Japanese sentiment. For someone who worked so hard to turn swords into plowshares, a call to arms did not come easily. But Liang Shiyi had steeled himself for the inevitable and was at peace with his conscience.

Family reunion Celebrating Dingmin's wedding, July 1931

National Emergency

"I trust you can handle everything yourself," Liang Shiyi said to his second lady as she was leaving Hong Kong for Beiping in October 1931. Ever since the Nationalist army entered the city of Beiping in 1928, Liang's residence at Ganshiqiao Lane was partially occupied by the troops of the triumphant army. After Zhang Xueliang became the commander of the garrison in Beiping in June, the troops were ordered to leave the occupied residence and return to their barracks. The second lady had the responsibility of supervising the restoration of the residence to livable conditions when she arrived in Beiping.

"If I need help, I can always call Haoyin and Zuzhang," the second lady replied, referring to her eldest daughter and son-in-law who lived in Beiping. However, she had an even more important mission in mind. She would go to Beiping to make preparation for the second marriage of her son Dingshu in the following month. It was an event she anticipated with pleasure, regardless of the amount of work involved in the preparation.

More than a year before, Dingshu met a girl who was attending Ginling College for Women in Nanjing. A native of Wuzhou, she went home to visit her parents in the summer and Dingshu took the opportunity to go to Wuzhou to be with her and meet her parents. With the encouragement of her parents, the girl was engaged to Dingshu after a brief courtship. When Dingshu went back to Guangzhou, his fiancee took a trip to Beiping to visit her elder sister who lived there. She was so charmed by the historical relics of Beiping she decided to stay with her sister's family until her wedding. Dingshu would be pleased to live in the comfortable residence in Ganshiqiao Lane if he could find a job in Beiping. Luckily, he was able to secure a position as special assistant in the Beiping office of the Ministry of Railways. Their wedding date was set for November when Dingshu arrived in Beiping.

Liang Shiyi decided not to attend Dingshu's wedding because of pressing business in Hong Kong. When Dingshu passed by the city on his way to Beiping, he dutifully asked his father, "Do you think you might change your mind about going to Beiping?"

425

"No, I don't think so," Liang Shiyi replied. "The Military Government in Guangzhou is currently negotiating in earnest with the Nanjing government to form a unity government. Tang Shaoyi has approached me for suggestions. It's my fervent hope that they succeed so people of all political persuasions can join in the common cause of fighting the Japanese aggression. The negotiation is in a critical stage and I want to be readily available if I'm consulted again."

Shortly after Dingshu left for Beiping, Dingji was sent by the Shanghai Commercial and Savings Bank to Guangzhou to set up a new branch office there. After staying at home in Hong Kong for four years, his parting with the extended family was particularly painful for Madam. Dingji's two sons and two daughters were her pride and joy—the boys especially. She said to her daughter-in-law, "Do come home often with the children. I like to have them around."

"Of course," Dingji's wife replied, "but Guangzhou is not that far away. You can come visit us from time to time.

"I'm almost a fixture here," Madam told her. "Nothing can make me leave my comfortable living quarters."

Dingji was in fact quite eager to be on his own, and so was his wife. The young family packed up and moved to Guangzhou in December. In addition to becoming the General Manager of the Guangzhou branch of his bank, Dingji was elected a member of Board of Directors of the Banking Association in Guangzhou.

* * *

The negotiation between the Nanjing and Guangzhou governments finally ended in an agreement expanding the Nanjing government to allow representation from more political factions. The Guangzhou government was to be dissolved. In late December, Chiang Kaishek resigned as the Chairman of the Nationalist Government while retaining his military leadership. On New Year's Day, 1932, a unity government was formed to accommodate politicians in both Nanjing and Guangzhou. Liang Shiyi was delighted, not only at the prospect of unity, but at the announcement that Ye Gongchuo, his friend and confidant, had been named Minister of Railways in the reshuffle.

On January 18, 1932, the government called for a National Emergency Conference to be convened in Nanjing on February 1. The purpose of the conference was to gather a group of government officials and elder statesmen to chart a course in resisting Japanese aggression. Three days later, Liang Shiyi received an invitation to attend the conference. He immediately jumped at the opportunity and left Hong Kong with his eighth lady. They arrived in Shanghai on January 25 amid the highly charged anti-Japanese atmosphere.

"Look at the store fronts, at the signs boycotting Japanese goods," his eighth lady said to Liang as their car passed along Nanjing Road.

"Yes," Liang replied, "the people rise to take action themselves while the government is hesitant."

The action of the people was not lost to the Japanese in Shanghai. On January

22, the commander of the Japanese fleet in Shanghai sent a message to the Shanghai municipal government, requesting it to suppress all anti-Japanese organizations and movements. The next day, a large fleet of Japanese military vessels arrived in a show of force. Three days later, the Japanese consul in Shanghai sent an ultimatum to the Shanghai municipal government, requesting the suppression of all activities promoting the boycott of Japanese goods. He demanded a reply before 6 p.m. on January 28. The Shanghai municipal government ordered the dissolution of all anti-Japanese organizations and stopped people from organizing volunteers to fight the Japanese. As a result, two popular newspapers were forced to close. Two hours before the deadline of the ultimatum, the Shanghai municipal government notified the Japanese consul that it had complied with the terms of the ultimatum. They thought the crisis was temporarily averted.

However, shortly before midnight, the Japanese army attacked the Chinese garrison stationed in Shanghai and occupied Zhabei, a Chinese-controlled area near the International Settlement. The Chinese garrison acted in self-defense without waiting for orders from Nanjing. The unexpected stiff resistance offered by the Chinese garrison enraged the Japanese and the conflict escalated.

Two days later, the Chinese government decided to move its national capital temporarily to Luoyang in Henan Province because Nanjing was threatened by the battle in Shanghai. The government also announced the postponement of the National Emergency Conference.

More reinforcements for Japanese units arrived in Shanghai in early February, and the Japanese fleet coordinated the attack. Three days later, the envoys from Britain, the United States, France and Italy tried to negotiate a peace. The Chinese side accepted the offer but the Japanese refused. On February 8, Japanese marines launched a major attack on Wusong and Zhaibei. The Chinese army fought gallantly and inflicted heavy casualties on the Japanese. China claimed its first victory in the battle of Shanghai.

But that victory was short-lived. On February 18, the Japanese sent another ultimatum, asking the Chinese army to retreat 20 kilometers in forty-eight hours. The Chinese army refused and the Japanese ordered an all-out attack. Several days later the envoys of Britain, the United States and France proposed to mediate. The Chinese and Japanese commanders were invited to meet on a British battleship to discuss terms. This time, the Chinese refused to accept the conditions imposed by the Japanese.

The fighting became heavy in early March as Japanese reinforcements continued to arrive. The Chinese troops were forced to withdraw from Wusong on March 3. The Japanese announced that Japanese interests in Shanghai were being protected and when that was accomplished, they would accept a cease-fire.

* * *

The Chinese garrison stationed in Shanghai was the 19th Route Army whose officers were mostly Cantonese. Liang Shiyi knew many of them well, particularly

General Cai Tingjia. He met with them to offer his help in coordinating supplies for the army during the battle. In one of their conversations, Cai said to Liang, "The Japanese thought its army could overrun us like they did in Manchuria. When they met strong resistance and suffered heavy casualties, they tried to find a face-saving way to negotiate with us. It's a good lesson that we should never seek peace at any price."

Playing his last card, Liang Shiyi, in the capacity of a private citizen, cabled James Ramsey MacDonald, the Prime Minister of Great Britain, enlisting his help to stop Japanese aggression. Liang had met MacDonald in his tour of Europe several years earlier and had since corresponded with him on a few occasions. He warned MacDonald of the Japanese intention to subjugate China, which sooner or later would be in conflict with British interests. He hoped the British Prime Minister could at least help China get better terms in the truce negotiation if he would do nothing else.

As a cease-fire became imminent, Liang Shiyi said goodbye to his relatives and friends in Shanghai and returned to Hong Kong.

"I have done all I can to help," Liang Shiyi told his eighth lady, "It's time for us to go home."

"How about the National Emergency Conference?" His eighth lady asked. "I thought that's why you came here."

"It's been postponed indefinitely." Liang replied.

On March 10, the Chinese government announced that the National Emergency Conference would be held in Luoyang in April. When Liang Shiyi received the news in Hong Kong, he decided not to attend because of the chaotic conditions of railway transportation disrupted by the battle of Shanghai.

The National Emergency Conference finally took place at Loyang on April 7 and ended five days later. A total of 144 members attended the conference, issuing a communique calling for an independent foreign policy and the expansion of national defense. Liang Shiyi was disappointed at the empty promises of the conference which was heralded as the gathering of patriotic statesmen to chart a course to resist Japanese aggression.

The merchants in Shanghai welcomed the prospect of a truce by reopening their businesses in April. While Japan agreed to a truce, it refused to accept a fixed date for withdrawing its troops. Japanese soldiers continued to construct a defense perimeter on the front line. On April 30, the League of Nations asked Japan to withdraw from Shanghai. After further negotiations, a truce agreement was signed on May 1 and ratified by both governments two weeks later. The Shanghai municipal government reclaimed the Zhabei district on May 15. The Japanese completed its withdrawal from Shanghai on June 13. After the Shanghai truce agreement was ratified, government agencies in Luoyang gradually moved operations back to Nanjing.

* * *

Liang Shiyi's mood was buoyed by the soft breezes of April and by the reunion with his brother. Shixu had come back from Guangzhou for the wedding of his eldest

428

son in Hong Kong. The two brothers took this opportunity to discuss family matters in great length. As Liang Shiyi left the wedding ceremony on the roof garden of the China Building, he suddenly felt the pain of recurring rheumatism when he walked from the elevator. He knew the torch of leading the expanded family must soon be passed to his brother.

No one in the extended family was prepared for the shocking news when Dingji called from Guangzhou in June. Since the long distance call between Hong Kong and Guangzhou was instituted only recently, the sound was not good. In a barely audible voice, Dingji told his father that his second son had died of cholera. In spite of repeated warnings of danger from his mother, the boy had apparently drunk unboiled water from the tap in school after a hot summer day. The dreadful disease had mercilessly claimed the life of Dingji's six-years-old son.

Yisheng returned home from Beiping in August after graduating from Yenching University. She soon found out that numerous obstacles could prevent a woman from finding a job in a man's world. She must be content to wait and see if her father could give her a helping hand. She was soon joined by her cousin Wosheng in the ranks of the unemployed. Wosheng had received a doctorate in chemistry from the University of Munich in Germany and wanted to find work in academic circles or in industry, which were almost off limits to women. Both would have to wait for a suitable entry.

Wosheng told her uncle about her boyfriend she met at the University of Munich and her wish to marry him. A native of Zhejing Province, her boyfriend had completed a doctorate in Chemistry in Germany. However, he continued to stay on to help his professor for a few months. Unlike Wosheng, he had already gotten an offer to be assistant professor at Zhejiang University. Liang Shiyi gave her his tentative approval, but he wanted to know more about the background of her boyfriend. He knew someone teaching at Zhejiang University who could help.

Dingmin had accepted a job as an electrical engineer with an American firm in Shanghai because his wife wanted to be near her family in Suzhou. As he and his wife passed by Hong Kong on their way, they brought with them the good news that they were expecting their first child in a few months.

Dingji also came to Hong Kong for the family reunion, but he had a secret mission in mind. A week earlier, he received a letter from his widowed sister Zangzheng who was in Beiping. A fine gentleman had proposed marriage to her and she had accepted. Could her brother gently break this delicate news to their parents? Dingji decided to approach his father privately when the family was in a festivity mood.

"I shared the pain of Zangsheng when her husband passed away," Liang Shiyi said to Dingji after hearing the news. "I understand her need to remarry. She has my blessing, though I cannot bring myself to announce it to the world. Who is her intended?"

"Morrison Yung, son of Yung Wing," Dingji replied. Liang Shiyi remembered the name Yung Wing, the first Chinese graduate of Yale University who married an

American school teacher and returned to China to spearhead the development of the state-owned industries. While he was reminiscing, Dingji asked: "Should I break the news to mother?"

"By all means," Liang Shiyi replied. "She will have to accept the fact whether she likes it or not, as we all must."

After this serious business, Liang Shiyi joined his young nephews and nieces in new parlor games Wosheng brought home from Germany. While they were in the thick of gaming, a servant interrupted, saying a messenger had an important letter for Liang, and was insisting Liang sign for the letter. When Liang found out that it came from the Japanese consulate in Hong Kong, he refused to accept the letter and turned the messenger away. Then he told his surprised family, "The Japanese are trying to corrupt my soul. Quite a few old literati and Beiyang generals were approached by the Japanese and were offered huge sums of money to support the Japanese cause in China. Do they think that I will become a traitor to my own country by accepting their bribe?"

* * *

As the anti-Japanese sentiment rapidly grew, a group of civic leaders in Shanghai planned to organize a "Stop the Civil War League" for the purpose of rallying public opinion to stop the war against the Communists and divert the military resources to national defense. Remembering Liang's strong voice in support of stiff resistance against the Japanese when he was in Shanghai the previous February, they invited Liang to be one of the sponsors of this new organization. In view of the failure of the official National Emergence Conference to take any meaningful action, Liang gave his consent to support this private organization.

Liang Shiyi felt that if the "Stop the Civil War League" was to be of any value, it would have to go beyond an empty declaration of principle. He thought of some practical steps to put the issue in the forefront of the national agenda by direct involvement in mediating the fighting between the supporters of the Communists and those in power in Nanjing. Since this was a touchy subject, he was waiting for the appropriate setting to present his plan to others.

In August 1932, the Stop the Civil War League called a meeting of its members in Shanghai. Liang thought it was time for him to bring his plan to the attention of a few close friends in the League even though he did not plan to attend the meeting. It happened that Zhu Qinglan, former governor of Guangdong and a staunch supporter of Sun Yatsen, came to Hong Kong for business before leaving for Shanghai. Liang asked Zhu to take his plan to Shanghai and discuss it discreetly with a few close associates at the League. Unfortunately, Zhu made his plan public in Shanghai by mistake and Liang suddenly became the center of controversy.

Chiang Kaishek had held the opinion that the government must suppress internal armed insurgencies before it could fight the war against Japan effectively. His view was not shared, even by some members of the Nationalist Party. As an outsider, Liang thought the civil war was futile and could drag on for years while the Japanese invasion was imminent. In his opinion, there were people of good will on both sides. Some intermediaries might be able to persuade them to find common ground to turn their guns toward the Japanese. Such an opinion immediately aroused the suspicion of Chiang supporters who vigorously impugned his motive. But Liang Shiyi did not find it necessary to explain his position. He was the ultimate conciliator.

* * *

The Japanese intention in Manchuria became perfectly clear when Japan created the puppet state of Manzhouguo (the Manchu state) on March 9, 1932. Puyi, the last emperor of the Qing Dynasty, was made its Chief Executive, with a group of leftover literati as ministers, a prelude to crowning him emperor of the puppet state.

After much debate, the League of Nations finally sent an investigative commission to Manchuria. Headed by Lord Lytton, the Acting Viceroy of India, the commission spent six weeks, from April 22 to June 4, in Manchuria. After stopping at Beiping and Tokyo to meet Chinese and Japanese officials, the investigation team returned to Geneva, Switzerland, to complete its report.

On September 15, Japan recognized the puppet government in Manchuria. It tried to present a fait accompli before the investigative commission made public its report on October 3. Undeceived by the facade, the report to the League of Nations condemned Japan as an aggressor and rejected its claim that Manzhouguo was a spontaneous development of the Manchus. But except for moral sanctions, the League did nothing. The Japanese reaction was singularly arrogant and insulting. It stepped up military operations in China and eventually withdrew from the League of Nations. The Chinese people watched helplessly as the Japanese army in Manchuria marched forward through the passes of the Great Wall into northern China.

Last Hurrah

It was a most pleasant occasion for the celebration of the Lunar New Year in 1933. Except his youngest daughter, Shiyi's children were grown and no longer lived at home in Hong Hong, but Liang Shiyi and Madam kept the tradition of greeting members of the extended family that morning. They were joined by their son Dingji and his family who had come from Guangzhou for the occasion. Of course Shixu's family were also there to exchange pleasantries.

Liang Shiyi spoke to Shixu about one of their brothers-in-law who had recently retired to his native village, "I got a letter from Xinghai a few days ago. He said, because of his ill health, he preferred to stay in Sanshui so that he would die in his native land." Then Shiyi casually commented, "I have no such desire. I want to die for the right cause, wherever it takes me."

Madam overheard the remark and was shocked. She disliked anything unpleasant and was superstitious about any reference to death. She suddenly interrupted, "It's a bad omen to talk about death on New Year's Day. Let's change the subject to something more cheerful."

Liang Shiyi calmly replied, "A person will die sooner or later. There's no harm in talking about it." Madam was repelled and turned to other members of the family.

Actually Liang Shiyi had a lot of good news. Two months earlier, a granddaughter had been born in Suzhou, the first child of his son Dingmin; and Dingshu and his wife in Beiping were expecting their first child any day.

Shiyi's three older grandchildren now surrounded him to attract his attention as son Dingji tried to lead them away. It was picture perfect for a happy family portrait. However, Shiyi was greatly troubled by the national news. The Japanese army, entrenched in Manchuria, was poised to invade Rehe Province, threatening the northern region of China.

Liang Shiyi's eighth lady understood his melancholy mood and suggested they take a walk in the garden to ease his mind. As they followed the path to see the full bloom of the winter plum, Liang remarked to her, "In the twilight of my life, nothing much matters to me, personally. However, I cannot sit still and let our country be conquered by Japan." Then he added, "Centuries ago, the officials of the Song

432

Dynasty tearfully committed suicide to prove their loyalty when the fate of their last emperor was doomed. Wouldn't it be better if they had continued to fight as long as they lived?"

"You look very tired," His eighth lady said, trying to divert him from such serious thoughts. "Why don't you take a nap after lunch?"

"That's a good idea," he replied as they walked back toward the house where a banquet to celebrate the New Year was waiting.

Liang Shiyi tried to mollify Madam by striking a cheerful note, "You will be happy to know Wosheng will be married sometime this spring. We're going to set the date soon." Then he turned to Shixu, "I will rely on you to make all the arrangements for our niece's wedding."

"It's my pleasure," Shixu replied. He thought of their solemn promise to bring up the daughter of their deceased brother and felt as if a weight had been lifted from his shoulder.

Several days later, Liang Shiyi was busy writing in his study when his youngest daughter Yisheng came to the door. She apologized for the intrusion but she wanted to give him a telegram from Dingshu, announcing the birth of his first child, a daughter. He showed Yisheng the draft of a poem he was just about copy onto a large sheet of paper.

"I composed this poem last week," Liang told her. "It expressed some of my random thoughts. I must now change 'my little granddaughter' to 'my two little granddaughters' before copying." When he finished his refined calligraphy, he wrote after the poem: "To my daughter Yisheng" before signing his name.

Yisheng looked at her father's writing and marveled at the sentimental poem and the refined calligraphy. She read aloud:

I reckoned my snowy white hair when I awoke from my nap amid a dream.
It matters not that I found a plum on the slope or a willow near the stream.
Fifteen hundred miles separate my two little granddaughters from me.
Forty years have elapsed since I became a historian in Hanlin Academy.
Though my modest ideas once startled the nation like a torrential flood,
I have only my remaining life to defend my country with sweat and blood.
My friends and followers, I implore you to sharpen your sword without fear.
Dry your tears and mount your horses to drive out the invaders who are near.

* * *

As the Japanese army was advancing in Rehe Province, the Japanese government secretly planned to set up a puppet government in Beiping. An emissary was sent to Beiping to persuade Duan Qirui to head this new government. Duan Qirui refused to cooperate, but Japanese pressure was mounting. Sensing the danger of a Japanese take-over of the north China through a puppet Chinese ruler, Chiang Kaishek invited Duan Qirui to join the Nationalist cause and move to Shanghai. After arriving on January 22, Duan Qirui wrote to Liang Shiyi to see if he could come to Shanghai for a reunion.

Liang Shiyi felt he could strengthen Duan's resolve to join the common cause of resisting the Japanese invaders. He decided to go to Shanghai as soon as traveling arrangements could be made. Before his departure, his brother Shixu told him that the plan for Wosheng's wedding had been finalized. It was set for April 9, a Sunday, to be held in the roof garden of the China Building on Queen's Road Central. It was expected that Shiyi would return to Hong Kong in time for her wedding.

Liang left Hong Kong with his eighth lady by boat on March 1 and arrived in Shanghai two days later. His daughter Yusheng and her husband Guo Jinkun, who lived in Shanghai, were on hand to greet him upon his arrival. They saw to it that his needs were taken care of in every way. In anticipation of extensive political and social activities, they had rented a mansion for him in the French Concession.

A day after his arrival, he gave an interview to a young reporter from the *Current News Journal* and answered questions for two hours. He indicated he would stay in Shanghai for about a month to assess the military situation in north China before making any other move.

What do you know about military operations?" The reporter asked.

"Thirty years ago, I was the editor of a series of military textbooks: *Strategies of the Beiyang Army*," Liang reminded him. "Perhaps I can make some modest contributions to the war of resistance against the Japanese."

"Isn't public finance your greatest strength? What do you have to say about that in order to sustain a war of resistance?" The reporter asked again.

"I will speak on this subject to the Bankers' Association tomorrow," Liang replied.

"Tell me candidly, please. What is your political ambition?" The reporter could not resist in asking this last question.

"As I speak to you, Chengde, the capital of Rehe Province, is overrun by the Japanese army. I am acting strictly as a private citizen to save our country in time of crisis. I can honestly tell you that I have no personal ambition in the twilight of my life." Liang had spoken from his heart.

For a couple of weeks, a steady stream of visitors showed up at his door after he had made his round of courtesy calls. He was in high spirits when he and his visitors discussed ways to resist the Japanese aggression. He felt the excitement of his youth, when he and his friends struggled to save the country from foreign domination. It was deja vu.

* * *

Liang Shiyi was visibly shaken when, on the morning of March 10, he received word from his son-in-law Zuzhang from Beiping that his old friend Guan Mianjun was critically ill. Liang immediately cabled Guan Mianjun to cheer him up. "I will visit you in a month after my brief stay in Shanghai," Liang stated. In the same evening, a reply from Zuzhang brought the sad news that his father had died.

Words could not express Liang Shiyi's feeling about Guan Mianjun's death. They had been friends and allies since the days of their sojourn in Hanlin Academy. As poor but promising scholars, they had great dreams of bringing peace and prosperity to China. Now Guan Mianjun was dead and Liang had a premonition that his own end was near. It was a sad commentary that their ambitions were not to be achieved in their lifetimes. His only consolation was that their personal friendship had been strengthened by the marriage of Guan's son to his own daughter.

Two days later, he felt a stomach pain after hosting a dinner in a restaurant honoring Dingmin's father-in-law who had come from Suzhou to visit him. Within a week, his health took a turn for the worse. His relatives were alarmed. They cabled his brother Shixu in Hong Kong and his eldest son Dingji in Guangzhou and urged them to come immediately. Together they arrived in Shanghai on March 31 and found Liang Shiyi seriously ill. The next day he was hospitalized for observation and further examination.

Before Shixu left Hong Kong for Shanghai, he knew that neither he nor his brother would be available for Wosheng's wedding on April 9. It was imperative that the wedding take place as scheduled before anything should happen to his brother. He advised Wosheng to move the wedding ceremony to Guangzhou where his youngest sister Fugui and her husband could take charge. Shixu also told Dingmin, who happened to be in Hong Kong on business, to comfort his mother who had just been told of his father's illness.

"Do you want to go to Shanghai to be at father's side?" Dingmin asked his mother as more bad news about his father's illness arrived.

"No, I shall remain in Hong Kong," Madam said firmly. "I have gone through good times and bad with your father. But I am now old and weak, and cannot weather any emotional trauma. You should go back to Shanghai to be with your father. Our servant Maisan will provide comfort and support for me at time of crisis."

So it was arranged that Wosheng and her fiance would go to Guangzhou as soon as possible. That left very little time for Fugui to make the wedding arrangements in Guangzhou. On the night of April 2, Fugui received a telegram from Shixu with a terse message, "Brother's illness turned grave. The wedding date scheduled for April 9 must be moved forward." In a frantic move, Fugui consulted with Wosheng and her fiance who decided to have their wedding on April 5. Learning that Dingmin had booked his passage on S.S. *Empress of Japan* sailing for Shanghai on April 7, Wosheng and her fiance arranged to join him for their honeymoon trip.

On April 5, a simple but solemn wedding ceremony was held in the presence of dozens of relatives and friends, including children. Many thoughts of her past went through Wosheng's mind as she walked down the isle. Her wedding ceremony had been scaled down, not once, but twice. Her two uncles, to whom she was indebted for her upbringing, were not able to attend. She only wished to forget all the commotion as she reached her intended who was smiling brilliantly at her.

After a brief reception, the newlyweds took a late train to Hong Kong. Fugui immediately cabled Shixu to report the success of the wedding which, she was sure, would please her brothers. She could not help but think about Wosheng's mother who hadn't had contact with the Liang Family for almost two decades. Fugui had heard that she and her family had moved to Singapore a few years earlier and there the trail lost. She would no doubt be pleased to know her daughter had married a respectable and ambitious young man.

* * *

Liang Shiyi had a good day at Baolong Hospital in Shanghai when his longtime friend and protege Ye Gongchuo came to visit him on the morning of April 5. He remarked to Ye and Shixu that it was the day of Qingming Festival when people went to the countryside to visit the cemeteries in honor of their ancestors. Then he recited a few familiar poems for such an occasion. Suddenly something dropped from Liang's hand to the floor and Ye saw that his friend was unconscious. A nurse was immediately summoned to check Liang's pulse and heartbeat. To the relief of his family and friends, he regained consciousness a few hours later. By then his son Dingshu had arrived from Beiping to be at his side. The doctor belatedly confirmed that Liang Shiyi had liver cancer and that it had spread. He was not expected to live for long.

That evening Shixu went to see him with the news of Wosheng's wedding. "I'm very happy indeed," he told Shixu. "I entrust the family affairs to your good hands, and I have no more worries." After speaking to Shixu, he fell into a deep sleep.

Wosheng and her husband had left Hong Kong with Dingmin onboard the *S.S. Empress of Japan*. It was not exactly the kind of honeymoon they had planned.

After the captain's dinner on the evening of April 8, the band played many pieces of Johann Strauss which reminded Wosheng and her husband of the days when they visited Vienna. They waltzed until midnight before walking out onto the deck of the starboard side. Leaning against the railing, they marveled at the full moon in a clear, dark sky. They felt a strong breeze and huddled together for warmth. As they embraced each other, they closed their eyes to make a wish. When they reopened their eyes, Wosheng was buoyant with hopes and dreams.

She was surprised when her husband soberly told her, "I have seen a bright comet which suddenly fizzled and disappeared on the horizon."

"It's all your imagination," Wosheng replied as she looked at her watch. "It's almost one-thirty and the air is getting chilly. Let's go back to our stateroom. Our ship will dock in Shanghai in less than twelve hours."

On the evening of April 8, in the Baolong Hospital in Shanghai, Liang Shiyi was fighting for his life. When the nurse came to check his pulse, his son Dingji held his other hand while his brother Shixu touched his feet. Liang Shiyi murmured, "Aba," referring to his eighth lady, but he did not finish the sentence. He died at 1:30 a.m. on April 9, 1933.

Afterword

After the death of Liang Shiyi, a two-volume chronicle entitled *Annals of Mr. Liang Yansun of Sanshui* was compiled by his friends and admirers, and edited by an alumnus of Fenggang Academy. Published in 1937, it was a tribute to Liang Shiyi, whose "courtesy name" was Liang Yansun, a name his friends used deferentially. This chronicle recorded the highlights of Liang Shiyi's public career and family activities from 1869 to 1933. Major historical events of that period were also included, along with some official communications and documents not generally available.

It was not uncommon for a man of Liang Shiyi's stature to leave such a legacy in the form of a chronicle. The Chinese elite had a sense of history and they wanted their voices and feelings known to future generations. Liang Shiyi's chronicle is notable only for its thoroughness in its documentation. Historians can exercise their own judgment on the merit of his actions.

For over half a century, Liang Shiyi's last surviving concubine, Liang Tan Yuying, devoted her life to perpetuating his memory. Before her death in Hong Kong in December 1986, she had entrusted her collection of Liang Shiyi's papers, including some of the correspondence from his illustrious friends, to a classics scholar of the old school. He edited these materials to produce a photographic volume, *Private Papers of Liang Shiyi as Collected by Liang Tan Yuying*. It was published posthumously in 1987 as a final tribute to her husband.

It is fortunate that such papers have been preserved. Of course, the most important state documents had already been included in the *Annals*, but the private papers collected by his surviving concubine show the human side of Liang Shiyi and his relations with family and friends. It includes a poem by Liang Shiyi dedicated to her during their honeymoon, and a memoir written by her, describing in detail the life in the Liang family.

Liang Shiyi was an inspiration to his loved ones and admirers. Ye Gongchuo, his most intimate friend and associate who lived to an old age in Shanghai, dictated the manuscript of a book to defend Liang's legacy even as his own health was failing. This book, *Liang Shiyi and Chinese Diplomacy Related to the Pacific Conference*, offered a spirited defense of Liang's foreign policy regarding the Washington Conference of Pacific Powers during his brief tenure as Premier in early 1922. Liang's surviving concubine played no small role in the ultimate publication of Ye Gongchuo's book in Hong Kong in 1970, as indicated by the end note she wrote for the publication.

* * *

Some British diplomats of the early Republic regarded Liang Shiyi as the Machiavelli of China. In their view, he was expedient in his acquiescence, if not acceptance, of authoritarian rule, something he sometimes felt necessary in his efforts to save the Republic from disunity and chaos. Those same diplomats might have been unduly influenced by malicious gossip, as well as the self-serving, fabricated stories about Chinese officials fed to them by Edmund Backhouse, a brilliant linguist and Chinese scholar. These British diplomats were so blinded by class prejudice they could not imagine Edmund Backhouse, who attended all the right schools and belonged to all the right clubs, could be so devious and dishonest. Only in retrospect, has Backhouse been found to be a compulsive and habitual liar. His hidden life was exposed in a book by the British historian, Hugh Trevor-Roper, in 1976. Liang had the misfortune of attracting the attention of Backhouse and, because of the trickery of this British Baronet, was blamed for what he didn't do as well as what he did.

More appropriately, Liang Shiyi might be compared to Henry Clay, the prominent nineteenth-century American. Like Henry Clay, Liang Shiyi thought of himself as a defender of the people's interest and gladly devoted his career to public service. He was a consummate insider in politics who attempted to steer his country out of harm's way at a time of social and political upheaval. Just as Henry Clay was hailed for his role in securing the Missouri Compromise, Liang Shiyi was hailed for his successful negotiation of the abdication of the Qing Emperor. Both men commanded the loyalty of their followers to an unusual degree.

Liang Shiyi was assailed by his critics for supporting Yuan Shikai's monarchical movement just as Henry Clay was accused of bargaining for high office in supporting John Quincy Adam for President of the United States. The charges of Liang Shiyi's involvement in helping Yuan leave office in a peaceful transition, without suffering indignity, caused damage to Liang throughout his public life. Like Clay, Liang Shiyi earned the hatred of powerful leaders who would never forgive him. Nevertheless, Liang worked hard for the cause of national unity and the promotion of national economic development. He spoke on every appropriate occasion, in and out of government, on behalf of national unity. Like Clay, he was best known as the Great Compromiser, but few people realized the significance of compromise in defusing full-scale civil war for at least a decade and a half. Such compromises not only saved the blood and treasures of the Chinese multitude, but also allowed progressive forces to survive and thrive in an inhospitable land. Liang Shiyi was well aware of the obstacles confronting him, and accepted the reality that he could affect so little the actions of others in the imperfect world. However, he truly believed that if the coalition of North and South, no matter how quarrelsome and divided at times, were allowed to survive through peaceful successions of its leaders, the people would eventually rise to demand the rule of laws and to form a more perfect union.

For better or for worst, Liang Shiyi left an indelible imprint in China's tortuous struggle for modernization.

References and Acknowledgements

The following references have been invaluable in providing background material for this novel. Specific citations are acknowledged in the commentary.

1. An Anonymous alumnus of Fenggang Academy, editor, *Annals of Mr. Liang Yansun of Sanshui, Volumes 1 and 2* (in Chinese). Private Publication, Hong Kong, 1939. Reissued as a monograph in the "Modern Chinese Historical Sources Series," with an introduction by Wu Xiangxiang, who identified Cen Xuelu as the anonymous editor. Wenxing Book Co., Taipei, Taiwan, 1962.

This chronicle of Liang Shiyi highlights his public career and family activities as well as major historical events during his lifetime. Its editor, Cen Xuelu, was a former private secretary of Liang Shiyi who had full access to his collection of papers, including some official communications and documents not available elsewhere. Because of the thoroughness of its documentation, this chronicle provides the basic information for the framework of the current novel.

2. Chen, Fen, chief editor, *Collected Historical Sources on Liang Shiyi, Premier in the Beiyang Government* (in Chinese), sponsored by Historical Sources Research Committee of the Political Consultative Council, Sanshui County, Guangdong Province. Chinese Literature and History Publishers, Beijing, 1990.

The major articles of this publication were based on two primary sources: *Annals of Mr. Liang Yansun of Sanshui, Volumes 1 and 2* (Item 1 on this list) and *Liang Shiyi and Chinese Diplomacy Related to the Pacific Conference* (Item 13 on this list). Other articles include memoirs written by Liang Shiyi's contemporaries, both friends and foes, which provide different points of view of Liang Shiyi's career.

3. Fitzgerald, C. P., *China: A Short Cultural History, Third edition*. Frederick A. Praeger, Publishers, New York, 1961.

This book provides a concise description of the foundations and major developments of Confucianism, Daoism and Buddhism in China. It is the source of such expositions in the novel.

4. Hsu, Immanuel C. Y., *The Rise of Modern China, Third Edition*. The Oxford University Press, London, 1985.

This comprehensive history of China from the beginning of the Qing Dynasty to the present provides important background information not adequately covered by Liang Shiyi's chronicle. The following topics have been especially helpful in providing historical background for the novel: the civil service examination system in the Qing Dynasty; the hierarchical structure of officials and gentry-scholars; the Opium War and its aftermath; the Taiping Rebellion; the self-strengthening movement; the Sino-Japanese War of 1894; the

441

"one hundred days of reform" in 1898; the Boxers Movement in 1900; the revolution of 1911 and the new Republic in 1912; the Beiyang government and warlords in the early Republic period; the May Fourth Movement in 1919; the Northern Expedition in 1927 and the Nationalist government in Nanjing in 1928; and the Japanese invasions of China in 1931 and 1932.

5. Hui-Lan Koo, *Hui-Lan Koo* (Madam Wellington Koo)—An Autobiography as told to Mary Van Rensselaer Thayer. Dial Press, New York, 1943.

This autobiography of the wife of Wellington Koo, former Chinese diplomat and Premier, depicts her social life in China and abroad, and provides many anecdotes of political events between the two World Wars. Some anecdotes in this work were cited in the novel.

6. Liu, Shaotang, chief editor, *Journal of Important Events of Republic of China*, (in Chinese). Literary Magazine Publishers, Taipei, Taiwan, 1973.

Volume 1 of this journal contains brief daily entries of important events of the Republic of China from 1912 to 1941. It is a convenient source to check the dates of major historical events cited in the novel.

7. MacKinnon, Stephen Robert, "Liang Shih-i and the Communication Clique," *The Journal of Asian Studies, Volume XXIX*, Number 3. May 1970.

The article gives detailed descriptions of the development of Chinese railways in general and the contribution of Liang Shiyi and his colleagues in particular. Such descriptions were helpful for the chapters on Liang's contribution to railway administration. The citations of foreign opinions toward the Chinese bureaucrats, including two articles in *The Times of London* in 1908 and 1909, came from this article.

8. Selle, Earle Albert, *Donald of China (as told by William Henry Donald, 1875-1946)*. Harper, New York, 1948.

William Donald, an Australian reporter in China, was an active participant in Chinese politics. His description of his dealing with Sun Yatsen's and Yuan Shikai's circle of friends is particularly interesting. Some conversations between Donald and his friends in China that are pertinent to the events in the novel are direct quotes.

9. Spence, Jonathan D., *The Search for Modern China*. W. W. Norton & Company, New York, 1990.

This is another comprehensive history of China from the beginning of the Qing Dynasty to the present. It provides important background information for this novel on the following topics: the Opium War and its aftermath; Hong Xiuquan and the Taiping Heavenly Kingdom; the Sino-Japanese War of 1894; the "one hundred days of reform" in 1898; the Boxers Movement in 1900; the revolution of 1911 and the new Republic of 1912; Beiyang government and warlords in the early Republic period; the May Fourth Movement in 1919 and its social and political consequences; the soviet influence in Chinese politics after the Russian Revolution; the Northern Expedition in 1927; and the Japanese involvement in China. Some insights of Chinese politics from Western sources have been cited in the novel.

10. Su, Wenzuo, editor, *Private Papers of Liang Shiyi as Collected by Liang Tan Yuying* (in Chinese). Private Publication, Hong Kong, 1987.

The photographic volume of the private papers of Liang Shiyi contains letters and short notes from some of Liang's illustrious friends in their own handwritings. It also contains an article by Liang Tan Yuying, the last surviving concubine of Liang Shiyi, which describes the life in the Liang family in detail. It has been an important source of information for this novel.

11. Swanberg, W. A., *Luce and His Empire*. Charles Scribner's Sons, New York, 1972.

An early chapter gives a vivid description of the Boxers Movement in 1900 and the subsequent killing of foreign missionaries and Chinese Christians. Its quotations of comments by Voltaire and Mark Twain about foreign missionaries in China are cited in the novel.

12. Trevor-Roper, Hugh, *Hermit of Peking: The Hidden Life of Sir Edmund Backhouse*. Penguin Books, New York, 1978. Originally published under the title *A Hidden Life: The Enigma of Sir Edmund Backhouse*. Macmillan Publishing Co. Ltd., London, 1976.

Although this book is primarily an expose of Edmund Backhouse, it contains materials related to Liang Shiyi and his times. For twenty years after the death of the Empress Dowager Cixi in 1898, Backhouse and his compatriots crossed path with Liang Shiyi in unexpected ways. This book is well researched and contains materials from the archives of the British Foreign Office describing the involvement of Liang Shiyi with some British diplomats at that time. Such materials were used to present the British view about Liang Shiyi and to verify the description of same events in Liang's *Annals*.

13. Ye, Gongchuo, as told to Yu Chengzhi, *Liang Shiyi and Chinese Diplomacy Related to the Pacific Conference* (in Chinese). Private publication, Hong Kong, 1970.

This monograph contains firsthand information about the purported actions of the Chinese government related to the Washington Conference in 1922. It is based on a careful research of Chinese archives to exonerate Liang Shiyi, who was the Premier of China at that time. It is an important source of information for that period.

14. Yuan, Jingxue et al, *Private Life of Yuan Shikai* (in Chinese). East West and Culture Publishing Co., Hong Kong, 1963.

The booklet consists of articles by a daughter and a son of Yuan Shikai, plus several memoirs by his former subordinates and friends. The principal contribution is a detailed and candid description of the private life of Yuan Shikai written by his daughter Yuan Jingxue, including the life in their native village of Zhangde and in Zhongnanhai, the former Imperial Winter Palace in Beijing. It provides some interesting information otherwise unavailable elsewhere.

Appendix: Major Events in Liang Shiyi's Life and Times

A. Highlights of Liang Shiyi's Career

Member of Hanlin Academy (1894-1903), with periods on leave of absence
Principal Lecturer, Fenggang Academy in Sanshui (1896 and 1901)
Chief of Editorial Bureau, Office of Commissioner of Northern Ports (1903-1904)
Counselor to the Special Envoy Plenipotentiary to India (1904-1905)
Expectant Counselor, Ministry of Foreign Affairs (1905-1906)
Head, General Railway Bureau, Ministry of Posts & Communications (1907-1911)
Associate Vice President, Bank of Communications (1908-1911)
Minister of Posts and Communications (December 1911-end of Qing Dynasty)
Chief Secretary to the President, Republic of China (February 1912-1914)
President and Chief Executive Officer, Bank of Communications (1913-1916)
Acting Minister of Finance, (June-September 1913)
Controller, Maritime Customs Bureau (1914-1916)
Head, Domestic Bonds Bureau (1914-1916)
Political exile (July 1916-February 1918)
Speaker of the Senate (August-December 1918)
Chairman and Chief Executive Officer, Bank of Communications (1918-1922)
Members of two Presidential Commissions (1919-1920)
Head, Domestic Bonds Bureau (1920-1921)
Premier (December 1921-January 1922)
Political exile (June 1922-December 1924)
Member of Rehabilitation Conference (1925)
Chairman, Finance Commission for Rehabilitation (1925-1926)
Chairman and Chief Executive Officer, Bank of Communications (1925-1928)
Member, Chinese Tariff Commission (1925-1928)
Political exile (July 1928-June 1931)
Member, National Emergency Conference (1932)

B.Chronology of Chinese Rulers in Liang Shiyi's Lifetime—1869-1933

Reigns of Qing Emperors

Emperor Tongji (1862-1874), under Empress Dowager Cixi
Emperor Guangxu (1875-1908), under Empress Dowager Cixi
Emperor Xuantong (1909-1912), under Empress Dowager Longyu

Provisional and Beijing Governments in the Republic Era

Sun Yatsen, Provisional President in Nanjing (January-March 1912)
Yuan Shikai, Provisional President in Beijing (March 1912-October 1913)
Yuan Shikai, President (October 1913-June 1916)
Li Yuanhong, President (June 1916-July 1917)
Feng Guozhang, Acting President (August 1917-October 1918)
Xu Shichang, President (October 1918-July 1922)
Li Yuanhong, President (July 1922-June 1923)
Regency Period without a President (July-October 1923)
Cao Kun, President (October 1923-November 1924)
Duan Qirui, Temporary Chief Executive (December 1924-December 1926)
Zhang Zuolin, Marshall & Head of Government (January 1927-June 1928)

Nationalist Government in Nanjing

Chiang Kaishek, Chairman (October 1928-December 1931)
Lin Sun, Chairman (from January 1932)
Chiang Kaishek, Generalissimo of the National Military Council (from March 1932)

C. Liang Shiyi's Extended Family

Liang Shiyi's Siblings (Children of Liang Zhijian and his Wife)

Eldest brother (b. 1868)—died in Infancy
Liang Shiyi (b. 1869), married the daughter of Gao Zuoqing & six concubines
First sister (b. 1871)—married to the Ou family
Third brother (b. 1873)—died in infancy
Second sister (b. 1875)—married to the Lin Family
Third sister (b. 1877)—married to the Lu family
Fourth brother, Liang Shixu (b. 1879)—married the daughter of Deng Zishan
Fifth brother, Liang Shixin (b. 1885)—married the daughter of Jian Chaoliang
Fourth sister (b. 1887)—married to the Ou family

Liang Shiyi's Spouses

Wife (Madam)—the daughter of Gao Zuoqing (m. 1887)
Second lady—from the Pan family (m. 1894)
Third lady—from the Zheng family (m. 1906)
Fourth lady—from the He family (m. 1910)
Fifth lady—from the Cai family (m. 1917)
Sixth lady—from the Zheng family (m. 1918)
No seventh lady out of deference for his mother's order in her family
Eighth lady—from the Tan family (m. 1919)

Liang Shiyi's Children and Their Spouses (until his death in 1933)

Eldest daughter, Haoyin, by his second lady (b. 1896)—married Guan Zuzhang
First son, by his wife (b. 1897)—died in infancy
Second son, Dingji, by his wife (b. 1898)—married Zheng Shungu
Third son, Dingwu, by his second lady (b. 1898)—drowned in 1913
Second daughter, Huaisheng, by his wife (b. 1900)—married Ou Shao'an
Third daughter Yusheng, by his second lady (b. 1900)—married Gou Jinkun
Fourth son, by his wife (b. 1903)—died in infancy
Fourth daughter, Zangsheng, by his wife (b. 1904)—married Rong Xianxun (d. 1930); second husband Morrison Yung
Fifth son, Dingshu, by his second lady (b. 1907)—married Margarita Huang (d. 1929); second wife He Yubo
Sixth son, Dingmin, by his wife (b. 1908)—married Zhong Huilian
Fifth daughter, Yisheng, by his second lady (b. 1909)

Index of Chinese Names

Guo Jinkun	郭錦坤	Juren	舉人
H		**K**	
Han Dynasty	漢朝	Kang Youwei	康有為
Han, ethnic	漢人	Kangxi	康熙
Hankou	漢口	Koo, Hui-Lan	顧黃彗蘭
Hanlin	翰林	Koo, Wellington	顧維鈞
Hanyang	漢陽	Kowloon	九龍
Harbin	哈爾濱	**L**	
He Yubo	何予博	Li Dazhao	李大釗
He Yuguo	何韜高	LiDuanfen	李端棻
Hebei	河北	Li Hongzhang	李鴻章
Heilongjiang	黑龍江	Li Jingqu	李經楚
Henan	河南	Li Lianying	李蓮英
Hexiwu	河西務	Li Yuanhong	黎元洪
Hong Kong	香港	Liang Boyin	梁伯尹
Hong Rengan	洪仁幹	Liang Dingji	梁定薊
Hong Xiuquan	洪秀全	Liang Dingmin	梁定閩
Hongxian	洪憲	Liang Dingshu	梁定蜀
Hu Hanmin	胡漢民	Liang Dingwu	梁定吳
Hu Shi	胡適	Liang Fugui	梁福桂
Hu Weide	胡惟德	Liang Haoyin	梁好音
Hu Yufen	胡燏棻	Liang Hongzhu	梁鴻矗
Huai (Army)	淮軍	Liang Huaisheng	梁懷生
Huairou	懷柔	Liang Qichao	梁啟超
Huang Xing	黃興	Liang Rucheng	梁汝成
Huang Yanpei	黃炎培	Liang Ruji	梁汝楫
Huangpu	黃埔	Liang Shixin	梁士訢
Huantong	宣統	Liang Shixu	梁士訏
Huazhizi	花之寺	Liang Shiyi	梁士詒
Hubei	湖北	Liang Shuming	梁漱冥
Hufangqiao	虎坊橋	Liang Tang Yuying	梁譚玉櫻
Hunan	湖南	Liang Wosheng	梁我生
J		Liang Yansun	梁燕孫
Jian Chaoliang	簡朝亮	Liang Yisheng	梁議生
Jiangsu	江蘇	Liang Yusheng	梁興生
Jiangxi	江西	Liang Zangsheng	梁藏生
Jilin	吉林	Liang Zhijian	梁知鑑
Jinan	濟南	Liaoning	遼寧
Jinshi	進士	Lin Yutang	林語堂

Tang Hualong	湯化龍	Yang Du	楊度
Tang Jiyao	唐繼堯	Yang Shiqi	楊士琦
Tang Shaoyi	唐紹儀	Yang Shizang	楊士驤
Tianjin	天津	Yang Xiuqing	楊秀清
Tieshizi Hutong	鐵獅子胡同	Yang Xiu	楊修
Tongji	同治	Yangzi River	揚子江
W		Ye Gongchuo	葉恭綽
Wang Chonghui	王寵惠	Yenching	燕京
Wang Jingwei	汪精衛	Yihetuan	義和團
Wang Wenshao	王文韶	Yinchang	廕昌
Wang Zhixiang	王芝祥	Yongzheng	雍正
Wang, C. T.	王正廷	Yuan Jingxue	袁靜雪
Wei Dynasty	魏朝	Yuan Keding	袁克定
Weihaiwai	威海衛	Yuan Shikai	袁世凱
Weng Tonghe	翁同龢	Yueyang	岳陽
Wu Jinglian	吳景濂	Yung Wing	容閎
Wu Peifu	吳佩孚	Yunnan	雲南
Wu Tingfang	伍廷芳	**Z**	
Wu Xiangxiang	吳相湘	Zeng Guofan	曾國藩
Wu Yusheng	吳郁生	Zhaibei	閘北
Wu Zi Bei	無字碑	Zhaize	載澤
Wuchang	武昌	Zhan Tianyou	詹天佑
Wuhan	武漢	Zhan Yunpeng	靳雲鵬
Wusong	吳淞	Zhang Hu	張弧
Wuxi	無錫	Zhang Jian	張謇
Wuzhou	梧州	Zhang Shaozheng	張紹曾
Xi'an	西安	Zhang Tianbo	張憩伯
Xianfeng	咸豐	Zhang Xueliang	張學良
Xiang (Army)	湘軍	Zhang Zhenfang	張鎮芳
Xiangshan	香山	Zhang Zhidong	張之洞
Xiliang	錫良	Zhang Zhongxiang	章宗祥
Xinjiang	新疆	Zhang Zuolin	張作霖
Xiong Xiling	熊希齡	Zhangde	彰德
Xiucai	秀才	Zhao Bingjun	趙秉鈞
Xu Shichang	徐世昌	Zhao Qinghua	趙慶華
Xu Tong	徐桐	Zhejiang	浙江
Y		Zheng Hongnian	鄭洪年
Yan Weiqing	顏惠慶	Zheng Lequan	鄭樂泉
Yan Yangchu	晏陽初	Zheng Shungu	鄭順姑

Zheng Xuan	鄭玄
Zhengding	正定
Zhengzhou	鄭州
Zhenjiang	鎮江
Zhili	直隸
Zhong Huilian	鍾慧廉
Zhong Wenyao	鍾文耀
Zhonghua	中華
Zhongnanhai	中南海
Zhou Enlai	周恩來
Zhou Shouchen	周壽臣
Zhou Xuexi	周學熙
Zhou Ziqi	周自齊
Zhu Qinglan	朱慶瀾
Zhu Qiqian	朱啟鈐
Zhu Xi	朱熹
Zhuang Yuan	狀元

Mayhaven Publishing
P O Box 557
Mahomet, IL 61853
Fax: 217 586 6330

Interesting Books for Interesting People